JOURNEY UNDER THE MIDNIGHT SUN

Keigo Higashino

TRANSLATED BY ALEXANDER O. SMITH
WITH JOSEPH REEDER

First published in Great Britain in 2015 by Little, Brown
This paperback edition published in 2016 by Abacus

Originally published in Japan as *Byakuyako*

Abacus
An imprint of
Little, Brown Book Group
Carmelite House
50 Victoria Embankment
London EC4Y 0DZ

An Hachette UK Company
www.hachette.co.uk

www.littlebrown.co.uk

ONE

Sasagaki left the station and headed west along the tracks. Despite being October it was still dreadfully muggy, yet the ground was dry so when a truck sped by it sent up clouds of dust. He frowned and rubbed his eyes, his feet falling heavy on the pavement. By all rights, he should have been spending the day at home enjoying some leisurely reading – in fact he'd been holding off on a new thriller just for the occasion.

A park came into view on the right, large enough to accommodate two pick-up softball games side by side. There was a jungle gym, swings, a slide – all the standard equipment. This, Masumi Park, was the largest in the area by far. On its far side stood a seven-storey building. Nothing unusual about the exterior, but Sasagaki knew that inside it was almost entirely hollowed out. Before joining the metropolitan police he'd been stationed with the local force here in the eastern part of Osaka, and he remembered a thing or two about his old beat. A crowd of onlookers had already gathered in front of the building, which was ringed by several squad cars.

Sasagaki didn't head straight for the building, but took a right on the street before the park. The fifth building from the corner was a tiny shop with a frontage of barely more than two metres. A sign out front proclaimed GRILLED SQUID. The squid in question were grilled on a stand set in the front of the shop, behind which a chunky woman of around fifty sat reading the newspaper. Sasagaki glanced beyond her to see shelves loaded with sweets. The place was a popular after-school hangout, but he didn't see any children today.

'One, please,' Sasagaki called out.

The woman hastily folded her newspaper and stood. 'I'll have that right up.'

Sasagaki smoked Peace brand cigarettes. He stuck one between his lips now, lit it with a match, and glanced at the newspaper where she'd left it on the chair.

MINISTRY OF HEALTH ANNOUNCES SEAFOOD MERCURY RESULTS, read one headline. Beneath it in smaller text: *Even large quantities produce levels below recommended limits.*

Back in March, a judge had handed down a decision in the Minamata disease trial down in Kumamoto, clearing the way for the resolution of three other large public health trials in one blow: Minamata disease up in Niigata, one on extreme environmental pollution in Yotsukaichi, and Itai-itai disease. All of the cases had been decided in favour of the claimants. Now pollution was on everyone's mind. In a nation that ate so much fish, worry spread fast that mercury and PCBs could be getting into the food supply.

I hope squid's safe, Sasagaki thought.

The specialised griddle for baking the squid consisted of two hinged steel plates which pressed together, cooking the squid and its blanket of flour and egg between them. The aroma made his belly twitch with hunger.

The woman opened the griddle, revealing an oblong, flattened squid to which she applied sauce – just a light brushing – before cutting it in half. She wrapped the pieces in a single sheet of waxy brown paper and held it out.

Sasagaki glanced at the little sign that read SQUID: FORTY YEN and took out a few coins.

'Thanks,' the woman grunted cheerily before sitting back down with her newspaper.

Sasagaki was walking away when another woman stopped to say hello to the squid lady. A housewife from the neighbourhood, a backward glance told him. He paused. She was carrying a shopping basket in one hand.

'What do you think it is? Must be something big,' the housewife said, pointing towards the abandoned building.

'Never seen so many cop cars around here,' the squid lady noted. 'Maybe some kid got hurt.'

Sasagaki turned around. 'Sorry, did you say "kid"?'

'Oh, they were always playing in there. I said it a thousand times, sooner or later one of 'em's going to get hurt, and it looks like I was right. Unless you heard different?'

Sasagaki ignored the question. 'Why would kids be playing in a place like that?'

'Why do kids play anywhere?' The squid lady shrugged. 'I always said someone should do something about it. It's not safe.'

Sasagaki finished off his squid and started towards the building, just another guy going to join the crowd of onlookers.

He ducked beneath the rope some uniformed officers had stretched across the front of the building. One of the officers glared at him, but backed down when Sasagaki patted his jacket over the pocket where every detective kept his badge.

Sasagaki went in to the foyer through a gap in the makeshift doors of plywood and scrap lumber. He'd expected it to be pretty dark inside and he was right; the air was heavy with mould and dust. He stood, blinking, hearing voices nearby.

Eventually his eyes adjusted and Sasagaki realised he was standing in what would have been an elevator bank. Two elevator doors stood off to the right behind a pile of loose construction materials and tangled electrical wires.

Straight ahead of him was a wall with a square, unfinished hole in it for a doorway. The blackness beyond was too dark to penetrate, but Sasagaki guessed he was looking at what would have been a car park.

There was a room to the left, set with another temporary plywood door, the words NO TRESPASSING scrawled on it in chalk. The door opened and two familiar faces emerged, both of them detectives in his unit.

'Hey. Enjoying your day off?' the older detective, a man by the name of Kobayashi, said. He was two years Sasagaki's senior. The younger man, Detective Koga, had joined Homicide less than a year before.

'I had a bad feeling when I woke up this morning,' Sasagaki said. 'Wish I'd been wrong for a change.' He lowered his voice. 'How's the old man's mood?'

Kobayashi frowned and shook his head. Koga gave a wry smile.

'That's what I figured,' Sasagaki said. 'Well, no rest for the wicked. What's he up to in there?'

'Dr Matsuno just got here.'

'Right.'

Kobayashi cleared his throat. 'We're going to take a look around outside, OK?'

'Have at it.'

Sasagaki watched the two leave. *Sent out to do questioning, no doubt.* Putting on his gloves, he slowly opened the door. The room was sizeable, a little over twenty square metres. Thanks to the sunlight slanting in through the windows it wasn't as dim in here.

Detectives stood in a huddle in the shadow opposite the windows. There were a few faces he didn't recognise, probably people from the local station. The others he knew all too well. Was tired of seeing them, to be honest. The first to acknowledge him was Captain Nakatsuka. He had a buzz cut and wire-frame glasses with the top half of each lens tinted light purple. The deep wrinkles between his eyebrows never went away, even when he smiled.

No greetings or jibes about being late. Nakatsuka just motioned him over with a jerk of his jaw. A sofa upholstered with black suede had been pushed up against the wall. It was big enough to seat three adults, if they were friendly.

The body was lying on the sofa. Male.

Dr Hideomi Matsuno of Kinki University was in the process of examining the body. He had been a medical examiner in Osaka for more than twenty years.

Sasagaki craned his neck to take a look at the corpse.

Age, he guessed, was about mid-forties, maybe fifty. Height, just shy of one seventy metres, and a little plump for that. He was wearing a brown jacket, but no tie. Designer clothes, top-of-the-line and impeccable save for the wine-red bloodstain on his chest that had spread to about ten centimetres in diameter. There were a few other stab wounds, but nothing else bleeding much.

It didn't look as if there had been a struggle. His jacket was in order and his hair, drawn back into a knot behind his head, wasn't dishevelled in the least.

The diminutive Dr Matsuno stood and turned to the huddle of detectives. 'Well, it's a homicide. Stab wounds in five places. Two on the chest, three on the shoulder. The only fatal one was here, on the lower left chest, several centimetres left of the sternum. The weapon passed between the ribs, straight into the heart. A single thrust.'

'He died immediately?' Nakatsuka had asked the question.

'Within a minute, tops. Haemorrhaging from a coronary artery put pressure on the heart. Classic case of cardiac tamponade is my guess.'

'Any blood splatter on the killer?'

'I doubt there was much.'

'And the murder weapon?'

The doctor stuck out his lower lip and shrugged. 'Something thin and sharp—a blade. Maybe a little thinner than your average fruit knife. I can tell you right now it wasn't a cleaver or any of your typical survival knives.'

'Time of death?' Sasagaki asked.

'You've got rigor mortis over the entire body, lividity has settled nicely, corneas are opaque. I would say anywhere between seventeen hours to an entire day. You'll have to wait for the autopsy to get any closer than that.'

Sasagaki looked down at his watch. It was two-forty, meaning the victim had been killed between three in the afternoon and ten at night on the previous day.

'Well, let's get the autopsy going,' Nakatsuka said.

'Works for me,' Dr Matsuno agreed.

Koga came in and announced, 'The wife's here.'

'Took her long enough,' Nakatsuka grunted. 'Let's get her to ID him now, then. Bring her in.' Koga nodded and went back outside.

Sasagaki leaned over to one of the other detectives in the huddle and whispered, 'How'd they know who he was?'

'He was carrying his driver's licence and a business card. Runs – ran a local pawnshop.'

'Pawnshop? They take anything from him?'

'Don't know. They can't find a wallet, though.'

There was a noise by the door and Koga ushered in the widow. The detectives took a few steps back from the body on the sofa.

The woman's checked black and burnt-orange dress made the room seem several shades darker. Her high heels must have been nearly ten centimetres and her long hair was set in a perfect perm, as though she had just stepped out of the beauty salon.

Large eyes, lined with thick eyeshadow, turned towards the sofa along the wall. She brought both hands to her mouth and made a noise like a hiccup. For a few seconds she didn't move at all. Finally, she took a few hesitant steps towards the body. Stopping just in front of the sofa, she looked down at the man's face. Sasagaki could see her chin tremble slightly.

'Is that your husband, ma'am?' Nakatsuka asked.

She didn't answer, just cradled her cheeks in her hands, then gradually slid her hands up to cover her face before her knees buckled and she crumpled on the floor. A bit put on, Sasagaki thought. Then came the sobs, muffled through her long fingers.

Yosuke Kirihara was the deceased's name, proprietor of the unsurprisingly named Kirihara Pawnshop. The shop, which also served as a home, was about a kilometre away from the building where his body had been found.

They carried the body out immediately after the widow, Yaeko, made the ID. Sasagaki was helping the Department of Criminal Identification guys get the body on the stretcher when something caught his eye. 'Think our boy had been out eating?'

'What makes you say that?' Detective Koga raised one eyebrow.

Sasagaki pointed to the victim's belt. 'His belt's fastened two holes wider than he usually fastens it.'

'Hey, you're right.'

Mr Kirihara had been wearing a brown Valentino belt with clear buckle marks near the fifth hole from the end, which was slightly widened from use. But now the belt had been loosened to the third hole from the end.

Sasagaki had one of the young Criminal Identification officers take a photo of the belt and, once the scene had been cleared, the detectives spread out to start questioning the neighbours, leaving only Criminal Identification, Sasagaki, and Captain Nakatsuka inside.

Nakatsuka stood in the centre of the room, taking another look around. He'd assumed his customary deep-thought posture: left hand on his waist, right hand to his forehead. 'Sasagaki,' he said. 'What do you make of it? What kind of killer we looking at here?'

'Haven't the faintest idea,' Sasagaki replied with a shrug. 'Except, whoever it was, the victim knew him.' The tidiness of the man's clothes and hair, the lack of any signs of a struggle and the frontal stab wound told him that much.

'So the question is: what were they doing in a place like this?'

Sasagaki went around the room again, scanning the floors and wall. It seemed like it had served as a temporary office while the building was under construction. The black sofa the body had been lying on was probably left over from that. There was also a steel desk, two folding chairs and a meeting table with folding legs left abandoned against the wall. The exposed metal was rusting, and a thick, floury layer of dust covered everything. Construction had stopped two and a half years ago.

Sasagaki's gaze stopped on the wall above and to the side of the black sofa where a square hole for some kind of duct opened just below the ceiling. Normally the duct would have been covered with a grating, but that had been removed, if it had ever been put on in the first place.

If hadn't been for the duct, they might not have discovered the body until much later. According to the local detectives, the kid who found the body was a third-grader from the neighbourhood elementary school. After Saturday classes ended at noon, the boy and four of his classmates had come to the building – not to play dodgeball or tag, but to explore the building's labyrinthine ventilation ducts. Sasagaki had to agree that crawling on all fours through the narrow, twisting passages would probably seem like a grand adventure to a boy.

Apparently, at some point along the way, one of them had taken a wrong turn. Separated from the other boys, he had crawled blindly through the ducts, panicking, until he eventually reached the abandoned office. At first, the boy had thought the man on the sofa was sleeping. He'd crept out of the air duct as quietly as he could so as not to wake him and the man hadn't moved at all. He'd gingerly stepped closer and that was when he saw the blood.

The boy had run home and told his family at about one in the afternoon. It took another twenty minutes or so until his mother actually believed him. The record showed that her phone call to the station came at 1.33 p.m.

'A pawnbroker, huh?' Nakatsuka said suddenly. 'You think the job requires meeting someone in a place like this?'

'If it was someone who didn't want to be seen, or someone he didn't want to be seen with.'

'Could be, but why here? If he wanted to meet someone in secret, there are all sorts of places he could've gone. And if he was worried about prying eyes, why not pick a place farther from home?'

'True.' Sasagaki rubbed his chin. He could feel stubble against his palm. He had rushed out of the house this morning without time to shave.

'His wife was something, though.' Nakatsuka changed the subject. 'He was fifty-two and she was ... what? Just over thirty? Practically a girl when they would've met.'

'A working girl,' Sasagaki muttered quietly.

Nakatsuka shook his head. 'She had the make-up for it. Done up to the nines, and this place is hardly a stone's throw from her house. And how 'bout that performance?'

'You saying her tears were as fake as her lashes?'

'Your words, not mine,' Nakatsuka smiled, then his face went hard. 'They should be done questioning. Sasagaki, you mind seeing her home?'

'Sure thing.' Sasagaki gave a light bow of his head and headed for the door.

Most of the onlookers outside had gone, replaced by a gaggle of newspaper reporters. It looked like one of the television stations was there, too.

Sasagaki glanced over the parked police vehicles and spotted Yaeko Kirihara in the back seat of the second car from the front. Kobayashi was sitting next to her and Koga was in the passenger seat. Sasagaki walked over and rapped on the rear door window. Kobayashi opened the door and stepped out.

'How's it going?'

'We've gone over pretty much everything. Honestly, she's still a little ruffled,' Kobayashi said, covering his mouth with his hand.

'Did you have her check his belongings?'

'I did. Wallet's missing. And a lighter.'

'She remembered a missing lighter?'

'A Dunhill. They're expensive.'

Sasagaki grunted. 'When's the last time she saw him?'

'He left the house some time between two and three yesterday. Didn't say where he was going. She got worried when he didn't come back in the morning and was about to call the police when she got the call they'd found him.'

'Anything about someone inviting him out?'

'She doesn't know. Says she can't remember if there was a phone call before he left the house, either.'

'Anything unusual about him when he left?'

'Nothing out of the ordinary.'

Sasagaki scratched his chin. There was nothing here to go on. Nothing at all. 'I figure she doesn't have any guesses who it might be?'

Kobayashi frowned and shook his head.

'She know anything about the building?'

'Asked that. She knew it was here but had no idea what kind of place it was. She says this was her first time in it today, and she'd never heard her husband talk about it before.'

Sasagaki smiled wryly. 'Well, we established a whole lot that didn't happen.'

'Sorry.'

'Nothing to apologise about.' Sasagaki rapped the younger detective on the chest with the back of his hand. 'I'll take her on home. You don't mind if I borrow Koga to drive?'

'No problem.'

Sasagaki got into the back of the car with the widow and told Koga to head for the Kirihara place. 'Drive around for a little while first. Don't want the press picking up on location.'

Koga nodded and took off.

Turning to Yaeko, Sasagaki introduced himself. Her only reply was to nod, apparently uninterested in learning the detective's name.

'So no one's at your house now?'

'Just someone watching the shop. And my son should be back from school,' she said, looking down at the floor of the car.

'You have a son? How old?'

'He's in fifth grade.'

That would make him ten or eleven. Sasagaki looked back at Yaeko. She had done her best to cover it up with make-up, but her skin was rough, and some wrinkles were noticeable. It wouldn't be unusual for her to have a son that age.

'I heard that your husband went out without saying anything yesterday? Was that a frequent occurrence?'

'Sure. But just for drinks, most times. I assumed that's what he was up to yesterday, and didn't pay it much mind.'

'And staying out all night? Did that happen sometimes?'

'On the rare occasion.'

'And he wouldn't call, even when he stayed out?'

'Hardly. Oh, I asked him to call plenty of times, but he'd just say "yeah yeah". I guess I'd got used to it. Still, I never – I never thought ...' Yaeko pressed her hand to her mouth.

After they had driven around for a while, they stopped next to a telephone pole with a street sign that read ŌE 3. It was a narrow street with terraced houses lining either side.

'It's right up there,' Koga said, pointing ahead through the windscreen. About twenty metres in front of the car Sasagaki saw the sign for the Kirihara Pawnshop. The street was empty. The media obviously hadn't figured out who the victim was yet.

'I'll take her in, you can head back,' Sasagaki said as he stepped out of the car.

The corrugated shutter at the front of the shop was lowered down to the height of Sasagaki's chin. He ducked under and went inside after Yaeko. The entrance was lined on either side with display cases. The name 'Kirihara' was written in gold brushstrokes across the frosted glass of the door.

Yaeko opened it and went inside. Sasagaki followed.

'Hey there,' the man at the front counter said when they walked in. He was around forty years old, slender build, with a pointed chin. His hair was black and perfectly combed into a parting on one side.

Yaeko gave a little sigh and sat down in what Sasagaki assumed was a chair for customers.

'Well?' The man looked between Sasagaki and Yaeko.

Yaeko put a hand to her forehead. 'It was him.'

'What?' The man's face darkened. 'He was killed?'

She nodded her head and mumbled yes.

'That's crazy!' The man shook his head in astonishment. He looked off to one side, blinking, collecting his thoughts.

'Sasagaki, Osaka PD. I'm sorry for your loss.' He showed the man his badge. 'You work here?'

'Yeah, um, here.' The man opened the drawer and handed over a business card.

Sasagaki bowed his head and took the card. He noticed that the man was wearing a platinum ring on the pinky of his right hand. Flashy for a guy.

The card said the man's name was Isamu Matsuura, the manager.

'You been here long?' Sasagaki asked.

'Yeah. About five years, I guess.'

That didn't seem like very long to Sasagaki. He wanted to ask the guy where he had worked before, how he'd got the job, but decided to leave that be for today at least. He would be back soon enough. Probably more than once.

'I heard that Mr Kirihara went out yesterday afternoon?'

'That's right. Around two-thirty, I'd say.'

'And he didn't give any indication of where he was going?'

'Nope. He likes to do things on his own, rarely talks to us about anything to do with work.'

'And you didn't notice anything unusual about him when he went out? Was he dressed differently, carrying anything out of the ordinary?'

'Not that I noticed.' Matsuura shrugged and gave the back of his neck a scratch. 'Though he did seem to be concerned about the time.'

'How so?'

'Well, I thought I saw him check his watch. But maybe I'm just imagining that.'

Sasagaki took a cursory look around the shop. Behind where Matsuura stood was a sliding screen door, tightly closed. That would be the living room. There was a place to take off your shoes to the left of the counter, in front of a short hallway leading into the residential part of the building. There was a door on the left wall just inside the hallway, which struck Sasagaki as possibly a storage closet, though the placement was a bit odd.

'How late were you open yesterday?'

'Well,' Matsuura took a look at the big round clock on the wall. 'We usually close at six, but I think we didn't really have everything done until seven or so.'

'And you were the only one manning the shop?'

'Yeah, that's pretty typical when the boss is out.'

'What did you do after closing?'

'I went right home.'

'Where's that?'

'Over in Teradacho.'

'That's a bit of a hike. You come by car?'

'No, I take the train.'

Even considering time for changing trains, it would take about thirty minutes to get from here to Teradacho. Leaving the shop by seven would get him home by eight, at the latest.

'Any family, Mr Matsuura?'

'No, it's just me. Got divorced six years ago, so I'm going it alone. Got an apartment.'

'And yesterday, after you got home, you were alone?'

'Yeah.'

No alibi, Sasagaki noted, but he kept his face blank.

'So, you're not often watching the shop?' Sasagaki asked, this time turning to Yaeko, who was still sitting, a hand pressed to her forehead.

'I wouldn't have the slightest clue what to do,' she said in a thin voice.

'Were you out yesterday?'

'No, I was home all day.'

'You didn't step out for anything? Shopping, maybe?'

She shook her head. Then she stood, weakly. 'If you don't mind, I'd like to lie down for a bit. It's hard even just sitting up.'

'Of course. You go right ahead.'

Yaeko took off her shoes, nearly stumbling, and opened the door to the left. Sasagaki saw a staircase beyond it. One mystery solved, he thought. She closed the door and he heard her ascending the steps. When he could hear her footsteps no longer, Sasagaki took a step closer to Matsuura. 'When you heard that Mr Kirihara hadn't come home, was that this morning?'

'Yeah. Me and his missus were worried. Then we got that call.'

'That must've been quite a shock.'

'Of course, yeah. Tell you the truth, I still don't believe it. I mean, who would kill the boss? Maybe it was a mistake?'

'Can't think of anyone who might've wanted to do something like this?'

'Not a one.'

'In this line of business, you must get a lot of different kinds of customers. You're sure there wasn't anyone with a bone to pick? Maybe about money?'

'Well, we have some strange customers, that's true. People blame their troubles on us when we're the ones loaning *them* money. But none of them strike me as the killing sort.' Matsuura shook his head. 'I can't think of anyone who would do something like that.'

'I understand you want to look out for your clients, but it's important for our investigation that we look into any possibility, no matter how slight. I was hoping you could show me a list of your recent customers?'

The man gave a weak frown. 'A list?'

'You must have something. How else would you know who you'd loaned money to? Keep track of your collateral?'

'Yeah, we got a ledger.'

'Think you could let me take a look? I'll take it back to the station, have them make a copy, and bring it right back. You have my word no one else will see it but us.'

'I'm not sure I got the authority ...'

'I'll be happy to wait while you get permission from Mrs Kirihara.'

Matsuura frowned for a little while before finally nodding. 'All right. I'll let you have it, but please, be careful with it, OK?'

'Thank you. You sure you don't need her permission?'

'It's fine. I'll tell her later. It's not like I'm going to get in trouble with the boss.'

Matsuura swivelled his chair ninety degrees and opened the door of the cabinet next to his knee. Sasagaki saw several thick files standing on end. He was leaning forward to take a closer look when, out of the corner of his eye, he saw the door to the stairs open. Sasagaki froze.

A boy of about ten years old was standing in the doorway. A skinny kid, in a sweatshirt and jeans.

Sasagaki hadn't heard the boy on the stairs at all. When their eyes met, the darkness deep in the boy's eyes made Sasagaki swallow.

'You Mr Kirihara's boy?' he asked.

The boy didn't respond. Instead, Matsuura looked around and said, 'Yeah, that's him.'

Still without a word, the boy stepped out into the shop and began putting on his sneakers. His face was expressionless.

'Where you going, Ryo?' Matsuura asked. 'You should stay home.'

The boy ignored him and walked out.

'Poor kid. I can't imagine what he's going through,' Sasagaki said.

'Yeah,' the man agreed. 'Even a kid like that, it's gotta be tough.'

'A kid like what?'

'Er, it's hard to explain,' Matsuura pulled one of the files from the cabinet and placed it on the counter in front of Sasagaki. 'Here you go. The latest ledger.'

'Thanks.' Sasagaki took it and flipped through the pages of men and women, skimming down through the list of names, but all he could see were the boy's dark eyes.

The autopsy report arrived at Homicide the following afternoon.

The time and cause of death matched what Dr Matsuno had said at the scene, but the contents of the stomach gave Sasagaki pause. There were undigested remains of buckwheat, onions and herring, consumed two to two and a half hours prior to death.

'If that's true, what are we to make of the belt?' Sasagaki asked Nakatsuka, who was sitting nearby with his arms crossed.

'The belt?'

'Yeah, it had been loosened two notches. Like you do after eating a big meal. But this was two hours later. Wouldn't he have tightened it back up?'

Nakatsuka shrugged. 'I don't see what's noteworthy about that. Maybe he just forgot.'

'That's the thing,' Sasagaki said. 'When we checked out his pants, it turned out they were big in the waist for a man his size. If he loosened his buckle two notches, they would've been slipping when he walked.'

Nakatsuka's eyebrows knit together as he glanced at the autopsy report on the conference table. 'So why do *you* think he loosened his belt?'

Sasagaki took a look around the room before leaning in closer.

'Because the victim had some business there that required him loosening his belt. Then, when he tightened it back up, he missed the usual spot. Of course, we don't know if it was him tightening it or his killer.'

'What business would require him to loosen his belt, exactly?' Nakatsuka looked up innocently.

'C'mon. He was dropping his trousers.' Sasagaki grinned.

Nakatsuka leaned back in his chair with the sound of squeaking metal.

'You suggesting a grown man would go to some place that dirty and dusty just to squeeze some titties?'

'I admit it wouldn't be my first choice,' Sasagaki said.

Nakatsuka waved a hand like he was swatting away a fly. 'It's an interesting story, but I think you're letting your gut get ahead of your evidence. We need to find out where the victim was before he got killed. There was buckwheat in his stomach? I'd check the local soba places first.'

'Yes sir,' Sasagaki said, turning to leave the room.

It didn't take long to find the soba shop Yosuke Kirihara had visited that day. According to Yaeko, he frequented a place by the name of Saganoya on the shopping street near the train station. A detective paid the shop a visit and was able to find a witness who could place Mr Kirihara there around four in the afternoon on Friday. He'd eaten the herring soba. Calculating back from the state of digestion put the time of death between six and seven in the evening. That meant they would be looking at the time period from five to eight for establishing alibis.

However, there was the statement from Matsuura and Yaeko that the deceased had left the pawnshop at two-thirty. That left the hour or so before he arrived at Saganoya unaccounted for. The walk from his house to the restaurant was only ten minutes, even at a leisurely pace.

The answer to that question came on Monday, with a single phone call to the police station from a female employee of the local Sankyo Bank branch. Apparently Yosuke Kirihara had visited the bank before closing hours on Friday.

Sasagaki and Koga went out to the bank, located across the street from the south side of the train station.

The woman who'd called was a cashier with a short fringe complementing a round, cheery face. She sat down with the detectives at a meeting table usually reserved for discussing customer accounts. It was separated from the rest of the bank floor by some free-standing dividers.

'When I saw his name in the paper the other day I wondered if it was the same Kirihara I knew. So I checked the name again when I came in this morning and got permission from my boss to give you a call,' she told the detectives, sitting with her back perfectly straight.

'Around what time did Mr Kirihara come to the bank?' Sasagaki asked.

'A little before three.'

'What did he come about?'

Here, she hesitated slightly before she was able to overcome her instinctive reluctance to reveal customer information. 'He closed out a CD account and withdrew the money.'

'How much?'

She hesitated again, wetting her lips. She glanced at her boss out of the corner of one eye and said in a quiet voice, 'Exactly one million yen.'

Sasagaki's eyes widened. It wasn't the kind of money one typically walked around with.

'And he didn't say anything about how he was going to use the money?'

'No, I'm afraid not.'

'Did you see what he did with the money? Did he put it away somewhere?'

'Not exactly. I know I handed it to him inside a bank envelope, but other than that ...' She frowned, trying to remember.

'Had Mr Kirihara done anything of the sort before? Closed accounts with a lot of money in them?'

'No, not as far as I know. I've been in charge of his accounts since the end of last year.'

'How did he seem to you when he took the money out? Was he unhappy about anything, or possibly excited?'

She frowned again. 'He didn't look too distraught, no. In fact, I think he said something about coming back to make a deposit soon.'

After reporting back to headquarters, Sasagaki and Koga paid a visit to the pawnshop to ask Yaeko and Matsuura whether they knew anything about the money Kirihara had withdrawn. But they were still a block away when they stopped. They could just see the front of the shop, and the long line of mourners gathered on the road outside.

'Oh, right.' Sasagaki sighed. 'The funeral's today.'

The two detectives watched the shop from a distance. Yaeko appeared at the door at the head of the procession that would carry the casket out to the waiting hearse. Her complexion didn't look as good as it had the first time Sasagaki met her and she seemed smaller, physically, yet at the same time somehow even more alluring. *The strange attraction of a woman in mourning*, Sasagaki thought.

Yaeko was clearly accustomed to wearing kimonos. Even her footsteps seemed calculated to make her look good. *If she's trying to play the part of the beautiful young widow, she's doing a knockout job.* Their investigation had already revealed that she'd once worked as an escort over in the nightclub district in Kitashinchi.

From behind, her son appeared, carrying a framed photograph of his father. *Ryo, that was his name.* Sasagaki had yet to exchange words with the boy.

Ryo's expression was as blank as the last time the detective had seen him. There was no trace of emotion in his dark, sunken eyes. They looked like eyes made of glass, vacantly following the motion of his mother's feet.

The detectives waited until evening before trying the pawnshop again. As before, the metal shutter in front of the store was half-closed when they arrived. This time, however, the door behind it was locked. Sasagaki tried the doorbell. He could hear the sound of a buzzer from inside the shop.

'Think they're out?' Koga asked.

'If they were, wouldn't they have put the shutter down all the way?'

Finally, they heard the sound of the door being unlocked. It opened slightly and Matsuura stuck his head out. 'Detective!'

'We had a few questions,' Sasagaki said. 'Is now a good time?'

'Let me check with Mrs Kirihara. Be right back.' He shut the door behind him.

The two detectives exchanged glances.

A few moments passed until the door opened again and Matsuura welcomed them inside. Sasagaki stepped in first. He could smell the scent of funeral incense in the air.

'The funeral go OK?' Sasagaki asked. He'd spotted Matsuura in the circle of casket-bearers.

'Yeah, we got through it somehow. I'm pretty beat, though,' he said, smoothing back his hair. He was still in a black suit, but he had removed his tie. The top two buttons of his shirt were undone.

The door behind the shop counter slid open and Yacko emerged. She'd changed from her mourning clothes into a navy blue dress and let down her hair.

'Sorry to trouble you after the day you've had,' Sasagaki said.

She shook her head. 'Have you found anything out?'

'We're still gathering information. Actually, we came across something I wanted to check with you. Although' – Sasagaki pointed towards the door behind her – 'if you don't mind, I'd like to offer some incense. Always good to give the Buddha his due.'

Yaeko looked startled for a moment and glanced at Matsuura before saying, 'Of course, I don't mind at all.'

'Thank you, I'll only be a moment.'

Sasagaki took off his shoes and stepped up to the raised floor behind the counter. His eyes darted towards the door off to the side, the one that hid the stairs going up to the first floor. There was a small bolt lock on the door and it was pulled shut, making it impossible to open from the other side.

'Excuse the odd question,' Sasagaki said, 'but what's that locked for?'

'Oh,' Yaeko said, 'that's to stop thieves from coming in through the top floor at night.'

'Pardon, the top floor?'

'The houses in this part of town are so close together, they jump from roof to roof. A watch-seller nearby us had it happen to him not so long ago. My husband put the lock on.'

'I take it there's nothing of value upstairs, then?'

'The safe is down here,' Matsuura said from behind him. 'And we keep everything from our customers down here, too.'

'Does that mean no one is upstairs at night?'

'No, we sleep downstairs,' Yaeko said.

'I see,' Sasagaki said, scratching his chin. 'And you always lock it this early in the evening?'

'Oh, no,' Yaeko said, coming up beside him and unlocking the door. 'I just locked it out of habit earlier.'

Which means no one's upstairs, Sasagaki thought.

He opened the sliding door in front of him to find a small room with a tatami-matted floor. There seemed to be another room behind that, hidden behind another sliding door. *The downstairs bedroom*, Sasagaki thought. He didn't imagine much happened in there other than sleeping, especially with Ryo sharing the same room.

The family altar was up against the western wall. Yosuke Kirihara smiled out of a small frame set to one side. The photo was of him at a younger age, wearing a suit. Sasagaki lit a stick of incense and placed it in the tray on the altar. He pressed his hands together and sat with his eyes closed for a full ten seconds.

Yaeko came with tea. Still on his knees, Sasagaki bowed his head and thanked her for the tea. Next to him, Koga took his own cup.

Sasagaki asked Yaeko if anything had occurred to her about the case or the events of the day her husband died. She shook her head immediately. Seated out in the shop, Matsuura was quiet, too.

Gradually, Sasagaki swung the conversation around to the topic of the million yen Kirihara had taken out of the bank. Yaeko and Matsuura both looked surprised at this.

'He didn't say anything to me about one million yen,' Yaeko said.

'I didn't hear anything about that either,' Matsuura said. 'The boss took care of most of the business side of things, but if he was dealing with something that big, I think he would've at least mentioned it.'

'Did your husband spend any money on entertainment? Anything potentially expensive, like gambling?'

'No,' Yaeko said, 'he never gambled. He didn't really have any hobbies to speak of.'

'Work was his hobby,' Matsuura added from the side.

'Right, well then ...' Sasagaki hesitated a moment before asking, 'How about any ... other kinds of ... entertainment.'

'I'm sorry?' Yaeko frowned.

'Basically, what I mean is, women. Did he go out to clubs, anything like that?'

Yaeko nodded, understanding. Sasagaki had feared he might be touching a nerve, but that didn't seem to be the case at all.

'I don't think he had a woman on the side, if that's what you mean. He wasn't the kind to be able to do that sort of thing.' She sounded very sure of herself.

'So you trusted him, in other words?'

'I wouldn't call it that ...' Yaeko said, her words trailing off as she looked down at the floor.

Sasagaki asked a few other questions before standing to go. He hated to leave empty-handed, but there didn't seem to be much else here for them at present.

As he was putting on his shoes, he noticed a pair of scuffed sneakers off to one side of the door. *They must belong to Ryo, which means he's home ...*

Sasagaki glanced at the door with its sliding lock, and wondered what the boy was doing upstairs, all alone.

The continuing investigation gradually revealed the path Yosuke Kirihara had taken on the afternoon of his death. Already established was his departure from home at two-thirty, followed by a trip to Sankyo Bank near the station to withdraw the one million yen, then a late lunch at Saganoya where he ate the herring noodles. He'd left Saganoya just after four.

At issue was what happened next. An employee at the shop was under the impression that Kirihara had walked, not towards, but away from the station when he left. If he hadn't come to the vicinity of the station to get on a train, then his only other reason for being there would have been to get the money.

The investigation team began questioning people in two areas: around the station, and near the building where the body had been found. The station team was the first to find anything.

A customer matching Kirihara's description had visited a local cake shop called Harmony. There he had asked for 'that pudding with lots of fruit on it,' the employee reported, by which he'd meant Pudding à la Mode, a speciality of the chain. However, as it happened, they were all out of Pudding à la Mode that day. The customer had asked if there were any other shops where he might get something similar nearby.

The employee had directed him to another branch of the same shop in town, showing him the location on a map.

'That's right next to where I'm headed,' Kirihara was reported to have said. 'I wish I'd asked sooner.'

The other Harmony in question was located in West Ōe 6. A visit confirmed that someone matching Kirihara's description had come to the shop in the early evening on Friday. He'd purchased three Puddings à la Mode, but the employee wasn't sure what for, or where he'd gone after that.

The purchase revealed two things to the investigation team: one, Kirihara was going to meet someone, and two, that someone was most likely a woman. Finally, a name surfaced: Fumiyo Nishimoto – the only female customer on the ledger at Kirihara Pawnshop with an address near the cake shop.

Sasagaki and Koga went to pay Fumiyo a visit.

Her apartment building, a squat two-storey affair with a sign that read YOSHIDA HEIGHTS, stood in a cluster of small houses that looked as if they had been thrown together from corrugated tin siding and whatever lumber happened to be lying around at the time. Black splotches marked the building's sooty grey walls and serpentine lines of concrete had been plastered over the many cracks.

Fumiyo's unit was listed in the ledger as No 103. The walkway leading down the line of ground floor apartments was dim and dank – open on one side to the air, but too close to the neighbours to get any sunlight. A rusted bicycle was parked at the corner of the building, half-blocking the entrance.

Avoiding the washing machines that squatted outside each doorway, Sasagaki looked for Fumiyo's unit. He found a piece of paper tacked to the wall beside the third door down, on which 'Nishimoto' had been written in permanent marker. He knocked.

'Yes,' came a girl's voice from inside. The door didn't open. 'Who is it?'

'Is your mom home?' Sasagaki asked through the door.

There was no answer until the voice said again, 'Who is it?'

Sasagaki looked at Koga and smiled wryly. Clearly the girl had been told not to open the door to strangers – a practice he normally would have applauded, except right now it was interfering with his investigation.

Sasagaki kept his voice loud enough that the girl could hear, but hopefully not the neighbours. 'We're with the police. We have some questions for your mother.'

Silence.

By her voice, Sasagaki pegged her as a pre-teen, maybe in middle school or about to finish elementary school. He could imagine her freezing when she heard the word 'police'.

Then came the sound of the door being unlocked. It opened, but the chain was still on. Through the narrow gap he saw a girl's face with wide eyes. Her skin was remarkably white and as smooth as porcelain.

'My mother's not home yet,' she said, a tone in her voice that put Sasagaki in mind of words like 'resolute'.

'Out shopping, maybe?'

'No, she's at work.'

'What time does she usually come home?' Sasagaki asked, glancing at his watch. It was just past five.

'Any time now,' the girl told him.

'Right,' Sasagaki said. 'We'll just wait outside, then.'

The girl nodded and shut the door. Sasagaki reached inside his jacket pocket and pulled out his cigarettes. 'Kid's got a good head on her shoulders,' he said in a low voice.

'I'd agree,' Koga said. 'That, and—'

He was about to say something else when the door opened again, this time without the chain.

'Could you show me your police thingy?' the girl asked.

Sasagaki blinked. 'Sorry, my what?'

'Your badge.'

'Oh, right.' He smiled. 'Here,' he said, holding out his badge displayed in his wallet, next to a photo ID.

The girl looked between the photograph and Sasagaki's face for a moment before saying, 'You can come in.' She opened the door.

'No, that's OK,' Sasagaki said, a little surprised. 'We're fine outside.'

The girl shook her head. 'The neighbours will wonder.'

Sasagaki glanced at Koga. He resisted the urge to grin.

The detectives stepped inside. As Sasagaki had guessed it was a small apartment for a family. The room beyond the door was a tiny kitchen-diner with a wooden floor and a small sink. Behind that was another room, only slightly larger, floored with tatami mats.

The girl offered the detectives a seat at the simple table in the front room. There were only two chairs. The pink-and-white checked tablecloth was plastic, with cigarette burns near the edge.

After the detectives had sat down the girl went into the back room and sat up against a closed closet door, where she began reading a book. There was a white label on the cover, indicating it was from a library.

'What're you reading?' Koga asked. She held the book up so he could see. He smiled. 'That's quite the book for someone your age.'

'What is it?' Sasagaki asked him.

'*Gone With the Wind*.'

Sasagaki nodded, impressed. 'I saw the movie.'

'Me too,' Koga said. 'It was pretty good. Never even occurred to me to read the book.'

'I don't read much these days myself.'

'You and me both. Not even manga, not since *Ashita no Joe* ended.'

'What, Joe's already done?'

'Yeah, back in May. Now that *Star of the Giants* is done too I'm all out of reading material.'

'It's just as well. Grown men shouldn't go around reading manga.'

'I guess.' Koga shrugged.

The girl didn't even look up from her book while the detectives chatted. It was as if she'd sensed that they were just saying whatever came to mind in order to fill the silence.

The thought must have occurred to Koga, too, because he said nothing further. Presently he began rapping his fingers restlessly on the table but stopped at a withering glance from the girl.

Sasagaki busied himself looking around the house. Furniture and appliances had been kept to a bare minimum. There was nothing that could be considered a luxury item in the place. There wasn't even a desk for studying or bookshelves. A small television sat by the window, but it was incredibly old, with a little bunny-ear antenna on top. He imagined it was probably a black-and-white set, one of the ones where, even after you turned on the switch, it took forever for the picture to come on. When it did, there were jagged lines across everything.

It wasn't just the lack of material possessions. The place seemed unusually austere for a house with a little girl living in it. The fluorescent lights on the ceiling were old, but even that didn't fully explain the bleak mood.

Two cardboard boxes were stacked right next to where Sasagaki was sitting. He pried open the lid of the top box with his fingertips, taking a peek inside. It was filled to the brim with rubber frogs. They were the kind that had a little tail you could squeeze to make the legs inflate, making the frog 'jump'. He'd seen them for sale at stalls during street festivals.

'What's your name, miss?' Sasagaki asked the girl. Normally he wouldn't use 'miss' when talking to a schoolchild, but for her it seemed appropriate.

'Yukiho Nishimoto,' the girl said, her eyes never leaving her book.

'Yukiho? How do you write that?'

'The characters for snow and ear, like an ear of rice.'

'Nice,' Sasagaki said. 'That's a nice name, isn't it?' He looked over at his partner.

Koga nodded. The girl continued reading.

'Have you ever heard of a shop called Kirihara?' Sasagaki asked. 'It's a pawnshop.'

Yukiho didn't answer right away. Then she licked her lips and said, 'My mom goes there sometimes.'

'Have you ever met the man who runs the shop?'

'I have.'

'Has he ever come here?'

Yukiho frowned. 'I think so,' she said.

'But not when you were home, is that it?'

'He might have. I don't really remember.'

'Any idea why he visited?'

'No.'

Sasagaki reconsidered questioning the girl right now. He had a feeling this would be only the first of many opportunities he would have to talk to her. He resumed looking around the room. He wasn't looking for anything in particular, but his eyes widened a little when he saw the waste basket next to the refrigerator. It was filled to the brim, and perched on top was some packaging paper with a mark on it from Harmony, the cake shop.

Sasagaki looked over at the girl. Their eyes met but she quickly went back to reading her book. He had the distinct impression that she'd been looking at the rubbish, too.

A short while later the girl looked up again. Then she closed her book and walked past them towards the door.

Sasagaki perked up his ears. He heard footsteps, sandals dragging across the ground. Koga's mouth opened slightly.

The footsteps approached the door and stopped. There was the sound of a key in the lock.

'It's open,' Yukiho called out.

'Why didn't you lock it? It's not safe,' said a voice as the door opened. A woman wearing a turquoise blouse came in. She looked in her mid-thirties, with her hair in a bun behind her head.

Fumiyo Nishimoto noticed the detectives immediately. She quickly looked between her daughter and the strange men in shock.

'It's OK, they're police,' the girl said.

'Police?' An unguarded look of fear washed over Fumiyo's face.

'Sasagaki, Osaka Police,' Sasagaki said, standing. 'This is my partner, Koga.'

Fumiyo was noticeably taken aback. Her face had gone pale, and she was clearly unsure what to do. She stood with a paper bag in her hand, the door still hanging open behind her.

'We're investigating a case and had some questions to ask you, Mrs Nishimoto. Sorry to drop in when you were out.'

'What sort of case?'

'It's about the guy from the pawnshop,' Yukiho said.

Fumiyo held her breath for a long moment. From the looks on their faces, Sasagaki ascertained that they both knew about Kirihara's death and, furthermore, had discussed it together at some length.

'Please, have a seat,' Koga said, offering his chair to Fumiyo. Wringing her hands, she sat down at the table across from Sasagaki.

A fine-featured woman, Sasagaki thought. A little soft under the eyes, but with make-up she'd definitely qualify as a looker. But hers was a cold beauty. The resemblance to her daughter was striking. Sasagaki could imagine any number of middle-aged men falling for her. With Kirihara at fifty-two, there could well have been something between them.

'Pardon the intrusion, but are you married?'

'My husband died seven years ago. He was working at a construction site, there was an accident ...'

'I see, I'm sorry. Where are you working now?'

'At an udon shop in Imazato.'

The name of the shop was Kikuya. Her hours there were from Monday to Saturday, eleven a.m. to four p.m.

'The udon there any good?' Koga asked with a smile, but Fumiyo's face remained hard.

'I suppose,' was all she said.

'I'm sure you've heard that Mr Yosuke Kirihara passed away?' Sasagaki said, getting to the topic at hand.

'Yes,' she said in a small voice. 'It was quite a shock.'

Yukiho went around behind her mother into the back room, where she sat against the closet like before. Sasagaki watched her go before looking back at Fumiyo.

'The things is, it's very likely that Mr Kirihara was involved in an incident. We were trying to track down exactly where he went last Friday afternoon and heard that he might have visited you here.'

'What, my house? No I—' Fumiyo began, haltingly, when her daughter chimed in, 'Isn't he the one who brought the pudding?'

Fumiyo's bewilderment was almost painful to watch. She moved her thin lips for a moment before saying, 'Yes, that's right. Mr Kirihara did come here on Friday.'

'Around what time?'

'I think it was ... ' Fumiyo looked past Sasagaki's right shoulder to the small clock atop a two-door fridge. 'A little before five, I think. Right after I got home.'

'And what was the purpose of his visit?'

'No reason in particular. He said he dropped in because he was in the area. He knows I'm a single mother and we're having a rough time making ends meet. He always dropped by now and then to give advice.'

'He said he was in the area? That's a little odd,' Sasagaki said, pointing at the wrapping paper from Harmony in the trash pail. 'He brought that, didn't he? Apparently he went all the way to the station to buy it. Not really in the area, is it?'

'Well, that may be, but I'm just telling you what he told me. He said he was dropping in because he was in the area,' Fumiyo said, her head drooping.

'Right, well, let's just leave that as that, then,' Sasagaki offered. 'Until when would you say he was here?'

'He left just a little before six, I think.'

'Just before six? Are you sure?'

'I'm pretty sure.'

'So that would mean he was here for about an hour? What did you discuss?'

'Nothing in particular. Just life.'

'That's a fairly broad topic. Did you talk about the weather, money, anything specific?'

'Well, he did mention the war ...'

'You mean the Pacific War?'

Sasagaki had read in the files that Kirihara had served in World War II. But Fumiyo shook her head.

'No, some war going on now, overseas. He was saying it was sure to drive up the price of oil again.'

'Oh, right, the Middle East.' That would be the Yom Kippur War that had just kicked off at the beginning of the month.

'He was saying it would wreck the economy. And we might not be able to get oil or anything made from it. The world would descend into a fight to see who had the most money and power – that's what he said.'

Sasagaki nodded, watching Fumiyo's downcast eyes as she spoke. It seemed to him that she was telling the truth. The question was why Kirihara had bothered to tell her that. Was he suggesting that he had money and power, so she should stick with him? According to the ledger at the pawnshop, Fumiyo Nishimoto had never once returned money to retrieve any collateral. She was destitute, and Sasagaki realised it was probably in the pawnshop's best interests to keep her that way. There might have been an angle by which Kirihara benefited personally, too.

He glanced over at Yukiho. 'And where was your daughter at that time?'

'She was at the library. Weren't you, honey?'

'Yeah,' Yukiho replied.

'Is that when you borrowed that book?' Sasagaki turned to ask the girl directly. 'Do you go to the library often?'

'Once or twice a week,' she told him.

'On your way home from school, maybe?'

'Yeah.'

'Do you have some set days you go, like, every Wednesday and Friday?'

'No.' She shook her head. 'I just go whenever I need something to read.'

'And that doesn't make you worry?' he asked the mother. 'I mean, don't you want to know where she is when she comes home late from school?'

'But she's always home right after six,' Fumiyo said.

'Is that when you came home on Friday, too?' Sasagaki asked Yukiho directly.

The girl nodded.

Sasagaki turned back to the mother. 'And did you stay home after Mr Kirihara left?'

'No, actually, I went out shopping. Marukaneya.'

Marukaneya was the name of a supermarket a couple of minutes away by foot.

'Did you run into anyone you know there?'

Fumiyo thought for a moment before saying, 'Yes, Mrs Kinoshita. She's the mother of one of Yukiho's classmates.'

'Would you happen to have her number?'

'Yes, I think so.' Fumiyo picked up the address book sitting next to the phone and put it on the table. Her finger went to an entry marked *Kinoshita*. 'That's her.'

Sasagaki watched Koga jot the number down in his notebook before continuing.

'Was your daughter already home when you left for the supermarket?'

'No, she hadn't come back yet.'

'And what time did you return?'

'A little after seven-thirty, I think.'

'By which time your daughter had come home, correct?'

'Yes, she had.'

'And you didn't leave the house after that?'

'No.' Fumiyo shook her head.

Sasagaki looked over at Koga to see if he had any more questions. Koga shook his head.

'Right, well, I'm sorry to have taken so much of your time. I'm afraid we might be back again later with more questions,' Sasagaki said, standing.

Fumiyo saw the two detectives to the door. Seeing that the daughter had remained behind, Sasagaki had one more question for her. 'Mrs Nishimoto, I have a rather delicate question to ask, if you don't mind.'

'Yes?' she said, her earlier unease returning to her face.

'Did Mr Kirihara ever invite you out to dinner? Or did you ever meet outside of your home?'

Fumiyo's eyes widened, but she firmly shook her head. 'No. Not even once.'

'I see. I was just wondering why Mr Kirihara had taken an interest in you and your household.'

'I think he was just a sympathetic man, that's all. Detective, am I a suspect?'

'We're just establishing his whereabouts on the day he died, that's all.'

Sasagaki thanked her for her time and the detectives left. They had walked until the apartment was out of sight when he turned to Koga and said, 'Something stinks.'

'Sure does,' the younger detective agreed.

'Why did she try to deny Kirihara had been there at first? And why didn't Yukiho help her hide it? You think she realised that I'd seen the pudding wrappers and there was no point lying?'

'I wouldn't put it past the kid.'

'What did she say? She finishes work at the udon place and gets home around five? And that's when Kirihara comes, right? Meanwhile, Yukiho is at the library and she only comes home after Mr Kirihara's already left. The timing is just a little too clean.'

'You think Fumiyo was his lover and she had her daughter stay out until they were done?'

'Could be. But if she was his lover, I'd imagine he'd have been supporting her somehow. You wouldn't think she'd be reduced to making rubber frogs in her spare time.'

'Maybe he was just in the process of winning her affections.'

'Could be.'

The two detectives hurried back to the station.

'It could've been an impulsive act,' Sasagaki said after he finished giving his report to Nakatsuka. 'I think it's likely that Kirihara showed the million yen he had just got from the bank to Fumiyo.'

'And she killed him because she wanted it? But if she'd killed him at the house there's no way she could've got the body to where we found it,' Nakatsuka pointed out.

'True, so maybe she needed some reason why they had to meet there. I can imagine that they walked together.'

'And forensics thinks a woman could've made those injuries.'

'And I doubt Mr Kirihara would've been expecting it coming from her.'

'Looks like we'll have to check out Fumiyo's alibi next,' Nakatsuka said, his tone grave.

At that point Sasagaki was pretty sure that Fumiyo was guilty. The way she had been acting was far too suspicious. And with the time of death somewhere between five and eight o'clock, she would have had plenty of time to do the deed.

Which made the news that Fumiyo Nishimoto had an alibi come as a something of a shock.

The park in front of the Marukaneya supermarket had a swing set, a slide, and a sandbox. It wasn't big enough to play catch, but it was just the right size for mothers to leave their children to play while they saw to the grocery shopping. This led to the park's other main use, as a place for housewives to meet, swap gossip, and take turns babysitting.

Around six-thirty in the evening on the day Yosuke Kirihara was murdered, a Mrs Yumie Kinoshita had met Fumiyo Nishimoto inside the supermarket. Fumiyo had already finished her shopping and was heading for the cash register. Yumie Kinoshita had just come into the shop and her basket was still empty. They exchanged a few words and parted ways in the front of the store.

It was already past seven when Yumie Kinoshita finished her shopping and left the store, upon which she got on the bicycle she'd left out front in order to ride home. As she was getting on the bike, she'd noticed Fumiyo in the park. She was on the swing set, gently swinging, lost in thought.

When asked if she was sure the person she saw was Fumiyo Nishimoto, Yumie Kinoshita replied that she was absolutely confident it was.

There was one other person who'd seen Fumiyo on the swings that evening, an older man who ran the *takoyaki* stand in front of the supermarket. He said she had stayed there, swinging, until it was almost closing time at eight. His description matched Fumiyo's age and appearance exactly.

Meanwhile, new information had come in concerning Kirihara's whereabouts after his visit to Fumiyo. A pharmacy owner of the pawnbroker's acquaintance had spotted him walking alone just after six. He had thought to call out to him but noticed that he seemed to be in a hurry. The location of the sighting was exactly midway between Fumiyo's apartment and the building where the body had been discovered.

With the time of death falling somewhere between five and eight, it was theoretically possible for Fumiyo to leave the swings, make straight for the building, and commit the murder. However, most of the investigative team agreed it seemed highly unlikely. It was already pushing it to stretch the time of death to eight. The most likely time for Kirihara's death had been placed between six and seven in the evening.

There was another piece of evidence that strongly suggested the murder hadn't taken place after seven-thirty, this being the available light at the scene of the crime. There were no lights in the room where the body was found. Though sunlight crept in during the day, at night it would be pitch dark. If the lights in the building across the road were on it would be light enough in the room to make out someone's face, at least once one's eyes had adjusted. However, those lights had been turned off at seven-thirty that night. It still would have been physically possible for Fumiyo to commit the murder had she brought a torch, yet, given the unusual circumstances that would entail, it was hard to imagine Kirihara being caught off his guard.

Though she was their main suspect at the time, the team was forced to admit that the probability that Fumiyo had murdered Kirihara was low.

While suspicion faded on Fumiyo Nishimoto, another investigator uncovered new information concerning Kirihara Pawnshop. His team had been going through the list of customers in the shop ledger, contacting each until they found someone who had visited the shop on the evening Kirihara was murdered.

The person in question was a middle-aged woman who lived by herself in Tatsumi, a neighbourhood several kilometres to the south of Ōe. Widowed when her husband had died two years earlier, she'd been making regular visits over the last several months, having chosen a pawnshop far from her home so friends wouldn't see her going in. On that Friday she had brought a pair of watches to Kirihara Pawnshop at five-thirty in the afternoon.

According to her statement, though the shop had seemed open, the door was locked. She had rung the doorbell, but no one had answered. She had then gone to a nearby market to buy things for dinner, dropping back by the pawnshop on her way home. This was around six-thirty.

Again, the door was locked. This time she didn't bother ringing the doorbell, but gave up and went home. She pawned the watches three days later at a different shop. As she wasn't in the habit of reading the newspapers she hadn't learned of Kirihara's murder until hearing it from the detectives.

Suspicion then turned naturally towards Yaeko and Matsuura, who had both previously stated that the pawnshop had been open until seven. Once again Sasagaki and Koga paid a visit to Kirihara Pawnshop – this time with two other detectives in tow.

Matsuura's eyes went wide when he saw the crowd at the door. 'What's this about?'

'Is Mrs Kirihara in?' Sasagaki asked.

'Yeah, but—'

'Would you mind calling her?'

Matsuura frowned and opened the sliding door behind him a little, calling in, 'More detectives here to see you.'

There came a sound of someone moving and the door opened the rest of the way. Yaeko appeared, wearing jeans and a knitted top. Her eyebrows drew together when she saw the detectives in the shop. 'Yes?'

'Sorry to trouble you. But we have a few questions,' Sasagaki said.

'It's no trouble, but I'm not sure what I can help you with.'

'Maybe you could come with us,' the detective behind Sasagaki said. 'Just to the café around the corner. We won't take much of your time.'

Yaeko frowned, but she put on her sandals. Sasagaki noted with interest the worried look she gave Matsuura before leaving with the other two detectives.

Once they were gone, Sasagaki walked up to the counter. 'And I have a question for you, Mr Matsuura.'

'Yes?' he said, smiling pleasantly even as his back stiffened.

'It's about the day of the murder. In our investigation we found something that contradicted one of your earlier statements,' Sasagaki said, his words deliberately measured.

'What sort of a contradiction?' Matsuura asked, the smile tightening on his face.

Sasagaki told them what they'd heard from the woman in Tatsumi. Matsuura's smile faded as he spoke.

'What are we to make of this? You said that the shop was open until seven that day. But now we have someone saying that the door was locked between five-thirty and six-thirty. Doesn't that seem strange to you?' Sasagaki stared the man in the eye.

Matsuura looked away, his gaze drifting up towards the ceiling. 'Well now, let's see ...' He moved as if to cross his arms, then clapped his hands together with sudden realisation. 'I know! I was in the safe.'

'The safe?'

'Yeah, it's at the back. We keep all the things from the customers there, anything of value. You can come take a look later if you want, but it's quite large. Like a bank vault. Anyway, I had to check on some things, so I was in there. You can't hear the door buzzer from inside, see.'

'And no one was watching the store while you were inside?'

'Well, usually the boss is here but since I was alone I'd locked the door.'

'And what about the wife and son?'

'They were both in the living room,' Matsuura said.

'Wouldn't they have heard the doorbell ringing?'

'Right, well,' Matsuura's mouth hung open for several seconds before he said, 'they could've been watching television in the back and not heard it.'

Sasagaki looked at Matsuura's bony-cheeked face for a moment before saying to Koga, 'Try ringing the doorbell.'

'Right,' Koga said, stepping outside. The buzzer went off above Sasagaki's head. The noise was almost painful.

'That's quite loud,' Sasagaki said. 'They would've had to be pretty engrossed in whatever show they were watching to have missed that.'

Matsuura's face twisted, eventually ending up in a wry smile. 'Well, Mrs Kirihara's never been that interested in the business here. She usually doesn't even greet customers when they come in. Ryo's never been one for helping out, either. They probably heard the buzzer but just ignored it.'

'Ignored it, right,' Sasagaki said, but what Matsuura was saying did have a ring of truth to it; neither Yaeko nor her son seemed very enthusiastic about the business.

'Am I a suspect, detective? I mean, do you think I killed the boss?'

'Let's not get ahead of ourselves,' Sasagaki said, waving his hand. 'We hit a contradiction in our investigation so we had to look into it. That's standard procedure.'

'I see, I guess. Not that being a suspect would bother me much,' Matsuura added, showing yellowed teeth. 'I got nothing to hide.'

'Not that we suspect you, but it always helps us to have something a little more concrete for an alibi. I don't suppose you have anything that can prove you were here on that day between six and seven?'

'Well you could ask Mrs Kirihara or the kid ... but that's not enough, is it?'

'A witness who has nothing to do with the case would be preferable.'

'So now we're conspirators, is that it?' Matsuura said, his eyes narrowing.

'We're just considering all the possibilities here,' Sasagaki said with a shrug.

'Well, that's messed up. What do I have to gain by killing the boss? He might have talked like he was a high roller, but I know there's not much money here.'

Sasagaki didn't answer. He was happy to have Matsuura get angry and maybe say more than he should. But the man had already calmed down. 'Between six and seven, right?' he said quietly. 'I don't suppose talking on the phone counts?'

'You talked to someone on the phone? Who?'

'Someone from the union, about our meeting coming up next month.'

'Did you call him?'

'Erm, no, he called me.'

'Around what time?'

'Once at six. Then again about a half-hour later.'

'He called twice?'

'That's right.'

Sasagaki arranged the timeline in his head. If Matsuura was telling the truth, that would give him an alibi between six and six-thirty, which made it unlikely he had been the murderer.

Sasagaki asked for the name and phone number of the union man who had called. Matsuura pulled out a box of business cards and had begun looking through them when the door to the stairs opened. A boy's face appeared in the gap. His eyes met with Sasagaki's and he quickly shut the door. The detectives could hear his footsteps hurrying back up the stairs.

'It looks like the Kirihara boy is in.'

'What? Oh, yeah, he just got home from school.'

'Would you mind if I took a look?' Sasagaki said, indicating the stairs.

'You want to see upstairs?'

'If you don't mind.'

'No, yeah, sure, no problem.'

Sasagaki told Koga to take down the number of the man who'd called, then take a look at the safe. He leaned down to take off his shoes and stepped up behind the counter.

Opening the door, he took a look up the stairs. They were dimly lit and smelled of plaster dust from the walls. Years of sock traffic had polished the wooden stairs to a shiny black. Placing a hand on the wall for balance, Sasagaki cautiously climbed the steps.

At the top he found a narrow hallway running between two rooms. One side was closed with a sliding door, the other with a *shoji* screen. There was a small door at the end of the hallway that was either a closet or a toilet, Sasagaki decided.

'Ryo? It's Detective Sasagaki. I was hoping to have a word.' Sasagaki stepped into the hallway.

For a while no answer came. Sasagaki had just taken a breath to call out again when he heard something clatter from behind the sliding door. Moving quickly, he took a step forward and opened the door. Ryo was inside, sitting at his desk, his back facing the detective.

'Mind if I come in?'

Sasagaki stepped into the small tatami-matted room. This was the south-west corner of the house and sunlight came streaming in through the windows.

'I don't know anything, OK?' Ryo said, his back still turned.

'That's fine. It's all helpful. Mind if I sit down?' Sasagaki asked, pointing towards a cushion on the floor. Ryo looked over his shoulder and nodded.

Sasagaki sat and looked up at the boy. 'Sorry about your dad.'

Ryo said nothing. He didn't even turn around.

Sasagaki looked around the room. It was clean to the point where it felt a little barren for a kid's room. There were no posters of girls in bathing suits on the walls, no model racing cars. There was no manga on the bookshelf, either, just an encyclopedia and two science books for kids: *How Cars Work*, and *How Televisions Work*.

Sasagaki's eyes lit on a frame on the wall. It contained a piece of white paper cut in the shape of a sailboat. The paper had been cut so deftly that even the rigging was reproduced perfectly. Sasagaki had seen some cut-paper pictures at an art show once and this seemed far more intricate.

'That's pretty impressive. You make that?'

Ryo glanced at the frame and nodded his head slightly.

'Wow,' Sasagaki said. His surprise was genuine. 'That takes some skill. You could sell those if you wanted to, you know.'

'What did you want to ask me?'

Apparently Ryo wasn't one for exchanging small talk with middle-aged men.

'Right,' Sasagaki said, shifting on his cushion. 'Were you home that day?'

'That day?'

'The day your father died.'

'Oh, yeah. I was here.'

'What were you doing between six and seven?'

'In the evening?'

'Yeah. Do you remember?'

The boy scratched his neck before saying, 'Watching TV downstairs.'

'By yourself?'

'No, with my mom.'

Sasagaki nodded. He had been unable to detect any hesitation in the boy's voice. 'Sorry,' he said, 'but would you mind facing me so we can talk?'

Ryo sighed and slowly turned his chair around. Sasagaki was half expecting a look of defiance from the boy but when he turned around he felt nothing of the sort. The boy's eyes were blank, almost inorganic – the eyes of a scientist. Sasagaki felt as though he was being observed.

'You remember what show you were watching?' Sasagaki asked, trying to sound as casual as possible.

Ryo gave him the name of a television series popular with boys. Sasagaki asked him what the episode had been about. Ryo thought for a moment then gave him a perfect summary of that night's action. Sasagaki had never even seen the show but he found he could picture it quite readily just from the boy's description.

'Until when were you watching TV?'

'About seven-thirty.'

'And afterwards?'

'I had dinner with Mom.'

'Right. You must've been worried when your father didn't come home.'

'Yeah,' Ryo said in a small voice. Then he sighed and looked out of the window. Sasagaki found his eyes drawn outwards too. The sun was setting, casting a red glow across the sky.

'Well,' Sasagaki said at length, 'sorry to bother you in the middle of your homework. Keep at it.' He stood and gave the boy a clap on the shoulder.

Sasagaki and Koga went back to headquarters and compared

notes with the two detectives who had questioned Yaeko. There weren't any noticeable contradictions between what she had said and Matsuura's statement. She too had claimed she was in the back with Ryo watching television when the customer came. She said she might have heard the buzzer ring, but she didn't remember, and besides, she generally didn't answer the door as it wasn't her job to greet customers. She claimed she didn't know what Matsuura had been up to while she was watching television. The description of the programme, too, matched Ryo's. It would have been fairly simple for Yaeko and Matsuura to agree on a story in order to establish each other's alibis, but with Ryo in the picture it changed everything. Nobody said it in as many words but the general feeling in the department was that the three of them were telling the truth.

Proof came soon afterwards. There was a record of the calls Matsuura had claimed came to the pawnshop at six and again at six-thirty. The man from the union had confirmed that it was Matsuura he talked to on the phone.

They were back to square one. The painstaking, methodical questioning of regulars to the pawnshop continued. The only progress made was that marked by the days on the calendar. In baseball, the Yomiuri Giants won nine games in a row, and Leo Esaki won the Nobel Prize in physics for his co-discovery of electron tunnelling. As a direct result of the Yom Kippur War, oil prices were on the rise. Throughout the country, the feeling spread that something was about to happen.

Just as the investigation team was starting to get impatient, new information came in from the detectives looking into Fumiyo Nishimoto.

Kikuya was a nice little udon shop with a wooden lattice door, over which hung a navy-blue *noren* curtain with the name of the shop written in large white letters across it. It looked popular, with a good crowd for lunch and no sign of business tapering off even after one in the afternoon.

Around one-thirty, a white van parked on the street a short

distance away from the shop. Large letters on the side of the van announced it as the property of Swallowtail Inc.

A man got out of the driver's seat. He looked to be around forty years old, of a stocky build, with a shirt and tie on beneath a grey jacket. He walked quickly into Kikuya.

'Like clockwork,' Sasagaki said with a glance down at his wristwatch. 'One-thirty on the dot.' He was sitting in a café across the road from Kikuya looking out through the window.

Sitting next to him, Detective Kanemura said, 'I can also tell you what he's ordering right now: tempura udon.'

'Oh yeah?'

'I'd bet money on it. I've been in there with him a few times already. Terasaki always gets the same thing.'

'You'd think he'd get tired of it.' Sasagaki looked back over at the shop. All this talk about udon was making his stomach rumble.

Though Fumiyo's alibi had been corroborated, she was not yet entirely free from suspicion. The team was fixated on the fact that she was the last person Kirihara seemed to have met before going to his death. If she was involved in his murder, that pointed towards a collaborator. So they had cast a net, looking for anyone who might fit the description of the pretty widow's young lover, when they had found Tadao Terasaki.

Terasaki made his livelihood as a wholesaler of cosmetics, beauty supplies, shampoo and detergent. He made deliveries to other retailers but also took orders directly from customers, which he would fulfil by personally delivering the goods to their doorstep. His outfit, Swallowtail Inc., was a company in name alone. Terasaki was the owner and sole employee.

Terasaki had first come to the attention of the team through the questioning of Fumiyo Nishimoto's neighbours. A housewife had seen a man in a white van pay several visits to Fumiyo's apartment. She remembered seeing the name of some company on the van, something about butterflies, but hadn't been able to remember the exact name.

They began a stakeout near Yoshida Heights but the van never showed up. When they did find it, it was in an entirely different location: Kikuya, the udon shop where Fumiyo worked. A white van paid the shop a daily visit.

From the company name on the van it was easy to track down the man's identity.

'He's out,' Koga announced. It had been his job to watch the door. All three detectives looked across the street. Terasaki had left the shop, but he wasn't going back to his van. He was just standing there. This, too, they had expected from Kanemura's report.

A few moments later Fumiyo came out of the shop wearing a white work apron. She talked a while with Terasaki then went back inside the shop, leaving Terasaki to return to his van alone. Neither of them seemed to be worrying too much about being seen.

'Let's move,' Sasagaki said, crushing his cigarette into the ashtray on the table as he stood.

Terasaki was just opening the van door when Koga called out to him. He turned, a startled look on his face. When he noticed Sasagaki and Kanemura coming from behind, his expression hardened.

Terasaki was willing enough to talk to them. They asked if he'd like to go to the café, but he said he'd prefer to talk right there in the van, so all four of them piled in: Terasaki in the driver's seat, Sasagaki in the passenger's seat, and Koga and Kanemura in the back.

Sasagaki asked whether he had heard about the death of the pawnshop owner in Ōe.

'I read about it in the paper, or maybe it was on TV,' Terasaki said, his eyes fixed on the road ahead. 'What's that got to do with me?'

'The last place Mr Kirihara visited before he died was the home of a Mrs Fumiyo Nishimoto. You do know Mrs Nishimoto, don't you?'

Terasaki swallowed noticeably. 'Nishimoto ... the woman who works at that noodle shop right? Yeah, I know who she is.'

'Well, we think she might have something to do with what happened.'

'Ridiculous,' Terasaki snorted, the corners of his mouth curling up into a smile.

'Is it?' Sasagaki asked.

'How could she have anything to do with that?'

'Mr Terasaki, you say you only "know who she is", so why go out of your way to protect her?'

'I ain't protecting nobody.'

'A white van's been spotted several times near Yoshida Heights, along with a man driving it who pays regular visits to Mrs Nishimoto's apartment. That man is you, isn't it, Mr Terasaki?'

Terasaki was clearly flustered. He wet his lips and said, 'She's a customer, so what?'

'A customer?'

'You know, cosmetics, detergent. I bring the things she orders. That's all.'

'You know, Terasaki, if you're lying, we'll uncover the truth soon enough. We have a witness who says you visit her apartment frequently. I can't imagine she needs that many cosmetics.'

Terasaki crossed his arms and closed his eyes.

'Start lying now, Mr Terasaki, and you'll just have to keep lying. It's hard to keep it up, you know. And we'll be watching you every minute of the day. All we have to do is wait until you visit Fumiyo Nishimoto again. So what would you do? Just give up on ever seeing her again? I think that'd be pretty tough on both of you. Look, why don't you just tell us the truth? You're in a relationship with Mrs Nishimoto, aren't you?'

Sasagaki waited patiently for Terasaki to make the next move.

After a long silence, he sighed and opened his eyes. 'So what's it to you? I'm single, and she's a widow.'

'So you're confirming the relationship?'

'Yeah, we're seeing each other. And not some fling, either. It's serious,' Terasaki said.

'Since when?'

'I have to tell you all that?'

'Humour me,' Sasagaki said with a smile.

'Since about six months ago,' Terasaki told him, a reluctant look on his face.

'What started it?'

'Nothing special. We saw each other at Kikuya, and got friendly, you know.'

'Did she ever talk to you about Mr Kirihara?'

'All I know is he ran the pawnshop she visited.'

'Had you heard about his visits to her apartment?'

'Yeah, I heard about that.'

'And how did that make you feel?'

Terasaki's eyebrows drew together and he made an unpleasant face. 'What's that supposed to mean?'

'You didn't think Mr Kirihara might have had an ulterior motive for seeing her?'

'What would be the point of thinking that? For one thing, Fumiyo's not that kind of girl.'

'And yet she was indebted to Mr Kirihara by the sound of it. He might have even helped her financially. That would make it pretty hard for her to resist if he put the pressure on, wouldn't you think?'

'Well, I never heard about it if he did. What are you getting at, anyway?'

'I'm just trying to imagine a very likely scenario. Here we have a man who's frequenting the apartment of the woman you're seeing. Because of her situation she can't easily brush him off. He's happy to help her, but he wants more and he lets her know it. I can't imagine you'd feel too good about that, being her lover.'

'So what – I lost my cool and killed him? Do I look that stupid?' Terasaki's voice echoed loudly in the van.

Sasagaki held up a hand. 'I'm just imagining a possible scenario, that's all. I'm sorry if I touched a nerve. Incidentally, do you remember where you were on the twelfth of this month from six to seven in the afternoon? It was a Friday.'

'What, you want an alibi now?' Terasaki said, rolling his eyes.

'Something like that,' Sasagaki said with a smile. People were quick to mention alibis lately thanks to a popular detective show on TV.

Terasaki took out a small appointment book and flipped back through the pages.

'Let's see, on the evening of the twelfth I was in Toyonaka making a delivery.'

'Around what time was this?'

'I got to the customer's house around six.'

Which would give him a perfect alibi, Sasagaki thought. *Another miss.*

'And the delivery went smoothly?'

'Actually, no. I guess there was a bit of a miscommunication,' Terasaki said, slightly mumbling his words. 'She was out when I got there. So I just left my business card at the door and went home.'

'They weren't expecting you?'

'I thought I'd told her I was coming on the phone. I guess she didn't hear me.'

'So you went home without seeing anyone, is that correct?'

'Yeah, but I did leave my card.'

Sasagaki nodded, thinking that there were any number of ways he could have got his card there.

Sasagaki took down the address and phone number of the house in Toyonaka and let him go.

Back at the station, Nakatsuka wanted to know if Sasagaki thought he was guilty.

'Fifty-fifty,' was Sasagaki's honest reply. 'He doesn't have an alibi and he has a motive. I think, if he were in league with Fumiyo Nishimoto, he could've pulled it off pretty smoothly. The thing that bothers me is that, if they were the killers, then they were acting far too nonchalant about it afterwards. Normally you'd expect them to avoid seeing each other until things died down. But they didn't change a thing. Terasaki was still going to eat lunch at her noodle shop every day. It doesn't make sense.'

Nakatsuka listened in silence, but his sour frown alone was proof enough of his agreement.

The team launched into a full investigation on the proprietor of Swallowtail Inc. Terasaki lived by himself in an apartment building about a fifteen-minute drive to the south. He'd been married once, but it had ended five years earlier in an amicable divorce.

He was well thought of by his customers. He worked quickly, was happy to take difficult requests, and his prices were low. The small retailers he worked with loved him. None of this, of course, cleared his name of murder. On the contrary, the investigative team was interested in how, by all indications, he seemed to be running a shoestring operation, never rising into wealth through his efforts.

'I could see him murdering Mr Kirihara because he was putting the moves on Fumiyo, but I can also see him lured in by the one million,' the detective assigned to look into Terasaki's financial situation said during a team meeting. Many of the other investigators agreed.

They had already confirmed Terasaki's lack of an alibi. When they went to the house where he claimed to have left his business card they found that the woman who lived there had been at a relative's that day and had not come home until eleven at night. She had found Terasaki's business card under her door, but there was no way of telling when he had left it there. When they asked whether she had been expecting him to come that day, she told them, 'He said he'd be coming around then, but I don't think we agreed on that day in particular.' Then she added, 'Actually, I remember telling Mr Terasaki on the phone that the twelfth wasn't good for me.'

This last part was particularly significant. If Terasaki had known she would be out that day, it would have made her house an excellent choice to visit in an attempt to create an alibi.

The prevailing opinion in the investigative team was gradually turning against Terasaki.

However they still lacked any substantial evidence. None of the hairs recovered at the scene of the crime matched Terasaki's, nor did any of the fingerprints. There were no witnesses. If Fumiyo and Terasaki had been conspirators, they would have had to be in communication on the day of the murder, yet there were no signs of that either. Some of the older detectives thought they should just interrogate him until he confessed, but as it stood, they didn't even have enough to get a warrant.

A month had passed without any progress. Whereas before the detectives had been spending their nights either on stakeouts or sleeping under desks, now they had started to go home, and Sasagaki went home for the first real bath he had taken in weeks. He was married, living in an apartment by Yao City Station, about an hour to the south-east of their current headquarters. His wife, Katsuko, was three years older than he was. They had no children.

Sasagaki was woken from sleep early the next morning by the sound of Katsuko hurriedly dressing. He looked at the clock. It was just after seven.

'You going someplace?' Sasagaki asked from the futon.

'Oh, sorry, I didn't mean to wake you. I'm just going to the supermarket.'

'You're going shopping? This early?'

'You have to line up now or you won't get anything.'

'Won't get any what? What are you going to buy?'

'Toilet paper, of course.'

'Huh? Toilet paper?'

'I went yesterday too. They're limiting it to one bag per person, you know. You're lucky I don't make you go with me.'

'Why do we need so much toilet paper?'

'If you don't know about the oil shortage, I don't have time to explain. I'll see you later,' Katsuko said, slipping into her cardigan and snatching up her wallet as she ran out of the door.

Sasagaki's head was a confused swirl. He'd been so full of the investigation lately he had very little notion of what was going on in the world outside. He'd heard about the oil shortage, but he didn't see what that had to do with toilet paper, or why people were queueing up this early in the morning to get it.

He decided he would ask Katsuko when she got home and tried closing his eyes again.

The phone rang moments later. He twisted under the cover and reached for the black rotary phone squatting by his pillow. His head hurt a little and he hadn't quite got his eyes all the way open yet.

'Yeah? Sasagaki speaking.'

About ten seconds later he leapt from the futon, all thoughts of sleep having fled his mind. The phone call had been to tell him that Tadao Terasaki was dead.

Terasaki had died on one of the main expressways through Osaka. He hadn't quite made it around a curve and had slammed into the divider, a classic case of falling asleep at the wheel.

His van had been stocked with a large quantity of soap and detergent. People were hoarding supplies and it came out later that Terasaki had run himself ragged trying to get as much stashed away for his customers as he could.

Sasagaki and a few other detectives searched Terasaki's apartment for anything that might link him to the murder of Yosuke Kirihara, but no one could deny the feeling of futility that had come over the operation. Even if they did find something, their prime suspect was beyond prosecution.

Finally, one of the detectives found something in the van's glove compartment: a Dunhill lighter. It was a tall model, with pointed corners. Everyone on the team remembered a similar lighter having gone missing from Kirihara's possessions when he was found.

However, Kirihara's fingerprints were not found on the lighter. In fact, no prints were found at all. It appeared to have been wiped with a cloth.

They showed the lighter to Yaeko, but she only shook her head. She said it did resemble her husband's, but she couldn't be absolutely sure.

They brought in Fumiyo Nishimoto for more questioning. The detectives were growing increasingly agitated and impatient for a confession, no matter what it took. The detective doing the questioning went so far as to make it sound like the lighter they'd found had belonged to Kirihara.

'So, what?' the detective pressed Fumiyo, waving the lighter in her face. 'Did you take it out of the victim's pocket and give it to Terasaki? Or did Terasaki take it out of the dead man's pocket himself? Well, which was it? Hmm?'

Yet Fumiyo continued to deny any involvement. Nor did she flinch or show any sign of breaking. Though a certain amount of shock would have been natural after Terasaki's sudden death, there was nothing in her attitude that suggested any bewilderment at all.

We made a mistake, Sasagaki thought, sitting in a side room where he could listen to the interrogation. *Somewhere along the line we took a wrong turn and it's leading us nowhere.*

TWO

Toshio Tagawa took a look at the sports page and thought about the game, his foul mood of the night before coming back over him.

The Yomiuri Giants had lost; there was nothing he could do about that. What bugged him was how it had gone down.

At the critical moment, Nagashima had just choked. This was the hitter that had taken the Giants to victory so many times before, and now his batting was so weak it hurt to watch. It was always Shigeo Nagashima who came through in a pinch, always the man they called 'Mister Giants' who gave a swing the fans could get behind, even when he was struck out.

But something had clearly gone wrong. To be honest, the warning signs had already been there two or three years back. But Tagawa, a Nagashima fan since childhood, had just looked away, unable to accept the harsh reality of what he was seeing. *Everybody gets older. The day comes when even the best players have to leave the field.* He looked at the photo in the newspaper of Nagashima having just been struck out and realised he might be at a critical juncture this year. The season was just getting started, but there would be rumours of retirement by summer. If the Giants stopped winning, it was almost certain. Tagawa wasn't too hopeful about their prospects, either. They had charged through nine years at the top of the Central League, but he couldn't help thinking that the cracks were beginning to show in the team – cracks epitomised by Nagashima.

He glanced sideways at an article about the Chunichi Dragon's latest win and closed the paper. The clock on the wall showed it was four. He doubted anyone else would come today. Not many people paid rent on the day before payday, anyway.

Tagawa was mid-yawn when he noticed someone standing outside the office. He could just see glimpses through the spaces between the apartment flyers he'd taped up on the window. He couldn't see a face, but he could see their shoes – sneakers, a child. Maybe some kid on his way home from elementary school killing time by checking out the apartment listings, Tagawa thought.

However, several seconds later, the door opened. A girl wearing a cardigan over a blouse peeked in, almost fearfully. Her eyes were large, like a cat's. Tagawa guessed she was in her last years of elementary school, maybe sixth grade.

'Can I help you?' he asked. His voice sounded soft even to his own ears. If this had been one of the typical area brats, the kind with scuffed-up knees and worn faces, he doubted he would have sounded half as nice.

'My name's Nishimoto,' the girl said.

'Nishimoto? Where from?'

'Yoshida Heights.'

The girl's crisp diction and bright voice was remarkably refreshing to Tagawa's ears. All the kids he knew talked as brutishly as you'd expect from their muddled heads and bad upbringing.

'Yoshida Heights . . . ' Tagawa pulled a file off the shelf.

Eight families lived in Yoshida Heights. The Nishimoto unit was in the middle on the ground floor, No 103. Tagawa noted that they were two months behind on the rent. It had been about time for him to give them a call, in fact.

'So, um.' He turned back to the girl. 'You're Mrs Nishimoto's daughter?'

'Yes,' the girl said.

Tagawa glanced back down at the file. The Nishimotos' unit only listed two residents: Fumiyo Nishimoto and her daughter, Yukiho. When they had moved in ten years earlier, Fumiyo's husband, Hideo, had been on the rental agreement, but he had died soon afterwards.

'You come to pay the rent?' Tagawa asked.

Yukiho looked down at the floor before shaking her head. *Didn't think so*, Tagawa thought to himself. 'So what's this about?'

'I was hoping you could open the door for me.'

'What, the door to your apartment?'

'I didn't bring my key with me and I can't get in.'

'Oh.' Finally Tagawa understood the reason for the girl's visit. 'So your mother locked the door and went out?'

Yukiho nodded. When she looked up at him, there was an allure to her face that made Tagawa forget for a moment that the girl was only in elementary school. He swallowed. 'And you don't know where she is?'

'She didn't say she'd be going out ... that's why I didn't take my key with me.'

'Right, I get you.'

Tagawa looked at the clock. It was still a little too early to close up shop. His father, who owned the estate agency, was off at a relative's place since the day before, and wouldn't be back until late tonight. Still, he couldn't just stay here and give the master key to the girl. It was in the agreement with the property owner that someone from the estate agency would always be present when a master key was being used.

Normally he would have just told the girl to wait until her mother came home, but when he saw the forlorn look in her eyes, he couldn't bring himself to turn her away.

'Right, well, hold on, I'll walk there with you.' He stood and walked over to the safe with the keys for the rental properties.

Tagawa trailed Yukiho Nishimoto's slender figure across the patched and cracked pavement on the ten-minute walk to Yoshida Heights. He noticed that she wasn't wearing the usual school backpack. Instead she was carrying a red vinyl handbag.

When she walked, he heard a bell ringing from somewhere on her person. He wondered where the bell was, but couldn't see it from behind her. Looking at her like this, he could tell now that she wasn't particularly well off. The soles of her sneakers were worn thin, her cardigan was covered with pills, and a few holes were opening here and there. Even the fabric of her checked skirt looked spent.

And yet she gave off a kind of refined aura he was sure he'd never seen before, certainly not in these parts. It made him wonder where it came from. He knew Yukiho's mother, an introverted, unremarkable woman, filled with the same vulgar desperation as everyone else who lived around here. It surprised him that a girl could grow up with a mother like that and still turn out the way she was.

'Where's your school?' Tagawa asked from behind her.

'Ōe Elementary,' she said, turning her head slightly to answer while she walked.

'You're kidding.'

Ōe Elementary was the public school that nearly all the kids from the neighbourhood went to. Every year a couple of them would get picked up for shoplifting or simply disappear when their parents skipped town to escape loan sharks or the like. When you walked by the place in the afternoon it smelled like old lunch and when school finished the local hustlers would come out on their bicycles trying to sell the kids crap to part them from their allowances. It was that kind of school. Not that any of the kids that went to Ōe Elementary would get taken in by a street hustler.

He found it hard to believe that this girl went there. Of course, given what he knew about her household's financial situation, sending her to private school would have been out of the question. He imagined she must be pretty popular in school.

They reached the building, and Tagawa knocked on the door to No 103, calling out, 'Mrs Nishimoto?' There was no answer. 'Looks like she's still out,' he said, glancing in Yukiho's direction.

The girl nodded. Again he heard the sound of a bell jingling.

Tagawa slid the master key into the lock and turned it clockwise. There was a click as the door unlocked. That was the instant he first had a premonition that something was wrong. It started in his gut and spread through his chest. Still he grabbed the knob and pulled the door open.

He'd only taken one step in before he saw the woman lying down in the far room. She was wearing a thin yellow sweater and jeans, asleep on the tatami mats. He couldn't see her face, but he knew for certain it was Fumiyo Nishimoto.

So she was home, he thought, when he noticed a strange smell in the air.

'Gas!'

He stopped Yukiho from coming in with one hand, and covered his mouth and nose with the other. His eyes went to the kitchen. A pot sat on the stove and the knob was turned on, but no flame came from the burner.

Holding his breath, Tagawa quickly turned off the gas and opened the window over the kitchen counter. Then he rushed into the back and opened the window in the far room, taking a sidelong glance at Fumiyo lying next to the tea table before sticking his head out and taking a deep breath. He felt a tingling sensation in the back of his skull.

He turned back to look at Fumiyo Nishimoto. Her face was a light blue and there was no warmth to her skin at all. *We're too late,* was his first thought. He spotted a black telephone in the corner of the room, picked up the receiver, and put his finger on the dial when he hesitated, wondering if he should dial 119 for an ambulance or just 110 for the police to come and pick up the body.

He stood for a moment, unable to decide. The only dead person he'd seen until then was his grandfather.

He dialled 1, 1, then rested his finger on the 0.

Just then, Yukiho's voice asked from the doorway, 'Is she dead?'

He turned to look at her. The light from the door behind her meant he couldn't see the expression on her face.

'Is my mother dead?' the girl asked again. There were tears in her voice.

'I don't know,' Tagawa said, his finger shifting from the 0 to the 9 before giving the dial a final twist.

It was several minutes after the bell rang before he heard the sound of talking, giggling, and running feet.

Camera cradled in his right hand, Yuichi Akiyoshi crouched and watched. Students were just beginning to spill from the front gate of the Seika Girls Middle School. He held his camera up to his chest and stared at each of them in turn.

His hiding spot was in the back of a pickup truck parked along the side of the road about fifty metres away from the gate. It was a perfect location. Most of the students leaving the school would have to pass him on the way home and the tarp over the back of the truck provided good cover. Given his objective for the day, it was the best vantage point Yuichi could have hoped for. If he could get the shot he wanted it would be worth having skipped out on sixth period to come.

The girls at Seika Girls Middle School wore sailor uniforms. In the summer the uniforms had white tops with a light blue collar and their neatly pleated skirts were the same light blue. Yuichi watched those skirts flutter around the legs walking by. Some of the girls still looked as if they could be in elementary school, but others had already taken that first step into womanhood. Whenever one of the latter came near the truck he wanted to take a picture, but he resisted. He didn't want to run out of film before the main event.

He'd been watching the girls pass by for about fifteen minutes before he spotted Yukiho Karasawa. Hurriedly he lifted his camera and began tracking her through the lens.

As always, Yukiho was walking with her friend, a lanky girl with wireframe glasses. She had a pointed jaw, a pimpled forehead, and her body was lumpy in all the wrong places.

Yukiho Karasawa, on the other hand, was a beauty with lustrous, chestnut brown hair down to her shoulders. She tossed it to one side with her fingers in an utterly natural motion. There was something luxuriously feline about her eyes and a winsome smile played across her slightly pouty lower lip. She was slender, too, except for the decidedly feminine curves of her chest and hips. This last aspect of her physique had been singled out by her many fans as a top selling point.

For Yuichi, however, Yukiho's nose was her best part and the most deserving of a close-up shot. He steadied his grip on the camera and smiled.

Yuichi's house was at the very end of a long line of terraced houses facing a narrow street. The place had been standing for thirty years already and an odd mix of miso soup, curry and other spices had infused the old roof and wall posts with their scent. Yuichi always thought of it as an embarrassingly working-class kind of smell.

'Fumihiko's upstairs,' his mother called from the kitchen. He glanced down at the chopping board in front of her and sighed inwardly. *Potato tempura again.* Ever since one of her relatives back home had sent them potatoes they'd been eating them nearly every meal.

Upstairs he found his friend Fumihiko Kikuchi sitting in the middle of his bedroom, flipping through a movie pamphlet from a trip Yuichi had made to the cinema a few days earlier.

'You saw *Rocky*, huh. Any good?' Kikuchi asked, looking up at Yuichi. The pamphlet was open on a close-up of Sylvester Stallone's face.

'Yeah, it was cool.'

'Cool. Everyone says it's pretty good.'

Kikuchi resumed looking at the pamphlet. Yuichi figured he probably wanted it but didn't say anything. He didn't want to give the pamphlet to Kikuchi – if he wanted it, he could go and see the movie and get one himself.

'I wish movies weren't so expensive,' his friend mumbled.

'Yeah.'

Yuichi pulled his camera out of his duffel bag and put it on the desk, then sat down on his chair, hugging the back. Kikuchi was a good friend, but he didn't like talking about money with him. Kikuchi lived alone with his mother, and you could tell just by looking at him that they had it pretty rough. Yuichi felt lucky that his dad was still healthy and working with the railroad company.

'You taking pictures again?' Kikuchi asked, looking at the camera. By his grin, it was clear he knew exactly what Yuichi's subject had been.

'Yeah,' Yuichi said, grinning back.

'Get any good ones?'

'I hope so. Actually, I'm pretty sure I did, yeah.'

'Big bucks,' Kikuchi said with an arch of his eyebrows.

'I don't know. They don't sell for that much. And it costs money to print them. I'll be lucky if I come out ahead.'

'Hey, man, cash is cash. You got yourself a marketable skill there. I'm jealous.'

'I wouldn't call it a skill, really. I don't even know how to use the camera, at least not how you're supposed to. All this stuff just fell into my lap.'

The room that Yuichi was now using as his own had previously belonged to his uncle, his father's younger brother. His uncle was into photography, and as a result he owned a lot of cameras. He even had the equipment to develop and print black-and-white photos. When his uncle got married and left, he'd given some of his stuff to Yuichi.

'Cool that you have someone who gives you things like that.'

Yuichi's mood darkened as he anticipated more envy from Kikuchi. He didn't know why Kikuchi always steered their conversation to money – except this time, Kikuchi changed the topic on his own.

'Remember those photos your uncle took that you showed me the other day?'

'The ones from around town?'

'Yeah. You still got those?'

'Sure.'

Yuichi reached for the album at the end of the bookshelf. This was another of the things his uncle had left. It had a few photographs inside, all of them black-and-white scenes taken on the streets near his house. He handed Kikuchi the album and Kikuchi began to pore over each photograph with great interest.

'What are you so into those for?' Yuichi said, looking down at his slightly chubby friend where he sat on the floor.

'No reason, really,' he said, pulling one of the photographs from the scrapbook. 'Hey, think I can borrow this one?'

'Which one's that?'

Yuichi looked at the photograph in Kikuchi's hand. There was a narrow street with a couple walking down it. A poster taped to an electrical pole hung loose in the wind, and there was a cat curled up on a plastic bucket in the foreground.

'Whatcha want that for?' Yuichi asked.

'There's a friend I want to show it to.'

'Who?'

'I'll tell you once I show it to him.'

'Why?'

'Come on, let me borrow it. You're not using it, are you?'

'No, it's cool, it's just a little weird,' Yuichi said, looking at his friend's face as he handed him the photograph.

After dinner that night, Yuichi went up to his room and began developing the photographs he'd taken that afternoon. Using his closet as a darkroom, he could take the film out of the camera in there and place it in a special container so he could do the rest out in the light. Once the photos were fixed, he took the film out of the container and took it down to the sink on the first floor to wash it.

As he washed the film, Yuichi held it up to the fluorescent light over the sink. He smiled when he saw that the negative perfectly captured the sheen of Yukiho Karasawa's hair. *Good*, he thought. *This will make the customers happy.*

Eriko Kawashima made a habit of writing in her diary each night before she went to bed. She'd started at the beginning of fifth grade, which meant she had been at it for a whole five years now. The trick to keeping a diary was not to pressure yourself into always being dramatic. Simple was OK. Even if all you wrote was 'nothing much happened today', that was fine.

But today she had lots to write about. For the first time she'd gone to Yukiho Karasawa's house after school.

Eriko had known who she was since their first year in middle school. Yukiho had the face of an intellectual and an elegant, trim figure. Eriko saw something in her that she didn't see in any of the other girls, or even in herself. What she felt when she looked at her was almost longing. She'd often wondered if there was some way they could be friends.

Which was why Eriko felt like celebrating when they were finally put in the same class in their third year of middle school. Mustering her courage, she had approached Yukiho right after the opening ceremony and introduced herself.

She'd been so afraid of a dirty look, or even worse, silence, that the girl's reaction startled her.

Yukiho smiled. 'Yukiho Karasawa,' she said.

Yukiho was even more womanly close up. And she was sensitive. Just being with her opened Eriko's eyes to all kinds of things she'd never noticed before. Yukiho had a natural talent for making conversations interesting, which made Eriko feel like she was more interesting, too. Though Eriko thought of herself as still a girl, in her mind and in numerous diary entries, Yukiho was always a 'woman'.

As always with someone so popular, Eriko had competition for Yukiho's friendship. At times she would feel a slight pang of jealousy, as though they might take something very important away from her.

Worst of all was when the boys at a nearby middle school noticed Yukiho and started following her around like she was some kind of celebrity. The other day during gym class some of the boys had climbed up the chain-link fence by the sports field to watch them. When they spotted Yukiho they hooted and hollered until the teacher made them leave.

And today, on their way home from school, there had been someone hiding in the back of a truck by the school gate taking pictures of her. Eriko had only caught a glimpse of him: an unhealthy-looking boy with a pimply face, the type of guy whose head was always filled with vulgar fantasies. When Eriko thought that the pictures he was taking of Yukiho might be fuelling those fantasies it made her want to puke, but Yukiho didn't seem to pay any mind at all.

'I just ignore them. They'll soon find better things to do.'

Then she ran her fingers through her hair, almost as if she was doing it on purpose.

'But doesn't it make you feel gross? I mean, they're taking pictures of you without even asking.'

'It is a little gross, but it's better than calling them out because then you end up having to talk to them and then it's like you know them.'

'I guess.'

'It's really better to just ignore them entirely.'

Yukiho walked right past the truck while Eriko stayed as close by her side as she could in hopes that she might get in the way of a photograph or two.

It was soon after this that Yukiho invited Eriko to her house. Yukiho had forgotten to return a book she'd borrowed and thought Eriko might want to come and pick it up. Eriko didn't care about the book, but she wasn't about to pass up a chance to visit Yukiho's home.

She got off the bus at the fifth stop and walked for about two minutes. Yukiho Karasawa's house was in a quiet residential area. It wasn't large, but it had a very nicely tended garden in front.

Yukiho lived alone with her mother, who came out to greet Eriko. The woman looked old enough to be Yukiho's grand-mother, and it put Eriko in mind of an unpleasant rumour she'd recently heard.

'Please make yourself at home,' the woman said softly, leaving them in the living room.

'Your mom seems nice,' Eriko said when they were alone.

'Yeah.'

'I saw the sign by the door. Does she teach the tea ceremony?'

'Yeah, flower arranging too. I think she even gives *koto* lessons.'

'Wow,' Eriko said. 'She's a superwoman. Is she teaching you all of that?'

'Just tea and flowers,' Yukiho said.

'That's so cool. It's like you get to go to finishing school for free.'

'I don't know,' Yukiho said. 'She might not look it, but she's a pretty strict teacher.' She poured a little milk in the tea her mother had brought them and drank.

Eriko followed suit. It was a fragrant black tea, not the kind that came in those little teabags at the corner store.

'Say, Eriko,' Yukiho said, staring at her with her big eyes. 'Have you heard anyone saying things lately about me. About my ele-mentary school.'

Eriko blinked. 'Um, well ...'

A little smile came to Yukiho's lips. 'You have heard, then, haven't you.'

'No. I mean maybe I heard a little, but—'

'It's OK, you don't have to hide it. I guess the stories are really making the rounds, huh,' she said.

'N-not really. Hardly anyone's heard. That's what the girl who told me said.'

'Yeah, but the fact that she told you means that it's out there. Eriko?' Yukiho put her hand on the other girl's knee. 'Can you tell me what you heard?'

'Nothing much, really. Nothing interesting, at least.'

'I bet they said I used to be really poor and I lived in a dirty little apartment in Ōe?'

Eriko swallowed.

Yukiho went on, 'And that my mother died mysteriously?'

Eriko looked up. 'You know I don't believe any of that,' she said, her voice earnest.

Yukiho smiled. 'It's OK. You don't have to pretend. And it's not all a lie, anyway. I'm adopted. I came here just before starting middle school. My mother you just met isn't my real mother.' She spoke easily, as if what she was saying wasn't that big a deal. 'It's also true that I lived in Ōe. And I was really poor. My dad died a long time ago, that's why. And my mom died when I was in sixth grade.'

'Oh no!' Eriko said. 'How?'

'Gas poisoning,' Yukiho said. 'It was an accident. But some people said it might have been suicide. That's how poor we were.'

'Oh,' Eriko said, really unsure of what to say now. Yukiho wasn't acting like she had just made some weighty confession. *Of course*, Eriko thought, *she's probably just playing it casual so she won't upset me.*

'My mother now is actually a relative of my father's. I used to come here by myself to play a long time ago and when I became an orphan she took me in. I guess she was lonely, living all by herself.'

'Wow, that must've been really hard.'

'A little. But I was also really lucky. I mean, normally they put you in some kind of institution.'

'I guess, yeah.'

Eriko wanted to say something sympathetic but she felt as if no matter what she said it could only earn Yukiho's disdain. How could she, who had lived a completely normal, easy life, understand anything of her friend's pain?

Eriko was impressed at the grace with which Yukiho seemed to have carried herself this far. She wondered if somehow all of those hardships were what made her shine from the inside as she did.

'What else were they saying about me?' Yukiho asked.

'I don't know. I really didn't want to hear any more.'

'Whatever it was, I'm sure there was some truth to it. And some parts they just made up ...'

'You really shouldn't worry about it,' Eriko told her. 'The ones talking are just jealous of you, Yukiho.'

'I'm not worried. I was just wondering who started the rumours.'

'Who cares?' Eriko didn't really want to talk about this any more.

In fact, there was one more part to the story Eriko had heard. Yukiho's real mom had been someone's mistress, they said, and when the man she was seeing got murdered, she became a suspect. That's why she killed herself. She was afraid of getting caught.

Of course, she wasn't about to tell that part of the story to Yukiho.

Yukiho had taken up patchwork lately and she showed some of the things she'd made to Eriko. There was a pillow cover and a pouch whose bright colour selection revealed Yukiho's good taste. There was one other piece, as yet unfinished, with a different colour scheme – a bag, or maybe a purse, made entirely with cooler colours, like black and navy. 'Sometimes dark can be fun, too,' Eriko said, and she really meant it.

The composition teacher always did her best to keep her eyes on either the textbook or the blackboard, never the students. She taught class mechanically, just trying to get through that forty-five minutes of hell, praying nothing would happen. No students were called on to read aloud to the class, no questions were asked.

The Ōe Middle School Year 3 Class 8 classroom was divided into two sections. Those students with even a slight interest in listening sat towards the front half of the class. Those without any interest sat in the back, doing whatever they felt like doing. Some of them played cards, some chatted loudly, and others just slept.

A few teachers had started off punishing such behaviour in their classes, but over the span of a month or two the punishments stopped. It just wasn't worth the consequences. Once, an English teacher had scolded a kid for reading a manga in class, taking the comic book away and swatting him on the head with it. Several days later a masked assailant attacked the teacher on a back street, breaking two of his ribs. It was clearly payback, but the student who had been scolded in class had an alibi. On another occasion, a young maths teacher had screamed and nearly fainted with shock when she went to the chalk tray of her blackboard and found it lined with condoms, all clearly used and still containing semen. She was pregnant and the fainting spell had nearly caused her to have a miscarriage. She had gone on sick leave the next day. No one expected her back until the current third years graduated.

Yuichi Akiyoshi sat almost exactly in the middle of the classroom, allowing him to pay attention or join the miscreants in the back depending on his mood.

Toshiyuki Muta walked in halfway through class with a loud rattling of the door, not seeming to notice the stares as he casually made his way to his own seat in the very back, next to the window. Once Muta sat down, the class resumed as though nothing had happened.

Muta put both his feet up on his desk and pulled a magazine out of his bag – a porno mag.

'Hey, Muta, no jacking off in class,' one of his friends whispered, and an eerie smile flickered across Muta's stony face.

Class finished and Yuichi pulled a large envelope out of his bag and walked over to where Muta was now sitting cross-legged on top of his desk. He had his back to Yuichi, making it impossible for him to see his face, but judging from the smiles of the other kids around him, he was in a good mood. This was important. They were talking about the latest craze, a videogame called *Brickout*. Yuichi figured they'd probably be ditching school again to hit the local arcade before the day was finished.

One of the boys sitting across from Muta noticed Yuichi approach and jerked his head towards him. Muta turned around. He'd shaved off his eyebrows, leaving two dark blotches on his forehead. Beneath, his eyes were like little sharp pinpoints of light shining out of the craters in the rugged landscape of his face.

'Here,' Yuichi said, holding out the envelope.

'What's that?' Muta said in a low voice. His breath smelled of cigarettes.

'I went to Seika yesterday.'

Muta snatched the envelope out of Yuichi's hand.

The envelope contained three photos of Yukiho Karasawa. Yuichi had woken up when it was still dark that morning to make the prints. He was proud of his work. Even though they were black and white, you got a real sense of the colour of her hair and skin.

Practically licking his lips, Muta looked up at Yuichi and half of his mouth curled upwards in an unsettling smile. 'Not bad.'

'They're pretty good, right? It wasn't easy,' Yuichi said with relief that his customer seemed satisfied.

'Why are there only three of them?'

'I just brought the ones I thought you'd like for now.'

'How many more you got?'

'Five or six good ones, I guess.'

'Bring the rest tomorrow,' Muta said, slipping the envelope inside his school uniform jacket. Clearly he wasn't intending to give them back.

'It's three hundred yen a photo, so that's nine hundred,' Yuichi said, pointing at the envelope.

Wrinkles formed in the space between Muta's shaven eyebrows and he glared sidelong at Yuichi. The angle made the scar under his right eye look even more impressive.

'I'll pay when you bring the rest. You're good with that, right?'

The implication was clear. If Yuichi had any complaints he was welcome to take them up with Muta's fist. Yuichi nodded and walked away.

'Hang on a second,' Muta called out from behind him. 'You know Miyako Fujimura?'

'Fujimura?' Yuichi shook his head. 'No.'

'She's at Seika. Third year. Different class than Karasawa.'

'Never heard of her,' Yuichi said, shaking his head again.

'I want you to take some of her, too. I'll pay the same price.'

'But I don't even know what she looks like.'

'She's a violinist so she's always in the music room playing violin after school. You can't miss her.'

'Can you even see inside the music room?'

'Guess you're going to go have to find that out for yourself,' Muta said, turning back to his friends. Clearly, Yuichi had been dismissed. He knew better than to ask any more questions. Muta had been known to fly into mad rages over less.

Muta had first taken an interest in the classy, rich girls attending the famous Seika Girls Middle School about halfway through the first term. Chasing after them was the latest pastime for his gang although it wasn't clear that any of them had actually ever scored.

The whole photography project had been Yuichi's initiative, though he'd only had the idea because he heard Muta and his buddies talking about wanting pictures. Yuichi needed pocket change to support his hobby, so the arrangement worked out well.

Muta's first request had been for photos of Yukiho Karasawa and Yuichi got the sense that he was genuinely interested in her; Muta never turned down any photo with her in it, even ones that were a little blurry.

So it came as a surprise to hear him mention another girl's name. Maybe he had switched targets, having decided Yukiho Karasawa was out of his league. Either way, it didn't make much difference to Yuichi. Work was work.

Yuichi had finished eating and was in the process of cramming his lunchbox into his bag when Kikuchi walked up, carrying a large envelope in his hand.

'You want to come with me up to the roof?' Kikuchi asked.

'What for?'

'That thing we talked about the other day,' the boy said, opening the envelope so Yuichi could look inside. It was the photo he had lent him.

'OK,' Yuichi said, his interest piqued. 'Sure, let's go.'

The roof was unoccupied. Until recently it had been a popular hangout for the bad kids, but after a large quantity of cigarette butts had been discovered there, the guidance counsellor had taken to making frequent patrols on the roof, and so no one ever came there any more.

After a few minutes the door to the stairs opened and a boy emerged. He was in Yuichi's class, but they had hardly ever spoken. His name was Ryo Kirihara and Yuichi had long since categorised him as one of those gloomy kids you just avoided. He didn't seem to have any friends, never stood out in class, never said anything. During lunch and recess he would always go off by himself and read.

Ryo walked over to them and stopped a short distance away. There was a sharp light in his eyes Yuichi had never noticed before and for a second he felt his heart race.

'What do you want?' Ryo said bluntly. Yuichi realised that Kikuchi must have called him up here.

'I wanted to show you something,' Kikuchi said.

'Yeah?'

'Here,' Yuichi said, taking out the photograph.

A wary look on his face, Ryo stepped closer and took the photo. He took one glance at the black-and-white scene and his eyes went a little wider. 'What's this?'

'I just thought it might be useful for you. You know, as evidence.'

Yuichi took a sidelong glance at Kikuchi. *Evidence?*

'I don't know what you're talking about.' Ryo glared at Kikuchi.

'Come on, that's your mom in the photo, isn't it?'

'What?' Yuichi blurted. Ryo shot him a withering glare then turned his sharp eyes back to Kikuchi. 'No way. That's not her.'

'Take another look. It totally is. And the guy with her, he's the one that worked at your place, right?'

Ryo took a closer look at the photo and slowly shook his head. 'Honest, I got no idea what you're talking about. And that's not my mom. Stop wasting my time.' He gave the photo back to Kikuchi and started to walk away.

'This was taken by the station,' Kikuchi called out. 'Near your house! It was four years ago. I could tell by the movie poster on the telephone pole. See? It's for *Johnny Got His Gun*.'

Ryo stopped. 'Drop it,' he said, looking back over his shoulder. 'It's got nothing to do with you.'

'I was just trying to help out,' Kikuchi said, but all Ryo did was glare at both of them before heading down the stairs.

'I thought it was pretty good evidence,' Kikuchi said after Ryo had left.

'Evidence for what?' Yuichi asked.

Kikuchi looked at his friend, surprised for a moment. 'Oh right, you didn't go to the same elementary school he did. You don't know.'

'Don't know what?' Yuichi asked, growing irritated.

Kikuchi looked around before replying, 'That big park up by the station? You remember the building next to it? The one they left half built?'

'What about it?'

'Well, four years ago, they found Ryo's dad in there. Murdered.'

Yuichi's mouth hung open.

'His money was gone, so they said it was probably a mugging. You should've been there. The cops were all over town for days.'

'They catch the guy who did it?'

'They found someone they thought might've done it, but they never knew for sure. He died.'

'What, someone kill him too?'

Kikuchi shook his head. 'Car accident. But when the cops checked his stuff, they found the same kind of lighter that Ryo's dad had.'

'That sounds like pretty good evidence to me.'

'Maybe, maybe not. They couldn't prove that it was the same one that belonged to Ryo's old man. And that's where it gets interesting. See, people started wondering if it wasn't his wife who did it.'

'Whose wife?'

'Ryo's mom, dumbass. They say she was going at it with the guy who worked in their shop and Ryo's dad got in the way.'

The story was that Mr Kirihara ran a pawnshop out of his house, and the 'other guy' was an employee who worked there. The whole thing seemed a bit unreal to Yuichi, like something on TV. Besides, he wasn't really sure what was meant by 'going at it'.

'So, what happened?' Yuichi asked.

'Well, the rumours kept flying, but there was never really any proof, so I guess people forgot about the whole thing. I barely remembered it myself. Until I saw this.' Kikuchi held up the photograph. 'Take a look. See that place behind the couple? That's one of the hotels people go to *to do it*. Doesn't it look like they just walked out of there together?'

'What does this have to do with what happened four years ago?'

'Everything, man! This is evidence that Mrs Kirihara was having an affair with the guy at the shop. That means she had a *motive* for killing her husband. That's why I wanted to show it to Ryo.'

Yuichi shook his head. Kikuchi spent way too much time reading books.

'OK, but Ryo isn't going to suspect his own mom,' Yuichi pointed out.

'I get that, but there's some things you just got to get to the bottom of, even if the truth hurts,' Kikuchi said, excitedly. It sounded like another line from one of those books he was always reading. 'Anyway, I'm gonna prove that this is Ryo's mom somehow. Then he can't ignore it. I bet if I brought this to the police they'd fire up the investigation again. I even know one of the detectives who was on the case. Maybe I'll show it to him.'

'Why are you so obsessed with this?' Yuichi asked.

'It was my little brother who found the body.'

'Your brother? Seriously?'

Kikuchi nodded. 'Yeah, he came and told me, so I went to look for myself. It was there, the body, really. I told my mom, and she was the one who called the police.'

'No way.'

'So because we found the body the police had us in for questioning like a hundred times. And they weren't just asking about how we found the body, either.'

'What do you mean?'

'The guy had his money stolen, right? Well, it turns out that sometimes the killer's the one who takes the money, but sometimes it's someone else.'

'You mean—'

'Like whoever found the body might've snatched the money before telling the police!' A little smile came to Kikuchi's mouth. 'The cops didn't stop there, either. They suspected my dad might've killed him, then had us find the body, see?'

'That's crazy.'

'I know, but it's totally true, just because we were poor. My mom used to go to Ryo's shop, too. That had the cops real excited.'

'But they cleared you, right? They didn't arrest your dad, did they?'

Kikuchi snorted. 'No, but they suspected him,' he said. He didn't elaborate any further.

After class Yuichi went back to the Seika Girls Middle School. He walked along the fence surrounding the school, stopping when he heard the sound he'd been listening for: a violin.

He looked around and once he was confident the coast was clear he climbed on to the fence and moved along it until he could see in through the window the music was coming from.

There was a girl inside sitting at a black piano, her hands on the keys. Her back was turned to Yuichi.

Yes! Yuichi thought, and shifted, craning his neck to see beyond the piano. There was a girl standing there in her sailor uniform, playing violin.

Miyako Fujimura.

She looked shorter than Yukiho. Her hair was short, too. He wanted to get a closer look at her face and was just craning his neck further when the sound of the violin abruptly stopped and, to his horror, the girl ran up to the window.

The window opened right in front of Yuichi and the girl stared straight out at him, a victorious smile on her face. Yuichi froze, unable even to climb down the fence.

Then Miyako Fujimura shouted something at him. Her voice hit him like a ton of bricks and he let go of the fence, tumbling when he hit the ground. Thankfully, he'd managed to land feet first.

The girl was still screaming inside the classroom. Yuichi ran for his life.

It was only later when he caught his breath that he was able to process what the girl had shouted at him through the window.

'Cockroach.'

On Tuesday and Friday evenings, Eriko went to English lessons with Yukiho from seven to eight-thirty. The lessons had been Yukiho's idea, of course.

The class was only a ten-minute walk from school, but Eriko always went home first to eat dinner before going. While she was doing that, Yukiho stayed at school to practise with the theatre club. Eriko was like Yukiho's shadow these days, following her everywhere, but she had stopped short at trying to join the theatre club.

One Tuesday night after class the two were walking back home as usual. They were nearing school when Yukiho said she had to call home and went into a phone booth. Eriko looked at her watch. It was almost nine o'clock. They'd stayed too long after class finished, chatting.

'Thanks for waiting,' Yukiho said as she came out of the booth. 'Mom told me to hurry home. How about we take a shortcut?'

'Sure.'

Normally the two of them walked along the main road where

the buses ran, but tonight, they took a back road they usually avoided because there weren't many lights, which made it really dark, and there weren't many homes, just empty car parks and warehouses. They were just passing by the storehouse for a lumberyard when Yukiho stopped.

'Hey,' she said, 'see that thing over there? Isn't that a school uniform?' Yukiho pointed towards something white lying on the ground next to a stack of wood.

'I don't know,' Eriko said, craning her neck. 'Maybe it's just a piece of cloth or something.'

'No, that's definitely a uniform.' Yukiho walked over and picked it up. 'See? What'd I tell you?'

She was right. It was torn, but it was definitely one of their school uniforms – the light blue collar was unmistakable. A small name tag was attached: MIYAKO FUJIMURA.

A nasty tingle ran down Eriko's spine. She didn't know why, but she wanted to leave this place soon as possible.

But Yukiho just stood there, looking around until she noticed that the door on the side of the storehouse was slightly ajar. Bravely, she walked up to it and looked inside.

'Let's go home,' Eriko called out, but Yukiho gave a little scream and stepped away from the door, clapping her hand to her mouth.

'What?' Eriko asked, her voice shaking.

'Somebody's inside,' Yukiho said. 'I think they might be dead.'

It was Miyako Fujimura. Her arms and legs had been tied and her mouth was gagged, but she wasn't dead. She was unconscious when help arrived, but came to soon afterwards.

After discovering her, the two girls had run back to the main road and, convinced they'd seen a body, called the police. Then they waited by the phone booth, holding hands and trembling.

Miyako was naked from the waist up. Everything from the waist down had been taken off except for her skirt. The rest of her clothes were scattered on the ground nearby along with a black plastic bag. The first responders carried her into the waiting ambulance, but the girl said nothing. Even when she saw Eriko and Yukiho she didn't react and her eyes were vacant.

Eriko and Yukiho were taken to the nearby police station where they were asked some simple questions. It was their first time in a police car – an event that would have been cause for excitement under any other circumstances. But after what they had witnessed they were just happy to be safe.

The man asking them questions was a middle-aged detective, with white hair parted in the middle. He looked like the kind of man you might see behind the counter at a sushi bar, but the way he talked, and even the way he sat in his chair, were completely different. He seemed as if he was doing his best to be gentle with them, but the sharp look in his eyes made Eriko shrink in her seat.

The detective wanted to know everything that had led up to their discovery of Miyako and whether they knew anything about what had happened to her. Eriko and Yukiho told the policeman everything they could remember, frequently exchanging glances while they talked to make sure they got it all right. The detective just nodded and listened to them, but when he asked whether they knew anything about what had happened, Eriko and Yukiho had nothing to say.

'Have you ever seen anyone unusual on your way home from school?' a female officer sitting next to the detective asked. 'Maybe someone who might have looked like he was waiting for somebody? Have you ever heard stories about anything like that from your friends?'

'No, nothing,' Eriko said.

'Except,' Yukiho said, 'there's been people looking inside the school, and taking pictures of us on our way home.' She looked at Eriko. 'Remember?'

Eriko nodded.

'Was it always the same person?' the detective asked.

'No, there were a few of them. I don't know if all of them were taking pictures, though,' Yukiho said. 'But I think they're all from the same school.'

'Wait, these are students you're talking about?' The female officer's eyes widened.

'I think they're from Ōe Middle School,' Yukiho said. She sounded so sure of it, Eriko was surprised.

'Ōe? How could you tell?' the female officer asked.

'I used to live there. I'm pretty sure those uniforms are from the middle school.'

The female officer exchanged glances with the detective.

'Do you remember anything else?' the detective asked.

'Well, I know the name of the one who took my picture the other day. He had his name tag on his shirt.'

The detective's eyes narrowed like an animal closing in on its prey. 'What was the name?'

'Akiyoshi, I'm pretty sure. Written with the characters for autumn and good luck.'

This all struck Eriko as extremely odd. Judging from her attitude the other day, she'd thought Yukiho was completely ignoring them. Yet she had been paying enough attention to even catch the boy's name. Eriko didn't remember seeing anything like that at all.

'Akiyoshi ... Right,' the detective said, writing the name down. He whispered something in the female officer's ear. She stood and walked out of the room.

'There's one last thing I want you to take a look at before we let you go.' The detective brought out a plastic bag and put it on the table. 'We found this in the warehouse. I wonder if either of you have seen it before?'

The bag contained a small figurine that looked like part of a key chain, except the chain was broken off halfway.

'No, sorry. I've never seen that,' Eriko said.

Yukiho's answer was the same.

'Hey, your key chain's broken.'

It was lunch hour and they were at the store to buy some snacks. Yuichi was standing in line behind Kikuchi when Kikuchi pulled out his wallet. He used to have a keychain attached to it with a little figurine at the end, but now there was just a short piece of chain. The figurine was gone.

'Yeah. I just noticed last night.' Kikuchi made a sour face. 'Sucks. You wouldn't think the chain'd break that easy.'

Yuichi almost said that it was because it was cheap but swallowed his words. 'Cheap' was a forbidden word when he was talking with Kikuchi.

'Speaking of yesterday,' Kikuchi said, lowering his voice, 'I saw *Rocky*!'

'Hey, cool,' Yuichi said, even though he was thinking: *I thought you said the tickets were too expensive.*

'We got free tickets,' Kikuchi added, as though he had read Yuichi's mind. 'Some customer gave them to my mom.'

'You lucked out.' Kikuchi's mom worked at a market near the school.

'Anyway, when we checked the tickets, we found out that they were only good until yesterday. Guess that's why they gave 'em to my mom in the first place. Man, we only just made the last show.'

'So, how was it?'

'It was great!'

For a while they just talked excitedly, trading notes on the movie.

They were just getting back to class when one of Yuichi's classmates told him that their homeroom teacher had been looking for him. Their teacher taught science and everyone called him Bear.

Yuichi found Bear waiting for him, a serious look on his face.

'Some detectives from Tennoji are here. They want to talk to you.'

Yuichi's mouth gaped. 'With me? About what?'

'They say you were taking pictures at the Seika Girls Middle School?' Bear glared at Yuichi with dark eyes.

'I – no, uh—' Yuichi stammered. He might as well have confessed on the spot.

'I don't believe it,' Bear said, scowling as he stood. 'What will you idiots think of next? You're an embarrassment to the whole school.' He walked out of the room, motioning with his jaw for Yuichi to follow.

Three men were waiting for them in the school office. One of them was the guidance counsellor. He was glared at Yuichi through thick glasses.

Yuichi had never seen the other two men before. One was middle-aged and the other was a little younger. They were both wearing plain dark suits. *These must be the detectives*, Yuichi thought.

Bear introduced Yuichi to the detectives, who were looking him over from head to toe.

'So you're the one they say has been taking pictures of the students by the Seika Girls Middle School?' the middle-aged detective said. His voice was calm, but there was a growl beneath the surface that was more frightening than anything Yuichi had ever heard from any teacher. Yuichi shrank in his seat, wanting to disappear.

'I, er— ' He tried to talk, but his tongue felt like it was tied in knots.

'One of the girls saw your name tag,' the detective said, pointing at Yuichi's shirt. 'It's a pretty unusual name. Guess that's why she remembered it.'

No way, Yuichi thought.

'Well? Were you taking pictures? Tell the truth, now.'

The younger detective joined in glaring at Yuichi. Meanwhile, the guidance counsellor was practically simmering in his chair.

'Yes,' Yuichi said, lowering his head. He heard Bear give a big sigh.

'You should be ashamed of yourself,' the guidance counsellor scolded him.

'Let us handle this,' the detective said, holding a hand up to the guidance counsellor before looking back at Yuichi. 'Were you taking photos of a particular student?'

'Yes, sir.'

'You know her name?'

Yuichi nodded. His voice was caught in his throat.

'Think you could write it here for me?' The detective pushed a piece of paper and a pen over to Yuichi.

Yuichi wrote Yukiho Karasawa's name on the paper. The detective took a look at it and nodded.

'Anyone else?' the detective asked him. 'You just took pictures of her?'

'Just her, sir.'

'She your favourite or something?' the detective asked, a knowing smile spreading across his face.

'Not *my* favourite exactly. More like my friend's. I was just taking the pictures for him.'

'Why couldn't he take them himself?'

Yuichi looked down at the floor and bit his lip. The detective watched him, then chuckled. 'You were selling the pictures?'

Yuichi flinched.

'I don't believe it,' Bear muttered next to him. 'Of all the stupid—'

'You the only one taking pictures?' the detective asked. 'No one else was doing the same thing?'

'I don't think so, sir.'

'What about the kids on the fence by the athletics field? You one of them, too?'

Yuichi looked up at the detective. 'That wasn't me. Honest, sir. I only took the pictures.'

'So who was on the fence, then? Any idea?'

Yuichi was sure it was Muta and his gang, but he didn't say anything. Who knew what they would do to him if they heard he'd squealed.

'Understand: if you're hiding something it's not going to go well for you.' The detective gave him a meaningful look. 'But right now what I want you to tell me is what you were doing yesterday after school. Be as detailed as you can.'

'Huh?' Yuichi blinked. 'Did something happen?'

'Akiyoshi!' Bear shouted. 'Answer the man's question!'

'It's OK,' the detective said. There was a faint smile on his face when he turned back to Yuichi. 'One of the students from Seika got pretty roughed up near school yesterday.'

Yuichi felt the muscles in his face freeze. 'I didn't do anything.'

'We're not saying you did. But we were talking to the students at Seika, and your name came up.' There was nothing threatening in the detective's tone, but Yuichi could hear the meaning behind his words: *you're our prime suspect, kid*.

'I don't know anything, really!' Yuichi shook his head.

'OK, then tell me what you were doing yesterday and where you were.'

'Yesterday ... on the way home from school I stopped at the bookshop and the record shop,' Yuichi said, recalling. That had been a little after six, and after that he had spent the entire night at home.

'Was your family home?'

'Yeah. I was with my mom. Dad came home around nine.'

'So no one other than your family was there?'

'No, sir,' Yuichi said, worried that they might not take his family's word for it.

'So, what to do?' The detective talking turned to the younger detective. 'Mr Akiyoshi here says he wasn't taking those photos for himself, but I'm not sure what reason we have to believe him.'

'I really was taking them for my friend.'

'If that's the case, you should probably tell us your friend's name.'

Yuichi was in a fix. If he didn't tell them, he was sure they would suspect he did it.

'Don't worry,' the detective said suddenly, 'we won't tell anyone it was you who told us.'

His timing was uncanny. It was as if he had peered right into Yuichi's thoughts. Hesitantly, he gave them Muta's name. As soon as he said it, the guidance counsellor's face fell. Probably because that was the name that always came up whenever there was trouble at the school.

'And he only asked you for pictures of Miss Karasawa? He didn't want pictures of any of the other girls?'

Yuichi hesitated for a moment, but decided not to hide anything. It wasn't like he had much left to lose. 'Actually, just the other day he asked me about one other one. Her name's Miyako Fujimura. I don't know her, though.'

A change came over the detectives' faces.

'And did you take her picture?' the detective asked him in a low voice.

'Not yet, sir,' Yuichi said, immediately regretting his choice of words.

The detective nodded.

'I don't ever want to hear about you taking any more pictures, you got that?' Bear growled next to him. 'If you hadn't been out there being an idiot you wouldn't be sitting in here right now, understand?'

Yuichi nodded silently.

'There's one more thing I wanted to check with you,' the detective said, pulling out a plastic bag. 'Have you ever seen this before?'

A small figurine was in the bag. Yuichi gaped. There was no doubt in his mind it was Kikuchi's missing key chain.

'Looks like you have seen it.'

If he told them who it belonged to, would Kikuchi become a suspect? But, if he lied, things might get worse for him, quick.

'Well?' the detective asked again, rapping his fingers on the table. The sound felt like needles pricking at Yuichi's skin.

Yuichi swallowed and told them.

It was Thursday morning when the announcement came. All students were to leave school by no later than five o'clock, even if they had after-school activities. They were reminded of the new rule again by their teacher in homeroom.

It seemed only natural to Eriko. When she thought about what she'd seen the other day, she felt like even five was too late, and every student should go home right when classes ended.

But all the other students complained. It was a testament to how well they had covered up the incident. It was safe to say that no one else in the school knew what had happened two nights ago in the storehouse so close to campus.

Of course there were rumours, and some bore a resemblance to the truth. One was that a pervert had attacked a student on the way home from school. But even then, they could have made that up just from reading the announcement. Eriko couldn't imagine any of the teachers talking, and neither she nor Yukiho had said a word. No one even knew that they were the ones who had found the victim.

It had been Yukiho who suggested they keep it to themselves. She had called Eriko that night after they got home.

'Miyako must be in shock, having that happen to her. If people start talking about it ... I mean, what if she does something? What if she kills herself? So I was thinking we should keep it to ourselves. Maybe we can stop the rumours from starting.'

It was a wise suggestion, Eriko thought. She told her friend that she had planned on staying quiet, too.

Miyako Fujimura had been her classmate in second year. She was a good student with a cheerful personality, a natural leader in class. She wasn't Eriko's favourite person, however. Miyako had a tendency to lash out whenever she felt her pride was being injured, which was often. She also never thought twice about saying bad things about people. There were others who felt the same way about her, Eriko was sure. If they heard about what had happened, they would be right up there in front, leading the rumour mill.

That day at lunch Eriko ate with Yukiho at their desks by the window. No one else was around.

'So the story is that Fujimura's off because she was in a traffic accident,' Yukiho told her in a quiet voice.

'Really?'

'Nobody suspects anything yet. I don't know how long that will last, though.'

When she had finished lunch, Yukiho took out her patchwork and looked out of the window. 'Doesn't seem like any of those boys are here today.'

Eriko looked up. 'Which boys?'

'The ones that are always on the fence.'

Eriko looked outside. It was true. During lunch break, the boys could usually be seen out there, hanging on the fence like geckos, but today the fence was clear. 'Maybe they heard about what happened and their teachers told them not to come.'

'Could be.'

'I wonder if one of them did it?' Eriko said quietly. 'I don't hear anything good about that school. I'm glad I don't go there.'

'I don't know,' Yukiho said. 'I'm sure some of the kids there aren't bad. They just don't have any other choice if their families can't afford to send them anywhere else.'

'Well, sure, but ...' Eriko's voice trailed off. She looked down at Yukiho's hands and smiled. She was almost done sewing the purse she'd shown her the other day at her house. 'You're almost finished.'

'Yep. Just the final touches left.'

'But why do the initials say RK?' Eriko asked. 'Shouldn't it be YK for Yukiho?'

'This is for my mother. Her name's Reiko.'

'Oh, that's nice,' Eriko said, watching Yukiho's fingers deftly work the needle.

It was clear that the police suspected Kikuchi. He was questioned in the school office by detectives on Thursday morning, though he never told anyone what they asked, or what he told them and he was called out of class again on Friday morning. He made his way to the door, weaving through the desks, making eye contact with no one.

'I heard someone attacked one of the girls at Seika,' one of the kids said after Kikuchi had left the room. 'And they think it's him. They found something of his at the scene.'

'Who told you that crap?' Yuichi asked.

'Somebody heard the teachers talking about it. It sounds like it was real bad.'

'What do they mean, "attack"? Did he rape her?' another boy asked, his face alight with curiosity.

'Yeah, probably. And took her money too,' the first boy added meaningfully.

Yuichi sensed the other kids listening, nodding, understanding. They all knew that Kikuchi's family wasn't rich.

'But Kikuchi says he didn't do it, right?' Yuichi said. 'Wasn't he at the movies when it happened or something?'

They weren't listening to him. 'He totally did it,' said another student, and several of the kids agreed. A circle had formed and Yuichi was surprised to see Ryo joining in. He usually avoided gossip, though Yuichi wondered if his interest wasn't more about the photo Kikuchi had shown him the other day.

Yuichi watched them for a while, until his eyes met Ryo's. Ryo returned his gaze for just one or two seconds before he slipped out of the circle and returned to his desk.

On the Saturday, four days after the assault, Eriko and Yukiho went to visit Miyako Fujimura at home. It had been Yukiho's suggestion that they go.

They waited in the living room, but Miyako didn't appear. Instead her mother came down and told them that Miyako still wasn't receiving any visitors. She sounded genuinely sorry.

'Was she badly hurt?' Eriko asked.

'No, not too bad ...' Miyako's mother gave a short sigh.

'Do they know who did it?' Yukiho asked. 'The police have been asking us a lot of questions.'

The mother shook her head. 'No, not yet. I'm sorry they've been after you so much.'

'No, it's fine. I was just wondering if Miyako might have seen who it was,' Yukiho said, her voice barely more than a whisper.

'No.' The mother shook her head. 'Whoever it was put a bag over her head from behind, so she couldn't see a thing. Then they hit her, and she blacked out.' Miyako's mother's eyes were red and she put her hands to her face. 'I was worried because she was coming home late every day, staying after class to get ready for the school festival. I think she felt responsible because she was in charge of the band, so she stayed even later than the other kids—'

Eriko truly hoped the woman didn't cry. She wanted to leave. Yukiho must have felt the same way, because she looked at her and said, 'Maybe we should go home.'

'Yeah,' Eriko said, gathering her things.

'I'm really sorry she couldn't see you,' the mother said. 'After you came out all this way.'

'It's no problem. We just hope she gets better soon,' Yukiho said.

'Thank you. Oh, and ...' Miyako's mother looked up at both of them. 'I know what you saw, and that her clothes were taken off, but they didn't touch her, you know. Her body, I mean.'

Eriko understood what she was trying to say. She exchanged surprised looks with Yukiho. Neither of them had used the word, but they had both assumed Miyako had been raped.

'Of course,' Yukiho said, in a voice that made it sound like they had never even suspected such a thing could happen.

'Also, I know you've both done a really good job keeping this to yourselves and I was hoping you could continue to do so. I'm afraid if people start talking they might say things that could hurt her ... hurt her future.'

'We understand,' Yukiho said crisply. 'We won't tell anyone, I promise. And if we hear any rumours, we'll deny them right away. Please let Miyako know her secret is safe with us.'

'Thank you. I'm glad she has such good friends. We won't forget this,' the mother said, tears in her eyes.

Suspicion over Kikuchi had lifted by Saturday – at least that was what Yuichi heard when he came in to school on Monday morning. Word was that Muta had been called in to talk to the detectives that morning.

Yuichi went to Kikuchi to get the whole story, but his friend just stared at him before looking back at the blackboard and saying, his voice rough, 'Yeah, I'm off the hook. It's done. Over.'

'Well, that's good, right?' Yuichi said brightly. 'How'd you get them off your back?'

'I proved I went to the movies that night.'

'How?'

'See ...' He folded his arms across his chest and gave a deep sigh. 'I don't see how that's any of your business. Unless you wanted me to get arrested?'

'What are you talking about? Of course I didn't want you to get arrested.'

'Then maybe you could just drop it, OK? I don't even want to think about it. Makes me sick to my stomach.' Kikuchi kept his eyes on the blackboard the whole time, without a single glance at Yuichi. It was obvious he was upset with him. Maybe he had an inkling of who had told them the keychain was his.

Yuichi racked his brain trying to come up with a way to mend relations. Then he got an idea. 'Hey, Kikuchi, remember that photo? If you wanted to look into that some more, I'll go with you.'

'What're you talking about?'

'That photo with Ryo's mom and the guy. I thought that whole thing sounded pretty cool.'

'Oh, that.' Kikuchi frowned. 'I've given up on that. I mean, it's got nothing to do with me. It was a long time ago, too. No one even remembers any of that any more.'

'But didn't you say—'

'Besides,' Kikuchi cut him off, 'I lost the photo. Maybe I threw it out by accident when I was cleaning my room the other day.'

'No way—'

When Yuichi saw the stony look on Kikuchi's face his words left him. He didn't look sorry he had lost the photograph one bit.

'It's not like you cared about that picture anyway, right?' Kikuchi said, looking at him. Actually, it was more of a glare than a look.

'Well, no, I guess not.' Yuichi shrugged.

Kikuchi stood and left his desk. Talking time was over.

Yuichi watched him go, a mix of emotions in his chest. Then he felt someone else's eyes on him. He turned and saw Ryo looking at him. The boy's cold, calculating stare gave Yuichi a chill.

It was over a moment later. Ryo looked back down at his desk and started reading a book. There was a patchwork bag on the desk next to his book, embroidered with the initials 'RK.'

Yuichi was walking home from school that afternoon when someone ran up and grabbed him on the shoulder. He looked around to see Muta glaring at him, rage in his eyes. Two of his friends were behind him. They all had the same look on their faces.

'Come on,' Muta growled in a low voice that made Yuichi feel like his heart was being squeezed out of his chest.

They dragged Yuichi into a narrow alleyway. Muta stood directly in front of him with his two cronies holding Yuichi on either side. Muta grabbed Yuichi by his collar, lifting him up until Yuichi had to stand on tiptoe.

'You sold me out,' Muta said.

Yuichi shook his head furiously. His face was drawn tight with fear.

'You squealed.' Muta bared his teeth as he brought his face closer to Yuichi's. 'You're the only one who could have.'

Yuichi kept shaking his head. 'I didn't say anything. Honest!'

'Liar,' the boy to his left said. 'We're going to fuck you up.'

'Tell the truth!' Muta gave Yuichi a violent shake.

Yuichi felt his back pressed up against the wall, the coolness of the concrete through his shirt.

'Honest. It's not a lie! I didn't say a word.'

'Really?'

'Really!' Yuichi pleaded.

Muta glared at him for a moment, then suddenly released him. The boy to his right swore under his breath.

Yuichi put a hand to his own throat and swallowed. *That was close.*

But the next moment, Muta's face twisted into a wicked grin. There was no time to react, not even time to shout. With the first hit, Yuichi was down on all fours.

He could feel the side of his face stinging and belatedly realised he'd been punched.

'It was you!' Muta shouted, and Yuichi felt something enter his mouth. He was already lying with his back on the ground by the time he understood it had been the tip of Muta's shoe.

There was a cut in his mouth, and he tasted blood. *Tastes like sucking on a coin*, he thought, as a staggering pain washed over him. Yuichi put his face in his hands and curled into a ball as the boys kicked him in the ribs, over and over.

THREE

Tomohiko Sonomura opened the door to a loud ringing of bells over his head. The café he'd been told to go was a tiny place, with a small bar and two dinky tables, one of which only sat two.

He looked around, hesitating a moment before taking a seat at the smaller table – the other table being occupied. They'd never spoken, but Tomohiko recognised him as Murashita from Class 3. He was rail-thin, and his high cheekbones gave him an almost foreign look. It was the kind of face Tomohiko imagined girls went for. His hair was long and wavy, too. He wouldn't have seemed out of place in a band. He was wearing a black leather waistcoat over a grey shirt, and tight jeans as if to show off his long, skinny legs.

Murashita was reading a copy of *Shonen Jump*. He looked up once when Tomohiko walked in but quickly went back to his manga. He might have been there waiting for someone but clearly it wasn't Tomohiko. There was a coffee cup and a red ashtray on the table. Smoke drifted up from a lit cigarette in the ashtray. He didn't seem to be worried that the guidance counsellor would find him all the way out here. It was two stops away on the subway from the station closest to their high school.

There was no waitress, just a greying man who came out from behind the counter and put a glass of water on Tomohiko's table. The man smiled but didn't say a word.

Tomohiko asked for coffee without even looking at the menu. The man nodded and went back behind the counter.

Tomohiko took a sip of water and glanced back at Murashita, who was still reading his manga. When the radio on the counter switched from playing Olivia Newton-John to the theme song to

Galaxy Express 999, he frowned. Apparently Murashita preferred Western music to local fare.

It occurred to Tomohiko that Murashita might actually be waiting for the same person he was.

Tomohiko looked around the café. Usually places like this had a *Space Invaders* game in the corner, but there was nothing of the kind here. Tomohiko didn't mind. He was already sick of *Space Invaders*. The rhythms of the game – when to shoot, how to score big – were already ingrained in his fingers. Put him in any arcade and he was confident he'd be at the top of the scoreboards in no time. If anything still interested him about *Space Invaders*, it was the code that made the game run but he'd almost finished learning all there was to know about that, too.

Out of boredom he opened the menu. He realised that this was, in fact, a speciality coffee shop. There were dozens of brands listed, some he'd even heard of. He was glad he hadn't looked at the menu before ordering, otherwise he never would've had the balls to just order coffee. No, he would have ended up getting the Colombian, or the mocha, and spending an extra fifty or a hundred yen. Even little outlays like that hurt, these days.

The jacket had clearly been a mistake, maybe the worst yet, Tomohiko thought. He and a friend had gone into a men's boutique shop to shoplift when the guy at the register caught them. His technique was simple: he pretended to be trying on a pair of jeans so he could stuff the jacket he'd brought into the changing room into his own bag. But when he brought the jeans back to the shelf and tried to leave, the guy at the register headed them off at the door. He remembered feeling like his heart had stopped.

Thankfully, the guy was more interested in making a sale than turning young punks over to the authorities. He treated Tomohiko as a customer who'd 'mistakenly placed an object for purchase in his personal bag'. No police were called and their parents and the school didn't hear about it, but he had to pay for the jacket to the tune of twenty-three thousand yen. Of course he didn't have that much money on him, so the employee took his student ID and told him to go and get the money from home. Tomohiko ran home and scraped together all the money in his room, fifteen thousand yen, and borrowed another eight from his friend to pay for the jacket.

Of course, he'd come out of the whole thing with a trendy new jacket, so he couldn't really call it a total loss. Except for the fact that the jacket wasn't something he would have actually paid money for. He'd just grabbed it off the shelf when he thought no one was looking. Since then he'd regretted not having that twenty-three thousand at least a hundred times. He could have gone on a shopping spree. He could have gone to see a movie. But now, except for the money his mom gave him for lunch every day, his personal funds had been reduced to zero. Worse than that, he still owed his friend eight thousand.

Tomohiko took a sip of the two-hundred-yen coffee the man had brought him. It was good.

I hope this isn't a waste of time, he thought, looking up at the clock on the wall. He'd come here to hear about a 'job opportunity'. That was how Ryo Kirihara had described it.

It was five o'clock on the dot when Ryo showed up.

Ryo looked at Tomohiko first when he walked in. Then his eyes went to Murashita and he snorted. 'Why aren't you guys sitting together?'

Murashita closed his manga and scratched his head. 'Yeah, I thought he might be here to see you too, but I figured it was better to read my manga than make a fool of myself.'

'Same here,' Tomohiko said.

'Maybe I should've told you guys there'd be someone else,' Ryo said, sitting across from Murashita. He looked over at the counter. 'I'll take a Brazil,' he called out.

The old man nodded. Ryo must be a regular.

Tomohiko picked up his coffee and moved over to the big table. Ryo motioned him to sit down next to Murashita.

Ryo looked at the two of them, squinting, tapping the table with his right index finger. Tomohiko didn't care for the way he was looking at them. Like he was sizing them up.

'Eat any garlic lately?' Ryo asked.

'Garlic?' Tomohiko's eyebrows drew together. 'No. Why?'

'It's complicated. But as long as you haven't, you're cool. How about you, Murashita?'

'I ate some dumplings about four days ago.'

'C'mere.'

Murashita leaned over the table, bringing his face up to Ryo.

'Breathe,' Ryo said.

Murashita coughed a little.

'Harder,' Ryo directed him.

Murashita breathed out a big breath and Ryo gave it a good sniff. He nodded and pulled a piece of peppermint gum out of his pocket.

'You'll want to chew this once we get going.'

'Sure, whatever,' Murashita said, growing a little irritated, 'but what are we going to do? Spit it out, come on. I don't like this mystery crap.'

Tomohiko felt relieved he wasn't the only one completely in the dark.

'I told you already. You're going to go someplace, and talk to some girls. That's it.'

'Man, I don't get it, I thought—'

Murashita was interrupted by the arrival of Ryo's coffee. Ryo lifted up his cup, took a long sniff of the aroma, then slowly took a single sip. 'Outstanding, as always.'

The old man smiled as he retreated behind the counter.

Ryo turned back to them. 'Look, it's not rocket science. You two will do just fine. That's why I picked you.'

'Just fine at what?' Murashita asked.

Ryo pulled a red box of cigarettes out of the breast pocket of his denim jacket, put one in his mouth, and lit it with a Zippo.

'What I mean is, they'll like you.' A thin smile spread on his lips.

'They ... you mean the girls?' Murashita asked, his voice low.

'Yeah, the girls. Don't worry. They're not ugly or all wrinkled or nothing. Just totally normal girls. Maybe a little on the older side, but that's a good thing.'

'And our job is to talk to them?' Tomohiko asked.

Ryo blew smoke at him. 'That's right. There's three of them, by the way.'

'Can you be a little more specific? Who are these girls and where are we talking to them and what are we supposed to talk to them about?' Tomohiko asked, his voice growing a little louder.

'It'll be obvious when we get there. And as far as what you'll be talking about – whatever comes up. You can talk about your hobbies or whatever you feel like. They'll like that,' Ryo said, smiling.

Tomohiko shook his head. He felt he had even less idea what they'd be doing now that it had been explained to him.

'I'm out,' Murashita said abruptly.

'Yeah?' Ryo said. He didn't seem that surprised.

'I don't like it. It doesn't feel right.' Murashita stood.

'I'm paying three thousand three hundred yen an hour,' Ryo said, raising his coffee cup. 'Three thousand three hundred and thirty-three, to be exact. That's ten thousand in three hours. You can't tell me you've had a better offer than that.'

'OK, now I know it's illegal,' Murashita said. 'Look, I stay out of that stuff.'

'Nothing illegal about it. And as long as you keep this to yourselves, you won't get any trouble. Guaranteed. And I can promise you one other thing: When you're done, you'll thank me. You can go read the help-wanted ads from cover to cover and you won't find anything sweeter. Anyone would want to do this. But not everyone can. See, you two are the lucky ones. Because I spotted you.'

'I don't know …' Murashita gave Tomohiko a hesitant look.

More than three thousand an hour, ten thousand in three hours – that was hard for Tomohiko to pass up. 'I'll do it,' he said. 'But on one condition.'

'What's that?'

'I want you to tell me who we're meeting and where. So I can psych myself up.'

'There's no need for any of that,' Ryo said, stubbing out his cigarette in the ashtray. 'But fine, I'll tell you once we're outside. But

I'm not taking just you, Tomohiko. If Murashita's dropping out, I'm calling the whole thing off.'

Tomohiko looked at Murashita, who grimaced. 'You sure we're not going to get in trouble for this?'

'Not unless you want to,' Ryo said. Maybe it was the irritation in Tomohiko's face that pushed Murashita, but eventually he nodded. 'OK. I'm in.'

'Smart boy.' Ryo stood, thrusting one hand into the back pocket of his jeans to pull out a brown leather wallet. 'Bill, please.'

The man raised an eyebrow and pointed at the table, making a circle with his finger.

'Yeah, all together.'

The man scribbled on a piece of paper and passed it over to Ryo.

Tomohiko watched as Ryo pulled a thousand-yen note from his wallet and regretted not ordering a sandwich.

The kids didn't wear uniforms at Tomohiko's high school, thanks to the efforts of his predecessors back during the student protest days. They had organised and staged a demonstration against the uniform code and they had actually won. There was a standard, school-approved uniform you could buy, but it wasn't compulsory, and only about one in five students bothered with it at all. Particularly after their first year, nearly everyone just wore whatever they felt like. It was also against the rules to get a perm, but hardly anyone paid any attention to that either. The same went for make-up, which was why some of the girls came in to school looking like they'd just stepped out of the pages of a fashion magazine, an invisible cloud of perfume trailing them as they took their seats. As long as it didn't interfere with the class, the teachers turned a blind eye.

Civilian clothes helped the kids blend in when they hit the town after school was out, too. If a shop assistant gave them trouble, they could just say they were college students. Which was why, on a sunny Friday like today, hardly any of them went straight home after school.

The only reason Tomohiko wasn't out there today was because of the shoplifting incident. He was broke.

That was why Ryo had found him, earlier that afternoon, sitting in the back of the empty classroom, reading *Playboy*. Sensing someone, Tomohiko looked up.

Despite the fact that Ryo was in the same class as Tomohiko, they'd hardly exchanged a word in the two months since school started. Tomohiko wasn't a recluse; on the contrary, he was already friends with about half the class. It was more Ryo who seemed to put up walls between himself and the other students.

'You free today?' Ryo spoke first.

'Yeah, why?'

That's when Ryo lowered his voice and told him about the job.

'All you have to do is talk a little and I'll pay you ten thousand. Not bad, huh?'

'What, just talk?'

Ryo held out a piece of paper. 'If you're interested, be here, five o'clock.'

'The girls should be there already,' Ryo told them. When he wanted to he had a way of talking without moving his lips much.

They'd left the café and got on the subway. The carriage was mostly empty and there were seats to go around but Ryo remained standing by the door, possibly to avoid being overheard.

'So who are they?' Tomohiko asked.

'Let's call them ... Ran, Sue, and Miki,' Ryo chuckled, using the names of the members of a singing group that had broken up the year before.

'Come on, you said you'd tell us.'

'I didn't promise names. And besides, it's better for you if there aren't any names. I haven't told them who you are, either, or what school we go to. So let's keep it that way.'

There was a hard light in Ryo's eyes that made Tomohiko suddenly nervous.

'What are we supposed to do if they ask?' Murashita wanted to know.

'I really don't think they will but if they do just tell them it's a secret. Or make up a fake name if you want.'

'Just what kind of girls are these?' Tomohiko asked, changing tack.

Unexpectedly, Ryo broke into a grin. 'Housewives.'

'Whoa! What?'

'*Bored* housewives. No hobbies, no jobs, no one to talk to all day. They get frustrated. And their husbands sure as hell don't talk to them. So they want to chat with some young guys. No harm in that, right?'

Tomohiko was reminded of a recent skin flick with something in the title about 'apartment block wives'. He hadn't actually seen it.

'And they're paying ten thousand, each, just to talk? I don't know—'

'Hey,' Ryo cut him off, 'don't worry so much. They're paying, just take the cash.'

'So why me and Murashita?'

'Because you got the look. I mean, you know you do, right?'

The way Ryo spoke was so unflinchingly straight, Tomohiko found himself stunned into silence. It was true he thought he had the face for the big screen if he wanted to go there. He dressed the part, too, despite being broke.

'That's why I said not everyone can do this job,' Ryo said, nodding at the evident wisdom in his own words.

'And they're not old?' Murashita said.

Ryo grinned. 'Not *that* old. I'd say probably somewhere between thirty and forty?'

'That's pretty old, man. What are we supposed to talk to them about?' Tomohiko was starting to get nervous.

'Don't even think about that. Just keep the conversation harmless and you'll be fine. Oh, you'll want to comb your hair when we get off the train. Get some hairspray on that too.'

'I don't have any,' Tomohiko said, and Ryo opened his duffel bag to reveal a stash of hairspray and brushes. He even had a dryer.

'I figured, why not go all out? Make you guys into some leading men, right?'

At Nanba station they switched from the Midosuji line to the
Sennichimae line, taking that to Nishinagahori station.
Tomohiko was familiar with the place. This was where the central
library was located. In the summer, kids studying for college
admission tests would be lined up to use the study rooms.

They walked right past the library, going several minutes further before Ryo stopped in front of a small, four-storey apartment
building. 'This is the place.'

Tomohiko looked up and swallowed.

'What's with the face? Try to loosen up.'

Ryo chuckled and Tomohiko absently massaged his cheekbones
with his fingers.

There was no elevator, so they walked up the stairs and Ryo
pressed the button by No 304.

'Yes?' came a woman's voice over the intercom.

'It's me,' Ryo said.

The door opened almost immediately. A woman wearing a skirt
and black shirt with more than a few buttons open at the neck was
holding the doorknob. She was short, with a small face and short
hair.

'Hi.' Ryo smiled.

'Hello,' she replied. Her eyes were dark with make-up and two
bright red round earrings hung from her ears. She might have
been dressed young, but there was no mistaking her for a twenty-
year-old. There were tiny wrinkles beneath her eyes.

She looked over at Tomohiko and Murashita behind him. He
felt like she was scanning them from top to bottom, like the light
on a photocopier.

'Your friends?' she asked Ryo.

'I told you they were the real deal.'

The woman smiled at that. She opened the door wider and
invited them inside.

Tomohiko followed Ryo in. A dining room and kitchen were
just inside the entrance. There were chairs set at the table but no

cupboards or pieces of furniture other than the shelves built into the wall, and no cooking utensils in sight, just a small, one-person refrigerator and a microwave sitting on top of that. It was clear that no one actually lived here. It must have been rented for the occasion.

The short-haired woman opened a sliding door to the back of the room, revealing a wide space that had been made by removing the divider between two smaller Japanese-style rooms. At one edge of the room sat a simple, steel-frame bed.

There was a television in the centre of the room where two more women were sitting. One had her brown hair in a ponytail. She was thin, but Tomohiko's eyes were drawn to the ample swell beneath the breast of her knee-length jersey dress. The other woman was wearing a denim miniskirt and jacket. Her face was rounder and her shoulder-length hair had a gentle wave to it. She was probably the plainest of the three, but that might just have meant that the other two had on too much make-up.

'We were wondering if you'd ever get here,' the woman with the ponytail scolded Ryo. She didn't sound particularly angry.

'Sorry. It took a while to get everyone ready,' Ryo apologised, smiling.

'What, you had to lie to them about the old ladies they were going to meet?'

'Never!' Ryo said, stepping into the room. He sat down cross-legged on the tatami-matted floor and indicated with his eyes for Tomohiko and Murashita to join him.

The two other boys sat. Then, almost immediately, Ryo stood again and the short-haired woman took his place, leaving Tomohiko and Murashita surrounded.

'Beer good?' Ryo asked the women.

The three women agreed that beer would be great.

'Beers all around, then,' Ryo said, without waiting for Tomohiko and Murashita to reply. He went back into the kitchen, where they heard him taking bottles out of the refrigerator.

'Do you drink a lot?' ponytail asked Tomohiko.

'Sometimes.'

'I'll bet you can hold your liquor,' she said.

'Not really.' He tried to smile as he shook his head.

Tomohiko noticed the women exchanging glances. He wasn't entirely sure what it meant, but it seemed like they weren't dissatisfied with Ryo's selections. He breathed an inward sigh of relief.

It was a little dark in the room. Tomohiko glanced over at the window to see that the shutter had been pulled down on the outside. The only light in the room came from a single bulb that hung from the ceiling beneath a wicker lampshade. He assumed it was to hide the women's age, but even in the dim light, when he looked at the woman with the ponytail, he could tell her skin was completely different from that of the girls in his class. It was even more obvious this close.

Ryo brought in three tall bottles of beer, five glasses, and a tray with peanuts and other snacks. Placing these in the middle of the room, he went right back to the kitchen. When he returned, he was carrying a large pizza.

'You two are hungry, right?' he said, looking at Tomohiko.

The women filled the boys' glasses and everyone brought their glasses together in a toast that Tomohiko wasn't convinced was necessary. Back in the kitchen, Ryo was going through his duffel bag. He didn't seem to be joining them.

'You have a girlfriend?' ponytail asked Tomohiko.

'Not right now.'

'Really? Why not?'

'Because ... I don't know, because I don't have one.'

'But I'm sure there's lots of cute girls at school.'

'I guess,' Tomohiko said.

'I know what it is. You're picky. I bet you could have any girl you wanted. You should just start asking them out.'

'I doubt that. Hardly any of them seem worth it, anyway.'

'Really? That's too bad,' ponytail said, placing her right hand on Tomohiko's thigh.

As Ryo had predicted, the conversation was completely harmless. They traded words without meaning until Tomohiko started wondering how it came to be that you could get paid for something like this, and why he hadn't done it sooner.

The short-haired woman and ponytail talked the most. The one with the denim jacket just sipped her beer and listened. There was something a little stiff about her smile, Tomohiko thought.

The women were quick to keep the boys' glasses filled to the brim. Tomohiko kept drinking whatever they poured. Ryo had told them on the way there that if they were offered alcohol or smokes they should just accept.

After about half an hour, Ryo interrupted, saying, 'I don't want to kill the conversation, but how about a little movie?'

Tomohiko grinned. He was already pretty buzzed.

'Ooh, something new?' the short-haired woman asked, her eyes gleaming.

'Oh, it's new all right. I hope you like it.'

Tomohiko had noticed Ryo back at the dining room table setting up a small projector and had just been about to ask what it was for.

'What's the movie?' Tomohiko asked.

'Watch and find out,' Ryo said with a grin, flicking on the projector switch. A beam of light shot across the room where they sat, making a square on the wall in front of them. The white plaster of the wall made a pretty good movie screen. Ryo said, 'Sorry, could you get the light?'

Tomohiko reached out and turned off the switch to the overhead light. At the same time Ryo started the film.

It was a colour 8mm reel. There was no sound, but it was obvious what kind of film it was from the first frame. The scene opened on a man and a woman, completely naked. Tomohiko gaped. There were parts of them plainly showing that he knew they never let you see in normal movies. He felt his heart beat suddenly faster. He had seen photos of this kind of stuff before, but this was his first time seeing the images move.

'Wow, look at that!'

'I didn't know you could do it *that* way.'

The women were commenting and giggling. It was clear they weren't talking to each other, but to Tomohiko and Murashita.

The woman with the ponytail leaned closer to Tomohiko and whispered in his ear, 'Have you ever done something like that?'

'No,' he said, hearing the quavering in his own voice.

The first movie was over in about ten minutes. Ryo deftly swapped reels on the projector. While he was doing that, the short-haired woman said something like, 'It's pretty warm in here,' and started taking off her shirt. She was only wearing a bra underneath. The light from the projector made her skin glow white.

The woman in the denim jacket stood abruptly. 'Um, sorry—' she said, then her voice faltered.

From beside the projector, Ryo asked, 'You need to go?'

She nodded.

'I see. That's too bad.'

With everyone watching, the woman in the denim jacket stepped out through the dining room towards the door, taking care not to meet anyone's eyes.

Once she'd left, Ryo closed the door behind her and came back into the room.

The short-haired woman was giggling. 'I think the movie was too exciting for her.'

'Maybe she just felt left out because you weren't playing, Ryo?' the woman with the ponytail said, lightly chastising him.

'I was paying attention,' Ryo said. 'I just think she wasn't ready.'

'That's a shame. After we invited her and everything,' the short-haired woman said.

'Who cares?' said ponytail. 'Let's watch the next one.'

'Right away.' Ryo flicked the switch on the projector again.

It was halfway through the second show when ponytail took off her dress and leaned over until her bare arm was against Tomohiko's. In a soft voice she whispered, 'You can touch, if you want to.'

Tomohiko felt all his blood go to his crotch, though he wasn't sure whether it was because there was a practically naked woman right next to him, or because of the movie. All he knew was he wasn't getting paid just to make small talk.

His mouth was dry, but he forced himself to swallow. It wasn't that he wanted to run away from the job. He just wasn't sure he could do it.

Tomohiko was still a virgin.

Tomohiko's house was near Bishoen Station on the Hanwa line, a little two-storey wooden house on the first corner after a short walk down a shopping street.

'You're back late. Dinner?' Tomohiko's mom asked when he came in just before ten. He used to get an earful if he was home after seven, but that had changed since high school started. Now his mom hardly spoke to him at all.

'Already ate,' he called back, before going into his room and shutting the door.

Tomohiko's room was a small room on the ground floor. Originally a storage space, when he started high school his parents had cleaned out their things, repainted the walls, and given it to him.

He immediately sat in his chair and flicked the 'on' switch on the large contraption squatting atop the desk. This was a daily ritual. The contraption was a personal computer. If you were to buy it outright in a store it would have cost nearly a million yen. Of course he hadn't bought it. His father, who worked at an electronics manufacturer, had used his connections to get one on the cheap in the hope that he'd be able to learn how to use it but he'd given up after two or three attempts. When Tomohiko showed interest, the computer became his, and after poring over books and hours of trial and error, he was now able to write simple programs.

Tomohiko turned on the tape recorder sitting next to the humming computer and tapped on the keyboard. The tape recorder lurched into motion, a warble of electronic static emitting from its speaker.

The tape recorder was for memory storage. Longer programs would be converted to magnetic signals, recorded on the cassette tape, and then read back into the computer's RAM when it needed to access them. Cassette tapes were a huge improvement over the old punch cards, but it still took a considerable amount of time to read in data.

Tomohiko stepped away from his desk, returning to the keyboard twenty minutes later. He smiled. The shimmering fourteen-inch monochrome monitor displayed the words:

WESTWORLD

And below that:

PLAY? YES=1 NO=0

Tomohiko pressed the 1 key and Return.

Westworld was Tomohiko's first creation, a simple computer game inspired by the Yul Brynner film. The game featured enemies that chased you, the player, as you navigated the twisting corridors of a maze in search of the exit. As he played, Tomohiko thought up ideas to make gameplay even more interesting. Whenever he had a particularly good one, he would interrupt the game and start rewriting the program. What had begun as a very barebones game grew increasingly complex and the joy he felt was, in a way, like watching something living grow.

For a while his fingers sped over the numeric keypad, controlling the movements of the character on screen. But though his fingers moved as fast as ever, he was having trouble getting his mind into the game. He quickly grew bored. It didn't even bother him that much when he made a slight error and was caught.

Tomohiko sighed and pulled away from the desk. Leaning back in his chair, he looked up at the wall where he had hung a swimsuit poster. The barely concealed breasts and thighs filled his vision and, imagining touching that water-flecked skin, he felt a stirring in his groin, despite his world-changing experience of only hours before.

Yes, it had been world-changing, he decided, revisiting it in his mind. The intensity of it had faded somewhat, but he was certain it wasn't a dream or his imagination running wild.

The sex had started after the third 8mm reel, Murashita on a futon with the short-haired woman, Tomohiko on the bed with ponytail. The two high school boys did as they were instructed, as their partners led them through the first sexual experience of their lives. (It was after they left the apartment that Murashita had confided to Tomohiko that he, too, had been a virgin.)

Tomohiko came twice inside ponytail. The first time he hadn't really been sure what was going on. But the second time he'd gained enough distance from the act to fully appreciate it. The energy of a release he'd never felt masturbating blasted through his entire body and he felt as though he must have drained himself of semen by the time it was over.

Part way through the women had discussed swapping partners but ponytail hadn't seemed that interested, so it never came to pass.

It was Ryo who suggested they wrap things up. Tomohiko glanced at the clock and saw that exactly three hours had passed since their arrival at the apartment.

Ryo hadn't participated. Nor had the women invited him to, which made it seem as though this had already been established beforehand. Yet he did not leave the apartment, either. While Tomohiko and Murashita were busy entwining themselves into sweaty little piles of limbs, breasts and buttocks, Ryo sat at the dining room table. After Tomohiko came the first time he had looked towards the kitchen in a daze to see Ryo in the dim light, staring at the wall, quietly smoking a cigarette.

Once they'd left, Ryo took them to a nearby café where he handed them eight thousand five hundred yen each. The boys protested almost in unison that they'd been promised ten thousand.

'I deducted expenses. You had beer and pizza, right? You got off cheap at one thousand five hundred.'

Murashita agreed this was reasonable, so Tomohiko couldn't really protest. That, and he was still flying high after his first experience with a woman.

'So,' Ryo said, a gleam in his eye. 'You boys have a good time?'

If you're interested, this could be a regular gig. I expect to hear from the ladies again before long.' He beamed with satisfaction for a moment, then his face hardened and he added, 'Just one thing: I don't want you meeting them on your own, got it? We need to do this businesslike to avoid any *accidents*. Get any funny ideas and try to solo this, and I guarantee you things will go badly. I want you to promise me right now you won't meet either of them on your own. Deal?'

Again Murashita promised right away, which made it hard for Tomohiko to even feign hesitation. 'Fine. No meeting them on our own,' he had said.

Tomohiko could still see the way Ryo's lips had curled in a satisfied smirk.

He stuck his hand into the back pocket of his jeans and pulled out a piece of paper, which he laid on the desk in front of him. It was a telephone number, with a name written beneath it: *Yuko*. Ponytail had slipped it into his hand just before they left.

Namie Nishiguchi was a little drunk. She wondered how many years it had been since she had been out drinking alone and couldn't come up with an answer.

That's how long it's been.

No one had so much as tried to hit on her.

She went back to her apartment and turned on the lights, catching her own reflection in the sliding glass doors that opened out on to the veranda. She'd left the curtains open, she realised. She walked over to the doors, acutely aware of her reflected denim skirt and jacket and red T-shirt. None of it matched and it looked terrible on her. She could pull out her old clothes all she wanted in an attempt to look younger, but the result was painfully inadequate. Those high school boys, she was sure, would agree.

She closed the curtain and tossed off her clothes. Down to her underwear, she sat in front of her dresser, seeing a woman's face looking out of the mirror at her. The lacklustre skin, the eyes devoid of any sparkle that she could see. It was the face of a woman who lived without purpose; aged without purpose.

She reached over and grabbed her handbag. Fishing out cigarettes and a lighter, she lit one and blew smoke at her dresser
mirror. The smoke cast a gauze-like veil over her face for a
moment and she found herself wishing she could always wear a
veil like that. It would hide the wrinkles.

The film she'd half-watched in the apartment flickered in the
back of her mind.

'C'mon, you should try it! Just once can't hurt!'

That had been Kazuko Kawada, her co-worker, two days earlier.

'You won't regret it, I mean that. Anything has to be better than
the usual humdrum, right? Don't *worry*. You'll have fun. Women
our age need to be around boys every once in a while or we get
stuck in a rut.'

Normally, she would have refused on the spot. But there was
something pushing at Namie's back this time. The idea that she
was ready for change – that she had to make a change, or she'd
regret it for the rest of her life – had been growing on her recently.
Hesitantly, she accepted the invitation, much to Kazuko's appar-
ent delight.

And yet Namie had fled. She'd stood on the threshold to another,
bizarre world, and found herself unable to step in. Meanwhile
Kazuko and the other woman had practically been oozing
pheromones in front of those boys. It made her want to vomit.

She didn't think what they were doing was bad. In fact, she
understood how, for some women, what they were doing could be
genuinely refreshing. She just wasn't that kind of woman.

Her eyes went to the calendar on the wall. She'd wasted her day
off. When she imagined her boss and the other women needling
her, asking her if she'd gone on a date, she felt her stomach sink.
*I'll go to work early tomorrow, get there before anyone else does. That way
I'll be working when they come in and they won't talk to me. I'll just set
my alarm a little earlier than usual . . .*

Namie ran the brush through her hair two or three more times
before her hand suddenly stopped. *My watch!* She opened her bag
and dug around inside, but couldn't find it.

Great!

Namie bit her lip. That apartment was the last place she wanted to leave her watch.

It wasn't a particularly expensive watch, which was why she never thought twice about where she wore it. She always imagined she wouldn't care if she lost it, but after years of failing to lose it, she'd grown attached to the thing.

She remembered taking it off after going to the bathroom. She'd been washing her hands at the basin and taken it off from force of habit.

She reached out for the phone to call Kazuko. If she didn't know where it was, she'd have to call that Ryo kid.

She knew Kazuko would get on her case about her walking out that afternoon, but she had to do something. She checked the number in her address book and dialled.

Fortunately, Kazuko was at home. 'Well, well,' she said, more chiding than surprised.

'I'm sorry about earlier,' Namie said. 'I just ... I just couldn't get in the mood.'

'It's OK, really,' Kazuko said. 'It was a bit much for you, I understand.'

Which means you think I'm a coward. Namie swallowed her pride and told her about the watch.

'Sorry, we didn't find anything,' was Kazuko's reply. 'I'm sure the others would have told me if they had.'

Namie sighed over the phone.

'Are you sure you left it there? Should I get someone to check?'

'No, that's all right. You know, maybe I left it someplace else after all.'

'OK, if you're sure. If you don't find it, let me know.'

'I will. Sorry to call so late.'

Namie hung up, a big sigh escaping her lips. *What do I do now?*

She could just give up on the watch. Had she left it anywhere else, she already would have. Anywhere but *that* apartment. Why had she worn that watch anyway? She had other watches.

After a few more drags on her cigarette, she put it out, her eyes fixed on a single point in space.

There was a way out of this. Namie worked it through in her head. It was crazy, but maybe not too crazy, and not that hard to pull off, either. At the very least, it wouldn't be dangerous.

The clock on her dresser read just past ten-thirty.

It was after eleven when Namie left her apartment. Late to avoid being seen by too many people, but not so late she'd miss the last train home.

The subway was nearly empty. She sat, seeing herself reflected in the glass on the other side of the car. She was wearing black-rimmed glasses, a sweatshirt and jeans – nothing that would stand out, but also nothing to hide her thirty-plus years. She felt much more comfortable like this, she decided.

At Nishinagahori she walked down the street she'd taken with Kazuko earlier that day. Kazuko, who had been practically frolicking the whole way, wondering what kind of boys would come. Namie had joined in her laughter, even as she felt her enthusiasm begin to fizzle out.

She was able to find the apartment without any difficulty. She went up the stairs and stood in front of No 304. She tried the doorbell, her heart beginning to race in her chest.

There was no answer. She tried again, with the same result.

She breathed a sigh of relief, but immediately tensed, looking down the hall from side to side to ensure the coast was clear before she opened the panel to the water meter off to one side of the door.

'Once they get to know you, they show you where the key's hidden,' Kazuko had told her that afternoon.

Namie groped with her fingers behind the water pipe and touched metal. Another sigh of relief escaped her lips.

She opened the door cautiously. The light inside was on, but there were no shoes in the entranceway. *Guess no one's home.* Even so, she was careful not to make a sound as she stepped into the apartment. The dining room table, clean last she had seen it, was littered with objects. They looked like some kind of tiny electronic devices and meters, though Namie wasn't sure exactly what. Possibly someone had been fixing a stereo, or even the projector.

Regardless, it was clearly a work in progress. She swallowed. She would have to find that watch before whoever it was came back. She first went into the bathroom and searched around the basin. But the watch wasn't where it should have been. She wondered if someone had found it, and if so, why they hadn't given it to Kazuko.

She grew worried. One of the high school students might have found it and not told anyone. Maybe they wanted a keepsake. Or they might have thought they could get some quick cash for it at a pawnshop.

Namie's skin prickled. She was getting angry, but she didn't know what to do.

She took a few deep breaths and considered the possibility that she might have been mistaken. Maybe she hadn't left the watch by the basin. She could have brought it back to the room with her and set it down somewhere.

Leaving the bathroom, she went into the back room with the tatami mats on the floor. The room was perfectly clean. Probably the work of that boy they called 'Ryo'. The boy was a mystery to her. Obviously young, yet somehow aged on the inside far beyond his years.

The dividers that had been removed during the day were back in place, so she couldn't see the half of the room with the bed. Gingerly, she slid the divider open.

The first thing she saw was a television screen. It was sitting in the middle of the room, displaying an image that was clearly not regular television. She leaned forward.

Several polygonal shapes were moving on the screen. At first she thought it was a simple test pattern, like the ones they showed on stations that had finished broadcasting for the day, but she soon realised that wasn't it. Something shaped like a rocket seemed to be moving through a field of circular and square objects that drifted across its path.

A videogame, she thought. She had played *Space Invaders* a few times herself. But the way the shapes were moving on the screen wasn't as smooth as the way the *Space Invaders* moved. Yet there was still something compelling about the way the rocket sped past the obstacles. It was so engrossing that she didn't notice the sound of footsteps behind her.

'I wouldn't have taken you for a videogame fan,' said a voice, and Namie gave a little cry of surprise. She whirled around to see Ryo standing in the room behind her.

'I – I'm sorry,' she managed to say. 'I left something here, and, well, Mrs Kawada told me where the key was and—'

The boy didn't seem to be listening to her. Pushing her to one side, he sat down in front of the screen. Then, picking up the keyboard on the table and putting it on his knees, he started typing with both hands.

Soon the motion of the objects on the screen changed. The obstacles began to move faster and became more varied in shape. Ryo kept hitting the keys as the rocket sped past obstacle after obstacle.

It took Namie a few moments to realise the rocket's motions were no longer automated. Ryo was controlling it now, typing instructions to move it forward, backward, and side to side across the screen. Finally, the rocket hit one of the round obstacles head on. The rocket disappeared, and in its place a large X grew on the screen, followed by the words:

GAME OVER

Ryo swore under his breath. 'Still not fast enough,' he said. 'Not even close.'

Namie had no idea what he was talking about. She knew only that she wanted to leave the apartment as soon as possible. 'I should probably go,' she said.

Without looking around, Ryo asked, 'You find what you're looking for?'

'I guess I must've left it someplace else. I'm sorry.'

He grunted.

'Goodnight,' Namie said. 'I'll show myself out.'

She turned and was walking towards the door when she heard him behind her.

'You've been working at that bank for ten years? I never took you for a banker.'

She stopped and turned to see him standing up. He held out his right hand, the watch dangling from his fingers. It had been a gift from her employer, engraved with her name and the name of the bank where she worked.

'It's yours, isn't it?'

For a moment she almost tried to deny it, but then changed her mind. 'Thanks.'

Ryo walked back to the dining room table in silence. In the midst of the electronics was a shopping bag from the supermarket. He sat down, reached into the bag, and took out two cans of beer and a pre-packaged meal.

'Dinner?' she asked.

He didn't answer. Instead, he seemed to get an idea and lifted one of the cans. 'Beer?'

'No, I'm fine, thanks.'

'Right.' He opened the can, sending a tiny spray into the air. He took a sip before it could spill over the side, all the while paying absolutely no attention to Namie.

She grew bolder. 'You're not angry?' she asked. 'That I came in here, I mean?'

Ryo's eyes turned slowly in her direction. 'Nope.' He began unwrapping the dinner.

Namie could have left right then, but something held her back. He knew where she worked now, but she still knew nothing about this boy. More, she was afraid that if she left without saying anything, the knot she'd carried in her stomach since that afternoon might never go away.

'And you're not angry about before?'

'When you walked out on us?' He shook his head. 'Nah. It happens.'

'It wasn't that I was scared,' Namie said. 'I was never really that interested from the start, but I felt like I had to accept the invitation—'

Ryo was waving his chopsticks at her. 'Look, I really don't care.'

Namie's mouth snapped shut and she stared at the boy. He ignored her and began to eat. His meal looked like some variation on fried pork cutlets with rice.

'Maybe I will have a beer,' Namie said.

He jerked his head to indicate the remaining can was hers. Sitting down across from him, she opened it and drank a gulp.

'You live here?' she asked.

Ryo ate in silence.

'You don't live with your parents?' she asked again.

'What is this, an interrogation?' He snorted.

'Why do you do what you do? Is it the money?'

'Is there anything else?'

'You don't have sex?'

'I do when I need to. If you hadn't gone home today, I would have done it with you.'

'Bet you're glad you didn't have to, then.'

'I wasn't glad to lose the money.'

'Look at you, a big businessman. This is all just a game to you, isn't it? You're like a little boy.'

'What did you say?' Ryo glared at her. 'Say that again.'

Namie swallowed. She hadn't expected the look she was seeing in his eyes, and she felt embarrassed to have flinched.

'I said you're a little boy. What do you think these ladies are, your toys? No wonder you don't have sex with them. I bet you can't even get them off before you blow your wad.'

Ryo took another sip of beer. No sooner had he set down the can than he was out of his chair, rushing her with feral speed.

'Wait! What are you—' she managed to shout before he had her off the chair and on her back in the living room. She hit the tatami mats hard enough to knock the wind out of her and leave her gasping for breath.

She tried to sit up and he was on her again. He'd already undone the zipper on his jeans.

'You want this? C'mon! Use whatever lips you want, baby, I ain't picky!' He gripped her face in his hands and thrust his penis towards it. 'What's the matter? I'm gonna blow my wad fast, right? Show me what you got!'

His penis was growing erect, twitching. She saw a vein in clear relief running down its side before she managed to get her hands on his thighs and push, struggling to turn her head away.

'What's the matter?' he growled. 'My little-boy cock scare you?'

Namie closed her eyes and groaned. 'Stop – please, I'm sorry.'

Several seconds later, she was released to fall back on the floor. Ryo was walking back towards the dining room table, zipping his fly as he sat down and went back to eating. It was as if nothing had happened. Only the way he jabbed at his food with his chopsticks gave any hint of his irritation.

Namie steadied her breath and smoothed back her hair. Her heart was still racing. Her eyes flickered to the television in the next room. The same two words still hung on the screen:

GAME OVER

'Why?' she asked. 'There are so many other jobs you could do. Why this?'

'I'm just selling something people want. What's wrong with that?'

'Just selling something ... right.' She stood and walked towards the door, shaking her head. 'I guess I'm too old to understand.'

She was past the table and at the door putting on her shoes when he called out to her. 'Hey, lady.'

She looked around, one foot still raised in the air.

'Interested in a job opportunity?'

'What kind of opportunity?'

'Nothing crazy,' he said. 'I got something needs selling.'

It was Tuesday of the second week in July and summer vacation was so close Tomohiko could taste it in the air.

He went up to get his graded English exam when his name was

called and immediately wished he hadn't. He'd been ready for a disappointment, but this was worse than he'd imagined. Every subject this term was the same. He didn't have to look hard for the reason: he hadn't studied for exams one bit. This was unusual for him. He might have a little bit of a bad streak, and there was the shoplifting every now and then, but for the most part Tomohiko took school seriously.

It wasn't that he hadn't tried. He'd sat down at his desk to take a stab at learning the bare minimum he thought he'd need to pass his exams. But his mind was so thoroughly elsewhere that no matter how hard he attempted to focus on his studying, his thoughts dragged him away.

Which all led to the test result he held in his hand.

Better not let Mom see this one. He sighed and crammed the paper into his bag.

After classes Tomohiko headed to the café in the lounge at the New Japan Air Hotel in Shinsaibashi. It was a sunny, spacious place, where you could look out through large windows at the hotel's central courtyard.

As always, Yuko Hanaoka was there, reading a book at a corner table. She had on a white hat that hung low over thick-rimmed sunglasses.

'Why are you hiding your face? What's up?' Tomohiko said, sitting across from her.

The waitress came over before she had a chance to respond. Tomohiko was about to wave her away, when Yuko whispered, 'No, order something. I want to talk here.'

Tomohiko raised an eyebrow at the tension in her voice and ordered an iced coffee.

Yuko reached out for her Campari soda, already two-thirds gone, and drained the rest. She sighed. 'How long till school's out?'

'End of the week.'

'You working over summer vacation?'

'You mean ... my regular job?'

She smiled a little. 'Of course. What else would I be asking about?'

'I don't plan to, no. Lot of hours, not a lot of money. Why bother?'

She pulled a pack of Mild Sevens out of her white handbag. Lifting the cigarette to her lips, she paused, a flash of irritation crossing her face.

Tomohiko's iced coffee came. He drank half of it down in one gulp. He was terrifically thirsty.

'Why aren't we going to the room like always?' he asked in a low voice.

Yuko lit her cigarette and blew out a long stream of smoke. Then she stubbed it out in the glass ashtray even though there was hardly a centimetre of ash at the end.

'There's a problem.' She glanced around the café then stared right at him. 'I think the old man found out.'

'What old man?'

'My husband, you idiot.' She shrugged as though she were trying to make light of it and failing.

'You mean he found out about us?'

'Not everything. But it's only a matter of time before he does.'

'Whoa …' Tomohiko felt the blood rush to his face.

'It's my fault,' Yuko said. 'I should have been more careful.'

'How'd he find out?'

'A friend of my husband's saw me talking with a young man. Having a little too much fun. You get the picture.'

Tomohiko looked around, suddenly conscious of the other people in the café.

Yuko chuckled. 'According to him, he suspected before his friend said anything. I was acting different, he says. He's right, you know. I do feel like I've changed in a lot of ways since I started seeing you. Maybe that's why I forgot to be careful.' She scratched her head through her hat.

'So, what, did he interrogate you or something?'

'He wanted to know who it was, of course. He wanted a name.'

'You told him?'

'Of course not. I'm not that stupid.'

'I wasn't saying that!' Tomohiko drank the rest of his iced coffee. Still thirsty, he gulped down his glass of water.

'I just played dumb. He doesn't have proof. Not yet, anyway. He'll get it, though. Knowing him, he might even hire a private detective.'

'That's not good.'

'No, it's not. And there was something else I noticed.'

'What now?'

'My address book. I think he was looking at it. I had it hidden in my dresser drawer ... it had to be him.'

'Don't tell me you wrote my name in there.'

'No name. Just a phone number. But he might have figured it out anyway.'

'Can you get someone's name and address from a number?'

'I don't know. I bet if you really needed to you could find a way. He's pretty well-connected, my husband.'

Tomohiko was beginning to form an image of Yuko's husband in his mind and it frightened him. He'd never imagined what it might feel like to be the target of a grown man's anger. Now that he knew, he didn't like it.

'So what do we do?' Tomohiko asked, his mouth already dry again.

'I don't think we should see each other. Not for a while at least.'

Tomohiko nodded listlessly. Even as a junior in high school he saw the sense in what she was saying.

'But, since we're here anyway,' she said, downing the last drop of her Campari soda and picking up the bill, 'shall we?'

Their relationship had already been going on for a month, beginning with the encounter at the apartment. Yuko Hanaoka had been the woman with the ponytail.

It wasn't that he'd fallen for her, Tomohiko told himself. He just couldn't forget how his first time had felt. When he masturbated, it was her he'd see in his mind's eye. The sheer intensity of the act had swept away all his other fantasies. He'd lasted three days before he called her. She was only too eager to suggest they meet.

He'd first learned her full name between the sheets of a hotel bed. She was thirty-two years old. Tomohiko told her things, too. His real name, what school he went to, his home phone number. He tried not to think about his promise to Ryo. The reality of it was that her skills in bed had disarmed him to the point where he had trouble thinking straight about anything.

'It was my friend who invited me to that party,' she told him. 'You remember, the one with short hair? Anyway, it sounded like she'd been a few times before, but that was my first time. I was so nervous. I'm glad it was you, Tomohiko,' she said, snuggling under his arm. She knew how to make him melt like that.

Tomohiko was surprised to hear that she had paid twenty thousand yen for the party. That meant Ryo had taken more than half for himself. No wonder he had been so businesslike about the whole thing.

Tomohiko met with Yuko two or three times a week. Her husband was always busy, she said, so she could come home a little late without raising any suspicions. On her way out of the hotel she would slip him five thousand yen, telling him it was his 'allowance'.

Even though he knew that sleeping with another man's wife was wrong, Tomohiko was drunk on the attention and the sex. Their regular routine continued, even when his finals loomed close. Which was what had landed him in his current quandary with his grades.

'I don't know if I like not being able to see you,' Tomohiko said. They were in bed.

'You think I'm happy about it?' she said from beneath him.

'Isn't there something we can do?'

'I don't know. I just don't think now is the best time.'

'So when will be a good time?'

'I don't know that either. The sooner the better, of course. I'm not getting any younger.'

Tomohiko embraced her slender body and went at it again. Thinking this might be their last time, he didn't want to leave anything undone. He wanted to pour all of his energy into her. Again and again she screamed, each time arching her body backwards like a drawn bow, her hands and legs extending, trembling.

It was after the third round that she announced in her usual languid voice that she had to go and pee.

'Sure,' he said, rolling away. She sat up in bed, naked, but then she gave a little gasp and lay back down again. Tomohiko thought she must have felt faint. It had happened many times before. But this time, she wasn't moving. He wondered if she'd fallen asleep and gave her shoulder a shake. She didn't stir. A horrible scenario flashed through Tomohiko's mind. He got out of bed and tried tapping her eyelids with his fingers. There was no response.

He began to tremble violently.

No way. This isn't happening!

He held his hand to her chest. He couldn't feel a heartbeat.

Tomohiko was almost home when he realised he still had the hotel room key in his pocket. He gritted his teeth. If the key wasn't in the room the hotel staff would suspect something. He shook his head. *They'll suspect something when they find a woman's dead body in their bed.*

Tomohiko had considered calling the hospital from the hotel room. But then he would have to admit that he was with her. He couldn't do that. Besides, what was the point in calling a doctor, he thought. She was already gone.

He had changed quickly, gathered everything that was his, and fled the hotel, trying to avoid everyone he could on his way out.

He was already on the subway when the realisation dawned on him that running hadn't solved a thing. There was someone who knew about him already, possibly the worst person of all: Yuko's husband. He would put two and two together and realise that a high school student named Tomohiko Sonomura had been with his wife and he would tell the police. Once the police were on it, the truth would come out in a matter of hours.

It's over, he thought. *Once word gets out, I'm ruined for life.*

He arrived home to find his mother and younger sister in the middle of dinner. He told them he'd already eaten and went straight to his room. Sitting at his desk, he thought about Ryo Kirihara.

If the police found out about Yuko, they'd find out about what was going on in that apartment and that would be bad news for Ryo. What he was doing was enabling underage prostitution. He was a pimp – even if his prostitutes happened to be boys, and his johns women in their thirties.

I need to talk to him.

He ran out of his room and picked up the hallway phone. The television was still blaring in the living room. He prayed that whatever his mom and sister were watching, it was interesting enough to hold their attention for five minutes.

Ryo answered immediately. 'What's this about?' he asked, his tone revealing that he already expected something was up.

'It's bad,' was all Tomohiko could say before his tongue twisted in his mouth.

'What's bad?'

'It's hard to say over the phone. And it's kind of a long story.'

Ryo was silent. Finally he said, 'This better not be about those women.'

Tomohiko's mind went blank. All he could hear was Ryo sighing on the other end of the line.

'Right. Let me guess: ponytail?'

'Yeah.'

Ryo sighed again. 'No wonder she hasn't been coming lately. So, what, she work out a business deal with you?'

'No, there was no deal.'

'What was there, then?'

Tomohiko rubbed his mouth. He couldn't think of what to say.

'Whatever. You're right, this isn't something to talk about over the phone. Where are you now?'

'Home.'

'Be there in about twenty minutes,' Ryo said and hung up the phone without waiting for a reply.

Tomohiko went back to his room and tried to think. But his head was a swirl and time kept slipping by.

It was twenty minutes later on the dot when Ryo arrived. Tomohiko went to the door and opened it. 'Hey, you ride a bike?' he asked, nodding towards Ryo's motorcycle out front.

'That's hardly important right now,' Ryo said, pushing past him.

They went into his room and Tomohiko sat at the desk. Ryo sat cross-legged on the floor, right next to a square of blue cloth covering a lump about the size of a small television. This was Tomohiko's personal computer – his pride and joy and usually the first thing he'd show friends who came to visit.

'OK, talk,' Ryo said.

'I'm not sure where to start.'

'How about we start with the part where you broke your promise.'

Tomohiko cleared his throat and slowly began to tell the story of what had happened.

Ryo listened without expression, but it was clear that he was angry. When Tomohiko got to the events of that day, his mouth gaped open.

'Dead? You mean she actually died?'

'Yeah. I checked her, man, more than once. I'm pretty sure.'

Ryo spat under his breath. 'That alcoholic bitch.'

'What?'

'You heard me. She must've got too excited and it got to her heart. That's what happens when you're over forty and you drink like you're in college.'

'But she was only thirty-two,' Tomohiko said.

Ryo broke into a grin. 'Idiot. No, trust me. She was an old lady with a thing for little boys. You're the sixth I introduced her to, you know.'

'But I – but she never said—'

'Oh please, really?' Ryo said, his look of disappointment turning swiftly into a glare. 'Where is she now?'

Tomohiko summed up the situation as quickly as he could, adding that he was pretty sure there was no way they'd be able to fool the police on this one.

Ryo groaned. 'OK, I think I get the picture. If her husband was on to you, you don't really have many options. Guess you're going to have to let the police question you,' he said, and the way he said it made it sound like an order.

'I know,' Tomohiko said. 'But I have to tell the truth. Everything. Even about the apartment.'

Ryo frowned and rubbed his temples. 'That's not going to work. That makes things a lot more complicated, understand?'

'But if I don't tell them about it, how will I explain how we met?'

'Easy. Tell them you were hanging out in Shinsaibashi and she picked you up.'

'I'm not sure I can lie to the police like that. I mean, what if they press me hard and I slip up?'

'Well, if you do …' Ryo slapped his hands down on his knees. 'Then I'm sure the people backing me will have something to say about it.'

'What do you mean?'

'You think I'm running this operation solo?'

'Yakuza?'

'Something like that.' Ryo stretched his neck to both sides until it made an audible pop. The next instant, he had his hands on Tomohiko's collar. 'Listen,' Ryo snarled. 'If you know what's good for you, you won't say anything more than you have to, or you're gonna learn there's people in this world a hell of a lot scarier than the cops.'

Tomohiko swallowed.

Ryo released him and stood, his speech finished.

'Ryo …'

'What?'

'I – never mind.' Tomohiko's eyes went down to the floor.

Ryo snorted and turned to leave, knocking the cloth off Tomohiko's computer.

'Hey,' Ryo said, his eyes widening. 'This yours?'

'Yeah.'

'Not a bad rig,' Ryo said, kneeling down to examine it more closely. 'You program?'

'Basic, mostly.'

'What about assembly language?'

'A little,' he said, startled that Ryo knew about computers.

'You write anything big?'

'Just a game or two.'

'Show me.'

'What? Now?'

'Just show me,' Ryo said, grabbing Tomohiko's collar again, this time with one hand.

Blanching, Tomohiko pulled a folder off of his bookshelf and handed it to Ryo. This was a collection of flow charts and code, describing the programs he'd written in detail.

Ryo pored over it for a few minutes. Then he closed the file and, at the same time, his eyes. He sat without moving for a long moment.

Tomohiko almost asked him if he was OK, when he saw Ryo's lips move as if he was talking to himself.

'Tomohiko,' Ryo said suddenly. 'I need your help.'

'What?'

Ryo turned to look him square in the face. 'You do exactly what I say and I'll get you out of this. You won't have to talk to the police. That woman dying and you will have nothing to do with each other.'

'How?'

'Can you follow instructions?'

'Yeah, sure, anything,' Tomohiko said.

'What's your blood type?'

'What?'

'Your blood type, are you deaf?'

'O.'

'Perfect. You used a glove, right?'

'A condom? Yeah, of course.'

'Good,' Ryo stood back up and extended a hand toward Tomohiko. 'The key, please.'

It was in the evening two days later when the detectives came. There was one in his forties wearing a white open-necked shirt, and another wearing a light-blue polo shirt.

'We'd like to have a few words with your son, Tomohiko,'

open-neck asked his mom. He didn't say what it was about. Tomohiko's mom was aghast.

They took Tomohiko to a nearby park. The sun had already set but the benches were still warm from the day. Tomohiko sat down next to open-neck. Polo shirt remained standing, facing him.

Tomohiko had tried to avoid saying anything on their way there. He just let himself look as nervous as he really was. 'It's suspicious if a high school student acts like it's no big deal to talk to detectives.' That had been Ryo's advice when he briefed him two days before.

Open-neck held up a photograph. 'You know this woman?'

It was Yuko. It looked like it might have been taken on a vacation somewhere. She was standing with the ocean behind her, smiling at the camera. Her hair was cut a little shorter than he remembered it.

'That's Mrs Hanaoka,' Tomohiko said.

'But you know her first name too, don't you?'

'Yuko, I think.'

'That's right. Yuko Hanaoka.' The detective put the photograph away. 'How do you know her?'

'Whatcha mean?' Tomohiko said, mumbling his words a little. 'I just know her.'

'Which is why I'm asking *how* you know her,' open-neck said. He spoke softly, but there was a ring of irritation to his voice.

'My advice,' polo shirt said, 'be honest, kid.' He had a mean smile on his face.

'I was in Shinsaibashi, 'bout a month ago. She came up and talked to me.'

'What did she say?'

'That if I was free, maybe I could get some tea with her.'

The detectives exchanged glances.

'Did you go?' open-neck asked.

'Yeah. She said it was her treat.'

Polo shirt snorted at that.

'So you had tea, what then?'

'That's it. We hung out at a café for a bit, and then I went home.'

'OK. That wasn't the only time you met her, though, was it?'

'No . . . We met twice after that.'

'How did that go down?'

'She called saying she was in Minami and if I had some time, maybe I could come down and we could have tea again. Something like that.'

'Your mom answer the phone?'

'No, I did. Both times.'

That answer didn't seem to please the detective. He stuck out his lower lip and asked, 'So you went?'

'Yeah.'

'What happened then? Don't tell me you just had tea?'

'Actually,' Tomohiko looked up at him, 'I had iced coffee. And we talked a little. Then I went home.'

'And that was everything?'

'Yeah. Was I supposed to do something else?'

Open-neck scratched his head and stared at Tomohiko, trying to read his expression. 'Look, your school's coed, right? You must have a girlfriend or two. Why bother hanging out with some old lady?'

'I had some free time, that's all.'

The detective grunted. 'What about cash? She give you anything?'

'I didn't take anything, sir.'

'You mean she offered you money, but you didn't take it?'

'That's right. The second time we met, she tried to give me five thousand yen, but I didn't take it.'

'Why not?'

'It just . . . I hadn't done anything to earn it, I guess.'

Open-neck shook his head and shot polo shirt a look of disbelief.

'Where was this café where you met?' polo shirt asked.

'The lounge at the New Japan Air Hotel.'

Here he told the truth, as he was pretty sure one of Yuko's husband's friends had seen them there.

'So you're telling us you went to a hotel just to have tea? No going up to the room afterwards for some hanky-panky?' polo shirt asked, his voice rough. Clearly he didn't think much of any high school student who entertained bored housewives to pass the time.

'No, we just drank and talked. Like I said.'

Polo shirt snorted.

'How about the night before last?' open-neck asked. 'Where did you go after school?'

'The night before last?' Tomohiko wet his lips. This was it. 'I was hanging out at Asahiya – you know, the bookstore in Tennoji.'

'And what time did you go home?'

'Seven-thirty.'

'And you were home after that?'

'Yeah.'

'You see anyone other than your family?'

'A friend came over around eight. He's in my class at school, name's Ryo.'

Open-neck made a note of that. 'How long was he at your house for?'

'Until nine.'

'Nine. And what did you do after that?'

'Just watched TV, and talked on the phone with a friend ...'

'Who were you talking to?'

'A guy named Morishita. We went to middle school together.'

'When did you talk?'

'He called around eleven, so we probably talked until after midnight.'

'He called you?'

'That's right.'

There was a trick here. Tomohiko had actually called Morishita first, when he knew he'd be out at work, and told his mom he wanted him to call when he came home. This was all according to Ryo's instructions.

The detective's eyebrows knitted together and he asked for

Morishita's phone number. Tomohiko told him on the spot. He had it memorised.

'I got another question. What's your blood type?' open-neck asked.

'My blood type? O. Why?'

'O? You're sure?'

'Yeah, I'm sure. My parents are both O, too.'

Tomohiko detected a sudden drop in the detectives' interest in him. He remembered Kirihara asking him his blood type, too, but he'd never explained why.

'Um,' Tomohiko asked hesitantly. 'Did something happen to Mrs Hanaoka?'

'You don't read the paper?' open neck said.

Tomohiko had seen the little column in the evening paper the night before, but he shook his head.

'She died. The night before last, at a hotel.'

'What?' Tomohiko acted surprised. He hoped it wasn't too obvious. 'How?'

'Who knows?' The detective stood from the bench. 'Thanks; you were a big help. We might have more questions for you later, but that's all for now.'

'Oh – OK.'

'Let's go,' open-neck said to polo shirt. They walked off without a single glance in Tomohiko's direction.

It wasn't just the detectives who paid a visit to Tomohiko.

Four days after talking to the detectives he was walking away from the front gate of the school when someone tapped his shoulder from behind. He looked around to see an older man with slicked-back hair and a bland smile on his face.

'Tomohiko Sonomura?'

'Yeah?'

The man's right hand slid out in a practised motion. He was holding a business card which read IKUO HANAOKA.

Tomohiko could feel the colour drain from his face. He knew he should act cool, but his body stiffened.

'I was hoping we could have a chat?' The man spoke in a deep baritone, the kind that rumbled in the chest.

'OK.'

'Let's talk in the car,' the man said, pointing to a silver-grey sedan parked by the side of the road. Tomohiko got into the passenger seat.

'Some detectives from the Minami station visited you, right?' Hanaoka said, sitting in the driver's seat.

'Yeah.'

'I thought so. See, I was the one who gave them your name. Your number was in my wife's address book, but I guess you already knew that. Sorry if they caused you any trouble, by the way, but there were a lot of things that just weren't adding up.'

Tomohiko was under no illusion that the man had any real concern for him. He held his tongue and listened.

'The detectives said she called you a few times?' He smiled with his lips, but not his eyes.

'Yeah. We talked, in a café.'

'So they said. And she was the one who called you, not the other way around?'

Tomohiko nodded. He heard Hanaoka chuckle.

'She always had a soft spot for pretty boys. At her age, getting all giddy over the little rock stars. And look at you. You're young; your face fits the bill. I bet you were *just* her type.'

Tomohiko clasped his hands together on his knees. There was something viscous about the man's voice, like tar. He could almost feel the jealousy oozing out of the cracks between his words.

'So you just talked?' he asked.

'That's right.'

'She never invited you to do ... anything else? Like go to a hotel?' Hanaoka was acting innocent, but there was nothing light about his tone.

'Not even once.'

'That's the truth?'

'Yes, sir.' Tomohiko nodded seriously.

'Then there was something else I was hoping you could tell me. I was wondering if you knew anyone else she met like that.'

'You mean, other than me?' Tomohiko shrugged. 'No.'

Tomohiko could feel Hanaoka's gaze, a grown man's eyes, staring daggers at him.

Just then, someone knocked on the window by Tomohiko's head. He looked up and saw Ryo looking in. Tomohiko opened his door.

'What are you doing, Tomohiko? The teacher's looking for you,' Ryo said.

'What?'

'He's in the office. You better get there quick.'

Tomohiko met Ryo's eyes for a moment, then looked back at Hanaoka. 'Um, are we done?'

'Yeah, we're done,' Hanaoka said, though it was clear from his tone that he was far from satisfied.

Tomohiko got out of the car and walked back towards the school with Ryo.

'What did he ask you?' Ryo asked in a whisper.

'He wanted to know what we did.'

'You play dumb?'

'Course.'

'Good. Very good.'

'What's going on, Ryo? What did you do?'

'You don't need to worry about that.'

'Yeah, but—'

Ryo gave him a whack on the shoulder. 'He might be watching us, so you'd better get inside. Go out the back when you leave.'

The two of them stood in front of the gate to the school.

'OK,' Tomohiko said.

'See ya.'

Tomohiko watched Ryo leave and then went inside as instructed.

He never did see Yuko Hanaoka's husband again. Nor did

the detectives from Minami Precinct ever pay him a second visit.

On a Sunday in the middle of August, Ryo took Tomohiko back to the apartment in Nishinagahori.

This time Ryo opened the door himself with one of many keys dangling from the ring in his hand.

'In you go,' Ryo said, removing his sneakers.

The dining room and kitchen were largely unchanged from the last time Tomohiko had been there: same cheap table, chairs, refrigerator and microwave. The only difference was a noticeable lack of perfume in the air. Ryo had called him the night before, saying he wanted to show him something, laughing and saying 'it's a secret' when Tomohiko asked what it was. The laugh threw him more than anything. It was a genuine laugh, the kind he'd never heard from Ryo before.

Tomohiko had frowned when he heard they were going back to the apartment.

'Don't worry. I won't ask you to sell your body,' Ryo said. He laughed again, but there was no warmth in it this time.

Ryo went in first and opened up the divider between the two back rooms. This was where he'd first met Yuko. No one was there today, but when he saw what was his eyes went wide.

'Thought you'd like it,' Ryo said with a grin.

Four computers were set up on a low table, along with a dozen peripherals.

'Where'd you get all these?' Tomohiko asked, amazed.

'I bought them. How else?'

'You know how to use these, Ryo?'

'I do OK. But I need your help.'

'Me?'

'That's why you're here.'

Just then, the doorbell rang. Tomohiko stiffened. He hadn't been expecting anyone else to be here.

Ryo stood. 'That'll be Namie.'

Tomohiko went over to the cardboard boxes stacked in the

corner of the room and peeked inside the one on top. It was packed full of new cassette tapes. If all of the boxes were full of these, that made a considerable number of tapes.

The front door opened and he heard someone coming in. 'Tomohiko's here,' Ryo said. A woman answered him.

She came in, a plain-faced woman, probably a little over thirty years old. She looked somehow familiar.

'Long time no see,' she said.

'Huh?' Tomohiko gaped and the woman laughed.

'She's the one who went home early. You remember,' Ryo said.

'You mean – oh!' Tomohiko looked back at her. She didn't have much make-up on today, which made her seem even older – or rather, how she probably really looked.

'Don't bother her with too many questions, OK? Her name's Namie. She's our accountant. That's all you need to know,' Ryo said.

'Why do we need an accountant?'

Ryo took a folded piece of paper out of his jeans pocket and handed it to Tomohiko. On it in black ink had been written:

Unlimited Designs
Sellers of all varieties of games for personal computers.

'Unlimited Designs?'

'That's the name of our company. We sell games on cassette tapes through the mail.'

'OK.' Tomohiko nodded, a picture starting to form in his head. 'Those might sell.'

'They will sell. No doubt about it,' Ryo said.

'Where do we get the software from?'

Ryo walked over to one of his computers and pulled a long sheet of paper out of the printer beside it. 'Our big seller,' he said, showing it to Tomohiko.

A program was written out on the paper. It was long and complicated, beyond Tomohiko's talents. At the top was written the word *Submarine*.

'Where did you get this game? Did you make it?'

'Does it matter? Namie, you come up with a good name yet?'

'I came up with something. I'm not sure if you'll like it or not.'

'Try me.'

'*Marine Crash,*' Namie said a little hesitantly.

'*Marine Crash,*' Ryo repeated, hands across his chest. 'Great, let's go with that.'

Namie smiled, looking relieved.

Ryo glanced at his watch and stood. 'I'm going to the printers.'

'The printers?' Tomohiko asked. 'What for?'

'You can't sell anything without advertising it first,' he said, putting on his sneakers as he went out of the front door.

Tomohiko sat cross-legged in the back room, scanning the code for the program. Namie was sitting at the desk, punching something into a ten-key calculator.

'Hey, Namie,' he said. 'Do you know what the story is with Ryo?'

'What do you mean? I thought you were friends.' Her hand stopped.

'I know him, he goes to my school. But I never even noticed him until he invited me here the other day. He doesn't have any friends and I've never seen him do much in class – and yet he's doing this in his free time?'

Namie turned around to look at Tomohiko. 'There's more to life than school, you know.'

'Sure, but, it's just – he's so hard to pin down.'

She shook her head. 'I'm guessing it's better not to pry too deep when it comes to Ryo.'

'Hey, I'm not prying. I was just wondering, that's all. I mean when—' Tomohiko stopped, unsure of how much he should say.

'When Yuko died?' she offered, her voice calm.

'Yeah,' he nodded, relieved. 'How did that just go away? It's like black magic or something.'

'Do you really want to know?'

'Yeah, of course I do.'

Namie frowned and scratched behind her ear with a ballpoint pen. 'From what I heard, they found the body around two in the afternoon the day after she checked into the hotel. They sent someone to speak to her since it was past checkout time, and no one was answering the room phone. They found her lying completely naked on the bed.'

Tomohiko nodded. He could imagine that scene particularly well.

'The police got there right away, but they decided pretty quickly it hadn't been murder. Their opinion was she had a heart attack in the middle of sex. Time of death was estimated as some time after eleven o'clock the night before.'

'Eleven o'clock?' Tomohiko shook his head. 'That doesn't sound right—'

'Room service saw her,' Namie said, staring at him.

'What do you mean, they "saw her"?'

'She phoned the front desk around eleven o'clock and asked for some shampoo. They brought it to her door, and Yuko answered.'

'No way. When I left that hotel—' He stopped because Namie was shaking her head.

'Room service clearly stated that they gave the woman in the room shampoo at eleven o'clock.'

Tomohiko's mouth hung open. If they wore Yuko's sunglasses and big hat, anyone could have taken that shampoo. *Even—*

Tomohiko looked at Namie. 'It was you, wasn't it.'

Namie smiled and shook her head. 'No, not me. Do I look like the kind of person that could pull something like that off? I'd be too nervous to talk clearly.'

'Then who?'

'Another thing not to think about too much,' Namie said crisply. 'Isn't it enough to know that someone, somewhere saved your ass?'

'Sure, but—'

'One other thing,' Namie said, lifting a finger. 'The police, they pulled you out of your home for questioning, but then they just left you alone. Care to know why?'

'OK, why?'

'Because they know whoever was having sex with Yuko that night had type AB blood.'

'They found blood on her?'

'Semen, in her,' Namie said without blinking. 'Semen from someone with AB blood.'

'That doesn't make sense.'

'But that's what they found. AB type semen inside her vagina.'

The word 'inside' struck a chord in Tomohiko's mind and he gasped. 'What blood type is Ryo?'

'AB,' Namie said, turning back around to the desk.

Tomohiko put a hand to his mouth. He felt sick. A chill ran down his spine, in spite of the summer heat.

'You mean he ... with her—'

'Sorry, we're not having that discussion,' Namie said, her voice cold.

Tomohiko couldn't think of anything to say. He noticed his fingers were trembling.

The door opened.

'We're all set,' Ryo said walking in. He handed the paper in his hand to Namie. 'Exactly on budget, am I right?'

Namie took a look at it and smiled, a little stiffly, Tomohiko thought.

Ryo seemed to notice the atmosphere in the room had changed. He looked between the two of them, then went over to sit next to the window and have a cigarette.

'What happened?' Ryo asked, flicking his lighter.

'Hey,' Tomohiko said, looking up at him.

'Yeah?'

'I just wanted to say ...' Tomohiko swallowed; his mouth was dry. 'I'll do anything. OK? Whatever you need. I'm good for it.'

Ryo stared a long time at Tomohiko's face before looking toward Namie, who nodded. A cold smile spread across Ryo's lips, and he took a long drag of his cigarette. 'Of course you are.'

He turned to look out the window at the darkening blue sky.

FOUR

It had been raining most of the evening, the kind of thin, autumnal drizzle that wasn't enough to warrant an umbrella, but quietly dampened hair and clothes until you were drenched. Yet, occasionally, breaks would appear in the grey clouds above, offering glimpses of the night sky. *The foxes will be holding a wedding tomorrow*, Masaharu thought, recalling something his mother always said when the weather was odd like this.

He'd stashed a folding umbrella in his locker back at the university, a fact he only remembered after he was through the front gate, by which time it wasn't worth the trouble of going back to retrieve it. He'd only get wetter.

Masaharu glanced at the hands of his favourite quartz-crystal watch. It was five minutes after seven – he was late. He knew she'd forgive him for not showing up on time, but that was beside the point. The fact of the matter was, he couldn't wait to see her.

He held a newspaper over his head to keep the rain off his hair. The previous year he had taken up the habit of buying a newspaper on the day after the Yakult Swallows won a game. He was still a Swallows fan, even though the last time he'd lived in Tokyo was in high school. Sometimes he felt like he'd been born a fan. He even remembered watching games way back when they were still called the Atoms.

Last year the Swallows had won a miraculous league victory under Manager Hirooka. But this year, it was as though they were an entirely different team. By September, they had already established themselves at the bottom of the rankings. This meant Masaharu was buying fewer papers. It was a bit of good luck that he happened to have one today.

He reached the house several minutes later, pressing the doorbell beneath the nameplate that read Karasawa.

Reiko Karasawa answered the door. She was wearing a purple dress, its thin fabric making her aging body seem painfully bony. On his first visit, back in March, she'd been wearing a dark grey kimono that suited her nicely, but since the start of the rainy season in early summer she'd switched to wearing dresses. Masaharu wondered if she'd go back to kimonos when the winter came.

'I'm sorry,' she said when she saw him. 'I just heard from Yukiho. She's tied up with preparations for the school festival and says she'll be about thirty minutes late.'

'That's no problem at all,' Masaharu said, a bit relieved. 'I'm just glad I'm not late.'

'You're always very punctual. I just wish some of that would rub off on Yukiho,' Reiko said.

Masaharu smiled and glanced down at his watch, muttering to himself about having some time to kill.

'Oh, you're not waiting out there,' Reiko said. 'Please, come in. I'll get you something cool to drink.'

She invited him into the living room on the first floor. The room had originally been a traditional Japanese-style room, with tatami mats, but with the addition of a few pieces of rattan furniture Mrs Karasawa had converted it to a Western-style sitting room. Masaharu had been in here once, six months ago, and never again since.

His introduction to the Karasawas had come via his mother, who was one of Reiko's tea ceremony students. Reiko's daughter, Yukiho, a junior in high school, was looking for a maths tutor, and Masaharu, an engineering undergrad with a strong math background, was looking for extra income after his last student passed his college entrance exams. The timing was perfect, and the money was nice – though Masaharu soon found that just the chance to be close to Yukiho was enticement enough.

Reiko brought him some barley tea in a glass cup – another relief. The last time he'd been invited to the sitting room she'd made him green tea in a traditional bowl and he'd sweated buckets, having absolutely no idea of the proper way to drink it.

He picked up the glass. His throat was parched, and the cool tea felt good going down.

'I'm terribly sorry,' Reiko apologised again as she sat down across from him. 'I don't see why she can't just leave early.'

'Oh no, it's fine, really. I think it's important for students to spend time with their friends, especially in high school.' Masaharu hoped the sentiment sounded appropriately grown-up.

Yukiho Karasawa attended the Seika Girls High School, which put her on the fast track to attend the attached Seika Girls College. If she could maintain a good GPA, she'd be able to matriculate with only an interview. Depending on which department she wanted to get into, however, admissions could be tough. Her choice, English Lit, was one of the most competitive, so in order to ensure she got in she had to be at the top of her class in every subject. She had accomplished this in everything but maths.

'Looking back on it, I really feel we made the right choice getting her into Seika,' Reiko said. 'That way she can actually enjoy her senior year instead of struggling through those horrible exams they have to take in public school.' She picked up her own barley tea with both hands.

'Absolutely,' Masaharu agreed. He felt that the exam regimen was needlessly brutal, and often shared his feelings with the parents of those he'd tutored before. 'I think that's why a lot more parents are taking the private school option, even as early as elementary school.'

'As well they should. I've advised my nieces and nephews to do the same. Even if they have to test to get into a school, better to get through that early, I say.'

Masaharu nodded, then a thought occurred to him. 'Yukiho didn't switch over to private until middle school, did she.'

Reiko was quiet for a moment, a contemplative look in her eyes. The moment stretched until Masaharu began to worry he might have touched on a sore subject. Finally she looked up at him and said, 'If I'd been there when she was still in pre-school, I might have advised her mother to consider it earlier, but of course I didn't even meet the child until she was in second grade or so. Not that she was really in a financial situation to attend a private school in those days.'

Masaharu had heard that Yukiho was not Reiko Karasawa's natural daughter when he first took the tutoring job. Yet the subject of her real mother and Yukiho's adoption hadn't ever come up. He now found he was curious to learn more.

Reiko must have sensed this because she said, 'Yukiho's real father was my cousin. He died in an accident when she was very little, and her mother had trouble making ends meet. She was working at least two jobs and I think it was very challenging for her to raise a child at the same time.'

'What happened to her mother?' Masaharu asked, and immediately regretted it.

A dark cloud had come over Reiko's face. 'She died in an accident, too,' the older woman said quietly. 'Yukiho was in sixth grade at the time. Yes, it was in May, as I recall.'

'A traffic accident?'

'No.' Reiko shook her head. 'Gas poisoning.'

'Gas?'

'She put a pot on the stove and fell asleep. Apparently, the flame blew out, and she succumbed without ever waking. I think ... she must've been very tired in those days.' Her thin eyebrows drew together in sorrow.

Masaharu had heard of similar stories, though a switch in recent years to natural gas had dramatically reduced the chances of carbon monoxide poisoning.

'I just wish it hadn't been Yukiho who found her. To think of the shock that poor girl must have had.' She shook her head, a pained expression on her face. 'It was a tragedy.'

'Yes,' he agreed. He realised he had probably already asked more than he should on the subject, but found that hearing the story had only piqued his curiosity. He debated letting the conversation die, but with Yukiho out of the house, this might be his only chance. Taking a sip of his tea, he quickly asked, 'Was she alone when she found her?'

'No,' Reiko said, without looking up at him. 'The door had been locked, so she had to go get the real estate agent to open it for her. They went in together.'

That must have been an unlucky day for him, too, Masaharu thought, imagining the man's shock at finding the body, and realising the girl he was with was now an orphan.

'I can't imagine losing all of my family to accidents,' he said.

'None of us can, which is probably for the best. I went to the funeral and Yukiho was there, clinging to the coffin as though she could stop her mother from leaving, the poor girl. I've never heard her cry so loudly since.' Reiko's eyes closed as her thoughts went back to that day. 'When I saw her there, I knew I had to do something.'

'Is that when you decided to adopt her?'

'Yes.'

'Did she have no other relatives?'

'To tell the truth, I never spoke much to her mother, and was never that close to her family. But I saw Yukiho many times before her mother died. She would come by herself to visit me here.'

Masaharu wondered why Yukiho would go by herself to a relative's house, especially one who wasn't close to her mother. He was about to ask, when Reiko told him she'd first met the girl at an observance for her late father.

'We only spoke briefly, but when she heard I was teaching the tea ceremony she seemed very interested. She asked so many questions that I invited her to come visit some time and see for herself. I think it was only a few weeks later that she actually came, much to my surprise. I hadn't been entirely serious in inviting her, you see. It's not many young girls who want to learn the tea ceremony. But she seemed genuinely interested and I thought I could use the company, living alone as I was, so I began teaching her, half for fun at first, you understand. She started coming every week, on the bus, all by herself. She would drink my tea and tell me about things that happened at school. In time, I came to look forward very much to her visits and missed her on the weeks she couldn't make it.'

'So she's been learning the tea ceremony since elementary school?'

'That's right. It wasn't long afterwards that she showed an interest in flower arrangement, too. She was watching me put together a vase and would occasionally help out with a flower or two. She even wanted me to teach her how to put on a kimono.'

'Sounds just like finishing school,' Masaharu said, smiling.

'Quite right. Of course she was only a child, so it was a kind of play for her, I think. She even copied the way that I spoke. When I told her I was embarrassed, she said that if she only listened to the way her mother talked at home, her own language would be "lower class", so she was visiting me to polish it up. Can you imagine?'

Several things were adding up for Masaharu as he listened. He now had an explanation for Yukiho's elegance – the way she moved, the way she talked – so unusual for a high school girl. It impressed him that her refinement wasn't forced on her, either. She'd sought it out herself.

'Now that you mention it, she doesn't really have a strong Osaka accent, does she.'

Reiko smiled. 'Like yourself, I grew up in the Tokyo area. She seemed to like my own lack of an accent.'

'I can appreciate that. I've never been very good at sounding like a local, either.'

'I think that's why she likes talking with you. She says she doesn't want to catch a bad accent from the other people around her.'

'Funny to hear that coming from someone who was born here.'

'Well, she's never been proud of where she's from.'

'Oh. Well, that's too bad, I suppose.'

'As long as she's proud of who she is,' Reiko pressed her lips. 'That said, there's something which does trouble me. She's spent so much time with an old lady like myself, I worry that it might have sapped away at her liveliness. I wouldn't want her to go wild, of course, but a little bit of spreading one's wings is necessary. If you ever get the chance, do take her someplace. Try to get her out of her shell. She needs that.'

'Me? Are you sure?'

'I'd rather it be someone I can trust.'

He smiled. 'Right, well, I'll think of something.'

'Please do. I think she'd enjoy that.'

Reiko didn't say anything more for a while, so Masaharu took another sip of his tea. It was not a boring conversation – far from it. It was clear that her foster mother did not know everything there was to know about her daughter. Yukiho Karasawa was not as old-fashioned as Reiko seemed to think, nor as well behaved.

One event stuck out in Masaharu's mind, something that had happened in July. The two-hour lesson was over and they were drinking coffee and chatting. Masaharu always talked about life at university at these times. He knew she liked to hear about that.

They had been talking for about five minutes when the phone rang. 'It's someone from some English speech contest,' Reiko said, calling her to the phone.

'Right,' Yukiho had said, and gone down the stairs.

It was about time for him to leave, so Masaharu had finished his coffee and gone downstairs to find Yukiho talking on the phone in the hallway, a serious look on her face. A bit hesitantly, he waved to indicate he was leaving and she waved back, her expression changing quickly to a smile.

'So Yukiho's going to be competing in an English speech contest? That's impressive,' Masaharu said to Reiko when she saw him to the door.

'If she is, this is the first I've heard of it,' Reiko had said.

As per his usual Tuesday routine, Masaharu had gone to a ramen shop near the station and ate a late dinner. He was just tucking into some dumplings and watching the little television in the shop when he happened to look up and see a young woman walking quickly along the road outside. Masaharu stared – it was Yukiho.

There was something unusually urgent about her as she stepped out into the street and hailed a taxi.

It was already ten o'clock. *Something must have happened*, he thought.

Worried, Masaharu used the phone in the ramen shop to call the Karasawa residence. The phone rang several times before Reiko picked up.

'Is something the matter?' she asked, when she heard his voice. She sounded more startled than concerned.

Masaharu hesitated. 'Um, is Yukiho there?'

'Certainly, would you like to speak with her?'

'What? She's right there?'

'No, she's up in her room. She had some club event she has to get ready for tomorrow. They're meeting very early in the morning so she went to bed early. But I should think she's still awake.'

Masaharu thought for a moment. 'No, that's all right,' he said. 'I'll talk to her next week. It's nothing urgent.'

'Are you sure?'

'Yeah. You should just let her get to sleep.'

'Right. Well, I'll tell her you rang tomorrow morning.'

'Yes, thank you. Sorry to trouble you this late at night.' Masaharu hung up quickly. His armpits were damp with sweat.

So Yukiho's sneaking out of her house late at night ... to go where? He wondered if the phone call she'd received before he left had something to do with it and hoped his call hadn't blown her cover.

Yukiho phoned the next day.

'Sorry,' she said, 'you called last night? I had some club stuff this morning and went to sleep really early. What's up?'

'It's not a big deal,' he said. 'I just thought something might be up and called to check in on you.'

'Oh? What sort of something?'

'Something that would have you hailing a cab at ten at night. You looked worried.'

This made her skip a beat. When she spoke again it was in a low voice. 'You saw me?'

'From the ramen shop, yeah,' Masaharu said, chuckling.

He heard her sigh. 'Thanks for not telling my mom.'

'I didn't think it would go well for you if I did.'

'No, it wouldn't have. Not at all,' she said, laughing.

'So what happened? I'm guessing the phone call you got has something to do with it.' He judged from her tone that whatever it was, it hadn't been anything too serious.

'You're a sharp one,' she said, lowering her voice again. 'Actually, one of my friends attempted suicide.'

'What? Really?'

'She got dumped ... I don't think she even really thought about it that much. Anyway, me and a couple of her other friends went to see her. I just didn't want Mom to worry about it.'

'Yeah, I can see why. How's your friend?'

'Fine, thanks. I think just seeing us helped a lot.'

'Good to hear.'

'It's crazy, isn't it? Wanting to die just because of a boy?'

'That I have to agree with.'

'Anyway,' Yukiho said, brightening, 'please don't tell my mom?'

'The thought never crossed my mind.'

She had thanked him and hung up.

Masaharu shook his head, chuckling to himself as he thought back to that day. The Yukiho on the phone had been so different from the one in lessons, the Yukiho her mother thought she knew. *It's hard to know what's really going on inside some people*, he realised, *especially young girls*.

Don't worry, he wanted to tell the woman in the rattan chair across from him, *your daughter isn't as hopeless as she seems*.

He'd just finished his barley tea when he heard the front door open.

'Sounds like she's home,' Reiko said, standing.

Masaharu stood behind her and checked his reflection in the sliding glass doors leading to the garden. *Idiot*, he thought to himself, *what are you so nervous about?*

For his undergraduate thesis, Masaharu was working on an implementation of graph theory in robot control systems at Laboratory No 6 of the Electrical Engineering Department at the University of Northern Osaka. Specifically, he was trying to get a computer to interpret three-dimensional objects using only unidirectional visual input – to see and understand the physical world through a pair of robotic eyes.

He was at his desk, debugging, when someone called him from behind.

'Hey, Masaharu. Check this out.'

It was a grad student named Minobe. He was sitting in front of a personal computer from Hewlett-Packard, his eyes focused on the display.

Masaharu came over and stood behind him, looking at the monochromatic image. On it were three square shapes above a longer, rectangular shape.

He had seen this before. It was the game they called *Submarine*. The goal was to sink your opponent's subs as quickly as you could. You played by trying to guess your opponent's location from co-ordinate data on three axes. If you took too long with your attack, your enemy might suss out your position first and sink you with a torpedo.

The game was something that the students and grad students in Lab No 6 had put together during their free time. All work was shared, from flow-charting the program to typing it in – an underground project for the whole laboratory that some of the students took more seriously than they took their own thesis work.

'What about it? It's *Submarine*,' Masaharu said.

'Is it? Take a closer look.'

'Huh?'

'See the pattern they're using to show the coordinates? It's different. Same with the shape of the submarine itself.'

Masaharu squinted at the screen, looking at the parts Minobe pointed out. 'Hey, you're right. Did one of the guys change the program?'

'Nope. None of us, at least.'

Minobe pressed the button on the tape player next to his computer and took out the tape. He showed it to Masaharu. The tape had a printed label that read *Marine Crash*.

'What's that?'

'Nagata over in Number Three loaned it to me.'

'Where'd he get it?'

'Take a look.' Minobe produced a train pass out of his jeans pocket. He pulled a folded piece of paper out of the pass holder. It looked like something torn out of a magazine. Minobe spread it out on the table.

SELLERS OF ALL VARIETY OF GAMES
FOR PERSONAL COMPUTERS

Below was a list of titles, all games, each followed by a simple explanation and a price. There were about thirty games in all. The cheapest were around one thousand yen, and the most expensive a little over five thousand.

Marine Crash was in the middle of the list, printed in a bold font with a comment next to it that read '★★★★ Fascinating'. Three of the other titles were bold, but this was the only one with four stars. Apparently, *Marine Crash* was the star of the line-up, all sold by a company called Unlimited Designs. Masaharu had never heard of it.

'So, what, they're selling these by mail order?'

'Yeah. I've seen them around. Never paid it much attention, but it sounds like Nagata's known about it for a while. One of his friends actually ordered this *Marine Crash*, so he borrowed their copy and checked it out. Guess what? The game's exactly the same.'

Masaharu shook his head. 'What the hell's going on?'

'*Submarine*,' Minobe said, leaning back in his chair with a squeak of metal, 'is our original game. Well, OK, maybe not entirely original, since we based it on that MIT game, but the implementation was entirely ours. What do you think the chances are that someone else could have had the exact same idea, and make it in practically the same way?'

'Not high. What does it mean?'

'Someone in our group leaked *Submarine* to this Unlimited Designs place.'

'No way.'

'You got a better explanation? We're the only ones with the program, and everyone's real careful about lending it out.'

Masaharu fell silent. Minobe was right. The evidence that someone was selling a rip-off of their game was right in front of him.

'Maybe we should hold a meeting,' Masaharu said.

'Good idea. How about after lunch? We get everybody's heads together, we might figure something out. Assuming the person responsible doesn't lie outright.' Minobe frowned and pushed up his glasses with the tip of his finger.

'I'm just having trouble imagining any of the guys selling out like that.'

'You can trust them if you want, Masaharu, but one thing's for certain: there is a traitor in our midst.'

'I don't know. What if it was leaked by accident? Somebody could've stolen the program from somebody when they weren't watching.'

'So, the thief wasn't one of us, but someone close to one of us?'

'That would make sense,' Masaharu agreed, though he objected to the word 'thief'. It wasn't like they'd taken a wallet. This felt different, somehow.

'Anyway, we'll have to talk to the group,' Minobe said, folding his arms.

Six people, Minobe included, had been involved in *Submarine*'s creation. All of them gathered during lunch break that day at Laboratory No 6. Minobe explained the situation, but no one had a clue how it could have happened.

One of the seniors in the group was talking. 'I mean, no one in our group would have leaked it. If any of us wanted to sell it, wouldn't they have gone to the rest of us first? You know, talk to the other guys, sell it together?'

Minobe asked if anyone had loaned the program to anyone. Three of the students said they'd let friends play it but none of them had left their friends alone with the tape long enough to copy it.

'That leaves only one other option, then,' Minobe said. 'Somebody's program was stolen without them knowing it. Think back, think hard. If it wasn't one of us, then somebody we know gave or sold it to these jokers.'

The meeting ended and Masaharu returned to his seat to mull things over. There wasn't even a chance anyone else had taken his tape. He always kept his copy of *Submarine* along with his other data tapes in his desk at home. On the rare occasions he took them out, he never let them leave his sight, not even at the laboratory.

More than the mystery, however, the situation intrigued him for an entirely different reason. *Submarine* was a program they had made as a lark, a game entirely for their own amusement, until someone out there had the idea that it could be sold and people would pay good money for it. What had started as a program had become a product. It was an entirely novel idea and maybe, he thought, it was a very good one.

Two weeks after his chat with Reiko, Masaharu was at the public library with his friend Kakiuchi, who was researching a paper. Kakiuchi was in the same hockey team at school. He was looking through old newspapers – archival editions with condensed print – when he started to chuckle.

'Check this out,' he said, pointing at an article. 'I remember this. My parents had me standing in line every morning to get toilet paper.'

The article was from November 2, 1973. The photo showed at least three hundred people crowding into a supermarket north of Osaka for toilet paper during the peak of the oil shock. Kakiuchi's research was on electrical power demand.

'They lined up in Tokyo, too?' Kakiuchi asked.

'Yeah, though I think it was more about detergent there. My cousin said he used to get sent out on shopping missions.'

'Yeah, look at this: a housewife bought forty thousand yen worth of detergent in a western Tokyo supermarket. Not your mom, I presume?' Kakiuchi said with a grin.

Masaharu laughed. 'Nah, we'd already moved by then.' He'd been in the first year of high school that year, too busy adjusting to his new life in Osaka to pay much attention to the news.

He wondered suddenly what grade Yukiho had been in. He guessed she'd have been in fifth grade. He had trouble picturing her at that age.

Then he remembered what Reiko had said about Yukiho's mother dying when she was in sixth grade. *That would make it 1974.* Pulling the May 1974 paper out of the stack, he spread it out on the table. He scanned the headlines: DIET ASSEMBLY IN SESSION, ENVIRONMENTAL PROTECTION LAWS AMENDED, ADVOCATES FOR WOMEN'S RIGHTS PROTEST THE EUGENIC PROTECTION ACT. There was a little bit about the Japan Consumer Alliance having paved the way for the first Seven Eleven to open in Tokyo's Koto ward.

Masaharu turned to the society pages, his eye travelling down the tightly packed text until he found a small article with the headline GAS POISONING DUE TO EXTINGUISHED FLAME?

'The body of Fumiyo Nishimoto (age 36) was found in her Yoshida Heights apartment in Ōe, a district in Osaka's Ikuno ward. Mrs Nishimoto was discovered by an employee of the real estate agency responsible for her building, who called an ambulance to the scene. According to a report by Ikuno ward police, the apartment was filled with gas at the time of discovery, leading them to conclude that Mrs Nishimoto's death was due to gas poisoning. It is thought that a pot of soup on the stove had boiled over, extinguishing the flame and filling the apartment with gas without alerting Mrs Nishimoto.'

The story matched exactly what he'd heard from Reiko, except the paper didn't mention Yukiho being there, probably out of consideration for her age at the time.

'Find something interesting?' Kakiuchi asked.

'Yeah, kind of,' Masaharu said, pointing to the article and telling him about his student.

'Wow.' Kakiuchi pulled the paper closer and read through the article himself. 'Ōe, huh? That's Naito's hood.'

'Really? He's from over there?'

'Yeah, pretty sure.'

Naito was a younger kid on their ice hockey team, one year behind them.

'Maybe I'll ask him about it,' Masaharu said, taking down the apartment building name he found listed in the article.

It was another two weeks before he got around to talking to Naito, a short, skinny fellow with great skating skills, even though his weight made his body checks kind of a joke. Still, he was a nice guy who was always willing to lend a hand, which secured him a place of authority on the team.

By contrast, Masaharu had hardly come to practice since senior year began. And he had only started hockey in the first place because he was afraid he'd get fat sitting around programming all day and track didn't appeal to him.

He caught Naito while the team was out training on the athletics field.

'Yeah, the lady who gassed herself? I remember that. It was a while ago, though,' Naito said. 'It happened next to my house, actually. Well, not right next to it, but walking distance.'

'So it was, like, the talk of the town?'

'People knew about it, sure. Though what really got everyone's attention were the rumours that it wasn't an accident.'

'You mean she did it on purpose? Suicide?'

'Yep,' Naito said, looking at him. 'So what's it got to do with you?'

'It's less me, and more a friend.' He explained the situation to Naito.

Naito's eyes went wide. 'Wow. You're teaching her daughter, then? That's a coincidence.'

'But what about these rumours? Why'd they think it was a suicide?'

'I don't know all the details. I was just in high school.' Naito scratched his head, then his eyes lit up. 'Wait, maybe that guy'd know something about it.'

'What guy?'

'The guy at the real estate agency I'm renting my parking space from. I remember him talking about the gas thing once. He was one of the ones who said it was a suicide.'

'The article said it was a real estate agent who found the body. Think it might have been him?'

'Hey, could be!'

'Think you could find out?' Masaharu said. He knew it was asking a lot of a guy he barely knew, but he was an upperclassman compared to Naito and the school sports teams took seniority very seriously.

Naito scratched his head again. 'Sure, no problem,' he said, giving Masaharu a nervous smile.

On the evening of the following day, Masaharu was sitting in the passenger seat of Naito's Toyota Carina.

'Sorry to put you through the trouble,' Masaharu told him as they started rolling.

'Hey, I don't mind. It's near home, anyway.' Naito smiled.

Naito had been as good as his word about helping. When he called the estate agency the man there told him it wasn't him but his son who'd discovered the victim of the gas poisoning five years before. His son was now running a new branch of the agency in Fukaebashi. Masaharu was holding a piece of paper with a simple map to the shop and a phone number.

'So, you're pretty serious about this tutoring thing, huh?' Naito said. 'I mean, that's why you're doing this, right? Finding out as much as you can about your kids?' He shook his head. 'I can't imagine ever going that far out of my way for a job.'

Masaharu didn't say anything to dissuade him from his theory though, in truth, he wasn't sure why he was doing this. Of course he understood the pull that Yukiho had on him. But that didn't mean he needed to know everything about her. Masaharu was generally of the opinion that the past didn't matter.

Maybe it was because he didn't understand her in the present, he thought. They talked together like old friends and yet she seemed so distant. He didn't understand why, and it aggravated him.

After a while they left the main road and went on to a side street where they found the local branch of Tagawa Real Estate right next to the freeway ramp.

Inside, a skinny man was sitting at a desk, filling in some forms. He looked at them as they walked in and asked if they were looking for an apartment.

Naito told him they were there to ask about the accident. 'I talked to the guy at your branch in Ikuno and he said the boss here, Mr Tagawa, was the one who saw what happened.'

'I'm Tagawa,' the man said, looking at them a bit suspiciously. 'That's ancient history, though. What concern is it of yours?'

'There was a girl with you when you found the body, right?' Masaharu asked. 'Yukiho Nishimoto?'

The man nodded warily. 'Are you a relative?'

'Actually, she's my student. I'm tutoring her.'

'Oh yeah?' the man said. 'Where is she these days? She was an orphan after her mother died, if I remember right.'

'She was adopted by a relative. Her last name's Karasawa now.'

The man nodded. 'She doing OK? I haven't seen her since then.'

'She's great. She's a junior in high school now.'

'Yeah, guess she would be. Time flies, huh?'

He took a cigarette out and put it in his mouth. Masaharu saw the box – they were Mild Sevens, one of the new, supposedly 'lighter' cigarettes. He was surprised a man this guy's age would be so trendy.

'She talk about what happened at all?' Tagawa asked, blowing a puff of smoke.

'Not much, just that you'd really helped her out,' Masaharu lied.

'Well, that's true enough, but it sure was a surprise.' Tagawa leaned back in his chair, hands behind his head, and began to tell them the story of how he discovered Fumiyo Nishimoto's body.

'Worse than finding the body was what came after,' he said after finishing his story. 'The police had all kinds of questions for me. They wanted to know how things looked when I entered the apartment. Did I touch anything other than the window and the stove, that kind of thing. They wanted to know if I touched the pot at all, or if the door really had been locked. It was a real pain.'

'Was there something strange about the pot?'

'Not that I saw. They were saying that if the soup had really boiled over it would've made more of a mess on the stove. Of course, it must have boiled over, because it put out the burner, right?'

Masaharu tried to picture the scene in his mind. He'd left a pot on the stove too long when he was making instant ramen once or twice and it had made quite a mess.

'Still, it sounds like the girl's doing well. If she lives in a home that can hire a private tutor and all. That's good. She had it pretty rough with that mother of hers.'

'Was there some kind of problem?'

'Yeah, poverty. Mrs Nishimoto definitely didn't have an easy life. She had a job working at some noodle place and it was pretty tough for her just to pay rent. They'd always be behind a few months.'

Compared to Masaharu's own experience, this was like hearing about life on another planet.

'Maybe that's why that kid always seemed older than her years. More aware, you know? I don't even think she cried when we found her mom lying there.'

'Really?' Masaharu looked at the man's face, remembering what Reiko had said about Yukiho sobbing at the funeral.

'What about the rumours?' Naito asked. 'Weren't people saying it was a suicide?'

'Yeah,' Tagawa grunted. 'There were some things that made it suspicious, I guess. I remember the detective talking about it.'

'What sort of things?'

'Well, they said something about Mrs Nishimoto taking cold medicine – about five times the normal amount, based on the wrappers they found in the trash.'

'Was that enough to kill her?'

'No, but the cops said that she might've taken it to fall asleep. You know, turn on the gas, take some sleeping pills? But it can be hard to get sleeping pills, so she went for the cold medicine.'

'Desperate times,' Masaharu said, nodding.

'She'd got into the alcohol, too. There were three open jars of sake in the garbage – the cheap stuff you get out of vending machines. And she supposedly wasn't a big drinker.'

'Right.'

'That, and the window,' Tagawa said, growing more talkative as the memories surfaced. 'Somebody thought it was strange that everything was locked up tight. There weren't any ventilation fans in the kitchens in that building, so if people cooked something, they usually opened the windows.

'But,' Masaharu said, 'it still could have just been an accident, right?'

'Sure, which is why they didn't investigate the suicide theory much. They didn't have any smoking gun, and there were other ways to explain the cold medicine and the sake, like what the girl said.'

'What did Yukiho say?'

'Just that her mom had a cold that week and that she'd sometimes drink sake when she felt a chill. The detective still thought it was too much cold medicine to explain away, but there's no way to really know without being able to ask her. And the big thing is, if it was a suicide, why would she bother putting soup on the stove? Anyway, they decided it was an accident, so that's that.

'The police said that if we'd found her thirty minutes earlier, she might have been saved. Think about it – thirty minutes. That's just bad luck. Whether it was suicide or an accident, you got to think she was destined to die that day.'

Long, slightly chestnut-coloured hair fell down across Yukiho's face. With her left hand, she brushed it back behind her ear, but a few strands remained. Masaharu wanted to kiss her pale white cheek. He'd wanted to since his first day with her.

She was working on a problem, trying to figure out the equation of a line formed by the intersection of two planes. Her mechanical pencil flew across the page.

'Done,' she said, well before time was up. Masaharu carefully checked the formulae. Her writing was precise, each number and symbol a work of art in miniature.

'Good job,' he said, looking back up at her. 'Perfect, actually. I can't find anything to complain about.'

'Well,' she said, smiling, 'that's a first!'

He chuckled. 'Look,' he said, 'it seems like you've got the general idea about dealing with coordinates in space. If you can do this one, everything else is just a variation on the same pattern.'

'Sounds like a fine time for a break! I just bought some tea.'

She stood and left Masaharu to sit by her desk and look around the room. He was never really sure what to do with himself while he waited. What he wanted to do was poke around, open her little drawers, pore through the notebooks on her shelf. Even a minor discovery, like what brand of cosmetics she used, would be progress. Yet the thought that she might catch him stayed his hand. He didn't want her to think badly of him.

He'd actually brought a magazine for just this sort of moment – a fashion magazine he'd seen on the stand that morning at a shop by the station – but he'd left it down in his duffel bag on the floor below. He'd been using the bag since his first year in hockey club and the years were showing so it stayed near the entrance while he was tutoring.

His eyes wandered to a small pink radio sitting in front of a bookshelf. A few cassette tapes had been stacked next to it. He scanned down the labels: Yumi Arai's 'Off Course' – all pop music and pretty new. The sight of the cassettes reminded him of something else: the stolen *Submarine*.

They still weren't any closer to finding out how the game had got leaked. Minobe had even tried calling the company from the ad, but that hadn't got him anywhere.

'I asked them where they got the program from and they just said they couldn't answer any questions. It was a woman on the phone, so I asked her to pass me to one of their tech guys, but he was no more help than she was. I'm guessing they were guilty and just didn't want to admit it. I bet they stole their other games, too.'

'What if we just showed up on their doorstep?' Masaharu suggested.

'Doubt that would help,' Minobe said, shaking his head. 'We start whining about stolen software, they won't even let us in.'

'What if you brought a copy of *Submarine* and showed it to them?'

Minobe shook his head again. 'What proof do we have that *Submarine* is the original? They could just say we copied their *Marine*-whatever game.'

Masaharu wanted to pull his hair out. 'But then there's nothing to stop them from stealing more programs!'

'Exactly,' Minobe said. 'We're going to need copyrights for these things before long. That's what my friend over in the law school said. I asked him how much money we could get if we could prove our program was stolen and he said nothing – not without any copyright laws on the books.'

'Great.'

'I still want to find out who did it,' said Minobe, then he added, in a cold voice, 'and make them pay.'

Minobe suggested that they write up a list of everyone they had shown *Submarine* to, or talked about *Submarine* with. 'Someone would've had to know about *Submarine* in order to want to steal it,' was his reasoning. Everyone came up with every name they could think of and before long they had a list several dozen names long. There were other people at the laboratory, friends from school clubs and teams, friends from high school, and others.

'One of these people must be connected in some way to Unlimited Designs,' Minobe said, sighing as he scanned the long list of names.

Masaharu understood his sigh all too well. He was doubtful they'd find anything like a direct connection. The program could have been passed from person to person dozens of times before it reached the company selling it. Unless they got very lucky, it would be nearly impossible to trace.

'Well, the place to start is for each of us to talk to the people we spoke about *Submarine* with. Someone's bound to come up with a lead.'

For his part, Masaharu had hardly mentioned *Submarine* to anyone, less out of security concerns and more because he never imagined anyone outside his department would be interested in something that was essentially part of his research. Besides, without fancy graphics, the game wasn't anywhere near as interesting as something like *Space Invaders*.

In fact, the only time he'd ever shown the game to anyone was when he'd talked about it to Yukiho one afternoon when she asked him what he studied at the university. He'd begun by telling her about his thesis work but soon realised that image analysis and graph theory wasn't that interesting to a junior high school student so he brought up the game. It worked well. Her eyes lit up the moment he mentioned it.

'Making a game sounds like fun,' she'd said. 'What kind of game is it?'

He wrote a picture of the *Submarine* screen on a piece of paper and explained the game to her. She listened very intently and said she was impressed he'd made something like that by himself.

'Oh, it was a group effort,' he'd told her, though not before feeling a rush of pride.

'But you understand how it works, don't you?'

'Sure, mostly.'

'See? Impressive.'

Masaharu felt something stir in his chest, a reaction to her gaze on him and her praise. The feeling that came from someone like her respecting his achievements was intoxicating.

'I'd love to try it some time,' she'd said.

This, he felt, had to happen, but as he explained to her, he didn't have his own computer and couldn't take her into the lab. She seemed disappointed.

'What I need is a rich friend with a computer,' he joked.

'A computer's all you need to play the game?'

'And the tape with the program on it.'

'The tape? What kind of tape?'

'It's just a regular cassette tape, except it holds data, not music.'

She seemed fascinated and asked if he could show her one some time.

'Sure,' he said, 'but it just looks like a regular cassette tape. Like the ones you have.'

'I'd still like to see it some time.'

'Sure thing.'

Fully expecting to disappoint her, Masaharu brought the tape with him the next time he came.

'Wow, it really is a regular cassette tape,' she said, looking at the tape in her hand.

'Like I said.'

'I never knew you could use these tapes for something else like that,' she said, handing it back to him. 'You should put that in your bag right away. I'm sure it's very important.'

'Hardly that important,' he said, though privately he thought it really was. He went back downstairs to put the tape in his duffel bag by the door.

This was the extent of Yukiho's contact with the program. Neither of them had mentioned it again. Nor had he mentioned their exchange to Minobe and the others. The idea that she'd stolen the program was laughable – in fact, he'd never even considered the possibility until now.

Of course, had she been of a mind to, Yukiho could easily have taken the tape out of his duffel bag that day. All she would have had to do was pretend to go to the bathroom and sneak down to the ground floor. But what would she do with it then? Stealing the tape wouldn't be enough. If she didn't want him to notice, she would have to duplicate the tape within the two hours of their lesson and return the original to the bag. Possible, if she had the equipment, but he knew she didn't own a personal computer and making a duplicate data tape wasn't as simple as copying your friend's tape of pop music.

Though it *was* an amusing pastime to imagine her as the thief, Masaharu thought as the door opened.

'What are you grinning about?' Yukiho said as she walked in with two teacups on a tray.

'Oh, nothing,' Masaharu said. 'That smells nice.'

'It's Darjeeling.'

She put the teacups on the desk and he took one and took a sip a bit too fast, spilling a little on his jeans as he tried to set down the cup.

'Well, that was dumb.'

He pulled a handkerchief out of his pocket, dislodging a folded piece of paper, which fell out on the floor.

'Are you all right?' Yukiho asked.

'I'm fine. It wasn't much.'

'You dropped something.' She picked the paper off the floor, but when she looked at it, her almond eyes went wide. 'What's this?'

She held the paper out to Masaharu. It had a hand-drawn map and a telephone number with the words 'Tagawa Real Estate' below.

Oops.

'Tagawa Real Estate? In Ikuno?' she asked. Her earlier good humour seemed to have vanished.

'No, not in Ikuno,' he said quickly. 'It's in Higashinari ward. See here, it says "Fukaebashi"?' Masaharu pointed at the map with his finger.

'But that must be a branch of the one in Ikuno. I'll bet the son of the owner opened that.'

'Huh, no kidding.' Masaharu tried not to let his bewilderment show on his face.

'Are you looking for an apartment?'

'No, I just went with a friend.'

'Oh.' Her eyes had a faraway look to them. 'I've just remembered something strange.'

'What do you mean?'

'Tagawa Real Estate, the original one in Ikuno, managed the apartment building I lived in as a child. I used to live there, you know, in Ōe.'

'Really?' Masaharu tried to focus on his teacup, not meeting her eyes.

'Have you heard about when my mother died? My real

mother, I mean,' she said, her voice calm and somehow deeper than usual.

'Uh, no, I haven't,' he said, shaking his head.

She chuckled. 'You're a bad actor. I know you know. The other day, when you talked to my mom for a long time, she told you then, didn't she.'

'Well, OK, maybe a little,' he said, setting down his cup and scratching his head.

Yukiho took a couple of sips of her own tea and breathed a long sigh of steam.

'May twenty-second,' she said, 'was the day my mother died.'

Masaharu nodded silently.

'It was a little cold that day. I wore a cardigan my mother had knitted for me to school. I still have it, you know – the cardigan.'

She glanced over at the dresser in the corner. Masaharu could only imagine what painful memories it contained.

'It must've been quite a shock,' Masaharu said, immediately regretting saying something so bland.

'It was like I was dreaming – a nightmare, of course,' Yukiho said, an awkward smile flashing briefly across her lips. 'I went to play with some friends after school that day. That's why I was a little late getting home. If I hadn't gone to play, I might have been home an hour earlier.'

Masaharu understood what she was trying to say. That one hour had changed her life.

Yukiho bit her lip before continuing. 'When I think about that—'

Masaharu tensed, hearing the tears in her voice. He thought maybe he should pull out his handkerchief, but didn't dare move.

'Sometimes, I feel like I killed her,' she said.

'You should never think that. You didn't come home late on purpose, Yukiho.'

'That's not what I mean. My mother had it very hard those days. She was giving up sleep to work. That's why she was so tired that day. I think if I'd been more helpful, if she hadn't had to work so hard ...'

Masaharu held his breath as he watched a large tear trace a path down her white cheek. He wanted more than anything else to hold her. *I'm an idiot*, Masaharu cursed himself. Because ever since talking to Mr Tagawa at the estate agency and hearing about what had happened, a horrible thought had been growing in the back of his mind.

The unusual number of cold medicine packages, the sake cups, the locked window – everything pointed towards suicide. The only thing that didn't make sense was the pot that had boiled over – boiled over, but not enough to leave a mess, according to the police. Not enough to put out a burner.

Maybe it had been a suicide, but then someone had come by and spilled soup out of the pot in order to make it look like an accident. The one who could have done that was Yukiho. She could have spilled the soup then opened the cold medicine boxes and the cups of sake.

Why make it look like an accident? Because she was afraid of what people would think? Yet the scenario raised another frightening question. If Yukiho had returned home earlier, before coming with the estate agent, had her mother already been dead at that time? Or could she still have been saved? Hadn't Mr Tagawa said that had they been there thirty minutes earlier, they might have been able to save her?

What if the young Yukiho had, upon walking in on her own mother on the brink of death, seen not tragedy, but opportunity? What if, in her weekly visits to Reiko Karasawa's house, Yukiho had realised that if something ever happened to her own mother, she could rely on this elegant lady to take her in?

The thought was not a place Masaharu wanted to linger long. And yet there was something grimly compelling about the scenario. He couldn't get it out of his head.

Now, seeing her tears, Masaharu chastised himself for having such a twisted mind. This was a human being sitting before him, a real, vulnerable girl. She could never have done something so cold.

'It's not your fault,' he said. 'You shouldn't think that. You wouldn't want your mother to be sad where she is now.'

'I just wish I'd had a key,' Yukiho whispered between sobs.

'It was just bad luck.'

Yukiho shook her head and stood, going to her school uniform where it hung on a hanger in the closet. She pulled a key out of the pocket. 'That's why I always keep a house key with me now,' she said. She held the key up to show him.

'That keychain looks ancient,' Masaharu said.

'It is. I've had it for ever. Except, that day, I forgot it at home.'

As she put the key back in her pocket, her hand brushed against the closet door, making the tiny bell on her keychain ring.

FIVE

The noise hit them as soon as they were through the ticket gates. Students from a nearby university – all of them boys – were practically falling over each other to hand flyers to the girls from Seika Girls College. 'Join our tennis club!' they shouted. 'Join our skiing club!' Their voices had long since gone hoarse.

Eriko succeeded in making it out of the station without accepting a single flyer. She and Yukiho exchanged glances and laughed.

'That was impressive,' said Eriko. 'I wonder how many different schools were there.'

'Today's the most important day of the year for them,' Yukiho told her. 'A word of advice: never settle for a flyer boy.' She brushed back her long hair.

The school buildings of Seika Girls College stood in the middle of a residential area that was mostly newer houses, with the occasional sprawling old walled-in property. It was a small college with only three departments: English Literature, Home Economics, and Athletics – meaning that there were usually very few students in what was ostensibly a college town. This kept things quiet, with the exception of recruitment day, when students from nearby men's universities competed to attract girls from Seika to join their clubs. Boys from nearby Eimei University were thickest on the ground. They loitered along the street leading to the school, casting about with hungry eyes for likely targets. When they spotted a freshman, they launched into their pitch.

'You don't even have to really be in the club if you don't want to,' shouted one as they passed. 'Just come to the parties. You don't even need to pay dues!'

It took the girls almost twenty minutes to navigate a path that only took five on a normal day. They seemed to be attracting far more than their share of attention, but Eriko knew all too well the boys were there for Yukiho, not her. So had it always been, ever since they were in middle school.

The frantic invitations died down once they were through the college gates. Eriko and Yukiho headed for the gymnasium. Opening ceremonies would be held here this year.

Folding chairs stretched out in long rows behind department names posted on placards. The two girls sat down in the row for English Lit. There should have been about forty new students in the department, but only half the seats were filled. Students weren't under any particular obligation to attend the opening ceremony, which meant that most would be arriving late, just in time for official school club recruitments, Eriko imagined.

The opening ceremony consisted of greetings from the president and the department heads. The speeches were painfully boring; it was all Eriko could do to stifle her yawns.

Outside the gymnasium, tables from each school club had been lined up on the campus lawn. There were some boys from Eimei here too, though energy levels were far more subdued than they had been that morning at the station.

'Going to join any clubs?' Eriko asked Yukiho as they walked outside.

'Maybe,' she said, passing her uninterested gaze over several of the club posters.

'There's an awful lot of tennis clubs – and skiing,' Eriko noted. It seemed those two activities made up about half of all the clubs. She guessed these clubs were less about community and school spirit, and more about skipping out on class and scoring free trips to the mountains.

'Not interested,' said Yukiho.

'No?'

'I'd just get sunburned.'

'True.'

'Did you know that your skin remembers the exact amount of

ultraviolet radiation it's absorbed? Even if a tan fades, the damage is done. And when you get older, you'll pay in wrinkles. They say tans are for the young, but if you ask me, the young are the last people who should be getting tans.'

Eriko looked over at her friend, her skin as white as the 'yuki' meaning 'snow' in her name, and agreed that she had something worth protecting.

The boys began their approach, like fruit flies to a banana. They invited them to play tennis, go skiing, play golf, go surfing – all things that would give you a serious tan, Eriko thought bemusedly. Yukiho wasn't paying them any attention. She had stopped, her eyes looking up at a poster. The sign read:

Ballroom Dance
(A joint club with Eimei University)

Two girls, new recruits by the look of them, were talking with the members by the club table. There was no sports paraphernalia here – everyone behind the table, Seika girls and Eimei boys both, wore dark, stylish jackets. They seemed more adult and refined than the students in the other clubs.

The boys had already noticed Yukiho stopping and one of them approached almost immediately.

'Might you be interested in a dance?' he asked. He was handsome, and there was a deliberate precision to his words.

'A little,' Yukiho said honestly. 'But I've never tried it before, and I really don't know much about it.'

'Everyone has to start somewhere,' the boy said. 'But don't worry, you'll be dancing in a month.'

'Would it be all right just to watch?'

'Of course.' He led Yukiho over to the desk as they talked and introduced her to the girl members from Seika. Almost as an afterthought, he looked back around at Eriko. 'How about you?'

'No, I'm fine.'

'OK!'

He went straight back to Yukiho, afraid that other boys might angle in on his catch, Eriko thought. Already three other boys were crowding around her.

'Why don't you audit?' said a voice from behind Eriko. She jolted to one side and glanced around to see a taller boy looking down at her.

'No, really,' she said, 'I'm fine.'

'Why not?' he asked with a smile.

'I just don't think dancing is my thing. I'm not suited for it. And if they found out, my family would go into shock.'

'There's no such thing as being suited or unsuited for dancing. Isn't your friend going to audit too?' He glanced towards where Yukiho was standing near the club table. 'Come along, just once. Take a look. If you don't like it, you don't like it – we won't force you to join just because you came to watch.'

'Really, it's OK.'

'You don't want to dance?'

'It's not that. In fact, I think it would be nice to be able to dance. I just don't think I'm cut out for it.' She shook her head. 'No, I'm definitely not.'

'Oh, I doubt that,' the tall student said, giving her a suspicious look. But his eyes were smiling.

'I – I'd get dizzy right away.'

'Dizzy?'

'Seasick. I'm just not very good at swaying from side to side.'

The boy raised an eyebrow. 'What does that have to do with dancing?'

'Well,' Eriko said, lowering her voice, 'don't the boys whirl the girls around a lot? Like that scene from *Gone with the Wind* when Scarlett dances with Rhett Butler. Just watching that made me feel a little sick to my stomach.'

Eriko had meant to be serious, but it was hard to keep a straight face when the boy started to laugh midway through her explanation.

'A lot of people get nervous when you mention the word "dance", but that's the first time I've ever heard *that* excuse.'

'But I'm not joking. I really am worried.'

'I don't believe it.'

'Honest!'

He shook his head. 'You owe it to yourself to at least see what you're so frightened of,' he said, taking Eriko by the hand and pulling her over to the club table.

Yukiho had just finished signing up to audit. She was smiling at something the three boys behind the table were saying. When she saw Eriko get dragged over, her eyes widened in surprise.

'Another for auditing,' the tall student said.

'What's Kazunari doing recruiting?' whispered one of the girls at the table.

'I believe this fine young lady has misconceptions about dance that need correcting,' he said, flashing white teeth at Eriko.

Dance club ended precisely at five, after which several of the boys from Eimei would invite new recruits who showed potential out to a café. This café date was the sole purpose for which many of them had joined the club in the first place.

Tonight, Kazunari Shinozuka was in a hotel in Osaka. He was sitting on a sofa next to the window, his notebook open on his lap with a list of twenty-three names. *Not bad*, he thought. It wasn't an outrageously large number, but it was more than the year before. The question was how many would actually join.

'There were a lot more boys this year than usual,' came a voice from the bed.

Kanae Kurahashi lit her cigarette and blew out a stream of grey smoke. Her bare shoulder was exposed, though she held a blanket over her breasts. The dim light of the nightstand lamp left the exotic features of her face in shadow.

'You think?'

'Don't you?'

'Seemed the same as always to me.'

Kanae shook her head. Her long hair swayed. 'No, today was definitely different. And I know who's to blame.'

'Do tell.'

'That Karasawa girl. She's joining, right?'

'Karasawa?' Kazunari traced down the names in his notebook with a finger. 'Yukiho Karasawa ... English Lit.'

'You don't remember her? That's hard to believe.'

'No, I remember her. Though I don't remember her face that well, to tell you the truth. We had a lot of people audit today.'

Kanae snorted. 'Guess she's not your type.'

'What type is she?'

'A perfect lady. You like the ones with imperfections, the bad girls. Like me.'

'I like a well-bred lady as much as the next man. Anyway, what makes you so sure she's a "lady"?'

'You should've seen Nagayama. He was practically beside himself, saying she was definitely a virgin.' Kanae chuckled.

'That proves nothing except that he's an idiot.'

Kazunari took a bite of the sandwich he'd ordered from room service and thought back on the students who came to observe the club that day.

It was true that he didn't really remember Yukiho Karasawa that well. They'd only exchanged a couple of words and he hadn't spent much time watching her move, so he'd never picked up on this 'perfect lady' thing Kanae was going on about. He did remember Nagayama being excited, but hadn't known why at the time.

The girl he remembered was Eriko. She was the kind of girl who didn't put on any make-up, wore practical clothes, spoke plainly ... and was still beautiful for it.

He'd seen her waiting for a friend – that was Yukiho, now that he thought of it – to finish writing her name on the sign-up sheet. She didn't seem to notice the other people walking by her or shouts from the other tables. It was almost as if she enjoyed the act of waiting. She made him think of a weed that had suddenly bloomed and now stood swaying in the breeze by the roadside, a tiny flower without a proper name – at least none anyone knew.

And he had reached out to pick that flower. Being the head of the dance club, he wasn't responsible for recruiting. But Eriko was unique. Her reactions to the things he said were completely unexpected, each one. He found the way she talked and the way she looked entirely fresh.

He'd thought about her all during the class audit that day, though he couldn't explain why. His eyes kept being drawn to her.

Maybe it was because she looked the most serious of all the potential recruits that day. While others had sat in the folding chairs they'd put out, she stood until the very end. Kazunari had walked up to her once the session was over to see what she thought.

'It was incredible,' Eriko said, clasping her hands together. 'I used to think ballroom dancing was old-fashioned, but watching them move – it was like they were born to dance.'

'No one's born to dance,' said Kazunari.

'They could have fooled me.'

Kazunari shook his head. 'None of us could dance when we started, and most of us won't go on to be dancers.'

'Then why do it at all?'

He smiled. 'You'd be surprised how many opportunities come up to dance. But even if you only got one, wouldn't you want to be ready for it? Know how to dance, and you'll dance through life.'

'I like that,' Eriko smiled.

'It's just something cheesy the old dance coach used to say.'

'It's not cheesy.' Eriko shook her head. 'It's excellent encouragement, and I won't forget it.'

'You mean you'll join the club?'

'I will. We decided to join together.' She looked over at her friend Yukiho.

'Great. Then we look forward to having you.' Kazunari looked towards the other girl.

'Thank you.' Yukiho bowed curtly before meeting his eyes.

It was the first time he'd seen Yukiho Karasawa straight on. She was pretty, he had to admit, with very delicate features. But there was something else, too. *There are thorns in her eyes* – that was the only way he could express it. For a moment, he thought she might have felt left out because he spoke to her friend first and not to her, but as she smiled, he realised the thorns were always there.

A true lady would never have eyes like that.

Two weeks had passed since the opening ceremony. It was Friday afternoon and Eriko and Yukiho were on the train to Eimei University for their fourth dance club practice since school began.

'Please let me dance well today,' said Eriko, hands pressed together before her in mock prayer.

'You *are* dancing well,' Yukiho said.

'Hardly. My feet won't go the way I tell them to. I keep feeling like I'm going to trip over myself.'

'Don't let Kazunari hear you saying that. You're his beacon of hope, you know.'

'Thanks. That just makes it worse.'

'They say you're the only one he's ever personally recruited. You have a reputation to live up to,' Yukiho said, giving her a teasing look.

'Stop it, Yuki, I'm really bad under pressure. That, and I have no idea why he picked me in the first place.'

'Because he likes you, silly.'

'Erm, no, sorry. That sort of thing might happen in your world, but not in mine. And isn't he dating Kanae?'

'Ah yes, the lovely Miss Kurahashi.' Yukiho nodded. 'They've been a thing for quite some time, apparently.'

'Nagayama says they've been dating since they were freshmen.'

'I guess he moves quick when he sees something he likes.'

'Actually,' Eriko said, 'I heard Kanae made the moves first.'

Yukiho shrugged to indicate she couldn't care less. 'She sure hasn't gone out of her way to hide the fact that Kazunari's her property.'

Kazunari and Kanae's relationship was public knowledge. If the new recruits hadn't known it going in to the first day of dance club practice, they knew it soon after by the way the two talked to each other and the way they danced close, hands on hips, faces practically touching.

If it had been an intentional display on Kanae's part, she'd certainly made her point. Eriko barely knew Kazunari and even she felt a little jealous when she saw them together. Not that she had a chance in the first place. Kazunari was the eldest son of the senior managing director of Shinozuka Pharmaceuticals, one of the top pharmaceutical companies in Japan, and the current CEO was his uncle – which made him nobility as far as she was concerned.

They got off the train. Outside the station, a warm breeze brushed her cheeks.

'I'm probably going to have to leave before the end of class today,' said Yukiho. 'Sorry in advance.'

'Going on a date?'

'I wish. Just an errand.'

Eriko shrugged. Yukiho had started doing these errands a while ago, leaving Eriko to fend for herself. Eriko had asked her once where she went, and Yukiho had refused to speak to her for nearly a week. It was, to date, the only time their friendship ever soured. She hadn't asked again.

Kazunari had been too lost in thought to notice the tiny droplets gathering on the windscreen. Just when he realised it was raining, it started coming down harder, obscuring his view of the road. He reached to the left side of the steering wheel for the wiper lever, then, realising his error, shifted his grip and went for the right side. Even imported cars that managed to put the steering wheel on the right still had their levers reversed. His month-old Volkswagen Golf was no exception.

Outside the school gate he saw students running for the station, paper bags and satchels held over their heads in lieu of umbrellas.

Then he saw Eriko. She was walking at her usual pace, seeming not to care that her white jacket was getting wet. Her constant companion, Yukiho Karasawa, was conspicuously absent.

Kazunari pulled over towards the kerb, slowing until he matched Eriko's speed. She didn't seem to notice. She just kept the same pace, a mysterious smile on her lips. Kazunari gave two taps of his horn and she looked up. He lowered the left-hand passenger window.

'Hey! Need a lift? You look like a drowned rat!'

Eriko didn't seem to appreciate the joke. Her expression hardened, and she started walking faster. Kazunari gave it a little more gas to keep pace.

'Hey, don't run! What's wrong?' he called out.

She walked even faster.

She's taking this the wrong way, he realised.

'Hey Eriko! It's me, Kazunari,' he called out, and finally she stopped and turned with a surprised look on her face.

'Believe me,' he said as she came over to the side of the car, 'if I was out cruising for chicks, I'd do it when it wasn't raining.'

She smiled, the rain running through the matted hair on her forehead and down her cheeks to drip from her chin.

Eriko had a floral-patterned handkerchief. She used it to wipe her hands and face, then ran it over her neck. She'd taken off her drenched jacket and placed it over her bare knees. Kazunari told her she was welcome to put it on the back seat, but she declined on the grounds that it would only get his seat wet.

'Sorry, I didn't realise it was you. It was too dark to see your face.'

'That's OK. The way I was calling out like that, no wonder you got the wrong idea.' Kazunari eased the car around a tight corner. He was taking her home.

'It's just, sometimes it happens and you have to be careful.'

'Strange men in cars call out to you often?'

'Well, no, not me. But when I'm walking with Yukiho ...'

'Speaking of which, where is she?'

'She had an errand to run.'

'That explains why you were alone. Still,' Kazunari glanced over her, 'why were you walking? Why weren't you running? Everyone else around you was.'

'Well, I wasn't in a particular hurry.'

'But you were getting wet.'

'If I ran, it would just make the rain hit my face harder. Like that,' she said, pointing at the windscreen. What had been a light drizzle was now a full-on downpour. Droplets bounced off the glass and rivulets streaked behind the sweeping path of the wipers.

'But wouldn't it reduce the amount of time you were getting rained on?'

'Believe me, I've thought about this. At the speed I run, it'd only cut three minutes off the trip, tops. I don't want to run along a wet road for three minutes. I might trip and fall.'

Kazunari laughed.

'I'm not kidding. I trip all the time. I even fell over today in class and stepped on Yamamoto's foot. He pretended it didn't hurt, but I saw the look in his eyes – the look of a man in true pain,' Eriko said, rubbing her legs where they emerged from her pleated skirt to warm them.

Kazunari chuckled. 'Getting used to the dancing?'

'A little. But I'm still terrible at it. Yukiho, she's practically a pro already.' She sighed.

'You'll get better in no time.'

'I wonder. It'd be nice.'

Kazunari stopped at a red light and took a sidelong glance at Eriko. She had hardly any make-up on, as usual. In the light from the street lamps, her skin looked perfectly smooth. *Like porcelain*, he thought. A few strands of wet hair were stuck to her cheek. He reached out and brushed them aside. She flinched away.

'Sorry, you had some hair on your face.'

Eriko brushed her hair back behind her ears. Even in the dim car interior, he could see her blush. The light turned green and the car lurched back into movement.

'How long have you worn your hair like that?' Kazunari asked, his eyes on the road ahead.

'This?' She put a hand to her wet head. 'Since not long before graduating from high school, I guess.'

'I thought so. That's a Seiko cut, right? Like the singer's? Pretty popular these days – maybe too popular. Everyone's got it, whether it suits them or not.'

It was a semi-long cut, with a fringe left to hang and the sides brushed back.

'You don't think it suits me?'

'Well ...' Kazunari shifted gears before saying, 'To be brutally honest, no, not really.'

'Oh.' Eriko began brushing her hair back with her hands again. 'You like it?'

She shrugged. 'I don't really care that much. It was Yukiho's idea.'

'Her again. Please don't tell me you do everything she says.'

'Of course not.'

Kazunari glanced over and saw Eriko looking down at her lap. An idea occurred to him. He glanced at his watch. It was a little before seven.

'Do you have plans tonight? I forget if you have a part-time job or anything.'

'No, nothing. Why?'

'Think you might join me for a little?'

'Where are you going?'

'Don't worry, it's nothing weird,' Kazunari said, putting his foot down.

He stopped at a phone booth and made a quick call, but he didn't tell Eriko who he was calling. He saw her looking a little worried and smiled.

They stopped in front of a building – their destination was on the first floor. Eriko took one look at the sign and took a step back. 'A beauty salon? Why?'

'I've been going here for years,' he told her. 'They're very good. You don't have anything to worry about.' He put his hand on her back and gently pushed her towards the open door.

The hairdresser was a man in his thirties with a little growth of bristle beneath his nose. Several awards hung on the wall – apparently he was something of a celebrity in the beauty salon world. 'Ah, there you are,' he said when he saw Kazunari walk in.

'Sorry it took so long.'

'Not at all. I can always spare a few minutes for you, Kazunari.'

'I was hoping you might have an idea for her hair,' Kazunari said, indicating Eriko with his hand. 'Something that suits her.'

'Excellent,' said the hairdresser, taking a long look at Eriko's face, his imagination working. Eriko blushed.

'Also,' Kazunari turned to the hairdresser's female assistant standing nearby, 'maybe give her a little make-up? Something to go with the new look?'

'Absolutely,' the assistant said, her eyes sparkling.

'Kazunari?' Eriko said feeling extremely out of place. 'I actually don't have that much money with me today. And I never wear make-up—'

'Don't worry about that,' he said. 'Just sit and let them work their magic.'

'But I'm afraid my folks will worry – I didn't tell them I was going to a beauty salon.'

Kazunari looked back at the assistant. 'Can we borrow your phone?'

She brought them the phone sitting on the counter. It had a long cord so customers could take calls while having their hair done. Kazunari held it out to Eriko.

'Go ahead, call home. Tell them you're stopping for a haircut. I'm sure they'll understand.'

She took the receiver. The hesitation was plain on her face, but she seemed to have accepted that resistance was futile.

Kazunari sat on the sofa in the corner of the shop to wait. A part-time employee who looked like she was still in high school brought him coffee. He was surprised to see the girl's hair was very close-cut up the sides, almost a buzz cut, and wondered if that was going to be the next fad.

Kazunari couldn't wait to see Eriko's transformation. If his instinct was right they would be uncovering her true potential tonight.

He wasn't sure what it was that drew him to Eriko but he'd been obsessed from the moment he laid eyes on her. All he could say for certain was that their relationship – if that's what this was – was one *he* had initiated. There had been no introduction. She hadn't come on to him. He had spotted her, and that satisfied him greatly. He couldn't say the same about any of the girls he'd dated thus far.

Now that he thought about it, the same thing was true about

more than just girls in his life. His toys, his clothes – everything had always been given to him before he even had a chance to want it on his own. He wondered if he ever would have wanted any of it, really.

His choice of an economics major at Eimei had been his parents' suggestion and he'd only chosen that school because several of his relatives were alumni. He hadn't chosen to join the dance club, either. It had been the only club allowed to him. His father was of the opinion that clubs in general were detrimental to studies. Dance was permitted because it would give him a leg up in the social situations he was sure to face in his future with the family company.

I didn't even choose Kanae.

A beautiful recruit from Seika, Kanae had had everyone vying to be her partner during the first recital, but she had made a bee-line for Kazunari and told him, in no uncertain terms, that she wanted him to pick her. Not that he had minded at the time. He'd had his eye on her already and once they were partners, the rest was easy. A few late nights at practice and they were in love.

Am I in love?

Kazunari had to admit the possibility that what he felt wasn't love. That maybe he was just excited to be sleeping with a pretty girl. As evidence, whenever there was something else – anything else – to do, he would let her slide. It wasn't hard for him to do this. All she asked of him was that he call her at least once a day, but he often felt even that was too much.

Nor was it clear that she loved him. Maybe she just liked the access to brand-name fashion his wallet provided. She talked a lot about their future, but what if it wasn't about being his wife? What if it was just about being part of his family?

At any rate, he had already decided it was high time to break things off. She had clung particularly close to him in practice today, marking her territory. He'd had just about enough of that.

He smiled and took a sip of coffee when he noticed the assistant approach.

'All done,' she announced.

'How are we looking?'

'You'll have to see for yourself.' She winked.

Eriko was sitting in the hairdresser's chair in front of a large mirror. Kazunari walked over slowly. When he saw her reflection he actually caught his breath. Her hair had been cut to just over shoulder-length. It was curved to show the bottom of her ears, yet not in a boyish way at all. The look was very feminine, and with just a dusting of make-up her face was stunning. They had really brought out the beauty of her skin. Her eyes stirred something inside him.

'Wow,' he breathed.

'It doesn't look funny?' asked Eriko.

'Far from it.' He shook his head firmly and looked over at the hairdresser. 'That's really impressive.'

'I had excellent material to work with,' said the hairdresser, smiling.

'Try standing,' Kazunari said.

She stood, looking up at him a bit nervously.

Kazunari gazed at her for a long while before he asked, 'Any plans tomorrow?'

'Tomorrow?'

'Saturday. You have morning classes?'

'I didn't take any Saturday classes ...'

'Perfect. Going anyplace? Meeting any friends?'

'No, nothing, but—'

'Then you're with me. We have a few places we need to go.'

'What? Where?'

'You'll find out tomorrow.'

Kazunari looked between Eriko's face and her new haircut. The transformation was more dramatic than he'd dared to imagine. She had a unique, individual beauty, and his mind jumped ahead to tomorrow's date as he began to imagine what ensemble would work well with her new look.

Eriko walked into class on Monday morning to find Yukiho already there. Her friend looked up at her and her eyes went wide. There was a long silence.

'What happened to you?' Yukiho managed at length. The surprise in her voice was something entirely new to Eriko.

'It's a long story,' Eriko said, sitting down beside her. She noticed other students taking astonished looks in her direction. Yes, this was definitely new territory. The attention felt great.

'When did you get your hair cut?'

'Friday.' She smiled. 'In the rain.'

As Eriko related the events of the day, Yukiho's usual calm and collected veneer broke into surprise, which eventually transformed into a smile.

'I knew Kazunari had a thing for you,' she said.

'Maybe,' Eriko said, her fingers playing with a strand of hair by her cheek.

'So where'd you go on Saturday?'

On Saturday afternoon, Kazunari had taken her to a boutique selling expensive designer clothes. He walked in like he owned the place and talked to the assistant there as if they were old friends. It was the hairdresser's all over again. 'Show us some clothes that that will suit her,' he said.

The elegantly dressed assistant – it turned out she was the owner – immediately sprang into action. Giving orders to her staff, she had them bring out ensemble after ensemble. For more than an hour Eriko had the run of the dressing room.

When she'd heard they were going to a boutique, Eriko had pictured getting herself something modest, a simple dress she could wear at formal occasions, but when she saw the price tags on the clothes she was trying on, she nearly fainted. She didn't have anywhere near that kind of money, and if she had she certainly wouldn't be spending it on clothes.

She whispered this to Kazunari, and he shook his head. 'Don't you worry,' he told her, 'this is my treat.'

'No, I can't accept. It's too expensive.'

He smiled. 'A word of advice: when a man says he's going to give you something, accept it. Don't worry. I'm not looking for any favours. I just think a beautiful girl should have beautiful clothes.'

She blushed. 'But you paid for the hairdresser's yesterday and everything.'

'Of course I did. After all, it's your hair and I practically forced you to cut it. There's an upside for me too, you know. I can't be seen walking around with a girl wearing a Seiko cut and dressed like an insurance salesman.'

'Was I really that bad?'

'To be brutally honest, yes.'

Eriko sighed. She had considered herself fashionable.

'Right now, you're just building your cocoon,' said Kazunari from the other side of the changing room door. 'You have no idea how beautiful you'll become. I just want to give you that chance. I want to help you see.'

'Hmm, I'm not convinced this caterpillar's coming out a butterfly.'

'You will, I guarantee it,' he said, handing her another outfit and closing the curtain.

She eventually allowed him to buy her a single dress. Kazunari urged her to try one or two others, but she put her foot down. She was worried how she would explain even one dress to her mother, especially after the surprise when she'd got home from the hairdresser's the day before.

'Just tell her you bought it at a clothes swap at school,' Kazunari said with a laugh. Then he added, 'It really looks good on you, you know. You look like an actress.'

'Hardly,' Eriko said, blushing as she looked in the mirror because he wasn't entirely wrong.

'It's like a Cinderella story,' Yukiho said, shaking her head as Eriko finished her account. 'I really don't know what to say.'

'I know, I thought I was dreaming, too. And ... I'm a little worried.'

'What could you possibly be worried about?'

'It's just, the makeover and the clothes ... It's a lot to get from someone.'

'But you like him, don't you?'

'I think so.'

Yukiho shook her head, and said, gently, 'If you could see your smile right now, you'd know.'

The following day was Tuesday practice at Eimei, where Eriko's new look caused a stir amongst the other members of the dance club. It wasn't just the girls, either. The Eimei boys flocked to her when she walked in, all wanting to know what had happened – did she get a new job over the weekend? Did she join a new club? Did she get dumped, or did she shack up with someone new?

For the first time in Eriko's life, people were talking about her, not Yukiho. A circle had formed around her. When she looked up, Yukiho was standing a little way off, smiling. It was all a bit unreal. Part of her wondered if the sudden shift might make Yukiho jealous, but another part of her was even more jealous of Yukiho for having had this attention since the day they met.

Not everyone was pleased with her sudden transformation. Some of the older girls were pointedly ignoring her. Kanae had given her a particularly dark look and muttered something about children playing dress-up. This reaction was still something of a relief. Apparently she hadn't caught on to the fact that it was her own boyfriend who had brought this change upon Eriko.

Still, she had clearly upset the balance of power in the club, and retribution was swift. Even before practice started, one of the sophomores called Eriko over.

'Think you can tally up the club's accounts?' asked the long-haired girl, handing her a brown bag. 'Everything's in here: the ledger and all our receipts from last year. Just write down the dates and the amounts and work it out by month. Got it?'

'When do you need this by?'

'By the end of practice today, if you can.' The sophomore glanced back over her shoulder. 'Kanae's orders.'

'Right ... OK.'

Once the sophomore left, Yukiho came over to Eriko. 'I can't believe it,' she said. 'You're not going to have any time left over for practice. I'll help.'

'No, it's OK. It shouldn't take too long.'

Eriko looked inside the bag; it was stuffed with receipts. She pulled out the ledger and took a look, but it seemed like no one had bothered to record anything for the last two or three years.

Something fell out of the book – a plastic card.

'Sankyo Bank. That must be the club bank account,' Yukiho said. 'That's a silly place to keep the ATM card. Someone could steal it.'

'But they couldn't use it without the PIN number, right?' Eriko said. Her father had recently got an ATM card, so she knew the basics.

'I guess,' said Yukiho, though she didn't sound entirely convinced.

Eriko went to a corner of the practice hall and began making entries. It took much longer than she had expected. Yukiho came over and helped her midway through, but once they were done writing everything in the ledger and going through the calculations to make sure it all added up, there really was no time left over for practice. 'I don't see why we bothered coming at all,' said Yukiho with a sigh.

Crestfallen, the two girls walked down the gymnasium hallway to deliver their work to Kanae, who'd said she'd be in the locker room. Almost everyone else had already left. They were a little way down the hall when they heard a voice coming from behind one of the doors.

'Don't treat me like I'm an idiot.'

Eriko stopped in her tracks. The voice was unmistakably Kanae's.

'I'm not,' said another voice – Kazunari's. 'I'm being honest with you because I respect you.'

'You call that respect? I call it making a fool of me.'

The door flew open, and Kanae stormed out, a scowl on her face. She didn't seem to notice the two girls standing outside the door as she charged back down into the practice hall. Eriko and Yukiho exchanged glances. Neither of them wanted to call out to her.

Next Kazunari emerged. When he saw the two of them, he gave a wry smile. 'Fancy meeting you here. I'm guessing you heard that?'

'Shouldn't you go after her?' Yukiho asked.

'No,' he said flatly. 'You're on your way home too, right? Need a lift?'

'Actually I've got somewhere I need to go,' Yukiho said. 'But I'm sure Eriko could use a ride.'

'Yuki—'

'I'll make sure Kanae gets the ledger next practice,' Yukiho interrupted her and took the bag from Eriko's hand.

'You sure you don't want a ride, Yukiho?' Kazunari asked.

'I'm good,' she said with a smile, walking off in the same direction Kanae had gone.

Kazunari sighed. 'She's going to try to smooth things over with Kanae, no doubt.'

'Are you sure it's OK?' Eriko asked. 'You don't need to go?'

'No, it's fine. Everything's fine.' He put a hand on her arm. 'It's over.'

Eriko smiled, and her reflection smiled back. The black miniskirt she had on was much shorter than anything she ever would have worn before, and was showing far too much leg, she thought. She did a little twirl. *He'll like this.*

'What do you think?' she asked the shop assistant. Ever since her date with Kazunari the other week she'd become far less bashful about talking to people in shops. The assistant took a look at Eriko and beamed.

'It's amazing,' she said.

'I'll take it.' It wasn't anything too expensive, but it really fitted her. She had more confidence about picking the right clothes now, too.

Outside, it was already getting dark. She walked towards the station, quickening her pace.

The month of May was already half gone. She counted in her head. This was her fourth new outfit this month. She was going out to buy things by herself more frequently these days. She was still a little shy about taking Yukiho along on these shopping expeditions, and besides, she had fun walking until her feet hurt, trying to find clothes she thought Kazunari might like.

She walked past the display window of a department store and caught her own reflection. She wondered if the Eriko of two months earlier would even recognise her now. She was more concerned about her appearance than she had ever been before in her life. There was a constant dialogue going on in the back of her mind these days, wondering how she would look to other people, how she would look to Kazunari. She was learning how to put on make-up, and spent hours poring over fashion magazines, trying to imagine what might work for her. It was clear that the more effort she put into it, the better she looked in the mirror. That made her happy.

Yukiho even told her one day that she was blooming into something different. 'It's like you're changing every day, like a butterfly coming out of its cocoon.'

'Oh, stop, you're embarrassing me.'

'But it's true,' Yukiho said, nodding.

Eriko wanted to leave her cocoon. She was ready to emerge a real woman. She'd already gone on more than ten dates with Kazunari by that time. He'd officially asked her to go out with him the day of his fight with Kanae. He pulled over on the way to her house to ask the question.

'Are you going out with me because you broke up with Kanae?' Eriko had asked.

Kazunari shook his head. 'I meant to break up with her for a while now. You were the push I needed.'

'She's not going to be happy when she hears.'

'We'll just keep it a secret for a while. As long as we don't say anything, no problem.'

'People will find out.'

'Don't worry about it. I'll deal with it.'

'But ...' Eriko began, but she had nothing more to say.

He'd kissed her.

Since that moment Eriko felt as though she'd been living in a dream. She worried almost daily that something so good couldn't last this long. They had, for the time being, been able to conceal their relationship from the other people in the club. Eriko had only told Yukiho. No one else knew. As evidence, in the last two weeks, no fewer than two of the other Eimei boys had asked Eriko out on dates. Even as she turned them down, she wondered at how completely things had changed for her. Getting asked out had been almost unthinkable just a month earlier, and getting asked out twice?

She worried about Kanae – she'd only come to two practices since the breakup. Surely part of it was that she didn't want to see Kazunari, but Eriko wondered if Kanae suspected that she was his new girlfriend. They'd passed each other once or twice in the hall at school, and each time she'd felt sharp eyes on her. Eriko would always say hello, as a matter of politeness, but Kanae would never respond. She hadn't mentioned it to Kazunari, but it was only a matter of time before they'd have to talk about it.

Other than that, Eriko was happy. There was a spring in her step, and she often found herself smiling for no reason.

Shopping bag tucked under her arm, Eriko was almost home – an old two-storey house she'd lived in her entire life. She looked up at the sky and saw that the stars had come out. *It'll be a sunny day tomorrow*, she thought. Tomorrow was Friday and she had a date with Kazunari. She wanted to wear her new miniskirt.

Then she realised she was smiling again, and blushed in spite of herself.

The phone rang three times before he heard the click of the receiver being picked up. 'Kawashima residence.' It was Eriko's mother.

'Hello, it's Kazunari. Kazunari Shinozuka. Is Eriko home?'

There was a moment of silence. His heart sank.

'I'm sorry, she's out right now,' said her mother.

Kazunari had been expecting this. 'Do you know when she'll be coming back?'

'Sorry, I'm not exactly sure.'

'She always seems to be out whenever I call. Is something the matter?' It was his third attempt to reach her this week.

'She's been at a relative's a lot lately,' her mother said.

He heard the hesitation in her voice. It irritated him.

'Could you have her call me when she gets back? Kazunari from Eimei. She has the number.'

'I will, Kazunari.'

'Thanks.'

'Actually ...'

'Yes?'

Eriko's mother paused for several seconds before she said, 'I'm sorry, but to tell you the truth, I'd rather you didn't call us any more.'

'What?'

'I know you two were seeing each other for a while, but ... she's still just a child. Please find somebody else. It's what she wants.'

'What do you mean? Did she really say that? She doesn't want to see me any more?'

'No ...' Another pause. 'It's just, she *can't* see you any more. I'm sorry. It's just not possible. Please understand, it's not the best time for our family. Goodbye.'

'Hold on!' he shouted, but she'd already hung up.

Kazunari stepped out of the phone booth utterly confused.

He hadn't heard from Eriko in more than a week. They had last spoken on the previous Wednesday. She'd told him she was going clothes shopping the next day, so she could wear something new for practice on Friday. But on Friday she didn't show.

Yukiho had called the club to tell them that a professor had asked them to stay after class, and she and Eriko would be missing practice that day.

That night, Kazunari called Eriko at home, only to be told she was visiting relatives and wouldn't be home that night. He called on Saturday, too. She was out than as well. Her mother's voice on the phone seemed strained and Kazunari got the distinct impression his phone call wasn't welcome.

Eriko had stopped coming to dance practice entirely. Yukiho wasn't coming either, so he couldn't even ask her what was going on. Today was Friday again and he had slipped out halfway through practice to call.

Kazunari racked his brain for a reason why Eriko should suddenly not like him – if that was even the case. What had her mother meant by it being 'not the best time'?

Kazunari was on his way back to the practice hall when one of the girls in class ran up to tell him they'd just received a strange phone call.

'What do you mean, strange?'

'It was somebody asking for the head of the Seika Girls College dance club. When we said that Kanae was out, they asked for the Eimei University rep.'

'Who was it?'

'They wouldn't say. They're still on the line.'

'Right,' he said, heading toward the office on the first floor of the gymnasium. The phone was there, lying off the hook. He picked up the receiver.

'Hello?'

'Is this the head of the dance club?' a man asked. His voice was low, but he sounded young.

'Yes. Who is this?'

The man ignored his question. 'There's a girl over at Seika by the name of Kanae Kurahashi, right?'

'What's this about?'

'I want you to let her know that she needs to pay up, quick.'

'I'm sorry, is this about money?'

'That's right. A hundred and twenty thousand up front, and a hundred and thirty thousand when the job is done, that was the deal. Tell her to dig into that club money she's got if she has to.'

'I'm sorry, when what job was done?'

'Sorry, pal, that's none of your business.'

'Then you'd better call her yourself.'

The man laughed. 'Aw,' he said, 'but you're the best person to give her the message.'

'What's that supposed to mean?'

The man hung up.

Kazunari shrugged and replaced the receiver on the hook.

Two hundred and fifty thousand yen was a lot of money. What

had Kanae needed that cost that much? The man on the phone hadn't sounded like a particularly upstanding citizen, either.

Kazunari wasn't eager to call Kanae and ask what was up. They hadn't spoken since they broke up. And besides, his head was too full of Eriko right now.

When practice was over, Kazunari drove home to find an envelope waiting for him in his private mailbox. It had been sent by express mail, but lacked the name of a sender. The letters of his own address looked like they'd been written by someone using a ruler, with strange, sharp-cornered characters.

He went into his room, sat down on his bed, and opened the envelope, an uneasy feeling spreading through his chest.

It contained a single photograph.

Kazunari stared at it in bewilderment.

After a few moments, the photograph slipped from his fingers to the floor.

Yukiho arrived five minutes late. Kazunari gave a little wave when he saw her. She saw him right away and walked up.

'Sorry I'm late,' she apologised.

'No problem, just got here myself.'

The waitress wandered over and Yukiho ordered milk tea. It was midday on a weekday and the restaurant was nearly empty.

'Thanks for coming out,' said Kazunari.

'Of course,' she replied. 'But, like I told you on the phone, if it's about Eriko, I really can't say much.'

'You need to protect her, I understand.'

Yukiho looked down at the table. She had long eyelashes. Some of the people in the club said she looked like one of those French porcelain dolls. The comparison was admittedly apt, with the exception of her Asian eyes.

'Of course,' he said, 'if I already knew what happened, there wouldn't be much point keeping it from me.'

She looked up, startled.

'I got a photograph in the mail. Sent anonymously.'

'A photograph?'

Kazunari slipped his hand inside his jacket pocket. 'I'd rather not show you if you haven't already seen it.'

'Wait,' Yukiho said quickly. 'In the back of the truck?'

'That's right.'

Yukiho covered her mouth with one hand. She looked as though she might burst into tears, but the waitress had just come back with her tea, so she held it in.

'You saw it?' he asked.

'Yeah.'

'Where?'

'Eriko's house. They sent one to her family. I couldn't believe it.' Yukiho's voice was trembling.

'What is this all about?' Kazunari said, his hand clenching into a fist on the table.

He looked out of the window, willing himself to calm down. It was drizzling slightly. It wasn't yet June, but the rainy season might already have started. He remembered the day that he took Eriko to the hairdresser's. It had been raining then, too.

'Can you tell me what happened?'

'Isn't it obvious? *That* happened.' She pointed at his pocket.

'That doesn't tell me anything. Where did it happen?'

'Near her house. On Thursday, the week before last.'

'Thursday, you're sure?'

'Absolutely.'

Kazunari pulled out his calendar and looked at the date. Just as he had thought. It was the day after her last phone call – the day she said she was going to buy some clothes.

'Has anyone called the police?'

'No.'

'Why not?'

'Her parents didn't want word getting out; they said it would be worse if everyone heard about it. And, you know, I think they're right.'

Kazunari hit the table with his fist. He could understand how her parents felt and yet the thought that they were powerless to do anything frustrated him.

'If they sent her a photo and they sent one to me, then this wasn't just a random attack. Do her parents understand that?'

'Yes,' Yukiho said, 'but who would do such a thing?'

'I have an idea,' said Kazunari softly.

'What? Who?'

'I think you can guess.'

They exchanged looks. It seemed Yukiho understood.

'But, how could a woman – I mean, she couldn't—'

'She hired somebody who could.'

Kazunari told Yukiho about the phone call he'd received the Friday before. 'The photo came right after the phone call, so I connected the two right away. And the man on the phone said something strange about Kanae using club money.'

He heard Yukiho catch her breath. 'To pay the man?'

'Yeah, I know. It's hard to believe, so I looked into it.'

'You asked Kanae?'

'No, I couldn't. But I had another way. I called the bank and asked whether anything had been withdrawn.'

'But didn't Kanae have the bank book?'

'She did, but I had another way to get the information.'

A man from Sankyo Bank was a friend of the family and he had asked him for a favour.

'So,' Kazunari lowered his voice, 'I found out that on Tuesday, two weeks ago, a hundred and twenty thousand was withdrawn by card. When I checked this morning, I found that another hundred and thirty thousand had been withdrawn at the beginning of the week.'

'But there's no way of knowing that it was Kanae who took out the money. It could have been someone else.'

'As far as I could tell, no one except for her has had access to the card these past three weeks. And the only person who touched it before that is you,' he said.

'Right, when Eriko and I were doing the books for the club. But I gave the bank book and the card back to Kanae two or three days after that.'

'And she's had it ever since. Which makes it pretty clear that she hired somebody to attack Eriko.'

Yukiho breathed out a long sigh. 'I just … I can't believe it.'

'Neither can I.'

'But this is still just guesses, Kazunari. You don't have proof. Someone could have just happened to take that money out of the account.'

'Well, it's an extremely odd coincidence if they did. I think this needs to go to the police.'

Yukiho scowled. 'Like I said, Eriko's family really doesn't want this getting out. If the police get involved – even if they find out who did it – it's not going to change what happened, and it's not gonna make things any easier for her.'

'That doesn't mean we can just let this slide. I won't let it.'

Yukiho stared at him. 'I really don't think it's your decision to make.'

Kazunari blinked. He hadn't been expecting her to say that. He caught his breath and stared at her for a moment, until she said, 'I have a message for you from Eriko: *Goodbye.*'

'Wait, that's the message? She sent *you* to say goodbye.' His hand clenched back into a fist on the table. 'I need to see her.'

'You can't.' Yukiho stood. She had hardly touched her tea. 'I really didn't want to have to be the messenger here.'

'Yukiho—'

'Goodbye,' she said and began to walk towards the exit, but then she stopped. 'I won't be quitting dance club, by the way. I wouldn't want her to think it was her fault.'

Once she was out of sight, Kazunari took a deep breath and looked out the window where the rain was still falling.

The only things on TV were boring talk shows and the news. Eriko reached for the Rubik's Cube lying on top of the futon. Despite it having been such a big hit the year before, hardly anyone remembered the toys now. It had been fun when everyone was saying they were impossible to solve, but once the solution started making the rounds, even elementary school kids could do it in a matter of minutes. Not Eriko though, who was still struggling after four days with the infernal thing. Yukiho had brought it over for her and even taught her the basics, but she still wasn't making any progress.

I'm no good at anything.

A knock came at the door. 'Yukiho's here to see you,' said her mother.

'OK.'

She heard footsteps approaching. The door opened slowly and Yukiho's face peeked through. 'Were you sleeping?'

'Not with this to solve. Are you kidding?' she said, holding up the Rubik's Cube.

Yukiho smiled and came in. 'Here,' she said, holding up a box. It was cream puffs, Eriko's favourite. 'Your mom said she'd bring us tea in a bit.'

'Great,' Eriko said. 'Did you see him?'

'Yeah,' Yukiho said. 'I did.'

'Did you tell him?'

'I did. It wasn't easy.'

'I'm sorry I had to ask you to do that.'

'No, it's OK.' Yukiho reached out and gently took Eriko's hand in her own. 'How do you feel? Still getting headaches?'

'No, it's much better today.'

Her attacker had used chloroform, which had given her headaches since the attack. Though according to the doctor, the psychological effects would be worse than anything physical.

Eriko had woken that night in the bed of a pickup truck to find her mother next to her, weeping. When Eriko hadn't come home, her mother had left to meet her at the station, only to come across the truck, abandoned by the side of the road beneath a street light.

The photograph came several days later. There was no sender and no letter with it, yet the envelope seemed infused with a hatred that made Eriko tremble.

She understood what she had to do. She would never try to stand out from the crowd again. She would always hide behind her friends, behind Yukiho. Just as she had always done. That was really best.

There was one saving grace to the night. Strange though it was, she hadn't been raped. Apparently, the criminal's only objective had been to take her clothes off and take a picture. This was part of why her parents had decided not to tell the police. Once word got out, everyone would assume she *had* been raped. She would be marked for life.

Eriko remembered something that happened back when she was in middle school – the night she and Yukiho had found one of their classmates, abandoned, naked from the waist down.

She remembered the girl's mother telling them that only her clothes had been removed – nothing else. Even they hadn't believed her, but now that the same thing had happened to Eriko, she knew it was possible, just as she knew she would never be able to convince anyone else.

'I hope you feel better soon. I'm here for you, whenever,' said Yukiho. She held Eriko's hand tighter.

'Thanks, Yukiho, you're the only friend I have.'

'It's OK. We'll make it through this.'

The two girls sat quietly. The nightly news had come on TV and the newscaster's voice echoed in the silent room.

'... the victim – a businessman in the Tokyo area – said the money was taken out of his account without his knowledge. He only discovered the theft when he went to the bank to attempt to make a withdrawal, and discovered that instead of the two million yen he expected to find, the balance was zero. An inquiry by the bank found that the money had been withdrawn in seven separate transactions by ATM card at a branch of the Sankyo Bank in Fuchu, the last transaction taking place on April 22. Apparently, the victim *had* applied for a cash card from the bank, which he never used. The card was safely in his office desk. Police believe that someone forged a copy of the card and are investigating—'

Yukiho leaned over and flicked off the switch.

SIX

Tomohiko Sonomura glanced both ways to make sure no one was looking at him, drew a deep breath, and walked through the automatic doors.

He immediately felt as if his wig might slip and had to resist the urge to reach up and adjust it. Ryo had given him explicit instructions not to do so. The same went for his glasses. Drawing undue attention to either might give away his disguise.

There were two ATMs at the Sankyo Bank's Tamatsukuri branch. One was currently occupied by a middle-aged woman in a baggy purple dress. She was taking a long time at it; perhaps she wasn't used to the machine. Occasionally she would look around, searching in vain for a bank employee who might explain it to her, but the cashiers had already locked up for the day. After four it was just the machines.

Tomohiko worried that the plump lady might look to him for help, which would force him to call off the whole operation. This made him reluctant to approach the ATM next to her, but there were no other customers, and it would be even more suspicious if he simply stood there waiting. He realised he should probably turn around and walk out, but then he probably wouldn't get another chance to go through with the test until tomorrow and he really didn't want to wait that long.

Slowly, he approached the open machine. Next to him, the woman was still frowning, jabbing at the buttons with her finger.

Tomohiko opened his bag and reached inside. His fingertips touched the card and he was just pulling it out when the woman turned in his direction. 'Excuse me, I'm trying to put money into this thing, but it's not working.'

Keeping his face down, Tomohiko waved dismissively and shrugged.

'They keep telling me these things are easy to use,' she said, 'but I'll be damned if I can make head or tail of them.' Tomohiko shrugged again and shook his head. Whatever he did, he couldn't speak to her.

The doors to the bank whisked open and Tomohiko heard the woman's friend call in, 'What's taking so long? We're going to be late if you don't hurry.'

'This isn't working,' the woman called back. 'It's not giving me the deposit thingy. You ever use one of these things?'

'Never,' her friend replied. 'Why don't you just come back when one of the tellers is here? It can wait, can't it?'

'Yeah, but I had my banker make me a card and everything. It seems silly not to use it. He kept saying the machine was much easier than waiting for a teller at the window, but I don't know.' She sighed and took a step back from the machine. 'Ask me, they'll get rid of these things in a couple years and everything will back the way it was.' The woman walked out, muttering under her breath.

Tomohiko breathed a little sigh and went back to his bag – a black purse with sequins along the top edge. Slowly, he pulled out the card. In size and shape it was identical to a Sankyo Bank ATM card, but the face was blank, save for a single magnetic strip. There was nothing printed on it at all: no account number, no name, not even a logo. Which was why he had to make sure the card stayed out of sight of the security camera.

Tomohiko looked up at the keypad, and pressed the button for a withdrawal. The light next to a small label that read PLEASE INSERT CARD lit up. Feeling his heart begin to race, Tomohiko slid the white card into the slot.

The machine asked him for his PIN.

Here goes.

His hands went to the number keys and input the sequence 4-1-2-6. He pressed the 'Enter' button.

There was an interminably long interval during which nothing happened. If the machine did anything out of the ordinary, he would have to leave right away. But the moment passed, and the machine asked him how much money he would like to withdraw. Tomohiko resisted the urge to leap for joy and keyed in two hundred thousand yen.

Several seconds later he was the proud owner of twenty ten-thousand-yen bills and a receipt. He retrieved the blank card and stepped quickly out of the bank.

The flared skirt he wore wrapped around his legs just below the knees, making it hard to walk naturally. There were a lot of cars on the road in front of the bank, but not many pedestrians, which helped. His face felt tight under a layer of make-up, as though his skin had been smeared over with glue.

The van was waiting about twenty metres away along the side of the road. The passenger side door slid open when he got near. Tomohiko glanced around, hiked up his skirt, and got in.

Ryo shut the manga he'd been reading, Tomohiko's well-worn copy of *Urusei Yatsura*, and turned the key in the ignition. 'How'd it go?'

'Take a look,' Tomohiko said, showing him the purse and its haul of fresh banknotes.

Ryo glanced at the money, put the van in low gear, and pulled out into traffic. His expression didn't change.

'Sounds like we cracked the code, then,' he said, his eyes looking straight ahead. There was no trace of pleasure in his voice. 'Not that I had any doubt.'

'Neither did I, but man, when it worked, I started shaking,' Tomohiko said, scratching his thigh. The pantyhose made his legs itch powerfully.

'You watch out for the security camera?'

'Yeah, no problem there, I made sure not to look up. Just—'

'Just what?' Ryo glanced over at him.

'There was this lady there ...'

Tomohiko briefly explained their exchange in the bank.

Midway through his story, a cloud came over Ryo's face. He slammed on the brakes and pulled the van over to the side of the road. 'What did I tell you?' he said, angrily. 'I said if anything out of the ordinary happened, anything at all, you were supposed to get out of there.'

'Yeah, I know, but I thought it wouldn't be a problem.' Tomohiko was unable to hide the quaver in his voice.

Ryo grabbed Tomohiko by the collar of his blouse. 'I don't want you thinking on your own like that. This is life or death, man. And it's not just your ass on the line.' His eyes flashed.

'She didn't see my face,' Tomohiko said in a squeaky voice. 'I didn't talk, either. Honest. There's no way she knew I was a guy.'

Ryo's face twisted into a scowl. He swore under his breath and let go of Tomohiko's collar. 'Idiot.'

'What?'

'Why the hell do you think I made you put on that getup anyway?'

'It's my disguise, right?'

'That's right. And who's that disguise supposed to fool? The bank people, the police, right? When they find out we used a forged card the first thing they're going to do is check the security tape. They're going to see you, and ten out of ten of them will think you're a woman. You've got a delicate build and a face that started a fan club in high school.'

'But the camera didn't see my face—'

'Maybe not, but it definitely got an eyeful of the chatterbox. So what the police will do is they'll go find her. And when they find her – which they will, because she was trying to use the machine, and they probably have a record of that – they'll start asking questions. They're going to want to know if she remembers anything about the woman standing next to her. What if she says, "But officer, it wasn't a woman at all. It was a man in woman's clothes." So much for your disguise then.'

'She won't say that. Look, I swear, she didn't notice a thing.'

'How can you know for sure? Women always pay way more attention to other people than they should. She might even remember the brand of the handbag you were carrying.'

'I still don't see how that's a problem.'

'As long as there's a possibility she noticed something, it's a problem. You can't just hope that you'll get lucky if we're going to do this for real. We're not talking about ripping a jacket off of some boutique.'

'I know, I'm sorry.' Tomohiko bowed his head.

Ryo sighed and put the van back into low gear. Slowly, they pulled away from the kerb.

'Still,' Tomohiko said, a little gingerly, 'I really don't think we have to worry about that lady. She was completely focused on that machine.'

'Whatever. The disguise was a total waste of time.'

'C'mon, man—'

'You didn't talk to her at all, right? Not a single word?'

'Right. That's why—'

'That's why it was a waste of time,' Ryo said in a low voice. 'What kind of person says absolutely nothing when someone asks them a question? The police are going to know you had a reason why you couldn't speak. Then someone's going to get the idea that maybe you couldn't speak because your voice would give away the fact that you were a guy dressed up like a woman.'

Tomohiko's mouth flapped open, then shut again without saying a word. Ryo was right, as always.

'Sorry,' he said.

Ryo's eyes were on the road. 'I'm not telling you this again.'

'Yeah. You won't have to. Promise.' Tomohiko said. He knew all too well that Ryo did not look favourably on people who made the same mistake twice.

Bending himself like a contortionist, Tomohiko wriggled his way into the back seat of the van. He pulled his own clothes out of the paper bag there and began to change, balancing himself against the swaying of the vehicle. He felt a strange sense of freedom as he took off the tights.

Ryo had assembled the pieces of his disguise: clothes, shoes, handbag, wig, glasses, and make-up. He hadn't said where or how he got them and Tomohiko hadn't asked. There were many things he had learned not to ask Ryo about over the years.

He had just finished taking off the make-up when the van stopped. They were in front of a subway station.

'Drop by the office tonight,' Ryo said.

Tomohiko was supposed to go out with some friends to catch the new sci-fi animation, *Gundam*, that was playing in all the theatres.

'Yeah,' he replied. 'I was planning on it.' Tomohiko opened the door and stepped out of the van. He waited until the van took off, then went down the stairs to the subway.

The lecture on high-voltage engineering was a pitched battle against sleep. Word had got out earlier in the term that the professor didn't take attendance and it was easy to cheat on the exams, so the classroom, which could easily seat fifty, held only a dozen or so students that morning. Tomohiko sat in the second row from the front, trying to maintain consciousness while the white-haired professor spoke in a slow drone about the mechanisms of arc discharges and glow discharges. Tomohiko took notes. If he didn't keep his hand moving, he felt like he would slam head first into his desk.

Tomohiko was, to all appearances, a serious student. At the very least, that was what everyone in the electrical engineering department at Shinwa University thought. He had an excellent attendance record in all of the classes he signed up for. The only ones he skipped were the classes on law, art, and general psychology – courses that had nothing to do with his major. As he was still a sophomore, he had quite a few of these required curriculum courses left to suffer through.

And there was really only one reason Tomohiko paid such close attention to his courses in his major: because Ryo had ordered him to. It was a cost of doing business, he had said.

Ryo had a big influence on Tomohiko's initial choice of electrical engineering, too. Because his scores in maths and science were good as a senior, Tomohiko had been contemplating engineering or physics. But he hadn't yet chosen a major when Ryo said, 'From here on out, it's all about computers. Learn everything you can about them and that will help me out, too.'

In those days, Ryo had been keeping up his business selling games by mail, with considerable success. Tomohiko had been helping all along on the programming side. But Ryo's interest in Tomohiko's choice of major wasn't about maintaining the status quo. He wanted to expand.

If it was so important, Tomohiko said to him once, why didn't Ryo apply to college himself? Ryo's scores in the sciences had been as good as or better than Tomohiko's.

Ryo had smiled. 'If I had enough time to go to college, I wouldn't be working this job.'

It was the first time that Tomohiko had realised Ryo wasn't planning on going to college. It made his choice easier, in a way. He wouldn't just be learning about computers and electrical engineering for his own benefit. He'd be helping Ryo out too.

That, and Tomohiko had a debt that would take years to repay, if he ever repaid it at all. What had happened in his junior summer of high school had left a deep scar in his mind.

So it was that Tomohiko paid attention in class and, much to his surprise, whenever he brought his notebooks to the office, Ryo would read them avidly. Sometimes he would open a textbook beside them, going back and forth between the notes and the text. It was safe to say that, though Ryo had never attended a single class at Shinwa University, he knew more about the subject material than most of the actual students.

Ryo had a new passion these days: magnetic-strip cards, like ATM cards and credit cards. He first got involved with the cards right after Tomohiko matriculated and spotted an interesting device while touring his department's offices. Called an encoder, the device could read and write data on magnetic strips.

When Ryo heard about it, his eyes sparkled. 'You could make a duplicate of an ATM card with that.'

'Yeah, you could,' Tomohiko said. 'But what would be the point? You'd still need a PIN.'

'A PIN, huh?' Ryo seem to be mulling something over for a while after that.

It was two or three weeks later when he came into the computer software office carrying a cardboard box about the size of a portable stereo. The box contained an encoder. It had a slot for magnetic cards, and a panel to display the information they contained.

'How did you get your hands on that?' Tomohiko asked, but Ryo just shrugged and grinned.

Shortly after obtaining the encoder, Ryo forged his first ATM card. Tomohiko didn't know whose the original had been, but whoever it was, they never knew about it. Ryo only needed it for a couple of hours to make the copy.

Ryo used the card twice to withdraw a total of almost two hundred thousand yen. To Tomohiko's amazement, Ryo had been able to decipher the PIN from the data encoded on the card itself.

There was a trick involved with this – something Ryo had figured out even before he got the encoder. Ryo had shown him how to read the data off the strip without special equipment, as a demonstration. The method was so simple even a child could do it, but Tomohiko had to admit it had taken a genius to figure it out.

For his demonstration, Ryo had prepared some magnetised iron filings. These he dusted on to the magnetic strip of the card. Tomohiko gasped.

The filings had formed themselves into a striped pattern along the strip.

'It's like a kind of Morse code,' Ryo explained. 'I did this a few times on cards I already knew the PIN to and figured out the pattern. All I had to do this time was work it in reverse. Even if you don't know the PIN, you can read it from the pattern.'

'So all you have to do is steal a cash card and dust some filings on it?'

'Easy money.'

Tomohiko shook his head, speechless.

Ryo must have thought this was funny because he gave a rare belly laugh. 'There's nothing secure about these things at all. Those guys at the bank go on and on about how you have to keep your bank book safe and not share any personal information, but get one of these ATM cards and you might as well have the keys to the safe.'

'And the banks don't know about this?'

'Oh, I'm sure a few people know they've got a disaster on their hands. But it's too late to do anything about it now, so they're keeping it to themselves. They're just waiting for the next shoe to drop,' said Ryo. He laughed out loud again.

Despite the potential to abuse his discovery, Ryo didn't act on it right away. For one thing, he was busy with his software business, and for another, getting your hands on someone else's ATM card was still difficult. After that one duplicate he made the first night, he didn't mention cards at all for some time.

Until he had another, even bigger idea. 'You know,' Ryo said one day, 'I was thinking about it and I realised, there's no need to steal ATM cards at all.' He was sitting at the desk in their small office, drinking a cup of instant coffee.

'What do you mean?' Tomohiko asked.

'All you really need is a valid account number. You don't even need a PIN. I'm kind of surprised I didn't think of it sooner.'

'Think of what?'

'It's like this.' Ryo leaned back in his chair, putting his feet up on the table. He picked up a business card lying on the desk. 'Say this is an ATM card. Put it into an ATM, and the machine reads the data on the strip, right? Now, we know that the strip contains an account number and a PIN. Of course, the ATM doesn't know if it's the card's real owner putting the card in or not. That's why it makes you input a PIN. Input the same number recorded on the magnetic strip, and it spits out your cash. So say we got a blank card, with nothing on the strip, and we fill it in with the necessary data, which is just an account number, then any PIN we want.'

Tomohiko's eyes lit up.

'The card is different from a real card,' Ryo continued. 'But the machine has no way of knowing the PIN on the card isn't the actual PIN the customer chose. All it looks to see is whether the code on the magnetic strip is the same as the number the person punches in.'

'So if you get someone's bank account number—'

'You can make a card to take their money,' Ryo finished his sentence, the corner of his lip curling upward.

Tomohiko got goosebumps all over his body. *We could really do this.*

They went to work immediately.

First, they did a deeper analysis of the codes on the card. Each began with a starting code, then there was the ID code, the acknowledgment code, the PIN, and the bank identification code all in a line.

Next, they rooted through waste bins at various bank branches, picking up receipts with people's account numbers on them, and used the patterns they had studied to encode those account numbers and PINs of their own choosing into seventy six-digit-long series of letters and numerals.

After that they used the encoder to encode these series on to magnetic strips, attached the strips to plastic cards, and they were done. The white card that Tomohiko used to withdraw money from the bank that day was their first prototype. They had chosen the account to steal from by picking the account number on the receipt that showed the largest amount of money remaining, reasoning that they'd have the best chance of the account holder not noticing a strange drop in their balance.

Though what they were doing was clearly a crime, Tomohiko felt no guilt. For one, the whole process of making the forged cards felt so much like a game, it was hard to take it too seriously. For another, they never saw the person they were stealing from. More than anything, though, it was because of something that Ryo once said.

'Say a man throws away an apple he doesn't want. I could come along and pick up that apple and no one would care, right? Now say he puts that apple down, meaning to eat it later. If I come along and see the apple, I might pick it up, because what's the difference between the first and the second apple to me? None. If he isn't watching his apple, he may as well have thrown it away. You snooze, you lose.'

The idea had wormed its way into Tomohiko's subconscious

until it felt like his own, and every time he thought about it, a wave
of fear and anticipation washed over him.

Tomohiko headed straight for the office after classes ended for the
day. They called it an office, but it was really a single unit in an old
apartment building, which didn't even have a sign out front.

The place held many memories for Tomohiko. The first time he
came here, he could never have guessed how familiar he would
become with the place.

He reached No 304, pulled the key out of his pocket, and
opened the door. Ryo was sitting at the table in the small dining
room immediately through the door. This was his base of operations.

'You're early,' he said, twisting a little in his chair to look
around.

'I came straight here,' Tomohiko said, taking off his shoes. 'The
noodle shop by the station was full.'

A computer sat on top of the table, an NEC PC8001. The
words 'Hello World' were displayed on its green-tinted screen.

'This the word processor?' Tomohiko asked from over Ryo's
shoulder.

'Yeah, we just got a new chip and software.'

Ryo's hands moved over the keyboard in a blur. He would type
in the regular English alphabet, but the screen displayed Japanese.
Using what was called a front-end processor, it first converted letters into syllables called *hiragana*. When he pressed the space key,
it further converted the *hiragana* into *kanji* – Japanese characters.
Whenever there was a question about which character to use, the
screen gave him numbered choices. The whole process took about
ten seconds to produce a single word.

Tomohiko scoffed. 'Quicker to just write it out by hand.'

'The system is on a floppy disk, and it has to call up a database
every time you convert characters, so yeah, it's going to take time.
If you could put the entire processor into memory you'd definitely
get a speed boost, but this computer's not going to be able to hack
that. Still, I'm impressed with the read/write speed.'

'Can't say I'm going to miss cassettes much,' Tomohiko said.

'Yeah,' Ryo muttered. 'The only problem left is finding the software.'

Tomohiko picked up the 5¼-inch floppy from the desk. He knew exactly what Ryo was thinking. When they'd started selling the computer games, the response had been incredible. He remembered the breaking point, the day when the orders piled up and the money started rolling in. 'This will be big,' Ryo had predicted, and he was right.

Sales continued well for some time afterwards. They had made quite a bundle. And yet they had reached another impasse. They had competitors now, for one thing. But their biggest enemy was copyright law.

Until now, they had been able to sell pirated versions of popular games like *Space Invaders* openly through ads, but the writing on the wall was clear that this would no longer fly. There were movements to penalise software copiers. Some companies had already been served with a legal notice, and their own company had already received a warning by mail.

'If any of these cases go to trial, they're going to ban copying programs,' Ryo predicted. The US had already enacted copyright reform in 1980. Programs were now 'a unique expression of the intellectual thought and creative expression of their creator', and copying them was a crime.

With that business model gone, the only way they could keep going was to make programs themselves. Yet they lacked both the necessary capital and the know-how to make that happen.

'Oh right, here,' Ryo said, and pulled an envelope out of his pocket.

Tomohiko looked inside. The envelope held eight ten-thousand-yen bills.

'Your share from today,' Ryo said.

Tomohiko tossed the envelope, cramming the bills into his jeans pocket. 'What's our next play?'

'What do you mean?'

'You know ...'

'With the ATM card?'

'Yeah.'

Ryo crossed his arms. 'If were going to try to make any money off of that, we better be quick about it. Waste too much time, and they'll come up with countermeasures.'

'The zero-PIN system, was it?'

'Right.'

'But that's going to cost them a ton.'

Ryo looked up at him. 'You think we're the only ones who've found the weak spot in ATM cards? Pretty soon what we did today will be happening all over the country. Then even the stingy banks will have to do something.'

'Yeah ... ' Tomohiko sighed.

A zero-PIN ATM card was just what the name suggested: a card with no personal identification number recorded on its magnetic strip. Instead, a customer's PIN was stored remotely, and each time they wanted to use their ATM card, the machine would have to contact the bank's central computer to verify the transaction. Though it was much slower and more expensive for the banks than the old way, it made their system for forging cash cards obsolete.

'What we did today was too dangerous, anyway. Even if we were able to fool the security cameras every time, we'd eventually slip up somewhere,' Ryo said.

'Yeah,' Tomohiko agreed. 'Not to mention people going to the police when they notice their balance—'

'Ideally,' said Ryo, cutting him off, 'we want to make it so they don't even know we're *using* forged ATM cards.'

It was clear Ryo was already thinking about the next scheme, but that was as far as he got when the doorbell rang. They exchanged glances.

'Namie?' Tomohiko asked.

'She wasn't supposed to come today. That, and she should still be at the bank,' Ryo checked his watch. 'Whatever. Go see who it is.'

Tomohiko walked up to the door and looked through the peephole. A man in grey overalls stood outside. He looked around thirty years old.

Tomohiko opened the door a crack. 'Yes?'

'Uh, hi,' the man said, a blank, bored look on his face. 'Building maintenance. I'm here to check on the ventilation fans.'

'You have to do this right now?'

The man nodded without saying anything. *There's a worker bee if I ever saw one*, Tomohiko thought, closing the door to undo the chain.

When he opened the door again, the number of people outside had multiplied. A large man in a navy blue jacket, and a younger man wearing a green suit were standing right in front of the door. The man in the overalls had stepped back behind them. Sensing danger, Tomohiko tried to shut the door, but the big man put his hand out to stop it from closing.

'We'll be coming in,' the big man announced.

'Who the hell—' Tomohiko said as the man forced his way inside. The breadth of his shoulders was impressive, and there was a faint citrus smell clinging to the fabric of his clothes.

The man in the green suit followed close behind. He had a scar next to his right eyebrow where it looked like he'd got stitches for a cut.

Ryo looked up without standing from the table. 'And you are?'

The big man didn't answer. He stepped in without taking off his shoes, took a look around the room, then planted himself in the chair Tomohiko had been sitting in a moment before.

'Where's Namie?' the man asked Ryo, a mean look in his eyes. His jet-black hair was smoothed back across his head.

'Can't say,' Ryo said, shrugging. 'Who's asking?'

'Where's Namie?'

'Did you need her for something?'

The big man glanced back at the one in the green suit, who came forward, also wearing his shoes, and went straight into the back room. The big man's eyes went to the computer on the table. He stared at the screen a moment. 'What's that?'

'A Japanese word processor,' Ryo said.

The man grunted and seemed to lose interest immediately. He resumed looking around the room. 'You make much money doing this?'

'If you do it right,' Ryo said.

The man chuckled, his shoulders rocking. 'Looks like you're not doing it right, then, huh.'

Ryo and Tomohiko exchanged glances.

The green suit was poking through their cardboard boxes. The back room had been converted into a storeroom.

'If you're looking for Namie, you should try coming on Saturday or Sunday. She's not usually here during the week.'

'We know,' the man said, pulling a pack of cigarettes out of his vest pocket. He stuck one in his mouth and lit it with a Dunhill lighter.

'You hear from her lately?' he asked, blowing smoke.

'Not today. Would you like me to give her a message if she calls?'

'No need.'

The man was about to flick ash from his cigarette on to the table, when Ryo quickly stuck out his hand to catch the ash.

The man raised an eyebrow. 'You trying to prove something, kid?'

Ryo shook his head. 'We have a lot of electronics here. I don't want ash getting into anything.'

'So get an ashtray.'

'I don't have one.'

The man's face twisted into a cruel smile. 'Oh?' he said, tapping more hot ash into Ryo's open palm. Ryo didn't flinch. 'I say you do.' He jabbed the lit end of his cigarette into Ryo's palm.

Tomohiko could see every muscle in Ryo's body tense, but his face remained blank. His hand remained motionless above the table as he stared the man in the eyes.

'You're a tough guy, is that it?' the man asked.

'Not particularly.'

'Suzuki,' the man called into the back. 'You find anything?'

'Nothing,' the green suit replied.

The man put his cigarettes and his lighter back into his pocket, then he picked up a ballpoint pen and wrote something on the corner of a software manual that was lying open on the table.

'If you hear from Namie, you call this number. Ask for "the electrician".'

'And your name?'

'Knowing my name isn't going to do you any good.' The man stood.

'What if we choose not to call?' Ryo asked.

The man smiled and breathed out through his nose. 'Why would you do something stupid like that?'

'Namie might not want us to.'

'Listen.' The man pointed at Ryo's chest. 'There's nothing in it for you if you call us. But if you don't call us, you stand to lose ...' He looked around the small apartment. 'Everything. Or enough that you'll regret it for the rest of your life. Any questions?'

Ryo looked the man in the face for a moment and shook his head. 'Nope.'

'Good. Glad to see you're not an idiot,' the man said, giving the guy in the green suit – Suzuki – a look. Suzuki left the back room and went out the front door.

The man pulled out his wallet and handed a ten-thousand-yen bill to Tomohiko. 'Make sure he gets that hand looked at.'

Tomohiko's fingers trembled as he took the money. The man chuckled, a deep, ugly sound.

Once they were gone, Tomohiko locked the door and fastened the chain. He turned around to Ryo. 'You OK?'

Ryo went into the back room without answering and opened the curtain.

Tomohiko walked over beside him and looked outside. A black Mercedes was sitting out in front of their apartment building. A moment passed, and the men emerged from the building. The big man and the one named Suzuki got in the back, and the man in the overalls got in the driver's seat.

Once the Mercedes had left, Ryo said, 'Try calling Namie.'

Tomohiko picked up the phone on the dining room table. He

tried her apartment. The phone rang for a long time, but no one answered. He put the receiver back down and shook his head.

'I guess if she were at home, they wouldn't be coming here looking for her,' Ryo said.

'Does that mean she's not at the bank either?' Tomohiko wondered out loud.

'Maybe she took the day off,' Ryo said, opening up the door of the mini refrigerator and pulling out an ice tray. He dumped the ice into the sink, and picked a single cube.

'Your hand OK?'

'I'll be fine.'

'Who were they? Yakuza?'

'That's a safe bet.'

'What does Namie have to do with the yakuza?'

'Who knows?' Ryo said, picking up a fresh piece of ice. The first had already melted to water in his palm. 'You should probably go home, Tomohiko. Give me a call if you find anything out.'

'What're you going to do?'

'I'm staying here tonight. Namie might try to call.'

'I should stay—'

'Go home,' Ryo said immediately. 'They might've left somebody to watch. If we both stay here, they'll start to wonder what we're up to.

He was right.

'You think something happened at the bank?'

Ryo shrugged. He poked at the burn on his left hand and winced.

It was already past dinner time when Tomohiko got home. His father was in the TV room watching a baseball game, and his younger sister was in her own room.

Tomohiko's parents had very little to say about the way Tomohiko lived his life. They were happy that their son had got into the electrical engineering department at a well-known university and that he seemed to be paying attention in class and getting good marks, unlike many of his peers. He had explained his work with Ryo by telling them that he had a part-time job at a computer shop.

His mom put out some fish, vegetables, stewed meat and miso soup for him. Tomohiko got his own rice. He wondered what Ryo would be doing for dinner that night.

Though they had known each other for three years, Tomohiko knew very little about Ryo's upbringing and family. About the only thing he did know was that Ryo's father used to run a pawnshop, and that he died when Ryo was still young. He didn't think he had any siblings. His mother was still alive, but it was unclear whether he was living with her. Nor did he have any close friends, at least as far as Tomohiko was aware.

The same went for Namie Nishiguchi. They entrusted her with the accounting side of their business, but never talked much about her private life. He knew that she worked at a bank, but didn't even know what she did there.

And now yakuza were looking for her.

He wondered what that was all about.

Tomohiko finished his dinner and was about to go up to his room when he heard the news on the television start. The ball game was over.

'A middle-aged man was found bleeding from a stab wound to the chest around eight o'clock this morning,' the newscaster was saying. 'A passer-by discovered the man and notified the police. The man, identified as a Mr Mikio Makabe, was taken to the hospital, but died of his wounds shortly after arriving. Witnesses reported seeing a suspicious male carrying a large knife in the area just before the attack. Police are now in pursuit of the man as a suspect in the stabbing. Mr Makabe had been on his way to work at the Taiko Bank's Showa branch not more than one hundred metres from the place he was found. Next—'

Everything up to that part had made Tomohiko think that it was just another random mugging – they'd been on the rise recently. But when he heard the name of the bank branch, he froze. *That's where Namie works.* Tomohiko went into the hallway and picked up the phone. He hammered the buttons, his heart racing.

Ryo didn't pick up at the office. Tomohiko let it ring ten times before hanging up.

He thought for a moment, then went into the living room to watch the news on the off-chance there might be an update on the stabbing. He sat down next to his dad, feigning interest in the other news stories so his dad wouldn't start talking to him about his 'future'. The news was almost over when the phone rang, jolting Tomohiko to his feet. 'I'll get it,' he called, running into the hallway.

'Sonomura residence.'

'It's me.'

'I just tried calling you,' Tomohiko said, lowering his voice. 'You see the news?'

'Yeah. What's it mean?'

'It'll take too long to explain over the phone. Think you can get out?'

'What?' Tomohiko glanced back at the living room. 'You mean now?'

'Yeah, now.'

'I think so.'

'Good. We need to talk about Namie.'

'You hear from her?' Tomohiko asked, gripping the receiver.

'She's sitting right next to me.'

'What?'

'I'll explain later. Just come, quick. And not to the office ...' Ryo gave him the name of a hotel and a room number.

Tomohiko swallowed. It was the same hotel where he used to meet Yuko Hanaoka, the older woman he'd dated in high school.

'Be right there,' he said. He repeated the room number to himself and hung up.

He was still in time to catch the train. It was a route burned into his memory. Yuko had been his first, and for a long time after, his only. He hadn't even kissed another girl until hooking up with a classmate at a party last year.

Once inside the hotel he made straight for Room 2015.

'Who's there?' came Ryo's voice from inside.

'The Kyoto Alien,' Tomohiko replied. It was the title of one of their poorer-selling computer games.

Ryo opened the door. He looked tired, with stubble on his chin. He indicated for Tomohiko to come into the small, twin room.

There was a table and two chairs by the window. Namie was sitting in one of the chairs.

'Hi,' she said. She was smiling, but she looked tired, too.

'Evening,' Tomohiko replied and sat down on the nearest bed, its sheets still perfectly smooth. 'Right, so ...' He looked up at Ryo. 'What's going on?'

Ryo had his hands in both pockets of his cotton trousers as he leaned up against the wall by the table.

'Namie called about an hour after you left. She said she couldn't work for us any more, so she wanted to return our ledger and documents. She's running.'

Tomohiko looked over at her. 'This have something to do with the guy at your bank who got killed?'

'Something,' Ryo said. 'It wasn't Namie who killed him, by the way.'

'I didn't think it was,' Tomohiko said, though the possibility had crossed his mind for a second.

'Apparently that honour goes to one of the fine gentleman who paid us a visit,' Ryo told him.

Tomohiko swallowed. 'Why?'

Namie sat silently with her head drooping. Ryo glanced in her direction, then turned back to Tomohiko. 'Remember the big guy with the navy blue jacket? His name's Enomoto. Namie was ... helping him out.'

'You mean with money?'

'Yeah, money. But not her own. She was using the bank's online system to siphon money into his account.'

'How much?'

'She doesn't know exactly how much. Some of the bigger transfers were in the two million range, though. And that went on for over a year.'

'You can just do that?' Tomohiko asked Namie.

She didn't look up.

'Yes, you can,' Ryo answered on her behalf. 'But it's not fool-proof. Someone caught wind of it. Makabe.'

'The guy on the news.'

Ryo nodded. 'Except he didn't know Namie was behind it when he brought it to her attention. So Namie told Enomoto someone was on to him. Well, Enomoto didn't like losing his golden-egg-laying goose, so he called in a hit.'

Tomohiko's heart was thudding in his chest.

'The good news,' said Ryo, 'is that Namie's involvement never came to light. The bad news is: this Makabe guy's dead and it's basically her fault.'

Namie's shoulders were shaking. She was crying.

'Couldn't you have put it a little nicer?' asked Tomohiko.

'No point trying to paint it any other way.'

'Yeah, but—'

'It's all right,' Namie said. She looked up. There was determination in her eyes. 'It's the truth, anyway. Ryo's right.'

'Which is why Namie realised she needed to cut ties with Enomoto,' Ryo explained, pointing to where two suitcases sat, both bulging. 'Now they're after her. If she disappears, they killed Makabe for nothing. That, and Enomoto needs more money, apparently. She was supposed to send it over today around noon.'

'He's got a few businesses he's running. But none of them are doing very well,' Namie muttered.

'So why'd you help him in the first place?'

'Doesn't matter now, does it,' Ryo said, frowning.

Tomohiko scratched his head. 'OK, then, what are we going to do?'

'We're going to get her out of here,' Ryo said. 'Problem is, we don't exactly know where to, yet. If she stays, Enomoto or the police will track her down eventually. So I'm going to find a place today or tomorrow where she can stay for an extended period of time.'

'You think you can?'

'I have to,' Ryo said, opening the fridge and pulling out a beer.

'I'm sorry,' Namie said. 'Sorry to both of you. If the police catch me, I promise I won't tell them you helped.'

'You got money?' Tomohiko asked.

'Enough,' she said. There was a bit of hesitation in her voice.

'That's where Namie's a genius,' Ryo said, beer in hand. 'She saw this day coming, and set up no fewer than five secret personal accounts, funnelling money away to each of them. It's impressive.'

'It's not something I'm proud of,' Namie said, putting a hand to her forehead.

'Having money is better than not having it,' Tomohiko said.

'Truth,' Ryo said, taking a gulp of his beer.

'So what should I do?' Tomohiko asked, looking between the two.

Ryo fixed Tomohiko with a stare. 'I want you stay here for two days with her.'

'What?'

'We can't let her go outside. Someone has to go shopping for her. You're the only one I can ask.'

'OK, I guess.' Tomohiko brushed back his hair and looked over at Namie. She returned his glance. Her need was plain to see in her face. 'Right,' he said. 'I'm on it.'

For food on Saturday, Tomohiko brought some boxed bento lunches he had bought in a department store food court back to the hotel room. They contained an assortment of rice and vegetables, broiled fish, and fried chicken. He used some of the hotel teabags to make green tea and they ate at the small table. 'Sorry you have to eat this stuff,' Namie said. 'You could just eat at a restaurant or something, you know.'

'Nah,' Tomohiko said, 'I'd rather eat here with you than eat alone. And these bento boxes aren't that bad.'

'They aren't, are they,' Namie said, smiling.

When they'd finished eating, Tomohiko pulled some pudding he'd bought out of the refrigerator. Namie gave him a girlish smile.

'You're very thoughtful, you know. You'll make a good husband someday.'

'You think?' Tomohiko grinned as he took a mouthful of his pudding.

'You don't have a girlfriend, do you?'

'No. I had one last year for a while, but we broke up. Which is to say, she dumped me.'

'Really, why was that?'

'She said she liked guys who knew how to have fun. I guess I was too quiet for her.'

'Well, she doesn't know what she's talking about,' Namie said, shaking her head. Then, just as suddenly, she chuckled. 'Not that I'm qualified to say anything about anyone's love life,' she said, exploring the surface of her pudding with the tip of her spoon.

After a moment she looked up. 'You're wondering about Enomoto, aren't you?' she asked. 'Why did I get tangled up with him?'

'Hey, it's none of my business—'

'No, it's OK. It's a ridiculous story anyway,' Namie said, setting down her half-eaten cup of pudding. 'Got any smokes?'

'Just Mild Sevens. The light ones, with the filter.'

'That'll do.'

She took a cigarette from him, lit it, and took a deep drag. The white smoke curled up into the air.

'About a year and half ago, I got into a little bit of an accident with my car,' she began, looking out the window. 'It was just a scrape. And it wasn't exactly my fault, either. Except I could have picked a better van to run into.'

Tomohiko raised an eyebrow. 'Yakuza?'

Namie nodded. 'They got out of the van and surrounded my car, right there in the middle of the road. For a second, I didn't know what was going to happen. That's when Enomoto showed up. He was in another car, but he seemed to know the guys that were on me. He worked it out so I would only owe them for repairs.'

'Let me guess, the repairs cost millions?'

Namie shook her head. 'No, more like a hundred thousand. Enomoto even apologised for not being able to work out a better deal. You might not believe it, but he was a real gentleman back then.'

'You're right, I don't believe it.'

'No, really. He dressed beautifully and always said he wasn't "one of them".'

'So wait, you two were dating?' Tomohiko asked.

Namie didn't answer right away. Instead she dragged at her cigarette, her eyes following the smoke trail.

'I know this sounds like an excuse, but he was really nice. I thought he really loved me. And, to tell the truth, that was the first time I'd ever felt that.'

'So you wanted to do something for him, I get it.'

'It was more that I was afraid he'd lose interest. I wanted to show him I could be helpful.'

'By stealing for him?'

'It was stupid, I know. He said he needed it for a new business, and of course I didn't doubt a thing.'

'But you had realised he was yakuza, right?'

'Mostly. But by then, it really didn't matter.'

'What do you mean?'

'I mean, as long as he was with me, I didn't care what he was.'

Tomohiko grunted and stared at the table. Namie snubbed out her cigarette.

'For some reason I keep hooking up with the wrong men. I guess it's just my luck.'

'Something like this happen before?'

'Sort of. Got another cigarette?'

He offered his pack. She took a cigarette and lit it.

'I used to date this bartender. At least. he said he was a bartender, but he hardly ever went to work. He loved gambling, so he would borrow money from me and throw it all down the drain. Once my savings hit rock bottom, he left. Guess he didn't have a use for me any more.'

'When was this?'

'Three years ago, maybe?'

'Three years ...'

'That's right, it was just before we first met. It's part of why I went in the first place.'

Went to a place to have sex with young men.

'I told Ryo about it once, a while ago. I don't think he listens to me much, though. He's probably sick of my boy troubles by now.'

'Yeah?'

'I would be, if I were him. Besides, he doesn't like it when people make the same mistake twice.'

'That's true enough.' Tomohiko agreed. 'Mind if I ask you something?'

'What?'

'Was it easy making those transfers at the bank?'

'That's a tricky question,' Namie said, crossing her legs and taking a few puffs. She seemed to be pondering her explanation. By the time she spoke, her cigarette had burned down close to her fingers. 'I suppose you could say it was easy, yes. Which is what made it risky.'

'What do you mean?'

'Well, all you really have to do is forge a transfer slip.' Namie scratched the side of her forehead, the cigarette dangling precariously between her fingers. 'Write an amount and the account the money is destined for, get two other people to put their stamp on it, and that's it. One of those people is the section chief and he's not at his desk all the time, so it's pretty easy to grab his stamp without him knowing. The other person's stamp was easy to forge.'

'Isn't there anyone checking that stuff?'

'There's a daily ledger that shows remaining balances. The head of accounts is supposed to watch that, but as long as you have the stamp you can just forge documents saying they checked it. That holds them off for long enough.'

'What do you mean, long enough?'

'Well, it has to do with the money I was using. It came from a special pool set aside for temporary payments.'

'What're those?'

'Say someone sends money from their bank to a customer at another bank. What happens is the receiving bank pays their customer immediately, then settles accounts with the sending bank later. The money they use to pay transfers up front is called "temporary funds", which every financial institution has set aside in a special pool. That's what I had my eye on.'

'Sounds pretty technical.'

'Well, to a point, yes. In order to manipulate temporary funds you need specialised knowledge, so only the people who have been working it for a long time know what's going on. At my branch, that was me. In theory, accounting was supposed to check everything two or three times after I did my work, but in practice everything was pretty much left up to me.'

'So they weren't checking it when they were supposed to be?'

'Right. For example, at our bank, if you transfer more than a million yen, you have to record the amount and the destination in a special ledger and get the section chief's permission to borrow the key you need to access the terminal where everything happens. The results of the transfer are printed out in a daily report from the computer the following day and the section chief is supposed to check those. However, they hardly ever do. Which is why, if you hide the illegitimate transfer slip and the daily report for that day, and make sure your boss only sees slips and reports from regular days, no one raises a fuss.'

'OK. It sounds pretty complicated, but I gather the point here is that your boss is lazy.'

'Yeah, though that only goes so far.' Namie let out a big sigh. 'It was only a matter of time before somebody like Makabe found out.'

'Which you knew. But that didn't stop you from doing it, huh.'

'Yeah. It was like I was addicted.' Namie flicked the ashes from her cigarette into the ashtray. 'All you have to do is hit some keys on the keyboard and these huge sums fly every which way. You start feeling like you have some kind of magic power. But it's all an illusion.'

Tomohiko had told his parents the night before that he'd be

staying nights at work for a few days, and one of the twin beds became his. He took a shower, put on the hotel bathrobe and got under the covers. Namie went into the bathroom after him. The lights in the room were off, except for the little footlight at the bottom of the bed.

He heard Namie get out of the bath and into the other bed. Though his back was to her, he felt acutely aware of her presence just an arm's reach away. A faint smell of shampoo drifted through the air.

Tomohiko lay still in the darkness. His mind was racing, trying to figure out ways of getting Namie out of there safely. Ryo hadn't called them at all that day.

'Tomohiko?' He heard Namie behind him. 'You asleep?'

'No,' he replied, eyes closed.

'Me neither.'

That came as no surprise. She would soon be fleeing for her life to destinations unknown.

'Do you ever think about her?'

'Who?'

'Yoko.'

'Oh.' The name sent a shiver down his back. He tried to keep the emotion out of his voice. 'Sometimes.'

'I thought so,' Namie said. 'Did you love her?'

'I don't know. I was pretty young.'

He heard Namie laugh. 'You're still pretty young.'

'I guess.'

'And I – I just ran.'

'From the apartment that day? Yes, you did.'

'You two probably thought I was some kind of reject. To go all the way to that apartment only to turn tail and run.'

'Not particularly.'

'Sometimes, I regret leaving.'

'Really?'

'I do. I think maybe if I'd just stayed and let things happen it would have changed me, somehow. I know it sounds funny, but I think maybe I would have been reborn.'

Tomohiko lay in silence. There was a weight to her words he didn't fully understand, but something told him he was about to.

The air in the room felt heavy. She spoke again. 'I wonder if it's too late.'

'Namie ...' *Might as well go for it.* 'You saying what I think you're saying?'

She was silent. *Now I've done it*, he thought.

'You don't think I'm too old?' she said after a long silence.

Tomohiko breathed an inward sigh of relief. 'You haven't changed a bit in three years,' he said.

'So was I already too old three years ago?'

He laughed. 'That's not what I meant.'

He heard Namie get out of bed. Seconds later, she was crawling under his covers.

'Rebirth would be nice,' she whispered into his ear. 'But I'll settle for this.'

Ryo showed up on Monday morning and began by apologising to Namie. He hadn't been able to find a safe house for her yet but thought she should move to another hotel for the time being. This one was a few hours away to the north, in Nagoya.

'It'll only be temporary.'

'That's not what you said last night,' Tomohiko protested. Ryo had called late with news that he'd found a good place and they would be leaving in the morning.

'Things changed. I'm sorry. But you won't have to put up with it for long, I promise.'

'I'm OK with that,' Namie said. 'I lived in Nagoya before, so I know the place.'

'That's part of why I picked it,' Ryo said.

A white sedan was parked in the underground lot at the hotel. A rental, Ryo told them. If he went anywhere in his van, Enomoto or one of his goons was sure to find out.

'Here's a ticket for the bullet train. And a map to your hotel,' he said, handing an envelope and a printout to Namie once they were in the car.

'Thank you for everything,' she said.

'One other thing – you should probably take this with you.' Ryo held out a paper bag.

She looked inside the bag and chuckled.

Tomohiko craned his head over to take a look. Inside the bag was a curly-haired wig, big sunglasses, and the kind of face mask people wore when they had colds.

'I'm guessing you're going to use an ATM card to get the money out of your accounts,' Ryo said, turning the ignition. 'When you do, you're not going to want to look like yourself. And whatever you do, make sure the camera doesn't see your face.'

'You're very thorough. Thanks.' Namie took the paper bag and managed to cram it into one of her already overstuffed suitcases.

'Give us a call when you get there,' Tomohiko said.

'I will,' Namie said, and she smiled at him.

The car drove out of the car park.

Once Namie was on the train, Tomohiko and Ryo went back to the office.

'I hope she makes it,' Tomohiko said.

Ryo shook his head. 'You hear the Enomoto story?'

Tomohiko told him he had.

'Stupid, isn't she?'

'I wouldn't say that.'

'Enomoto had her pegged from the start. He wanted to use her position at the bank. That whole thing with the traffic accident? Enomoto planned that from the get-go. You see? Stupid. She's always been that way, too. She falls for some guy and can't think straight.'

Tomohiko swallowed. He had nothing to say, except his stomach felt like he'd just swallowed a ball of lead. He wasn't sure he would have realised the set-up either.

Tomohiko went home early that day and waited for a call from Namie, but none came.

Four days later he read in the newspaper that Namie Nishiguchi's body had been discovered at a hotel in Nagoya. She'd been stabbed with a knife in the chest and stomach.

Namie had filed for a two-day vacation from work. When she didn't show up on the third day, people started looking. They found five bank books in her possession. As of Monday, the money in those accounts was well over twenty million yen. By the time her body was found, they had been emptied.

The bank investigated and found out about her illegal transfers. The accounts she had used led the police to arrest one of the directors at the bank on suspicion of embezzlement, making him a suspect in her murder in the process.

The money she withdrew from those five accounts just before her death was never found. A security camera at the ATM where she had made the withdrawals showed a woman dressed in the same wig, sunglasses, and mask that had been found in her luggage.

Tomohiko threw down the newspaper, ran to the bathroom and emptied the contents of his stomach.

SEVEN

Makoto Takamiya stared at the patent application in his hand: *Physical Properties of Eddy-Current Testing Coils.* He'd just finished talking on the phone with the technician who'd written the application. Makoto stood and looked over towards the wall where four 'data entry technicians' – their official title – sat with their backs to him in front of a row of computer terminals. The technicians were all women, three temp workers dressed in civilian clothes and one full-time employee in an official Tozai Automotive uniform.

While the company had previously kept all patent information on microfilm, they were currently in the process of transferring everything over to floppy disk to enable computer-based searches. Lately, more and more companies were using temp workers for these kinds of tasks. Though the temp agencies were probably running foul of the Employment Security Act, the previous administration had given them legal status and established a 'Temporary Staffing Services Law' in an attempt to afford them some protection.

Makoto walked towards the woman sitting on the far left. She had long hair tied behind her head in a braid – 'so as not to interfere with my typing,' she had told him once.

Chizuru Misawa looked between her screen and the paper stand next to it, her fingers flashing over the keys with blinding speed. The movements of the women were so fast and so precise, it sometimes gave one the impression of watching robots on an assembly line.

'Ms Misawa?' said Makoto.

Chizuru's hands stopped as though a switch had been thrown.

There was a beat before she turned to look in Makoto's direction. She was wearing large-lens glasses, with black frames. There was a hardness in her look that came from staring at the screen for so long, but when she saw Makoto, her expression softened.

'Yes?' A smile came to her lips. Her pink lipstick matched the milky white of her skin well, Makoto thought. Though her roundish face gave her a young look, he had learned through previous conversations that she was only a year younger than him.

'I was wondering what other applications we've had for eddy-current testing coils.'

'"Eddy-current", you said?'

'Yeah.' Makoto showed her the title of the paper in his hand.

She quickly jotted down a memo. 'Sure thing. I'll take a look, and if I find anything, shall I print it out and bring it your desk?' she asked crisply.

'That'd be great. Sorry to interrupt you.'

'All part of the job,' Chizuru said with a smile. That was her catchphrase. It might have been the catchphrase of all the temp workers, but Makoto wouldn't know. He'd only spoken directly to her.

Back at his seat, one of his co-workers asked him if he was ready to go on break. 'Not quite,' replied Makoto, shaking his head. 'Break' entailed lingering by the vending machines that dispensed drinks into a paper cup. Unusually for a Japanese company at the time, Tozai Automotive didn't believe in making their female employees serve tea to their male counterparts.

Makoto had been in the Patent Licensing Division of Tozai Automotive's Tokyo headquarters for three years now. Tozai Automotive made starters, spark plugs, and other electrical components for vehicles. Patent licensing was responsible for managing the intellectual property rights for all of their products. Specifically, they helped their own researchers file patent applications for new technologies, and devised strategies and countermeasures when they had to dispute another company's patent claim.

Chizuru arrived at Makoto's desk with some printouts a short while later. 'I think these are what you were looking for?'

'Thanks so much,' Makoto said, glancing over the sheets. 'Have you taken a break yet?'

'No.'

'Great, let's get some tea. My treat.' Makoto stood and walked towards the door, looking over his shoulder to make sure Chizuru was following him.

The vending machines were in the hallway. Makoto got a cup of coffee and stood to drink it by the windows a short distance away. Chizuru came over, holding her cup of lemon tea in both hands.

'That must be tough hitting the keyboard all day like that. Don't your shoulders cramp up?' Makoto asked.

'It's harder on the eyes than the shoulders, staring at the screen all day long.'

'I can imagine.'

She smiled. 'Oh, my eyesight has got much worse since I started this job. I was fine without glasses before.'

'Sounds like an occupational hazard.'

He'd noticed that Chizuru took off her glasses when she was away from the terminal. Her eyes looked much larger without them.

'It must wear you out, having to shuttle back and forth from company to company,' he said.

'At least I'm in data entry. The IT guys have it worse. They're always pulling all-nighters before deadlines. Since the regular employees are using the computers during the day, they have to do all of their debugging and fixing at night. I heard one guy had overtime of more than a hundred and seventy hours.'

'Is that even possible?'

'Depending on what they're working on, it can take two or three hours just to print out the program. So he'd bring a sleeping bag to sleep in front of the monitor. He said he'd trained himself to wake up when the printer stops moving.'

'That's crazy,' Makoto shook his head. 'I hope they get paid for all of that.'

Chizuru chuckled dryly. 'They only hire temp workers because they're cheap. Kind of like ... disposable lighters.'

'I admit, I didn't really know how bad it was. I'm surprised so many people stick with it.'

'We have to eat.'

Makoto gave her a sidelong glance, watching her lips purse as she sipped her tea. 'What about our company?' he asked. 'We treating you OK, I hope?'

'Tozai is one of the better ones. Clean workplace, and good atmosphere,' she said, but then her brows knitted. 'I probably won't be able to work here much longer, though.'

'Really? Why?'

Makoto's heart thudded in his chest. This was unexpected news.

'I'll be finished with my allotted amount by next week. My initial contract is only for six months, and even if I did a final check through, it won't take me much longer than a couple of days.'

Makoto crushed his empty paper cup. He felt like he should say something, but he didn't know what.

'I wonder what kind of company I'll get next,' Chizuru said, a faint smile blooming on her face as she stared out the window.

After work that day, Chizuru had dinner at an Italian restaurant in Aoyama with her friend Akemi, another temp assigned to Tozai. They were both the same age, and unmarried, so these dinners had become something of a weekly tradition for them.

'Guess we'll be saying bye-bye pretty soon,' Akemi said. 'When I think about the mountain of patents we got through, I'm kinda impressed.' She sipped from a glass of white wine and stabbed a piece of octopus out of her salad with a fork.

Chizuru smiled. Though her friend always wore make-up and feminine clothes, the way she ate and often the way she talked were very rough. 'It's my downtown roots,' she was fond of saying.

'Still, the pay wasn't bad,' Chizuru noted. 'Especially compared to that steel company. They were terrible.'

'Yeah, I'm kinda hoping we don't get another one like that for a while.' Akemi frowned. 'The bosses were a bunch of idiots. They had absolutely *no* idea how to use us. I think they thought we were slaves or something. It was certainly slave wages.'

Chizuru smiled and took a sip of wine. Somehow, listening to Akemi bitch about things was an excellent outlet for her own stress.

'So what will you do?' Chizuru asked. 'Off to the next place right away?'

'That's the question, isn't it?' Akemi skewered a slice of courgette and rested her chin on her other hand. 'I think I might quit.'

'No kidding? Boyfriend pressure?'

'Yeah,' Akemi frowned. 'He says he doesn't mind me working all the time, but I'm not sure he really means it. You know, we're always ships passing in the night with our schedules the way they are, and trying to set up a date night is like pulling teeth. Besides, he says he wants children, which of course would mean I can't work any more, so why not quit now, I say.'

Chizuru had started nodding halfway through. 'Yeah. You can't keep working these hours for ever anyway.'

'Yup.' Akemi popped the courgette into her mouth.

She was due to get married next month. Her fiancé was a salary-man five years older than her. They'd had an ongoing argument about whether she should keep working after they got married, and it sounded like a decision had finally been made.

The pasta arrived. Chizuru had the sea-urchin cream spaghetti, and Akemi the garlic pepperoncini. It was Akemi's stated belief that a life lived in fear of stinking like garlic wasn't worth living.

'What about you, Chizuru? Going to keep at it for a while?'

'I don't know,' she said, using her fork to twine her spaghetti into a ball. She let it rest on the plate for a while. 'I'm thinking I might go back to my parents' house for a bit.'

'Sapporo, right? It's nice up there,' Akemi said.

Chizuru had come down to Tokyo for college, and hadn't been home for more than a couple of days at a time since.

'When would this be?'

'When Tozai finishes up, I guess.'

'So, soon. Like next weekend soon.' Akemi said, shovelling some pepperoncini into her mouth. She swallowed and said, 'Hey, isn't Mr Takamiya getting married that Sunday?'

'What, really?'

'Yeah, I'm pretty sure I overheard some people talking about it.'

'No kidding. Someone from the company?'

'I don't think so. Some college sweetheart, I heard.'

'Right,' Chizuru said, mechanically putting spaghetti in her mouth. It tasted like nothing.

'I don't know who she is, but she's done well for herself. They don't make many men like that.'

'Look at you, talking like you're not about to get married yourself. Or is he your type, Akemi?' Chizuru teased.

'It's less about type and more about the financial package that comes with it. His parents are big landowners, you know.'

'I had no idea.'

Despite the many times they'd got tea together, they had rarely discussed private matters.

'Yeah they're quite the elites. His house is out in Seijo and they own all kinds of land around there. An apartment building, too. It sounds like his father passed away, but they're living just fine on rental income. Heck, the lack of a father-in-law is probably a bonus.'

'You're certainly well-informed,' Chizuru said, looking across the table at her.

'Oh, the talk's made the rounds of the entire patent team. Apparently more than a few of the women had set their sights on him. Too bad they can't all be college sweethearts.' Akemi seemed to have enjoyed the entire spectacle, possibly because she hadn't ever been in the running herself.

'I think even if he weren't rich or good-looking he'd be a catch,' Chizuru said. 'I mean, he's always been a gentleman to the temps. You know how rare that is.'

Akemi waved her hand. 'See, now you're just showing your own inexperience. It's only the rich families that produce that kind of class. The money comes first. Looks and style follow, every time. Put the same kid in a poor family and you can kiss all that good-bye. I bet he'd be all bucktoothed, too.'

'Maybe you're right,' Chizuru said, laughing.

The main dish arrived and the conversation drifted on to their fish and other matters, and never once returned to the subject of Makoto Takamiya.

It was a little after ten o'clock when Chizuru got back to her apartment. Akemi seemed like she wanted to go for a nightcap, but Chizuru turned her down, pleading fatigue.

She opened the door and flicked on the switch, filling her one-room apartment with pale fluorescent light. The sight of the clothes, bags and magazines lying scattered throughout the room increased her weariness tenfold. She'd been living in the same apartment since sophomore year at college, and at times it felt like her room was a physical catalogue of all her worries and break-downs.

She flopped into the bed in the corner without even bothering to change. The bed frame creaked loudly as she landed on the mattress. *Nothing's new. Everything's just getting older.*

Makoto's face floated through her mind.

She hadn't been completely unaware that he had someone in his life. She'd heard one of the women, an employee in the licensing division, say something about it not too long ago. But she'd never known how serious it was, and she'd never asked. There wasn't anything she could have done about it, anyway.

There was really only one thing she liked about being a temp worker, and that was meeting people – especially men. Each new posting was a chance to meet Mr Right, even if nothing had panned out so far. She even suspected the female employees at some companies of purposely arranging things, like where the temp workers sat, to minimise their chances of meeting men.

But not at Tozai Automotive. She'd only been one day on the job when she met the man of her dreams: Makoto Takamiya. His looks were what first caught her attention, not that he would have passed for a model or a movie star. It was the quality of upbring-ing he exuded with every act, as though he existed on a higher level of being. She had known her share of young dandies, but most of them just dressed the part. He was the genuine article.

The more she worked with Makoto, the more she realised her first impressions had been spot on. He was kind to the temp workers, to the point that he'd even stuck up for them more than once when things went wrong due to bad instructions or overly optimistic schedules.

She'd gone so far as to imagine they might get married one day.

He seemed to like her too. At least he was aware of her. He never said as much, but the way he acted, the furtive glances, the way he talked – all told the same story.

And yet she had been mistaken. She thought back to their tea break that day, and laughed at her own stupidity. She'd been this close to saying something truly embarrassing.

This is it, she'd thought when he asked her to go on break with him. *He's finally going to ask me on a date.* But the question never came, and when she played the only card she had left and told him she'd be leaving soon, she'd got nothing more than a 'good luck'.

Of course, after hearing what Akemi had to say about him, she realised his unavailable status had been plainly obvious to everyone but her. *Someone a week away from getting married isn't going to think of a temp as anything more than a co-worker, if they think of them at all. The only reason he was nice to me is because he's nice.*

She decided it was better not to think about him any more. Sitting up with some effort, she reached for the phone by her pillow to call her parents in Sapporo. She wondered how they'd react when she told them she was coming home.

A crisp breeze blew in through the bay window. It had been deep into the rainy season when he'd first come to see the place, Makoto thought, but that was already three months ago. 'Perfect day for moving,' his mother said, pausing from wiping the floor. 'I was worried about the weather, but the movers will certainly be happy with this.'

'They're professionals,' Makoto said. 'They don't care about the weather.'

'I doubt that. Didn't Yamashita's new wife move in last month during the typhoon? They said it was hell.'

'Well, a typhoon is another matter. Besides, it's already October.'

'It can rain in October,' she said. She'd gone back to wiping when the doorbell rang.

'Who could that be?' Makoto wondered out loud.

'Isn't it Yukiho?'

'But she has a key,' he said, picking the intercom off its hook on the wall. 'Yes?'

'It's me.'

'Oh, hey. You forget your key?'

'Well, no—'

'Don't worry, I'll buzz you in.'

Makoto pressed the button to unlock the front door to the building, then he went to make sure the door to their unit was open and waited there for Yukiho to arrive. He heard the door open and footsteps before she came around the corner in a green cardigan and white cotton trousers. She had her jacket over one arm – it was particularly hot for autumn.

'Hey.' Makoto smiled at her.

'Sorry I'm late. I had some shopping to do.' Yukiho showed him the supermarket bags in her hands. He saw cleaning products, sponges, and rubber gloves.

'I thought you finished cleaning last week?'

'Well, yes, but it's already been a week, and once the furniture gets in, there's going to be new dirt everywhere.'

Makoto shook his head. 'Exactly what my mother said. She's got a whole truckload of sponges and soap in there already.'

'I'd better get helping, then!' Yukiho hurriedly took off her sneakers.

Makoto raised an eyebrow. He'd never seen her in anything other than high heels. In fact, this was the first time he'd seen her in something other than a dress or skirt. He commented on it and she gave him an exasperated look. 'On moving day? How am I supposed to help in a skirt?'

'That's right,' said his mother from inside. She came to the door, her sleeves rolled up past her elbows. She was smiling. 'Hello, Yukiho.'

'Hello.' Yukiho gave a little bow of her head.

'I apologise on behalf of my son. He's never had to clean his own room, and I'm afraid it's left him a little clueless about exactly how much work it is. I'm sorry the burden will probably fall on you, Yukiho. I hope you're ready!'

'Oh, I'm ready.'

The two women went into the living room and began setting up a base of operations. Makoto listened to them chat for a bit, then went back over to the bay window and looked down at the road outside. The truck from the furniture store should be there any moment now. The people from the appliance shop would follow an hour later.

This is it, Makoto thought. In two weeks, he'd be the head of a household. It hadn't really hit him until now, and he was surprised to find that he was a little nervous.

In the room behind him, Yukiho was on her knees in an apron, wiping the tatami mats. Even in work clothes, she was a beauty.

Four years, he thought. That was how long they'd been dating. They'd met in the college dance club: he a senior at Eimei University and she a new recruit from their sister school, Seika Girls College.

Of all the recruits that year, Yukiho had shone the brightest. With her face and proportions she would have been perfectly at home on the cover of a fashion magazine. The first time he laid eyes on her she stole his heart, though Makoto was only one of several boys with a thing for her. Though he wasn't seeing anyone at the time, he had been reluctant to ask her out. She'd already turned down several of the other guys in the club, and he didn't want to suffer the same fate.

He might never have got up the courage if Yukiho hadn't come to him for help with her dancing – she was having trouble getting a certain step right. So it happened that he found himself with the perfect excuse to steal away time with the object of everyone's desire.

It was not long after they started practising together that he began to think Yukiho might be interested in him, too. So one day he decided to ask her out for a date.

Yukiho had stared at him for a long time before saying, 'Where did you have in mind?'

Resisting the urge to start dancing, he had said, 'Wherever you like.'

They had gone out for dinner and a musical, and he saw her home afterwards. They had been dating now for four years.

And yet they might never have gone out in the first place if she hadn't asked him to teach her that step, Makoto thought. If it had been another girl who'd asked him for help, he could be marrying her in two weeks' time. There had been plenty of girls who'd caught his eye back in those days. Even Yukiho's friend Eriko had left enough of an impression on him that he still remembered her name, although he hadn't seen her since she quit halfway through her first year.

Fate is a curious thing, he thought.

'So why'd you ring the intercom?' Makoto asked Yukiho as she was wiping down the kitchen counter.

'I didn't want to just barge in,' she replied, her hands never stopping their work.

'Why not? That's why I gave you a key.'

'But we're not married yet.'

'I don't think anyone's keeping track of that.'

'Yes, but if we didn't observe these rules the occasion wouldn't be so special,' his mother chimed in with a smile at the bride-to-be.

Yukiho smiled back at the woman who would become her mother-in-law in two weeks' time. Makoto sighed and looked back out of the window. His mother had liked Yukiho from the first time they met. It was another thread binding him together with Yukiho, he thought. All he had to do was follow these threads, and things would go well.

And yet another woman's face was stuck in the back of his mind, where his bride's should have been. He wasn't thinking of her on purpose. In fact, he tried to forget her, but when he closed his eyes, there she was.

Makoto rubbed his temples and frowned when he heard a noise from the street outside.

The furniture had arrived.

At seven o'clock the following evening, Makoto was sitting at a café in Shinjuku Station.

At the next table over, two men were talking loudly in Osaka accents about baseball. The subject, of course, was the Hanshin Tigers and their unexpected transformation from a long period of being also-rans to contenders for this year's title. Everyone in the western half of the country was excited. At Tozai, one of the section leads – apparently a closet Tigers supporter until now – had established a company fan club and was taking people out for celebratory drinks nearly every night after work. Makoto, himself a Giants fan through-and-through, sighed inwardly, realising that this commotion probably wouldn't end any time soon.

Yet it was nice hearing Osaka accents again. After attending college in the city, he'd spent four years living by himself in an apartment in Senri, a suburb to the north of Osaka proper.

He'd just taken his second sip of coffee when the man he was waiting for appeared. He was decked out in a perfectly tailored grey suit: the quintessential businessman.

'How does it feel to be saying goodbye to bachelor life?' Kazunari Shinozuka asked, sitting down across from him. He ordered an espresso.

'Sorry to call you out here like this,' Makoto said.

'No skin off my nose. Mondays are pretty light for me,' he said, crossing his long legs.

The students who took ballroom dancing tended to come from respectable families. Kazunari's family was in charge of a large pharmaceuticals company. His family home was in Kobe, but he had come up to Tokyo to work in the family company's local branch.

'I'm guessing you're busier than I am,' Kazunari said.

'I guess. We just got our furniture and appliances delivered yesterday. I'm going to start sleeping there alone tonight.'

'Ah, the nest is nearly complete! Now all you need is a bride.'

'Her stuff arrives next Saturday.'

'Well, congratulations,' Kazunari said with a bright smile, 'it's finally happening.'

'I guess so,' said Makoto. He looked away and took another sip of coffee.

'So what did you want to talk about? You sounded pretty serious on the phone yesterday. I got a little worried.'

'Yeah, sorry about that.'

'So what's so important you couldn't tell me over the phone? Having second thoughts about leaving the good bachelor life behind already?' Kazunari laughed.

He'd meant it as a joke, but Makoto couldn't smile. In a sense, Kazunari was right on the money.

Kazunari frowned and leaned forward. 'Hey, now.'

Just then, the waitress arrived with his espresso. He sat back in his chair, but his eyes were still fixed on Makoto.

'You're kidding, right?' He asked once she'd left again. He hadn't even looked at his coffee.

'Unfortunately, no.' Makoto crossed his arms, returning his friend's look.

Kazunari's eyes widened and his mouth hung open a little. His eyes went around the café before looking back at Makoto. 'It's a little late to change your mind, don't you think?'

'Yeah, I know. I just worry I'm not ready.'

Kazunar's expression froze. Then he slowly began to nod. 'Don't worry. I hear most guys feel like running when the day gets close and the responsibility really settles in. You're not alone.'

Makoto shook his head. 'It's not that.'

'Then what?' Kazunari asked, and Makoto couldn't meet his gaze this time.

He was afraid his friend would laugh if he told him the truth. And yet, if he couldn't tell Kazunari, who could he tell? Makoto took a sip of water. 'There's someone else,' he said.

Kazunari didn't respond for a while. Nor did his expression change.

Makoto was about to repeat himself, when Kazunari asked, 'Who?' There was a hard look to his eyes.

'Someone at work ... for now.'

'What do you mean "for now"?' Kazunari asked, lifting an eyebrow.

Makoto explained about Chizuru Misawa.

'And you've only seen her at work, never in private?' Kazunari asked once Makoto had finished.

'Of course. I can't exactly ask her out on a date.'

'No, you can't. Which raises the question, how do you know how she feels about you?'

'I don't.'

'Well then,' Kazunari said, a light smile coming to his lips, 'I advise you to forget about her. To me, it sounds like nerves.'

Makoto smiled at that. 'I figured you'd say that. In fact, if I were in your place, I'd tell me the same thing.'

'Yeah, sorry,' Kazunari said. 'I know you already know what this is. And I don't mean to make light of your feelings. You were right to come to me.'

'I understand that I'm being an idiot, yes.'

Kazunari took a sip of his espresso.

'So when did this start?' he asked.

'When did what start, exactly?'

'When did you start having feelings for her?'

'Oh.' Makoto thought for a moment before replying, 'Around April of this year, I guess. Which would be the moment I first saw her.'

'That's already half a year ago, then. Why didn't you do something about it earlier?' There was a hint of irritation in Kazunari's voice.

'Do what, exactly? The wedding was already planned. And more than that, I didn't trust my own feelings. Like you said, I thought it was just a fleeting thing. I told myself I needed to get rid of it, quick.'

'But you couldn't, and here we are,' Kazunari said with a sigh. He scratched his head. His hair had a slight curl to it back in the student days, when it was longer, but now it was cut short. 'This is quite the bomb to drop two weeks before the big day.'

'I know, and I'm sorry. There was no one else I could talk to.'

'Oh, I don't mind,' said Kazunari, but his frown remained unchanged. 'As a practical matter, we still don't know how this woman feels, do we. About you, I mean.'

'No, we don't.'

'In which case, and this may be a strange thing to say, but the only problem here is how you feel.'

'Exactly. And how I feel is, I'm not sure it's right to get married feeling like this. I just can't picture even going to the ceremony.'

'I hear you.' Kazunari sighed again. 'What about Yukiho? How do you feel about her? You cooling off?'

'No, that's not it. I mean I still feel the same—'

'The same less-than-a-hundred-per-cent, then?'

In lieu of responding, Makoto drained his glass of water.

'I don't want to say anything too outrageous, but your instincts are probably right. I can't see how it would be best for either of you if you got married feeling the way you do now.'

'So what would you do in my position?' Makoto asked.

'Avoid all women for at least a year before marriage.'

Makoto laughed quietly. He might have laughed louder at his friend's dry sense of humour if the truth in what he said hadn't been such a hard pill to swallow.

'And yet, if my attentions did stray to another woman before I tied the knot ...' Kazunari let his eyes wander up towards the ceiling before he returned his gaze to Makoto. 'I would call it off.'

'Even two weeks before the wedding?'

'Even on the day before.'

Makoto was silenced by the weight of what Kazunari was saying.

But his friend grinned. 'Which I can only say because it's not me in the hot seat. I know it's not that easy. And there is the matter of exactly how strongly you feel about this other girl.'

Makoto nodded slowly. 'Thanks, I think I get you.'

'Everyone plays by their own rules,' Kazunari said. 'You come to your own decision. I won't second-guess you either way.'

'I'll let you know when I know.'

Kazunari laughed. 'You might want to make your mind up soon.'

The hand-drawn map led them to a spot right next to the Isetan department store in Shinjuku. There was a sign for a bar – the kind of place that had been there for decades – on the third floor.

'I suppose we should be grateful they're doing this, but they could've picked a trendier place,' Akemi said, as they got on the elevator.

'That's what you get for letting a bunch of balding engineers throw you a party,' said Chizuru.

'I guess,' Akemi said, frowning.

The bar door slid open automatically as they approached, letting a blast of noise out into the hall. It was still before seven, and yet the place was already overflowing with drunken revellers. A salaryman type was sitting just inside the door, his necktie hanging loose down his chest.

A voice from the back of the bar called to them. There were already a few tables full of familiar faces from the Patent Licensing Division, many of them already flushed with alcohol.

'Remember: this is *our* party,' Akemi whispered in Chizuru's ear. 'If they make us pour their beer for them, I'm kicking over the table and going home.'

Chizuru laughed, but she didn't think that was how it was going to play out today. She had already spotted Makoto Takamiya at one of the tables.

There were the standard greetings and a toast. *All part of the job*, Chizuru thought, putting on her best smile. Part of her mind was already projecting forward to the end of the party. She knew from prior experience that even men who would never dream of coming on strong to a woman who worked at their own company acted differently towards temp workers – after all, they wouldn't be around to cause any aftermath – and there were no women at the table today to keep things in line.

Makoto was sitting across and a little way down from them. He was already eating and had a glass of beer in front of him. Never the talkative sort, today he seemed to be in full listening mode.

Still, Chizuru kept sensing his eyes on her throughout the night. She thought she caught him looking away once or twice, but then again, maybe it was just her mind playing tricks on her.

You're being too self-conscious, Chizuru told herself.

Gradually the conversation came around to Akemi's upcoming marriage.

'I don't know about having a kid at a time like this, with all that's going on. That said, if I have a boy, I'm naming him Tiger after the Hanshin Tigers,' Akemi said after she'd had a few drinks, making everyone laugh.

'Isn't Mr Takamiya getting married too?' Chizuru said, trying to make her voice sound as natural as possible.

'Er, eh, yes,' Makoto said, seeming a little embarrassed, which set off another round of laughter.

'The day after tomorrow!' a man named Narita, who was sitting across from Chizuru chimed in, giving Makoto a clap on the shoulder. 'If you're going to make a move, better make it quick, because this bachelor's going off the market!'

'Congratulations,' Chizuru said.

Makoto thanked her quietly.

'Congratulations!' Narita echoed loudly, his voice a little slurred. 'Congratulations for proving beyond a shadow of a doubt that some guys get all the luck!'

Makoto gave a self-effacing laugh and said, 'Well, that's hardly true, but thanks all the same.'

'Nope!' Narita smiled and shook his head. 'It's completely true.' He looked over at Chizuru. 'Listen to this, Ms Misawa. This guy is two years younger than I am and he's already got a home of his own. Should that even be legal?'

'It's not technically mine, and it's not even a house.'

'Objection!' Flecks of spittle came out of Narita's grinning mouth. 'I said "home", not "house", and I think an apartment you live in without paying rent counts as a home of your own.'

Makoto sighed. 'It's in my mother's name. She's just letting me live there. So, technically, we're squatting.'

'See, his mommy owns an apartment! If that's not luck, I don't know what is.' Narita looked to Chizuru for some sign she agreed, while filling his own cup back up to the brim with sake. He tossed it back and kept talking. 'Now when you say someone owns an apartment, you usually think a little two-room, three-room place, right? But not when it comes to this guy's family. They own the entire *building*!'

'Enough, already,' Makoto said. He was still smiling, but it was clear to everyone but Narita that his patience for the conversation was already wearing thin.

'No, I'm definitely putting my foot down. Especially when you consider that his bride-to-be is practically a beauty queen.'

'Narita!' Makoto frowned. He picked up the bottle of sake and topped off the man's glass in an attempt to silence him.

'Is she that pretty?' Chizuru asked.

'Oh, gorgeous,' Narita said. 'Could be an actress, no problem. And she does tea and flower arrangement too, right?'

'A bit,' Makoto admitted.

'See what I mean? Speaks English too, fluently. Damn, man, what's with all your good luck?'

'Easy there,' said the section chief at the end of the table. 'There's plenty of luck to go around. You'll get yours soon enough, Narita.'

'Yeah? I'd like to know when.'

The section chief nodded sagely. 'Middle of next century, at the latest.'

'That's over fifty years from now! I don't need luck when I'm dead!'

Chizuru joined in the laughter, glancing towards Makoto. For a moment, their eyes met. Something in his eyes made it look like he was trying to tell her something – *or I'm overthinking things again.*

The farewell party ended at nine o'clock. As the group began shuffling out of the door, Chizuru called Makoto over. 'I brought you a gift, for your wedding.' She pulled a thin, wrapped package out of her bag. 'I was going to give it to you at work today, but I never found the time.'

'Oh, you didn't have to do that,' he said, opening the package to reveal a blue handkerchief. 'Thanks, this is really special.'

'Thank you for the last six months,' she said, giving a little bow.

'I didn't do anything to earn that, but you're welcome. Where are you off to next?'

'I'm going to go home, take it easy for a while. I'll be leaving for Sapporo the day after tomorrow – your big day, in fact.'

'Oh,' he said, nodding as he put the handkerchief back inside the wrapper and slid it into his jacket pocket.

'Your wedding's going to be at that hotel in Akasaka, right? I'd come to watch through the window, but I think I'll have to settle for waving from the train instead.'

'You heading out early?'

'Yes, I'm staying at a hotel in Shinagawa tomorrow night, so I can get going first thing.'

'Which hotel?'

'The Parkside.'

Makoto looked like he wanted to say something, but he was interrupted by a voice from the elevator. 'What's taking you two so long? Everyone's downstairs already.'

Makoto smiled and turned towards the door. Chizuru followed behind him, like she had on so many tea breaks over the last six months. Like she never would again.

Makoto went home that night to the family home in Seijo. Once he officially moved out, only his mother and her parents – his grandparents – would be living there. It was his mother's side of the family that owned all the land. His late father had moved in with them, and even taken his mother's family name of Takamiya.

'Only one more day!' his mother announced cheerily when he arrived. 'Tomorrow will be busy. I have to go to the hairdresser's, and pick up some jewellery I had on order. I expect everyone up bright and early!' She spread a newspaper over the antique dining room table and began to peel an apple over it.

Makoto sat across from her, pretending to read a magazine with one eye on the clock. *Eleven*, he thought. *That's when I need to call.*

'Makoto's the one getting married,' his grandfather said from where he sat on the sofa. 'I don't see why *you* have to get all dressed up.' A chessboard was laid out in front of him, and he cradled a pipe in his left hand. He was already over eighty years old, but he walked with a straight back, and his voice still had a ring to it.

'I disagree. This will be my only chance to attend my own child's wedding. I think I should be allowed to dress up for the occasion, don't you?'

Her last 'don't you' was directed towards Makoto's grandmother, who was sitting across from her husband, working on her knitting. She just smiled and said nothing.

His grandfather's chessboard, his grandmother's knitting, and his mother's cheerful prattle – this was family life as Makoto had known it since he was a child. He loved that even tonight, two days before his wedding, it was no different. The house never seemed to change, nor did the people inside it.

'To see my own grandchild getting married makes me feel ancient,' his grandfather noted, thoughtfully.

'It still feels a little early to me,' his mother said. 'You're both so young, though I suppose you've been together for four years now and there wouldn't be any difference if you waited longer.'

'And this girl, Yukiho. She's a good one. I'm happy for you,' said his grandmother.

'Yes, a good girl. Good head on her shoulders,' his grandfather agreed. 'Very solid for someone so young.'

'I liked her from the moment Makoto brought her home. Girls with a proper upbringing are just *different*,' said his mother, arranging apple slices in a bowl.

Makoto thought back to the first time he had brought Yukiho home to meet his family. His mother had been taken first by her looks, and second by the fact that she lived with an adopted mother. She empathised with that, and when she learned that the foster mother had taught Yukiho not only how to keep house but the tea ceremony and flower arrangement as well, her opinion of her had only grown.

Makoto ate two of the apple slices, then stood. It was almost eleven. 'I'm going upstairs.'

'Don't forget, we're having dinner with Yukiho tomorrow night,' his mother said.

'Dinner?'

'Yukiho and her mother are staying at the hotel tomorrow, so I phoned them and asked if they'd like to eat together.'

'You can't just decide these things on your own,' Makoto said, surprised at the sharpness in his voice.

'You had other plans? You were going to meet Yukiho tomorrow night anyway, weren't you?'

'What time?'

'I reserved a table at the restaurant at seven. The French place in that hotel is quite famous, you know.'

Makoto left the living room in silence. He climbed the stairs and made for his own room. Other than the clothes he had bought recently, nearly all of his possessions were still here in this room. He sat down in front of the desk he'd used since coming home from college and picked up the phone lying on top of it. It was his own private line, and they still kept it connected.

He checked the list of numbers on the wall and started dialling. Kazunari picked up after two rings.

'Hello?' He sounded disgruntled. He'd probably been in the middle of a relaxing evening listening to classical music in his room. Kazunari lived alone in an apartment in Yotsuya, right in the middle of Tokyo.

'Hey, it's me.'

'Hey.' Kazunari's tone lightened a little. 'What's up?'

'Can we talk?'

'Go ahead.'

'OK, this is kind of big, and I'm guessing it's going to come as a bit of a shock. Just promise you won't freak out.'

He was pretty sure Kazunari had already guessed what he was about to say, but there was silence from the other end of the line. Makoto listened to the hiss of the telephone line in his ear. The noise had been steadily getting worse over the past few months. Sometimes it was so bad he couldn't hear who he was talking to.

'This about what we talked about the other day?' Kazunari finally said.

'Yeah.'

'Oy.' Makoto heard him laughing, though it didn't sound like he was smiling. 'You're wedding's in two days, isn't it?'

'You said you'd call it off the day before if you had to.'

'I did say that,' Kazunari said, breathing a little loudly into the phone. 'You serious?'

'I am.' Makoto swallowed and said, 'I'm gonna tell her how I feel tomorrow.'

'And by her, you mean this temp worker? Chizuru, was it?'

'Yeah.'

'So you tell her how you feel, then what? You going to propose?'

'I haven't thought it through that far. I just want her to know how I feel … and I want to know how she feels. That's all.'

'What if she doesn't feel anything at all?'

'Then at least I'll know.'

'You mean you'll go marry Yukiho the next day, like nothing ever happened?'

'Not the most upstanding thing I've ever done, I know.'

'Nah,' Kazunari said, 'I think you gotta do what you gotta do. What's important is that you don't leave any regrets.'

'I'm glad to hear you say that.'

'The problem,' Kazunari went on, 'is what to do if she says she likes you too.'

'Well—'

'Think you can just throw it all away?'

'I can.'

He heard Kazunari breathing on the other end of the line.

'That's going to be harder than you might think, Makoto.

You're going to be putting a lot of people through a lot of hell, and you're going to hurt a few of them. Most of all Yukiho.'

'I'll make it up to her. I'll do whatever I have to.'

They were both silent for a while, with just the crackling hiss of the telephone line between them.

'Well, sounds like you've made up your mind. I've got nothing to say.'

'Sorry to put you through this, man.'

'Don't worry about me. I'm just wondering what the day after tomorrow is going to be like. Gives me goosebumps.'

'Yeah, I'm nervous too.'

'I bet you are.'

'On that note, I need to ask a favour of you. Are you free tomorrow night?'

The day that would decide his fate dawned cloudy. After eating a late breakfast, Makoto had gone to his room and sat staring at the sky. He hadn't been able to sleep very well, and his head was pounding.

Makoto had been racking his brains for a way to get in touch with Chizuru. He knew she was staying in a hotel in Shinagawa that night. If it came to it, he could try seeing her there, but if at all possible he wanted to meet her during the day and lay it out.

Yet he'd never seen her outside the office, so he didn't know her address or phone number. Their company didn't keep records of that information for temp workers in the usual places, either. His section chief or division chief might know, but he wasn't sure how he could ask them. That, and it was a Saturday. There wasn't any guarantee they'd have her contact information at home.

There was only one route left to him. He would have to go to work and try to find her contact information there somehow. It was a Saturday, but there were doubtless some people there over the weekend. No one would look twice at him for coming to work to find some things.

Makoto stood from his chair, ready to go, when the doorbell rang. A bad premonition made his heart beat faster, and a minute later, his fears were confirmed when he heard the sound of his mother's felt slippers coming up the steps.

'Makoto,' he heard her say from the other side of the door. 'Yukiho's here.'

'Be right there.'

He went down to find his fiancée in the living room, having tea with his grandparents. She was wearing a dark brown dress.

'Yukiho brought some cakes. Would you like one?' his mother asked. She seemed to be in an unusually cheerful mood.

'I'm fine. What's up?' he asked, turning to Yukiho.

'There are some things I needed to buy for the honeymoon. I thought you might like to come with me,' she said in a cheery sing-song. Her almond-shaped eyes glittered like two jewels. She had the look of a bride, and it sent a sliver of pain through Makoto's chest.

'Right, well, hmm. I was going to drop by the office.'

'The office? Today?' His mother frowned, wrinkles forming between her brows. 'I can't believe they make you come in to work on the day before your wedding.'

'It's not work, exactly. There were just some things I want to take a look at.'

'We could go on the way,' Yukiho said. 'Didn't you say that people from outside the company were allowed to visit on week-ends?'

'Well, that's true, but—' Internally, Makoto was panicking. Her offer to come along had caught him by surprise.

'Always the company man,' his mother said, frowning. 'What's more important? Your family or your job?'

'Fine, fine, you know, it's really not that important, I'll just put off going today.'

'I don't mind, honestly,' Yukiho said.

'No, it's OK. Really,' Makoto smiled at his betrothed. The confession to Chizuru would have to come that night, at the hotel.

He had Yukiho wait while he got changed and went up to his room. He fished a jacket out of his dresser and phoned Kazunari.

'It's me,' he said as soon as his friend picked up. 'Remember that back-up plan we discussed?'

'No dice on the contact info, huh?'

'Unfortunately no. And now I have to go shopping with Yukiho.'

He heard Kazunari sigh on the other side of the line.

'I'm really sorry to put you through this.'

'Hey, man, it's fine. OK. Nine o'clock.'

'See you then.'

He hung up the phone, got changed, and opened the door to find Yukiho standing in the hallway. She had her hands behind her back and was leaning up against the wall, looking at him with a curious smile on her lips.

'I came to see what was taking so long,' she said.

'Sorry, I was picking out my clothes. You coming?' He walked past her and started down the stairs.

'What's the back-up plan?'

Makoto almost missed a step. 'Oh, you were listening?'

'Well, I overheard.'

'It's nothing, just work,' he said, continuing down the stairs. He was afraid of what she might ask next, but no further questions came.

They went shopping in Ginza, hitting all the famous department stores and a few high-end boutiques.

She'd claimed she needed to buy things for travel, but to Makoto it didn't look as though Yukiho was intending to buy anything. When he pointed it out, she shrugged and smiled. 'To tell you the truth, I just wanted to spend some time together. You know, a date on our last day as an unmarried couple. Nothing wrong with that, is there?'

Makoto sighed. There *was* something wrong with it, but nothing he could tell her.

He watched Yukiho window-shop, and thought back on the last four years. It was true that he'd stayed with her because he loved her. But he couldn't pin down a particular reason for deciding to marry her. Was it because of the depths of his affection for her?

Makoto thought that, unfortunately, that probably wasn't the case. He'd only first seriously considered marriage two years earlier, on a morning when Yukiho called him from a small business hotel in the city.

When he got there she was waiting for him with a look on her face more serious than he'd ever seen before.

'What's wrong?' he asked. 'And why are you staying at this place?'

She let him into the room and pointed towards the table without saying a word. There was a clear tube there, about half a cigarette in length. It was filled with a small amount of liquid. 'Don't touch it, look at it from the top,' she said.

Makoto looked, and saw two red circles on the bottom of the tube. He reported this to Yukiho, and she thrust out a piece of paper to him.

It was the instructions for a pregnancy test. Two circles meant positive.

'It says I'm supposed to check with my first pee after I wake up in the morning. I'm staying here because I wanted you to see.'

Makoto must have frowned, because she added in a bright voice, 'Don't worry. I'm not going to demand we have it or anything. And I can go to the hospital by myself.'

'Are you sure?'

'Of course. We're not ready to have a kid.'

A wave of relief had washed over him when he heard her say that. He'd never even imagined being a father before that moment, and he certainly didn't feel ready.

True to her word, Yukiho went to the hospital by herself and had an abortion. No one was told. He didn't see her for a week, but when he did, she was the same old Yukiho. She never spoke about it again. He tried to bring the subject up once or twice, but each time, she would seem to sense it before he spoke, and shake her head no.

'It's OK. We don't need to talk about it.'

This event marked the time when he began to seriously contemplate marriage. If they'd slipped up once, they could slip up again. Taking responsibility for her, legally, was taking responsibility as a man. It had all seemed very important at the time, but now, looking back, he wondered if he hadn't made the biggest decision of his life for the wrong reasons.

Makoto pretended to drink his coffee while he kept an eye on his watch. It was a little after nine.

The two families, his and Yukiho's, had been eating since seven, though much of that time had been passed listening to his mother talk. Yukiho's adoptive mother Reiko Karasawa was an elegant woman, with intellectual substance. She smiled warmly and was a good listener. It pained Makoto to think he might be betraying her the next morning.

It was nine-fifteen when they left the restaurant. His mother made the suggestion he thought she would – it was still early, why didn't they all go out to a bar?

'I'm sure the bars are all crowded,' Makoto said. 'Let's go to the lounge on the first floor.'

Reiko said that sounded pleasant. She wasn't much of a drinker.

They took the lift down to the first floor and headed for the lounge. Makoto checked his watch. Nine-twenty.

Just as they were heading into the lounge, a voice called out 'Makoto,' from behind them. Makoto turned and saw Kazunari walking over.

'Hey!' Makoto said, feigning surprise.

Kazunari stepped up close to him and clapped him on the shoulder. 'You were so late, I thought you'd called the whole thing off,' he whispered.

'Dinner ran long,' Makoto whispered back.

They pretended to say a few more things, then went back to Yukiho and the others. 'Some people from Eimei University are getting together nearby,' Makoto announced. 'I'm going to go say hi.'

'You have to go? On tonight of all nights?' his mother said, a displeased look on her face.

Reiko came to his rescue. 'Why not? It's important for a man to spend time with his friends.'

Makoto smiled at her.

'Don't stay out too late,' Yukiho said, watching his eyes.

Out of the lounge, Makoto fled the hotel with Kazunari, who had his favourite Porsche parked out front.

'If we get caught for speeding, the ticket's on you,' said Kazunari as he took off.

Parkside Hotel was a five-minute walk from Shinagawa Station. Makoto got out of Kazunari's Porsche at the front entrance to the hotel just a little before ten o'clock.

He went straight to the front desk and asked whether they had a guest by the name of Chizuru Misawa. The man, with his hair perfectly cut, said politely that she did have a reservation. 'But,' he added, 'Ms Misawa has yet to check in. She was supposed to be here by nine.'

Makoto thanked him and walked away from the front desk. He looked around the lobby, found a sofa in view of the front desk, and sat down.

'She's going to be here any moment,' he whispered to himself, and the thought made his heart beat faster.

Chizuru arrived at Shinagawa station at ten minutes to ten. It had taken her much longer to clean up her place and pack than she'd expected. She crossed the crosswalk in front of the station through a crowd of people as she headed towards the hotel.

The main entrance to the Parkside was along the road, but in order to go in you had to first walk through a garden in the front. Heavy bags in her hands, Chizuru made her way along the winding walkway. Small spotlights illuminated the flowers in the neatly kept beds on either side of the path, but she wasn't in the mood to stop and appreciate them.

Beyond the garden, taxis were pulling in one after the other, dropping off guests. Chizuru reflected that most people coming to a hotel like this would be coming by car. Not even the porters were looking out for pedestrians like her.

Which was why she was surprised when a voice called out, 'Excuse me, miss?' from behind her just as she was nearing the doors to the main lobby.

She turned and saw a young man in a dark suit. 'I'm sorry, but are you on your way to check in?' he asked.

'I am,' she said warily.

'I'm with the police,' he said, flashing her a badge on the inside of his jacket. 'I was hoping we could talk. I have a request for you, actually.'

'Me?' Chizuru gaped.

The man beckoned her to follow him into the garden. Shrugging, she followed him.

'Are you staying here alone tonight?' he asked.

'Yes. What's this about?'

'I was wondering, is it absolutely necessary you have to stay at this particular hotel?'

'Well, I have a reservation here, and I'm taking a train early tomorrow morning, so I need to be near the station.'

'Of course. If I could get you a room at the hotel just behind this one, would that work? It's closer to the station.'

'I'm still not sure why you're asking me this.'

'A suspect in the case we're working on is staying at this hotel tonight. We need to keep an eye on him and, unfortunately, a large group has just checked in, and we can't get a room to use for our investigation.'

'So you need my room?'

'That's right,' the man said. 'It's difficult for us to switch with a customer who's already checked in, and we don't want to risk tipping off the person we're watching.'

'I see, I guess,' she said, looking the detective over. He seemed very young. *Maybe a new recruit.* But his suit was well pressed, and she got the impression he was very serious about his request.

'If you're willing to help, we'll pay for your stay and give you a lift to your hotel,' he said. She thought she detected a hint of an Osaka accent in his words.

'By the hotel behind this one, you mean the Queen?' Chizuru asked. It was at least one rank above the Parkside.

'Yes, we have a forty-thousand-yen room there,' he said.

There's no way I could ever afford a room like that, she thought. Her mind was made up. 'Then what are we waiting for?'

'Thanks so much. Here, I'll take those,' he said, reaching out for her luggage.

It was already past ten-thirty and Chizuru was nowhere in sight.

Makoto had picked up a newspaper somebody left behind to read, but he kept one eye on the front desk. The desire to see her face had already overtaken his desire to confess as quickly as he could. He'd been here more than half an hour and his pulse was still racing.

A woman walked up to the front desk. For a second his heart jumped, but then he saw her face and his eyes went down to the floor.

'I don't have a reservation, but do you have any rooms?' he overheard her say.

'Just one?' the man at the front desk asked.

'Yes, please.'

'How about a single room?'

'That'll be fine.'

'We can get that for you. We have a standard room for twelve thousand yen, a room overlooking the pool for fifteen thousand, and a room for eighteen thousand with a nice view of the skyline. Do you have a preference?'

'Oh, the standard is fine.'

Makoto quickly lost interest in the conversation. He glanced towards the door then back at his newspaper. He read the words but his mind was elsewhere. Only one article held his interest for more than a few seconds: a story about members of the Japanese Communist Party having their phones tapped by the police. It had sparked a debate about invasion of privacy and the legality of wiretapping. The politics didn't interest Makoto; what caught his attention was how the wiretapping was discovered.

Apparently the owner of the tapped phone line had contacted the phone company because there was a lot of noise on the line and occasionally the volume of calls would drop so dramatically he couldn't hear who they were talking to.

I hope my phone back home isn't tapped, he thought, chuckling to himself. It certainly had the same symptoms. Not that anyone had anything to gain by tapping his phone.

He was folding the newspaper when the man from the front desk walked over.

'You were waiting for Ms Misawa?' he asked.

'Yes?' Makoto said, half standing from his chair.

'We just had a phone call. She's cancelled her reservation.'

'What?' Makoto felt his skin grow hot. 'Where is she?'

'I'm afraid he didn't say,' the man shook his head.

'He?'

'Yes, sir,' the man nodded.

Makoto began walking towards the front door. He didn't know what to do. The only thing that was clear was that waiting here wouldn't do him any good. He walked out the front doors, and got into the first taxi in line.

In the cab on the way back to Seijo, Makoto started to laugh. *Clearly it wasn't meant to be*, he thought. Maybe she caught an earlier train. Maybe the guy who called was her fiancé and Makoto never had a chance in the first place. Either way, it felt bigger than coincidence. It felt like destiny.

But thinking back on it, no supernatural power had been required to keep him apart from Chizuru. He'd had plenty of chances to confess how he felt and let every one of them slip by.

He pulled out a handkerchief and wiped the sweat off his brow. He looked down at it as he put it back in his pocket. It was the blue handkerchief Chizuru had given to him. Then he closed his eyes and thought about what he needed to do to prepare for the ceremony and reception tomorrow. When the cab driver woke him, they were outside his home.

EIGHT

Two people walked in just before closing time: a short man of about fifty and a skinny high-school boy. *Father and son*, Tomohiko thought immediately. The kid had a familiar face. He'd been in the shop several times before. He never asked any questions, never bought anything. He just stared at the computers on display and went home. There were a few others like him, come to ogle the high-end machines. As a rule, Tomohiko didn't try to engage them; he didn't want to spook them off. 'They're welcome to window-shop as much as they like,' Ryo always said. 'When that first big pay cheque lands, or their parents offer to buy them something to celebrate a good report card, they'll be back.'

Ryo was the manager, and if he was happy, Tomohiko was happy.

The father peered through wireframe glasses at the centrepiece of their display – a computer Tomohiko had seen the boy staring at before. They stood side by side, looking at it, whispering, until the father leaned in to read the price tag. 'What?' he exclaimed, his voice loud in the quiet shop. The son, desperate to keep him from walking out, immediately switched to damage control, telling him about all the other, cheaper options.

Tomohiko watched his screen, feigning disinterest while continuing to observe them out of the corner of his eye. The father had a distant gaze as he moved down the rows of computers and peripheral devices, as though he were surveying the landscape of some foreign country. He was dressed casually, a wool cardigan over a turtleneck sweater, but he still smelled like a company man. Middle-level management in some industrial complex, Tomohiko guessed.

Hiroe Nakajima looked up from the parts shipment she was

examining to give Tomohiko a look to say *shouldn't you talk to them?*

Tomohiko nodded. *I know, I know.*

He waited for the right moment and then stood, smiling. 'Can I help you find something?'

The father's expression turned to a look of guarded relief. The boy, on the other hand, averted his eyes towards a shelf of boxed software.

Not very sociable, that one.

'My son's been asking for a computer,' the father said, a thin smile on his face. 'But to be honest, I have absolutely no idea what to get.'

'Do you know how he'll be using it?' Tomohiko asked, glancing at the kid.

'How're you going to use it?' the father asked.

'Word processing, message boards, that kind of stuff,' the boy replied quietly, still looking down at the floor.

'Any games?' Tomohiko asked.

The boy gave an almost imperceptible nod.

'Well ...' He looked back at the father. 'What's your budget?'

'I was hoping we could get away with something around a hundred thousand yen.'

'A hundred thousand isn't going to buy anything, I told you,' the boy said.

'Just a moment,' Tomohiko went back to the computer at his desk and typed something. A list of the store's inventory came up on the screen. 'I've got an 88 that should work.'

'Eight-eight?' The father frowned.

'An NEC-88 series. It just went on sale in October. The price for the computer body is about a hundred thousand, but I think I can cut it down a bit for you. It's not a bad system. The CPU clock runs at fourteen megahertz, and it has sixty-four kilobytes of RAM, standard. Add a monitor, and I can probably get that for you at around a hundred and twenty thousand.'

Tomohiko picked a brochure off the shelf behind him and handed it to the father. He took it, leafed through the pages, and passed it to his son.

'You need a printer?' Tomohiko asked the son.

'Yeah, probably,' he muttered.

Tomohiko went back to their stockroom list.

'I have a Japanese thermal that runs at about sixty-nine thousand eight hundred.'

'So a hundred and ninety thousand altogether?' The man made a sour face. 'That's way over budget.'

Tomohiko grinned sheepishly. 'Actually, you'd also have to get some software to go with that.'

'Software?'

'Programs to make the computer run. Without those, it's just a box. Unless you program?' He glanced at the boy, who didn't respond.

'You mean those don't come with the computer?'

'Not usually. You need different programs for different uses, so not everyone wants the same package.'

The man grunted.

'We can probably throw in a standard word-processing program, though,' Tomohiko said as he punched some numbers into his calculator. He showed the resulting number to the father: 199,800. 'How about this for a total? You won't get a better deal anywhere else, I guarantee it.'

The man frowned, clearly unwilling to part with that kind of cash.

His son, however, was thinking in entirely the opposite direction. 'How about the NEC-98?'

'The 98 series runs at at least three hundred thousand yen. With peripherals, you're looking at a price tag of over four hundred thousand.'

'Four hundred thousand? For a toy?' The father shook his head. 'Even that 88 thing is overpriced.'

'Well, let me know what you'd like to do. If your budget is fixed at one hundred thousand, I might be able to find something for you, but you'd be losing a lot of functionality. Might have to go with an older model, too.'

The father was clearly struggling, but finally, the pleading look in his son's eyes won him over. He turned to Tomohiko. 'We'll take the 88.'

Leaving Hiroe to handle the payment, Tomohiko left the shop, which was nothing more than a converted apartment. If it hadn't had a 'Limitless Computers' sign on the door, it would have been impossible to distinguish from any of the other units. The unmarked apartment next door served as their stockroom.

The stockroom had a work desk and a simple area for greeting guests with a low table and two sofas. Two men turned to look at Tomohiko when he walked in. One was Ryo, and the other was a man he'd seen a few times named Kaneshiro.

'Sold the 88,' Tomohiko said, showing the slip to Ryo. 'Nineteen ninety-eight with a monitor and printer.'

'Good,' Ryo said. 'More room for the 98s.'

The room behind them was filled with cardboard boxes stacked nearly to the ceiling. Tomohiko checked the numbers printed on the side of the boxes as he walked between the stacks.

'Nice little operation you got here,' Kaneshiro said. 'How many hundred-thousand-yen customers you get a week?' There was a faint mocking tone to his voice. He had turned away so Tomohiko couldn't see his face, but he could picture his smile all the same, with those hollow cheeks, and squinting, sunken eyes. He reminded Tomohiko of a skeleton wearing a grey suit two sizes too big.

'I like keeping things manageable,' Ryo replied. 'Low return, low risk.'

Kaneshiro gave a low, rolling laugh. 'You did well enough for yourself last year, and I didn't hear you complaining then. You wouldn't have got this place open if it wasn't for that job I gave you.'

'Look,' Ryo said, 'I told you I'm not interested in crossing that bridge blindfolded again, now that I know how narrow it is. One misstep, and I lose everything.'

'You're exaggerating. Besides, we're not stupid. Things are under control this time, nothing to worry about.'

'Regardless, I'm not interested. You're going to have to take your business elsewhere.'

Tomohiko wondered what Kaneshiro's business was. A few possibilities occurred to him, none of them particularly legal.

It took him a while to track down all the boxes: a computer, monitor, and printer. Tomohiko carried them to the door one at a time. Ryo and Kaneshiro had fallen to silently staring at each other, so he didn't get to hear any more of their conversation.

'Ryo,' Tomohiko called as he was about to leave. 'Think I can close up shop?'

'Go ahead. Doubt we'll get any more tonight.'

Tomohiko nodded and left. Kaneshiro hadn't looked at his face once during this exchange.

Tomohiko handed the packages to the father and son and started to close the store.

'Want to go get dinner?' he asked Hiroe.

'That guy's here, isn't he,' Hiroe said with a frown. 'The one that looks like a corpse.'

Tomohiko grinned.

'Who is he, anyway?' she asked, frowning. 'What's his connection to Ryo?'

'That's a better topic for somewhere else,' Tomohiko said, putting on his coat.

Outside the shop, Tomohiko and Hiroe ambled down the pavement. December was just getting started, and there were Christmas decorations here and there. Tomohiko wondered what they would do for a Christmas Eve date this year. It was a tradition. Last year, he'd made reservations at a French restaurant in a big hotel, but so far he hadn't had any good ideas. Either way, he'd definitely be spending it with Hiroe – their third Christmas Eve together.

Tomohiko had met Hiroe back in sophomore year in college. He'd had a part-time job at one of the big electronics stores, where he was in charge of microcomputer and word processor sales. At the time, there were very few people with any knowledge of those things whatsoever, so Tomohiko was highly valued. It was supposed to be a behind-the-counter position, but he often did service calls, too, since there was no one else to do them.

He'd picked up the job when Unlimited Designs went on hiatus after their initial success. Companies selling software had sprung up like mushrooms after the rain, trying to jump on the computer game boom, and crapware was ubiquitous. Most of the places had shut down after a wave of customer complaints, and Unlimited Designs had been caught in the backlash.

Tomohiko had been grateful for the break – and the chance to expand his social life. Hiroe worked on the same floor as Tomohiko, selling phones and fax machines. They ran into each other a lot, and began chatting during their breaks. Their first date came about a month later, and before long they were going steady.

Hiroe was not what you would call a beauty. She was short, with a round face, and moved less like a girl and more like a skinny boy. But she had a softness to her manner that put people at ease, and just seeing her made Tomohiko's worries go away.

Their relationship hadn't been all smooth sailing. Two years ago they'd slipped up and Hiroe ended up pregnant. She decided to get an abortion. They lay in bed the night after the operation and he held her body close as tears rolled down her face. But she never once cried about it after that night.

Tomohiko still carried the pregnancy test she'd used in his wallet, a clear tube about the size of a cigarette cut in half. When you looked at it end-on, you could see two concentric red rings on the bottom, which meant positive. Tomohiko carried it with him right next to a pack of condoms as a reminder. He would never put Hiroe through that again.

He'd shown it once to Ryo and much to his surprise, Ryo asked to borrow it 'to show to someone'. He returned it to him a couple of days later without offering any further explanation.

'Men are weak,' Ryo had said off-handedly. 'A woman just has to whisper the word "pregnant" and they'll do anything.'

To this day, Tomohiko had no idea what Ryo had used it for.

Tomohiko and Hiroe went into a tiny bar, already mostly filled with salarymen. The only open table was at the very front. Tomohiko sat across from Hiroe and they draped their coats across the chair next to them. There was a television above his head; he could hear the sounds of a talk show.

A middle-aged woman wearing an apron came to wait on them and Tomohiko ordered two beers and a few dishes. The sashimi at this place was solid and the appetisers were pretty good too.

'I met Kaneshiro last spring,' Tomohiko said, taking a sip of beer to wash down some squid. 'Ryo introduced me to him. He looked a lot healthier back then.'

'A little meat on his bones?'

Tomohiko chuckled. 'Something like that. He was dressing up a little more back then, too. Came on strong, wanting us to write a program for a game.'

'What kind of game?'

'Golf.'

'You mean you wrote a whole game, from the ground up?'

Tomohiko drank down the rest of his beer. 'It was a little more complicated than that.'

His mind wandered back. The whole project had smelled fishy from the get-go. The first thing Tomohiko had seen was the specs for the game and a partially completed program. Kaneshiro wanted them to take what they already had and polish it into working shape within two months.

'Why make it this far and have someone else do the rest?' Tomohiko had asked.

'Because the programmer working on it died. Heart attack. The company didn't have any other good programmers on staff. They got afraid they were going to slip even further behind schedule, and so they brought it to me,' Kaneshiro had told him. Tomohiko remembered how he used to talk: calm, professional. That hadn't lasted very long.

'Well?' Ryo had asked Tomohiko. 'It's unfinished, but the basic system is there. Filling in the missing pieces shouldn't be too hard.'

Tomohiko wasn't as confident. 'What about debugging? We might be able to get the thing working in a month or so, but getting it to run smoothly? That's at least another couple of months.'

'Please, see what you can do,' Kaneshiro had pleaded with them.

'There's no one else I can go to.' It was the only time Tomohiko ever saw him ask nicely.

They took the job. The pay was good, maybe good enough that they could start up Unlimited Designs again.

The game was an ambitious attempt to make the most realistic golf game possible. Players chose clubs and swings based on their position, and checked the lie of the green for putting. In order to get all the nuances rights, Tomohiko and Ryo had to give themselves a crash course in golf. Neither of them had known much about the game to start with.

The story was that the game they made would be available in arcades and cafés. Kaneshiro promised them that if things went well, it could be the next *Space Invaders*.

Tomohiko knew very little about Kaneshiro, mostly because Ryo had neglected to tell him anything about the man. However, after several discussions, it came out that Kaneshiro had some connection to Hiroshi Enomoto – the yakuza who had been dating their old accountant, Namie Nishiguchi, before he was hunting her down.

Namie's murder in a Nagoya hotel had never been solved. The paper trail of illegal transfers had led the police to suspect Enomoto, but there was never any conclusive evidence of murder, or even embezzlement. With Namie dead, it was difficult for the police to make any progress.

Tomohiko was reasonably certain that Enomoto had killed Namie. The lingering question was who had told him she was in Nagoya. Tomohiko had a theory for that one too, but not one he'd ever say out loud.

Tomohiko kept his discussion with Hiroe to the details of the golf game job. While they talked, a sashimi plate and some fried aubergine had arrived at their table.

'So you finished the golf game?' Hiroe asked, cutting into the aubergine with her chopsticks.

'In two months' time, as promised. A month later it was being shipped throughout the country.'

'It sold pretty well, right?'

'How did you know?'

'Because I'd heard of the game. I even played it a few times. I remember the approaches and putting being pretty difficult.'

It was strange to hear Hiroe using golf lingo.

'Well,' he said, 'I'd like to take credit for that, but I'm not sure that the game you played was the one we made.'

'Why not?'

'The golf game sold about ten thousand units across Japan. Except we only made about half of those. The rest were sold by a different company.'

'You mean someone copied you, like with *Space Invaders*?'

'Not quite. With *Invaders*, the copies only came out after the original game was a big hit. But with our golf game, the pirated version came out at almost exactly the same time as the official release from Megahit Enterprises.'

'What?' Hiroe stopped, a piece of aubergine centimetres away from her mouth. 'I'm guessing that wasn't a coincidence?'

'Hardly. Somebody got hold of the program before it was finished and started working on a copy before it was even released.'

'Wait, so which version were you working on? The original, or the copy?' Hiroe said, casting him a dubious look.

Tomohiko sighed. 'Do I even have to say?'

She shook her head. 'No, not really.'

'I still don't know how Kaneshiro got his hands on the program and design docs.'

'I'm surprised there wasn't any backlash.'

'Oh, there was. Megahit scoured the countryside looking for the source of the pirate edition – in vain, ultimately. Whoever was in charge of distribution used some pretty convoluted sales routes.'

Gang channels, he thought to himself. He didn't feel the need to explain that.

'Aren't you afraid you'll get in trouble?'

'So far, so good. If the cops come asking questions, we'll just have to play dumb. I wouldn't even be playing, really.'

Hiroe smiled. 'I had no idea you were involved with such shady dealings.'

'Yeah, well, I've had enough of shady.'

Tomohiko was pretty sure that Ryo had known exactly what the score was from the very beginning. He was far too sharp to let a low-level player like Kaneshiro pull the wool over his eyes. He hadn't seemed particularly surprised when Tomohiko came to him with his belated realisation that they had been making the pirated version of the game.

Tomohiko had to admit he hadn't been that surprised either, not after everything he'd seen Ryo get involved in over the years. Stealing someone's half-finished golf game seemed pretty tame by comparison.

He wondered again how much Ryo had made out of that forged credit card scheme back in the day, the one he'd helped with. He guessed it was considerably more than two hundred thousand yen.

More recently, Ryo had gone on a wiretapping spree. He didn't know who was making requests, or who Ryo was listening in on, but Ryo had come to him several times to talk about methods and technology.

Which was why it was refreshing to see him seemingly satisfied just to keep his computer shop running these days. Tomohiko hoped Kaneshiro didn't bring him anything too enticing – not that Ryo was one to be easily swayed. The problem was, Tomohiko didn't know what Ryo was really thinking, deep down. Ryo was his closest friend, and he didn't know him at all.

Tomohiko took Hiroe to the station and returned to the shop. The lights on the upper floor were on. He went up the stairs, and used his own key to open the door, peering in to see Ryo glued to a computer screen, a can of beer on the table next to him.

'Didn't expect to see you again today,' he said.

'Yeah, I wanted to talk to you about Kaneshiro,' Tomohiko said, pulling a folding chair off of the wall and sitting down. 'What did he want?'

'Money, what else? That golf game gave him a taste, and he's having trouble letting it go.' Ryo pulled the tab off another can of beer and took a slug. There was a small refrigerator by his feet that always contained at least a full case of Heineken.

'So what was it this time?'

'Something ridiculous,' Ryo said, snorting. 'I mean, there's risky, and then there's this. No way I'm touching it.'

Ryo had a hard set to his eyes, like when he was mulling over a problem. He might not be taking on whatever job Kaneshiro had brought, but it had definitely grabbed his interest.

'So, what was it?' Tomohiko asked.

Ryo chuckled. 'You don't want to know.'

Something about the way he said it made Tomohiko narrow his eyes. 'No way. Not the Monster?'

Ryo raised his beer in a mock toast.

Tomohiko sat, speechless.

'The Monster' was their nickname for the most popular game in history: *Super Mario Bros.*, for Nintendo's game console. The thing had stormed the charts, selling out across the country since going on sale in September, to the tune of two million copies and counting. Featuring a charismatic plumber who avoided obstacles and enemies in his quest to rescue a princess, the game had expanded on the simple single-path gameplay of its rivals by introducing numerous shortcuts and sidetracks. There was the element of a treasure hunt to the game as well. Not just the software, but strategy guides and magazines featuring the game were selling like hot cakes and with Christmas looming, sales were steadily on the rise. Tomohiko and Ryo both agreed that the *Mario* boom was here to stay, probably well into the next year.

'So what about *Mario*? Don't tell me he wants us to make a pirate version,' Tomohiko said.

'That's exactly what he wants,' Ryo said, chuckling. 'He's claiming it'd be easy, from a technical standpoint.'

'I don't know about easy, but the finished game *is* out already. You'd just have to copy the data in the cartridge and build a new board. It wouldn't be that hard with the right tools and a workshop.'

'Which is what Kaneshiro wants us to set up for him. He

already has a printer in Shiga prefecture that can do the fake pack-aging and instruction manual.'

'Shiga? Why so far away?'

'Some gang connection, most likely,' Ryo said.

'There's no way they could make it in time for Christmas.'

'He's not even thinking about Christmas. He's after the allowances kids get from their relatives on New Year's. Still, even if we started right now, the fastest they could get product on the shelves would be the end of January. By which time I'm betting that the kids will have blown their cash already.' Ryo grinned.

'If he was going to sell it wholesale, he'd have to find some place willing to pay cash—'

Ryo shook his head. 'That would just get the wholesalers breathing down your neck. You think they're not going to suspect something if someone comes in trying to sell them a whole ship-ment of a sold-out game? Once they check with Nintendo, it's over.'

'So what's the sales route?'

'The black market. And no middlemen, like with *Invaders* or the golf game. He was talking selling it straight to kids.'

'Except they're not, because you said no, right?' Tomohiko asked.

'Of course I did. I'm not going down with that ship.'

'Well, that's a relief,' Tomohiko said, pulling a Heineken out of the fridge for himself. He pulled back the tab, sending a white spray of foam into the air.

The man arrived on a Monday the week after Tomohiko and Ryo had talked about *Super Mario Bros*. Ryo was out on a purchasing run, so Tomohiko was handling all the in-store customers while Hiroe answered the phone. Half their business came from phone enquiries in response to their magazine advertisements. When Limitless first opened at the end of the previous year, it had just been Tomohiko and Ryo, and things frequently got hectic until they took on Hiroe in April.

Tomohiko had just sold an old model for half-price and was

feeling pretty good about himself when the man walked in. He was
of medium height and build, about fifty years old. His forehead
sloped back a little with a receding hairline. What hair remained
was slicked back. He was wearing white corduroy jeans and a black
suede jacket. He took off his gold-framed green-tinted shades and
slid them into his jacket breast pocket. Tomohiko was struck by
how pale the man's face looked. His mouth seemed permanently
fixed in a scowl and the way his lips curled up at the edges put
Tomohiko in mind of an iguana.

He first glanced at Tomohiko before his eyes went to Hiroe,
where they lingered for at least twice as long. Hiroe frowned, and
swivelled her chair so her back was facing him. He then went to
look over the computers and peripherals on the shelves. It was
clear from his expression that he had no intention of buying anything.

'Got any games?' he asked in a gravelly voice.

'What sort of game are you looking for?' Tomohiko asked, playing it by the book.

'A fun game,' the man said, 'like *Super Mario Bros.* Got anything
like that?'

'Sorry, we only carry computer software.'

'That's a shame,' he said, though he didn't look disappointed in
the least. A strange smile came to his lips.

'If that's the case, why not just buy a word processor?' Hiroe was
saying to someone on the phone, a bit loudly. 'Yes, you can save
files on a floppy.' Tomohiko knew what she was doing: she was
trying to send a signal that customers who weren't interested in
what they were selling were wasting their time. The man's mention of *Super Mario Bros.* had Tomohiko thinking he was there for
another reason entirely.

Hiroe hung up the phone and the man looked up, his eyes
going between the two of them, until his eyes settled on Hiroe.
'Ryo here?'

'Ryo?' Hiroe said, shooting Tomohiko a confused look.

'Ryo Kirihara,' the man said. 'He's the manager, isn't he? He
out?'

'Yes, he's out on a call,' Tomohiko said.

The man turned to Tomohiko. 'When's he coming back?'

'I'm not sure. He said he'd be late,' Tomohiko lied. He expected Ryo back any moment, but he was damned if he was going to let this guy meet him.

The man grunted and stared Tomohiko in the eye. Tomohiko resisted the urge to look away.

'Maybe I'll just wait here a bit, then,' the man said after a moment. 'You don't mind?'

'Not at all,' Tomohiko lied again. He really didn't have a choice. Maybe Ryo would have a way of turning the guy out. He wished he had half Ryo's talent when it came to being a hardass.

The man sat on a folding chair near the door. He started to pull a cigarette out of his jacket pocket, saw the no smoking sign, and put it back. A little ring on his pinky finger shone with a platinum gleam.

Tomohiko went back to sorting sales slips, but he kept making mistakes. He could feel the man's eyes on him. Hiroe had her back turned again, looking over orders.

'This is a nice shop,' the man said, looking around. 'Ryo's done well for himself. How's he been doing?'

'He's fine,' Tomohiko replied without looking up.

'Good to hear, good to hear. He always was a tough one.'

Tomohiko looked up. 'How do you know Ryo, exactly?'

'Oh, we go way back,' the man said, a crooked smile on his face. 'I've known him since he was a kid. Him, and his parents.'

'Are you a relative?'

'You could say that,' the man said, nodding at some deep meaning in his own words. He looked up at Tomohiko. 'He still gloomy?'

Tomohiko blinked.

'Gloomy – you know, a cloud hanging over his head?' the man explained. 'With those dark eyes. Never knew what that kid was thinking. I was hoping he'd brightened up along the way.'

'He seems normal enough to me.'

'Normal, huh?' The man chuckled. 'Well, that's good to hear.'

Something about the man's attitude made Tomohiko think that even if he was a relative, Ryo wouldn't want anything to do with him. Presently, the man looked at his watch, slapped his thighs and stood. 'Guess he's not coming. I'll try again later.'

'Want me to give him a message?'

'Nah, that's OK. I'll tell him in person.'

'Should I tell him you came?'

'I said no messages.' The man glared at Tomohiko and headed for the door.

Tomohiko shrugged. Ryo would know who it was when he described him, and besides, the man was leaving.

'Come again any time,' Tomohiko said to the man's back.

The man was reaching for the door handle when it turned on its own, and the door opened inwards. Ryo was standing outside the shop, eyes wide with astonishment. Tomohiko thought he detected the hint of a scowl before Ryo's expression hardened. It was like a shadow had fallen across his face. Tomohiko had never seen Ryo look like that. And yet, a moment later, he smiled.

'Matsuura!'

The man took a step back to let Ryo inside. 'Long time no see. You look good.'

Tomohiko watched as the two shook hands.

'He's an old friend,' Ryo explained before they headed off to the stockroom.

Tomohiko was confused. Ryo was all smiles, but that did nothing to explain the darkness he'd glimpsed the moment he first met Matsuura at the door. The negative energy pouring off of him was almost tangible. Definitely weird.

Later, Hiroe returned from taking tea to the next apartment.

'How were they?' Tomohiko asked.

'Laughing,' she said, shrugging. 'They were telling jokes to each other. Ryo, telling a joke. Can you believe it?'

'I can't.'

'I thought I was hearing things,' Hiroe said, rubbing her ear. 'You find out what this Matsuura wanted?'

She shook her head. 'They kept it to small talk while I was there. Whatever they're really talking about, they didn't want me to know.'

Worry stirred in his chest. Whatever they were discussing on the other side of that wall, it was trouble.

About thirty minutes later, he heard a door open outside. Ten seconds more and the shop door opened and Ryo stuck his head in. 'I'm going to see Matsuura off.'

Tomohiko saw Matsuura behind him, waving as the door closed.

Tomohiko and Hiroe exchanged looks.

'Wonder what that was about?' wondered Tomohiko.

'I've never seen Ryo look like that,' Hiroe agreed, her eyes wide.

Ryo returned a few minutes later. 'Tomohiko,' he said, sticking his head in the door. 'Next door.'

'Yeah, sure,' Tomohiko replied, but Ryo was already gone.

Hiroe raised an eyebrow at Tomohiko but all he could do was shake his head.

In the next apartment over, Ryo was busy opening the windows and airing the place out. The smell of cigarette smoke hung in the air. To Tomohiko's knowledge, Ryo had never let anyone smoke in the stockroom before. A leftover aluminium tray from some instant noodles had served as a makeshift ashtray.

'After all the guy's done for me, I figured I should at least let him light up,' Ryo said, by way of explanation.

First jokes, now he's making excuses?

Once the air was a little fresher and feeling thoroughly like December, Ryo shut the window and took a seat on the sofa. 'I'm sure Hiroe's imagining all kinds of things by this point, so if she asks, tell her Matsuura wanted me to sell him some computers wholesale.'

'Who is he, anyway?' Tomohiko said. 'I can't say I got the best vibes off the guy.'

'An old employee,' Ryo said.

'What, at Unlimited Designs?'

'Not my employee. My dad's. Back at the pawnshop. I told you about that, didn't I?'

Tomohiko nodded, surprised.

'After my father died, he kept working until we finally closed down. If Matsuura hadn't been there, we would've been out on the street.'

Tomohiko wasn't sure what to say. That was more information about Ryo's past in a few words than he'd heard the entire time they'd known each other.

'So what did this benefactor of yours come to talk about? And how did he know you were here, anyway? You call him?'

'No, I didn't know he was coming. He heard I was working here, apparently.'

'From who?'

The corner of Ryo's mouth twisted in a slight smile. 'Kaneshiro.'

Tomohiko frowned.

'Remember we were saying how hard it'd be to sell a pirated version of *Mario*? Well, they found the answer.'

'What's the trick?'

'No trick at all.' Ryo chuckled. 'It turns out their target audience already has a black market all set up.'

'Their target audience? You mean kids?'

'Yeah. Matsuura's a broker for a shady speciality shop these days, dealing in just about everything you can imagine. Whatever they think will sell, they buy. Lately, they've been putting a lot of energy into kids' software. Because *Super Mario Bros.* is so light on the shelves in regular stores, they don't even have to lower prices to move serious units.'

'But where does he source his carts? He got a pipeline to Nintendo or something?'

'Better.' Ryo flashed white teeth. 'Other kids. They shoplift the carts, or steal them from their friends, and bring them in to sell. Matsuura said he has a list of over three hundred of these juvenile offenders. He buys it from them at ten to thirty per cent of retail, and sells at seventy per cent retail.'

'And he wants to sell pirated *Mario* games at his store?'

'Not just at his store. Him and a bunch of like-minded brokers got a network set up. It's a regular pipeline of illicit goods. With a product like *Mario*, he claims he can move five or six thousand without even lifting a finger.'

'Ryo,' said Tomohiko, 'you said you weren't going to do this. You said it was too dangerous, and I *agreed*.'

A wry smile came to Ryo's lips. 'I did. That's why they sent Matsuura to win me over.'

'Please don't tell me it worked.'

Ryo gave a deep sigh. He leaned forward. 'Look, I'm doing this alone. You don't have to be involved at all. In fact, I don't *want* you involved. Hiroe either. Mum's the word as far as she's concerned, got it? '

'Ryo.' Tomohiko shook his head. 'What happened to "too risky"?'

'It's still too risky.'

Tomohiko began to protest, but when he saw the look of resolve in Ryo's eyes, his heart sank. 'OK,' he said, 'I'll help you.'

'No, you won't.'

Tomohiko sighed and looked away. This was not good.

While the rest of the country was shutting down for the year-end holiday, Limitless stayed open until 31 December to court two potential categories of customer: the first being the people who'd waited until the last possible minute to write their New Year's cards and came to buy a word processor in order to make their lives easier; the second small business owners who had to settle accounts at the end of the year, and showed up with a broken computer.

Thus went Ryo's rationale, but the fact was that, after Christmas, hardly anyone came to the shop, aside from the occasional kid who mistook them for a video game store. Tomohiko played cards with Hiroe to pass the time. They lined tricks up on the table and wondered out loud if people would soon stop playing games like Go Fish and Old Maid altogether.

Despite a lack of customers, Ryo kept busy – working on *Super Mario Bros.*, Tomohiko knew. He was already running out of excuses to give Hiroe.

Matsuura showed up again on the twenty-ninth. Hiroe happened to be out at the dentist, so Tomohiko was holding the fort alone. He hadn't seen Matsuura since his first visit to the shop. The man's face was still pale, his eyes hidden behind those green-tinted sunglasses. When Tomohiko told him Ryo was out, he again offered to wait in the folding chair by the door.

Matsuura took off his jacket – dark leather with fur around the collar – and hung it on the back of his chair before taking a look around the shop. 'I'm surprised you're still open this late in the year,' he commented.

Tomohiko told him it was Ryo's policy, and Matsuura laughed, his shoulders shaking a little. 'The boy's got it in his genes. His pops always stayed open until the last possible minute on New Year's Eve. Lots of people cleaning house around then, selling off stuff cheap.'

It was the first time Tomohiko had ever heard anyone other than Ryo talk about his father.

'Were you there when his father died?' Tomohiko asked.

Matsuura swung his eyes around to look at him. 'Ryo tell you about that?'

'A little. He said it was a mugging.'

His dad had been stabbed and left to die – that was about all Ryo had ever said about his father, and that was years ago. The story had piqued Tomohiko's interest, but Ryo had made it clear it wasn't a topic he wanted to discuss.

'I don't know if it was a mugging or not. I just know they never caught whoever did it.'

'I see.'

'He was killed in an abandoned building in the neighbourhood. Stabbed in the chest.' Matsuura frowned. 'They took his money, too. The thing is, he was carrying a lot that day, more than he'd ever had on him. That made the police think it was someone who knew him.' A grim smile had spread across Matsuura's face halfway through his story, prompting a question in Tomohiko's mind.

'Were you a suspect too?'

'For a while,' Matsuura said, his smile growing wider, though there was no warmth in it. 'See, Ryo's old lady was a real looker in those days. When the cops found out there was a single guy working at the pawnshop, well, it got their imaginations all fired up.'

Tomohiko blinked and looked back at him. *They suspected this guy was having an affair with Ryo's mom?*

'Wait, did you ... ?' Tomohiko began.

'Kill him? Absolutely not.'

'I meant about Ryo's mom.'

'Oh,' Matsuura said. He rubbed his chin for a moment then said, 'Nah. I was the hired help, that's all.'

'OK.'

'You don't believe me?'

'No, I believe you,' Tomohiko lied. It was a sure bet there had been something between Matsuura and Ryo's mom, though he fell short of suspecting him of murdering Ryo's father. 'Did they check out your alibi and stuff like that?'

'Of course. I'll give those detectives one thing: they were persistent. At first they didn't like my alibi, but luckily for me someone called the shop right around the time that his father was killed. And once they figured out it wasn't some kinda set-up, they finally gave up.'

'Lucky break for you,' Tomohiko said. The whole thing sounded like a mystery novel. 'How'd Ryo handle it?'

'Oh, everyone sympathised with him. And we told them he was with me and his mom when it happened, so the cops didn't pester him too much.'

Tomohiko raised an eyebrow. 'You told them?'

'Yeah,' Matsuura said, 'we told them he was with us 'cause he *was* with us.' He grinned, showing nicotine-stained teeth. 'Ryo ever tell you anything about me?'

'Well, he said that you worked at his father's pawnshop and that he owed you a lot. That you basically helped raise him, kept food on the table, that kind of thing.'

'He *owes* me, huh?' Matsuura's shoulders shook with a laugh. 'That's rich. He does owe me. More than he thinks.'

Tomohiko was about to ask what that meant when he heard Ryo

say, 'Talking about old times?' Tomohiko looked up to see Ryo standing in the entrance.

'What's the point talking about ancient history?' Ryo asked, undoing his scarf. 'What's done is done.'

'Actually, it was pretty interesting,' Tomohiko said.

'We were talking about alibis,' Matsuura said. 'You remember that detective, Sasagaki? That guy did not know when to give up. All those statements we gave him. I felt like we said the same thing a hundred times.'

Ryo sat down in front of the electric heater in the corner of the shop, warming his hands. He looked around at Matsuura. 'You need something?'

'Nothing particular. Just thought I'd drop by, wish you a Happy New Year.'

'Then maybe I should see you off. Sorry, but we've still got a lot of things that need doing today.'

'We?'

'Me and *Mario*.'

Matsuura chuckled. 'Yes, you do. Everything going well?'

'I'm on schedule.'

Matsuura gave a satisfied nod.

Ryo stood and wrapped his scarf back around his neck. 'We can continue our little chat next time,' Matsuura said to Tomohiko as they left.

It was a short while later when Hiroe came in. She had seen Ryo downstairs, waving off Matsuura's taxi.

'What's Ryo's connection to that guy?' Hiroe wondered. 'I mean, besides the fact that he helped them out after his father died? They seem pretty close.'

Tomohiko shrugged. He was rapidly losing confidence in his earlier conviction that there had been something between Matsuura and Ryo's mom. For one thing, it was hard to imagine Ryo not catching on. And then how could he explain Ryo's friend-liness to Matsuura now?

Hiroe looked up from the office desk. 'Is Ryo not coming back?'

'Maybe not, now that you mention it.'

Tomohiko left the shop and was about to go downstairs when he stopped. Ryo was on the staircase, his back turned to Tomohiko.

Tomohiko almost called out to him, but his voice caught in his throat. There was something odd about Ryo as he stood there looking out of the landing window. The headlamps of passing cars scanned over his body, framing his silhouette. There was a darkness to him that reminded Tomohiko of the time when Matsuura had first walked through their door.

As quietly as he could, Tomohiko went back to the shop.

Business hours at Limitless for the year 1985 ended at six o'clock on 31 December. They did a big clean-up of the office, then toasted the year, just the three of them. Hiroe wanted to know what everyone's New Year resolutions were.

Tomohiko said he wanted to make a computer game that was as much fun as a Nintendo game.

Ryo said he wanted to take time out for walks during the day.

'Miss walking to school?' Hiroe asked, laughing. 'Or are you just not getting enough exercise?'

'Nothing like that.' Ryo shook his head. 'It's just ... sometimes I feel like I spend my life under a midnight sun.'

'Come again?' Tomohiko asked.

Ryo shook his head, finished his Heineken, and looked at them. 'When are you two getting married?'

Tomohiko almost choked on his beer. 'Ah, I guess we haven't really thought about it?'

Ryo reached over and pulled open the drawer of his desk. Inside was a single page of printer paper and a small, flat box. Tomohiko had never seen the box before. It looked old; the corners had been worn smooth.

Ryo opened the box and pulled out a pair of scissors. They were long, with ten centimetres or more just in the blade, and sharp-looking tips. The metal shone with a silvery light, as though newly forged, yet they were clearly antique.

'Wow, nice scissors,' Hiroe breathed.

'They're German,' Ryo said. 'Somebody sold 'em to our pawnshop back in the day.' He picked up his scissors and snapped them open and shut a few times. The intersecting blades made a crisp sound in the silence of the shop.

Picking up the piece of paper, Ryo began to make little cuts, rotating the paper smoothly as he went. Tomohiko's eyes were glued to his fingers as his hands worked in perfect unison.

When he was done, Ryo handed the cut paper to Hiroe.

Her mouth opened in surprise. 'Amazing!'

It was two figures, a boy and a girl, holding hands. The boy was wearing a hat, and the girl had a ribbon in her hair.

'That's real impressive,' Tomohiko said. 'You're a man of many talents, Ryo.'

'Consider it an early wedding present.'

Hiroe thanked him, carefully setting the cut paper on top of a glass case on the table.

'So, Tomohiko,' Ryo said. 'Computers aren't going away any time soon. I'm guessing the shop will make you some good money.'

'What can I say, you run a tight ship,' Tomohiko said.

Ryo shook his head. 'Not me. The fate of this store is on your shoulders.'

'What's that supposed to mean?' Tomohiko laughed. 'Way to put pressure on a guy.'

'I'm not joking.'

'Ryo—'

The phone rang. Even though she was sitting farthest away, Hiroe got up and answered it by force of habit.

'Hello, thanks for calling Limitless.' A cloud came over her face. She handed the receiver to Ryo. 'It's Kaneshiro.'

'On New Year's Eve?' Tomohiko said.

Ryo held the phone up to his ear. 'Yeah? '

A moment passed before Ryo's face hardened. He stood, phone still in hand. His other hand went for the baseball jacket he'd hung on the chair. 'Right. The case and the packages, got it. Thanks.' He set the phone down and turned to them. 'I'm heading out.'

'Where to?'

'I'll explain later,' he said, picking up his scarf and wrapping it around his neck as he walked to the door.

Tomohiko got up to follow him, but Ryo was practically running. He didn't catch up until they were both on the street outside.

'Ryo!' he called out, stopping him. 'What happened?'

'Not what happened. What's going to happen.' Ryo was walking with long strides towards the car park where he kept his work van. 'Someone caught wind of pirate *Mario*. Criminal Affairs is going to raid the factory and the warehouse early tomorrow morning.'

'How'd they find out?'

'Somebody must have snitched.'

'But how could Kaneshiro possibly know that the police are coming?'

'The snitching works both ways.'

They reached the car park. Ryo jumped in the van and keyed the ignition. The engine turned over grudgingly in the cold December air.

'I don't know when I'll be back, so go ahead and close up without me. Don't forget to lock the door. Tell Hiroe whatever you need to.'

'You sure you don't need me to go with you?'

'Like I said, I don't want you anywhere near this.'

With a squeal of tyres, Ryo drove the van out of the car park, quickly disappearing into the night.

Tomohiko went back to the shop and found Hiroe waiting for him, a worried look on her face.

'Where'd Ryo run off to?'

'Some arcade game subcontractor found a problem in the code on a machine Ryo worked on before.'

'They found a bug on New Year's Eve?'

'This is big business time for game makers. Guess they wanted to get it sorted out before shops open back up after the break.'

Tomohiko was pretty sure that Hiroe wasn't buying the story, but at least she didn't press for more information. She frowned and looked out of the window.

Tomohiko and Hiroe turned on the television and watched some of the year-end retrospectives. There was a shot of the Tigers' manager being lifted into the air by his team – footage Tomohiko had seen at least a dozen times already. They sat barely saying a word, though Tomohiko felt sure Hiroe was as unable to focus on the TV as he was.

Ryo showed no signs of coming back.

'You should probably head home,' he said at length. The *Kohaku Utagassen* 'song battle' – an annual tradition on NHK public TV that brought all of the year's big acts together on one stage – was just starting up.

'I guess.' Hiroe hesitated for a bit. 'Are you going to wait for him?'

Tomohiko nodded.

'Keep warm, OK?'

'Thanks.'

'What about later?' she asked.

'I'll be over. Might be a little late, though.'

'OK. I'll get some soba noodles ready. It's tradition.' She slid into her coat and headed out of the shop.

Alone, Tomohiko's imagination ran wild. He half expected the police to break down the door. At some point he noticed that the programmes had gone from retrospectives to New Year's celebrations. He called Hiroe at her apartment and apologised that he might not be able to make it after all.

'Ryo not back yet?' she asked.

'No. Sounds like he's having a bit of trouble. I'm gonna wait just a little longer. Don't wait up for me.'

'I'm fine. I've got some movies to watch,' she said, the forced cheer plain in her voice.

Tomohiko was watching a movie himself, just after three in the morning, when the door to the shop opened. Ryo stood in the doorway, a sour look on his face. Tomohiko took one look at him and gaped. His jeans were covered with mud and the sleeve of his baseball jacket was ripped. He was holding his scarf in one hand.

'What the hell happened to you?'

Ryo didn't answer. He looked exhausted. He squatted down on the floor and hung his head.

'Ryo—'

'Go home,' Ryo said, his eyes closed.

'But—'

'Go. Home.'

Tomohiko shrugged and got his stuff together. All the while, Ryo sat unmoving.

'OK, I'll see you,' Tomohiko said. Ryo didn't answer.

Just as Tomohiko opened the door, Ryo called his name from behind.

'Yeah?'

Tomohiko turned, but Ryo just sat there staring at the floor. Just when Tomohiko was about to say something, Ryo said, 'Happy New Year.'

'Yeah, you too. You should go home and get some sleep.'

Ryo didn't answer.

Shrugging, Tomohiko opened the door and stepped out of the shop.

The discovery of a large volume of pirated copies of *Super Mario Bros.* was in the morning paper on 3 January. The cartridges had been found in a car park by the house of a videogame wholesaler who had gone missing.

Tomohiko's best guess was that the wholesaler was Matsuura. The police didn't know anything about the creation of the pirated software or the intended sales route, other than that yakuza were probably involved. Ryo's name was nowhere in the article.

Tomohiko tried calling Ryo at home, but no one picked up.

On 5 January, Limitless opened as scheduled. Ryo still hadn't shown up, so Tomohiko and Hiroe worked purchasing and sales themselves. It was still winter vacation from school, so they had a lot of high school customers.

Tomohiko called Ryo's apartment several times that day, but no one ever answered.

'You think something happened to him?' Hiroe asked.

'Knowing him, it's probably nothing to worry about,' Tomohiro assured her. 'I'll drop by his place on the way home.'

'Yeah, good idea,' Hiroe agreed, her eyes straying to Ryo's usual seat. His scarf was hanging from the back of the chair – the one he'd been wearing on New Year's Eve.

A tiny frame Hiroe had brought in hung on the wall just above the chair. Inside the frame she'd placed the intricate paper cut-out Ryo had made of the boy and girl holding hands.

A sudden thought struck Tomohiko and he opened the drawer to Ryo's desk. The box with the scissors was gone. For the first time it occurred to Tomohiko that he might not see Ryo again.

That day after work, Tomohiko stopped by Ryo's apartment. The shades were drawn and all the lights were off. He knocked on the door and rang the bell half a dozen times but there was no hint of anyone inside.

The next day, and the day after that, Ryo didn't come in to work. Eventually, his phone was disconnected. Tomohiko paid a visit to his apartment and found several men he'd never seen before loading his furniture and appliances into a truck.

'What are you doing?' he asked one of the men who looked like he might be in charge.

'Cleaning out this apartment. Got a request from the owner.'

'And who are you?'

'Handyman service,' the man said, giving Tomohiko a suspicious look.

'Did Ryo move?'

The man lifted an eyebrow. 'Ryo?'

'The guy who lived here.'

'Must have, if he's cleaning out the place.'

'You know where he's moved to?'

'We haven't heard anything about that.'

Tomohiko frowned. 'Aren't you taking the stuff somewhere?'

'Actually, we were told to get rid of it all.'

'Get rid of it? Everything?'

'Everything.' The man turned to shout some instructions to the rest of the crew. 'Sorry, but we're a little busy here.'

When Hiroe heard the news, the bewilderment showed on her face. 'Why didn't he say anything?'

Tomohiko shook his head. 'I'm sure Ryo's got a plan – he always does. We're just going to have to stick it out in the meantime and see what we can do by ourselves.'

'You think he'll call?'

'Of course he will. We just need to hang on till he does.'

Hiroe nodded, though she didn't look convinced.

Five days after they reopened, a man dropped by the shop in the afternoon. He looked around fifty, wearing an old herringbone jacket. He was tall for his age, with broad shoulders. There was a keenness to his eyes and a softness to his smile that Tomohiko immediately liked, even as he realised the man had not come shopping for a computer.

'You run this place?' the man asked looking over at him.

'Yes,' Tomohiko told him.

The man nodded. 'You're awfully young. Same age as Ryo, are you?'

Tomohiko's eyes widened a little.

'I've got a few questions, if you have a moment.'

'Sorry, were you looking for something?'

The man shook his head. 'I'm not a customer.' He pulled a police badge out of his jacket.

Tomohiko remembered when the detectives visited him back in high school. The man standing in front of him gave off the exact same aura they had. Tomohiko was glad he'd come while Hiroe was out.

'You here about Ryo?'

'OK if I sit down?' the man said, indicating the folding chair directly in front of Tomohiko.

'Be my guest.'

'Thanks.' The man sat, leaning back in the chair. He took a look around the shop. 'Quite the selection of stuff you have here. So kids actually buy these things?'

'We have a lot of adult customers as well, but they range as young as middle school.'

The man shook his head. 'The world never stops changing. I can't keep up.'

'Sorry, what did you want to ask me about?' Tomohiko asked, a little anxious.

The detective smiled, enjoying Tomohiko's discomfort. 'Your manager, Ryo Kirihara. You know where he is?'

'Did you need him for something?'

'I had some questions for him,' the detective said, smiling. 'He moved out of the apartment he'd been renting since last year; the place is stripped bare. Which brings me here, to you.'

Tomohiko had already decided he wouldn't gain much by misleading the guy. 'Actually, we've been wondering where he is, too. It's tough having your manager suddenly disappear on you.'

'When'd you last see him?'

'New Year's Eve. He closed up shop with us.'

'You talk to him since? A phone call, maybe?'

'Nope.'

'So he just up and vanished, without a word to his friends. Seems strange to me.'

'Strange isn't the half of it. We're kind of in a tight spot here.'

'I don't doubt it,' the detective said, rubbing his chin. 'You notice anything different about Ryo the last time you saw him?'

'Nothing particular,' Tomohiko said with a shrug, careful to keep his tone as casual as before. 'He seemed the same as always.'

The detective put his hand in his jacket pocket and pulled out a photograph. 'Ever seen this man?'

It was a shot of Matsuura from the waist up.

Tomohiko only had a second to decide how he was going to respond. *The fewer lies the better.*

'That's Matsuura. Didn't he used to work for Ryo's family?'

'He ever been by here?'

'A few times, yeah.'

'What about?'

Tomohiko shrugged. 'The only time I talked to him was the first time he came. He said he looked up Ryo for old times' sake.'

The detective gave Tomohiko a penetrating stare. Tomohiko met it without blinking.

'Did you see any change in Ryo the day Matsuura showed up? Anything at all that got your attention?'

'Not really, no. He seemed happy to see him. They talked like it'd been a while.'

'A while? That right?' The detective's eyes sparkled.

'Yeah.'

'You don't remember exactly what they were talking about, do you? Anything about the old days?'

'I didn't hear anything specific. Most of the time I had customers to deal with.'

Instinct told him it was better not to mention overhearing them talking about Ryo's father.

Just then, the door opened and a boy came in. 'Hi,' Tomohiko called out, smiling.

The detective stood. 'Thanks. I'll be back.'

'Has something happened to Ryo?' Tomohiko asked as he was standing.

The detective hesitated a moment before saying, 'I don't know what he's done, not yet. But he's got himself involved in something.'

'Something?'

The detective ignored him. He was looking up at the paper cutout in the frame on the wall. 'Ryo make that?'

'Yes.'

'The kid hasn't lost his touch. A boy and a girl holding hands? Cute.'

It occurred to Tomohiko that whatever the detective was here about, it went much deeper and much older than pirate *Mario*.

'Sorry to take your time,' the detective said, walking towards the door.

'Excuse me, sir?' Tomohiko said to his back. 'Might I ask your name?'

He stopped and looked around. 'Sasagaki,' he said, then with a wave of his hand he walked out of the door.

Tomohiko pressed his fingers to his forehead. Hadn't Matsuura mentioned a Sasagaki? Could he have been the detective who'd pestered them about their alibis all those years ago?

Tomohiko sighed and looked up at the paper cut-out. That and the scarf were the only things Ryo had left behind.

NINE

Monday mornings were when most managers in Tozai Automotive's Tokyo headquarters held their weekly meetings. The division chiefs would relate any news from the upper management meeting the week before and if any team leaders had things to report, this was the time for that, too.

This Monday in mid-April, Nagasaka, the chief of the patent licensing division, was talking about the Great Seto Bridge that had just been completed and opened to traffic the previous week down in the Inland Sea. Together with the Seikan Tunnel which had opened a month ago, connecting the main island of Japan to Hokkaido in the north, Japan was getting smaller, he said, and more people would be driving cars, which meant increased demand for parts and increased competition to supply those parts. The 'Japan getting smaller' bit was doubtless a phrase he had picked up in the management meeting.

When the meeting was over, everyone went back to their seats and started work. Some were manning the phones, others pulling out documents, and others hurrying out of the door. An average Monday morning.

Makoto Takamiya started his day just like any other. He began by cleaning up the patent applications he'd left from Friday. In order to give himself something to warm up with, he liked putting off less pressing work until the next week. Yet before he could even finish that much, the E team was ordered to assemble. The call came from Narita, who had just been promoted at the end of the previous year.

The E team was the group responsible for everything electronic: electrical systems, electrodes, and computers. There were five of them working under Narita.

They gathered around the boss's desk.

'This one's important,' Narita said, his expression a little hard. 'It has to do with our manufacturing expert system. You all know what that is?'

Everyone nodded except Yamano, a new recruit, who said, a little sheepishly, 'Sorry?'

'Do you know what an expert system is?' Narita asked.

'I've heard the term, but that's about it.'

'How about AI?'

'Artificial intelligence, sure,' Yamano said, though he didn't sound all that confident.

The world of computing had been making rapid advances, in particular in the field attempting to make computers function more like human brains. For example, when two people passed on the street, they didn't calculate the distance between them in order to avoid a collision. Rather, they used experience and intuition to adjust their speed and bearing. Adding that kind of flexible thinking and decision-making to computers was the goal of AI.

'Expert systems are one application of AI – in effect an attempt to replace experts in certain fields,' Narita explained. 'Now, a human expert in a particular field isn't just a walking bag of facts; they have the know-how to use those facts. If you can build that know-how into a system along with all the relevant data, and teach someone how to use it, then even a novice can make decisions like a pro – that's what an expert system lets businesses do. They're already used in fields like medicine and financial analysis.'

Narita looked at Yamano to make sure he was following.

Yamano nodded, though it was clear he was still a little unsure.

'We've been putting a lot of energy into these systems here over the last two or three years. Our company's been growing rapidly and there's a real age gap between our veterans and our new recruits. That means when our veterans hit retirement age we're going to lose all of our experts. Particularly in metallurgy, heat management and chemical processes in manufacturing, we need the knowledge and know-how of professionals, which makes losing our veterans really hard. Which is why we're building an expert system now so even our younger technicians can handle the job.'

'And that's your manufacturing expert system?'

'Precisely. We've been developing it in tandem with the manufacturing technology and systems development divisions. It's already on their workstations and usable, or it was supposed to be,' Narita said. 'Right?' He looked at the other three.

'It should be working,' Makoto said. 'You need a tech password in order to use it, though.'

The technological information search password was what kept the company's proprietary information out of the hands of anyone outside the company and any employee who didn't have clearance. Makoto's patent division members all had access because they needed to be able to search patent information to do their jobs.

'Anyway, that's enough explanation,' Narita said, lowering his voice. 'That doesn't have much to do with us. Since the manufacturing expert system is only being used within the company, it won't affect us in patents. At least, it shouldn't have.'

'But something happened?' one of the men asked.

Narita nodded. 'They just had a visit from somebody in system development. Apparently, there's a computer program that's been making the rounds of several mid-level manufacturers. A metallurgy expert system.'

Everyone exchanged glances.

'Is there some problem with the software?' Makoto asked.

Narita leaned forward. 'Someone on the team got a copy and systems development and manufacturing tech were looking through the program and they found some data that looked a whole lot like the metallurgy component of our manufacturing expert system.'

'Did someone leak our program?' one of Makoto's superiors asked.

'We can't say for sure, but it's definitely a possibility.'

'And we don't know who's distributing the software?' Makoto asked.

'No, we do. It's a software company in the city. In Tokyo. They were handing it out as PR.'

'PR?'

'Yeah, it's a demo version, apparently, with only a small subset of the usual data. You try it out and if you like it you buy the full package.'

Makoto nodded. It sounded like samples a cosmetics company might send out.

'The problem is,' Narita continued, 'in the event that part of our system did get leaked, and they designed their program based on our data, how do we prove it? And once we do, can we use legal means to shut them down?'

'And we're going to be looking into that?' Makoto asked.

Narita nodded. 'There's early precedent for enforcing copyright on software. But it's very hard to prove whether the contents were copied or not. It's a bit like plagiarism – it's hard to draw the line between coincidental similarity and theft. But we have to do what we can.'

'Yes, but,' Yamano said, 'if our expert system did get leaked, how did it happen? I thought all of our technical information was kept under lock and key.'

Narita grinned. 'There's an interesting story there about a certain company that developed a new kind of turbocharger. They made each of the components – all top secret – and after months they finally had a prototype put together. Then two hours later' – Narita leaned closer to Yamano – 'the exact same turbocharger arrived on the desk of the section chief in charge of turbo engine development at a rival company.'

Yamano's eyes went wide. 'Just like that?'

Narita was still smiling. 'That's the development race for you.'

Makoto smiled wryly at the naivety of the new recruit. He could sympathise – he'd heard a similar tale not long before.

It was a little after eight o'clock by the time Makoto returned to his apartment in Seijo. They had already started analysing the expert system, and that meant mandatory overtime.

When he opened the door, he thought he probably should have worked a little longer. It was pitch black inside the apartment.

He went through the foyer, hallway, and living room, turning on the lights in each room. Even though it was already April, the house had sat cold all day, and he could feel the chill of the floor even through his slippers.

Makoto took off his coat, sat down on the sofa, and loosened his tie. He picked a remote control off the table and pressed the big red button. Several seconds later, an image of a mangled railcar resolved on his thirty-two-inch big-screen TV. He'd seen the footage several times already, a news report of a train collision in a Shanghai suburb last month. The programme seemed to be talking about the aftermath of the accident. A hundred and ninety-three Japanese students on a school trip from a private high school in Kochi Prefecture had been on board. Twenty-six of them and the student leading the trip were dead.

The reporter was saying that talks between Japan and China on compensation for the loss were stagnating.

Makoto changed the channel, hoping to catch a ball game, but then remembered it was Monday and turned off the TV. The house felt even quieter than it had before he turned it on. He looked at the clock on the wall. The clock face had a floral pattern – it had been a wedding gift – and it read 8.20.

Makoto stood, undid the buttons on his shirt, and poked his head into the kitchen. It was spotless, not a single dirty dish in the sink, and the well-arranged utensils all glittered as if brand new. But he was less concerned with the cleanliness of the kitchen than learning what his wife was going to do about dinner that night. He wanted to know if she had made something before she went out, or was planning on cooking something when she came back. From the look of the kitchen, the answer was the latter.

He looked at the clock again. Only two minutes had passed.

Pulling out a ballpoint pen, he wrote a large X on today's date on the wall calendar to mark that he'd come home first. He'd started with the marks this month. He hadn't told his wife what they meant yet. He was saving that for the right time. It wasn't a particularly nice thing to do, but he felt that he had to record what was going on in some objective fashion.

There were already ten X marks on the page, and they were only halfway through the month.

He regretted for at least the hundredth time having permitted her to work and, at the same time, he hated himself for being so petty.

It had been two years since he married Yukiho.

As Makoto had expected, she was the perfect wife. She was good at everything, and everything she touched turned to gold. He was particularly impressed with her cooking. She was equally at home making French, Italian or Japanese, and it was always indistinguishable from something you might have in a restaurant.

'I hate to say this, but you are the century's most lucky man,' a friend said. Makoto had invited some people over to the house for a party after they got married. 'A beautiful bride, and yet she's not content to just be beautiful. She's also an amazing chef. When I think I live in the same world as you, I hate myself.' The sentiment – and the jealousy that lay beneath – was shared by the other guests.

Makoto praised her cooking too. For the first few months after they'd got married, he made a comment almost every day.

'My mother used to take me to some pretty good restaurants,' she responded the first time he paid her the compliment. 'I think you have to eat delicious things when you're young to have a true appreciation for food.' She blushed. 'So I'm glad you like mine.'

The shyness with which she had said it only endeared her to him more.

And yet those halcyon early days of their marriage were over in the space of about two months. It all started with a seemingly innocuous conversation.

'What do you think about playing the market?'

'The stock market?'

For a second, he didn't even know what she was talking about. Back then, the stock market had seemed so far removed from their lives. He was more bewildered than surprised.

'What do you know about stocks?'

'Quite a bit. I've been studying.'

Yukiho pulled several books on buying and selling stocks for beginners off of the bookshelf. Makoto didn't do a lot of reading, so he'd never even noticed them.

'Why do you want to buy stocks?' Makoto said, changing tack.

'It's just I have so much extra time sitting at home doing house-work. And the market's really good right now. It's a lot better than just parking the money in a bank somewhere.'

'Yes, but it's not without risk.'

'That comes with the territory. That's why they call it "playing" the market,' she said, smiling brightly. 'It's just a game.'

That turn of phrase – 'it's just a game' – troubled Makoto. He couldn't put his finger on it, but it almost felt like he'd been betrayed.

What she said next only strengthened that impression. 'It's OK. I know I won't lose. And I'll just use my own money anyway.'

'Your own money?'

'I have a little savings.'

'Well, I know that, but—'

He didn't like that expression either – her own money. They were married. Didn't their money belong to both of them?

'No?' Yukiho said, looking up at him. Makoto didn't say any-thing, and she sighed.

'I know, I know. I haven't even really come into my own as a housewife. I probably shouldn't start running off to other things quite so soon. I'm sorry. I won't mention it again.' Shoulders sag-ging, she picked up her books on stock trading and put them back on the shelf.

Makoto watched her thin frame from behind and thought what an ungenerous man he was. She'd never really asked him for any-thing before now.

'I have a few conditions,' he said. 'Don't go too deep, and never borrow money. Can you live with those?'

Yukiho turned around. Her eyes were sparkling. 'Really, you mean it?'

'Only if you can promise to follow the rules.'

'I will, I promise, thank you,' she said, hugging him.

And yet, as he put his hands around her narrow waist a bad premonition crept over him.

As it was, Yukiho kept her promise to him. She played the market and their fortune grew. Makoto didn't know how much money she started with, nor how much training she did. Yet whenever the stockbroker called the house and he heard them talk, it was clear she was dealing in sums of more than ten million yen.

For a while, her life centred on the stock market. She would go to a brokerage twice a day to keep a handle on the market. And because she never knew when her broker might call, she hardly ever left the house. When she did, she would make a phone call every hour. She read six newspapers, including a financial paper and one aimed at professionals in manufacturing.

'OK, that's enough,' Makoto said one day. Yukiho had just got off the phone with a broker and the phone had been ringing all morning. Normally Makoto would be at work so he didn't care, but that day was the anniversary of the company's founding and everyone had the day off. 'I can't even enjoy my day off. And we can't go anywhere because you're too busy trading. If we can't live a normal life, I don't see what the point is.'

It was the first time he'd ever raised his voice since they'd started dating. It had been eight months since their wedding.

Yukiho stood in silence for a moment, either surprised or in shock. When Makoto saw how pale she looked, he immediately felt sorry.

But before he could apologise, she did. 'I'm sorry. I didn't mean to be ignoring you. Please believe me. I just got carried away, that's all, because things are going well. I'm sorry. I'm a terrible wife.'

'That's not what I meant.'

'No, it's OK, I understand,' she said, picking up the receiver. She called the broker and, right then and there, told him to sell all of her stocks.

When she hung up, she turned around to look at Makoto. 'I can't do anything about the investment trusts right away. I'm so sorry.'

'Are you sure you're OK with this?'

'I'm fine. It feels good, to be honest. And I can't believe I was ruining your life over it.'

Yukiho sat down on her knees on the carpet and looked down at the floor. Her shoulders were trembling. A tear fell on the back of her hand.

'Let's not talk about it any more,' Makoto said, putting his hand on her shoulder.

The next day, everything in the house having anything to do with stocks was gone. Yukiho didn't even talk about them.

And yet it was clear that the spring had gone out of her step. She seemed bored. Because she wasn't going out, she stopped putting on make-up, and she hardly ever went to the beauty salon.

'Wow, I look terrible,' she said once, looking into the mirror and laughing weakly.

Makoto had even recommended she try taking some courses at a community college, but she didn't seem that interested in learning anything. She'd been taking tea ceremony, flower arrangement, and English lessons since she was in school – maybe that had something to do with it.

He knew what they really needed to do was have children. Raising a child would steal away all of that free time overnight. And yet, they couldn't. They stopped using birth control half a year after the wedding, but Yukiho showed no signs of getting pregnant.

Makoto's mother wasn't pleased. It was her belief that couples should have children early, when they were still young. She had, on more than one occasion, suggested they pay a visit to the doctor.

Makoto wanted to, too, for that matter. He even suggested as much to Yukiho, but she refused outright, an unusual move for her. When he asked her why, she said, her eyes a little red, 'What if the operation I had made it so I can't have kids? I don't think I could live with myself.'

'Even if that's what it is, we should find out. It might be something they can fix.'

But she only shook her head. 'Fertility treatments don't really work, you know. And if we can't have kids, so be it. Unless you don't want to be with a woman who can't bear children.'

'That's not what I'm saying. I don't care about children,' he sighed. 'Fine, we won't talk about it.'

Makoto understood how horrible it was to badger a woman about not being able to have a family, so he hardly ever mentioned it after that conversation. To his mother he said that they had both gone to the hospital, she'd had a check-up, and there were no problems.

But sometimes he would catch Yukiho muttering to herself, 'Why can't I have children?' And every time, the next thing she would say was, 'Maybe I shouldn't have had that abortion.'

All Makoto could do was listen in silence.

Makoto was lying back on the couch, staring up at the ceiling, when he heard the front door open. He sat up a little. The clock on the wall read nine.

He heard footsteps in the hall and the door flew open.

'Sorry I'm so late!'

Yukiho came in wearing a moss-green suit, juggling two paper sacks in her right hand and two plastic bags from the supermarket in her left. She even had a black shoulder bag over one arm.

'You must be starving! I'll get something ready right now.'

She put the grocery bags down on the kitchen floor and went into the bedroom, leaving a trail of perfume in her wake.

Several minutes later she came back out in her regular clothes, an apron in one hand. She tied it on as she went into the kitchen.

'I brought something we can eat right away, so it won't take that long. And there's some canned soup, too,' she called from the kitchen, still catching her breath.

Makoto had just started reading the newspaper but unexpectedly he felt anger growing inside him. He wasn't even sure what it was. If he had to say, it was her damn cheerfulness.

Makoto put down the newspaper and stood. He headed for the kitchen where he heard her bustling as she worked.

'Dinner out of a can again?'

'Sorry, what was that?' Yukiho asked over the din of the kitchen fan. That annoyed him even more.

Makoto stood in the entrance of the kitchen. Yukiho was boiling some water on the gas stove and looked at him curiously.

'After you made me wait that long, you're going to give me something reheated on the stove?'

Her mouth opened. She reached up and turned off the kitchen fan. Silence descended on the room.

'I'm sorry. Are you mad?'

'It would be one thing if this just happened every now and then,' Makoto said, 'but lately it's been every night. You come home late, and start with the can opener. Over and over.'

'I'm sorry. I just didn't want you to have to wait any longer—'

'Oh, I've already waited. More than enough. I was about to make myself some instant ramen. Of course, if you're just going to slap something out, I probably should've gone with the ramen.'

'Sorry. I know this isn't much of an excuse, but I've just been so busy – I know I haven't been treating you well.'

'Well, I'm glad business is going so great,' he said, feeling his mouth twisting into an ugly smile.

'Don't be like that. I really am sorry. I'll be more careful in the future,' she said, putting her hands on her apron and bowing her head.

'That's what you say every time,' Makoto spat, jamming his hands into his pockets.

Yukiho stood quietly, head drooping. What could she have said, anyway? *Maybe*, Makoto thought, *she's just waiting for the storm to pass*.

'Why don't you quit?' Makoto asked. 'It's impossible to be a housewife and hold a job at the same time. It must be hard for you, too.'

Yukiho didn't say anything.

Her shoulders began to shake. Grabbing the edge of her apron, she pressed it to her face. He heard a sob come from between her hands.

She apologised again. 'I know I'm no good. I really know. I'm just causing trouble for you. You're letting me do whatever I want to, and I'm not repaying you at all. I'm just, I'm no good as a human being. Maybe you shouldn't have married me,' she said, hiccuping between sobs.

Which of course meant that Makoto couldn't press her any harder. In fact, once again, he started to feel foolish for getting angry over something so small.

'Whatever, it's fine,' he said, putting away his anger like a sword into its sheath. Yukiho never talked back, so it never became a fight.

Makoto went back to the sofa and opened the paper. Yukiho called from the kitchen, 'Makoto?'

'Yeah?' He looked over at her.

'What about dinner tonight? I mean, I'd make something, but I don't have much on hand.'

'Oh,' Makoto said, his whole body feeling dull and weary. 'It doesn't matter. Let's eat whatever you bought.'

'You're sure?'

'There's nothing else, right?'

'I'll have it ready soon,' she said, disappearing into the kitchen.

Hearing the kitchen fan whirr back to life, Makoto shook his head, feeling like nothing had been settled at all.

About a month after their first wedding anniversary, Yukiho had surprised Makoto by asking if she could get a job. One of her friends in the apparel business was striking out and opening a shop on her own, and she had asked Yukiho if she wanted to be co-manager. Makoto asked her if it was something she really wanted to do and Yukiho said she did.

It was the first time he'd seen that look in her eyes, that sparkle, since she gave up on the stock market. When he saw that, he couldn't say no.

He admonished her not to overextend herself, and Yukiho expressed her joy in a stream of thank-yous.

The new store was in South Aoyama, a trendy part of town. The whole front of the shop was a wall of glass, giving it a bright atmosphere and allowing passers-by to look in and see the wares from the street. Makoto only learned later that the money they had spent on renovating the place had come from Yukiho.

Yukiho's partner was a woman named Naomi Tamura. She had a round face and a round body and there was the air of a commoner about her. True to her looks, she was a hard worker. At the shop Yukiho handled the customers, and Naomi brought out clothes and worked the register.

The shop saw customers by reservation only. In addition to giving the mystique of exclusivity, this provided Yukiho and Naomi time to find an outfit to match the customer's size and taste. It also allowed them to avoid having a large warehouse for merchandise, since they only needed to carry items for particular clients.

The question was how well they would be able to leverage their networks in order to bring in customers, but they never seemed to have trouble keeping a steady flow through their door.

Though Makoto worried that Yukiho would spend too much time on her business, it wasn't a problem at first. In fact, she put even more effort into housework after she started at the shop. Every night he returned from work to find a home-cooked meal waiting, and Yukiho rarely came home after Makoto.

However, about two months after the shop opened, Yukiho said something unexpected again. She wanted to know if Makoto wanted to become the owner of the shop.

'Owner? Me? Why?'

'The landlord's looking for money to pay off some inheritance tax and he asked us if we wanted to buy the place.'

'Do you want to?'

'More than that, I think it would definitely be the right move. With that location there's no chance the price will go down. And the number he's quoting is, frankly, a steal.'

'And if I don't buy it?'

'Then we really wouldn't have any other choice, I guess.' She sighed. 'I'd have to buy it myself.'

'You?'

'I'm sure the bank would lend me money for that location.'

'So you'd borrow money to buy the shop? You want it that badly?'

'If we don't buy it the owner's only going to try to sell it to someone else. We might even lose our lease. If they can get us out of there and tear the place down they can sell it for a lot more.'

Makoto thought for a while.

It wasn't out of their reach financially. Makoto's family had several plots of land in Seijo, all of which Makoto was set to inherit. He could sell off some of those and purchase the shop easily. If he proposed it in the right way, he didn't think his mother would object, either. As it was, they hardly used the land anyway.

On the other hand, he was opposed to Yukiho borrowing any money – if she did, he was afraid he would lose her to work entirely. Also, something didn't sit well with him with the idea of her owning a shop in her own name.

He asked her to let him think about it for a couple of days. Though, in truth, he had already made up his mind. Hardly a month into 1987, the shop in Aoyama was his. Rent from Yukiho's business now came into his account.

It was only a short while afterwards that Makoto learned how right Yukiho had been.

High demand for office space in central Tokyo led to rampant price hikes. Land increased by as much as two or three times in value in the space of weeks. Makoto received several offers to sell the shop and land, and whenever he heard the asking prices he had to pinch himself wondering if it all was real.

This was around the time that he developed a slight inferiority complex towards Yukiho. He began to think that in the home, in business, and more than anything else in sheer guts, he lacked what she had. He would never be her equal. He had no way of knowing directly how well she was doing in business. However, it was clear that growth was steady. She was already planning to open a second shop in Daikanyama.

Makoto lacked the courage to start something new. All he could do was cling to his company job, content to do the bidding of someone else. He had no inspired ideas to turn the land he had inherited to any good use, and he was even living in an apartment given him by his parents.

The stock boom of the year before only compounded his sense of failure. In February of the previous year, NTT had made its initial public offering, starting a new stock bubble in the process. It was common knowledge that anyone with any money had to be in stocks.

And yet they hadn't benefited from the boom at all, because he had criticised Yukiho for getting involved. She never talked about stocks after that. Yet just thinking about what must have gone through her mind when she saw prices taking off made him uncomfortable.

'Golf lessons?' Makoto looked over at his wife's face in the dresser mirror. He was lying in his bed, a semi-double. Her bed was a single. They'd slept in separate beds since moving in together.

'I thought if we went on Saturday nights we could go together,' Yukiho said, laying down a pamphlet in front of him.

'Since when are you interested in golf?'

'A lot of women are doing it now. It's great for couples, too. It'd be fun if we did it together.'

'Yeah.'

Makoto's late father had loved golf. Practically every day he had off, he loaded his large golf bag into the trunk of the car and headed out to the country club. Makoto remembered how lively his father looked at those times. Maybe he just liked getting out of the house, since he lived with his wife's family.

'There's an information seminar next Saturday. Let's go,' Yukiho said, getting into her own bed.

'Sure, let's go.'

'Great.'

'I have another idea for something we could do together.'

Yukiho laughed and slipped out of her bed, sliding into his.

Makoto reached out and turned down the lights by the head of the bed. He rolled over towards her and put his hands down the front of her white negligée. Her breasts were soft and bigger than you might think to look at them.

Except, his mind was elsewhere. He was hoping there wouldn't be a problem today, as there had been so often recently.

He worked her breasts, looking at her nipples, and then pulled the negligée off over her head. He started to remove his own pyjamas. She hadn't even touched him really, and already he was hard.

Completely naked now, he embraced her. She kept fit, even though he never saw her exercising. When he put his hands around her waist, she wriggled as though she was ticklish. Arms enveloping her, he kissed her neck and nibbled at her breasts.

His hand went to her panties. Lowering them down to her knees, he used his foot to peel them the rest of the way off. This was his usual technique.

He already had a premonition when his hand went to go between her thighs and his fingers brushed her pubic hair.

She wasn't wet at all. He stroked her clitoris, but no matter how gently he moved his fingers, there was no lubrication inside.

Makoto was fairly sure nothing was lacking in his technique. Until only recently, things had worked just fine.

Giving up on the clitoris, he moved his finger down, trying to penetrate her, only to find her closed tightly. When he tried to force his way in, she whispered, 'Ouch.' He could tell she was frowning, even in the dim light.

'I'm sorry, did that hurt?'

'It's OK. Come inside.'

'Not if my finger hurts.'

'No, it's OK, I can deal with it. It hurts more when you go slow like that,' Yukiho said, spreading her legs a little further.

Makoto moved until he was between her legs. Then, holding his penis in one hand, he pushed up against her vagina, thrusting his hips forward.

Yukiho gasped. He saw her gritting her teeth. Makoto blinked. He hadn't pushed that hard. He wasn't even inside.

He tried again and Yukiho groaned strangely.

'What's wrong?' he asked.

'It's just, my stomach hurts.'

'Your stomach?'

'I mean, lower down.'

'Again?' Makoto said.

'I'm sorry. But it's OK, it'll get better.'

'No, it's not OK.' Makoto said, picking up his underpants from the foot of the bed and putting them on. He put on his pyjamas, thinking, 'I guess tonight's a wash too.' This was the way it always seemed to go lately.

Yukiho was putting on her undergarments. She picked up her negligée and went back to her own bed.

'I'm sorry,' she said. 'I don't know what's wrong with me.'

'You know, we really should go see a doctor.'

'I know, it's just—'

'What?'

'I've heard that having an abortion can do this to you. The dryness . . . and the pain.'

'I've never heard of that.'

'Well, why would you have – you're a man.'

'Yeah, but—'

Makoto got the feeling that the conversation wasn't going to go any place good and turned away from her, pulling the covers up. He had already gone soft, but he was still horny. If they couldn't have sex, he at least wanted her to show her affection in other ways, but Yukiho wasn't the type to do that sort of thing. And it was hard for Makoto to ask.

A few minutes later, he heard her sniffling in bed.

It seemed like too much of a chore to try to console her, so he buried his face under the covers and pretended not to hear.

The Eagle Golf Driving Range had been built in the dead centre of a square residential area. A sign out front boasted a longest driving range of two hundred yards and the latest ball delivery system. Inside the green netting, tiny white balls flew in a swarm through the air.

The school was about twenty minutes by car from their apartment. They were there by four-thirty. The information session was from five, according to the pamphlet.

'Guess we got here early. I told you we should have left later,' Makoto said, turning the wheel of the BMW.

'I thought the roads might be crowded. Besides, we can watch other people hit. We might learn something,' Yukiho replied from the passenger seat.

'I'm not sure how watching amateurs practise is going to help.'

The country was in the middle of a golfing boom, and it was Saturday, which meant that the place was packed. You could tell just by looking at the car park, which was almost completely full.

It took some time to find a spot, but he did. The two got out and headed for the entrance. On the way in was a phone booth. Yukiho stopped in front of it.

'If you don't mind, can I make a phone call?' she said, pulling her schedule book out of her bag.

'Fine; I'll go take a look inside.'

'Great,' she said, the receiver already in her hand.

The entrance was as brightly lit as a twenty-four-hour diner and two young women in bright uniforms were greeting customers. A handful of people were killing time on the grey carpet of the lobby.

'Thanks; just write your name here. We'll call you as soon as there's an opening,' one of the employees said. She was talking to a slightly overweight man who didn't look as if he'd had much to do with sports in his life. He had a black golf bag next to him.

'Is it that busy?' the man asked, a scowl on his face.

'Yes, I'm afraid there's a wait of about twenty or thirty minutes.'

'Great,' the man said, grumbling as he wrote his name on the list.

Makoto walked up to the counter and mentioned he'd like to be in the information session. One of the employees told him with a smile that there would be an announcement and to please wait in the lobby.

Yukiho stepped through the doors and quickly walked up to Makoto.

'We have a little bit of a problem,' she said. 'At the shop. I think I should go.' She bit her lip.

On Saturday Naomi and a part-time worker ran things.

'Right now?' Makoto asked. His exasperation was plain in his voice.

Yukiho nodded.

'So what about golf school? You're not even going to stay for the information session?'

'No, I'm sorry, but you can stay. I'll take a taxi and if it's too boring, you can go home.'

'Oh, I will.'

'I'm really sorry. See you,' Yukiho said, taking off for the door.

Makoto watched her go, holding back the anger he could feel rising in his stomach. He knew that if he let it grow it was he who would suffer. He'd already had the pleasure several times.

He passed the time by checking out the golf shop in a corner of the lobby. Looking at the items there didn't do anything to increase his interest in the sport. Makoto hardly knew anything about golf. He had a general grasp of the rules and understood that the goal for most golfers was to get under a hundred on the course. Yet he had no concept of what that really meant or how big a score that one hundred represented.

He was checking out a set of driving irons when he felt someone's eyes on him. A woman was standing next to him in business slacks, facing in his direction.

He looked up and their eyes met.

It took a little while for him to be sure that it really was her before he finally gasped.

He was staring at Chizuru Misawa. She had cut her hair and looked a little different, but there was no mistaking her.

'Chizuru? What are you doing here?' Makoto asked.

'Practising golf,' Chizuru said, showing him the club case in her hand.

'Right, I mean, obviously,' Makoto said, scratching his cheek, even though it didn't itch.

'That's why you're here, isn't it, Mr Takamiya?' she asked.

'Yeah, kind of, I guess.' He was happy that she had remembered his name.

'You here alone?'

'Yes, you?'

'Yeah. Should we sit down?'

They managed to find two empty seats and grabbed them before anyone else came.

'What a surprise, meeting you here,' Makoto began.

'No kidding. For second I thought it was a case of mistaken identity.'

'Where are you these days?'

'Shimokitazawa. I'm working for an architectural firm in Shinjuku.'

'Still doing the temp thing?'

'Yeah.'

'Didn't you say you were heading back to Sapporo when your contract with our company ended?'

'I'm surprised you remember,' Chizuru said, smiling, showing white, healthy teeth. Her smile made Makoto think that short hair suited her well.

'So you didn't go?'

'No, I did, for a little. But I came right back.'

'I see,' Makoto said, looking at his watch. It was already four-fifty. The information session would start in ten minutes. He began to feel rushed.

That day resurfaced in his mind, two years and however many months ago. The night before his wedding to Yukiho, when he had sat there in the lobby waiting for her to show, and she never did.

He had been in love with her, he realised now, ready to give up everything to tell her. In that instant he had truly felt that she was the one he was destined for.

And she never came. He didn't know why. All he knew was that fate had lied. There was nothing fated about it.

But seeing her now, he realised the torch he carried for her had not been entirely extinguished. Just being near her made his heart soar. He felt elated, a sweet elation that he hadn't felt in so long.

'Where do you live these days, Mr Takamiya?' Chizuru asked.

'In Seijo.'

'Right, I think I remember you mentioning that before,' she said. 'It's been two and a half years now, hasn't it. Any kids?'

'No, not yet.'

'Not having them?'

'Not, or can't.' Makoto smiled wryly.

'Oh, I see,' Chizuru said, a look of concern passing over her face. 'How about you? Are you married?'

'No, still single.'

'Any plans?' Makoto said, watching her face intently.

Chizuru smiled and shook her head. 'Nobody to make plans with.'

Makoto felt relief at that, even as he had to ask himself what it mattered to him whether she was single or not.

'Do you come here lots?' he asked.

'Once a week. I've been taking lessons.'

She said she'd been coming for the last two months. She was taking beginner lessons every week on Saturdays at five. The exact same class that Makoto and Yukiho were considering.

Makoto said that he had just come to hear the information session about the same course.

'No kidding?' she said. 'I know that they look for new people every two months or so. So maybe I'll be seeing more of you.'

'I would imagine so,' Makoto said.

Makoto was confused about this coincidence. Mostly because when he came, he would be coming with Yukiho. He didn't want her to meet Chizuru. Nor did he want to tell Chizuru that she was coming either.

Just then they announced that everyone who had come for the information session should go to the reception desk.

'I guess I should get to my lesson,' Chizuru said, picking up her golf bag.

'I'll come see how you're doing afterwards.'

'Oh no, don't, I'd be too embarrassed,' she said smiling, the skin above her nose wrinkling.

When Makoto got home, Yukiho's shoes were in the entranceway. He heard the sound of something frying from inside.

He went into the living room and found Yukiho in the kitchen, apron on, making dinner.

'Welcome back. You're later than I expected,' she said loudly, moving the frying pan as she spoke.

It was already after eight-thirty.

'What time did you get back?' Makoto asked, standing in the entrance to the kitchen.

'About an hour ago. I came home early to make dinner.'

'OK.'

'Hang on, it's almost ready.'

'It's funny,' he said, watching Yukiho in profile as she made her salad. 'I met an old friend today.'

'Really? Someone I know?'

'I don't think so.'

'And?'

'Well, it'd been a while, so we decided to go have a little something to eat, and we ate at a restaurant by the golf place.'

Yukiho's hands stopped. She brought her hand up to her neck. 'Oh.'

'I figured you'd be late. What was the trouble at the shop?'

'Actually, I straightened that out pretty quick,' Yukiho said, rubbing the back of her neck. She smiled weakly. 'But of course you didn't expect me back. Why would you?'

'Sorry. I should've tried to get in touch.'

'Don't worry about it. I'll finish it up, so if you get hungry, go ahead.'

'Thanks.'

'So how was it?'

Makoto grunted non-committally. 'It wasn't anything special. They said they have a particular curriculum, and they follow it to the letter, stuff like that.'

'Did it sound like fun?'

'Kind of,' Makoto said. He wasn't sure how to explain it. Now that he knew Chizuru was going to the golf school, he didn't want to take Yukiho there. He was ready to give up on it, but he wasn't sure how to explain that to Yukiho.

'I don't know ...' he said, searching for the right words, when Yukiho cut him off.

'I know I suggested it, and I might sound silly saying this now, but maybe this isn't the best time.'

'What?' Makoto said looking at her face. 'Isn't the best time for what?'

'Well, we're opening that second shop, right? And we're look-ing for a new employee, but it's hard to find the right people – with all the big companies practically tripping over themselves to get good people, hardly anyone's interested in a little boutique like ours.'

'And?'

'Well, I talked it over with Naomi today, and it sounds like there's no getting around my coming in on Saturdays, at least for the time being. Hopefully it won't be every week—'

'You mean you'll only have Sundays off?'

'Something like that,' Yukiho said, looking up at him. She was clearly afraid he would get angry.

But he didn't.

'Doesn't sound like you'll be taking golf lessons, then.'

'I'm afraid not. Which is why I'm apologising because the whole thing was my idea in the first place. Sorry,' she said, bowing her head.

'Right,' Makoto said, crossing his arms and going over to the sofa. 'Guess that's that, then.' He sat down. 'Maybe I'll take lessons by myself.'

'You're not angry?' Yukiho said, a little surprised.

'Why should I be? I decided not to get angry about this kind of thing.'

'Phew. I was afraid that you were gonna get angry with me again. It's just we really don't have enough people—'

'It's OK, really. Just don't come telling me you want to join lessons later on, because you'll be too late.'

'I wont, I promise.'

'Good.'

Makoto picked up the television remote and pressed the button, thinking about when he might be able to make a call without Yukiho overhearing ...

Makoto had trouble sleeping that night. When he thought about his unexpected reunion with Chizuru, he felt hot, as if he had a fever. Her smile flashed in his mind; her voice rang in his ears.

Part of the information session included going to see an actual class in session. Makoto watched Chizuru and the rest of her class hitting the ball with their instructor giving them pointers. From behind. When she noticed he was there, Chizuru seem to stiffen and missed the ball several times. Each time she would turn in his direction and stick out her tongue at him.

Makoto asked her to dinner at the end of the lesson.

'There's nothing for me to eat at home, so I was planning on eating out anyway. I'd rather not eat alone,' he said, making an excuse.

She hesitated for just a moment before agreeing to go with him with a smile. Makoto didn't think she was just coming along to be polite.

Chizuru took the train to get to golf lessons, so Makoto gave her a lift in his BMW to a pasta place he'd been to several times before. He had never taken Yukiho there.

The lighting was dim and Makoto sat across from Chizuru. Thinking back on it, he realised that they had never gone out together when she was working at his company. Makoto felt relaxed. It felt right, in his gut, to be with her. When he was with her, conversation felt easy. He even felt like he'd become a better talker. She laughed often and talked a lot herself. As she spoke about her experiences at different companies, an idea struck Makoto so strongly it startled him.

'Why did you start golf? To stay fit?' he asked.

'I don't know. I guess I wanted to change something. Change myself, maybe.'

'Did you need to change?'

'There was something I felt I wanted to change, yes. I just felt kind of rootless drifting around like I do.'

Makoto smiled.

'What made *you* want to start?' she asked him.

'Me?' He searched for an answer. He didn't want to say that his wife had suggested it. 'I guess because I wasn't getting enough exercise.'

Chizuru seemed to accept this.

When they left the restaurant, Makoto offered to drive her home. She refused, of course, but didn't seem displeased, so Makoto pressed harder. She accepted.

He didn't know whether it was intentional or not, but all through dinner, Chizuru hadn't asked about Makoto's married life once. Nor did he talk about Yukiho or say anything that might suggest her presence whatsoever. Only once they got in the car and started driving did Chizuru ask, 'Was your wife out today?'

For some reason she seemed a little nervous when she said this.

'She works, so she's out quite a lot.'

Chizuru nodded. She didn't ask anything more about his wife.

Her apartment building was right along a train line. It was a small place, only three storeys high.

'Thanks so much. See you next week?' she said as she got out of the car.

'Maybe, though I'm not sure if I'm going to join the lessons yet,' Makoto said. At the time, he hadn't intended to at all.

'I see. I suppose you're busy,' Chizuru said, looking disappointed.

'Still, I hope we can see each other again. You don't mind if I call, do you?' Makoto asked. He had got her phone number during dinner.

'Of course not,' she said.

'Great. Well, see you.'

'Goodnight.'

When she got out of the car, Makoto felt a strong urge to grab her hand. He would grab her hand, pull her close and kiss her right there. But that was only in his imagination.

He saw her wave him off in his rear-view mirror as he drove into traffic.

He wondered if she would be happy if he started taking lessons – as his head sank into the pillow. He wanted to tell her as soon as he could. But he didn't have a chance to phone that night.

He would get to see her every week. Just thinking that made his heart leap like he was a young man again. He couldn't wait for next Saturday.

He rolled over and heard the steady breathing of sleep from the next bed.

That was all right. He wouldn't be waking her tonight.

'Meeting time,' Narita announced to the members of the E team one day in July. The thin drizzle of the rainy season was falling outside the window. The air conditioning was on full blast in the building, but Narita still had his sleeves rolled up above his elbows.

'We got some new leads from systems development about that expert system,' Narita said once everyone was there. His hands were filled with printed reports.

'Systems is of the opinion that if someone did steal our data there must've been an illegal access of our expert system, so they've been looking into that, and they finally found some traces of it the other day.'

'So it *was* stolen,' one of the more senior members of the team mumbled.

'Last November someone used one of our workstations to copy the entire manufacturing expert system. They have a record of the copy being made, and that record itself was overwritten. Which is why they never found it until now,' he added, lowering his voice.

'So it was somebody in our company?' Makoto asked, looking around at the other members.

'That's likely, yes,' Narita said, his face severe. 'They're going to look into it a little more before deciding whether or not to take it to the police. Of course we still can't prove that the expert system making the rounds is a copy of ours. We won't be able to do that until we've analysed the data down to the last byte. Still, it's looking more likely that that is the case.'

Yamano raised his hand. 'What if it wasn't somebody from inside the company? Couldn't someone have come in on a vacation day and used one of our workstations?'

'They'd still need an ID and password,' Makoto said.

'Actually, on that point,' Narita said, 'systems has been looking into that exact possibility. Whoever did this would've had to be very good with computers. A pro. Which leaves us with really only two possibilities. The first is that somebody inside brought in the thief. The other possibility is that somehow a thief got hold of somebody's ID and password. I don't think any of us have really been aware how valuable that information is, myself included. Somebody might have caught us with our pants down.'

Makoto felt his back pocket to make sure his wallet was still there. His employee identification card was inside. He had written the ID he used to access the workstations and the password on the back.

He remembered being told explicitly not to do that – write down the password and ID together in the same place where someone might see it – and thought he should probably erase them as soon as he got a chance.

'Whoa, at Tozai, too?' Chizuru said, taking a sip of coffee out of a paper cup.

'You mean this happens at other companies?' Makoto asked.

'Yeah, it's been going around lately. They say information is money these days. Pretty much every company has all their data on computers now, which works out great for people looking to steal information. You can take a whole stack of documents and put them on a single floppy. And you can search them with a few key presses to find exactly what you want.'

'I see how that would be good.'

'And Tozai just had an internal network, right? Imagine if they were like some of these places that have connections to external networks. There are more of those these days. That would let someone sneak in from the outside, which makes it even more dangerous. Apparently it's already been happening for a few years now in America. They call them hackers, the people who sneak into other people's computers to play tricks and steal stuff.'

He was impressed with Chizuru's knowledge, guessing it came from being at so many different companies. He reflected that it was she and other temp workers like her that had transferred all of his own company's patent information from microfilm to computer disks.

It was almost five o'clock. Makoto threw his empty cup in the bin. The lobby of the driving range was filled as usual with people waiting their turn. They hadn't been able to find empty seats so they were leaning against the wall as they talked.

'So, have you practised your approach since then?' Makoto said, changing topics.

Chizuru shook her head. 'No. I barely have time to come practise. How about yourself?'

'I haven't touched a club since class last week.'

'But you have a natural talent for it,' she said. 'I had such a head start, and you're already learning higher-level things than I am. I was never very coordinated, I guess.'

'They say that if you start off a little rough, you get better faster.'

'If you're trying to make me feel better, it's not working,' Chizuru said with a laugh.

It had already been three months since Makoto had joined lessons at the driving range. To date he hadn't missed a single class. For one thing, golf was far more interesting than he had anticipated, though his eagerness to meet Chizuru every week was his true motivation.

'Care to go anywhere after practice today?' Makoto asked. It had already become customary for them to go out to eat after lessons were over.

'I'm fine with any place.'

'How about Italian, then?'

'Sure,' she said, smiling.

'You know,' Makoto said, glancing around before continuing in a low voice, 'I was hoping I could see you some time on a day when we don't have practice. Just to talk, without worrying about the time.'

He was confident she wouldn't think this was an imposition. The question was how much she would hesitate. Meeting on a day when they didn't have practice was a very different thing from grabbing dinner on the way home from lessons.

'That'd be fine,' she said simply. It sounded natural, though that might have been an act. A smile lingered on her lips.

'Great, well, I'll think of a good day and let you know.'

'Just give me a little warning and I can move work around.'

'Sounds good.'

That one simple exchange had Makoto walking on sunshine.

Makoto's date with Chizuru was set for the third Friday in July. They would have plenty of time because it was the beginning of the weekend, and Chizuru would be able to get off work earlier that day.

There was another thing working in that day's favour: Yukiho was supposed to leave for a week-long purchasing trip to Italy that Thursday. She had been going to Italy once every few months of late.

Makoto came home on the Wednesday before Yukiho was set to depart and found her in the living room with her suitcase wide open getting ready for the trip. 'Hi,' she said when he walked in, but her eyes were on the calendar spread out on the table.

'Dinner?' Makoto asked.

'I made some stew, you go ahead. I'm a little busy right now.' She still didn't look at her husband.

Makoto went into the bedroom without saying anything and changed into a T-shirt and sweatpants.

He had felt the change in her lately. Until recently, she had been so distraught over not being able to be a good wife to him that she would cry. But now it was, 'Go ahead and eat.'

He wondered if it was her success at work that made her so stand-offish. *Or maybe it's because I've stopped demanding anything of her*, Makoto thought. Before, whenever something rubbed him the wrong way, he would get mad immediately, but lately, he hardly raised his voice at all. He was happy if each day went by uneventfully.

His re-encounter with Chizuru Misawa had changed everything. Since that day he had lost all interest in Yukiho, nor did he want her to have any interest in him. *This is what they mean when they talk about people drifting apart*, he thought.

Makoto went back to the living room and Yukiho said, 'Oh, I almost forgot. Natsumi is staying over tonight. It's better if we go to the airport together tomorrow.'

'Who's Natsumi?'

'You haven't met her? She's been working at the shop since the very beginning. We're going together this time.'

'OK. Where she's sleeping?'

'I cleaned up the guest room.'

So I guess it's all decided then, Makoto wanted to say, but he held back.

Natsumi arrived just after ten. She was a little over twenty, with a pretty face.

'I hope you're not planning on going like that,' Yukiho said when she saw Natsumi wearing a red T-shirt and jeans.

'I'll change into a suit tomorrow. This is going in my luggage.'

'I don't think you'll need a T-shirt and jeans. We're not going as tourists. You should probably leave them here.' Yukiho's voice had a severity to it that Makoto had never heard.

'OK,' Natsumi replied in a small voice.

The two women started talking in the living room, so Makoto went ahead and took a shower. When he came out of the bathroom, they had gone off to a different room.

Makoto pulled a glass and a bottle of Scotch out of the living room cupboard, grabbed some ice from the fridge, and sat down in front of the television. He had never been much of a beer drinker. Whenever he drank alone it was Scotch on the rocks. It had become a nightly routine.

The door opened and Yukiho came in, but Makoto didn't look at her. His eyes were fixed on the sports news.

'Makoto?' Yukiho said. 'Think you could turn it down? Natsumi can't sleep with that noise.'

'You can't hear it in there, can you?'

'You can. That's why I came to tell you to turn it down.' There were thorns in her voice. Makoto scowled, grabbed the remote and turned the volume down.

Yukiho was still standing there. He could feel her eyes on him. *So she wants to say something.* The thought crossed his mind that it could be about Chizuru. But that was impossible.

Yukiho sighed. 'Look at you, living the life.'

'What?' He looked up at her. 'What's that supposed to mean?'

'I mean just look at you, doing whatever you want, whenever you want. Drinking your Scotch, watching the ball game—'

'What's wrong with that?'

'Nothing's wrong. I'm just saying you're living the life,' she said as she turned to go into the bedroom.

'Hold on, what do you mean? If you have something to say, say it.'

'Keep your voice down. Natsumi will hear,' Yukiho said, furrowing her brow.

'You're the one who started it. I'm asking you what you meant.'

'Nothing, like I said,' Yukiho turned back around to face him. 'I was just wondering if you have any dreams? Ambitions? Or do you just plan on spending the rest of your life this way, getting old, never trying to make something of yourself?'

He felt his hair bristle and tightness come into his jaw. 'You think you have ambition?' he scoffed. 'You're just playing at being a businesswoman.'

'I am *running* a business.'

'Whose business? I bought that shop.'

'And I'm paying rent, aren't I? And who are you to talk? You bought it with money you got from your parents.'

Makoto glared at her. She glared right back.

'I'm going to bed. I have to get up early tomorrow,' she said.

'You should probably get to bed soon too. And don't drink too much.'

'Leave me be.'

'Goodnight!' She disappeared into the bedroom.

Makoto sat back down and grabbed the bottle of Scotch. He poured a long slosh into his glass. The ice was almost gone. He drank it down and somehow it tasted more bitter than usual.

When he opened his eyes, his head was pounding. Makoto frowned and tried to rub the fog out of his eyes. He could see Yukiho sitting at her dresser putting on make-up.

He glanced over at the clock. It was time to wake up, but his body felt as if it was made out of lead.

He went to say something to Yukiho, but couldn't think of anything. For some reason she felt impossibly distant.

He looked at her face in the mirror and blinked. Why was she wearing a patch over one eye?

'What's that for?' he asked. 'Why are you wearing a patch?'

Yukiho looked around slowly. Her face was like a mask. 'It's from last night.'

'Huh?'

'You don't remember?'

Makoto was silent. He tried to remember anything about last night. He recalled getting into a fight with Yukiho and drinking a little more Scotch than normal after that. But he couldn't remember what he'd done afterwards. He just had a vague memory that he'd got very sleepy. And yet he didn't remember how he had gone to bed. The pounding in his head was making it hard to remember much of anything.

'Did I ... do something?' Makoto asked.

'I was asleep last night and you came in and ripped the covers off ...' Yukiho swallowed before continuing. 'Then you shouted something and started hitting me.'

'What?' His eyes shot wide open. 'I didn't do that.'

'You most certainly did. My head, my face ...'

'I don't remember that at all.'

'You were drunk,' she said, standing and walking towards the door.

'Wait, no,' he called out her. 'I really don't remember it.'

'Oh? That's funny, because I'll never forget.'

'Yukiho ...' He tried taking a deep breath. His head was swirling. 'If I did that I apologise. I'm so sorry—'

Yukiho stood for a while, her head drooping, then she said, 'I'll be home next Saturday,' and opened the door and walked out.

Makoto let his head sink into the pillow. He looked up at the ceiling and tried to retrace what had happened the night before, but found nothing but darkness.

The ice clinked in the tumbler in Chizuru's hand. Her face was flushed beneath her eyes.

'This was really fun. I mean everything. The talking, the food,' she said, shaking her head as if in disbelief.

'I had a great time too,' Makoto said. 'It's been a long time since I've felt this good.' He leaned on the counter and turned towards her. 'It's because of you. Thanks.' It was an embarrassing thing to say in public, but thankfully the bartender was otherwise occupied and didn't seem to have heard.

They'd ended up at a hotel bar in Akasaka near the French restaurant where they'd eaten dinner.

'No, I should thank you,' she replied. 'I just feel like years of bumbling around has been swept clean.'

'What bumbling around?'

'Nothing, it's just I have a lot on my mind,' she said, sipping on the straw of her Singapore Sling.

'Me too,' he said shaking the ice to stir his Chivas Regal. 'I'm really happy I met you again. If I were a religious man, I'd praise God.'

This, too, was a brazen admission. Chizuru smiled and lowered her eyes.

'There's something I have to confess,' he said.

She looked back up, her eyes shimmering.

'I got married two years ago. But the very day before the wedding I made a decision, a huge decision, and it took me some place.'

Chizuru raised an eyebrow. Her smile faded.

'I need to tell you what happened.'

'OK.'

'Except,' he said, 'I'd rather that we were alone.'

Her eyes widened slightly, and he held out his right hand, open. The hotel room key was on his palm.

Chizuru looked down, silent.

'The place I went,' he said, 'was the Parkside Hotel. The hotel where you were supposed to stay that night.'

She looked up again. Her eyes were bloodshot.

'Let's go,' he said.

She nodded yes, her eyes never leaving his.

As they made for the room, Makoto told himself *this is right. Everything up until now was the mistake. I'm getting things back on the right path.*

They stopped in front of the room and he put the key in the door.

The client's name was Yukiho Takamiya. She was a beautiful woman; she could have been an actress. But her face was just as dark as all the others.

'So your husband's asking you for a divorce, is that it?'

'That's right.'

'But he's not telling you why, correct? He just doesn't think it's working any more.'

'Yes.'

'Do you have any idea why he's making this move?'

The client seemed to think for a moment before she said, 'I think there's another woman. I – I had someone look into it.'

She pulled several photographs out of her Chanel bag. They clearly showed a man and a woman meeting in a variety of places. The man had a company-man haircut and a company-man suit, and the young woman had a short bob. Both of them looked happy.

'Have you asked your husband who she is?'

'No, not yet. I thought I should talk to you first.'

'Right. Let me ask, do you want a divorce?'

'Yes. I knew it wasn't working, too.'

'Did something happen?'

'I think it's been since he started seeing her, but sometimes he can be violent – only when he's drinking, though.'

'That's no good. Does anyone know about this? I'm talking about a witness – someone who could corroborate this.'

'I haven't told anyone. Except once, when it happened, a girl from work had come to spend the night. She must remember.'

'Right.'

As she took notes, the lawyer thought there were a number of ways they could approach this. She took another look at the photograph. She knew the type: they looked like perfect gentleman, but treated their wives like dirt. It was her least favourite type.

'I just – I just don't believe it. I can't believe he would do something like this. He was so nice before,' Yukiho said, putting a white hand to her mouth and beginning to cry.

TEN

Imaeda frowned as he pulled into the car park. There were dozens of spaces, and nearly all of them were full. 'I thought the market bubble broke already,' he grumbled.

He found an open space at the far back, parked his Honda Prelude, and took his golf bag out of the trunk. It had a light coating of dust on it from two years spent in the closet. He'd taken up golf at the suggestion of one of his former co-workers, and had been genuinely interested in it for a little while, but ever since he'd gone freelance, his clubs had languished inside their bag. It wasn't that he was too busy; there just wasn't any compelling reason for him to go. Golf was a pack sport – no fit pastime for a lone wolf.

He strolled through the front entrance of the Eagle Golf Driving Range – the décor of the place always reminded him of a second-rate business hotel – and his shoulders slumped. The lobby was full of golfers in various stages of ennui, all waiting their turn on the range. He counted nearly ten.

He considered leaving and coming back again later, but realised that he'd likely face the same scene unless he returned in the middle of the week, which wasn't going to happen. Resigning himself to his fate, Imaeda went up to the front counter and put his name on the list.

Finding a free sofa seat, he sat and absent-mindedly watched television. A sumo bout was on: the big summer tournament. It was still early in the day, so only the lower-ranked wrestlers were competing. In the past they hadn't even shown these matches, but with the recent surge in sumo's popularity, fans were watching earlier and earlier in the day, giving some of the up-and-coming wrestlers coveted time in the spotlight. The sport's reversal of fortune could be largely credited to a handful of rising stars: Takatoriki, Uminomai, and the Wakataka brothers. Of the brothers, Takahanada had recently become the youngest wrestler in history to sweep all three *sansho* prizes awarded to top-division sumo wrestlers, before going on to defeat reigning *yokozuna* Chiyonofuji to become the youngest wrestler to ever win the Gold Star. Chiyonofuji was defeated by another of these up-and-comers, Takatoriki, only two days later, spurring the *yokozuna* to announce his retirement.

The times are definitely changing, Imaeda thought as he watched the screen. The media had been announcing the end of the bubble economy for weeks, and people who had amassed fortunes in stocks and land were now standing with mouths agape, watching as it all vanished into thin air. He had expected things would quieten down a bit, and none too soon. When people were dropping five billion yen for minor van Gogh paintings, something had to give.

And yet, a casual glance around the lobby was enough to tell him that young women were clearly still flaunting their cash. Traditionally golf had been strictly a men's sport and one enjoyed only by people who had attained a certain status, at that. Recently, however, younger, female players were a common sight on the greens and nearly half the people waiting their turn in the lobby today were women.

Which is precisely why I'm dusting off the clubs, he thought with a wry smile. He'd got a call from an old school friend four days earlier. His friend was taking two women, nightclub hostesses both, golfing, and had invited him along. Their planned fourth had backed out and his friend was looking to round out the number.

Imaeda didn't have a problem swallowing his pride and accepting the invitation. He needed the exercise and he never passed up an opportunity to meet girls. The only thing holding him back was the fact that he hadn't swung a club in years. Thus his visit to the range today, to brush up on his technique. His date on the golf course was two weeks away and he wanted to at least get to the point where he wouldn't embarrass himself.

He only had to wait thirty minutes before his name was called, which he supposed was pretty good considering the number of people in line. The woman at the counter handed him coins for the ball machine and a card indicating his stall number and he headed out on to the driving range.

His stall was at the far end of the first level. He put a coin into the nearest ball dispenser and got two baskets' worth to get him started.

He stretched a little bit to warm up before stepping into the stall, and decided to start with the seven iron – by far his favourite club. He wouldn't be doing a full swing at first, just a nice controlled shot.

It took him a little bit of trial and error, but he'd soon got the feel of it back in his muscles. After about twenty balls, he was starting to loosen up and take bigger swings. His body was moving smoothly, and he was catching the ball with the sweet spot on the clubface. Imaeda figured he was hitting 150, maybe 160 yards with the seven iron, and was starting to feel pretty good about himself. Taking a break hadn't set him as far back as he'd feared. Everything he'd learned in his lessons was coming back.

He had just switched to a five iron and hit a few balls when he felt someone's eyes on him – the man hitting from the stall beside his was watching Imaeda's shots while taking a break on the chairs. Imaeda didn't mind, but it did make it a little harder to focus.

As he settled his grip on the new club, Imaeda glanced in the man's direction. He was young, maybe not even thirty, and he looked oddly familiar. Imaeda stole another glance. Now he was sure he'd seen him somewhere before, but he couldn't remember where. Judging by the way the man was looking at him, he didn't recognise Imaeda at all.

He moved on to practising with the three iron. A short while later, the man got back up and started hitting balls himself. He was pretty good, and his form was excellent. He was using a driver and hitting the balls straight into the net two hundred yards away.

When the man twisted his neck a little to the right, Imaeda

spotted two black moles on the back of his neck and the memories
came rushing back.

Makoto Takamiya. Tozai Automotive.

Suddenly it all made sense. Seeing this particular man here
hadn't been a coincidence at all. The only reason Imaeda had
known about this practice range was because of a job three years
ago – the job on which he'd first seen Makoto.

No wonder he doesn't know me.

Imaeda wondered what Makoto had been up to in the intervening years, and whether he was still seeing that woman.

His three iron was giving him trouble, so Imaeda decided to
take a break. He bought a soft drink at the vending machine,
leaned back in his chair, and watched Makoto hit the ball. Makoto
was practising his pitch shot, aiming for a flag fifty yards away. He
hit a half-wedge and the ball floated upward, hung in the air for an
instant, and finally dropped down right by the flag. It was impressive.

Makoto turned around, perhaps sensing his eyes on him. Imaeda
looked away and took a sip of his drink, noting by the shadows
moving across the deck that Makoto was walking towards him.

'Brownings, aren't they?'

Imaeda looked up. 'Huh?'

'Your clubs. They're Brownings, right?' Makoto was pointing at
Imaeda's golf bag.

'Oh,' Imaeda checked the brand marker engraved on the head
of the irons. 'Yeah, they are. I'd forgotten.'

He'd bought them on impulse at a golf shop. The owner had
recommended them, talking at great length about why they were
the best clubs he had, perfect for someone with a slender frame –
but Imaeda hadn't really been listening. He'd bought them, he
remembered now, because he liked the name Browning. It
reminded him of a gun-obsessed phase he'd gone through.

'Mind if I have a look?' Makoto asked.

'Go right ahead.'

Makoto pulled out the five iron. 'Yeah,' he said, 'one of my
friends got really good all of a sudden, and he's using Brownings.'

'You think the club has much to do with it?'

'Well, he'd been plateaued for ever, and then he shot right up after he switched, so maybe. I started thinking I should spend a bit of time looking for the right fit for me too.'

'I'd say you're good enough already, seeing you hit.'

'Maybe out here, but not on a real course,' Makoto said, assuming the stance and giving a light swing. 'Hmm. The grip's a little narrower than I'm used to.'

'Why don't you try hitting a couple?'

'You don't mind?'

'Not at all.'

Makoto took Imaeda's clubs over to his stall and started hitting a few balls. The balls zinged away, just the right amount of spin on them.

'You've got it. That's some fine hitting,' Imaeda said. He wasn't just being polite, either.

'The club feels good,' Makoto said.

'Hit as many as you want. I need to practise with my woods anyway.'

'Really? Thanks.'

Makoto started swinging again. He hardly missed a shot. But that wasn't because of the clubs – his form was solid. Which made sense, since he'd practised for years at this very range. That girl had been taking lessons with him, too, Imaeda recalled. It took him a little while to dredge up her name: Chizuru Misawa.

Three years earlier Imaeda had been working at Tokyo General Research, a private investigations outfit with over seventeen offices throughout the country. Imaeda had been stationed at the Meguro office in southwest Tokyo.

Though they did their fair share of domestic cases, Tokyo General Research was unusual for its large number of corporate clients. They would frequently be asked to look into the management and earnings of a potential trade partner, or check whether a particular employee had been talking to headhunters. Once, they were asked to find out who the brash young CEO of a particular company was sleeping with, only to discover, much to their amusement, that he was sleeping with all four female members of the board.

Even with all this variety, the request that came from a man claiming association with Tozai Automotive was unusual: he wanted them to investigate a product by another company, a software developer by the name of Memorix. The product was a metallurgy expert system they had brought to market the year before.

He wanted Imaeda's team to look into the history of the software's development, the personal histories of the core members on the development team, and everyone in their social circles. The client hadn't mentioned why he wanted this information, but they had a vague idea. Clearly, someone suspected that Memorix had stolen code from Tozai's software and required evidence of the theft to prove it. A route connecting someone at Memorix to a conspirator inside Tozai would be the smoking gun they needed.

There were roughly twenty people at the Meguro branch of Tokyo General Research. Half of them were put on the job, including Imaeda.

Two weeks into the investigation, they had uncovered pretty much everything there was to know about Memorix. It had been founded in 1984, with former programmer Toru Anzai as CEO. Including part-time workers, they employed twelve system engineers who developed systems to meet the needs of various parts manufacturers.

There were several question marks surrounding the metallurgy expert system, the largest of these being the question of where Memorix had sourced the large volumes of metallurgical know-how and data. The story was that a certain mid-level metals manufacturer had given them technical assistance when they were developing the program, but when Imaeda and his team investigated further, they found that by the time Memorix had requested the assistance, the software was already complete – the manufacturer had only been hired to check the software.

The most obvious explanation was that they had simply used

data previously acquired from other clients. Memorix did a lot of work in cooperation with other companies, which gave them access to their partners' data.

Yet there was a problem with this theory. Whenever Memorix worked with another company, they drew up very precise contracts detailing exactly how information was to be handled, with severe penalties if any of their employees were found disseminating information outside of the company without permission.

There was no connection, however, with Tozai Automotive, and thus no contractual agreements. If Memorix had stolen software from Tozai, no one would be watching. The theft would be extremely difficult to prove, moreover, because the Tozai software had strictly been for internal use and never widely circulated. Even if the Memorix software bore a similarity to the earlier product, Memorix could simply claim coincidence.

As the investigation went on, one man came to their attention: a chief developer at Memorix named Yuichi Akiyoshi who'd joined the company in 1986. Development of the metallurgy expert system began shortly after his arrival and was mostly completed by the following year. It was hard to reconcile the speed. The typical production cycle for a piece of software like that was three years at the minimum. Imaeda's team came up with another theory: that Akiyoshi had already been in possession of the information forming the basis for the metallurgy expert system when he joined the company.

They knew very little about the man.

Akiyoshi lived in a rented apartment in north-west Tokyo but had never registered as a resident. Imaeda's team went to the company managing the apartment to check on any places he might have lived previously, learning that he'd come up to Tokyo all the way from Nagoya.

An investigator went down to Nagoya to check it out, only to find a tall, chimney-like building where the residence should have been. None of the locals remembered an Akiyoshi having lived at the previous building that had occupied the space. City Hall had a similar lack of records. No Yuichi Akiyoshi had ever registered as a resident in the area, nor could they find anyone living at the Nagoya address he'd listed in the contact information for his guarantor when he signed the lease on his current apartment. Everything pointed to Akiyoshi as having forged his rental documents. It was likely he was living under an assumed name.

In order to find out who he really was, they were obliged to resort to the basics: they began a stakeout.

First, they planted bugs in Akiyoshi's apartment when he was out one day: one in the living room and another on his phone. All the mail that arrived in his mailbox, other than registered mail and express packages, was opened and examined then they resealed the envelopes and put them back in the box. They would never be able to use any information gained this way in a trial, but for now, finding out who he was took precedence.

At first it seemed that Akiyoshi lived an entirely unremarkable life, just shuttling back and forth between office and home. No one paid him any visits, and there was nothing remarkable about his conversations on the phone. In fact, he hardly received any phone calls at all.

'What does this guy do for fun? Doesn't he have any friends?' Imaeda's partner said once as they were staring at the monitor in their van. The van had been disguised to look like a cleaner's delivery truck. A camera on top of the truck was pointed at Akiyoshi's apartment window.

'He might be running from someone,' said Imaeda. 'Keeping a low profile.'

'A murderer on the lam?' his partner said, grinning.

'We should be so lucky.' Imaeda smiled back.

It was a little while longer before they discovered that there *was* someone Akiyoshi contacted with some regularity. They were monitoring him in the apartment when they heard a loud electronic warble – a pager. Imaeda tensed and listened to the feed over his headphones, expecting Akiyoshi to phone someone.

Instead, he left the apartment and walked down the street. Imaeda's partner quickly started up the van and they followed him. Eventually Akiyoshi stopped at a public phone behind a bar and made a call. His face was expressionless while he talked, though he was keeping an eye on his surroundings, preventing them from getting too close.

The same sequence of events played out several times. After his pager rang, Akiyoshi would leave the apartment to place a phone call. They thought at first that he might have realised his phone was tapped, but then it would have made more sense for him to simply remove the tap. Instead, it seemed that Akiyoshi was in the habit of always using a public phone to make important phone calls. Nor did he use the same phone each time. After one or two visits to the same phone, he would switch booths, showing an unusual degree of thoroughness.

The big question was: who was ringing Akiyoshi's pager?

Yet before they could unravel that mystery, the investigation took a sudden turn.

One Thursday after work Akiyoshi took a train to Shinjuku. This was more than unusual – it was the first time he had gone anywhere since they started watching him. He went to a café near the west exit of the station. There, he met a man. The man was thin and short, in his mid-forties, with a face as impenetrable as a Noh mask.

Akiyoshi received a large envelope from the man. After checking the contents he handed the man a smaller envelope out of which the man took a small stack of bills. He counted them quickly and placed them in his jacket pocket before handing Akiyoshi a slip of paper.

A receipt, thought Imaeda.

Akiyoshi and the man spoke for several minutes before they both stood from the table. Imaeda and his partner split up, Imaeda following Akiyoshi and his partner following the man. To Imaeda's disappointment, Akiyoshi went straight home.

It turned out that the other man ran a small private detective agency in the city – 'small' meaning it was just him and his wife.

This confirmed the hunch Imaeda had formed the first time he saw him. There was just something about him that smelled like a man in their line of work.

Imaeda wanted to know what business Akiyoshi had hiring a private detective. If the agency had any ties to Tokyo General Research, a few well-placed questions would tell him what he wanted to know, but it turned out that the detective Akiyoshi had hired was running his operation almost entirely independently. They couldn't risk making contact. If the man got wind of their investigation, it would be all over.

They continued their stakeout.

Akiyoshi made his next move on the following Saturday.

Imaeda and his partner were watching the apartment when Akiyoshi came out, dressed in jeans and a windbreaker. There was something about the way his shoulders were hunched that made Imaeda think this wasn't just a trip to the convenience store.

Akiyoshi took a few trains, getting off in Shimokitazawa, a trendy suburb just west of central Tokyo. He cast his eyes around, wary of his surroundings, but didn't seem to have noticed he was being tailed. He had a small notebook in his hand, and would occasionally check something in it as he wandered the streets near the station. *He's looking for someone's house*, Imaeda thought.

Finally he came to a stop by a small, three-storey building near the tracks. It looked like an apartment building made up entirely of small, single-resident units. But Akiyoshi didn't go inside. Instead, he went into a café across the street. After a moment's hesitation, Imaeda sent his partner into the café, in case Akiyoshi might be meeting someone inside, and himself went into a nearby bookshop to wait.

An hour later, his partner came out of the café alone.

'He's not meeting anyone,' he said. 'It's a stakeout. He's waiting for someone who lives in that apartment building.' He nodded his head, indicating the building across the street.

Imaeda wondered if the private investigator hadn't found whoever lived in the apartment for Akiyoshi.

'Which means we're on stakeout, too,' Imaeda said. He sighed and went to look for a payphone so he could get someone back at the office to bring a car.

Akiyoshi left the café before the car arrived. Imaeda glanced at the apartment and saw a young woman just leaving. It looked as though she was walking towards the station, a bag of golf clubs in her hand. Akiyoshi followed the woman, keeping a good distance between them, with Imaeda and his partner behind him.

The woman was going to the Eagle Golf Driving Range. Akiyoshi followed her inside. Imaeda and his partner went in too. As they soon discovered, the woman was attending golf lessons. Akiyoshi watched her until lessons began, then took a brochure from the front desk and headed out. He didn't return to the practice range that day.

It didn't take them long to identify the woman. Her name was Chizuru Misawa, a temp worker with one of the large staffing agencies. They looked into her agency records and found that she had previously been assigned to Tozai Automotive. They had finally found their connection.

They renewed their stakeout on Akiyoshi, fully expecting him to make contact with Miss Misawa, until the investigation took another unexpected turn.

For a while, Akiyoshi did nothing out of the ordinary, until one Saturday when he went again to the driving range. He timed his visit for when Chizuru would be beginning her lesson. However, Akiyoshi didn't approach her. He merely sat, undetected, watching.

Eventually, another man approached and sat down next to Chizuru and began talking to her. It was clear from the way they spoke that the two were in a relationship.

This, apparently, was what Akiyoshi had come to see, because as soon as he saw the two of them sit down he left the practice range.

That day was the last time he ever approached Chizuru Misawa. Nor did he again go to the Eagle Golf Driving Range for as long as they watched him.

Imaeda's team looked into the man who was with Chizuru that day. His name was Makoto Takamiya, an employee of Tozai Automotive in the patent licensing division.

Fully expecting that they had hit the jackpot, they started to look into their relationship and their connection to Akiyoshi.

However, they could find absolutely nothing connecting the two to the stolen software. The only thing they did discover was that Makoto Takamiya was married and having an affair with Chizuru.

Eventually, with the detective's bills piling up, the client called off the investigation. Though Tokyo General Research handed off a thick file of findings to the client, it was unclear how useful the information would be.

Imaeda was willing to bet good money it had all gone straight into the shredder.

A wrenching metallic clang brought Imaeda back to the present. He looked up and saw Makoto Takamiya standing, dumbfounded.

'Man ...' He was staring at the club in his hand, his mouth agape. The end of the club had broken clean off.

'What happened?' Imaeda asked, looking around. The head of the club was lying on the floor some distance away from where Makoto stood. A few of the other golfers nearby had stopped swinging to look over. Imaeda stood up, walked over, and picked up the broken golf head.

'Wow, I'm so sorry. I have no idea how that happened,' Makoto said, holding the headless club in his hand. His face had gone pale.

'Metal fatigue, most likely,' said Imaeda. 'I've been abusing that five iron for years.'

'I don't understand. I wasn't even swinging it that hard.'

'I know, it's OK. Its number was up. It probably would've broken faster if I'd been swinging it. You're not hurt, are you?'

'No, I'm fine. Look, I'll be happy to pay for your club. I broke it, after all.'

Imaeda shook his head. 'No need. Like I said, that club wasn't long for this world.'

'No, I insist. And besides, I won't even be using my own money. I have insurance.'

'Insurance?'

'Golfer's insurance. I just have to fill out a few forms and they should cover the cost of a repair.'

'Even if the club isn't yours?'

'I think so. We can ask at the shop.'

Makoto took the broken club in his hand and started walking towards the lobby. Imaeda followed. The shop was in a corner of the lobby. Makoto walked in like he was familiar with the place and waved to the suntanned attendant behind the counter. He showed him the broken club and explained what had happened.

'Yeah, insurance should cover that,' the attendant told them. 'You just need to describe the place where it happened, attach a picture of the broken club, and the receipt from the repair shop.' He leaned over the counter and whispered, 'See, there's no way to prove the club isn't yours.' Then, more loudly, he added, 'We can get the forms for you, if you call the insurance company.'

'Great, thanks. How long will repairs take?'

'Well, we have to find the same size shaft, so two weeks, maybe?'

'Two weeks ...' Makoto shot Imaeda a worried glance. 'Is that OK?'

'Sure, no problem,' Imaeda said, smiling. Two weeks later would be after his golf date but the lack of one club wouldn't really affect the score either way. More than that, he didn't want to impose on Makoto any more than he already had.

They turned the club in for repairs and left the shop.

'Hey, Makoto,' a voice called out as they were heading back to the practice range. Imaeda looked around and his mouth tightened. He recognised this woman as Chizuru Misawa. A tall man was standing behind her, though his face was unfamiliar to him.

'Hey there,' Makoto said to them.

'All done with practice?' Chizuru asked.

'Almost, if I hadn't gone and broken this poor man's club.'

Makoto explained what had happened to Chizuru and the man. Her face clouded as she listened.

'How awful,' she sympathised. 'I bet that's the last time you'll loan your club to a stranger.'

'No, really,' said Imaeda, 'it's fine.' He looked towards Makoto. 'Is this your ... wife?'

Makoto nodded, smiling.

So the affair stuck, Imaeda thought bemusedly.

'I hope the club head didn't hit anyone on its way down?' the man standing behind Chizuru said.

'Luckily, it didn't. Here, let me give you my business card,' Makoto said, pulling his wallet out of his golf trousers and handing a card to Imaeda.

'Oh, thanks,' Imaeda said, pulling out his own wallet. He hesitated for a moment, unsure of which card to give him. He always carried several, each with different names and job titles. After a second's thought, he decided on his real card. There was no point using an alias here, and there was always a chance that Makoto or one of the other two might be a future client.

'A private detective?' Makoto asked, looking curiously at the card.

'Let me know if you ever need our services,' said Imaeda.

'Ooh, do you catch people having affairs and things like that?' Chizuru asked.

'Of course,' Imaeda nodded. 'That's probably our most frequent request.'

She laughed at that, then said to Makoto, 'In that case, maybe I should hold on to that card.'

'Probably a good idea,' Makoto said, grinning.

It is a good idea, Imaeda wanted to say. *Right now is the most dangerous time of all*, he thought, his eyes noting the prominent swell of Chizuru's belly.

Imaeda's office, which also served as his residence, was located in west Shinjuku, on the second storey of a five-storey building facing a narrow street. There was a bus stop right out in front, so you could get there in just a few minutes from the station. Still, that wasn't convenient enough for his clients. Whenever he explained the directions over the phone, he could hear the frustration on the other end. But he needed the business, so he always put in extra effort to sound welcoming. The end result was that most phone calls left him exhausted.

He knew it made more sense to move closer to a station. Clients usually had a lot on their mind when they first considered hiring a private eye. They could well change their mind in the several minutes it took to catch a bus. Yet, with the housing bubble, rents had gone through the roof. Imaeda still hadn't got used to the eye-popping sums of money he had to pay each month just for his tiny office. Increased rents meant increased fees for services, which put the pressure on him. One of his goals when he went independent was to keep his fees reasonable and his clients happy, but it was getting harder to do both.

It was a Wednesday in late June when a call came to his office from one Kazunari Shinozuka. Rain was falling in a fine drizzle outside the window, and Imaeda had just given up hope that any customers would show themselves that day.

Imaeda knew from the moment Kazunari introduced himself on the phone that he would be a client. There was that certain ring in his voice. A few minutes later he was giving him directions to the office.

Imaeda hung up and scratched his neck, thinking. Kazunari hadn't gone into specifics about his request over the phone, which left Imaeda to wonder what he needed. He knew Kazunari was single, which ruled out the usual adultery investigation. He didn't peg him as the sort to hire someone else to look into a lover's suspected infidelities, either.

Imaeda had first met Kazunari the day he ran into Makoto Takamiya at the driving range – Kazunari had been the man standing behind Makoto's wife, Chizuru. The three of them had arranged to meet that day for dinner. Imaeda hadn't gone so far as to invite himself along, but he had shared a cup of instant coffee with them in the lobby, which was when Kazunari had given him his business card.

He had since run into him twice more at the driving range. Kazunari was an accomplished golfer. They had spoken a little about Imaeda's work on those occasions. Though Kazunari hadn't seemed all that interested at the time, perhaps Imaeda had succeeded in sowing the seeds that led to today.

Imaeda pulled out a Marlboro and lit it with a disposable lighter. Putting his feet up on his cluttered desk, he leaned back and took a deep drag, sending a stream of smoke to drift up towards the dimly lit ceiling.

Kazunari Shinozuka wasn't your average salaryman. He was next in line for an executive position at his uncle's pharmaceutical company and that meant he couldn't rule out a corporate investigation. Just thinking about that possibility made Imaeda's heart race. He hadn't felt this excited in a long while.

Imaeda had gone independent from Tokyo General Research two years earlier. He didn't like the crappy working conditions and the low pay and after doing it for a couple of years he didn't see why he couldn't accomplish many of the same things himself. He certainly had all the connections he needed by that point.

And business had been good, for the most part. He was getting enough requests to support his own modest lifestyle. He was even saving a little and hitting the golf course once a month.

But he wasn't satisfied. More than half of his jobs were looking into affairs. The kind of corporate cases he occasionally got when he was working for Tokyo General were nowhere to be seen. This meant he was spending every day out on the streets, wallowing in the stench of love and betrayal, and while he didn't mind that per se, it was getting old. There was none of the tension he used to feel.

At one time, he had considered joining the police force. He passed the tests and had been accepted to the Academy, but he was discouraged by what he saw as the unnecessary harshness of laws and regulations that seemed meaningless to him at the time. He dropped out without graduating. That was when he was in his early twenties.

After that he drifted from one part-time job to another before finding the help-wanted ad for Tokyo General in the newspaper. *If I couldn't make it as a police officer, maybe I could make it as a private eye*, he thought half-jokingly to himself as he went for the interview. He was hired on the spot, but in the beginning, it was little more than part-time work. That went on for about six months before he became a full employee.

It was on his very first investigation that he realised how well suited he was for the job. Being a private eye held none of the glamour depicted in the movies and on TV. It was repetitive, lonely work. Without the authority of the badge, you could never walk in the front door to any case. And you had to protect the privacy of your client. You left no traces of your investigation and could allow nothing to leak. And yet the feeling of fulfilment when, at the end of long hours, you got what you were looking for wasn't something he'd ever found anywhere else.

The phone call from Kazunari started Imaeda thinking that maybe he could get some of that excitement back. He had a good feeling about this client.

Then he shook his head and stubbed out his cigarette. *Don't get ahead of yourself. You'll probably be following some woman again. Just like always.*

Kazunari arrived at twenty past two. He was wearing a light grey suit and his hair was perfect, despite the weather. He looked a good four or five years older than he had at the practice range and carried himself like a man with well-lined pockets.

'I haven't seen you much at the driving range,' Kazunari said, taking a seat.

'Yeah, I can never seem to make myself go when I don't have a date set up to play,' Imaeda told him as he went to pour coffee.

'We should go play a round some time,' Kazunari offered. 'I know a few good courses.'

'Sounds great. Definitely let me know if you're heading out.'

'I will. I'll invite Makoto along, too,' he said, taking a sip of his coffee. Imaeda detected that familiar stiffness in his movement and voice that every client had.

Kazunari put down his cup, took a breath, and said, 'I have a rather odd request.'

Imaeda nodded. 'Don't worry. Nearly everyone that comes here thinks their request is odd. How can I help?'

'It's about a woman,' he said. 'I'd like you to investigate her.'

'All right,' Imaeda said. He felt his heart sank a little. 'Your girl-friend, perhaps?'

'No, actually. We're not directly connected. Not like that, at least.' He reached into his jacket pocket and pulled out a photograph that he placed on the table. 'This is her.'

Imaeda picked up the photo.

It was a picture of a woman standing in front of a large house. From the white fur coat she was wearing, he guessed the photo had been taken during the winter. She had a natural smile and could easily have passed for a professional model.

'She's attractive,' Imaeda said.

'She is. In fact, my cousin is dating her now.'

'By cousin, do you mean your uncle – the CEO's – son?'

'Yes. He's a managing director at Shinozuka Pharmaceuticals.'

'How old is he?'

'Forty-five.'

Forty-five was a very young age to be managing director at a big company like that. Clearly the CEO's son had been fast-tracked along the way.

'Is he married?'

'No, not currently. His wife died in the Japan Air crash six years ago.'

'Oh, sorry to hear that. Did he lose any other family members?'

'No, she was the only one of them on board.'

'Any children?'

'Two, a boy and a girl.'

Imaeda looked back at the woman in the photo. She had large eyes, with a slightly feline curve to them.

'So, if his wife has passed away, am I right to assume that there's no legal issue with your cousin seeing this woman?'

'That's right. In fact, we all hope he finds the right person soon.'

'So,' Imaeda said, tapping his finger on the desk next to the photograph, 'you don't think *she's* the right person. There some kind of problem with her?'

Kazunari leaned forward in his chair. 'Frankly, yes, there is.'

'So what is it? If you don't mind telling me.'

Kazunari nodded and clasped his hands together, resting them on the table. 'Well, for one, she was married before. That in itself isn't a problem; the problem is who she was married to.'

'And who was that?' Imaeda asked, his own voice growing softer.

'Makoto.'

Imaeda sat up straight. 'Makoto Takamiya?'

'That's right. She's his ex-wife.'

'Well,' Imaeda said, shaking his head. 'That's a surprise.'

'I thought it might be,' Kazunari said, smiling. 'As I may have mentioned before, Makoto and I were in dance club together during college. The woman in that photograph was in our club, too. That was how they met.'

'When was the divorce?'

'That was in '88, so three years ago.'

'And Chizuru was the cause?'

'I don't know the details, but that's a good guess,' said Kazunari, a faint smile on his lips.

'So Makoto's ex-wife is dating your cousin now. Was their meeting a coincidence? I mean, did Makoto's ex-wife and your cousin meet at some other place and start dating without your knowledge?'

'No, I wouldn't call it a coincidence. I suppose you can say that I was the one who brought them together.'

'How so?'

'I took my cousin to her store, a clothes boutique in South Aoyama called R&Y. She told me it was named after herself and her mother, Reiko.'

Yukiho Karasawa had been running a couple of boutiques since before her divorce. Though Kazunari had never been a patron during the marriage, a short while after the divorce he'd received an invitation letter to a special sale. When he asked why she sent the invitation, she explained that Makoto had asked her to.

'Apparently, he thought I could help out her business. He still felt responsible, I guess, and wanted to do what he could to support her.'

Imaeda nodded. It was a common enough story. Every time he heard something like this, he wondered anew at the foolish generosity of some men. Sometimes, even when the fault in a divorce lay clearly with the wife, the ex-husband would try to lend a hand afterwards, despite himself. Women, on the other hand, typically wanted nothing to do with their husbands after they split up.

'I'd been wondering myself how she was doing after the divorce, and thought I might as well go, if only to check up on her. I mentioned the whole thing to my cousin and he said he wanted to come along too. He said he was looking for something he could wear on his days off that would still be a little classy.'

'And the rest is history, as they say?'

'Something like that, yes.'

Kazunari claimed that he hadn't realised his cousin, whose name was Yasuharu, was smitten with Yukiho at all at first. It was only later that Yasuharu admitted to him that it had been love at first sight. He even went so far as to say that he couldn't imagine being with any other woman. 'My cousin's always been a passionate sort of man. Once something catches his fancy, he's not one to put on the brakes, no matter what people might say. I didn't know this at the time, but apparently, ever since I brought him that day, he started visiting the boutique regularly. The maid says he owns more outfits than he can possibly wear.'

Imaeda chuckled. 'I think I get the picture. So, Yasuharu made the moves and scored?'

'Yes, and I believe my cousin is hoping they'll get married. Except she seems to be playing hard to get. He thinks it's their age difference and the fact that he has two children.'

'I'm sure that's a factor, yes. Also we have to remember that she's been burned once already. I'd expect some caution on her part.'

'Indeed.'

'So,' Imaeda stretched his arms and placed both hands on the table in front of him. 'What about this woman do you want me to look into? From what I've just heard, it sounds like you already know quite a bit about her.'

'You'd think so, but actually, that's not the case. In fact, there's quite a lot about her that's frankly mysterious.' Kazunari picked up the photograph. 'You know, if it would make my cousin happy, truly happy, then I'd say he should marry her. Sure, I hesitate a little when I think that she's my friend's ex-wife, but I'm sure I could get used to that with time. It's just ...' He turned the photo around so it was facing Imaeda. 'The more I see of her, the more uneasy I feel. I can't explain it. I just can't shake the feeling that there's something else to her, a darkness under the surface.'

'I would propose that every woman has a little darkness under the surface,' Imaeda said with a smile.

'It's more than that, I think. The way she smiles, she gives people the impression that it's a learned skill, a sort of noble way to cope with the pain and the bitterness. Even my cousin says that it's not her face that attracts him, it's the goodness he sees shining from inside her.'

'And you think she's faking that.'

'That's what I want you to find out.'

'That's a tough one. Are you sure you don't have any more, well, *tangible* reason for suspecting this woman isn't all she seems?'

Kazunari looked down at the floor for moment before looking back up and saying, 'I do.'

'And that is?'

'Money.'

'Ah.' Imaeda leaned back in his chair and shot a long look at Kazunari. 'I was wondering when we were going to get to that. You think she's after your cousin's money?'

To Imaeda's surprise, Kazunari shook his head.

'Actually, it's *her* money that concerns me. Makoto said he often wondered about it too. See, it was never really clear where her money was coming from. When she opened those boutiques Makoto didn't help her out at all. She had been into stocks for a while, but with the kind of money she would've needed to open stores in those locations ... it's hard to imagine an amateur investor doing so well in such a short time.'

'Does she come from a wealthy family?'

Kazunari shook his head again. 'Not from what I've heard. Her mother teaches tea ceremony, but she's just living on that income and what she gets from the government.'

Imaeda nodded. This was getting interesting. 'Do you suspect anything in particular? Maybe she has a patron of some sort?'

'I'm not sure. It's hard to imagine her having some secret patron, especially after she got married ... And yet, there is something there, something happening behind the scenes. I'm sure of it.'

'Behind the scenes, right.' Imaeda scratched the side of his nose with his pinky.

'And there's one other thing that bothers me.'

'Yes?'

'The people close to her,' Kazunari said, his voice growing quiet. 'All of them have met with some kind of misfortune.'

'Huh?' Imaeda blinked and looked back at him. 'Are you serious?'

'There's Makoto, of course. He may be happily remarried to Chizuru now, but the divorce was certainly a kind of misfortune.'

'Yeah, but that was his fault, wasn't it?'

'To all appearances, yes. But it's hard to say for sure.'

'Right, well, any other people who met with misfortune?'

'My ex-girlfriend,' Kazunari said, then he closed his mouth tightly.

'OK.' Imaeda took a sip of his coffee. It had gone lukewarm. 'What happened there, if you don't mind me asking?'

'Something bad. Almost the worst thing that could happen to a woman. That *event* was what drove us apart. So,' Kazunari continued, 'I guess you could say that I've met with misfortune, too.'

Imaeda parked on the street a good distance away from the shop. If anyone saw the beat-up Honda Prelude he'd driven, it would undo the impression made by the expensive suit and watch he'd borrowed from Kazunari.

'Are you seriously not going to buy me anything? Maybe there's something that's not too expensive,' Eri said. She was walking beside him in the best dress she owned.

'It's all too expensive,' he told her. 'Heart-attack-inducing levels of expensive, I'm guessing.'

'But what if I really *really* want something?'

'You have your own money. Spend it.'

'You're stingy, you know that?'

'Just be happy I'm paying you to come along.'

They arrived at the R&Y Boutique. The storefront was all glass windows, giving them a good view of the women's clothes and accessories within.

'Wow,' Eri breathed. 'Those do look expensive.'

'Watch what you say when we're inside.' He gave her a jab in the ribs with his elbow.

Eri worked at the bar next to Imaeda's office. She went to a professional school of some sort during the day, though Imaeda had no idea what she was studying. All he knew was that she was trustworthy and whenever he needed to go anywhere as a couple, he could pay her to come along. She seemed to like the work, besides. It was fun pretending to be someone else.

Imaeda opened the glass door and took a step inside. A faint, tasteful scent of perfume lingered in the air.

'Hello,' said a young woman, coming out of the back. She was wearing a white suit, and had on a canned smile, like a stewardess. She wasn't Yukiho Karasawa.

'Yes, the name's Sugawara. I made an appointment?' Sugawara was Eri's real last name. He used it because sometimes she would forget to respond when people called her by an alias.

'What can I help you find today?' the woman asked.

'Something for her,' Imaeda said, indicating Eri. 'Classy, good in summer or autumn, but nothing too fancy. Something she could wear to the office if she wanted. This is her first year at work, so I wouldn't want her standing out too much.'

'I see,' said the woman in the white suit. 'I think I have just the thing. Give me just a moment.'

As soon as her back was turned, Eri looked over at Imaeda. He shook his head. Another person emerged from the back of the shop. Imaeda turned to see Yukiho Karasawa coming towards them, weaving carefully through the clothes hanging on the racks. She had a pleasant, utterly natural smile on her face, and a soft, gentle light in her eyes. There was an aura around her, as though her desire to meet the needs of every customer who came into her shop was some visible, tangible thing.

'Hello,' she said, bowing gently, her eyes never leaving them.

Imaeda nodded back in silence.

'Mr Sugawara, correct? You heard about us from Mr Shinozuka?'

'That's right,' Imaeda said. He'd been asked how he heard about the shop when he called to make an appointment.

'Would that be Kazunari Shinozuka?' Yukiho asked, raising an eyebrow.

'Yes,' Imaeda replied, wondering why her first guess had been Kazunari, and not Yasuharu – the Shinozuka she was dating.

'Buying something for your wife?' she asked with a glance at Eri.

'No,' Imaeda said laughing. 'My niece. It's a present to celebrate her first job.'

'Oh, I see. My apologies,' Yukiho said, still smiling. Her long eyelashes fluttered, and a few strands of hair fell across her forehead. She lifted them away with her index finger, an utterly graceful gesture that put Imaeda in mind of women he'd seen in old foreign films.

If he remembered correctly, Yukiho Karasawa was only twenty-nine years old. He wondered how she managed to project that kind of refinement at such a young age. Imaeda thought he could understand how Yasuharu had fallen for her. He'd like to meet the man who wouldn't feel some twinge of longing in her presence.

The woman in the white suit brought several outfits for them to look at. She showed them to Eri, asking her what she thought.

'Take your time,' Imaeda told her. 'Talk it over with this nice lady here and pick the one that really suits you.'

Eri looked around at him, a curious smile coming to her lips. *Like you're going to buy me anything*, her eyes seemed to be saying.

'How is Mr Shinozuka doing these days?' Yukiho asked.

'Busy as always.'

'If you don't mind me asking, how do you know him?'

'He's a friend. We play golf together sometimes.'

'Ah, that makes sense,' she said, nodding. Her almond-shaped eyes went to Imaeda's wrists. 'That's a lovely watch.'

'What, this?' Imaeda self-consciously covered his watch with his right hand. 'It was a gift.'

Yukiho nodded again, yet he couldn't help but notice that something about her smile had changed. For a second, he wondered if she had somehow guessed it belonged to Kazunari, despite his assurances that he had never worn it in front of her. So how could she know?

'This is really a nice shop you've got here,' Imaeda said. 'You have a fantastic selection. You must be a very talented businesswoman. Remarkable for one so young.'

'Thank you. Though we do have trouble meeting some clients' requests.'

'You're just being modest.'

'No, it's true. But where are my manners? Would you like something to drink? I have iced coffee, and tea. Or something hot, if you prefer.'

'That's nice of you. I'll take a coffee. Hot, thanks.'

'Right away. Have a seat over there.' Yukiho indicated a corner of the shop with a sofa and a table.

Imaeda sat down on the sofa. It was Italian-made, with little clawed feet. The table doubled as a display stand. Beneath the glass top, necklaces, bracelets and the like were lined out for customers to see. There were no price tags, but these were clearly for sale. No doubt they were put here to catch the eye of shoppers who came over to take a break from the clothes.

Imaeda took a pack of Marlboros out of his jacket pocket and pulled out his lighter. The lighter, too, was a loan from Kazunari. He lit his cigarette and filled his lungs with smoke. Gradually he could feel his nerves relaxing. He hadn't realised how tense he was. *All because of one woman.*

He wondered where she got her seemingly natural elegance and grace. What had polished her to gleam so brightly?

An old two-storey apartment building floated in the back of

Imaeda's mind. Yoshida Heights. The building had somehow remained standing since the 1950s. Imaeda had paid the place a visit the week before in an attempt to gain some insight into Yukiho's past.

There were a few old houses nearby, pre-war structures, most of them. Some of the residents remembered the mother and daughter who had lived in Yoshida Heights No 103.

The mother's last name had been Nishimoto, making Yukiho's original name Yukiho Nishimoto.

Her father had passed away when she was still young, so she had lived alone with her mother, Fumiyo, who worked a few part-time jobs to make ends meet. Fumiyo had died of gas poisoning when Yukiho was in sixth grade. Officially, the death had been ruled an accident, but one of the older women living nearby had told him about the rumours of suicide.

'She was taking all kinds of medicine, you know,' she told him. 'And there were all these other strange things going on. The poor thing was so tired all the time, what with her husband passing and all. Still, they never found out what really happened,' she added in a hushed voice.

Imaeda went over to the apartment building to give it a closer inspection. Around the back, someone had left a window open, letting him take a good look inside. The unit was tiny, a small tatami-matted room next to a little kitchen. There was an old dresser and a wicker basket along the wall. Both had seen better days. A low table sat in the middle of the matted room, on which had been left some glasses and a few bottles of pills. Whoever lived there was elderly – nearly all the residents of Yoshida Heights were, according to what he had heard.

He tried to imagine an elementary school girl and her mother – probably in her late thirties – living in the tiny apartment in front of him. The girl would be doing her homework at the little table. Behind her, the mother moved wearily as she prepared supper …

Something tugged at his chest, and he remembered another thing the people who lived near Yoshida Heights had told him about. A murder.

The murder had taken place about a year before Fumiyo's death. The victim had been the owner of a pawnshop who paid occasional visits to Fumiyo, which had put her on the list of suspects. She was never arrested, however.

'But of course word got around that the police had paid her visit, so everyone figured she had something to do with it. I heard she had real trouble getting jobs after that, the poor lady,' an old man who ran a tobacco shop nearby told him.

Imaeda had gone to the library and looked through archival newspapers to find out more about the murder. A year before Fumiyo's death made it 1973. He also knew it had happened during the autumn.

The article wasn't hard to find. According to the report, the body had been discovered in an unfinished building located in a part of town called Ōe. The victim had been stabbed several times with something like a slender knife, but the murder weapon was never found. The victim, one Yosuke Kirihara, had left his house some time after noon that day and not returned. The wife had called the police. Though he typically carried little money on his person, he had just withdrawn a considerable sum of money before he was killed, making it likely that the murderer knew him. Imaeda searched for an article reporting that the case had been solved, but couldn't find one. The man at the tobacco shop had been right, then. The killer was never found.

If Fumiyo Nishimoto had been a regular at the pawnshop, he could see why the police would have suspected her. She could have approached the owner without alarming him, and caught him unawares with the knife. And yet the way public opinion had turned against her after the questioning made him think that, in a sense, Fumiyo Nishimoto had been a victim, too.

Imaeda looked up as someone approached him. The aroma of coffee hit his nostrils. A woman just over twenty years old, wearing an apron, had come over with a coffee cup on a tray. Beneath the apron she wore a tight-fitting T-shirt that showed off her curves.

'Thanks,' Imaeda said, reaching out for the cup. Just being in a place like this made even the coffee smell richer. 'Do you always have three people running the shop?'

'Most of the time,' the girl said. 'Though Miss Karasawa often spends time at another one of our boutiques.'

'Where would that be?'

'Daikanyama.'

Daikanyama was another trendy area, on the western edge of central Tokyo. 'Two stores, at her age?' Imaeda said. 'That's impressive.'

'Actually, we're about to open a third store selling children's clothes in Jiyugaoka.'

'Amazing. Miss Karasawa must have a goose tucked away somewhere that lays golden eggs.'

'She's a very hard worker. I wonder sometimes if she ever sleeps,' she added in a quiet voice, glancing towards the back. 'Enjoy,' she said, leaving him alone with his coffee.

Imaeda drank his coffee black. It was much better than the stuff they served at the café near his office.

It occurred to Imaeda that Yukiho might be more frugal than she appeared. Most successful businesspeople were. And she would have had plenty of time while living at Yoshida Heights to hone that part of her character.

When her mother died, a nearby relative, Reiko Karasawa, had taken Yukiho in. Reiko was Yukiho's father's cousin.

For his next trip, Imaeda had paid a visit to the Karasawa house. It was an elegant Japanese-style home, with a small garden. A sign hanging on the door announced that tea ceremony classes were held there regularly.

This was where Yukiho's foster mother had taught her tea, flower arrangement, and a number of other skills that would serve her well in her future life. He imagined it was during her time living here that the femininity she seemed to exude from her entire body had begun to bud.

Because Reiko Karasawa was still alive, he had to be circumspect in his questioning in the area. Still, he was able to gather that

Yukiho's life after moving to the Karasawa household wasn't anything out of the ordinary. Most of the residents remembered little about her other than that she was a 'pretty, well-mannered sort of girl'.

Someone else approached and he looked up to see Eri Sugawara wearing a black velvet dress. The hem sat alarmingly high up her shapely legs.

'You sure you can wear that to work?'

'It's a bit much, huh.'

'How about something like this?' the woman in the white suit said, showing her another outfit. It was a blue jacket, with a white collar. 'You can wear this with a skirt or knee-length pants if you prefer.'

'Hmm ...' Eri rubbed her chin. 'I like it – it's just that I already have something very similar.'

'Well, no sense getting two,' Imaeda said. He looked at his watch. It was almost time for them to leave.

'Do you think we could come back?' Eri asked him. 'You know, I'm starting to forget exactly what I already have.' This was her line, exactly as they had rehearsed.

'I suppose, though I hate having put them through all this trouble.'

'I'm really sorry. Thank you for showing me everything,' Eri apologised to the woman in the white suit.

'Not at all,' the woman replied with a saccharine smile.

Imaeda stood and waited for Eri to change back into her own clothes. Yukiho reappeared from the back.

'Couldn't find anything for your niece?'

He shook his head. 'I apologise. She has trouble making up her mind sometimes.'

'Not to worry,' Yukiho said. 'It's often difficult to find something just right.'

'Apparently so.'

'I've always thought that clothes and jewellery aren't meant to hide what's inside a person. They're meant to bring it out. That's why, when we help our customers find something, we like to talk to them so we can understand what they're like on the inside as well as the outside.'

'That's an interesting approach.'

'Someone who's been well raised can wear practically anything and make it look elegant. Of course ...' Yukiho stared directly at Imaeda before continuing, '... the opposite is also true.'

Imaeda nodded and looked away. Maybe his suit didn't fit him. Or maybe it was Eri who seemed unnatural.

Eri returned from the fitting room. 'All ready,' she said.

'I'd like to send you a postcard the next time we have a sale, if you'd write your address here for me,' Yukiho said, handing a piece of paper to Eri, who shot Imaeda an uneasy look.

'Your address is fine,' he said. 'You can let me know.'

She started to write.

'It really is a nice watch,' Yukiho said, her eyes on Imaeda's wrist.

'Yes, you seem to like it.'

'It's a Cartier Limited edition. In fact, I only know one other person who owns one.'

'You don't say,' Imaeda replied.

'We hope to see you again soon,' Yukiho said.

'Yes, soon.'

Outside, Imaeda gave Eri a ride back to her apartment and paid her ten thousand yen. 'Not bad just for trying on some fancy clothes, huh?'

'Are you kidding? That was torture. Next time I'm definitely making you buy me something.'

'If there is a next time,' Imaeda said to himself as he drove away. Today's visit hadn't strictly been part of his investigation. He just wanted to meet Yukiho Karasawa in person.

He sensed it would be dangerous to go back. Yukiho was clearly someone to watch out for, far more than he had realised.

Back at his office, he gave Kazunari a call.

'How did it go?'

'I think I understand what you're saying now, a little,' Imaeda told him.

'How so?'

'There *is* something mysterious about her.'

'You see?'

'And she's incredibly attractive. I can understand why your cousin fell for her.'

There was silence on the other end of the line.

'Actually,' Imaeda continued, 'there was one thing I wanted to ask you about: the watch you loaned me.'

'What about it?'

'Are you sure you never wore it in front of her? Or spoke to her about it in any way?'

'I don't think so. Did she say something?'

Imaeda related what Yukiho had said at the shop. He heard Kazunari groan.

'I'd be really surprised if she knew I had it,' he said. 'Except . . .' His voice grew quiet.

'Except what?'

'Actually, I did wear it once when she was around. But there's no way she could have seen it. And even if she had, I'd be amazed if she remembered.'

'Where was this?'

'Her wedding reception.'

'You wore it to her reception? What makes you so sure she didn't see it?'

'I talked a little with Makoto, but I never got that close to her. The only time I did was when the couple was going around the tables with a long taper, lighting the candles at each table – you know that thing they do at receptions sometimes. But the lights were down, and I have a hard time believing she could have either seen or remembered my watch.'

'Right, well, probably not something worth worrying about, then.'

'I wouldn't think so, no.'

Imaeda nodded, holding the receiver in his hand. Kazunari seemed like a bright enough man. If he didn't think she had seen the watch, he would have to take his word for it.

'I'm sorry to put you through all this trouble,' Kazunari apologised.

'All in a day's work,' said Imaeda. 'To tell you the truth, I'm a little interested in her now, too. Don't get the wrong idea, I don't mean I'm smitten with her. It's just ... there's definitely something going on there.'

On the other end of the line, Kazunari fell silent. After a moment, he said, 'Well, thanks, and let me know if you find out anything else.'

'Will do,' Imaeda said and hung up the phone.

Two days later, Imaeda was back in Osaka to meet someone he'd learned of while questioning people who lived near the Karasawa house.

A woman running a small bakery had told him he should look for 'Mrs Motooka's daughter – she went to Seika. She might know the Karasawa girl. She's about the same age as her, I should think. Sorry, I don't know for sure.'

The daughter's name was Kuniko, a regular at the bakery. The woman had told him she was an interior designer who did work for one of the large real estate agencies in town.

Back in Tokyo, he looked into the estate agency. It took some doing, but he managed to dig up Kuniko's phone number and gave her a call. Imaeda introduced himself as a freelance writer doing some research for a column he was writing for a woman's magazine.

'We're doing a special on women from elite girls' schools who've gone independent in the workforce. I was looking for women in the Tokyo and Osaka area who are making a name for themselves in business, and your name came up.'

Kuniko sounded surprised, but not displeased. She wanted to know who had given him her name.

'Sorry, but I can't say. Source confidentiality, and all that. I was wondering if I could ask you what year you graduated from Seika?'
'1981.'

Inwardly, Imaeda cheered. That put her in Yukiho Karasawa's year.

'Do you happen to know someone by the name of Ms Karasawa?'

'You mean Yukiho?'

'That's right – you know her?'

'Yes, though we weren't in the same class, ever. Was there something about her?'

Imaeda thought he detected a note of alarm in the woman's voice.

'Yes, actually, I had planned to interview her as well. She's running a few boutiques up here in Tokyo.'

'I see. I had no idea.'

'Anyway,' Imaeda said, 'I was hoping we might meet some time. I'd only need an hour, tops. I'd like to hear more about the work you do, and your lifestyle, things like that for the article – as long as you can fit it into your schedule.'

Kuniko hesitated a moment before agreeing.

Kuniko worked at an office several minutes' walk from the subway station in central Osaka, a part of town called Senba. It was known for its wholesalers and financial institutions and the streets were lined with business hotels. Even now that the economic bubble had burst, businessmen and women hurried along the streets, no one seeming to have a second to waste.

The office for her company, Staging Success, was on the twentieth floor of a building owned by the estate agency. Imaeda waited for her in the café in the shopping mall beneath the building.

The glass clock on the wall read five past one when a woman wearing a white jacket came into the café. She had on glasses, the frames a bit large on her face. For a woman, she was very tall and she fitted the image Imaeda had from talking to her on the phone to a T. She had slender legs, too, and was quite attractive.

Imaeda stood and introduced himself, handing her a business card that said he was a freelance writer. The name on the card was an alias.

She ordered a milk tea and sat down.

'Thanks for taking the time to see me,' he said.

'It's no problem, I only hope it's worth your time,' Kuniko said. She had a noticeably Osakan accent.

'I have no doubt it will be. I'm interviewing a number of people for this project.'

'I had a question about that, actually,' she said. 'Will my real name appear in the article?'

'Our general rule is to use aliases. Unless of course you wanted to request that we use your actual name?'

She shook her head. 'No, no. An alias is fine.'

'Right, let's begin, then.'

Imaeda took out his pen and notebook and started asking the kind of questions he might have asked if he had really been doing a report on graduates from girls' schools. Kuniko answered each question thoughtfully and Imaeda felt oddly guilty, so he tried to at least pay attention and be serious with his follow-up questions. As a result, he learned all about the merits of using an interior designer and the added value an estate agency gained by working with her team. It was all very interesting, actually.

Getting through his first questions only took about thirty minutes. Kuniko stopped talking for a moment to take a sip of her tea.

Imaeda had been waiting for the right moment to bring the conversation around to Yukiho. He had already laid the groundwork on the phone the other day, but was struggling for a natural segue when Kuniko asked, 'You said you were looking at Ms Karasawa as well?'

'That's right,' Imaeda said, a little surprised.

'She's running some kind of boutique?'

'Yes. In Aoyama, up in Tokyo.'

'My, she's really done well for herself,' Kuniko said. Her expression looked a little hard.

Apparently, this woman didn't have a very favourable impression of Yukiho. That was perfect – if he was going to start asking questions about Yukiho's past he wanted someone who wouldn't mince words.

Sticking his hand in his jacket pocket, he asked if she minded if he had a cigarette. She shook her head.

He put a Marlboro in his mouth and lit it – a calculated move to indicate that the real interview was over and now they were just chatting.

'It's funny you should mention her,' Imaeda said. 'We've actually been having a bit of a problem with her part of the story.'

Kuniko's eyes lit up. 'What sort of problem?'

'It's probably nothing,' Imaeda said, 'just, some of the people I've talked to don't have a very favourable impression of her.'

'Oh? In what way?'

'Well, I think because she's young and she's running a few stores, people are envious of her success. That, and I'm sure she had to step on a few people to get where she is. Comes with the territory.' Imaeda took a sip of his tepid coffee. 'You know, we're hearing comments like "she's tight with her money", or "she's not afraid to use people if her business will benefit", that sort of thing.'

'I see.'

'Of course, we're very interested in featuring her as a young female entrepreneur, but if it turns out she actually does have a bad reputation, well, some people in editorial think we should give her a pass. So now I'm wondering what to do.'

'I suppose it wouldn't be good for the magazine if something came out.'

'That's just it,' Imaeda said, stealing a glance at Kuniko's expression. She didn't seem to find this discussion of her former classmate's flaws uncomfortable. 'You were in middle and high school with her, was it?'

'That's right.'

'You remember anything about her from those days? Did she seem like the kind of person who might get into trouble later in life? I won't include any of this in the article, of course, so feel free to be honest.'

'I'm not sure,' Kuniko said, frowning. She glanced at her watch. 'Like I said on the phone, we were never in the same class together. But I definitely knew about her. Everyone in school knew about her. She was a minor celebrity.'

'You don't say?'

'Well, it's just,' she blinked a few times, 'looking like she does, she stood out. Some of the boys from a nearby school even made a fan club in her honour.'

'A fan club?' Imaeda chuckled. Having met her in person, he wasn't surprised.

'She was a good student, too, I hear. One of my friends had been in the same class as her since middle school.'

'So a real achiever, then.'

'Yes, but I don't know much about her first-hand. I don't think we ever spoke, even.'

'Did your friend have anything to say about her?'

'No, *she* never said anything bad about Yukiho. It was just talking about how lucky she was to be born so beautiful, things like that.'

'*She* never said anything bad ... but someone else did?'

Kuniko thought for a moment.

'There was a strange rumour going around about her in middle school,' Kuniko said. Her voice grew quieter.

'What sort of rumour?'

She shot him a suspicious look. 'You swear you're not going to put this in your article?'

'You have my word,' he said.

Kuniko took a breath. 'People said she was lying about her past.'

'In what way?'

'Well, they said that she was born into a really bad household, but she hid it and was just pretending to be well-to-do.'

'You sure they weren't just talking about her being adopted by a relative when she was little?'

Kuniko leaned forward slightly. 'There was that, yes, but the problem was the house where she was born. They said that her real mom made money through special ... arrangements with men.'

'I see,' Imaeda said, taking care not to seem too surprised. 'You mean she was someone's mistress?'

'Not just someone, several people. It was only a rumour, of

course,' she added. 'Except,' she continued, 'one of the men she was seeing was killed.'

Now Imaeda acted surprised. 'Really?'

She nodded. 'Apparently the police had Yukiho's mom in for questioning.'

That would be the pawnshop owner, Imaeda thought, staring at the tip of his cigarette. So the police hadn't had their eyes on Fumiyo Nishimoto just because she was a customer at the shop – if the rumour was actually true.

'Please don't tell anyone I told you this.'

'I won't, I promise.' Imaeda smiled at her. Then his face went serious again. 'Still, that's a pretty heavy rumour. There wasn't any trouble because of it?'

'Not that I ever noticed. I mean, word did get around, but it was only in our little circle. And besides, everyone knew who started the rumour.'

'They did?'

'Yes. It was a girl who had a friend or relative or something who lived near the house where Yukiho grew up, which is how she knew about it. I wasn't close to her myself, but I heard about it through a friend.'

'Was this girl also at Seika?'

'She was our classmate.'

'What was her name?'

'I'm not sure I should say.' Kuniko looked down at the table.

'Of course, I'm sorry,' Imaeda said, tapping his cigarette on the edge of the ashtray. He didn't want to raise any suspicions by probing too deeply. 'Still, that's quite a rumour to spread. Don't you think she would've been worried that it would get back to Yukiho?'

'Oh, it was pretty clear that they were enemies back then. This other girl was an over-achiever herself, so she probably thought of Yukiho as a rival.'

'Sounds like a classic girls' school story.'

Kuniko smiled. 'Thinking back on it now, it sure does.'

'So what happened to their rivalry in the end?'

'It's funny, actually,' Kuniko said, then she fell silent. After a long moment, she said, 'There was an incident, I guess you'd call it, and after that, they became friends.'

'An incident?'

Kuniko glanced around them. No one was sitting near their table. 'The girl who spread the rumour was attacked.'

Imaeda leaned forward. 'How do you mean, attacked?'

'Well, she was absent from school for days. They told us she'd been in a traffic accident, but I heard later that she'd been attacked on her way home from school one night and was resting to recover from the shock.'

'How exactly was she attacked, if you don't mind me asking?'

Kuniko shook her head. 'I don't know the details. Some people said she was raped, but there were others who said it didn't go that far. All I know is something bad must have happened to her. Someone who lived nearby said the police were coming around and asking questions.'

Something tugged at the back of Imaeda's mind. This was important, he was sure of it. 'And this incident brought the girl and Yukiho together somehow?'

Kuniko nodded. 'It was Yukiho who found her after it happened, apparently. And I guess she visited her at her house afterwards and brought her notes from class, that sort of thing.'

Imaeda's mind started racing. He tried to act calm, but he could feel his skin prickle.

'Do you know if Yukiho was alone when she found her?'

'No, I heard she was with a friend.'

Imaeda nodded and swallowed. His throat was dry.

That night he stayed at a business hotel near Umeda Station in the heart of Osaka. Imaeda listened to the tape of his interview with Kuniko Motooka, taking notes. She had never noticed the tiny recorder in his jacket pocket and he had managed to keep it running the entire time.

He thought about Kuniko going out to the newsstand every week to buy the magazine she thought her story would be in. He felt a little bad about it, but decided that at least he had given her something to dream about. He reached for the phone on the bed stand, pressing the buttons as he read the number out of his note-book.

The phone rang three times before Kazunari picked up.

'Hello? Mr Shinozuka? It's Imaeda. I'm in Osaka ... That's right. I'm calling because there was somebody I wanted to meet and I thought you could help me with her address or number.'

The name of the woman he wanted to meet was Eriko Kawashima.

The doorbell rang just as Eriko was taking clothes out of the dryer. She tossed her handful of sheets and underwear into the basket.

The intercom for the front door was on the wall in the dining room. She went in, picked it up and said, 'Hello?'

'Mrs Tezuka? It's Maeda from Tokyo.'

'Oh, be right there.'

Eriko took off her apron and walked to the front door. They had just bought this old house and she was getting familiar with the way some of the floorboards in the hallway squeaked when she walked across them. She'd been on at her husband to fix them for a while, but he had yet to rise to the challenge.

She opened the door with the chain still attached. A man was standing outside wearing a short-sleeved shirt with a blue tie. He looked a little over thirty.

'Sorry to drop in on you like this,' the man said, bowing. His hair was perfectly combed. 'Your mother mentioned I was coming, I hope?'

'Yes, she called.'

'That's good,' the man said with a relieved smile. He offered her his business card, which introduced him as Kazuro Maeda, an investigator with the Heart-to-Heart Marriage Counselling Centre.

She took the card, closed the door, and undid the chain before opening it again. Still she was reluctant to let him inside the house. 'I'm sorry, the house is a bit of a mess,' she said.

Maeda shook his head. 'Here is fine, if you don't mind.' He pulled a small notebook out of his shirt pocket.

Her mother had told her on the phone that morning that an investigator from a place specialising in prenuptial background checks would be visiting to talk to her. Apparently, he had gone to her family's home first.

'He wants to know about Yukiho,' her mother said over the phone.

'Yukiho? But she's divorced,' Eriko had said.

'Not for long, apparently.'

Her mother explained that someone interested in Yukiho had hired an investigator to look into her. 'He wants to talk to some of her old friends. I told him you were married and didn't live here any more, and he asked where you'd moved to. You don't mind if I tell him, do you?'

'No, it's fine, go ahead.'

Apparently the man was still at her mother's house, because she put down the phone for a while before returning to say, 'OK. Mr Maeda says if it's all right, he'll drop by later today.'

'OK, that's fine. Whatever.'

Normally she would have turned down a meeting with someone she didn't know. The only reason she didn't was because it concerned Yukiho Karasawa. They hadn't talked for years, and Eriko wanted to know how her old friend was doing.

Still, she was a little surprised that the investigator was asking about her so openly. She had always assumed that these investigations into potential partners happened under a veil of secrecy.

She gave him a general overview: how she and Yukiho had got to know each other in middle school, and gone to the same college and the investigator took notes.

'Can I ask who it is that wants to marry her?' Eriko asked during a pause in the questions.

Maeda looked surprised, then a wry smile came to his face. 'I'm sorry, but that's confidential for the time being.'

'For the time being?'

'Well, if all goes well, I'm sure you'll hear about it directly. However, at the current stage, there's always the possibility that things might not, er, get as far as that.'

'You mean this man has other options for brides?'

'Something like that, yes.'

Apparently this guy was some kind of high-roller if he was hiring investigators to look into a number of potentials.

'I'm guessing I shouldn't talk to Yukiho about this?' Eriko asked.

'It would be extremely helpful if you could keep this to yourself, yes,' Maeda told her. 'Not many people look favourably upon being investigated. Are you still in contact with Ms Karasawa, incidentally?'

'Not really,' she told him. 'We send each other New Year's cards, and that's about it.'

'I see. If you don't mind me asking, when did you get married?'

'Two years ago.'

'Did Ms Karasawa attend the wedding?'

Eriko shook her head. 'We had a ceremony, but we didn't do a big reception. It was just a little family party. I sent her an announcement, of course, but no invitation. She's all the way up in Tokyo, and the timing wasn't so great, so I didn't think it was appropriate ...'

'By timing, you mean ... ?' Maeda asked, then it seemed that a light went off in his head and he nodded. 'Of course. That was right after Ms Karasawa's divorce, wasn't it.'

'Yes. She'd written about it on her New Year's card.'

When she'd heard about the divorce, Eriko had wanted to call and ask what had happened. But then, she didn't want to open any fresh wounds, and so in the end they never spoke. She still didn't know the reasons for the divorce. All the New Year's card had said was that Yukiho was 'going back to the starting line, and beginning again'.

Eriko had spent a lot of time with Yukiho through their first two years in college, just as they had in middle and high school. They went shopping together, went to concerts together – they were practically attached at the hip. Eriko had clung to Yukiho even more after what happened to her as a freshman. She avoided dating anyone she didn't know and was scared to make new friends. In many ways, Yukiho became her lifeline to the outside world.

It wasn't a state of affairs that could go on for ever. Eriko knew that better than anyone. She couldn't keep Yukiho from living her own life. Though she never said as much, she'd clearly begun dating Makoto from dance club. It was only natural that she would want to spend more time with him.

Yukiho and Makoto's budding relationship reminded Eriko of someone else she didn't want to think about: Kazunari Shinozuka. When she thought of him, her heart sank into a deep, dark place.

Around halfway through sophomore year, Eriko began intentionally reducing the amount of time she spent with Yukiho. At first Yukiho seemed confused, but gradually she began to draw away, too. Maybe she thought that if they kept on the way they were, Eriko would never have a chance to find her own footing.

Of course, they were still friends and they kept in touch. They could talk for hours whenever they got together, and they occasionally called each other to chat on the phone, but no more than they talked with other friends.

After graduation the two of them grew even further apart. Eriko's parents had got her a job at a local bank and Yukiho went up to Tokyo and married Makoto.

'What sort of person would you say Yukiho is?' Maeda asked. 'Just your impressions are fine. Would you say she's nervous, or withdrawn? Is she detail orientated? Does she like to win? Simple things like that.'

'I'm not sure it's that simple to sum a person up.'

'Then maybe you could tell me about her in your own words.'

'Well ...' Eriko paused a moment to think. 'She's a strong woman. Not the go-out-and-get-'em type. A quieter kind of strength. When you're near her, you can feel her radiating a kind of power.'

'Anything else?'

'Well, she seemed to know everything, sometimes.'

'I see,' Maeda's eyes opened a little wider. 'That's interesting. A woman who knows everything. Was she very erudite?'

'No, it's just that she seemed to know a lot about people's true natures and the underside of the way the world worked. Talking

with her sometimes, I ...' She hesitated a moment before continuing, 'I learned a lot.'

'I see. And yet this woman-who-knew-everything failed at marriage. What do you think about that?' Maeda asked quickly.

Clearly, the investigator – and his client – wanted to know why
Yukiho had got a divorce and whether the cause had lain with her.

'It's possible,' Eriko said after a moment's thought, 'that she
made a mistake getting married in the first place.'

'How so?'

'I feel like – and this is unusual for her – that she got caught up
in the moment when she agreed to marry. I think that if she had
thought about it more, she might not have gone through with it.'

'You mean the man she married forced her hand?'

'Not forced, no,' Eriko said, careful to choose the right words.
'I just think, when people get married, ideally, they have to reach
a certain stable level in their feelings for each other – a balance.
And I'm not sure they had that.'

'You mean Ms Karasawa wasn't as enthusiastic about the relationship as Mr Takamiya?'

'It's hard to express it exactly,' Eriko said, frowning. 'But I
wouldn't call him the love of her life.'

'Interesting,' Maeda said, his eyes widening slightly.

Eriko immediately regretted having said it. 'I'm sorry, that's
entirely just my opinion. I'm probably completely off the mark.'

Maeda fell quiet, looking at her. Then, gradually, the smile
returned to his face. 'It's all right. Like I said before, I'm interested
in your impressions. I understand you weren't directly involved.'

'Even so, I think I should stop. I don't want to cause any trouble for her. I think you should be able to find other people who
know her far better than I do these days.'

Eriko reached for the doorknob.

'Just one more question ...' Maeda lifted his index finger.
'There was something I wanted to ask you about your time
together in middle school.'

'OK,' Eriko said warily.

'About a certain incident that happened in your last year of middle school, when one of your classmates was assaulted. Is it true that you were with Ms Karasawa when she discovered her?'

Eriko felt the blood drain from her face. 'What does that have to do with—'

'I was just wondering if you remembered anything about Ms Karasawa's reaction, anything that might illuminate her character.'

Eriko had already started shaking her head violently before he finished talking. 'No, nothing. I'm sorry, but I think we're done here. I have things to do.'

Apparently, she had made her point. The investigator took a step back from her door. 'I understand. Thanks for your time.'

Eriko closed the door without answering. She didn't want him to see her shaking, and pretending she was fine wasn't an option.

She sat down on the entrance hall mat. Dark memories filled her mind. It was incredible how many years had gone by and still the wound inside her felt raw. It had never healed. She'd just forgotten it was there.

It was only partially the investigator's fault for bringing up Miyako Fujimura, the girl who had been assaulted. In truth, just talking about Yukiho had already started the memories surfacing in the back of her mind.

Eriko wasn't sure what it was, but from a certain point she had started to imagine things about her old friend. At first she'd thought she was just obsessing about things, but gradually her suspicions and fears had coalesced into a story.

She never spoke about it to anyone. It was a horrible thing to think, so horrible she didn't want anyone else to know she'd thought it. She tried to forget, but the story had settled in her mind, lurking, indelible. She hated herself for thinking it. When she thought about Yukiho's kindness over the years, she felt like a beast by comparison.

And yet another part of her repeated the story over and over, like a mantra. Was it really just her imagination? Was there no kernel of truth to it?

Therein lay the true reason she had distanced herself from Yukiho back in college: she couldn't stand the weight of the doubt and the self-loathing she felt inside whenever she saw her friend's face.

Eriko put a hand on the wall to help her stand. She looked up and saw that she had left the front door unlocked. Reaching out, she turned the deadbolt and pulled the chain firmly shut.

ELEVEN

Imaeda made his way towards the café, a little place facing the main drag in Ginza. It was thirteen minutes to six in the evening. Shoppers and people on their way home from work crowded the street outside. A young couple was walking in front of him. Neither of them looked a year over twenty. The man was wearing a summer jacket – an Armani. He had seen them get out of a BMW parked down the street. *Probably something he bought when the economy was good*, Imaeda thought. He wouldn't shed a tear when kids barely old enough to drive were no longer able to buy luxury cars as they'd been doing over the last decade.

The ground floor of the café was a pastry shop. He walked up the stairs, checking his watch. Five-fifty. He'd arrived a little later than he wanted to. Imaeda made it a policy to show up to appointments fifteen to thirty minutes early, for the psychological advantage it gave him over the person he was going to meet, if nothing else.

He scanned the patrons but, failing to see Kazunari Shinozuka anywhere, picked a seat where he could look out through the window at the street below. The café was about half full.

A waiter with southeast Asian features came to take his order. Many establishments had turned to hiring foreign help during the bubble years when it became too expensive to hire locally. *Anything's better than dealing with the preening Japanese kids these days*, Imaeda thought. He ordered coffee.

Lighting a Marlboro, he looked down at the street through the window. There seemed to be more people walking outside than there had been just a few minutes ago. He heard businesses were cutting back on entertainment expenses but maybe the frugality was less widespread than he'd imagined. Either that, or Ginza was witnessing the last bright flicker of a dying flame.

Imaeda had only been watching for a minute before he picked a man out of the crowd who walked with long strides and had a beige suit jacket slung over one arm. It was five minutes to six. *I guess the elite don't believe in being late, either.*

Kazunari walked in and waved a hand in greeting as he approached the table, just as the waiter was bringing Imaeda his coffee. Kazunari sat and ordered an iced coffee for himself. 'Hot outside, isn't it,' he said, fanning himself with his hand.

'Very,' Imaeda agreed.

'Do you take summer vacations in your line of work?'

'Not usually, no,' Imaeda said with a smile. 'I tend to take my breaks whenever work is slow. Besides, summer is an excellent time to do a certain kind of investigation.'

'What kind would that be?'

'Adultery. For instance, if a woman has asked me to find out whether her husband is having an affair I advise her to tell her husband she wants to go visit her parents during the summer. If her husband shows any reluctance to going, she offers to go by herself.'

'I see. So if the husband does have a woman on the side—'

'It's too good an opportunity to pass up. While his wife frets away at her parents' house I photograph the husband and his lover on an overnight trip somewhere. I would say the rate that cheating husbands fall for that one is about 100 per cent.'

Kazunari laughed quietly. The stiffness Imaeda had seen in his face when he came into the café was fading.

The waiter brought Kazunari's iced coffee. He took a gulp.

'So, did you find anything out?' he asked. The way he said it made it clear he had been waiting to ask this question since the moment he walked in.

'I looked into a few things,' Imaeda told him. 'Though I'm afraid my report might fall a little short of what you were expecting.'

Imaeda pulled the file out of his briefcase and laid it on the table. Kazunari opened it at once.

Imaeda was confident he'd managed to cover everything he could about Yukiho Karasawa's upbringing, school history, and current life.

After a while, Kazunari looked up from the report. 'I had no idea her natural mother committed suicide.'

'Actually, you'll see I didn't write suicide. Though that was a prevalent theory at the time, they never found any decisive evidence to support it.'

'And yet given the conditions they were living under, suicide wasn't unthinkable.'

'No, it wasn't.'

'This is all a little surprising,' Kazunari said then. 'Or, maybe not.'

'Yes?'

'Everything about her gives the impression that she was brought up in luxury, but every once in a while you see something in her other than the refinement. An attitude she wears like armour. Have you ever had a cat as a pet?'

Imaeda shook his head.

'We had four when I was a kid,' Kazunari explained. 'They were all strays, nothing fancy. We tried to treat them all exactly the same, but their attitude towards us was different depending on how old they were when we took them in. A cat rescued as a kitten grows up never knowing life without human protection. They're trusting and easily spoiled. But a cat picked up when it's already grown – even though they might seem friendly, they never stop being wary. They'll live with you because you feed them, but they'll never completely let their guard down. I feel like that's how she operates sometimes.'

'Whatever Yukiho is, she's no house cat.'

'I'm sure if she heard me comparing her to a stray, her hair would bristle like one,' Kazunari said, the corners of his mouth softening.

'Of course,' Imaeda said, thinking of Yukiho's feline eyes, 'that quality of hers might be attractive to some people.'

'Oh, absolutely. Women can be scary that way, can't they.'

'You got that right,' Imaeda agreed. 'Incidentally, did you read the part about the stock trading?'

'Briefly, yes. I'm surprised you found out who her broker was.'

'She left some of her papers behind after the divorce.'

'At Makoto's place?' Kazunari asked, a cloud coming over his face. 'How did you explain the investigation to him?'

'Only in very broad strokes. I told him that the family of a man considering marriage to Yukiho wanted me to look into her past. Should I not have told him?'

'No, that's fine. If they get married he'll find out sooner or later anyway. How did he react to the news?'

'He said he hoped she'd found the right man.'

'You didn't tell him the man was someone he knew?'

'I didn't tell him, but I think he might've guessed that you were behind the investigation. It would've been too big a coincidence for a complete stranger to have come to me – a friend of her ex-husband – requesting an investigation into Yukiho Karasawa.'

'I'd better talk to him about it one of these days,' Kazunari said, half to himself, as he looked back down at the file. 'According to this, she did quite well for herself with the stocks?'

'Yes. The broker she worked with retired from his firm last spring, so all I had to go on was what he remembered.'

It had been a mixed blessing, Imaeda thought. If the broker had still worked at the firm, there was a chance he might have had access to more detailed information. Then again, he might have also been more reluctant to talk about a client.

'I've heard that even amateur traders were doing quite well up until around last year. Did she really buy two million yen's worth of Ricardo?' Kazunari asked.

'Her broker remembered that quite vividly.'

Ricardo, Inc. was originally a semiconductor manufacturer. They announced that they had developed an alternative for chlorofluorocarbons, giving them a leg up on the competition when the UN announced a ban on the use of CFCs in September of 1987. The Helsinki Declaration in 1989, recommending that all chlorofluorocarbon use should be abandoned by the end of the century, only buoyed the stock further.

What impressed the broker so much was that, at the time Yukiho purchased the stock, nothing had yet been made public about Ricardo's research. Even in the industry, few people knew what Ricardo was doing. Only after the press release announcing their discovery of the substitute was it revealed that several of the technicians who had been working at one of the few Japanese companies producing chlorofluorocarbons, Pacific Glass, had been headhunted by Ricardo to turbocharge their research.

'And Ricardo wasn't the only one,' Imaeda said. 'It's not clear what kind of information she was basing her purchases on but nearly every company whose stock Yukiho bought had a hit product of one kind or another just after her purchase. The broker said her success ratio was amazingly close to perfect.'

'Insider trading?' Kazunari asked, his voice dropping.

'That's what the broker suspected, too. He knew that Yukiho's husband worked for a manufacturer, and thought perhaps he had a route by which he was getting information on other companies' projects in development. Of course, he never confronted Yukiho with this.'

'What department did Makoto work in again?'

'The Patent Licensing Division at Tozai Automotive. Definitely a position that would give him a window into the research and development going on at other companies. But only things that had been made public. He wouldn't have had any easy or legal means of obtaining information on projects still under wraps.'

'So we're supposed to believe that she just had a knack for picking good stocks?'

'Oh, she definitely had a knack. According to her broker, she was very good at knowing when to let go of stocks, too. Just when it looked like prices might inch a little higher, she would sell them off and move to the next investment. That sense of timing isn't something most amateurs have, the broker said. And if it was blind luck – well, it's hard to consistently make money in the market based on your gut.'

'Which suggests that she did have access to privileged information – or someone working with her did.'

'It does seem that way.' Imaeda shrugged. 'But then, that's just *my* gut talking.'

Kazunari looked down at the file again. His eyebrow twitched. 'There was one other thing that bothered me.'

'Yes?'

'According to this report, she was buying and selling stocks pretty frequently through last year. And she's still trading now?'

'Yes. Though I think her shop keeps her too busy to spend as much time on it as she used to. She still dabbles, though.'

Kazunari shook his head. 'That doesn't fit with what I heard from Makoto.'

'He said something about her investments?'

'Just about how Yukiho had got deep into stocks back when they were still married. It got so bad that at one point they had an argument and she sold off everything. But maybe he didn't check closely enough.'

'It was the broker's opinion that Yukiho never gave up trading for any significant period of time since she started. At any rate, I was able to get a good picture of her financial situation as it stands now,' Imaeda said. 'Only one major question remains.'

'Where'd she get her seed money from in the first place?'

'Exactly. It's difficult to trace the money back without proper documentation, but according to the broker she started with a sizeable sum of cash. Not the kind of money you would expect a housewife to have.'

'Several hundred thousand yen, maybe?'

'Probably more.'

Kazunari crossed his arms and let out a little groan. 'Makoto said he had no idea how much she had stashed away.'

Imaeda nodded. 'You said her foster mother, Reiko Karasawa, didn't have much in the way of money. Certainly it would be hard for her to come up with a few hundred thousand yen.'

'Isn't there some way you can look into that?'

'I plan to. Just, it's going to take me a little time.'

'That's not a problem. Do what you need to do. Can I have this file?'

'Of course. I kept a copy for myself.'

Kazunari slipped the file into the slim attaché case he'd brought with him.

'I needed to give this back to you,' Imaeda said, pulling a paper bag out of his briefcase. He took out the watch he had borrowed and put it on the table. 'I've sent the suit back by courier. It should get there tomorrow.'

'You could have sent the watch with it.'

'No, I wouldn't want to be responsible if it'd got lost along the way. It's a limited edition Cartier.'

'Is it? It was a gift,' Kazunari said, glancing at the watch face before putting it into his jacket pocket.

'I wouldn't have known myself,' Imaeda said, 'if Yukiho hadn't pointed it out.'

'Right,' Kazunari said, rolling his eyes. 'I suppose it's important to know that sort of thing in her line of work.'

'I think it's a little bit more than that,' Imaeda said, playing the words for effect.

'What do you mean?'

Imaeda shifted forward and rested his hands on the table, his fingers crossed together. 'You mentioned that Yukiho hadn't responded enthusiastically to your cousin's proposal?'

'Yes?'

'I have an idea of why that might be.'

'Why?'

'It's simple, really,' Imaeda said, staring Kazunari in the eye. 'She's in love with someone else.'

Kazunari nodded several times before saying, 'I had a similar thought myself. But something tells me that you're basing this on a bit more than that. Do you know who the other man is?'

'Yes.'

'Well, who is it? Someone I know? In fact, don't tell me if you think it might cause problems.'

'Whether it's a problem or not depends largely on you,' Imaeda said, taking a drink of water. 'That is to say, it *is* you.'

Kazunari furrowed his brows quizzically. Then he chuckled, his shoulders shaking. 'That's very funny.'

Imaeda shook his head. 'I'm serious.'

Something in Imaeda's voice made Kazunari's face tighten. 'What makes you think that?' he asked.

'I suppose you'd laugh if I said it was a gut feeling.'

'I wouldn't laugh, no, but I also wouldn't believe you.'

'It's more than that. First, we have the watch. Yukiho clearly remembered its owner. Even though her chance to see it was so brief you didn't even remember it, she did. I believe it's likely she remembered because of her interest in you. And another thing: when I went to pay her a visit, she asked me who had introduced me and I gave her the name of Shinozuka. Normally you would expect her to assume it had been your cousin – Yasuharu Shinozuka. He's older than you, higher up in the company, and a frequent visitor to her store.'

'Maybe she was shy about mentioning him, in the wake of his proposal.'

'That doesn't fit what I know of her character. How many times have you visited her boutique?'

'Twice, I think.'

'When was the last time?'

He didn't answer, so Imaeda answered for him. 'More than a year ago, I bet.'

Kazunari nodded.

'So, as far as her shop is concerned, the only Shinozuka who really matters is her frequent customer, Yasuharu Shinozuka, wouldn't you say? If she had no special feelings towards you, I can't see why your name would've come out first. You said you've known Yukiho since college, correct?'

'Yes, from dance club practice.'

'Try to think back on that time, see if you remember anything that sticks out. Anything you might be able to interpret as her having special feelings for you.'

'You went to see her, didn't you?' said Kazunari, frowning. 'Eriko Kawashima.'

'I did, but I never mentioned your name and I made sure she wouldn't suspect anything.'

Kazunari sighed. 'How was she doing?'

'She seemed good. She's been married two years now. Her husband works at an electrical engineering company. They were introduced by a marriage service.'

'I'm glad to hear she's well,' Kazunari said. 'Did she have anything to say?'

'Well, she seemed to think that Makoto wasn't Yukiho's one and only. Which I took to mean that she thought Yukiho loved someone else.'

'And you think that someone else is me? No way,' Kazunari laughed and shook his head.

'Still,' Imaeda said, 'she seems to think it is.'

'I doubt that,' Kazunari said, his smile fading. 'Wait – she didn't say that, did she?'

'Not in so many words, but that was the impression I got.'

'It's dangerous to make too many assumptions like that.'

'I know. That's why I haven't written it in the report. But there's something there, I'm sure of it.'

Imaeda still remembered Eriko's expression when she had told him. It was the look of someone with a deep, abiding regret. She was afraid of something too, he realised. She was afraid he was going to ask who it was that Yukiho Karasawa loved. The moment he realised that, several pieces of the puzzle fell into place.

Kazunari sighed and grabbed his glass of iced coffee, drinking down half of it in one gulp. The ice made a clinking sound in the glass as he set it back on the table.

'Well, I'm afraid I have no idea who it might be, except I'm sure it's not me. She never confessed anything of the sort to me and she's never given me presents for my birthday or Christmas. I think the best I got was a chocolate on Valentine's Day, but then again, she gave one to all the boys in dance club.'

'Maybe your chocolate was special?'

'Not even a little.' Kazunari shook his head.

Imaeda stuck a finger in his box of Marlboros. There was only one left. He put it in his mouth and lit it, crushing the empty box in his left hand. 'There's another thing I didn't write in the report. Something that happened when she was in middle school.'

'What was that?'

'A rape. Actually, it's not clear whether it was technically rape, but it was definitely close.'

Imaeda explained how Yukiho and Eriko had discovered their classmate after she was assaulted and how their classmate had once been Yukiho's rival in school.

'So what about this incident bothered you?' Kazunari asked, his voice hard.

'Wouldn't you say it bears some resemblance to what happened when you were in college?'

'What if it does?' Kazunari said with evident displeasure.

'The assault in middle school had the effect of removing Yukiho's rival. That doubtless left an impression on her. One could imagine that she arranged for the same thing to happen to her romantic rival several years later in college.'

Kazunari stared hard at Imaeda's face. The look turned quickly into a glare. 'You have a dark imagination, detective. Eriko was her best friend.'

'Eriko certainly thought so. I wonder if Yukiho felt the same way? To be perfectly honest, I even suspect she had something to do with what happened in middle school, too. It would explain a lot.'

Kazunari held his hand up. 'I think that's enough imagining for now. I want facts.'

Imaeda nodded. 'Of course.'

Kazunari stood and reached for the bill sitting on the table, but Imaeda quickly put his hand over it. 'If I were to discover something that would prove what I just told you isn't just my imagination, but something that actually happened, do you think you would be able to tell your cousin?'

Kazunari took his other hand and, moving slowly, brushed

Imaeda's aside, taking the bill from the table. 'Of course,' he said.
'Provided there's proof.'

'Very well.'

'I hope to see proof of something in your next report.'

Bill in hand, Kazunari walked away from the table.

The phone call from Eri Sugawara came two days after he met
with Kazunari in Ginza. Imaeda had been on a stakeout for an
unrelated job at a hotel in Shibuya until eleven at night. It was
after midnight by the time he got home. He had just taken off his
clothes and was about to get into the shower when the phone
rang.

The first thing Eri told him was that she was worried. He could
tell from her tone that she wasn't kidding around.

'There are all these messages on my answering machine where
the caller just hangs up without saying anything. It's weird. It's not
you, is it, Imaeda?'

'Sorry, I'm not in the habit of making crank calls. Maybe it's
some guy from the bar who has a thing for you?'

'No, no one has a thing for me. And I never give my phone
number to customers, anyway.'

'It's easy enough to find out someone's phone number,' Imaeda
told her. For example, you could steal someone's phone bill out of
their mailbox. He had used that technique himself, though he
wasn't about to share that with Eri now. She sounded frightened
enough.

'And there's something else, too. It might just be my imagination,' she said, lowering her voice, 'but I have a weird feeling, like
someone's been in my apartment.'

'What?'

'When I got back from work just now, I noticed something was
off as soon as I opened the door. For one thing, my sandal had
fallen over on its side.'

'Your sandal?'

'Yeah, they're high heels. I left them in the entrance way and
one of them had fallen on its side. I never leave my shoes lying on

their side, never. No matter how much of a hurry I'm in, I always make sure they're in a neat pair.'

'So one of your sandals fell over and that's why you're calling me in the middle of the night?'

'It's not just that. There's something weird about my phone.'

'What about it?'

'I always leave it at a bit of an angle to the table, so I can grab it with my left hand while I'm in bed, but for some reason it was flush with the table edge.'

A thought flashed through Imaeda's mind, but he kept it to himself. 'Right. Listen, I'm coming over.'

'You're coming here? Now? OK, I guess.'

'Don't worry. I'll behave. Also, I don't want you using this phone until I get there. Understood?'

'Fine, but what's this all about?'

'I'll explain once I'm there. And one other thing. I'm going to knock on your door, but don't open it until you're sure it's me. Got it?'

'Right,' Eri said, her voice sounding considerably more worried than it had when she first called.

Eri's apartment was on a side street one block in from the main road, with a car park across the street. He ran up the outside staircase of the apartment building and knocked on the door to unit 205, saying his name. The door opened and Eri looked out, a scowl on her face. 'OK, you have to tell me what this all is all about.'

'I don't know. In fact, I hope it's just your mind playing tricks on you.'

'It's not.' Eri shook her head. 'After I hung up the phone, I could sense it. It was like my apartment wasn't my own any more.'

Now that's your mind playing tricks with you, Imaeda thought, but he just shrugged and stepped inside.

Three pairs of shoes were out in the hall: a pair of sneakers, a pair of pumps, and the sandals in question. The heels were rather high. It looked like it wouldn't take much to knock one over.

Imaeda took off his shoes and stepped inside. It was a small place, one room with a small sink attached. Eri had hung a curtain halfway across it so you couldn't see the whole apartment from the doorway. Beyond the curtain was a bed, a television, and a table. The air conditioner on the wall looked old, probably something that came with the apartment when she moved in. It was succeeding in blowing cold air into the room, but it was making an incredible racket in the process.

'Where's the phone?'

Eri pointed towards the bed.

Next to the bed was a small shelf with an almost perfectly square top on which rested a white telephone. He noted it wasn't cordless – probably wouldn't be much need for that in an apartment this small.

Imaeda took a black, blocky device out of his bag. An antenna stuck out of the top and the front side had a small meter and a few switches.

'What's that? Some kind of radio?' Eri asked.

'Just a little toy.' Imaeda clicked on the power switch and began to turn the frequency adjustment dial. At around 100 MHz, the meter started to react. At the same time a light on the front winked on. He brought the device closer to the phone, then further away. The meter went up and down as he moved.

He turned off the switch. Next he picked up the phone, looked at the base, then pulled a small tool pouch out of his bag. Fishing out a Phillips screwdriver, he began to undo the screws holding the cover on the base of the phone. As he'd expected, it didn't take much effort to loosen the screws, because someone else had recently taken this phone apart.

'Are you breaking my phone?'

'I'm fixing it.'

'What?'

He ignored her. Once all the screws were out, he carefully removed the cover. There was a small board inside with various circuits for the phone. His eyes went to a small box-like object attached to the board with tape. Grabbing it between his fingertips, he yanked it out.

'Are you sure you're supposed to take that out?'

Imaeda took another screwdriver and pried open the lid on the small box. It had a small mercury battery, which he dug out with the tip of his screwdriver. 'There, all done,' he announced.

'What is that thing?' Eri asked, terror creeping into her voice.

'It's nothing to be afraid of. Just a listening device – a bug,' Imaeda said, as he re-fastened the cover on her phone.

'What?' Eri's eyes went wide. She picked up the box. 'Who the hell would want to bug my phone?'

'That's what I want to know. Are you sure some guy isn't after you?'

'Pretty sure.'

Imaeda turned his bug detector back on and adjusted the frequency as he walked around the apartment. The meter didn't react at all.

'Looks like they weren't that serious about listening to you,' he said, turning off the device and putting it back in his duffel bag along with his tools.

'Serious enough. How did you know someone had bugged my phone?'

'You got anything to drink? I'm all hot from walking around.'

'Yeah, sure.' Eri went over to her mini-refrigerator and took out two cans of beer. She put one on the table and opened the other for herself.

Imaeda sat cross-legged on the floor and took a sip. He felt himself relax, which was a signal for the sweat to start pouring from his body.

'Basically, it was intuition via experience.' He set the beer down. 'You said it looked like someone had been in your room, and the phone was moved. Makes sense that someone might have done something to your phone, right?'

'When you put it that way, I guess it was pretty obvious.'

'I'd like to claim some special professional knowledge, but yeah, you're right,' he said, taking another sip of beer and wiping his mouth with his hand. 'You sure you don't know anyone who could have done this?'

'I'm sure. Positive.' Eri sat down on the edge of her bed.

'Which means,' Imaeda said, 'they were probably after me.'

'After *you*?'

'You said someone left messages on your phone? That got you worried, right? So what did you do? You called me. That might've been what they wanted you to do. In other words, they wanted you to make a phone call to the first person you thought might've left those messages.'

'What would that do for them?'

'They would learn who you talk to, who your friends are, who you call in times of need.'

'I can't see how knowing any of that would do anybody any good. I mean, they could've just asked me. They didn't have to bug my phone.'

'Clearly, they wanted to know more about you without you knowing they knew. Let's review the facts. Our snoop wants to know someone's name and identity. Their only lead is you. All they know is that the person they want to know more about is close to you somehow.' Imaeda finished his beer and crushed the empty can in his hand. 'Now who do you think knows you who wants to know me?'

Eri looked down at the floor and chewed the thumb of her hand that wasn't holding the beer. 'The people at that boutique we visited in South Aoyama?'

'An excellent guess,' Imaeda said. 'I believe you gave them your address? But I wrote nothing. If they wanted to know more about me, they would have to go through you.'

'But why would they care about you? You think they knew you were a detective?'

'There are a number of reasons they could've wanted to know,' Imaeda said, grinning. 'But that's grown-up talk.'

A picture of Kazunari's watch loomed in the back of Imaeda's mind. Yukiho obviously knew it was his. Of course she would want to know who this man was coming to her store wearing such an important timepiece. So she had hired someone in Imaeda's profession to follow up on their only lead: Eri Sugawara.

He thought back on his conversation with Eri over the phone just before he had come to her apartment. She had called him 'Imaeda' over the phone, which meant that it was only a matter of time before whoever placed the bug would find out that there was a man by that name who ran a private detective agency not far from this apartment.

'But I didn't give them my real address. I figured it would sound weird if I was supposed to be this little rich girl and my address had an apartment name like "Yamamoto Co-Op". I changed several things.'

'You did?'

'Yeah. I mean, I *am* a private detective's assistant. I know a few things.'

Imaeda reflected back on their visit to the boutique, trying to figure out where they had slipped up.

'Did you have your wallet with you that day?' Imaeda asked.

'Yeah, sure.'

'It was in your handbag?'

'Uh huh.'

'You tried on a lot of dresses that day; where did you put your bag while you were doing that?'

'I guess ... in the dressing room?'

'So you left it there when you went to look at other clothes on the racks?'

Eri nodded. She was starting to frown.

'Can you show me your wallet?' Imaeda held out his left hand.

'Hey, there's not a lot of money in there.'

'I don't care about the money. I'm interested in what's in there besides money.'

Eri reached inside the shoulder bag hanging from the corner of her bed and pulled out a black wallet. It was a slender leather one with a Gucci mark.

'That's quite a nice wallet you've got.'

'It was a gift, from the boss.'

'At the bar? You mean that guy with the whiskers?'

'That's the one.'

'Well, *that's* interesting,' Imaeda said, opening the wallet and checking the pocket for cards. Eri's licence was in there, along with her member's card for a local department store and a loyalty card for a hairdresser. He pulled it out and gave it a look. The address listed her apartment.

'You mean someone snuck a look at my wallet?' Eri said.

'It's possible. I'd give it a sixty per cent chance. Maybe more.'

'I don't believe it! Do people just do that kind of thing? I mean, does that mean they suspected me from the beginning?'

'It does,' Imaeda said. He was pretty sure Yukiho had suspected them from the moment she noticed the watch. He wouldn't put looking at someone's wallet past her. Those feline eyes glimmered in the back of Imaeda's mind.

'Then why did she have me write down my name and address before we left? Not to send me a postcard, I'm guessing?'

'They were probably just making sure.'

'Making sure of what?'

'They wanted to see whether you would write your real name and address. Which, as it turns out, you didn't.'

Eri looked sorry. 'I changed the numbers a bit, too.'

'Which is how she knew for sure that we hadn't just come to buy clothes.'

'I'm sorry. I shouldn't have tried to be clever.'

'It's OK. They suspected us anyway.' Imaeda stood and picked up his bag. 'Be careful to lock up tight. As I'm sure you know by now, the lock on your apartment isn't going to stop a professional who wants to get in. Keep the chain on when you're at home.'

'OK, got it.'

'See you,' Imaeda said, stepping into his sneakers.

'Are you going to be OK, Imaeda? You sure they're not going to attack you or anything?'

Imaeda chuckled. 'Who do you think I am? James Bond? No, don't worry. At worst they'll just send some evil-looking killer with steel jaws after me.'

'What?' Eri gasped.

'Goodnight,' Imaeda said, smiling. 'And don't forget to lock up.'

He stepped outside and closed the door behind him. But he didn't start walking right away. He waited until he heard the lock turn and the chain slide closed before leaving.

I wonder who will *show up?*

Imaeda looked up at the sky. It was still drizzling, but he didn't mind getting a little wet.

The following day, the drizzle turned to a downpour. This at least had the effect of cooling off temperatures, making the sweltering mid-August heat slightly more bearable that morning.

Imaeda crawled out of bed a little after nine and went out dressed in a T-shirt and jeans. Holding an umbrella with one bent rib above his head, he walked to Bolero, a small café right across the street from his apartment.

The wooden door had a tiny bell on it that rang when he walked in. Bolero was a small place, just four tables and a counter. Presently, two of the tables were taken and a man was sitting at the counter. Behind the counter, the balding owner nodded in greeting when he saw Imaeda come in.

Imaeda chose a table at the back. It was late for breakfast, and in the unlikely event that a big group came in, he could always move to the counter. He didn't have to order. In a few minutes, the owner would bring him the hot dog morning set: a hot coffee and a fat sausage on a bed of chopped cabbage that overflowed its bun.

There were a few folded newspapers in the rack next to his table. He saw the regular paper and a business paper – the man at the counter was already reading the sports pages. Imaeda sighed and fished out today's *Asahi Shimbun*. He had just leaned back in his chair and was about to open the paper when he heard the jingle of the bell on the door and reflexively glanced up to see another man come in.

The man looked about sixty, with white-speckled hair parted evenly down the middle. He was a big man, with a wide chest under his white shirt and thick arms emerging from his sleeves. He was at least one metre seventy tall, and stood straight, like a samurai in the movies.

Yet more than the man's appearance, it was his sharp gaze that went directly towards Imaeda which caught his attention. It only lasted a moment. The man looked away and walked over to take a seat at the counter. 'Coffee, please,' he said.

Imaeda had already gone back to reading his paper, but at those words, he looked back up again, surprised to hear an Osakan accent.

Just then the man looked back around at Imaeda and their eyes met.

There was nothing like threat or malice in the man's look. On the contrary, his eyes looked like they had seen their share of the dark, twisted things humans were capable of and taken it all in stride. Whoever the guy was, he was one cool customer, Imaeda thought, and he actually felt a shiver travel up his spine.

Imaeda went back to reading the headlines on the society pages. There was something about an accident on the highway involving an eighteen-wheeler. Still, his attention was only half on the paper.

The owner brought over his hot dog and coffee. Imaeda applied a liberal helping of ketchup and mustard to his dog before taking a bite. He liked the feel of the skin as it broke beneath his front teeth. Not so tough that eating was a chore, but firm enough that you felt that first bite. That particular degree of resilience was, in his opinion, the mark of a good hot dog.

Imaeda took pains not to look in the man's direction as he ate, just in case their eyes met again. He had just finished the last bite and was taking a sip of his coffee when he glanced towards the counter again to see the man turning his head back to his own cup of coffee.

He was looking at me.

Imaeda finished his coffee and stood. He stuck his hand in his pocket, pulled out a thousand-yen bill and put it on the counter. The owner set out his four hundred and fifty yen's worth of change in silence. During this time, the man hardly moved. He just drank his coffee, his back straight beneath his jacket. He moved rhythmically, like a clockwork automaton, never looking in Imaeda's direction.

Imaeda left the café and dashed across the road without

bothering to put up his umbrella. He ran up the stairs to his apartment, turning round to glance back at Bolero before going inside. The mysterious man was nowhere in sight.

Imaeda flipped the switch on the stereo system he had set up on a steel shelf against the wall, hearing the CD player whirr to life, followed shortly after by the sounds of Whitney Houston coming out of the speakers he'd mounted on the wall.

Imaeda took off his T-shirt in order take a shower – he usually showered before bed, but hadn't got around to it the night before and his hair was a mess. He was just unzipping his jeans when the doorbell rang.

A familiar sound, but there was something different about it today. Probably because he had a pretty good idea who was at his door, and it wasn't someone he wanted to talk to. The bell rang again.

Imaeda zipped up his jeans and put his T-shirt back on. Wondering when he ever would get the chance to shower, he went out to the entranceway, undid the lock and opened the door.

The man from the café was standing outside, a faint smile on his face. He was carrying an umbrella in his left hand, and a black travel bag in his right.

Imaeda didn't blink. 'Yes?' he asked.

'Mr Imaeda?' the man asked. His Osaka accent was strong. 'Satoshi Imaeda?'

'That's me.'

'I had a few questions for you, if you have the time.' The man had a deep voice that rumbled in his chest and wrinkles that looked as though they had been carved out with a chisel across his face, meeting between his brows. Imaeda realised that one of the lines was, in fact, a scar left by a blade.

'I'm sorry, but who are you?'

'The name's Sasagaki. From Osaka.'

'Well, you've certainly come a long way, so I'm sorry to disappoint you, Mr Sasagaki, but I was just on my way to work.'

'I won't take much of your time,' the man said. 'Just two or three questions.'

'Can you try another day? I'm really in a bit of a hurry here.'

'Not so much of a hurry that you couldn't enjoy a leisurely breakfast with the paper,' the man said, the corner of his mouth curling upwards.

'How I spend my time is none of your business. Goodbye,' Imaeda said, going to close the door. The man stuck his umbrella in to stop it from closing.

'I applaud your enthusiasm for your job. Unfortunately, I have a job to do too,' the man said, sticking his hand into the pocket of his grey trousers and pulling out a police badge.

Imaeda sighed and relaxed his grip on the doorknob. 'If you're a cop, why didn't you just say so?'

'Some people don't like us announcing ourselves out in the hall-way where the neighbours might hear. Now, might I ask a few questions?'

'Be my guest,' said Imaeda, showing him to the chair he had set out for visiting clients. Imaeda went back behind his desk. He had set the height on the client's chair a little on the low side, to give himself a height advantage when talking. He didn't hold out much hope that such Negotiation 101 tricks would work on today's visitor, however.

Imaeda asked for a business card, but the man said he wasn't carrying any – almost certainly a lie, but he didn't feel the need to dispute his claim now. Instead, he asked for him to show him his badge again.

'If it's a fake, I at least want to see whether or not you did a good job making it.'

'By all means,' the man said, offering Imaeda his badge. 'Knock yourself out.'

Imaeda looked over the name, and the small photograph next to it.

'I hope it passed inspection,' Sasagaki said, putting the badge away. 'I'm a detective in Homicide, Eastern Osaka.'

'So this is a murder investigation?' Imaeda asked. This did come as surprise.

'You could say that.'

'You could say what, exactly? I haven't heard anything about any murders connected to me.'

'Just because you haven't heard anything, doesn't mean it hasn't happened.'

'OK.' Imaeda held up his hands. 'So who died?'

Sasagaki smiled, the wrinkles forming a complex pattern across his face. 'I have some questions for you first, if you don't mind, Mr Imaeda. Answer them, and you'll have my gratitude.'

Imaeda narrowed his eyes at the detective. The man was rocking slightly in his chair, but his expression was unwavering.

'Fine, you first. What do you want to know?'

Sasagaki stood his umbrella on the floor in front of him and rested his hands on the handle. 'I believe you were in Osaka about two weeks ago? You did some snooping around in Ōe, a neighbourhood in Ikuno ward, if I'm not mistaken.'

Imaeda felt like he'd been jabbed in the gut. From the moment he'd heard the man was from Osaka, he had been wondering if this visit had anything to do with his recent trip.

'Well?' Sasagaki asked again, although it was clear from his face that he'd already knew the answer.

'I did,' Imaeda admitted. 'You're well informed.'

'When it comes to that particular neighbourhood, I can tell which of the stray cats are pregnant, and who the father was,' Sasagaki said, his mouth opening in silent laughter. All Imaeda could hear was the wind passing between his lips.

Sasagaki smiled after a moment had passed and asked, 'What were you there for?'

Imaeda's mind raced, trying to figure out this guy's angle. 'Work.'

'And what work is that?'

Now Imaeda smiled, if only to give the impression that he wasn't frightened. 'Don't tell me you don't already know what my job is, detective.'

'It's a very interesting line of work,' Sasagaki said, his eyes straying to the shelves packed with case files. 'A friend of mine runs a similar operation down in Osaka. Though I couldn't tell you how business has been.'

'That's why I went down to Osaka. For work.'

'So looking into Yukiho Karasawa's upbringing was part of your job?'

Now things are starting to come into focus, Imaeda thought. He wondered how they had managed to chase him down, and remembered the wiretapping incident from the night before.

'I'd really appreciate it if you could tell me exactly why Yukiho's past is so important to you,' Sasagaki said in a languid drawl, looking up at Imaeda.

'If you have a friend in my line of work, as you say, you know I can't reveal anything about my clients.'

'So someone hired you to look into Yukiho, then?'

'That's right,' Imaeda said, wondering why the detective referred to Yukiho Karasawa by her first name and not as 'Ms Karasawa', as he'd expect. Either that was just the way detectives talked, or the two were very close. Or else—

'This have to do with marriage talks?' Sasagaki suddenly asked.

'Huh?'

'I've heard someone proposed to her. I can imagine they'd want to look into her past a little first, given her business dealings.'

'What are you talking about?'

'Marriage.' Sasagaki gave him a curious smile. His eyes went across the desk and he pointed towards the ashtray he saw there. 'Mind if I smoke?'

'Go right ahead,' Imaeda told him.

Sasagaki pulled a box of Hi-Lites out of his shirt pocket. The box was crumpled nearly flat, and the cigarette he pulled from it was bent in two places. He lit it with a match from a familiar looking matchbook – it was from Bolero across the street.

The detective blew a long stream of smoke into the air, as if to indicate he was in absolutely no hurry at all. The smoke rose wavering in a cloud before dissipating towards the ceiling.

Clearly, he was giving Imaeda time to think. He had shown a few of his cards; now he was waiting to see what Imaeda pulled out of his sleeve. Showing up at the café had just been a way to let Imaeda know that he was being watched, a way to suggest he was holding the better hand. The detective's expression was blank, but there was a crafty look in his eyes as they followed the smoke.

Imaeda badly wanted to know what kind of hand the detective was holding. Why would someone in homicide be after Yukiho Karasawa? Though, Imaeda thought, he hadn't actually said it was Yukiho he was after. The only thing he knew was that the man clearly knew quite a bit about her.

'I'd heard the talk of marriage concerning Ms Karasawa,' Imaeda said after thinking about it for some time. 'But I'm not at liberty to say whether that has anything to do with my investigation.'

Sasagaki gave a satisfied nod, his cigarette dangling between his fingers. Slowly, he snubbed the butt out in the ashtray. 'Mr Imaeda,' he said, 'do you remember *Mario*?'

'Excuse me?'

'*Super Mario Bros*. A big seller several years back. One of those games for kids. Though I hear a lot of adults play them these days.'

'Oh, the Nintendo game. Yeah, I remember that.'

'Well, there was a man who tried to sell fake copies of the game down in Osaka. They'd made a pirate edition, see, and were on the verge of bringing it to market. They would have made a bundle if the police hadn't caught them in the nick of time and confiscated every last one of the fake game cartridges. But they never found the man who did it.'

'He ran?'

'That's what the police thought. That's what they still think.' Sasagaki opened his travel bag and pulled a folded flier out of it. He spread it open on the table and showed it to Imaeda. Beneath the familiar *Have you seen this man?* headline was a picture of a man in his fifties, his hair slicked back across his head. Beneath that was a name: *Isamu Matsuura*.

'I'll ask just in case, but have you ever seen this man?'

'Sorry, no.'

'I didn't think you would have,' Sasagaki said, folding the paper and putting it back in his bag.

'So you're after this Matsuura guy?'

'In a manner of speaking.'

'What's that supposed to mean?' Imaeda stared Sasagaki in the eyes, but the detective merely gave him a knowing smile.

With a start, Imaeda realised what it was that had been nagging him since Sasagaki started talking about *Super Mario Bros*. Why would a detective in homicide care about someone pirating a game? That was what he meant about the police 'thinking' Matsuura had run. Apparently, this detective thought he was dead – murdered. He wasn't looking for Matsuura, he was looking for Matsuura's body, and whoever killed him.

'Does this guy have something to do with Yukiho Karasawa?'

'Nothing direct. At least, not that I know of.'

Imaeda shook his head. 'OK, I'll admit it. I'm confused. Why should I care about any of this?'

'There was a man with Matsuura who disappeared at the same time he did,' Sasagaki said. 'It's highly likely this other man was involved in pirating the game as well. And ...' The detective paused, choosing his words carefully. 'He's likely to be somewhere near Yukiho.'

'*Near* her?' Imaeda said. 'What does that mean?'

'Exactly what it sounds like. He's hiding somewhere. Have you ever heard of something called a pistol shrimp?'

'You mean shrimp, like in the ocean?'

'That's right. The pistol shrimp digs out a little hole to live in. But every once in a while, something else comes and sets up camp in the shrimp's hole – a little fish, called a goby. The goby isn't a freeloader, however. In exchange for a place to live, he hangs out at the entrance to the hole and wags his tail whenever enemies approach, letting the shrimp know what's coming. It's what biologists call a symbiotic relationship.'

'Let me get this straight,' Imaeda said, holding out his left hand. 'Are you saying that there's a guy working with Yukiho Karasawa?'

If there was, the ramifications would be huge – but Imaeda didn't believe it. He'd been on her case for more than a month now, and never seen any sign of a collaborator.

Sasagaki grinned. 'It's just a theory,' he said. 'I have no proof.'

'Surely you have something you're basing this on?'

'Call it the intuition of a detective past his prime. It's not a horse I recommend putting any money on.'

He's lying, Imaeda thought. *He has proof, solid as a rock. Proof enough to bring him all the way up here to Tokyo.*

Sasagaki opened his bag again and pulled out a photograph. 'How about this man? Ever see him?'

He put the photograph on the desk and Imaeda reached out for it. The man was facing directly towards the camera. It looked like a photo taken for a driver's licence. He was about thirty years old, with a pointed chin.

The face looked familiar. Imaeda tried not to let his expression show it as he tried to think back to where he'd seen it before. He had a good memory for faces, but sometimes it took a little while to put everything together.

He stared at the photo for a few seconds more and, like that, the fog lifted. He knew exactly who he was looking at: alias, occupation, most recent address, everything. He almost yelped out loud, it was so unexpected, but he managed to restrain himself.

'Is this the guy working with Yukiho Karasawa?' he asked, taking care his voice remained casual.

'Maybe,' Sasagaki said with a shrug. 'You've seen him?'

'Maybe,' Imaeda replied, 'but maybe not.' He held the photo up and took a closer look. 'You mind if I take this into the next room? I want to check my files.'

'What do you think you'll find?'

'I'll bring it right back. Wait here,' Imaeda stood without waiting for Sasagaki's answer. He hurried into the next room, locking the door behind him.

This room was originally designed to be a bedroom, but he often used it as a dark room for developing monochrome photos. He pulled a Polaroid camera off the shelf. Then, placing the photograph he got from Sasagaki on the floor, he looked through the viewfinder on the camera, and bent his knees to get the focus right. Adjusting the lens would take too much time.

At just the right height, he pressed the shutter, and the flash filled the room with light.

Imaeda pulled the film out and put the camera back on the shelf. Then, shaking the developing picture in one hand, he pulled a thick file off another shelf. This file contained all the photographs he'd taken during his investigation of Yukiho Karasawa. He checked through quickly, making sure there was nothing in it that would get him in trouble if he showed it to Sasagaki.

He glanced down at his watch, checking that enough time had passed before peeling off the top paper. It was a perfect reproduction – he could even see the tiny specks of dust that had been on the original.

Placing his new photo in a desk drawer, Imaeda opened the door and took the original photograph and his file back into the room where the detective was waiting.

'Sorry, my mistake,' he said, placing the file on the desk. 'The face looked familiar, but looking through this I realised I was mistaken.'

'What's this file?' Sasagaki asked.

'Everything I have on Yukiho Karasawa. There's not many pictures, I'm afraid.'

'Might I take a look?'

'Go right ahead. Just, I'm not at liberty to tell you much about them.'

Sasagaki took out each of the photographs in the file and looked them over carefully. There were photos of the streets near the house where Yukiho Karasawa had grown up, and some shots he had taken of her broker without the man's knowledge.

When he had finished looking at them all, the detective looked back up. 'Some interesting photos in here.'

'See any you like?'

'I was just wondering why someone investigating a potential bride would need photos of her visiting a bank.'

'You'll just have to use your imagination on that one.'

In fact, he had taken pictures of the bank because Yukiho had a safe deposit box there. He'd discovered this when following her one day. The reason he took pictures of her going in and coming out was to see if there was anything different about her appearance. For example, if she came out wearing a necklace she hadn't been wearing when she went in, that would suggest she'd kept the necklace in a safe deposit box. It was a very primitive way of checking on someone's most valuable possessions.

'I was wondering if I could ask a favour of you,' Sasagaki said.

'Yes?'

'If, in your investigation, you should come across this man' – here, he held up the photograph – 'if you should see or hear of him, I want you to tell me. As quickly as you can.'

Imaeda looked between the photo and Sasagaki's wrinkled face. 'OK, but there's something I need to know,' he said.

'Yeah?'

'What's his name? And where's the last place he lived?'

For the first time, Imaeda noticed a look of hesitation pass across the detective's face.

'If you find him, I'll give you more information about him than you ever wanted to know.'

'All I want now is his name and his address.'

Sasagaki looked at Imaeda for a few seconds before nodding. Then he pulled a single sheet of paper off the memo pad on the desk and wrote something on it before placing it in front of Imaeda. It read:

Ryo Kirihara
LIMITLESS
2-42-12 Nihonbashi, Chuo Ward, Osaka

'What's Limitless? Some kind of company?'

'A computer shop. Ryo was the manager.'

Sasagaki wrote out another note with his own name and phone number on it.

'Sorry to take up so much of your time,' the detective said. 'I believe you said you had work to get to?'

'No problem,' Imaeda replied, unconcerned that the detective had called his bluff. 'I was wondering, though. How did you know I was investigating Yukiho Karasawa?'

Sasagaki smiled. 'I'm sure you'll figure that one out the next time you're out and about.'

'Out and about? You mean walking around, listening to my radio?' Imaeda made a motion like he was twisting the dial on his wiretap detector.

'Radio? I'm not sure I follow,' Sasagaki said, looking honestly confused.

'Nothing, forget I mentioned it.'

Sasagaki stood and walked towards the door, using his umbrella as a kind of cane. Just before he opened the door, he turned back around. 'I'm sure you don't need to hear this from me, but if I ever met him, I'd have a word of advice for the person who asked you to look into Yukiho.'

'Yes?'

Sasagaki's lips curled into a smile. 'Steer clear of that woman. Yukiho Karasawa is trouble.'

'Don't worry,' Imaeda said. 'He knows.'

Sasagaki gave a satisfied nod and walked out the door.

A group of women on their way home from some kind of community college class had taken over two of the tables. Imaeda considered changing locations entirely, but the person he was going to meet had probably already left the office, so he made do with the table furthest from the noise. He'd hoped that, with it being already one-thirty in the afternoon, the café would be relatively empty. Clearly he was wrong, and this was the spot for a late lunch after class let out. He'd remember that in the future.

Imaeda had only taken a few sips of his coffee when his old colleague walked in. Hitoshi Masuda looked a little thinner than he had when they last worked together. He was wearing a short-sleeved shirt and a navy-blue tie and carrying a large envelope in one hand.

Masuda spotted Imaeda immediately and walked over to the table.

'Long time no see,' he said, sitting across from him, but when the waitress came to take his order he told her, 'No, thanks, I'll be heading right back out.'

'Busy as always, I see,' said Imaeda.

Masuda shrugged. He was clearly in a foul mood. He set the brown paper envelope on the table. 'This what you wanted?'

Imaeda took the envelope and examined its contents. He counted more than twenty sheets of letter-sized paper. He scanned the papers and gave a deep nod. Everything looked familiar. Some of the sheets he had even written himself.

'This is it. Thanks.'

'Look,' Masuda said, leaning closer, 'I shouldn't have to tell you this, but please don't ask me to do this again. You know the rules against sharing office documents with someone outside.'

'I know, sorry. This is the only time I'll ask.'

Masuda stood, but he didn't immediately leave. 'Why do you need those now, anyway?' he asked, looking down at Imaeda. 'You find the missing piece to some old puzzle?'

'No. Just something I needed to check. That's all.'

'Right, whatever,' Masuda said, walking away. It was clear he didn't believe Imaeda in the least, and also clear he knew better than to stick his nose where it didn't belong.

Imaeda waited for him to leave before looking back at the documents. Three-year-old memories resurfaced in his mind. The pages were a copy of the report they had done on behalf of the client from Tozai Automotive – an investigation that had run up against a brick wall when they were unable to determine the true identity of the Memorix employee suspected of data theft: Yuichi Akiyoshi. They'd never found out his real name, his real work history, or even where he was from.

Thus Imaeda's surprise when Sasagaki had shown him a picture of Akiyoshi the other day, calling him 'Ryo Kirihara'.

Managing a computer shop fitted Akiyoshi's profile, and the date of Ryo's disappearance from Osaka roughly matched the timing of Akiyoshi's arrival at Memorix.

At first, Imaeda thought it was just a coincidence. The longer you did this kind of work, the greater the chances were that you'd run into the same people from an old case under completely unrelated circumstances.

Yet, as he thought things through, he realised it couldn't be unrelated. On the contrary, the request from Tozai Automotive and his current investigation were deeply intertwined at their very roots.

For one thing, the entire reason Shinozuka had asked him and not another PI to investigate Yukiho Karasawa was because he had run into Makoto Takamiya at the golf driving range. And the reason he went to that particular range was because, three years earlier, he had followed Akiyoshi there. That was when he'd first taken note of Makoto, who was clearly in a relationship with the woman Akiyoshi had been following, Chizuru Misawa, despite the fact that Makoto was already married to Yukiho at the time.

Detective Sasagaki had suggested that Ryo Kirihara and Yukiho Karasawa were somehow working together, and Imaeda wasn't buying the detective's claim that it was just a theory. He decided to reassess his investigation of three years earlier with the premise that Ryo and Yukiho did in fact have some kind of covert connection.

This hardly required any deep thinking at all: the connection was obvious. Yukiho's husband worked at Tozai Automotive in the Patent Licensing Division, a position with access to internal company data. He would have had both the ID and the password to access top-secret data on the company's systems. Imaeda had no doubt that Makoto took this responsibility seriously, but would he extend a wary eye to his wife? Couldn't she have got access to his ID and password somehow?

Three years ago, Imaeda and his team had been looking for a connection between Akiyoshi and Makoto, and found nothing. Which made sense, because the person they should have been watching was Yukiho.

Another question occurred to Imaeda at this point. Why had Akiyoshi, aka Ryo, been so interested in Chizuru? Was it because of her relationship with Makoto?

He could imagine a scenario where Yukiho had asked him to investigate her husband's infidelity. But why would she ask Ryo to do something like that? It would make more sense to go to a private investigator. Also, if he had been investigating Makoto's infidelities, why was he watching Chizuru? It had to mean that he already knew she was Makoto's lover. But if they knew that, why keep investigating at all?

As he leafed through the copy of the report, another curious thought occurred to Imaeda. It had been early April when Ryo first visited the Eagle Golf Driving Range in pursuit of Chizuru. But that day Makoto hadn't been there. Then, two weeks later, Ryo paid another visit to the driving range. This was the first time that Imaeda's team had spotted Makoto being on familiar terms with Chizuru.

That was also, to their knowledge, the last time Ryo ever visited the range. Except, Imaeda's team had continued observing Makoto and Chizuru, watching their relationship deepen. By the time their investigation had been called off at the beginning of August, the two were deep into an affair.

This struck Imaeda as odd. If Yukiho and Ryo were in contact, and Ryo knew that Yukiho's husband was growing closer to another woman, why hadn't Yukiho acted? She had to have known what was going on.

Imaeda took a sip of his coffee, remembering another similarly lukewarm coffee at the Ginza café with Kazunari. *What if*, Imaeda thought, *what if Yukiho didn't want to stop the affair? What if she wanted a divorce?*

This made sense on a few levels. To borrow Eriko Kawashima's turn of phrase, Makoto had never been Yukiho's one and only. What if her husband had fallen for another woman, and she had just decided to wait it out, let the crush bloom into a full-blown affair?

No, Imaeda thought, shaking his head. Yukiho wasn't the type to just let things happen like that. But what if Makoto's encounter with Chizuru, and everything that had developed since, had been part of Yukiho's plan?

That was a scary thought. He never would have even considered it if the woman involved was anyone but Yukiho. There was something about her that made him unable to entirely discount the possibility.

And yet he still doubted it was that easy to control someone's heart like that. Even if Chizuru Misawa were the most beautiful woman in the world, that wouldn't guarantee love at first sight. Of course, if there had already been something there, it would be much easier to ensure those feelings were given space to grow.

Imaeda left the café and found a payphone. Checking his notes, he dialled the number of Tozai Automotive and asked for Makoto Takamiya.

A couple of minutes later, Makoto was on the phone.

'Hello, it's Imaeda. I'm sorry to bother you while you're at work, but I was hoping I could ask you some questions.'

He heard hesitation on the other side of the line. Clearly this wasn't someone who enjoyed getting calls from private eyes at work.

'Questions about what?'

'Actually, it would be best if we could meet and talk in person.' Imaeda wasn't about to ask the man how he had fallen in love with his wife over the phone. 'Would you have time today or tomorrow evening?'

'Tomorrow, sure.'

'Right, I'll call you again to set up a time.'

'Fine. Oh, wait, there is something I needed to tell you.'

'Yes?'

'A couple of days ago,' Makoto lowered his voice, 'a police detective came to visit me. An older man from Osaka.'

'What did he have to say?'

'He wanted to know if anyone had been asking questions about my ex-wife recently, and I gave him your name. I hope that's OK.'

'Oh, sure.'

'I hope I didn't cause any trouble.'

'No, it's fine. Did you tell him what I did for work?'

Makoto said he had.

'Right, I'll keep that in mind,' Imaeda replied, before saying goodbye and hanging up.

Imaeda hadn't even considered the possibility that Sasagaki had gone through Makoto to get to him. *That was easy work for him*, Imaeda thought. Of course, that made him wonder who was tapping Eri's phone, if not the police. He had a pretty good idea.

It was already late when Imaeda returned to his apartment that night. He had run around checking on things for another job all afternoon, then stopped in for the first time in a long while at the bar where Eri worked.

'I always keep the chain on the door whenever I'm at home now,' she told him. She said she hadn't noticed any signs that anyone was in her place since that first day.

On his way back to his building, he had to step around an unfamiliar-looking white van parked on the street right outside the door. He walked up the stairs, swaying a little, his feet feeling heavy. He had reached his door and was fishing around in his pocket for his keys when he noticed a cart out in the hallway, with a large cardboard box folded flat on top of it. It was a big box, large enough to hold a washing machine. He wondered for a moment who had left it there, but not for long. His neighbours weren't the most polite people, and frequently left rubbish sitting out in the hallway for days. Imaeda had long since given up complaining. He didn't exactly have a great track record on that count himself.

Keys out, he unlocked the door, feeling the bolt slide as he turned the lock. The bolt seemed to slide faster than usual. He gave it a few seconds' thought before deciding he was imagining things.

Imaeda opened the door, flicked on the lights and looked around the room. Nothing was out of place. His room was as devoid of decoration as usual and covered with dust. The air freshener he used to cover up the smell of dirty clothes hung thick in the air.

He threw his stuff down on a chair and headed for the toilet. He had a good buzz on and was feeling a little sleepy and a little sluggish. When he turned on the bathroom light, he realised that the fan was already on. *That's a waste of electricity*, he thought dimly, fumbling for his zipper as he opened the door. The toilet lid was down, which also struck him as strange. As a long-time bachelor, Imaeda took pride in never lowering the lid. Closing the door behind him, he lifted the lid – and an alarm went off in his head.

Without being consciously aware of what it was, he knew he was in grave danger. He tried to close the lid, twisting his body to get out of the bathroom as quickly as he could.

But his body wouldn't move. He couldn't even breathe.

The bathroom spun around him. He felt his body hit something, but there was no pain. All his senses had been robbed from him too. He tried to move his arms, his legs, but he couldn't even twitch a single finger. Then he had the sensation that someone was standing next to him, but he couldn't be sure. *Maybe I'm just imagining things again.*

Everything went dark.

TWELVE

The rainy season had long since passed but still the rain in September was relentless, falling in a dusting of fine droplets that covered the city despite a forecast for clear skies that night. Noriko Kurihara walked past the shops outside Nerima Station in north-western Tokyo. The awnings would keep her dry for most of the ten-minute walk between the station and her apartment.

She passed by an electronics store and heard the sounds of 'Say Yes' by Chage and Aska – the theme song to a popular TV show – blaring out of some speakers. One of Noriko's co-workers had recently been lamenting the fact that the show was about to end, but Noriko didn't really care. She rarely watched television.

Past the shops there was nothing to shield her hair from the rain, so she pulled out a blue-and-grey checked handkerchief and draped it over her head. Just a little farther ahead she ducked into a convenience store where she bought some tofu and leeks. She was tempted to buy a disposable umbrella but balked at the price.

Her apartment stood right along the train tracks. Two bedrooms, for eighty thousand yen a month. If she had planned to live alone, a smaller place would have been fine, but she had expected to be living with a man. He had, in fact, slept over a few times. Now that was over, she was alone, living in a too-large apartment, but lacking the will to move again.

I should never have moved in the first place.

Rain soaked her apartment building's walls, turning them the colour of mud. She walked up the outside staircase, careful not to brush her clothes against the stucco walls. There were four units on each of the building's two storeys. Noriko's was at the far back on the first floor.

She unlocked the door and opened it. It was dim inside as always. No lights were on in the kitchen, or the living room beyond.

'I'm home,' she said, hitting the switch on the kitchen wall. She knew he was there because of the dingy sneakers tossed haphazardly in the entrance. He didn't own any other shoes.

She went through the living room and opened the door. This room was dark too, save for the wan light spilling from the computer monitor by the window. He was there, sitting cross-legged in front of it.

'Hey,' she said to his back.

His hand stopped over the keyboard. He twisted his torso and glanced at the alarm clock on the bookshelf before looking up at her. 'You're late.'

'My boss made me stay. You must be hungry. I'll make something. Tofu stew OK?'

'Whatever's fine.'

'Great, it'll just be a minute.'

'Noriko.'

She looked around the doorway. The man stood, walked over to her. He put his palm to her neck. 'You get wet?'

'A little. It's no big deal.'

He showed no sign of having heard her. His hand went from her neck down to her shoulder. She could feel his firm grip through her sweater. She fell into his embrace. He sucked on the skin below her ear. He knew all her spots. His tongue and lips moved cleverly, quickly. Noriko felt something like electricity run down her spine.

'I ... can't stand,' she managed to say.

He didn't answer. When she tried to sit, he kept a firm grip, holding her up. Then his hands shifted and he turned her around until she was facing away from him, lifting up her skirt and pulling down her stockings and panties. When he had them to her knees, he stepped on them, lowering them the rest of the way to the floor in a single motion.

With his hands around her waist she couldn't even sit, so she leaned forward and grabbed on to the door handle with both hands. The handle squeaked against the wood of the door.

Keeping his right arm around her waist, he began stroking her. Pulses of sensation shot through Noriko's body, and she threw back her head.

She heard him hastily taking off his trousers and underwear. Something hard and hot pressed against her. Then there was pressure, and a sharp pain that spread. She gritted her teeth and bore it. He liked taking her this way.

Even when he was all the way inside, the pain didn't stop. Then he started to move, and the pain increased. But that was as bad as it got. Noriko ground her teeth and then, suddenly, the pleasure hit and the pain disappeared so completely, it might as well have never been there.

He rolled up the front of her sweater and pushed up her bra, squeezing her breasts in both hands. His fingertips played with her nipples. She could hear him breathing, feel the warmth on her neck with each exhalation.

The orgasm approached slowly, like distant thunder. Noriko's arms and legs went taut. The man's thrusting became more violent, until his movements and the ecstasy inside her began to beat at the same frequency. Then lightning broke through her, and she cried as her body trembled. She lost her sense of balance and the world spun.

Noriko let go of the doorknob. She could no longer stand. Her legs were shaking.

The man pulled his penis out of her and she collapsed on the floor, shoulders heaving. A ringing sound filled her head.

Behind her, the man pulled up his underpants and trousers. He was still hard, but he uncaringly buttoned his pants over his erection. Then, as if nothing had happened at all, he returned to his computer. He crossed his legs and began to type in a smooth, natural rhythm.

Noriko slowly sat up, refastened her bra, and pulled on her sweater. She picked up her panties and stockings from the floor.

'Guess I should get dinner ready,' she said, putting her hand out to steady herself on the wall as she stood.

*

The man's name was Yuichi Akiyoshi. At least, that was what he had told her.

She had first met him on a chilly day in the middle of May that year. She'd been walking back to her apartment when she found him curled up on the side of the road. He was skinny, around thirty years old from his looks. He was wearing black denim jeans, and a black leather jacket.

'Are you OK?' she asked, peering down at him. The man's face was twisted in a scowl, his hair sticking to the sweat on his forehead. His right hand was clutched to his stomach, but with his other hand he waved her away.

'I'm fine,' he croaked.

He didn't look fine.

'Do you want me to call an ambulance?'

The man waved his hand again, and this time shook his head.

'Has this happened to you before?' she asked.

He didn't respond.

Noriko stood there for a moment, then said, 'Hold on a second,' before going up the stairs to her apartment. She went inside and poured hot water out of an electric kettle into the largest mug she could find, cooling it off with a little water from the tap, then brought it outside.

'Here, drink this,' she said holding the mug in front of his face. 'We've got to clean out whatever's inside your stomach.'

The man didn't reach for the cup. Instead, he said something that surprised her.

'You got any booze?'

'What?'

'Booze – whisky's best. If I drink it straight, the pain will go away. That's what worked before.'

'Don't be ridiculous,' she said. 'That'll just shock your stomach. Drink this first.' She offered the mug again.

The man frowned and glared at the mug for a few moments, then finally relented and reached out his hand. He took a sip of the warm water.

'Drink the whole thing. It will help clean you out.'

The man's frown deepened, but he said nothing, and drained the mug in one gulp.

'You feel nauseous?'

'A little.'

'You should probably try to throw up. Can you?'

The man nodded and slowly got to his feet. Holding a hand to his stomach, he began to walk towards the back of the building.

'Just do it here. It's nothing I haven't seen before,' she called out, but he ignored her and disappeared behind the apartment.

For a while, he didn't re-emerge, though she heard the occasional groan. Feeling that she couldn't just leave him, she stood and waited.

When he finally returned, he looked a little improved. He sat down on top of a bin by the road.

'Better?' Noriko asked.

'Yeah. A bit.'

Still frowning, the man crossed his legs and pulled a pack of cigarettes out of his jacket pocket. He put one in his mouth and lit it with a disposable lighter.

Noriko snatched the cigarette out of his mouth. He looked at her, still holding the lighter in his hand, his eyes widening.

'Did you know that when you smoke a cigarette your stomach secretes dozens of times more acid than normal? That's what makes people want to smoke when they're full. But if you smoke when your stomach's empty you could damage your stomach lining and get an ulcer.'

Noriko snapped the cigarette in two. Then she looked around for a place to throw it out before she realised the man was sitting on the bin.

'Could you stand up?'

He got to his feet and she tossed the cigarette into the bin. Then she turned to him and held out her hand. 'The box.'

'What box?'

'Your pack of cigarettes.'

The man grinned. Then he reached into his pocket and pulled

out the pack. Noriko took it and tossed it into the bin. She closed the lid and clapped her hands as though she was brushing off dust.

'You can sit back down now.'

The man regained his perch and looked over at her, interest in his eyes. 'You a doctor?'

'Not exactly,' she laughed. 'Though you're not too far off. I'm a pharmacist at a hospital.'

'Ah, that explains it.'

'Do you live near here?' she asked.

'Pretty close.'

'Do you think you can get home OK?'

'Yeah. Thanks to you, I'm right as rain,' he said as he stood from the bin.

'You should go get yourself checked out when you have a chance. Acute gastritis can be pretty scary.'

'The hospital near here?'

She blinked, not understanding. 'There's the General Hospital in Hikarigaoka. That's pretty close.'

The man started shaking his head before she'd finished speaking. 'I meant the hospital where you work.'

'Oh. That's the Imperial University Hospital, out west in Ogikubo.'

'Right,' the man said, beginning to walk. He stopped after a few paces and looked around. 'Thanks.'

'Take care of yourself,' Noriko replied. He raised a hand and started off again, this time disappearing into the night.

She hadn't expected to see the man again. Still, the following day at work, her thoughts kept drifting back to him. She didn't expect him to actually show up at her hospital, but even so, she couldn't resist the urge to take the occasional glance out at the waiting room, and every pharmacy request for stomach medicine for a male patient set her imagination wandering.

He didn't show up at the hospital, but they did meet again. It was exactly one week later, in the same place they'd met the first time.

The man was sitting on the bin and she was just getting home from the evening shift. It was eleven o'clock at night and she didn't recognise him in the darkness. The idea of a stranger sitting in front of her apartment building this late at night was creepy, frankly, and she had already hurried past him when she heard a familiar voice say, 'They must work you pretty hard at that hospital.'

She turned. 'You! What are you doing here?'

'Waiting for you. Thought I should thank you for the other day.'

'How long were you waiting?'

'I forget,' the man said, looking down at his watch. 'Guess I got here around six.'

'Six?' Noriko's eyes widened a little. 'You've been waiting here for five hours?'

'The last time I saw you was around six, so ...'

'Right. I'm on evening shift this week.'

'You don't say.' The man stood. 'Right, well, you're here now. Let's go get something to eat.'

She frowned. 'There's nothing open this late around here.'

'Shinjuku's only twenty minutes away by taxi.'

'I don't want to go that far. I'm tired.'

'That's too bad.' The man lifted his hands. 'Guess I'll have to take a raincheck.'

He waved and began to walk off. He had only made it a few steps before Noriko stopped him. 'Wait,' she said.

He turned.

'There's a Denny's down the street.'

The man took a sip of beer and declared it had been at least five years since he'd set foot in a Denny's. He had plates of sausages and fried chicken in front of him. Noriko had ordered one of the Japanese dishes off the menu.

It was then that the man introduced himself as Yuichi Akiyoshi from Memorix, which was a computer software company, or so it said on his business card.

'Basically, we take orders from other places and write software for them to run their computers.' That was all Akiyoshi ever said about the work his company did and he never talked about work again.

He seemed very interested in Noriko's work, however, wanting to know every detail. He asked about shifts, salaries, bonuses, and the kind of duties she was expected to perform. She expected it to bore him, but on the contrary, his eyes gleamed with interest.

Noriko had dated before, but she usually settled into the role of listener, mostly because she had no idea what sort of things a guy might want to hear. Small talk never came easily to her. But Akiyoshi seemed to know exactly what he wanted to hear, and he was always fascinated by what she had to say. At least it looked that way.

'I'll be in touch,' he had said when he left.

He called three days later. This time they met in Shinjuku. They had drinks at a bar and Noriko found herself talking to him about anything and everything again. He was full of questions. He wanted to know about her home town, how she was raised, what her school was like.

'Where are you from?' Noriko asked.

'Nowhere in particular.' He didn't seem happy about the question and she resolved not to push. All she knew about him was that he was from western Japan, probably Osaka, and even that she'd had to pick up from his accent.

They left Denny's and Akiyoshi saw her back to her apartment. All the while she was wondering should she just say goodnight, or should she invite him up? The closer they got, the louder the argument inside her head grew.

It was Akiyoshi who made the decision easy. There were just nearing the apartment when he stopped in front of a vending machine.

'Thirsty?' she asked.

'I just wanted some coffee,' he said, putting some coins into the slot. He looked up at the display and reached for one of the buttons.

'Wait,' she said. 'I could make you coffee.'

His finger paused in mid-air. He didn't seem particularly surprised, just nodded and gave the coin return lever a yank. The coins fell down with a clatter. He fished them out without saying a word.

Inside, Akiyoshi's eyes scanned her apartment. Noriko made coffee and worried he'd see something of her ex-boyfriend's.

He seemed to enjoy the coffee, and commented on how clean she kept her place.

'Oh, I never clean these days.'

'That why there's dust on the ashtray?'

She blanched. 'What ashtray?'

'Up on top of your bookshelf.'

'No,' she said at length. 'It has dust on it because I don't smoke.'

Akiyoshi grunted.

'We broke up two years ago.'

'Wasn't asking.'

'Right ... sorry.'

Akiyoshi stood. Noriko stood to show him out. But then his arm reached out to her and, before she could speak, he was holding her.

She didn't resist. When he brought his lips closer to hers, she leaned into him and closed her eyes.

The light from the overhead projector lit the presenter's face from below. He was from the Overseas OEM Department, a section chief, still in his early thirties.

'We have every reason to expect that the United States Food and Drug Administration will approve our hyperlipidemia medication Mevalon. The handouts you have describe our sales proposal for the US market.'

Sounds a little nervous, thought Kazunari Shinozuka. He watched as the man licked his lower lip and scanned the faces in the room.

They were in conference room 201 at the Shinozuka Pharmaceuticals main Tokyo office, having a meeting about overseas sales for their newest products. Seventeen people were in attendance, most of them from sales, but he spotted a section chief from research and another chief from manufacturing among them. The highest-ranking person in the room was managing director Yasuharu. He sat in the dead centre of a C-shaped configuration of desks and his eyes were shooting daggers at the speaker. He seemed to hang on every word, unwilling to miss the slightest syllable. Kazunari saw it as a bit of a show, but it was one Yasuharu couldn't afford to do without. He knew what people said about him riding on his father's coat-tails, and he knew well the danger of risking even a single stray yawn in a meeting like this.

The silence in the room lingered for a moment before Yasuharu spoke.

'The licensing agreement we were supposed to make with Slottermeyer is already two weeks late, according to the date we were given at the last meeting. What's the holdup?' He looked up from his handout and glared at the presenter. The rims of his glasses glinted under the fluorescent lights.

'About that.' A short man sitting in front of the presenter spoke. 'There were some difficulties with our export procedures.' His voice sounded strained, almost cracking.

'Why can't we just follow the same procedure we use for base powders. Like our exports to Europe?'

'Right, well, it's about the particulars in the handling of the base powders. There was a bit of a misunderstanding—'

'This is the first time I'm hearing about it. Did I receive a report?' Yasuharu opened the file in front of him on the desk. Not many of the board members brought personal files to meetings like this. As far as Kazunari knew, Yasuharu was the only one.

The short man exchanged a few words with the man next to him and the presenter, before turning back to Yasuharu.

'We'll send you all the related documents immediately.'

'Do that.' Yasuharu's eyes went back down to his file. 'So assuming that settles Mevalon, what about the antibiotic and the diabetes medicine? They should already have been submitted to the FDA for approval.'

'Wanan and Glucoz are both still in clinical trials. We should have a report by the beginning of next month.'

'Well, let's move on that as soon as we can, then,' Yasuharu said.

'I've heard some of our rivals are pushing for more industrial manufacturing rights acquisitions from overseas, and we don't want to fall behind.'

'Of course,' the presenter said. Several of the men around him nodded.

The meeting went on like that for an hour and a half. Kazunari was gathering up his things when Yasuharu walked over and whispered to him, 'My office, fifteen minutes. There's something I want to talk to you about.'

'Yeah, sure thing,' Kazunari replied quietly. Whatever it was, it didn't sound like company business, which meant Yasuharu was gearing up to break the rule both their fathers had set for them: no personal talk at the company.

Kazunari went back to his seat in Planning and Management, where he was deputy director – a post that had been created solely for his benefit. Until last year, Kazunari had gone through positions in general management, accounting, and HR. This was the standard course for a Shinozuka man. Personally, Kazunari would have preferred being down in the trenches with the new recruits rather than the sort of general administrative position he was in now. He had even requested reassignment once. But after a year in the company, he realised that as long as he was a member of the family that was impossible. In order to keep the complex system that was Shinozuka Pharmaceuticals running smoothly, management needed to wield a free hand when they ordered their underlings around. A Shinozuka doing grunt work would only be a rusty cog, gumming up the works.

Immediately next to Kazunari's desk was a small blackboard-style placard where he was supposed to write his current whereabouts. He erased '201' and wrote 'Gen. Management' in white chalk before getting up from his chair.

He knocked on the door and a low voice said, 'Come in.' Kazunari stepped inside to find Yasuharu sitting at his desk, reading a book.

'Hey, sorry to drag you in like this,' Yasuharu said, looking up.

'No problem.' Kazunari took a look around the room. They

were alone in the office, which wasn't particularly large – just a desk, a cabinet, and a simply apportioned meeting space.

Yasuharu grinned. 'Did you see the look on those overseas guys' faces? Bet they didn't imagine I remembered those licensing agreement dates.'

'I bet they didn't.'

Yasuharu shook his head. 'You got to wonder what they're thinking, not telling their direct supervisor about the slippage.'

'I'm sure they won't underestimate their manager in future.'

'Let's hope not. Anyway, I've you to thank for it, Kazunari.'

'Not at all,' Kazunari said, waving a hand dismissively.

It had been Kazunari who had told Yasuharu about the slippage in the licensing agreement date. He'd heard it from a guy who joined the company at the same time he had, and was now in the Overseas OEM Division. Gathering titbits of information from each department and passing them on to Yasuharu was another one of his tasks. It wasn't one he particularly relished, but it had been a direct request from the CEO – Yasuharu's father.

'You wanted to talk to me about something?' Kazunari asked.

Yasuharu shook his head. 'Don't sound so serious. It's not about work.'

A premonition rose in Kazunari's stomach, and he felt his right hand clench into a fist.

'Have a seat,' Yasuharu said, standing and pointing towards the sofa.

Kazunari waited for Yasuharu to sit down before joining him.

'I was just reading this, see,' Yasuharu said, laying a book on the table. The cover read *Etiquette for Ceremonial Occasions*.

'Should I be congratulating someone?'

'Unfortunately, no, it's not that kind of ceremony.'

'Did someone die?'

'Not yet. But soon.'

'Do you mind me asking who?'

'As long as you keep it to yourself. It's her mom.'

'Sorry? Her?' Kazunari asked, though he knew the answer.

'Yukiho,' Yasuharu said, his voice crisp despite a slight blush that came over him.

'What's wrong with Yukiho's mom?'

'Yukiho called the other day, said her mom collapsed at her house down in Osaka.'

'Collapsed how?'

'A brain haemorrhage. She just found out about it yesterday morning. One of her mother's tea students came over for a lesson and found her in the garden.'

'And she's been hospitalised?'

'They took her in right away. Yukiho was there when she called me.'

'I see,' Kazunari nodded. 'How's she doing?' he asked, though he knew the answer to that question, too. If Yukiho's mother was on the road to recovery, Yasuharu wouldn't be reading a book about funeral etiquette.

Yasuharu gave a slight shake of his head. 'I called just a short while ago. She still hasn't regained consciousness. The doctors aren't particularly hopeful either. Yukiho said this might be it. Never heard her sound so defenceless before.'

'How old is her mother?'

'Around seventy, I think. Yukiho's adopted, right? Thus the age gap.'

Kazunari nodded. He knew all about that.

'So why are you reading this, boss?' Kazunari asked, pointing to the book on the table.

'Don't call me that. At least not while we're talking about personal stuff.' Yasuharu said, an exasperated look on his face.

'I just don't see why you'd be so concerned about her mother's funeral.'

'You mean I shouldn't be thinking about the woman's funeral before she's cold?'

Kazunari shook his head. 'No, I just don't think it's your place to be worried.'

'Why not?'

'I know you proposed to her. But she hasn't responded yet, has she? That kind of leaves you, well …' Kazunari paused a moment, trying to find the right words. 'You're strangers, really. What I'm saying is, the death of someone's mother shouldn't have the General Manager of Shinozuka Pharmaceuticals running around learning about funeral etiquette.'

Yasuharu leaned back in his chair and grinned at the ceiling while Kazunari spoke. Eventually, he looked back down and said, '"Strangers" might be going a bit far. She might not have said "yes", but she hasn't said "no" either. If there wasn't a chance, she would have turned me down on the spot.'

'If there was a chance, she would've already given you her answer.'

Yasuharu shook his head again. 'You only say that because A: you're young, and B: you're not married. She and I know what it's like to be married. That's why, when the chance comes to make a household again you take things slow, cautious. Even more so when one of you is a widower.'

'I suppose that's true.'

'Also,' Yasuharu added, raising a finger, 'if we were strangers, she wouldn't have called me to tell me about her mother in the first place. I think the fact that she turned to me when the going got rough is an answer in and of itself.'

Which explained Yasuharu's chipper mood, Kazunari thought.

'Anyway, I think it's proper when a friend is going through a hard time to reach out and lend a hand. Not just as a member of society, but as a human being.'

'So that's what this is? She's going through a hard time? That's why she called you?'

'Well, you know how she is, tough and all. She wasn't talking through tears or asking me to come save her or anything like that. She just called to let me know what was happening. Still, I don't think it's a stretch of imagination to say this is a hard time for her. Osaka might be her home, but she doesn't know anyone down there any more. If her mother dies, then on top of the grieving she'll have to deal with all the funeral arrangements by herself. That might even give the great Yukiho Karasawa cause to panic.'

'See, that's the thing with funerals,' Kazunari said, looking his cousin in the eye. 'They're *always* being arranged by people who are grieving – that's why they have them all programmed out in advance for you. All she has to do is make a single call to the funeral home. After that, she can just leave it to the pros. All she has to do is follow their instructions, sign on the dotted line, and pay some money. Then, if she gets a free moment, she can collapse in front of the photo of the deceased and cry if she wants to. It's really not a big deal.'

Yasuharu drew his eyebrows together in exasperation. 'Well, that's a little cold. I thought you were supposed to be looking out for Yukiho, given that she was from your alma mater.'

'Her school just took dance lessons with my club, that's all.'

'Details, details. Regardless, you are the one who introduced her to me.' Yasuharu gave Kazunari a long stare.

Kazunari suppressed the urge to tell Yasuharu how much he regretted that now.

'Anyway,' Yasuharu said, crossing his legs and leaning back on the sofa, 'maybe this isn't the sort of thing one should really be preparing for in advance, but should something happen to her mother I thought I'd like to be ready. Of course, like you say, there is my position to think about. I'm not sure I'll even be able to go down to Osaka if her mother dies. Which is why I wanted to talk.' He pointed a finger slowly at Kazunari's face. 'Depending on the circumstances, I was hoping you might be able to go down to Osaka for me. You know the area. And Yukiho knows you.'

Kazunari had begun to frown before Yasuharu was finished. 'Don't make me do that, Yasuharu.'

'Why not?'

'Because it's mixing company business with private business. People will say I'm your personal secretary.'

'Supporting a member of the board is part of Planning and Management's official duties,' Yasuharu said, glaring.

'What does this have to do with Shinozuka Pharmaceuticals?'

'Who cares? What matters is who's asking you,' Yasuharu said severely, then he grinned and looked up at Kazunari. 'Yes?'

Kazunari sighed. *So now he likes being the boss.*

Back at his desk, Kazunari picked up the phone. With his other hand, he opened his desk drawer and took out his schedule planner. He flipped to the addresses in the back and opened it to the first page, finding the entry for Imaeda. He pressed the buttons on the phone, checking to make sure the number was right, held the receiver up to his ear, and waited. The phone rang a couple of times. He began to tap his desk with the fingers of his right hand.

After the phone had rung six times, it stopped. *Not again,* Kazunari thought. Imaeda's answering machine was set to pick up after six rings.

From the other side of the line, he heard the computerised voice of a woman who sounded like she had a stuffy nose telling him that no one was home, and to please leave a name, number, and short message—

Kazunari hung up before he heard the beep.

He cursed under his breath, loud enough that the female employee sitting across from him jerked upright in her chair a little.

What's up, Imaeda?

The last time he had met the private eye was mid-August. It had already been more than a month since then and he hadn't heard a thing. Kazunari had called several times, but Imaeda was always out. He'd even left two messages, telling him to call, apparently in vain.

Kazunari assumed he must be on vacation. It hardly seemed like the way to run a private detective business to him. In fact, he had specifically requested frequent reports when he first hired him.

Or, Kazunari thought, maybe he's followed Yukiho Karasawa to Osaka. It was certainly a possibility, though he would have expected a report all the same.

The paper sitting at the edge of the desk caught Kazunari's eye. It was the minutes from the meeting two days earlier. The meeting had been about a computer system that automatically determined the chemical compositions of substances. It was research Kazunari had a personal interest in, but this time he only mechanically scanned the page. His head was full of Yasuharu and Yukiho Karasawa.

Kazunari truly regretted having taken Yasuharu to her shop. He hadn't even really thought it through when he got the invitation from Makoto Takamiya. That had been a mistake.

Kazunari vividly remembered the time when Yasuharu first met Yukiho. There'd been nothing about him to suggest he had fallen in love. In fact, he seemed to be in a bad mood. Even when Yukiho talked to him, he only offered gruff responses. It was only later that Kazunari realised that was exactly how Yasuharu acted when he was falling head over heels.

Not that there was anything wrong with him falling in love – it was a good thing, to be sure. There was no reason why a forty-five-year-old man with two children had to live the rest of his life single. *Get remarried*, Kazunari thought, *but to the right person.*

Yukiho was not the right person.

He had never been able to put his finger on exactly why he didn't like Yukiho Karasawa. As he'd told the private eye, the mysterious way money seemed to move around her wherever she went was unsettling, yet even that felt like an excuse his rational mind had made up after the fact. In reality, it probably all went back to that first impression he had when they met at dance lessons.

Kazunari didn't want them getting married, but he would need a very good reason to convince Yasuharu. He could tell him that she was dangerous, that he should give her up, but he was sure he could talk himself hoarse and never win that way. No, that would probably just piss Yasuharu off.

Which was why Kazunari really needed Imaeda to dig up some dirt. He needed someone to pull back the curtains and reveal Yukiho for what she really was – everything hung on that.

Yasuharu's request flitted through the back of his mind. He might just have to go down to Osaka to meet Yukiho, support her in her time of need.

What a joke, Kazunari thought to himself. He remembered another thing: Imaeda's theory that Yukiho didn't love Yasuharu because she already loved someone else.

Me.

'What a joke.' This time Kazunari said the words out loud, keeping his voice hushed in the quiet office.

'I'll be away for two or three days,' Akiyoshi said as Noriko stepped out of the bath one evening.

'Where are you going?'

'Research.'

She stopped by the dresser. 'You're not going to tell me where?'

He hesitated a moment before mumbling, 'Osaka.'

'All the way to Osaka?'

'I'm leaving tomorrow.'

'Wait.' Noriko stepped away from the dresser and sat facing him. 'I want to go too.'

'Don't you have work?'

'I'll take a few days off. I haven't taken a single vacation day since last year.'

'This isn't a vacation.'

'I know. I won't get in the way. I'll do some sightseeing while you work.'

Akiyoshi furrowed his brow for a moment. Noriko could tell he was taken aback by her request. Normally she'd never be so forward, but when she heard him say Osaka, she knew she had to go. For one, she wanted to see where he was from. He'd never told her the first thing about his family and this was her chance to find out more.

'This isn't some kind of tour. My schedule could change at a moment's notice. To be honest, I'm not even sure when I'll be able to come back.'

'Not a problem,' Noriko said.

'Fine,' he relented at last. 'Do what you want.'

Noriko felt an almost painful stirring in her chest as he turned back to the computer. This was a big step. There would be no going back after this. Not that doing nothing was an option. If they kept on like this, they'd fall apart before too long, and she didn't want that. Despite the fact that they'd only been together two months, Noriko was in deep.

They had started living together when Akiyoshi quit his job. She never got a straight answer from him as to why he left. He just said he felt like taking a break.

'I've got savings, so I won't starve, not for a while at least. I'll have time to think about what's next.'

She knew him well enough to know that he wasn't the type to lean on anyone for help. Still it made her sad that he wouldn't discuss these decisions with her, let alone ask for her advice. She wanted to be more than that: not just part of his life, a *necessary* part.

Living together had been Noriko's suggestion. Akiyoshi hadn't seemed that enthusiastic about it at first, but it had only taken him a week to change his mind. His worldly possessions consisted of a computer and six cardboard boxes.

So, in a small way, Noriko had realised her dream. She was living with the man she loved. He was there beside her when she woke up in the morning. It was a happiness she wanted to last. Marriage wasn't an issue, she had decided. Not that she didn't want to get married – that would have been fine. But she didn't want to ruin what they had by pushing it, either.

Yet it wasn't long before unease began tugging at the back of her mind. It started one night, when they were having sex. They had been going at it as usual on her thin futon. Noriko climaxed twice before Akiyoshi let himself come – their usual pattern.

They'd never used condoms, not even the first time. He would thrust hard, pull out, and ejaculate into a wad of tissue paper. Noriko had never noticed anything unusual about it, until that night. She wasn't even sure what had tickled her suspicions. Maybe it was the look she saw in his eyes before he rolled over on his side.

She reached out to touch him between the legs.

'Knock it off,' he said, twisting away until his back was turned.

Noriko sat up and looked at him. 'You didn't come, did you.'

He didn't say anything. His expression didn't change. He just closed his eyes.

Noriko got off the futon and reached for the wastebasket.

'I said knock it off!'

She looked around to see him sitting up, glaring at her.

'Why do you want to do that for?' he growled.

'Why didn't you come?'

He scratched his chin and didn't reply.

'How long has this been going on?'

He didn't answer.

Noriko gasped. 'Wait. You *never* came?'

'What does it matter?'

'It matters!' she said, sitting down, nude, in front of him. 'It matters a lot! Is it me? You can't come with me?'

'No. Nothing like that.'

'Then what is it like? Tell me.'

Noriko felt the heat rise to her face. She was being made a fool of. It was wretched, and sad, and horribly embarrassing all at the same time. When she thought of all the times they'd had sex, it made her want to cover her face with her hands.

Akiyoshi sighed and shook his head. 'It has nothing to do with you.'

'What is it, then?'

'I've never been able to come inside a woman. I can't even if I want to.'

'Is that something like erectile dysfunction?'

'See, that's the problem with you medical people. You want to classify everything into a disease.'

'I don't believe it. You better not be joking about this.'

'No joke.'

'Have you seen a doctor?'

'Nope.'

'Why not?'

'Because it's not something I feel like I need to fix.'

'Of course you have to fix it!'

'Look, it's my dick and I'm fine with it. So leave me alone.' He turned his back to her again.

She wondered at the time if that was it and they would never have sex again, but three days later he came on to her again. She let him do what he wanted. *If he can't come, neither will I,* she thought, but the flesh wasn't so disciplined. After the release, there was no lingering glow, no sweet sleep, just embarrassment and sadness.

'It's OK,' he whispered, his voice unusually gentle as he stroked her hair.

Once he'd asked her if she could use her hands and her mouth. She did as she was told, curling her tongue and working her fingers rhythmically. But although he got an erection, there were no indications he would ever orgasm.

'That's enough. Stop. I'm sorry,' he said.

'No, I'm sorry.'

He shook his head. 'It's not your fault.'

'Why isn't it working?'

Akiyoshi didn't respond. He looked down at her hand, still gripping his penis. Eventually, he said, 'They're small, aren't they.'

'What?'

'Your hands. They're small.'

She looked down at her hands, but her head was filled with thoughts of another girl's hands on his cock, a girl he was comparing her to, a girl who could make him come.

His penis had already gone soft in her palm.

And so Noriko had been worried for several days when Akiyoshi said something wholly unexpected.

He wanted to know if she could get some cyanide.

'It's for a novel,' he said. 'I might as well do something if I'm just loafing around, so I figured I'd write a mystery. Anyway, I want to use cyanide in the novel, but I've never seen any and I was just wondering if you could get some. I'm sure they have some lying around in a big hospital like yours.'

'Well, I'd have to check, I'm not sure,' she said, trying and failing to imagine Akiyoshi writing a novel. In fact, she knew that the pharmacy did have some potassium cyanide in special storage. It wasn't for medicinal use, of course. Being a university hospital they had all kinds of poisons as part of their research collection. But only a select few at the hospital were even allowed near special storage.

'You just have to see it?'

'I just want to borrow it for a little.'

'I'm not so sure that's a good idea. This is cyanide we're talking about.'

'Look,' he said, 'I haven't figured out what I want to do with it yet. I have to see it first. Get some, if you can. Of course, if you can't, or you don't want to, I won't force you. I have another route.'

'What kind of route?'

'I have connections to a number of companies through my last job. I'm pretty sure one of them can get me some cyanide.'

Noriko was ready to put her foot down and refuse, but the mention of other routes gave her pause. What if someone untrustworthy gave it to him? What if something happened?

She sighed and shook her head. *This is a bad idea.*

It was mid-August when she placed the small bottle of potassium cyanide in front of him.

'Promise me you aren't going to use this.'

'Absolutely. You have nothing to worry about,' Akiyoshi said, picking up the bottle.

'Leave the lid on. You can look at it through the glass.'

He didn't answer. He seemed transfixed by the colourless powder inside the bottle. 'How much of this do you have to take for a lethal dose?'

'Two hundred to three hundred milligrams.'

'How am I supposed to tell how much that is just by looking at it?'

'Just picture a quarter-teaspoon or so.'

'Sounds potent. It dissolves in water, right?'

'It'll dissolve, but if you're thinking of having someone put it in a glass of juice or something, you'd probably need more than a quarter-teaspoon.'

'Why's that?'

'Because the victim would notice something strange on the first sip. It's very bitter, they say. Not that I've ever tasted any.'

'So you'd have to put enough in so they died on the first gulp? If it tastes so bad, wouldn't the victim just spit it out.'

'It has an unusual smell, too, so someone with a good nose might notice before they even take a sip.'

'Smells like almonds, right?'

'Yeah, but not the almond you're thinking of. It smells like the almond fruit. The nuts we eat are the seeds.'

'I think I read a book where someone dissolved cyanide in a solution then painted the back of a stamp with it ...'

Noriko shook her head and laughed. 'That's not very realistic. You'd need a lot more solution than that to reach a lethal dose.'

'How about mixing it in with lipstick?'

'That wouldn't make for a lethal dose, either. First of all, cyanide is highly alkaline, so it would make the skin sore. Also, that method wouldn't get the cyanide into the stomach, so there wouldn't be any toxicity.'

'How so?'

'Cyanide by itself is an inert substance. It has to get in the stomach in order to react with the acid there before it forms cyanide gas. That's what poisons you.'

'So you could poison someone with just the gas, right?'

'Sure, but it's difficult to pull off. For one thing, the killer might accidentally kill themselves. Cyanide gas can be absorbed through the skin, too, so it takes more precautions than just holding your breath.'

'No kidding. Guess I'd better give this some thought,' Akiyoshi said.

In fact, he spent the next two days sitting in front of his computer, thinking.

'Let's say you have access to the victim's home – the bathroom, specifically,' he said during dinner one night. 'You could sneak into their house before they came home, throw some potassium cyanide and sulphuric acid into the toilet, and close the lid. You'd have time to get out of there before killing yourself, right?'

'I would think so,' Noriko said.

'So now the intended victim comes home. They go into the bathroom. Unbeknownst to them, a chemical reaction is taking place inside their toilet, creating a large amount of cyanide gas.

They open the lid, the gas comes billowing out, and the victim breathes it in – how's that sound?'

Noriko gave it some thought, then agreed it would probably work.

'It's just a novel, so that's probably good enough. If you started getting into specifics, you'd never get through the scene.'

Akiyoshi didn't seem satisfied with that. Setting down his chopsticks, he pulled out a notepad and pen.

'I don't like doing things in half measures. If there's a problem with this scenario, I want you to tell me. That's why I'm coming to you with this.'

Noriko felt like she'd been slapped in the face. She sat back down. 'It's not that there's a problem with it. I think the method you describe could work fine. It's just that, in reality, it might not work one hundred per cent of the time.'

'Why not?'

'Because a closed toilet lid doesn't form a perfect seal. The cyanide gas would fill the toilet bowl, then start to leak. It might even leak out through the bathroom door, in which case the intended victim might notice something was off before they even went in. Actually, "notice" isn't the right word. If they breathed in a little bit of the gas, they might show signs of poisoning. Of course, if it was enough to kill them, I suppose that would be all right ...'

'But the leaked gas might not be enough to prove lethal, is what you're saying?'

'If the killer got unlucky, yes.'

'No, you're totally right, it's not a fail-safe plan,' Akiyoshi said, folding his arms across his chest. 'You'd need to do something to get a better seal on the toilet.'

'Well, it might be enough to just run the fan,' she said.

'The fan in the bathroom?'

'Assuming the victim lives in an apartment that has one of those. That would be enough to siphon off the gas that leaked and keep it from going outside the bathroom door.'

Akiyoshi thought in silence for a bit, then looked up at Noriko.

'Good. I'll go with that. Thanks for the help.'

'Good luck with the novel,' Noriko said, glowing. Any worries she'd had when he first asked her to get the cyanide had since faded, replaced by the elation she felt at his gratitude.

A week later she came home from work to find Akiyoshi gone. She thought maybe he'd gone drinking somewhere, but he didn't come home, even after the trains had stopped, and there was no call. She started to worry, realising that if something had happened to him, she'd have no way to find him. She didn't know any of his friends, and she couldn't even think of a place he might have gone. The only Akiyoshi she knew was the one who sat in her back room, staring at the computer.

It was close to dawn when he finally came back. Noriko was still up. She hadn't taken off her make-up. She hadn't even eaten.

'Where were you?' she asked almost as soon as he stepped through the door.

'Doing research for my novel. Sorry, there weren't any pay-phones around or I would've called.'

'I was worried!'

Akiyoshi was wearing jeans and a grimy white T-shirt. He set down a duffel bag by the computer and took off his shirt. His skin was gleaming with sweat.

'I gotta take a shower.'

'Well, hold on a second, I'll draw a bath.'

'The shower's fine,' he said, carrying his T-shirt in his hand as he walked towards the bathroom.

Back at the door, Noriko straightened his sneakers and noticed they were incredibly dirty. It was as though he'd been walking through the mountains all night.

She had a feeling that Akiyoshi would never tell her where he had been, and there was something about him that made it difficult for her to ask. She was sure of one thing, though: he hadn't been doing research for his novel.

A thought occurred to her. She could hear the shower running. Moving quickly, she went into the back room and opened the duffel bag.

On top were several file folders, like you might get in a filing cabinet. She pulled out the largest one, only to find it empty. All the other folders were empty, too, without any markings or writing, save for one that had a single sticker across the top that read IMAEDA DETECTIVE AGENCY.

Why would Akiyoshi have a file from a detective agency – an empty file at that? *Maybe he took out whatever was inside?*

She checked the rest of the bag. When she saw what was at the very bottom, she held her breath. It was the bottle of potassium cyanide.

Gingerly, she picked it out. It contained white powder, but only half as much as there had been when she gave it to him.

Her chest tightened and she felt sick to her stomach. Her heart pounded in her ears.

She heard the shower stop. Quickly she put the bottle and the folders back in the bag and zipped it shut.

Akiyoshi didn't say anything as he came out of the bathroom. He just went over to sit by the window and stare outside. There was a hard, dark look to his face that Noriko had never seen before.

She could ask him where he'd been, and he'd probably tell her something, but she knew it would be a lie. What had he used the cyanide for? Just the thought was enough to make her stomach churn with fear.

When Akiyoshi came for her, it was swift. He practically tore off her clothes, taking her more roughly than he ever had before, like there was something he was trying to forget.

He wouldn't orgasm, she knew, but he would keep fucking her until she did.

That morning, as the dawn light streamed in through the window, Noriko faked it for the first time.

The call came three days after Yasuharu had called him into the office to talk about Yukiho's mother. Kazunari had just returned to his desk from a long meeting when the phone rang. A small light on the phone indicated the call was from an outside line.

The caller introduced himself as Sasagaki, with the Osaka police. Kazunari couldn't recall ever talking to anyone with that name before, let alone a detective. From his voice he sounded like an older man, with a thick accent.

'I got your name from a Mr Takamiya. Sorry to bother you at work like this,' the man said, though from his tone he wasn't sorry at all.

'Can I ask what this is about?' Kazunari asked, an edge creeping into his own voice.

'I wanted to ask you some questions concerning a case we have under investigation. It should only take about thirty minutes, if you have the time.'

'What investigation is this?'

'It's best if I talk to you in person about that.'

Kazunari's interest was piqued. Whatever the case was, it must be important if the man was going to come all the way up to Tokyo to talk to him about it.

'This also involves a Mr Imaeda – a private detective. I believe you're acquainted with him?'

Kazunari's grip on the phone tightened and his legs tensed, as though his body were getting ready to run. How did this man know about Imaeda – or more specifically, his connection to the private eye? He knew people in that line of work didn't readily give up the names of their clients, not even when the police came calling.

A possibility occurred to him. 'Has something happened to Mr Imaeda?'

'I'd like to talk to you about that too,' the detective said. 'Can we meet?' His voice sounded louder now, his question carrying the weight of a command.

'Where are you calling from?'

'Across the street. I can see a white building, about seven storeys high – that's you, right?'

'Right. Go in and tell the receptionist you'd like to speak with Kazunari Shinozuka in Planning and Management. They'll be expecting you.'

'Got it, be right over.'

'I'll be here.'

Kazunari hung up the phone, then picked the receiver back up again to call the receptionist and have them show Sasagaki to room seven. This was the room board members used whenever they had private visitors to the company.

Sasagaki seemed unusually fit for his age, with short-cropped hair that was peppered with white. The man had stood when Kazunari knocked on the door, and he was still standing. Despite the steamy weather outside, he was wearing a brown suit and a tie.

'Thank you for seeing me,' the detective said, holding out his business card.

When Kazunari looked down at it, he blinked. It seemed a little bare. There was only a name – Junzo Sasagaki – an address, and a phone number. The address was in Yao City, Osaka. No police department affiliation, or even a title.

'I never put anything official on my business cards,' the man explained with a smile that deepened the wrinkles on his face. 'Somebody took one of my old cards once and went around pretending they were on the force.'

Kazunari listened in silence. It had never occurred to him to exploit a business card that way. He felt he was getting a glimpse of a world that operated by very different rules from his own.

'I still carry this, though.' Sasagaki reached into his jacket pocket and pulled out his badge.

Kazunari took a look, then motioned with his hand to the sofa. 'Please, have a seat.'

The detective nodded and sat down. He frowned a little when he bent his knees, revealing his age. No sooner had he sat down than a knock came at the door and one of the women from the office came in carrying a tray with two cups of tea. She set it down on the table, bowed, and left the room.

'Quite the office you have,' Sasagaki said, reaching out for his cup. 'Impressive companies have impressive reception rooms.'

'Thanks,' Kazunari said, even though, in his opinion, this reception room was rather austere. Despite its special status, the sofa and table set were the exact same ones they used in every other meeting room. The only thing that set it apart was the soundproofing in the walls.

'So,' Kazunari began, looking up at the detective. 'What's this all about?'

Sasagaki nodded and set his cup back down. 'I understand you're having Mr Imaeda do some work for you.'

Kazunari felt his jaw tighten.

'I understand your alarm,' Sasagaki said, 'but I really need you to be completely candid. You should know that it wasn't Mr Imaeda who told me about you. As a matter fact, he's gone missing.'

'What?' Kazunari blurted. 'Really?'

'I'm afraid so.'

'Since when?'

'Well ...' Sasagaki scratched his hair. 'That's not entirely clear. All I know is that around the twentieth of last month he called Mr Takamiya asking if he could meet that day or the next. Mr Takamiya told him to come the following day, and Mr Imaeda said he would call before coming. But no call ever came.'

'So no one's heard from him since the twentieth?'

'That's correct.'

Kazunari folded his arms across his chest and groaned despite himself. 'Why would he go missing?'

'That's what I mean to find out. As a matter of fact, I met with him not too long ago myself,' Sasagaki said. 'Concerning an investigation. I tried contacting him once later, but no matter how many times I rang, he never picked up. So I came up to Tokyo yesterday and paid a visit to his office.'

'And no one was there?'

Sasagaki nodded. 'Quite a few letters stacked up in his mailbox, too. I had the concierge let me into his unit.'

'What did you find?' Kazunari asked, leaning forward.

'Nothing much. No sign of an incident or any struggle. I let the local precinct know but I doubt they'll put much effort into finding him.'

'Might he have gone into hiding?'

'Possibly. But I don't think it's very likely.'

'Why not?'

'I just think it's *more* likely something happened to him.'

Kazunari swallowed. The inside of his mouth was bone dry. He took a sip of his tea.

'Was he involved in anything dangerous?'

'That's the question, isn't it?' Sasagaki reached into his pocket. 'Mind if I smoke?'

'Go right ahead,' Kazunari said, pushing the stainless steel ashtray from one corner of the table until it sat in front of the detective.

Sasagaki pulled out a Hi-Lite cigarette. *You don't see those much these days*, Kazunari thought, staring at the classic blue and white packaging.

The detective blew out a thick stream of white smoke.

'Based on what I picked up the last time I met Mr Imaeda, his biggest case involved the investigation of a particular woman. I'm sure I don't need to tell you who that is.'

The detective's friendly smile vanished, and Kazunari almost flinched at the sharp, lizard-like look in his eyes.

No point in playing dumb, he thought, even as he realised it was probably the detective's look that had disarmed him. *He might be craftier than I gave him credit for.* Kazunari nodded slowly. 'Yes, I know.'

Sasagaki nodded again.

'And you're the one who requested he investigate Miss Yukiho Karasawa?'

'You said you got my name from Takamiya,' Kazunari responded, ignoring the question. 'I don't see the connection.'

'It's not all that difficult,' the detective replied. 'Nor particularly pertinent.'

'Yes, but it still makes me wonder ...'

'So much that you can't answer my question?'

Kazunari nodded, meeting his gaze. Against a lesser adversary he might have tried to glare, but he was convinced it would have little effect on the battle-hardened detective.

Sasagaki smiled and took a drag on his cigarette. 'For various reasons, I too have a strong interest in Yukiho Karasawa. Which is how I noticed when someone else started looking into her. Naturally, I got curious about who that was, so I went to meet Miss Karasawa's ex-husband. Takamiya told me that there was talk she was getting married again and someone from the groom's family was looking into her. He gave me Imaeda's name.'

'And?'

Sasagaki picked up an old leather satchel and put it on his knee, opening the clasps. He pulled out a small tape recorder. A knowing smile on his face, he placed it on the table and pressed the play button.

There was a beep and then a voice, clear enough to understand over the hiss of the tape.

'Hi, it's Shinozuka, calling about the Yukiho investigation. I wanted to know how it's going. Give me a call.'

Sasagaki pressed the stop button and placed the tape recorder back in his satchel.

'I borrowed this from Mr Imaeda's answering machine the other day. I'm correct in assuming the Mr Shinozuka on the line was you?'

'Yes. That would've been from the beginning of the month.' Kazunari said with a sigh. He thought a moment about protesting this invasion of privacy, then discarded the idea as pointless.

'Right. So, I gave Mr Takamiya another call to ask him about you.'

'And he told you everything?'

'He told me enough. Anyhow, like I said, it's not that difficult a thread to follow.'

'As you say.'

'Let me ask again, it was you who requested the investigation into Miss Yukiho Karasawa?'

'Yes.'

'And who wants to marry her?'

'A relative of mine. But she hasn't given him an answer.'

'Mind telling me the name of this relative of yours?' Sasagaki asked, opening his notebook.

'Do you really have to know that?'

'That's what we do, in my line of work. We ask a lot of people a lot of questions. If you don't want to say, that's fine. No skin off my nose. I'll just have to go around asking a lot of other people a lot of questions until I find someone who can tell me who it is that wants to marry Yukiho Karasawa.'

Kazunari frowned. That would be a disaster, and the detective knew it. 'It's Yasuharu – my cousin.'

Sasagaki scribbled the name. 'I'm guessing that's Yasuharu Shinozuka, correct? And he works at this company?'

Kazunari told him his cousin was managing director.

'There are a few things I don't understand, if you don't mind?' Kazunari said.

'Not at all, though there may be some things I'm not at liberty to share.'

'You said you had interest in Yukiho Karasawa for various reasons. I was wondering if you could tell me what those reasons are?'

A wry smile spread across Sasagaki's face. 'Unfortunately, that's one of the things I can't share.'

'It's confidential?'

'To be frank, I'm just not ready to talk about it. There are still too many unknowns. You see, this whole thing goes back to a case that's eighteen years old.'

'Eighteen years?' Kazunari shook his head, trying to picture an investigation spanning such a long period of time. 'Can you tell me what that case was, at least?'

A brief moment of indecision passed across the detective's face. Then he blinked and said, 'Homicide.'

Kazunari straightened and breathed out a long sigh to steady himself. 'Who was killed?'

'You'll have to forgive me if I don't answer that,' Sasagaki said, holding his palms out to indicate he'd given all he could.

'But she – Yukiho was involved?'

'Let's just say it's likely she holds an important key to understanding what happened.'

'But wait,' Kazunari said. 'Isn't the statute of limitations already up, if it happened that long ago?'

'I'm afraid so, yes.'

'But you're still on the case?'

The detective picked up his box of Hi-Lites and jabbed a finger in, fishing out a second cigarette. Kazunari didn't remember when he had snuffed out the last one.

'It's a bit of a long story, as you might imagine, and it's not finished. Nor do I think it will ever reach its conclusion without me going back to the very beginning, if you follow.'

'I'd love to hear it.'

'Not today,' Sasagaki said with a smile. 'For one thing, it's eighteen years' worth of a tale, and I'm afraid we'd be sitting here a very long time in the telling.'

'Some other time, then?'

'Sure,' the detective said, looking him in the eye and taking a deep drag on his cigarette. 'Someday, when we have time.'

Kazunari reached for his tea and discovered that both their cups were empty.

'Would you like some more?'

'No, I'm fine. If you don't mind, though, I have another question for you.'

'Yes?'

'Can you tell me the real reason why you asked Mr Imaeda to investigate Yukiho Karasawa?'

'You already know that. I mean, it's nothing unusual. Lots of people in our position like to find out about potential spouses before the wedding.'

'I'm sure they do. What I don't get is, why you? I can understand if it were the groom's parents, but I don't think I've ever heard of a cousin going out of his way to hire a private eye. And there's another thing that makes it strange that you, in particular, would want to investigate Yukiho Karasawa. You're old friends with her ex-husband. Go back further and the three of you were in the same dance club in college. So you should know quite a bit about Miss Karasawa without going through the trouble of investigating her. And yet you did.

'That might be reason enough to wonder,' the detective

continued, 'but in all honesty, it was something else that piqued my curiosity about you. It was the tape I found in Imaeda's answering machine. Specifically, the way you said her name. It sent a shiver down my spine, Mr Shinozuka. Call it a hunch, but something in your voice made me think "this man fears Yukiho Karasawa", and I want to know why.'

The detective snuffed out his second cigarette. He leaned forward, placing both hands down on the table. 'I need you to tell me the truth. What was the real reason you asked Mr Imaeda to look into Yukiho Karasawa?'

Something had shifted about Sasagaki's demeanour. The authoritative weight was still there, but he no longer felt threatening. Rather, he seemed warm and eager to help. *He must use this face when he's questioning a suspect*, Kazunari thought. Immediately he understood that this, then, was the question the detective had come here today to ask. It didn't matter to him in the least who wanted to marry Yukiho Karasawa. It only mattered why Kazunari suspected she was dangerous.

He chuckled. 'Don't go barking up the wrong tree, detective. I was being honest when I told you I hired Mr Imaeda purely for my cousin's benefit. If my cousin hadn't wanted to marry Yukiho, then I couldn't care less what kind of woman she is or what kind of life she leads.'

'I see.'

'You were, however, right about one thing,' Kazunari continued.

'And that is?'

'She does scare me.'

'Ah.' Sasagaki leaned back in the sofa, looking him in the eye. 'And why is that?'

'Well, it's a little vague, and very subjective.'

'Not a problem,' said Sasagaki with a wry grin. 'I live for vague subjectivity.'

Kazunari explained everything to Sasagaki in roughly the same fashion as he had when he first spoke with Imaeda: he sensed someone or something behind her, a shadowy backer with lots of money, and not a lot of morals. Everyone who got involved with her ended up meeting misfortune.

Despite the tale sounding increasingly ridiculous as he told it, Sasagaki listened to every word, a serious look on his face as he puffed at his third cigarette.

'I see,' the detective said once he had finished. 'Thanks for sharing that with me.' He put out his cigarette and bowed his head in gratitude, giving Kazunari a good look at his greying hair parted right down the middle.

'I'm sure you think I'm letting my imagination run away with me.'

'Not at all,' Sasagaki said waving a hand in front of his face as if to brush away the mere suggestion. 'To be honest, I'm a little surprised you understand the situation as well as you do. It's impressive for someone your age to show such intuition.'

'You mean ... you think I'm right?'

'That I do,' Sasagaki said with a nod. 'I think you've seen right through to the truth of Yukiho Karasawa. Unfortunately, few people possess your keen eye, especially when it comes to her. Even I was blind for a very long time.'

'So my intuition about her, that's correct?'

'As far as I can tell,' the detective replied. 'Nothing good happens by getting involved with her, that's for certain. And I have eighteen years of experience to verify that.'

'Well, then, I'd sure like to introduce you to my cousin.'

'As I would like to meet him and warn him. Though I doubt he'd listen. You're the first person I've even been able to talk with openly about this.'

'What I wanted – the whole reason I hired Mr Imaeda in the first place – was to get something decisive on her. A smoking gun,' Kazunari said.

'You learn anything from his investigation?'

'Nothing, really. Just a few details about her stock trades. Imaeda was only getting started.'

Kazunari had already decided he would forbear mentioning what the private eye had said about him being the one Yukiho Karasawa truly loved.

'Well,' Sasagaki said in a low voice, 'this is only conjecture, but I think Mr Imaeda might just have found something decisive, as you say.'

'Proof of her backer?'

The detective nodded. 'The other day when I was looking through Mr Imaeda's place I couldn't help but notice he had nothing on Yukiho Karasawa at all in his files. Not even a single photograph.'

'What?' Kazunari's eyes widened. 'You mean—'

'Someone who was afraid of that particular investigation may well have played a part in Mr Imaeda's disappearance.'

Kazunari shook his head. The thought didn't even seem like a stretch, not any more. Yet there was still that faint whiff of unreality to it.

'And you believe that,' he muttered. 'You believe someone would go that far.'

'So you think she's bad, but not that bad?'

'Couldn't his disappearance be a coincidence? Maybe he got wrapped up in something else?'

'Doesn't fit,' the detective said with confidence. 'Mr Imaeda gets two newspapers delivered, and when I checked with the delivery people they said that a man called to stop delivery last month on the twenty-first, because he was going on a trip.'

'A man who could have been Mr Imaeda.'

'True. But given that he had no reason to go on a trip without informing you first, I don't think it was,' Sasagaki said, shaking his head. 'I think whoever made him disappear was trying to arrange things to attract as little attention as possible. If newspapers started piling up at his door, it wouldn't take long before his neighbours or the concierge started asking questions.'

'But if what you're saying is correct, then whoever did this is a hardened criminal. I mean, we'd have to assume that Mr Imaeda was killed, wouldn't we?'

An emotionless mask fell over the detective's expression. 'I think the chances of him still being alive are extremely small.'

Kazunari breathed out. This conversation was nerve-racking. His heart had been racing for what felt like hours.

'But there's still no way to directly connect whoever called the newspapers with Yukiho,' Kazunari said, even as he wondered at himself. *Why defend this woman I'm trying to expose?* Maybe, he thought, it was because whatever evils he was trying to lay at her feet, murder seemed like one step too far.

Sasagaki went for his other jacket pocket and pulled out a single photograph.

'Have you ever seen this man?'

'May I?' Kazunari took the photo from him.

The photo showed a young man with a thin face. He had broad shoulders and a cold look to his eyes that went well with the dark jacket he was wearing.

Kazunari had never seen him before in his life. He told the detective as much.

'I see. That's too bad.'

'Who is it?'

'A man I've been looking for. Can I borrow that business card I just gave you?'

Kazunari handed the detective back his business card. Sasagaki flipped the card over and wrote a name on the reverse side: *Ryo Kirihara*.

'Who's that?'

'A ghost.'

'Excuse me?'

'Mr Shinozuka, I'd appreciate it if you could commit this face and name to memory. If you should see or hear of him, anywhere, I want you to contact me immediately.'

'That's fine, but why should I see him? And you're the police. Wouldn't you have better luck putting up Wanted posters?' Kazunari asked with a shrug.

'I would, if I had anything to charge him with. And besides, I know the one place he's most likely to show up – one you're well acquainted with.'

'Where's that?'

'Near Yukiho Karasawa.' Sasagaki wet his lips. 'Ever heard about the goby and the shrimp?'

'Sorry? Shrimp?' Kazunari blinked.

'Never mind. Suffice it to say, Yukiho Karasawa and Ryo Kirihara have what biologists call a symbiotic relationship. One can't live without the other. They're a pair for life.'

Outside the window it was all rice paddies and farmhouses, occasionally interrupted by large billboards proclaiming the virtues of one manufacturing company or the other. It was monotonous, boring scenery. Noriko would have preferred looking at towns and streets, but they had put walls up as sound barriers wherever the bullet train passed through anywhere really interesting.

Elbow resting on the windowsill, Noriko glanced at the seat next to her. Akiyoshi was sitting motionless, his eyes closed. He wasn't sleeping, she realised, but engaged in some deep thought.

She looked back out of the window, feeling the tension weighing on her like a lump of lead in her stomach. *This trip was a bad idea.*

And yet this was probably her last chance to get to know him. She couldn't believe they had been together so long and she had so little to show for it. It wasn't for lack of interest on her part, although she did try to maintain the mindset that what was past was past. What mattered was the present. And right now, this man was something very important to her.

The scenery changed slightly. They were in Aichi prefecture now, proud home of Toyota. The number of billboards for car manufacturers increased. Noriko thought about her own hometown. She was from Niigata, on the north-west coast, across the Japan Alps from Tokyo. There had been a small automobile factory near her home, too.

Noriko had first come to Tokyo when she was eighteen, with no plans other than getting into university. She hadn't wanted to become a pharmacist; she'd just gone with the first programme that accepted her, and right after graduation she had slid into her current job at the hospital on a friend's recommendation. Those first five years after university had been some of her best, Noriko thought.

In the sixth year, she got a lover. He was an older man, thirty-five, working at the same hospital. It was serious – she was considering marriage. But there was one problem: he had a wife and children. He said he planned on divorce and Noriko had believed him. That was why she got her current apartment. It was a place for him to go once he left his wife. She wanted to give him a place to make a soft landing when he left his home.

But when she set her mind on their future, he started giving her excuses. He was worried about the kids, the alimony payments would be too big, it was better to take it slow, cautiously. Each word came like a blow to Noriko. She wasn't sleeping with him so she could hear about his family problems.

The split came in an unexpected fashion. She went to work at the hospital one morning to find him missing. When she asked another of the nurses on staff, she said that he'd quit the day before.

'He was swiping money from the patients,' she told Noriko in a hushed voice, her eyes gleaming with the joy of the gossip. How much more brightly they would have gleamed if she had known about the man and Noriko.

'Swiping?'

'He was making it look like there had been errors when handling the bills, and erasing the records of patients paying for their hospital stays. Then he took the money they paid and put it in his own wallet. After a few incidents of people who had already paid getting delinquency notifications in the mail, they found him out.'

Noriko watched the nurse's ruby-red lips smile as she felt her world crashing down around her. It was like a nightmare.

'How much did he take?' Noriko asked, desperately trying to keep her cool.

'About two million yen, I heard.'

'That much? I wonder what he was using it for?'

'Someone said he was using it to pay back the loan on his apartment. You know he bought right at the peak of the bubble,' she said, her eyes still bright.

Apparently, the hospital didn't mean to press charges. As long as he paid the money back they were going to sweep the whole thing under the rug. They didn't want word getting out to the press.

For the next few days, she heard nothing from him. She had trouble focusing on her work and began making so many slip-ups that her co-workers began to suspect something.

She considered calling him at home, but when she imagined someone other than him picking up the phone, she couldn't bring herself to dial the number.

One night, very late, her own phone rang. She knew it was him, although his voice on the other end of the line was hushed and thin.

'How've you been?' he wanted to know.

'Not good,' she told him.

'Yeah, I thought not.'

She could picture his pained smile.

'You've probably already heard, but I won't be going back to the hospital.'

'What are you going to do about the money?'

'I'll pay it. In instalments. They're giving me that much.'

'Can you pay it?'

'Well, I'm going to have to. There's no way around it, even if I have to sell the apartment.'

'It's two million, right?'

'Two point four, to be exact.'

'Can I help?'

'What do you mean?'

'I have some savings. I can probably handle two million.'

'I don't know—'

'No, you could pay it off, and then you could leave—'

Your wife, she was going to say, but he cut her off.

'No, I can't.'

She gasped. 'Can't what?'

'I can't let you help me like that. I need to do this myself.'

'But—'

'My wife,' he said, 'we borrowed money from her father to buy this place.'

'How much?'

'Ten million.'

Noriko felt a lump in her stomach. A bead of sweat trickled from her armpit.

'If I'm going to get a divorce, I have to do something about that first.'

'But you never said anything about that before.'

'What good would that have done?'

'What does your wife think about all this?'

'What do you care?' he said, sounding displeased.

'I care. Is she angry?'

Noriko was hoping that his wife would be so angry he might be forced to get a divorce. But his answer surprised her.

'Heh. She apologised.'

'To you? Why?'

'She was the one who wanted this apartment in the first place. I resisted quite a bit at first. The loan was going to be too difficult for us to pay back, I thought. Which is how we got to the current situation.'

'Oh ...'

'She's going to get a part-time job to help pay the money back.'

What a perfect wife. 'So,' she said after a moment, 'I guess I can't expect anything to happen with us any time soon.'

He was silent for a while. She heard him sigh. 'Can you just stop it with that?' he said.

'With what?'

'That pretending-to-be-angry thing you do. You knew the deal as well as I did.'

'What deal?'

'I was never going to get a divorce. That was just part of the game we were playing.'

Noriko was speechless. She wanted to get angry, to tell him how serious she had been. Except she knew how miserable she'd feel the moment she said it. Her pride wouldn't let her utter a word – which was of course exactly what he wanted.

Then she heard a voice behind him asking who he was calling at this time of night. It must be his wife.

'It's a friend; they called because they were worried about what's going on,' he told her.

A moment later he spoke again, his voice quieter than before. 'Right, anyway, so that's that,' he said.

That's what? Noriko wanted to say. But the emptiness that had spread to fill her entire body robbed her of her voice. Seeing that his work was done, he hung up without waiting for her reply.

It was the last time they spoke. She never even saw him again after that.

She got rid of all of the things he had left in her apartment. His toothbrush, his razor blade, shaving cream, condoms.

The only thing she forgot to throw out was the ashtray, the dust accumulating on it like the scar tissue forming over the wound he had left in her heart.

Noriko didn't see anyone for a while after that. It wasn't that she had decided to go it alone. Rather, she wanted more than ever to get married. She wanted to find the right man, have kids, and live the quiet, family life.

About a year after breaking up with the man from the hospital she paid a visit to a matchmaking service, intrigued by their new computer system that promised to help find the perfect match. She decided she could only find her life partner by cutting romance out of the equation. She had had it with romance.

A middle-aged woman with a kind smile asked her questions and typed her responses into the computer. Several times she paused to assure Noriko not to worry, she would find the right man.

As promised, the matchmaking service started introducing men they thought she would like. She looked at the results and chose six of them to actually meet. Five of them she only met once. They were the kind of people who made you depressed just seeing them. Disillusioned. Some of them looked nothing at all like their photographs. One guy had registered with the service as being unmarried, but it turned out he had a kid.

One man out of the six, however, she met for two more dates after the first. He was a little over forty, but serious enough, and Noriko started contemplating the idea of marriage. It was on the third date that she learned that he was living with his mother, who had dementia. Apparently he had specifically requested a woman with 'medical experience' on his application to the company.

'I wish you the best,' she said, and left him. She was being made a fool of. Not just her, but every woman.

After the sixth introduction, she stopped her contract with the matchmaking service, feeling as if she had wasted precious months of her life.

Six months later, she met Akiyoshi.

It was evening by the time they reached Osaka. They checked in at their hotel, and Akiyoshi took Noriko out for a tour of the town. Despite his hesitation at taking her when she had first proposed the trip, he seemed unusually generous today. Maybe, Noriko thought, it was the effect of coming home after a long time away.

The two of them walked downtown by the famous Dotonbori Moat and ate *takoyaki* octopus skewers – the local speciality. It was the first time they had ever taken anything resembling a trip. And while Noriko was still uneasy about what was to come, it made her happy. It was her first time ever in this part of the country.

'Is the place where you grew up far from here?' she asked as they shared beers at a restaurant overlooking the moat.

'Only five stations away by train.'

'That's close.'

'Osaka isn't all sprawled out like Tokyo is,' Akiyoshi said, looking out the window. A large neon sign for Glico chocolates shone outside.

'Say,' Noriko ventured after a moment of hesitation, 'would you take me there?'

He looked up at her, a wrinkle forming between his eyebrows.

'I'd like to see the town where you lived.'

'I think we've done enough touristy stuff.'

'But—'

'I have work to do,' Akiyoshi said, looking away. His mood was clearly dampened.

'I'm sorry ... ' Noriko said, her head hanging.

They finished their beers in silence. Noriko watched the people busily crossing a bridge over the moat. It was a few minutes after eight o'clock. The Osaka night was just getting started.

'It's a worthless place,' Akiyoshi said abruptly.

Noriko looked over at him. He still had his eyes out the window.

'A dull town. Dusty, dirty, filled with worthless people who squirm like so many insects. But their eyes are sharp, beady. A town where no one lets their guard down, not ever.' He finished his beer. 'You still want to go there?'

'I do.'

Akiyoshi thought for a moment, then putting down his beer glass he stuck his hand into his jeans pocket and pulled out a single ten-thousand-yen bill. 'You mind paying?'

Noriko took the bill and went over to the cash register.

Outside, Akiyoshi hailed a cab. He gave a destination to the driver, but the names were all unfamiliar to Noriko. Still, it was fascinating to hear him talk in the Osaka dialect. Just being here made him revert to his native tongue. Noriko had never heard him speak like that.

Akiyoshi barely said a word in the taxi. He just stared out of the window. Noriko worried that he might be regretting his choice.

The taxi went into a narrow, dark street. Akiyoshi had begun giving the taxi driver turn-by-turn instructions. Finally the taxi stopped, right next to a park.

They got out and Akiyoshi went into the park. Noriko followed. It was a big park, large enough to play baseball in, with swings, a jungle gym, and a sandbox.

'We used to play a lot here as kids.'

'Baseball?'

'Some. Dodgeball, too. Even a little soccer.'

'Do you have any pictures from then?'

'Nope.'

'Oh. That's too bad.'

'There was no other wide-open space like this around here, so this park meant everything to us. This park, and that . . . ' Akiyoshi said, pointing to the other side of the park.

Noriko turned around to look. An old building was standing right behind them.

'That building?'

'We used to play in there all the time.'

'What kind of games did you play in a place like that?'

'Time tunnel.'

'How?'

'The building wasn't finished when I was a kid. They'd built about half of it before abandoning the project. So only the rats and the neighbourhood kids ever went in.'

'Wasn't that dangerous?'

'Why would we play there if it wasn't?' Akiyoshi said with a grin. But the humour quickly faded from his face. He gave a little sigh and looked up at the building. 'One day a kid found a body in there. A man's body. He'd been murdered.'

Noriko felt a sharp pain in her chest. 'Did you know him?'

'A little,' he said. 'No one much liked him at all. I guess it comes with the territory when you run a pawnshop. Still, I didn't like him either. I doubt anyone was much surprised when he got it. Just about everyone in town was a suspect.' He pointed up at the side of the building. 'Check out the artwork.'

Noriko squinted in the dim light. It was hard to make out; the picture had mostly faded, but it was a man and a woman, naked, making love. It was a mural, though there was nothing particularly artistic about it.

'After the murder, the building was entirely off-limits until someone came along and actually rented the place. They covered it in plastic sheets and went to work finishing it. Their little artistic embellishment was hidden until construction wrapped and the sheets came off.'

Akiyoshi fished a cigarette out of his pocket and lit it with a match from the restaurant.

'Pretty soon, shady-looking guys started to show up. They'd go in one at a time, looking around to make sure no one was watching. I had no idea what was going on in there at first. None of the other kids knew either, and none of the grown-ups would tell us. But finally, one of us got some information. It was a place where men could buy women, he said. Pay ten thousand yen and they could do whatever they wanted to them, even what was in the painting on the side of the building. I didn't believe it at first. Ten thousand yen was a lot of money at the time, but even more than that, I couldn't imagine a woman who would do that kind of work.' Akiyoshi chuckled dryly, breathing out smoke. 'I guess I was still pretty naive. I was in elementary school, after all.'

'I think if I'd heard something like that in elementary school I would've been pretty shocked.'

'I don't think I was too shocked by it. But I did learn something. I learned what the most important thing in this world is.' Akiyoshi took another puff of his cigarette and tossed it to the ground, even though it was only halfway gone. He put it out with his shoe. 'Anyway, I doubt you care about any of that.'

'Akiyoshi,' Noriko said, 'did they ever catch the one who did it?'

'The one who did what?'

'The murder in the old building.'

'Oh, that,' Akiyoshi said, shaking his head. 'I've got no idea.' He started to walk. 'Let's go.'

'Where are we going?'

'There's a subway station down the street.'

They walked down the narrow, darkly lit road, side by side. The houses were packed in tight along the sides of the street – old terraced houses with their doors opening right on to the road.

After they had walked for a few minutes, Akiyoshi stopped. He was looking up at a house on the other side of the street. It was large for the area, a two-storey Japanese-style building. A metal shutter covering part of the front made it look as if they ran some kind of business there on the first floor.

Noriko glanced up at the upper storey. There was an old sign on it: KIRIHARA PAWNSHOP.

The letters were mostly faded.

'You know this place?'

'A little,' he said. 'Just a little.'

They had only gone ten metres from the pawnshop when a stocky woman about fifty years old came out of one of the houses. There were a dozen or so potted plants in front of the house, about half of them actually sitting on the street. The woman was wearing a tattered T-shirt and carried a watering can in her hand.

She looked up as the couple passed, curiosity in her eyes, and gave Noriko the once-over. Her eyes had the look of someone who didn't care whether she was caught staring.

Next her eyes slid over to Akiyoshi, but then she reacted in a very unusual way. She had just been stooping down to water one of her plants but now she stood straight up.

'Ryo?' she said, staring straight at Akiyoshi.

He didn't even look in her direction. It was as if he hadn't even heard her speak. His pace didn't quicken, he just kept going straight ahead, leaving Noriko no choice but to follow him. They passed in front of the woman, who was still staring at him.

'Looks just like him,' Noriko heard the woman mutter to herself as they passed. Akiyoshi didn't seem to hear that, either.

But the woman calling out that name, 'Ryo', stuck in Noriko's head. As they walked, she could hear it echo back and forth, growing louder and louder.

Noriko had to spend their second day in Osaka by herself. After breakfast, Akiyoshi left, saying he had some research to do and wouldn't be back until that night.

Not wanting to sit around the hotel all day, Noriko decided she would take a walk downtown, near the moat where they had gone for dinner. She passed an area with upscale boutiques, the kind that you might find in the Ginza in Tokyo, except in Osaka the fancy storefronts stood side by side with game arcades and pachinko parlours. They didn't seem to put as much value on appearances here in Osaka and business was business.

She did a little shopping, but was still left with plenty of time on her hands. She started feeling like she wanted to go back to the place where they had gone the night before – that park, and especially the pawnshop.

She took the subway from the main station in town. She still remembered the names of all the stops and was pretty sure she could find her way back to the park from the station once she got there.

After she had bought her ticket, a thought occurred to her and she stopped by a small station shop to buy a disposable camera.

Reaching her destination, she walked down the street, retracing their steps from the night before in reverse. The town looked remarkably different in the daylight. Many of the shops were open and there were a lot of people on the street. There was a strength in the eyes of the people she saw working in the shops and the passers-by. Not a mercantile energy so much as an attitude. Everyone was looking for something – a weakness. No one let their guard down. It was just like he said.

She walked slowly, taking pictures every now and then. She wanted this record of Akiyoshi's hometown for herself. She knew she could never tell him about it.

She arrived at the pawnshop to find it closed. In fact, it might have been closed for some time. She hadn't noticed at night, but seen in the daylight it had a distinctly abandoned feel to it.

She took a picture.

Then she came to the old building by the park. Some kids were playing soccer. She took more pictures, hearing their shouts as they played behind her. She even took a picture of the pornographic mural. Then she went around to the front of the building. It didn't seem as if they were doing any business here at all now. It was just another abandoned building, like so many that had been abandoned after the economic bubble burst, just a lot older.

Back on the main street, she grabbed a taxi back to the hotel.

It was after eleven that night when Akiyoshi returned. He looked as if he was in a terrible mood and exhausted.

'Did you finish your work?' she asked, somewhat fearfully.

He threw himself on the bed and took a big sigh. 'It's finished,' he said. 'Everything's finished.'

She almost said 'good', but something about the tone of his voice made it hard for her to speak. In the end, she said nothing and they went to sleep in silence.

Kazunari rolled over in bed. It had been too hot to sleep comfortably the last few nights and now his conversation with Sasagaki was stuck on a loop in his head. The whole situation strained belief – and yet, when he let it in, the reality of it hit him like a ton of bricks.

Though he might not have used the word 'murder', the old detective had all but said that Imaeda had been killed. At the time Kazunari had listened to everything Sasagaki told him as if it was a story about other people, not him – something he might have seen on television or read in a novel. Even though he knew, intellectually, that these events affected people directly around him, they lacked visceral impact when heard in the meeting room at Shinozuka Pharmaceuticals. Which was why he hadn't really worried when Sasagaki told him that he should be careful, too.

But once he was alone in his room with the light off, lying down in bed with his eyes closed, anxiety gripped him and he broke out in a cold sweat.

He knew Yukiho was dangerous. He'd just never imagined he might be placing Imaeda in harm's way by putting the private eye on her case. For the hundredth time he wondered just who Yukiho was.

And that man, Ryo Kirihara.

Sasagaki hadn't been very forthcoming about him – except that he and Yukiho were a pair and the detective didn't know where he was hiding, even after searching for nearly twenty years.

Two decades. Kazunari couldn't understand how something that had happened so long ago in Osaka could be having such an effect on his personal life in the here and now.

He opened his eyes, staring out at the darkness, and grabbed the remote control for the air conditioning off his bedside table. He pressed the switch and sighed as cool air filled the room.

Just then, the phone rang. Starting up, he turned on the lamp. His alarm clock showed that it was one a.m. For a moment he worried that something had happened to his parents – he had been living alone downtown since buying his apartment the year before.

He coughed to clear his throat and picked up the phone.

'Hello?'

'Kazunari. Sorry to call so late.'

Yasuharu. A feeling of dread came over him. The premonition quickly turned to certainty. 'Did ... something happen?'

'Yeah – the matter I mentioned to you the other day. I just got a call from Yukiho.'

Yasuharu's voice sounded hushed over the phone – and not just because it was the middle of the night.

'Her mother?'

'She passed away. Never regained consciousness.'

'I'm sorry to hear that,' Kazunari said, the words only a reflex.

'You good for tomorrow?' Yasuharu asked. It wasn't a question.

'You still want me to go to Osaka?'

'Yeah, I'm completely tied up. Some people from Slottermeyer are coming, and I have to see them.'

'I was supposed to be at that meeting.'

'Not any more. Get on the first bullet train you can, got it? Thankfully it's already Friday. I'll probably have to go out with our guests tonight, but I should be able to head down there Saturday morning.'

'What do we tell the boss?'

'I'll talk to him tomorrow. His old body can't take getting woken up at this time of night.'

The CEO – Yasuharu's father, Sosuke – lived in a residential area of Setagaya, on the western side of town, close to the house Yasuharu had moved into at the time of his previous marriage.

'You ever introduce him to Yukiho?' Kazunari asked, hoping he wasn't sounding too nosy.

'Not yet, no. But he does know I found a potential bride. You know how he is. He's probably too busy to worry about his forty-five-year-old son getting married anyway.'

Public opinion said Sosuke Shinozuka was a very open-hearted, generous man, and he'd never been very controlling with his son or with Kazunari when it came to private matters. But Kazunari had long understood that this was because his uncle was first and foremost a company man. He just didn't care about anything out-side of business. As long as his son's intended didn't do something outrageous to besmirch the family name, he honestly didn't care whom he took for his second wife.

'So, thanks for doing this,' Yasuharu said.

Kazunari wanted nothing more to do with Yukiho and yet he couldn't think of any good reason to refuse.

'Where in Osaka am I going?'

'I got a fax with the address of the funeral parlour and the mother's home, so I'll send that along. Your fax number is the same as the phone, right?'

'Yeah.'

'OK, I'll hang up. Give me a ring once the fax comes through.'

'Sure.'

Kazunari got out of bed. He looked up at the glass doors set in his bookshelf, behind which stood a bottle of Remy Martin and a brandy glass. He took the glass out and poured himself a finger, tipping it back without bothering to sit down. The brandy hit his tongue and he drank in the fragrance and the taste and the sting of the alcohol. His blood stirred. His nerves were ringing.

Ever since Yasuharu had come to him with his feelings about Yukiho, Kazunari had considered pulling an end-run by bringing his concerns to his father in hopes that he might talk to his uncle, Sosuke. But vaguely defined worries would lack the weight he needed to stop Yasuharu's marriage. Yasuharu was positioned to eventually become the most powerful member of their extended family, and he could already hear his father telling him to worry about his own life before he started worrying about Yasaharu's. Besides, his father had been recently appointed CEO of Shinozuka

Chemicals. He had enough on his plate without worrying about his nephew's family plans.

Kazunari arrived in Osaka just before noon. For a moment he just stood on the platform in the station, feeling the humidity and the heat on his skin. Even though it was already late in September he could feel sweat trickling down his back. Summer lingered longer down here than it did up in Tokyo.

He went down the stairs and out through the ticket gates. The main exit was right in front of him, and beyond that, a taxi stop. He was making a beeline for the first taxi when he heard a voice calling out his name. He stopped and looked around and saw a woman in her mid-twenties waving at him. She was wearing a dark navy suit with a T-shirt underneath. Her hair was in a long ponytail.

'Thanks for making the long trip,' she said, with a respectful bow that made her ponytail bob up and down like its equestrian namesake.

Kazunari had seen her before. She worked at the boutique in South Aoyama.

'I'm sorry, your name is?'

'Natsumi,' she replied, handing him a business card.

'How did you know I was coming?'

'Miss Karasawa told me. She said she thought you'd get in just before noon, but there was so much traffic, I'm afraid I was a little late.'

'No, not at all. Where is Yukiho?'

'Miss Karasawa is speaking with the funeral director at home. She asked me to take you directly there.'

'Lead on, then.'

Yasuharu must have called while I was on the train. He could hear him now, telling Yukiho, 'I'm sending you my best man to lighten your load. Don't you hesitate to order him around.'

'This must have come very suddenly,' Kazunari said as their taxi took off.

Natsumi nodded. 'We knew things were bad, which is why I

came down yesterday, but no one thought it would happen quite as soon as it did.'

'When did she pass away?'

'We got the call from the hospital last night around nine o'clock. Her condition had taken a turn for the worse and the hospital wanted to let us know. She was gone by the time we arrived.'

'How did Yukiho take it?'

'Not well,' Natsumi said with a frown. 'She's not the kind to wail and carry on, but I don't know how many hours she sat there, pressing her face into the comforter on her mother's bed. I've never seen her like that.'

'I'll bet she didn't sleep much last night, then.'

'Not at all, I think. I woke up once myself and walked down the hall past her room. The light was on and I heard her inside. I think she was crying.'

Whatever Yukiho Karasawa was hiding in her past, or her present for that matter, her grief was probably very real. From what Imaeda had told him, being adopted by Reiko Karasawa had given Yukiho a freedom she had never known.

Natsumi began giving specific directions to the driver and Kazunari noticed from her accent that the girl was originally from the area. He could see why, of her many employees, Yukiho had chosen to summon this one to help when the time came.

They went past an old temple and into a quiet neighbourhood where the taxi came to a stop. Kazunari made to pay the fare, but Natsumi adamantly refused.

'I was told that under no circumstances was I to let you pay,' she said with a smile.

Yukiho's mother's home was a traditional Japanese-style house with a tall wooden fence and proper gate. Kazunari pictured Yukiho as a high-schooler, waving to her adopted mother as she skipped, carefree, down the path. It was a beautiful image and one he wanted to hold on to, though he couldn't say why.

A small intercom hung by the gate. Natsumi pushed the button and Yukiho answered almost immediately.

'I've brought Mr Shinozuka.'

'Please bring him right in. The door's open.'

Natsumi looked up at Kazunari. 'In we go.'

He followed her through the gate. The front door was wooden with vertical slats, a standard in traditional construction. Kazunari couldn't remember the last time he had gone into a house like this.

He let Natsumi lead him down the hallway. His eyes took in the details. Everything was perfect. Even the wooden floorboards beneath his feet shone with a lustre that could only be the result of years upon years of polishing by hand. The wooden posts along the walls, too. He felt as though he was gaining, in a weird way, an insight into the person who had been Reiko Karasawa, the woman who had raised Yukiho.

He could hear talking from up ahead. Natsumi stopped and turned toward a closed sliding door in the hallway. 'Miss Karasawa?'

'In here,' said a voice from the other side.

Natsumi opened the door part-way and he heard Yukiho saying, 'Please show him in.'

Natsumi motioned with her hand, and Kazunari stepped into a room that was a curious mix of Japanese and Western sensibilities. There were tatami mats on the floor, but a carpet had been spread over them on which sat a table and two sofas. A man and woman were sitting in one of the sofas and across from them sat Yukiho. She stood when Kazunari entered.

'Thanks for coming all the way down here,' she said, bowing her head to him. She was wearing a dark grey dress and looked a great deal thinner than when he had last seen her, the picture of a woman in mourning. But although her make-up was light, and her face hung with weariness, there was an undeniable allure to her. *Genuine beauty never takes the day off.*

'I'm sorry for your loss,' he said.

She nodded, but if she said anything, her voice didn't reach his ears.

Yukiho turned to the couple on the sofa and introduced Kazunari as a business associate. The couple, as Natsumi had told him, were from the funeral parlour.

'I'm glad you're here,' Yukiho told him. 'We've been discussing arrangements for hours now and it's really all too much for me to decide.'

'I'm afraid I don't have much experience in this sort of thing either,' Kazunari said.

'All the same, two heads are better than one.'

'Then my head's all yours for what it's worth.'

The meeting stretched another two hours. Kazunari learned that they were planning a wake and that both the wake and the funeral itself would take place at the funeral parlour, a seven-storey building only ten minutes away by car.

When all the details had been decided upon, Natsumi and the funeral directors left for the funeral parlour, leaving Yukiho at home to wait for a package to arrive from Tokyo.

'What are you waiting for?' Kazunari asked her once they had gone.

'Mourning clothes,' Yukiho told him. 'I'm having one of the girls from the shop bring some down. She should be arriving at the station any time now.' She glanced at her watch.

'Have you told anyone from school yet?'

'No. I don't think I will, either. I hardly see any of them any more.'

'Not even anyone from dance club?' Kazunari asked.

Yukiho's eyes widened for a moment, as if he'd touched a sore spot. But the look faded quickly. 'No, nobody needs to come for this.'

'Right,' Kazunari said, crossing off an item in the list he had made in his notebook in the train on the way down.

'I'm sorry,' Yukiho said suddenly, 'I haven't offered you tea. Something cold, or coffee perhaps?'

Kazunari waved a hand dismissively. 'Don't worry about me.'

'It's no trouble at all. I have beer if you prefer?'

'Tea's fine. Cold if you have any.'

'I'll get you some oolong.'

Alone, Kazunari stood and looked around. Though the furnishings were mostly Western, he spotted a Japanese tea chest in one corner. He was no interior designer, but somehow it all seemed to fit.

There was a sturdy wooden bookcase along one wall filled with books. In between books on the tea ceremony and flower arrangement he spotted some old textbooks and a beginner's piano book. He imagined Yukiho sitting in the room, studying, and looked around for a piano but there was none to be found.

Spotting some sliding doors on the opposite side of the room from where he had entered, he opened them and peeked out into a small sunroom. A pile of old magazines sat in the corner. Kazunari stepped out into the sunroom and looked out at the garden. It wasn't very large, but the few twisted trees and rustic stone lantern were perfectly placed to create a little self-contained scene, the quintessential Japanese garden. It looked as if grass had once carpeted the space beneath the trees, but this had all withered. Tending to even a small garden was no mean feat for an elderly woman.

Several potted plants sat close to the house, most of them cactuses, the round ball-like ones, bristling with spikes.

'Isn't it miserable? I haven't done a thing with it,' he heard a voice say behind him. Yukiho had arrived carrying a tray with glasses.

'It's not too far gone,' Kazunari said. 'That's an impressive lantern you've got out there.'

'Too bad there's no one left to look at it,' Yukiho said, putting the tea down on the table.

'Have you decided what you're going to do with the house?'

'Not yet,' she said with a sad smile. 'I don't want to just let it go, though. Or let someone tear it down,' she said, resting her hand on a part of the sliding door where the frame had been scratched, giving it a thoughtful rub with her thumb. Then she looked up at Kazunari as though she had only just noticed him standing there. 'Thank you so much for coming down. I was afraid you might not.'

'Why wouldn't I?'

'I mean ...' She looked down at the floor before returning to meet his gaze and when she did, her eyes were red, and bright with tears. 'I mean, I know you don't particularly like me.'

Kazunari tensed. 'What possible reason would I have to not like you?'

'I don't know. Maybe you're mad that I divorced Makoto. Maybe you have another reason. I just sense it. You don't like me. You try to avoid me.'

'You're imagining things,' Kazunari said with a light laugh.

'You honestly mean that?' she said, taking a step in his direction so that the two were almost uncomfortably close.

'Really. I have no reason to dislike you.'

'I'm glad, then,' she said, closing her eyes. She gave a sigh of relief and Kazunari found himself disarmed by her nearness. She was standing close enough that he could feel the warmth of her breath on his skin. She opened her eyes. The redness had gone, leaving nothing but the impossibly deep brown of her irises, so deep he felt like he might topple and fall into them.

Kazunari looked away, and took a step back. Too close, and he could feel her latching on to him, unseen hooks burrowing into his skin.

'So,' he said, looking out at the garden. 'Your mother liked cactuses, did she?'

'She did, despite the fact they don't fit in at all. She used to give them away as presents.'

'What will you do with them?'

'Good question. They're pretty low-maintenance, but I can't just leave them there.'

'I'm sure you can find a home for them.'

'Care for a cactus, Mr Shinozuka?'

'I'll pass.'

She smiled. Then she crouched to better look out over the garden. 'They're like sad little children without their mother.'

A tremble passed through her shoulders. Soon, her whole body was shaking. He heard her sob. 'I don't have anyone either,' she said in a choked voice, and Kazunari felt a flutter in his chest as he stood behind her. He reached out and put a hand on her shoulder.

Her white fingers moved up till they lay across his hand. Her skin was cold to the touch. The quaking in her shoulders grew softer.

Then Kazunari felt a sudden, inexplicable rush of emotion, something that had been locked inside until now, unknown and inaccessible even to him. It grew, changed, becoming an impulse. His eyes went to the porcelain-white skin at the nape of her neck.

Just when it felt as if his last defences might come tumbling down, the phone rang. He took his hand from her shoulder, her fingers slipping away.

Yukiho stayed there for several seconds before she stood and walked over to the table.

'Hello? Junko? You just get in? Thanks for doing this. Could I have you take them by taxi?'

Kazunari listened, half in a daze, as Yukiho gave her assistant directions.

The funeral parlour was on the fifth floor. Just outside the elevator was a small space like a studio, with an altar at the back. Folding chairs waited in neatly arranged rows.

The woman from the shop in Tokyo had arrived there before them with Yukiho and Natsumi's mourning clothes. Natsumi had already changed.

'I'd better get changed myself,' Yukiho said, taking the hanger with her clothes on it and disappearing into the dressing room.

Kazunari sat on one of the folding chairs and looked up at the altar. He had overheard Yukiho request the best that money could buy, but Kazunari was hard-pressed to see how the altar in this room was different from any other he'd seen.

He thought back to earlier at Yukiho's mother's house and felt a trickle of sweat run down his spine. If the phone hadn't rung precisely when it had, he almost certainly would have put his arms around her, and who knew what would have happened then? He didn't even understand where the impulse to hold her like that had come from. How could he have let his guard down so completely after months of telling himself that Yukiho was bad news?

He resolved to not let himself slip again. He couldn't let her draw him in. Yet, a whisper in the back of his mind said *what if?* Maybe, just maybe, he had her all wrong. Those tears and those trembling shoulders weren't for show, he was sure of that. This was a person who could feel, who had felt, genuine emotions. He was forced to admit that the picture of her weeping over the cacti was utterly different from the one he had been carrying around for so long.

Maybe she really was that teary-eyed girl. Maybe that was the true Yukiho, and the one in his mind was just a warped image, grown out of years' worth of misunderstandings. Maybe Makoto and his cousin Yasuharu had been looking at the true woman all this time, the Yukiho he had never really seen until today.

Something moved in the corner of his vision. Kazunari looked up to see her walking towards him, resplendent in her mourning gown.

A black rose, he thought. *That's what she is*. He'd never seen a woman so vibrant, so brilliant. The black frame of her dress only served to increase her enchantment.

When she noticed him, a faint smile came to her lips. But her eyes were moist with tears – dewdrops on a black flower petal.

Yukiho drifted over to the reception counter that had been set up near the back of the hall. She exchanged a few words with the other women, who were going over the routines for greeting guests. Kazunari watched from a distance.

People started showing up to attend the wake. By and large they were middle-aged women, Reiko Karasawa's students in the tea ceremony and flower arranging, Kazunari surmised. One by one they came up and stood by the photograph of the deceased that had been placed on the altar. There, they pressed their hands together and, almost without exception, they cried.

Those who knew Yukiho came over to clasp her hands and share stories of her mother. And each time, in the middle of the telling, they would have to stop to weep. But Yukiho listened to every one of them, never hurrying them away, until it was hard for Kazunari to tell exactly who was comforting whom.

After Kazunari exchanged a few words with Natsumi about how the funeral would proceed, little remained for him to do. Food and beer had been set out in an adjacent room, but he felt out of place standing in there all by himself.

He began walking around aimlessly until he discovered a vending machine with some coffee by the stairs outside the room. He wasn't that thirsty, but he fished in his pocket for loose change.

He was buying his coffee when he heard women talking – Yukiho's assistants from the shop. They were standing on the other side of the doors to the stairs.

'Well, the timing on this worked out perfectly,' Natsumi was saying. 'I mean, it's a shame she passed and everything, but still.'

'No, I totally understand. She could've gone on a long time without ever regaining consciousness. That would've made it even harder,' Junko agreed.

'For a while there, I was afraid we'd have to delay opening in Jiyugaoka.'

'I wonder what the boss would've done if her mother hadn't died?'

'Oh, probably showed up for opening day and gone back down to Osaka, I guess. To be honest, that's what I was most afraid of. Imagine some of our repeat customers coming in to celebrate the opening and her not being there.'

'Close call, then.'

'I guess. Anyway, it's really better for everyone that this ended soon. Comas can be really tough when they go on for ever. She was over seventy, right?' Natsumi asked. 'I mean, I almost asked the boss if pulling the plug was an option.'

'Natsumi!'

He heard the girls giggle.

Coffee in hand, Kazunari slowly walked away from the door. Going back to the ceremony room, he set his cup down on the reception counter.

What Natsumi had said about pulling the plug echoed in the

back of his mind, demanding attention. *No, don't even think that*, he told himself. And yet the gears were already turning.

Reiko Karasawa had passed away just after Natsumi arrived in Osaka. She had been there with Yukiho when the call came, which gave Yukiho an alibi. But what if she had called Natsumi down there expressly so she *would* have an alibi. She could remain the picture of innocence while someone else crept into the hospital to play mischief with her mother's life-support system.

Ridiculous, Kazunari thought. But it stuck in his head, jostling for space with the name Detective Sasagaki had written on the back of his business card: Ryo Kirihara.

Natsumi had said she heard sounds from Yukiho's room that night. She had thought Yukiho was crying, but what if she had been making contact with the person she sent to do the deed? Kazunari glanced over at Yukiho. She was talking with an older woman, nodding sympathetically. Kazunari shook his head and went to get another coffee.

By ten at night the number of visitors to the wake had dwindled and Yukiho told her assistants to head back to the hotel.

'What about you, boss?' Natsumi asked.

'I'm staying here tonight. It's a wake, after all.'

There was a room for mourners to stay just off to the side of the hall.

'Will you be OK by yourself?'

'I'll be fine. Thanks for all your help today.'

The girls left and Kazunari realised he was once again alone with Yukiho. He cleared his throat. It felt like the air had grown thicker. He glanced down at his watch and was about to say he should be heading out too when Yukiho turned to him and said, 'You want something to drink? You have a little time, right?'

'Sure, I'm good.'

'Great,' she said, walking ahead.

There was a room in the back with tatami mats, looking like a traditional Japanese hotel room. An electric kettle and teapot had been placed on the table. Yukiho poured some tea.

'It's strange being here with you like this, Kazunari.'

'I know.'

'Makes me remember those dance club days. And the trip we went on before the big competition.'

They'd all gone on a retreat just before the competition in hopes they could brush up their form a little and leave their mark on the scoreboards.

'The boys were particularly well behaved,' she said. 'The girls were on full alert for a midnight raid, but it was all for nothing. A little disappointing, really.' She smiled. 'I'm joking of course.'

Kazunari took a sip of his tea and smiled back. 'You would have been off-limits anyway. You were already going out with Makoto.'

Yukiho laughed and shook her head. 'Oh, I'm sure he told you all sorts of things about me.'

'Not as much as you might think.'

'It's OK, I know how it is. And a lot of it was my fault. I think that's why he drifted, in the end.'

'He seemed pretty certain that the fault was his, though I'm sure these are matters that only the two of you will ever understand.' Kazunari cradled his teacup in the palm of his hand.

Yukiho sighed. 'I'm just no good at it.'

Kazunari looked up. 'No good at what?'

'Love,' she said, looking him in the eye. 'I don't know how to love a man.'

Kazunari looked away. 'I'm not sure that there *is* a proper way.' The air had grown heavier. Kazunari loosened his tie, almost gasping for air.

'I should go,' he said abruptly, standing.

'Oh. Sorry to have kept you so late,' she said.

He nodded and turned away. 'I'll see you tomorrow, then.'

'Thanks.'

He put his hand on the doorknob and had given it a turn when he felt something behind him. He didn't have to look around to know that Yukiho was standing right there. He felt the touch of her hand on his back.

'I'm scared,' she said quietly. 'I'm scared to be alone.'

Kazunari felt his heart wrench inside him. The impulse to turn to her came over him like a wave. But at the same time the warning lights in his mind had gone from yellow to red and a voice said *if you look into her eyes now, you're done.*

Kazunari opened the door. Then without looking around he said, 'Goodnight.'

As if those were the words to some magic spell, her presence and the hold it had over him disappeared like a puff of smoke. In its place he heard her voice, as dispassionate and collected as it had been before. 'Goodnight.'

Kazunari walked out of the room, hearing the door close behind him. Only then did he allow himself to look back over his shoulder.

He heard the click of the door into the overnight room locking.

Kazunari stared at the door for a moment.

Are you really alone?

He began to walk, his footsteps echoing in the empty corridor.

THIRTEEN

Sasagaki's coat whipped in the breeze as he stepped off the bus. It had been relatively warm until the day before, but this morning had brought a sudden chill to the city streets. Or maybe, he mused, it was just that Tokyo was a lot colder than Osaka.

He walked along the now-familiar route until he reached his destination, where he paused to check his watch. Four in the afternoon, right on time. He would have come earlier but he'd had to take a detour to a department store in Shinjuku to buy the contents of the small bag he carried in one hand.

He walked up the stairs to the second floor, feeling a little pain in his right knee. It had started bothering him several years ago – he couldn't remember exactly when – and had proven a reliable indicator of the changing seasons.

He stopped in front of a door with a plate that read IMAEDA DETECTIVE AGENCY. The plate sparkled, having been recently cleaned. Anyone who didn't know any better might think the agency was still in business.

Sasagaki pressed the doorbell and heard someone moving inside, probably checking him out through the spyhole.

He heard the door unlock and it opened to reveal a smiling Eri Sugawara. 'Hey,' she said. 'I thought you'd never make it.'

'The line was out the door,' he said, holding up the package.

'Oh, fantastic! You got it!' She took the bag from him and immediately opened it up to examine the contents. 'Mmm. That is one fine-looking cherry pie.'

'What is it with cherry pies?'

'It's the big thing right now. Because of *Twin Peaks*.'

'I'm not sure what that means,' the detective said, 'but wasn't tiramisu the big thing just a couple of months ago? When did that change?'

'Don't strain yourself trying to keep up with the trends, I'll handle that. But first, some pie. You want some? I put coffee on.'

'Coffee sounds nice.'

'OK!' Eri said brightly, heading into the kitchen.

Sasagaki took off his coat. The place had hardly changed from the time it had been a functioning agency. The steel shelves and cabinet were all in the same places. The only difference was that now there was a television in one corner and the number of knick-knacks had grown. These new arrivals belonged to Eri.

'How many days are you here this time?' she asked.

'Three, maybe four. Can't leave my place sitting empty for much longer.'

'How much can you really get accomplished in so short a time?'

'We work with what we have.'

Sasagaki pulled out a box of Seven Stars and lit one with a match. He threw the spent match in a glass ashtray sitting on Imaeda's desk. The surface of the steel desk had been perfectly cleaned. If Imaeda came walking back into the door, he could get right back to work. Except the desk calendar was still on August from the year before – the month when Imaeda disappeared. It was hard to believe it had already been over a year.

Sasagaki beat a little rhythm with his feet and hummed a tune, watching Eri go to work on the cherry pie. She always looked so cheerful and optimistic, but he knew she was in pain, deep down, and it bothered him. She must have accepted the fact that Imaeda was dead and yet that hadn't kept her from waiting for him to return.

It had been almost exactly a year ago when Sasagaki first met her. He'd come back to see if anything had changed with the apartment and found the young woman living there.

She had been extremely wary of him at first, but he'd introduced himself as a detective and told her that he had met Imaeda just before his disappearance, which seemed to warm her up to him a little.

Though she hadn't ever admitted as much, he suspected Eri had been involved in a romantic relationship with Imaeda. She was fervent in her efforts to find him. She had even got rid of her own apartment and moved into the office because she wanted to be able to keep tabs on anything with a direct connection to him. Here, she could read his mail and meet anyone who came to see him. Thankfully, the landlord didn't seem to mind. Having someone in the place was better than a missing tenant who didn't pay rent.

Since meeting her that first time, Sasagaki had always made a point of stopping in whenever he visited Tokyo. She was helpful, giving him tips about how to get around the unfamiliar city and keeping him up to date on the latest trends. She was a good conversationalist, too, and Sasagaki genuinely enjoyed the time spent talking with her.

Eri brought a tray with two mugs and two small plates, on to which she put two slices of cherry pie. She sat the tray down on Imaeda's steel desk.

'Dig in!' she said, holding a blue mug out towards Sasagaki.

'Thanks,' he said, accepting it and taking a sip. *Nothing like hot coffee to chase the chill out of the bones*, he thought.

Eri sat down in Imaeda's chair and took a bite of her cherry pie. She chewed enthusiastically, giving Sasagaki the thumbs-up.

'So, anything to report?' Sasagaki asked. Even though it was the same question every visit, he'd been working up the courage to ask it since he walked through the door.

The faintest cloud came over Eri's features. She set her fork back on the dish and took a sip of her coffee.

'Nothing you'd be interested in, unfortunately. I hardly get any letters any more and most of the calls are just new customers, looking to hire a private eye.'

She had kept Imaeda's phone line connected and listed. Eri was paying the bills.

'So nobody's dropping by the office these days?'

'Not really. There were a bunch of callers at the beginning of the year, but that tapered off.' Eri reached over to the desk and pulled a notebook out of the drawer. 'We had one more in the summer, and another in September. Both women. The one in summer was a repeater.'

'Repeater?'

'Someone who'd asked Mr Imaeda to do work before. Her name's Kawakami. She looked pretty disappointed when I told her Imaeda was on an extended stay in the hospital. I looked into it and she'd had him investigate her husband for cheating two years ago. He hadn't found any conclusive evidence at the time, so I wonder if she didn't want him to try again. Her husband probably got back into the action,' Eri said, looking cheery. Sasagaki had guessed before that part of the reason why she had helped with Imaeda's work was that she liked digging into other people's secrets. Her smile seemed to confirm that.

'What about the person who came in September? Another repeater?'

'No, not her. She wanted to know if someone had made a request here.'

'What's that mean?'

'Well,' Eri looked up from her notebook. 'Specifically, she wanted to know if someone named Akiyoshi had come in to make a request about a year earlier.'

Sasagaki frowned. The name Akiyoshi sounded familiar, but he couldn't quite place it. 'That's an odd question.'

'Not that unusual,' Eri said with a grin. 'This is something I heard from Mr Imaeda, but apparently some people who have affairs get to wondering whether their spouse has hired a detective to check up on them. I think she might've been one of those. She must have found some evidence that her husband had hired Imaeda, or at least visited the agency, and came to find out.'

'You sound pretty sure about that.'

'I have a sense for these things,' she said. 'Also, when I told her I would look into it and get back to her, she didn't give me her home address, but her work address. Suspicious, right? She doesn't want her husband to pick up the phone.'

'And what was this woman's name?'

'She told me it was Kurihara. I'm guessing that's her maiden name, the one she uses at work. A lot of women do that these days.'

Sasagaki shook his head. 'Well, I'm impressed. Eri, you'd make a good private eye. Heck, you'd make a good *police* detective.'

Eri laughed and shook her head at that. 'I'll tell you my next bit of conjecture, then. This Kurihara woman is a pharmacist at the Imperial University Hospital, see? So she's having an affair with a doctor. And the person she's having an affair with has a family. That's what I think. Double infidelity!'

'I think you've gone past conjecture and into fantasy,' Sasagaki said, managing to frown and chuckle at the same time.

It was already seven at night when Sasagaki walked into the lobby of his hotel in Shinjuku.

It was a drab place, dimly lit. Even calling it a lobby was being generous – there was just a long desk that served as the reception. A middle-aged man who didn't look particularly well suited for the hospitality industry stood behind it, a scowl on his face. It wasn't Sasagaki's first pick for lodgings but he didn't really have a choice if he was going to stay in Tokyo for several days. In truth, even this was a bit of a financial stretch, but he couldn't stand those new capsule hotels. The cramped quarters and shared facilities weren't easy on his old body: he felt more exhausted when he woke up than when he went to sleep. Even if it was plain to the point of desolate, he preferred a private room where he could relax.

He checked in and was surprised to hear there was a message for him. The receptionist passed him a white envelope together with his key.

Sasagaki opened the envelope and looked inside. Within was a piece of notepaper with a message that read: 'Call 308.'

Sasagaki frowned, wondering who it could be.

His room was 321, on the same floor as whoever had left him the message. He stopped in front of room 308 on his way from the elevator. After a moment's hesitation, he knocked and immediately heard the sound of someone shuffling to the door on the other side.

Sasagaki gaped when the door opened to reveal Hisashi Koga. 'Well, you sure took your time,' his former subordinate said.

'What?' Sasagaki said, stammering a little. 'What are you doing here?'

'This and that. Mostly waiting for you, old man. You eat yet?'

'No.'

'Great, let's go get something. You can leave your stuff in my room.' He took Sasagaki's things and opened the narrow closet in his room to pull out his jacket and coat. 'Got a preference for dinner?'

'Anything but French,' Sasagaki replied.

They ended up at a street corner place serving Japanese food with seating at four low tables on tatami mats in the back. They picked a table and sat across from each other. Koga mentioned he often came here when he was in Tokyo, and recommended the stew and the sashimi.

Koga ordered some beer and Sasagaki let him pour. He offered to pour for Koga, who refused and filled his own cup. After offering Koga a toast, Sasagaki asked, 'So what's this all about?'

'There was a meeting at Tokyo Police Headquarters. Normally the section chief would go, but he wasn't available so they sent me up here.'

'You're moving up in the world. Congratulations,' Sasagaki said, his chopsticks aiming for a particularly tempting piece of fatty tuna. It was as good as it looked.

Koga had gone from being one of Sasagaki's subordinates to head of Homicide in Osaka. Sasagaki knew there were some who viewed his rise through the ranks as nothing more than the achievement of a sycophant with a knack for aceing exams. But Koga had never shirked his duty. He worked as hard as anyone else at the station and studied harder for those advancement exams than the rest of them put together.

'I'm still at a bit of a loss,' Sasagaki said. 'Surely you have better things to do than chew the fat here with me. Not to mention stay at that cheap-ass hotel.'

Koga chuckled. 'It *is* pretty cheap-ass, isn't it? Why do you stay there?'

'Don't ask questions you already know the answer to. I'm not here on vacation.'

'That's the problem,' Koga said. 'If you were here on vacation, I'd have nothing to say. But when I think about the most likely reason you're up here, well, it's hard for me to smile. Your wife's pretty worried, too.'

'So Katsuko put you up to this? What does she think you are, her errand boy?'

'She didn't ask me to come up. We were just talking about things, and she mentioned it.'

'Same difference. She gave you your orders, admit it. Or was it Orie?'

'I think it's safe to say that everyone's concerned.'

'Great,' Sasagaki snorted.

In addition to their relationship at work, Koga and Sasagaki were now actually related after Koga's marriage to his wife's niece, Orie. On the surface it was a coincidence. Apparently the two of them had just happened to meet and fall in love, but Sasagaki had always suspected Katsuko of pulling some strings.

Their beer bottles drained, Koga ordered some sake. Sasagaki started on his stew. The miso flavouring was a Tokyo thing, but he found it pretty good all the same.

The sake arrived and Koga poured some into Sasagaki's cup, saying, 'So, still on about that old case?'

'It's my cross to bear.'

'Why this one? There are other unsolved cases out there. And this one stands a good chance of actually being unsolvable. What if that guy who died in the traffic accident was the killer? That seemed to be the prevailing opinion in the department.'

'Terasaki didn't do it,' Sasagaki said firmly, tossing back his cup. Despite the nearly two decades that had passed since the pawn-broker had been found stabbed to death in that abandoned building, he still remembered the names of everyone involved.

'We must have searched his place a hundred times, and there was never any sign of that million yen Kirihara was carrying. I don't buy that he hid it either, like some people are saying. Terasaki was deep in debt. If he came into that kind of money, he would have turned it around as quick as he could. Which leads me to think that he never had the money, which leads me to think that he wasn't the one who stabbed him.'

Koga nodded. 'I agree with your basic premise – I do. That's why I kept making the rounds with you even after Terasaki died. But there's making the rounds, and then there's walking in the same wheel rut for twenty years.'

'I know the statute of limitations is up on the case. But I'm not dying until I've cleaned it up, one way or the other.'

Koga tried to fill Sasagaki's empty cup, but Sasagaki stopped him and snatched the decanter from his hand. He filled Koga's cup to the brim before filling his own.

'You're right that it's not the only unsolved case. There are bigger, more brutal cases out there where we haven't caught so much as a hair off the perp's head. And none of them sit well with me. But the pawnbroker's different, because we had our chance and we blew it, and people have suffered for our mistake for years – people that had nothing to do with the pawnbroker at all.'

'What do you mean?'

'I mean we should have nipped this thing in the bud when we had a chance. And because we didn't, it grew and began to bloom into an evil, evil flower,' Sasagaki said with a frown, pouring back some sake.

Koga loosened his tie and undid the top button of his shirt. 'You're talking about Yukiho Karasawa.'

Sasagaki reached into his jacket pocket. He pulled out a folded piece of paper and placed it on the table in front of Koga.

'What's that?'

'Take a look.'

Koga unfolded the paper. A deep line formed between his thick eyebrows. 'R&Y Osaka Now Opening?'

'Yukiho Karasawa's store. It's a big deal. They finally made it down to Osaka, near Shinsaibashi. And take a look: the big opening's on Christmas Eve this year.'

'Is this that evil flower, then?' Koga asked, carefully folding the pamphlet and pushing it in front of Sasagaki.

'It's more like the fruit.'

'Remind me when you started to suspect Yukiho Karasawa? Or was she Yukiho Nishimoto at the time?'

'Still Nishimoto. You may recall that Fumiyo Nishimoto died the year after Yosuke Kirihara. That's what started it.'

'And yet that was ruled an accidental death. Which you never believed.'

'The victim drank sake, which she never drank, and took more than five times the normal dose of sleeping pills. I wouldn't call that accidental. Unfortunately, I wasn't on the task force, so I didn't have much say in how it was handled.'

'Wasn't there talk of suicide?' Koga crossed his arms, thinking back over the years.

'Yukiho's testimony put an end to the suicide theory. She said her mother always drank a little sake whenever she had a cold.'

'Most people wouldn't suspect an elementary-school-aged daughter of lying about her own mother's death.'

'No one else except for her said Fumiyo had a cold.'

'But why would she do that? What difference would it make to Yukiho whether it was a suicide or an accident? There was no life insurance payout. And what kind of kid thinks about that sort of thing in the first place?' Koga's eyes widened. 'Wait, you don't think Yukiho killed her own mother?' He was half-joking when he said it, but Sasagaki didn't smile.

'I wouldn't go that far. But she could have been involved.'

'How so?'

'Ignoring obvious signs that her mother was contemplating suicide, for one.'

'You think she wanted her mother to die?'

'Yukiho didn't waste much time moving in with Reiko Karasawa. They might've been talking about that move before the time came, even. Maybe Yukiho wanted to leave, but Fumiyo was holding her back.'

'You think she'd just abandon her mother like that?'

'She's capable, yes. And she'd have a reason to want to hide the fact that her mother had committed suicide: an accidental death and everyone around her is sympathetic. But if word got out it was suicide, it would colour their opinion of her, too. Not hard to figure which one she'd pick.'

'Look, Sasagaki, what you're saying makes sense ... but it all feels like a stretch, if you know what I mean.' Koga ordered two more bottles of sake.

'It took me a while following in Yukiho's footsteps before I started putting things together – hey, this is pretty good. What's this tempura?' Sasagaki asked, staring at the small piece of fried food between his chopsticks.

'What do you think it is?' Koga asked with a grin.

'I don't know, that's why I asked. Never tasted anything like it.'

'It's natto.'

'What, that rotting bean stuff they eat up here?'

'You got it,' Koga said. 'I knew you'd never eat it if you knew what it was.'

Sasagaki grunted. 'They're not so slimy when you do them up like this,' he said, taking another mouthful. 'Pretty good, actually.'

'See? It pays to not have any preconceived notions about things. You never know until you try.'

'You don't say?' Sasagaki said, drinking some sake. He could feel the warmth spreading down to his toes. 'Speaking of preconceived notions, that's exactly what tripped me up with this case. See, it was only when I started to realise that Yukiho wasn't your average kid and looked back on the case of the murdered pawnbroker that I realised I'd overlooked something vital.'

'What's that?' Koga said, a serious look in his eyes.

Sasagaki stared back at him. 'Footprints, for one.'

'Footprints?'

'Yeah, the footprints at the scene where the body was found. The place was covered in dust, so there were a lot of footprints on the ground. But I never paid much attention to them. You remember why?'

'Because we didn't find any that looked like they belonged to the murderer,' Koga replied.

Sasagaki nodded. 'The only footprints at the scene, other than those made by the leather shoes of the victim, were made by kids' sneakers. And we knew the kids played in there, and it was some kid from Ōe Elementary who discovered the body, so what's so strange about some sneaker marks? That was where I was wrong.'

'You mean the murderer was wearing kids' sneakers?'

'Don't you think it was a little careless to not even consider the possibility?'

Koga frowned. 'A kid couldn't have pulled that murder off.'

'Or maybe being a kid is *how* they pulled it off. Caught Kirihara off guard.'

'But ...'

'There's another thing I overlooked,' Sasagaki said, putting down his chopsticks and sticking up a finger. 'Alibis.'

'Go on.'

'When Fumiyo Nishimoto's alibi checked out we immediately started checking for an accomplice. That's when we hit on Terasaki, but there was someone else we should have looked at first.'

Koga rubbed his chin. 'Wasn't Yukiho at the library at the time?'

Sasagaki stared the younger detective in the face. 'Good memory.'

Koga chuckled dryly. 'Don't tell me you're one of the ones who thinks I care more about my rank than my work.'

'Never crossed my mind. I didn't think any of the other detectives remembered where Yukiho had been that day. But like you said, she was at the library. I looked into it and found out that that library is pretty darn close to the scene of the crime. She would've had to pass in front of that abandoned building on her way home.'

'I see where you're going with this, but come on – what age is that?'

'Eleven years old. Old enough to know the deal.' Sasagaki opened his box of Seven Stars and put one in his mouth. He began to look for a match.

Koga's hand shot out with a lighter. 'I'm not so sure,' he said, lighting the old detective's cigarette. The expensive lighter had a satisfying click.

Sasagaki nodded his thanks, then blowing a puff of white smoke he looked down at the lighter in Koga's hands. 'That a Dunhill?'

'Cartier, actually.'

Sasagaki snorted. 'Remember that Dunhill we found in Terasaki's car after the accident?'

'The one they thought might have belonged to the pawnbroker, right? Never did figure that one out, as I recall.'

'That was my theory, that it belonged to Kirihara. But Terasaki wasn't the murderer. I think it's more likely that someone who wanted to make it *look* like he did it snuck it into his place, or sold him some story and gave it to him.'

'And you think that was Yukiho?'

'That would make the most sense. I'd say it's even more likely than Terasaki just happening to own the same lighter as Kirihara.'

Koga sighed, a sigh that gradually turned into a groan. 'Look, I admire your flexibility in even considering the possibility that Yukiho is behind all this. It's true, we might have cut some corners because she was a kid. But without anything more conclusive, this is really just another theory. You have any evidence that she was the one who did it?'

'Well ...' Sasagaki said, taking a deep drag on his cigarette and slowly exhaling. The smoke floated over Koga's head before dispersing. 'I'd have to say no. I don't have evidence.'

'Then maybe you better rethink this whole thing from the beginning. And, I'm sorry, but the statute of limitations is up on the case. Even if you did find the real killer, there's nothing we can do.'

'I know that.'

'Well?'

'Well, listen,' Sasagaki said, snuffing his cigarette out. He glanced round, making sure no one was listening to them. 'This is bigger than the question of whoever killed the pawnbroker. I'm not just after Yukiho Karasawa.'

'Who else would you be after?' Koga asked, a sharp light in his eyes.

'I'm after both of them,' Sasagaki said, a wry smile on his face. 'The goby *and* the shrimp.'

The first patients were admitted for consultations at the Imperial University Hospital at nine, but there was always a considerable lag time before the first prescriptions came into the system.

Whenever one came through, they would work on it in pairs. One would measure out the medicine, the other would check for any mistakes and bag it. The checker would stamp the sealed package when the prescription was complete.

In addition to outpatient requests, they would get work from the wards as well. There were emergency medicine deliveries, and occasionally carting around IVs.

Today, there was someone else in the pharmacy besides Noriko and her partner: a man who sat in the corner staring at a computer terminal. He was a young assistant professor in the medical department.

For two years Imperial University had been taking steps to connect their computers with those at other research facilities. The biggest of these connections was a permanent online channel between their office and the central research facility of a pharmaceutical manufacturer. Whenever they needed to know anything about any of the drugs handled by that company, they could check the data instantly.

Anyone with an ID and a password could use the system. Noriko had both, but she had never touched the thing. Whenever she needed to know something about a medicine she called the pharmaceutical company up, the way they had always done. Most of the other pharmacists did the same.

The assistant professor currently working the terminal was engaged in a joint research project with the pharmaceutical company. Noriko agreed that their kind of system would be extremely handy for someone in his position – though it wasn't perfect.

They'd had a bunch of technicians in just the other day discussing the latest issue with the doctors on staff: a recent hacking attempt on their system. Noriko wasn't entirely sure what that meant, but it didn't sound good and it did little to instil faith.

After lunch she made the rounds helping inpatients with their daily dosages and talking to doctors and nurses about the drugs they were using. Then she went back to the pharmacy to measure out more dosages. Five o'clock came quickly.

She was just getting ready to leave when one of her colleagues stopped her – a phone call for Noriko, she said.

Noriko's heart fluttered.

'Yes?' she said, picking up the receiver. Her voice was a little hoarse.

'Noriko? Noriko Kurihara?' It was a man's voice, but not the one she had been hoping to hear. The voice was thin and made her think of illness. It was also somehow familiar.

'Yes?' she replied.

'I wonder if you remember me. It's me, Fujii. Tamotsu Fujii.'

'Mr Fujii?' She remembered. He was one of the men she'd met through the matchmaking service – the one with the mother suffering from dementia.

'Oh,' she said, 'how have you been?'

'Fine, fine. You sound well.'

'Yes, um, can I help you?'

'Well, I'm calling from very close to the hospital. Actually, I stepped in a few moments ago and saw you – have you been eating properly? You're a little on the skinny side.'

He chuckled, and the sound sent a chill down her spine.

'I was hoping we could meet up,' he said. 'Maybe have tea?'

Noriko rolled her eyes. *What, he wants another date?*

'I'm sorry, but I have plans today.'

'It would only be for a bit. There's something I really need to talk to you about. Can you spare even a little time? Thirty minutes?'

Noriko sighed loudly for effect. 'Really, I don't have time. I can't even have you calling me here like this. I'm going to hang up.'

'No, sorry, wait. At least answer one question, just one? Are you still living with that man?'

'What?'

'Just, if you're still living with that man you've been living with there's something I really need to talk to you about.'

Noriko cupped her hand over her mouth and the receiver, lowering her voice. 'What are you talking about?'

'That's what I want to tell you, in person.'

Noriko hesitated, but he had piqued her curiosity. 'OK. Where should I go?'

Fujii told her to meet him at a café just a few minutes' walk from the hospital, near Ogikubo Station.

She went in and saw him sitting at a table near the back. He was thin, with buggy eyes that made her think of a praying mantis. He was wearing a grey suit, his jacket hanging on the wall behind him.

'Long time no see,' Noriko said, sitting down across from him.

'I'm so sorry to call out of the blue like that.'

'What's this all about?'

'Please, order something first.'

'I'm fine. I need to leave soon, so please, just say what you have to say.'

'It's not that simple,' Fujii said, calling the waitress over and ordering a milk tea. He looked at Noriko and smiled. 'You liked tea, didn't you?'

She didn't remember anything she'd ordered on their last date. The fact that he did made her feel uncomfortable.

'How's your mom?' she asked, hoping to put him on the spot.

The man's face darkened and he shook his head. 'She died. A few months ago.'

'Oh. I'm sorry. Was it her illness?'

'Not really, it was an accident. She choked.'

'That's horrible. Choking on food is pretty common, though.'

'Well, it was cotton.'

'Cotton?'

'I only took my eyes off her for a moment and she started eating the stuffing out of a cotton comforter I'd put over her. I have no idea why she did it. When I took it out, it was larger than a soft-ball. Can you believe it?'

Noriko shook her head. *No, I cannot believe you're telling me this.*

'I was so overcome, I didn't know what to do for a little while, but then I realised that there was also a kind of relief, you know? I thought: now I won't have to worry about her all the time.' He sighed.

Noriko understood how he felt. She'd seen more than her share of families exhausted by having to take care of elderly relatives. Still, she wasn't sure what any of this had to do with her.

The waitress brought her milk tea. She took a sip and Fujii's eyes narrowed as he smiled. 'It's been a while since I've seen you drinking tea.'

Noriko looked down at the table.

'There was another thing I thought, probably inappropriately, after my mother died,' he continued. 'That is, I thought someone might think of dating me again. I don't mean just *anyone*, of course. I mean you.'

'That was a long time ago.'

'But I never forgot you. And I went to your apartment. It was about a month after my mother died. That's when I found out you were living with someone. It came as a bit of a shock. But I was also very surprised when I saw him.'

Noriko frowned and stared at him. 'Surprised? Why?'

'Well, it's just that I had seen him before.'

'No way!'

'It's true. I don't know his name, but I remember his face quite well.'

'Where did you meet him?'

'Well, that's the thing. I didn't actually meet him, but I saw him. Here, at the hospital, and near your apartment.'

'What?'

'It was around April of last year. To be perfectly honest, I was a little obsessed with you back then and, well, I'd make trips to the hospital just to see you, or hang out near your apartment. I'm guessing you never noticed.'

'I had no idea.' Noriko shook her head. The thought made the hair on the back of her neck rise up.

'But,' he continued, unaware of her reaction, 'it wasn't just me coming to see you. He was watching you, too. I know this is a little funny, me saying this, but he gave me a bad vibe. I even thought of telling you once. But I started getting busy at work, and with my mother, and I had no time to myself and, well, I guess I just let it slide.'

'And you're sure it was him?'

'He's the one living with you now, absolutely.'

'That's impossible,' she said, shaking her head. Her face felt drawn and taut, as if she were wearing a plaster mask. 'I'm sure you're mistaken.'

'I'm sure I'm right. I have a very good memory for faces. He was definitely the man I saw last year,' Fujii said with certainty.

Noriko picked up her teacup, but she didn't feel like drinking. Her head was a storm of thoughts.

'Of course, just because he was hanging out around you doesn't mean he's a bad person. Maybe he was like me, and he fell for you, you know. But, like I said, he gave me a bad vibe, and the thought of you two together, well, it made me worry. Not that it's any of my business, of course, so I held back until I saw you the other day – entirely by accident, you understand – and that got me thinking about it again. Thinking about you. So, that's why I'm here.'

Noriko was hardly listening to him by that point. His meaning was clear: break up with Akiyoshi and go out with him. But she wasn't interested in the least. Not only because it was ridiculous; she just wasn't in the right state of mind.

She wasn't sure what she said when she left the café. When she came to her senses, she was walking down the street at night. *April*, he had said. April of last year.

That didn't make any sense. She hadn't met Akiyoshi until May, and their meeting had been a total accident – or so she'd thought.

What if it wasn't?

She thought back to that night. Akiyoshi, hunched over with a pain in his stomach. Had he been waiting for her to come home? Had it all been an act to get close to her?

Why?

Assuming that Akiyoshi had some purpose in getting close to her, why had he chosen her? She wasn't so enamoured of herself as to think he had fallen for her looks. So she filled some other condition, then. Was it because she was a pharmacist? An unmarried thirty-something? Was it because she lived alone, or because she worked at the Imperial University Hospital?

Noriko gasped as a thought occurred to her. When she had signed up for the matchmaking service she'd given them a great deal of information about herself. If someone peeked at the data they could easily find someone who met certain criteria. Maybe Akiyoshi had got his hands on their data somehow. Hadn't he worked at a computer company? What if Memorix had been involved in making the matchmaking service's computer systems?

She looked up and noticed that she had already reached her apartment. A little shakily, she climbed the steps until she was standing in front of her unit. She unlocked the door and opened it, Fujii's warning ringing in her ears.

If we know the truth, there's nothing to be afraid of, she muttered to herself, staring into the dark apartment.

FOURTEEN

A hammer struck a bell inside her head: *ding, ding, ding!*

Then she heard the faint sound of laughter. That got her eyes open. She saw a ray of sunlight striking the floral print on the wallpaper, the morning sun sneaking through a gap in the heavy curtains.

Mika Shinozuka twisted her neck to look at the clock by her pillow. Her father had bought it for her in London. She'd set it for seven-thirty, one minute away from now. If she just lay there a little more, a cheerful melody would play and figurines would emerge from the clock face to begin a dance. She reached out and turned off the alarm.

Mika got out of bed and opened the curtains. The sunlight poured in through the big window, illuminating every corner of her room. She saw herself in the mirror on the dresser – pyjamas all wrinkly, hair a tangled mess, face like a lump of coalesced grumpiness.

Ding, the bell sounded again. Then she heard voices talking, too faint to overhear. She had an idea what they would be talking about, though, and immediately lost interest.

Mika went over to the window and looked out over the lawn, still green, though its colour was fading. Just as she had thought, her dad was teaching Yukiho how to play golf.

Yukiho stood holding the club in both hands. Then her father wrapped his arms around her from behind, holding her hands in his. It was like that comedy routine where one person does the arms for another person. Her father whispered something in Yukiho's ear and together they lifted the club. It swung up and slowly back down. It looked like her father's lips might brush the back of Yukiho's neck. He was so close. In fact, he probably had done that on purpose a few times already.

After they slowly swung the club together a few times he stepped back and watched while Yukiho tried to hit the ball. *Ding*. Sometimes she would hit it, but most of the time she would miss. Then she would get a sheepish look on her face and Mika's father would give her some advice. Then they would start over from the beginning with the comedy routine. This would go on for half an hour.

The same scene had played out the same way almost every day for the past week. Mika wasn't sure whether Yukiho had expressed an interest in starting golf, or whether her father had pushed her into it. Regardless, it looked like the two of them were doing their utmost to find something they could enjoy together as a couple.

Even though her father had flat-out refused when Mom once said she wanted to learn how to play.

Mika stepped away from the window and stood in front of her dresser, painfully aware of her fifteen-year-old reflection. She was skinny, without any womanly roundness. Her arms and legs seemed too long for the rest of her and her shoulder bones were pointy and stuck out at all the wrong angles.

In her mind's eye she saw an image of Yukiho's body superimposed over her own. She had seen Yukiho naked only once, when she had mistakenly opened the bathroom door, thinking no one was inside. Yukiho had just stepped out of the shower. She wasn't wearing anything, not even a towel.

Her body was perfect, made up of curves so precise they looked like something computer-generated, yet with the simple warmth of something turned on a potter's wheel. Her ample breasts were still firm, and tiny droplets of water hung on her pinkish white skin. What fat she had seemed to fit perfectly along the lines of her body, rounding out the curves. Mika had gasped. In the space of a few seconds the sight of Yukiho's body was burned into her mind.

Yukiho had taken it with utmost grace. She hadn't seemed flustered in the least or unhappy at all.

'Hello, Mika,' she'd said. 'Getting into the bath?' She had smiled, not even hurrying to cover herself.

It was Mika who'd lost it. She turned and ran without saying a word. Dashing into her room, she dove under the covers of her bed, her heart racing.

Mika frowned, remembering her embarrassment. The girl in the mirror made the same expression. Picking up her hairbrush, she started working at her hair until the brush became so entangled it stopped. She tried yanking it, and only succeeded in snapping off a few of her hairs.

She heard a knock at the door. 'Mika? Are you awake? Good morning.'

She didn't answer, and on the third knock, the door opened and Taeko gingerly peeked in. 'Oh, you are awake,' she said, stepping inside and immediately beginning to make the rumpled bed. Mika looked at her. She was the perfect image of a housemaid in an old movie: the dumpy body, the big apron around her waist, a sweater with the sleeves rolled up, her hair done up in a big bun on the top of her head.

'I wanted to sleep more, but the noise woke me up.'

'Noise?' Taeko said with a curious frown. Then she nodded. 'Ah, your father. Yes, he's been getting up early these days.'

'It's stupid. Why does anyone get up so early?'

'Well, they're both very busy, you know, and this is the only time they have together. Besides, exercise is good thing, I think.'

'He never would've been caught dead doing that when Mom was alive.'

'People change as they get older, you know.'

'Change how? Like they start marrying younger women? She's ten *years* younger than Mom was.'

'Mika, your father is still quite young himself. He can't live the rest of his life alone, can he? You'll go off and get married someday and your brother will leave, too.'

'You're not making much sense, Taeko. Talking about people getting old and then still being young.'

Taeko frowned a little. 'Come down soon, breakfast is ready.

Your father said he's not going to give you any more rides in the morning, even if it looks like you're going to be late.'

Mika snorted. 'Bet I know whose idea *that* was.'

Taeko said nothing and started to leave, but Mika stopped her before she had fully closed the door.

'You're on my side, right?' she asked.

Taeko looked taken aback for a moment before recovering with a chuckle. 'I'm on everyone's side, dear,' she said, closing the door.

Mika got ready for school and went downstairs to find the other three already at breakfast. Her father and Yukiho were sitting facing her and Masahiro, her brother, was in the chair next to hers. He was in fifth grade.

'I still don't feel like I know what I'm doing,' Yukiho was saying. 'I have to get the hang of at least the driver, or I'm going to be a real menace out there on the course.'

'Don't worry, it's always easier than it looks. Also, you say at *least* the driver, but the driver's the toughest one. Use that well and you're a pro. First step is to just get out there and try a round on the course.'

'I don't know, I'd be pretty worried,' Yukiho said with a shrug. She looked over at Mika. 'Hey there, good morning.'

Mika sat down without answering. Her father said 'good morning,' adding a stern look. She muttered a half-hearted 'good morning' back.

Ham, scrambled eggs, salad and croissants were spread out on the table.

'Wait just a bit, Mika, and I'll bring your soup,' Taeko said from the kitchen. It sounded like she was in there busily preparing something.

Yukiho set down her fork and stood from the table. 'That's OK, Taeko. I'll get it.'

'I don't want soup,' Mika said, grabbing a croissant and tearing off a bite. Then she snatched the milk glass from in front of Masahiro and took a swig.

'Hey, that's mine.'

'Don't be stingy.'

Picking up her fork, Mika dug into her ham and eggs. A bowl of soup appeared in front of her plate, courtesy of Yukiho.

'I said I didn't want any,' Mika said, not looking up.

'That's not how you talk to someone who does something for you,' her dad said.

'It's OK,' Yukiho said to her husband and an uncomfortable silence settled over the table.

Mika couldn't taste the food at all. Not even Taeko's ham and eggs, which was her favourite. And eating wasn't any fun. Her chest hurt near the top of her stomach.

'So, any plans tonight?' her father said to Yukiho, taking a sip of his coffee.

'Nothing in particular.'

'Then we should go out for dinner, the four of us. A friend of mine just opened an Italian restaurant in Yotsuya, and he's been asking me to come.'

'Italian? That sounds lovely.'

'You too, kids. If there's a show you want to watch, you can set the VCR.'

'Cool,' Masahiro said. 'I'll go easy on the snacks.'

Mika took a sidelong glance at her brother and said, 'I'm not going.'

She could feel the eyes on her from across the table.

'Why not?' her father asked. 'You have something you need to do? There's no piano lessons today and no tutor scheduled.'

'I just don't want to go. What, is this mandatory?'

'Why don't you want to go?'

'Why does it matter?'

'Because it matters. Look, if you have something you want to say, let's hear it.'

'Dear ...' Yukiho said. 'Actually, maybe tonight isn't the best idea. I've just remembered a few things that need doing.'

Her father glared at her, but fell silent. Yukiho's coming to her defence annoyed Mika even more. Throwing down her fork, she stood. 'I gotta go.'

'Mika!'

Ignoring her father, Mika grabbed her bag and jacket and went out into the hall. She was slipping into her shoes when Yukiho and Taeko came up behind her.

'Don't be in such a hurry that you get run over by a car, now,' Taeko fretted.

Yukiho reached down and picked her jacket up off the floor. Mika snatched it from her without a word. She was just putting her arms through the sleeves when Yukiho said with a smile to Taeko, 'I like that navy sweater, it's cute.'

'Very cute,' Taeko agreed.

'They make school uniforms so stylish these days. Back when I was in school we only got one choice and that was it.'

Mika felt the anger rise in her chest, though she didn't understand why. She took off the jacket. While Yukiho and Taeko watched, dumbfounded, she peeled off her Ralph Lauren sweater and tossed it on the floor.

'Mika, what're you doing?' Taeko asked.

'I don't feel like wearing it any more.'

'You'll be cold.'

'I don't care.'

Her father came out and asked, 'What are you going on about now?'

'Nothing. Bye.'

'Wait, Miss Mika!' Taeko said, but she could hear her father grunt 'Let her go,' behind her back as Mika ran for the front gate. The long, tree-lined path between their front door and the gate was one of her favourite spots in the whole world. Sometimes she lingered on it just so she could look at the trees, and the flowers, and note the changing of the seasons. But today, it seemed much too great a distance between her and freedom.

Mika couldn't say what bothered her so much. Every time she lost her temper with Yukiho, another Mika inside her head would ask, coldly, *Are you crazy?* And she would always answer, *No. I don't know. I'm just angry.*

She'd first met Yukiho that spring when her father had taken her and her brother to the boutique in South Aoyama. She remembered seeing a woman come to the door and thinking *Wow, she's pretty*. Her father said he wanted to buy his children new clothes, and Yukiho immediately began ordering her helpers around, bringing outfit after outfit for them to try on. There were no other customers in the place. It was like having their own private fitting boutique.

Yukiho treated them like fashion models, giving them various outfits to wear and try on in front of the mirror. Masahiro lasted about thirty minutes before he gave up and said he was tired of trying on clothes.

For Mika it was a dream come true – or it would have been, if she hadn't spent the entire time wondering who Yukiho was and exactly what kind of relationship she had with her father.

It was when they were picking out a party dress that she began to suspect that Yukiho might soon have a special relationship not just with her father but with all of them.

'You go to family parties, right, Yasuharu?' Yukiho said. 'Take her in this dress and it will positively *bowl* the other families over.'

Mika didn't like how Yukiho referred to her father as Yasuhiro, as though they were close friends. Nor did she like being thought of as an accessory to make other people look good. What bothered her most, however, was the sudden realisation that Yukiho might be joining them at the next 'family' party.

The discussion turned to what they should buy. Mika couldn't choose. Truth be told, she wanted it all.

'You decide, Dad,' she said eventually. 'I'm good with anything.'

'That's not making it very easy on me,' her father complained. Nevertheless, he picked out a few of the outfits. They were all fancy, good-little-girl dresses with long skirts that covered up the skin, the kind of things Mika's mother liked. Mika's mother had never really got over playing with dolls, and loved dressing her up in the most ridiculously frilly outfits. It made Mika happy to see that her father remembered.

After he was done, her father asked Yukiho what she thought.

Yukiho crossed her arms. 'I think she could get away with something a little brighter, a little more vigorous.'

'Really? Which would you choose?'

'Well ...' Yukiho said, pointing to a few of the other outfits, all of them tighter-fitting, with shorter skirts. They bordered on racy.

'She's still in middle school,' her father said. 'Aren't these a little grown-up for her?'

Yukiho smiled. 'Oh, she's more grown-up than you think.'

'I don't know about that,' her father said, scratching his head. He asked Mika what she thought.

Mika left it up to him, so her father decided to buy all the ones Yukiho picked, warning her that he'd hold her responsible if they didn't look good.

'Not to worry,' she told him, and smiled at Mika. 'You don't have to be a little doll any more, dear.'

The words felt like boots, stepping on something in Mika's heart, trying to rub out the memory of her mother. Thinking back on it, she realised that was the moment she started to hate Yukiho.

Later, their father would occasionally take Mika and Masahiro out to eat with him and Yukiho, or go on long drives together. Mika always thought her father was unusually bright and cheerful when they were with her. On family trips with her mother, he had always been silent, an unwilling participant, but in front of Yukiho, it was like he couldn't stop talking. He always wanted to ask Yukiho's opinion, to do the things she wanted to do. To Mika, he looked like a wimp.

One day in July their father laid the news on them. It wasn't a discussion or an opinion poll. It was an announcement: he was going to marry Yukiho.

Masahiro seemed a little spaced out by the news. He wasn't particularly happy, or concerned. Maybe, Mika thought, it just wasn't that big a deal to him. He had only been four years old when their mom died.

Mika had been honest. She said her only real mother was the one who had died seven years before.

'That's fine,' her father told her. 'I'm not telling you to forget your mother. I'm just telling you, a new person is coming to live with us. We'll have more family now.'

Mika was silent, but in her heart she was screaming *she's not family!*

Once that particular stone began to roll, there was no stopping it. Everything went the way Mika didn't want it to go. Her father was beside himself with happiness and she despised him for it. He seemed lesser now in her eyes, a fallen man, and Yukiho was to blame.

If someone had asked her exactly what she didn't like about Yukiho, Mika would have had a hard time naming it. It was just a feeling, a twisted lump in the pit of her stomach. There was no denying that Yukiho was beautiful, and smart, too. Mika respected that. She was a talented businesswoman. Mika didn't know any other women her age who ran not just one, but two boutiques. But when she was around her, she could feel her body tense. Something inside her warned her that she needed to be on guard. There was something about Yukiho, an aura hanging around her, that was unlike anything she'd felt before. She was like the sun, with her father and her assistants orbiting around her, but her light brought no warmth, just unhappiness.

Mika admitted the possibility that these thoughts were nothing more than her imagination. But if she was delusional, at least she had one person keeping her company: her older cousin, Kazunari Shinozuka.

Ever since her father had announced his engagement to the family, Kazunari had started visiting them at home. Out of all of their relatives, he was the only one who had spoken out against the wedding.

'You don't know what she's really like,' Kazunari had said once when Mika overheard them talking. 'At the very least, I can promise you she's not the kind of woman who puts the happiness of her family first.' He had sounded very serious.

But her father never listened, and, over time, he began avoiding Kazunari. She'd even seen him pretending not to be home once or twice when Kazunari came calling.

The wedding took place three months later. It wasn't a very fancy ceremony, and the reception was very laid-back, but they looked happy, as did nearly everyone in attendance. Everyone except Mika, who was filled with the gloomy bleakness of someone seeing a tragedy in the making, a terrible mistake that couldn't be undone.

They started their new life with a new mother in their house and, from the outside, it didn't look like much had changed in the Shinozuka household. But Mika could feel things shifting under the surface every day. One by one her memories of her real mother were being smothered. Their daily lives were changing bit by bit. And worst of all, her father was becoming a different person.

Her real mother had loved flowers. She always put seasonal arrangements in the entranceway, the hallway, and the corners of the rooms. There were flowers there now, too, bigger, and even more beautiful – eye-opening displays of floral magnificence.

But they weren't real. They were all expertly crafted from silk. Artificial flowers.

That's what this family is becoming, Mika thought. *An artificial flower.*

Sasagaki got off the Tozai Subway Line at Urayasu and began walking back towards Tokyo along Kasaibashi Street, taking a left just before he reached the Old Edogawa River. Along the narrow road stood a nearly perfectly square, white building, with a sign on the gate that read SH RESINS. There didn't seem to be a guard, so Sasagaki let himself in.

Cutting across a car park lined with trucks, he entered the building. Immediately on the right stood a small reception desk where a woman in her forties was busily writing something. She looked up and frowned suspiciously when she saw Sasagaki.

Sasagaki handed her his business card, and asked to meet Kazunari Shinozuka. The woman's expression didn't change when she saw the card. 'You have an appointment to meet the director?' she asked.

'The director?'

'Kazunari Shinozuka. He's our director.'

'Oh, right. Yes. I called before I came.'

'Wait please.'

She picked up a phone on the desk and dialled some numbers. After a few words, she set the receiver down and looked back at Sasagaki. 'He says please come straight to his office.'

'OK. Where is that?'

'Third floor,' she said, returning to her writing. He looked and saw that she was writing New Year's cards. From the personal address book on the desk next to her, it didn't look like she was writing cards on behalf of the company, either.

'Where on the third floor?' Sasagaki asked.

The woman seemed aggravated by this, and jabbed towards the hall behind him with her felt-tip pen. 'The elevator's there. Just walk down the hall until you get to the door with a sign over it that says "Director's Office".'

'Right, thanks,' Sasagaki said, but the woman had already gone back to her cards.

Sasagaki went up to the third floor to find there was only one hallway on the floor, going in a square around the building, with doors along on either side. Sasagaki walked, checking the plates above the doors. He found it at the first corner and knocked.

'Come in,' he heard a voice say from inside. Sasagaki pushed open the door.

Kazunari was just standing from his chair, a large window to his back. He was wearing a brown double-breasted suit.

'It's good to see you. It's been a while,' Kazunari said with a warm smile.

'Sorry I haven't been in touch. Have you been well?'

'I'm hanging in there.'

Kazunari guided him to a sofa in the middle of the room and sat across from him in an overstuffed armchair. 'How long has it been since we actually met?' he asked.

'Since September of last year. At Shinozuka Pharmaceuticals, I recall?'

'Yes, of course,' Kazunari said. 'I can't believe it's already been more than a year.'

'I actually called the pharmaceutical company first, but they sent me here.'

'Right, well, I left right after your visit,' Kazunari said, a downward cast to his eyes. He looked as though he wanted to say something, but was refraining.

'So you're director now?' Sasagaki said, as warmly as he could. 'That's quite the promotion. At your age, no less.'

Kazunari looked up at him, a dry smile on his face. 'Is that what this looks like?'

'Am I wrong?'

Kazunari stood without answering and went over to his desk. He picked up the phone and said, 'Can I get two coffees? Yes, right away.'

He set the phone back down and turned to Sasagaki. 'I believe I mentioned over the phone that my cousin got married.'

'October, was it?' Sasagaki said. 'I'm sure that was quite the affair.'

'It was rather subdued, actually. A small ceremony at a church, followed by a relatives-only reception at a restaurant in town. Considering it was the second time around for both of them, I think they wanted to keep it simple. That, and my cousin has children.'

'You attended?'

'I am a relative, so, yes. That said,' he sat back down in the armchair and sighed before continuing, 'I've no doubt they would rather not have invited me at all.'

'You never withdrew your objections.'

Kazunari nodded.

Sasagaki had kept in close touch with Kazunari over the phone through the spring. Both sides had something to gain: Kazunari wanted to learn more about Yukiho, and Sasagaki wanted to learn more about Ryo Kirihara. So far, both sides remained disappointed.

'You and I know more about her and what's happened than anyone else I know and yet we still have nothing to go on,' Kazunari said with a sigh. 'I couldn't open my cousin's eyes.'

'It was a tall order from the get-go. He's not the first man she's fooled,' Sasagaki said, adding, 'I was one of them.'

'Nineteen years ago, was it?'

'That's right.' Sasagaki took out a cigarette. 'You mind?'

'Go right ahead.' Kazunari pushed a crystal glass ashtray in front of him. 'Detective, I was hoping you could tell me everything today, the whole story. All two decades' worth.'

'That is why I'm here,' Sasagaki said, lighting a cigarette. A knock came at the door – the coffee had arrived. Kazunari stood to get it.

Sasagaki took a sip out of his thick-rimmed mug and began to talk. He started with the body found in the abandoned building, then the ever-changing list of suspects, ending with Tadao Terasaki's car accident that derailed the entire investigation. He filled in the details where necessary. Kazunari listened with his coffee cup in hand, but before long he put it down on the table and folded his arms across his chest. When Yukiho Nishimoto finally joined the story, he crossed his legs and took a deep breath.

'That pretty much wraps up what happened with the murder of the pawnbroker,' Sasagaki said, taking a drink of his coffee, which had by then gone lukewarm.

'So the case was thrown out as unsolvable?'

'Not right away, but without any new witnesses or information the general feeling was that it was only a matter of time before the case was put aside.'

'But you didn't give up, did you, detective?'

'To tell the truth, I almost did.'

Setting down his mug, Sasagaki began the rest of his story.

Unable to find any clear evidence of Terasaki's guilt, and unlikely to find any new suspects, the task force was drifting. There was talk of disbanding. Things on the streets had gone from bad to worse in the wake of the oil shock, and burglaries, arson and kidnappings were on the rise. Osaka police couldn't afford to dedicate much manpower to tracking down one single murderer. Especially not when it was looking likely that the man who did it was already dead.

Sasagaki himself was starting to think he had reached the end of the road. It would be the third unsolved case of his career. Each one had a particular smell to it. There were cases so chaotic you didn't know where to begin, which ended up being solved in a week. Then there were the cases that looked simple at first blush that ended up going nowhere. The Kirihara case was one of those.

So, a month after Terasaki's death, when Sasagaki started rereading all of the notes they'd taken from the very beginning, it was more out of boredom than any real hope he'd find something. He mostly skimmed the vast pile of documents, pages upon pages without a clue in sight, but his fingers stopped when he found the report detailing the testimony given by the boy who found the body. His name was Michihiro Kikuchi, nine years old at the time of the discovery. The first person he told about it was his older brother, a fifth grader. The brother had gone to the building to make sure he was telling the truth, then told their mother, who had called the police. The report was mostly an outline of what she had told them.

Sasagaki was very familiar with the details surrounding the discovery. The kids had been playing a game they called 'time tunnel', crawling through the ducts in the abandoned building, when Michihiro had got separated from the rest. He'd circled around in the ducts for a while until he came to a darkly lit room where he found a man lying on a sofa. Suspicious, he looked closer and saw blood. The interesting part was what happened next.

'He was scared,' the report said, 'and tried to leave, but there was a concrete block by the door that made it hard to open.'

Sasagaki found this strange. He thought back to the scene of the crime, remembering the door. It opened inwards, he recalled. It would have made sense for the murderer to place the block there to delay the discovery of the body, except that was impossible if you assumed he had then left the scene through the blocked door.

Sasagaki went to check it out. The name of the officer who'd taken the initial report was a captain named Kosaka from the local precinct.

Kosaka remembered the report in detail, but his explanation left something to be desired. 'Actually, that part of the testimony was a little vague,' he told Sasagaki with a frown. 'The boy didn't remember it very well. It was never clear whether the block was so close that the door didn't open at all, or whether it was far enough away that someone could have opened the door enough to squeeze through. The kid was too flustered to remember. That said, since the murderer clearly exited through the door, we just figured it was the latter.'

Sasagaki checked the forensics report on the matter, but they hadn't bothered mentioning exactly where the block was in relation to the door, except to note that it was hard to tell because the boy who discovered the body had moved it.

Sasagaki was forced to give up that particular line of inquiry until a year later when he began to suspect Yukiho's involvement following her mother's death. This made the position of the block more important because its distance from the closed door would determine the size of the person that could have passed through and Yukiho would have been able to squeeze through a very small gap.

Sasagaki decided to meet with the boy, Michihiro, and what he learned came as a considerable surprise.

For one thing, the boy claimed to remember what had happened the year before perfectly – even better than he had at the time. That made some sense, Sasagaki thought. It would have been challenging for a nine-year-old, flustered at the discovery of a corpse, to put together an accurate statement. But he would have matured quite a bit in the intervening year.

Sasagaki asked him to describe how he had gone through the door in as much detail as possible.

'Well, I couldn't get it open at all at first,' the boy told him. 'When I looked down, there was a big concrete block there, right up against the bottom of the door.'

'You're sure about that?'

The boy nodded firmly.

'Why didn't you ever say that until now? Is this something you remembered recently?'

'No, I said it at first back then when they were asking all the questions. But the police officer said it didn't sound right and then I started to wonder and I guess I got kinda confused. But when I thought about it later, yeah, I'm sure I couldn't open the door at all.'

Sasagaki gritted his teeth. This would have been critical testimony one year earlier, if the questioning officer hadn't talked the kid out of it. Sasagaki told his superior officer immediately. But his boss's reaction was cold. The kid's memory couldn't be trusted; not to mention that it was crazy to take a year-old testimony without a big pinch of salt.

Sasagaki's boss at the time the investigation began had been recently transferred away and his replacement was ambitious to a fault, the type who would rather make his name solving a new, flashier case than waste his time on the half-abandoned search for the murderer of a pawnbroker.

Sasagaki continued investigating on his own. He had a path to follow now. It would have been impossible for whoever killed Yosuke Kirihara to have left through the door, and all of the windows into the room had been locked from the inside. None of the windows were broken, nor were there any holes in the walls, which left only one possible explanation: the killer had left through the duct the boy had used to get in.

An adult probably wouldn't be able to fit through the duct, nor would they risk getting stuck without an extremely good reason to not just use the door. A kid who had been playing in the ducts, on the other hand ...

Sasagaki's sights were increasingly focused on Yukiho. At first, he tried to get some proof that she had played in the ducts with the other kids, but none of the ones who played there, and none of her friends, remembered ever seeing her go near the place. 'No girls would play in there,' one of the boys said. 'The place is super dirty and there's like dead rats and bugs and stuff. And your clothes get all messed up.'

Sasagaki had to admit, from what he knew of Yukiho, that it

didn't seem likely she'd have spent much time in the abandoned building. Another of the kids who said he used to play in there all the time wondered if a girl could even handle the ducts. According to him, there were a lot of really steep slopes inside them and places where you had to crawl up just using your hands for several metres, which meant you had to be pretty strong and pretty confident in your own athleticism.

Sasagaki took the kid to the building and had him try to leave by the duct in the room where the body had been found. He went outside to wait and about fifteen minutes later the boy was standing by an exhaust duct on the rear side of the building.

'Yeah, that was tough,' the boy said. 'There's a place halfway through where you really gotta climb. I don't know any girls with arms strong enough to handle that.'

Sasagaki was inclined to trust the kid's judgment on this point. There were girls in elementary school as tough as some of the boys, no question. But Yukiho Nishimoto wasn't one of them. He couldn't picture her crawling around like a monkey through the building ducts.

In the end he had to admit that it was possible his fantasies about an eleven-year-old girl killer were just that, and the boy's original testimony had just been incorrect.

'I agree. There's no way Yukiho Karasawa was playing games in air ducts,' Kazunari said. Sasagaki wondered if he called Yukiho by her college-era maiden name out of habit, or because he was reluctant to call her by his own last name.

'I hit a dead end.'

'But you did find an answer, right?'

'Of sorts,' Sasagaki admitted. 'I tried going back to square one, getting rid of all my preconceived notions about the case. That's when I saw something I hadn't seen up until that point.'

'Which was?'

'It's pretty simple, really,' Sasagaki said. 'Once you know a girl couldn't climb through those ducts, it means whoever did use them to escape the scene of the crime was a boy.'

'A boy …' Kazunari said, giving it a moment to sit before he asked, 'You don't mean Ryo Kirihara killed his own father?'

'Yes,' Sasagaki said. 'That's exactly what I mean.'

Sasagaki hadn't arrived at his conclusion immediately. It was a chance discovery on a visit to the Kirihara Pawnshop that first turned his suspicions towards Ryo.

He'd come back to the pawnshop to talk to Matsuura about Yosuke Kirihara's life. He kept the questions light – Matsuura had clearly had it with the investigation by that point and wasn't going out of his way to make Sasagaki's job any easier. It was already more than a year into the investigation, which would strain anyone's good humour.

'Detective,' Matsuura said at one point, 'I think you've squeezed just about everything you can out of us. There's nothing else.'

Sasagaki nodded, when a book sitting on the edge of the counter caught his eye. He picked it up. 'What's this?'

'That's Ryo's,' Matsuura said. 'He must have left it there.'

'Ryo read a lot?'

'Quite a bit, yeah. He used to go to the library all the time.'

'The library?'

Matsuura nodded, clearly wondering what the library had to do with anything.

Sasagaki put the book back on the counter, his heart pounding.

The book was *Gone with the Wind* – the same book Yukiho had been reading when he went to pay a visit to Fumiyo Nishimoto. If he was being honest with himself, it wasn't much more than a coincidence. Two kids of similar ages reading the same book probably happened all the time. Nor were they reading it at the same time. Yukiho had read it a full year earlier.

But the discovery stuck in his mind. Sasagaki paid a visit to the library, a small, grey building about two hundred metres north of the abandoned building where Yosuke Kirihara's body was found.

He showed a photograph of Yukiho to the librarian, a young woman with glasses who looked like she was only a few years past being a book-loving student herself. She nodded when she saw the photo.

'Oh, she used to come here all the time. I only remember her because she borrowed so many books.'

'Did she come alone?'

'Yes, always.' Then she frowned. 'Wait, well, no, sometimes she would come with a boy. A classmate, maybe? They looked about the same age.'

Sasagaki quickly pulled out another photograph, this one of the Kiriharas. He pointed his finger at Ryo. 'Was that the boy?'

The librarian squinted through her glasses. 'Well, that looks a bit like him, sure. It's hard to say for certain, though.'

'Were they always together?'

'Not always. Just sometimes. They would often come looking for the same book. And I remember they would play by cutting paper.'

'What do you mean?'

'The boy would make these shapes out of paper with scissors and show them to her. I remember having to talk to them because I didn't want little pieces of paper everywhere. But, I'm sorry, I really can't say for sure whether it's the boy in this picture.'

She'd given him proof enough. He remembered the paper cut-out he'd seen in Ryo's room.

So Yukiho and Ryo were meeting at the library. They had known each other at the time of the murder. That was enough to turn everything on its head. Sasagaki made a complete about-face in his thinking on the investigation.

Ryo could have easily navigated the ducts, and he already had a witness in the same class who said Ryo often joined in their games. According to the witness, Ryo knew his way around the abandoned building better than any of them.

That left Ryo's alibi. At the time of Yosuke Kirihara's death, Ryo had purportedly been with his mother, Yaeko, and the shop manager, Matsuura. But there was good reason to suspect they might be protecting him – a possibility no one on the task force had yet explored.

The only problem was motive.

What could bring a son to murder his own father? It had happened before in the history of the world, of course, but it wasn't commonplace. It would require a pretty compelling backstory and Sasagaki couldn't think of any that applied to Yosuke Kirihara and his son. The investigation hadn't uncovered any rift between the two. On the contrary, all the testimonies they had received made it seem like Yosuke Kirihara had genuinely cared for his son, and his son had loved him in return.

Sasagaki continued making the rounds and asking questions, but he had begun to seriously entertain the notion that it was all in his head. *When you wander in the dark too long, you start to see things that aren't really there.*

'I knew all too well that if I told anyone my Ryo theory, they'd think I was off my rocker and I would've got pulled off the case on the spot and probably given a nice long vacation,' Sasagaki said with a chuckle. He sounded as if he was only half-joking.

'So you couldn't find a motive?' Kazunari asked.

The detective shook his head. 'Nothing at the time. It was too much of a reach to think that Ryo had killed his father just because he wanted the money.'

'By "at the time" I take it you mean you found something later?' Kazunari said, leaning forward, but Sasagaki waved him back with his hands.

'Be patient, I'll get there. Just let me tell it in order. Basically, my own little private investigation fell apart at that point, but I kept tabs on Ryo and Yukiho. Not that I was on stakeout, mind you, but I made a point of asking around every once in a while to see how they were coming along, what schools they were going to, trying to keep a general picture forming in my head. I was sure I'd find the two of them together at some point.'

'Did you?'

Sasagaki gave a long sigh. 'It took a long time. No matter which way you looked at it, they were complete strangers.'

'But something happened?'

'In their last year of middle school.' Sasagaki stuck a finger into his box of cigarettes to find it empty. Kazunari opened the crystal case of cigarettes on the table. It was filled to the brim. Sasagaki nodded in thanks and took one.

'Does this have anything to do with the attack on Yukiho's classmate?' Kazunari asked as he lit Sasagaki's cigarette for him.

The detective looked at him. 'You know about that?'

'I heard about it from Mr Imaeda.'

Kazunari told the detective what Imaeda had told him, about the middle-school rape, and Yukiho being the one who discovered the victim. He added his own experience when he was in college and mentioned that Imaeda had suspected the connection might be Yukiho.

'He was a good private eye, then. I'm surprised he went that deep. Yes, that was the incident in question. Of course, I was looking at it from a slightly different angle from Mr Imaeda. The perpetrator was never caught, you see, but there was a suspect – another kid in the same grade. Except, he had an alibi and was cleared of suspicion. The problem was who the suspect was and whose testimony gave him an alibi.' Sasagaki breathed out a stream of silky smoke. The cigarettes were much more expensive-tasting than the ones he smoked. 'The suspect's name was Fumihiko Kikuchi, the older brother of the kid who found the pawnbroker's body. And the person to give the testimony establishing his alibi was none other than Ryo Kirihara.'

Kazunari gaped.

'Curious, right?' Sasagaki said. 'I found it hard to brush off as mere coincidence.'

'But what does it mean?'

'Well, I only heard about the rape a year after it happened, from Fumihiko Kikuchi himself. I had followed up with the family concerning the previous case a few times, so I knew both of the Kikuchi brothers pretty well. It was on one of those visits when we got to talking and he brought it up.

'To sum it up, when the rape happened, Fumihiko had been watching a movie. He didn't have any proof at first, but then Ryo Kirihara came to his rescue. There was a small bookshop across the street from the movie theatre and Ryo said he had been there with another friend and just happened to see Fumihiko going into the theatre. The officer taking the testimony checked it out with a friend, too, and decided it was true.'

'So he was let go.'

'He was. Fumihiko thought he just got lucky. But then, a little while later, he got a call from Ryo telling him he'd better be grateful and not to think about doing anything rash.'

'What did he mean by that?'

'Fumihiko had recently come into possession of a certain photograph that he thought showed Ryo's mom and an employee at the pawnshop having an affair. He said he'd shown it to Ryo.'

'So the wife and the assistant were a thing?'

'Seems like it.' Sasagaki tapped off his ash into the ashtray. 'Ryo made Fumihiko give him the photograph and promise not to go sniffing around about his father's murder any more.'

'They made a deal?'

'So it seemed, but the more he thought about it, the less Fumihiko thought it was so simple. Which is why he told me about it.'

Sasagaki remembered the teenager's face, covered with pimples.

'What wasn't simple about it?'

'He started wondering if it hadn't all been a set-up.' The cigarette had burned short between Sasagaki's fingers but he took another drag. 'See, the reason Fumihiko was a suspect in the first place was they found a keychain that belonged to him at the scene of the crime. But according to him, he had never been there before and the keychain wasn't one that could have easily fallen off his bag.'

'So Ryo stole the keychain and left it at the scene?'

'That's what Fumihiko thought might have happened. Which would peg Ryo as our middle-school rapist. He could have spotted Fumihiko with his friend at the movie theatre, then gone straight to the scene and done the deed. Then all he had to do was plant the fake evidence.'

'But did Kirihara know that Fumihiko was going to go to the movies that day?' Kazunari asked the obvious question.

'That's the problem right there,' Sasagaki said, lifting a finger. 'Fumihiko says he never told Kirihara about his plans.'

'Then the set-up would have been impossible.'

'Agreed, and that's where Fumihiko's line of conjecture hit a dead end.' *But I still think he had something to do with it*, Fumihiko had told him, a chagrined look on his face.

'Still, it piqued my interest enough that I checked the records on the rape incident, which is when I found out about Yukiho's involvement. That sent me back to Fumihiko with a few more questions.'

'Like what?'

'Mostly about how he came to go to the movies that day. It turns out the tickets were a gift – Fumihiko's mother was working at a cake shop at the time and one of her customers gave them to her. But it gets better: the tickets were for *Rocky*, which Fumihiko had expressed interest in several times, and they were only good for that day. He would have to go to the movies that night, or miss his chance.'

Kazunari shook his head with disbelief. 'Did you find out who the customer was who gave her the tickets?'

'I didn't get a name. But Fumihiko remembered his mom telling him it was a girl, around the same age as him, well-dressed.'

'Yukiho.'

Sasagaki gave him a grim smile. 'If we assume that Yukiho and Ryo pinned the rape incident on Fumihiko to keep his mouth shut about Ryo's mother's affair, everything falls into place. Though the collateral damage – Miss Fujimura in this case – seems exceedingly cruel.'

'I agree it's cruel, but the choice of the Fujimura girl might not have been entirely random.'

Sasagaki raised an eyebrow. 'How so?'

'They may have had reason to target her – this is something Mr Imaeda told me.'

The private eye had told Kazunari that the girl who was attacked had been Yukiho's rival in class, but that following the incident she had become a subservient member of Yukiho's clique.

'I hadn't heard any of that,' Sasagaki said with a grimace. 'So they were killing two birds with one stone.' He looked up at Kazunari.

'I hate to even suggest this, but there's a possibility that what happened to your friend in college wasn't entirely coincidental either.'

'You think Yukiho planned that one too.'

'I wouldn't rule it out.'

'Neither did Mr Imaeda. But why?'

'Probably because she believed that rape was the surest way to break someone's spirit.'

Kazunari shook his head. 'That's really something to say about a person, even Yukiho.'

'I know. But if I'm right, this all leads us back to the motive in the murder of Ryo's father.'

Kazunari's eyes widened and he was about to say something when the phone on his desk began to ring. He swore under his breath and stood from his chair to get the phone. He answered the call in a hushed voice and quickly returned to the armchair. 'Sorry about that.'

'You OK for time?'

'Yes, fine. That wasn't a work call, actually. It was regarding an issue I've been looking into,' Kazunari said, then after a moment's hesitation, he added, 'When you came in, you congratulated me on my promotion. Actually, this is more like a demotion. Are you familiar with the pharmaceutical company Yunix?'

'I've heard the name.'

'Well, something very strange started happening last year. Our company and Yunix are competitors in several areas and it came to light that some internal information from Shinozuka Pharmaceuticals was leaking out to their teams.'

'How did you find out?'

'Someone inside Yunix informed us. Of course, the company denied everything.' A thin smile rose on Kazunari's face.

'I suppose these things happen in research,' the detective said. 'But how does that relate to you?'

'According to the informant, *I* was the one who leaked the information.'

Sasagaki's eyes widened. 'That doesn't sound very likely.'

'It shouldn't, because it didn't happen,' Kazunari replied, shaking his head. 'I had no idea what to make of it. Nor was the identity of the informant ever revealed. They only communicated via phone calls and mail. But the information leak was verifiable enough. When the guys in the lab saw the materials the informant sent them, they went blue in the face.'

'But you didn't leak that information.'

'Of course not. Unfortunately, someone has made it look like I did.'

'Any idea who?'

'No,' Kazunari replied immediately.

'I see. Still, getting demoted over something like that seems a little harsh.'

'The board members didn't believe it was me either. But the company had to take some kind of action. And there were some who thought that because the trap was clearly set for me, that was reason enough to move me out of headquarters before more damage was done.'

Sasagaki listened, dumbfounded.

'That, and one other thing,' Kazunari said. 'There's at least one board member who would prefer to keep me at a distance.'

Sasagaki raised an eyebrow.

'My cousin, Yasuharu.'

'Ah ...' Sasagaki said.

'It was a good chance for him to get the one naysayer to his marriage out of the picture. This assignment was supposed to be temporary – but one wonders how long they intend "temporary" to last.'

'And you're looking into this?'

A hard look came over Kazunari's face. 'I need to find out how the information leaked.'

'Have you found anything yet?'

'A little,' Kazunari replied. 'Whoever did it accessed our computers. We have a pretty advanced system, with both the network connecting computers internally and an external network allowing us to share data with other research facilities outside the company. That's how the hacker got into our system.'

This was already straining Sasagaki's understanding of computers but he listened attentively.

Kazunari smiled, noticing the look on the detective's face. 'It's really not that complicated. Basically, the hacker used a phone line to get on to one of our internal computers. So far, I've determined the access came through computers at the Imperial University Hospital. In other words, the hacker first accessed the pharmacy system at Imperial University, then went from there into our system. But it's been very difficult trying to figure out where he accessed the Imperial University system from.'

The name of the hospital sounded familiar to Sasagaki, but he couldn't place it at first, until he remembered his recent conversation with Eri Sugawara about how a client at Imaeda's office had been a pharmacist at the Imperial University Hospital.

'Would a pharmacist at the hospital have access to those computers?' he asked.

'Yes, they would all have access,' Kazunari explained. 'Except, even though our computers are connected to these external networks, not all of our information is available through those channels. There are some walls put up here and there in the system, to protect sensitive material from getting out. Which means that our criminal would have a considerable amount of know-how. A pro.'

'A professional hacker?' Something was tugging at the back of Sasagaki's mind. He knew at least one professional when it came to computers. He also wondered if there was a connection between whoever set a trap for Kazunari Shinozuka and the pharmacist from the Imperial University Hotel who had gone to Imaeda's office. But it could well be a coincidence.

'Is something wrong?' Kazunari asked, a suspicious look in his eyes.

'No,' Sasagaki said waving his hand. 'It's nothing.'

'I'm sorry, that phone call really took us off track,' Kazunari said, stretching in his seat. 'Please, go on with your story.'

'Right, where was I?'

'You were talking about motives,' Kazunari said.

'Ah, right,' Sasagaki said, sitting up straight and taking a deep breath.

Saturday afternoon was like an air pocket, a little bubble of tranquillity protected from the rest of the world. Mika was in her room listening to music and reading magazines as she always had before things changed. An empty teacup and a saucer with a bit of cookie left on it stood on the bedside table. Taeko had brought them in for her about twenty minutes earlier.

'I'm heading out for a bit, Mika,' Taeko had said. 'You're in charge.'

'You'll lock the door, right?'

'Of course.'

'Fine. Bring a key, 'cause I won't answer even if you ring,' Mika had said, snuggling under the covers of her bed and opening a fresh magazine.

Mika was all alone in the big house. Her father was out playing golf and Yukiho was at work. Masahiro had gone off to their grandparents' for the night. After her mother died, Mika was often left to her own devices at home. It felt lonely a bit at first but these days she preferred it to company, especially if it involved being around Yukiho.

She was just getting up to swap in a fresh CD when she heard the phone ring in the hallway. Mika frowned. She welcomed calls from her friends but she doubted this was one of those. There were three lines in the house: one for her father, one for Yukiho, and the last one was for everyone to use. She'd been asking her father for her own line for some time now but hadn't made much progress.

Mika went out into the hallway to pick up the cordless phone from its cradle on the wall. 'Shinozuka residence.'

'Hello? Is a Mika Shinozuka there?' It was a man's voice.

'Speaking,' she said.

'I have an overnight delivery here from a Miss Tomoko Hishikawa? Would it be all right to bring that by now?'

That's strange, Mika thought. The delivery people had never called in advance before, but then again, she'd never received an overnight delivery before. She didn't wonder long, however, as her excitement over the prospect of something from her friend Tomoko drove all concern out of her mind. She hadn't seen her since Tomoko's father got transferred last spring and the family had moved down to Nagoya.

'Sure,' she said. The delivery man told her he'd be right over.

Several minutes later the doorbell rang. Waiting in the living room, Mika picked up the intercom. The security camera showed a man dressed in a delivery uniform. He was carrying a box about the size of an orange crate.

'Yes?' she spoke into the intercom.

'Package for Miss Shinozuka?'

'Come in,' Mika said, pressing the button to undo the latch on the gate.

She went out to the entrance hall and opened the door. The man with the box was standing right outside.

'Er, where should I put this?' he asked. 'It's a little heavy.'

'Right here is fine,' Mika said, pointing down at the floor of the entrance hall.

The man put the box down. He was wearing dark glasses, and a hat with a brim that went low over his forehead. 'Can I get your signature here?' He handed her a pen and took out a small sheet of paper.

'Where do I sign?' she asked, leaning forward.

'Right here,' the man said, also taking a step forward.

Mika was about to put her pen to the paper when the slip suddenly disappeared.

'Huh?' she said as something soft pressed over her mouth. Mika gasped in surprise and felt the world slip away.

Time seemed to be slowing down and speeding up in fits and starts. There was a ringing in her ears but only when she was awake enough to hear it. She kept fading out, like a radio with bad reception. She couldn't move at all. Her arms and legs didn't feel like her own. Everything seemed dreamlike and unreal, except for the pain. That was real. It took her a while before she realised the pain was coming from a specific place inside her body. It was so strong her entire body felt numb with it.

There was a man immediately in front of her. She could see his face clearly. He was breathing on her. Hot, quick breaths.

I'm being raped.

Part of her understood this, yet another part of her felt as if she were watching the horror unfold from a great distance. And there was another part of herself, a higher level of consciousness, wondering why she was so spaced out, why she wasn't reacting.

Then fear such as she'd never known before gripped her in its clutches. It was the fear of falling into a deep hole, of not being sure what was at the bottom. The fear of not knowing how long this hell would go on.

She wasn't entirely sure when it ended. She'd fallen unconscious at some point.

It was her vision that came back first. She saw flowerpots in a line. Cactuses – the ones that Yukiho had brought from her home in Osaka.

Next her hearing returned. She heard a car somewhere nearby and the sound of the wind blowing. With a start, she realised she was outside, in the garden. She was lying on the grass. She could see the net that her father had set up for practising golf.

Mika sat up. She hurt all over. She was cut and bruised and there was another, dull pain near her lower belly. It felt like something had scooped out her insides. The air was cold on her skin. Only then did she realise she was mostly naked. What clothes remained on her had been torn to rags. Her other consciousness was still there too, coldly observing, upset that her favourite shirt had been ruined.

She was still wearing her skirt, but she didn't have to look to know that someone had taken off her panties. She looked into the distance and saw the reddening sky.

'Mika!' a voice called out. She turned her head slowly to see Yukiho running toward her. Mika stared, lost in a dream.

Nothing seemed real. Nothing at all.

*

Noriko struggled to open the front door. The plastic handles of the convenience-store bag were digging into her fingers with the weight of a big bottle of mineral water and bag of rice. She stopped herself from saying, 'I'm home.'

Noriko put her bag down in front of the fridge and opened the door to the back room. It was dark, the air still and cold. In the back corner, the white computer case seemed to float in the dim light. She missed the glow of the monitor, the slight whirr of the fans.

Noriko returned to the kitchen and started to put away her shopping: veggies in the fridge, frozen stuff in the freezer, everything else on the shelf. Before she closed the refrigerator door, she pulled out a can of beer.

Making her way to the living room, she turned on the television and switched on the electric heater. She picked up a throw rug that lay in a ball in the corner and draped it over her legs while she waited for the room to warm up. There was a game show on TV pitting various comedians against each other. The one with the worst score would be forced to bungee-jump off a bridge. It wasn't the kind of show she would have been caught dead watching before but now she found she liked them because they were so ridiculous. She already had enough to think about, sitting alone in her cold, empty apartment.

She pulled back the tab on the beer and drank, feeling the coolness flow from her throat to her belly. It gave her goosebumps and she shivered. It felt good. She kept a supply of beer in the fridge in the winter. He liked to drink beer most when it was cold. He said it kept him sharp. Noriko hugged her knees to her chest. *I should eat dinner,* she thought. *Nothing special.* She could just warm up the stuff she'd bought at the convenience store. But even that seemed like far too much trouble. Inertia was working against her. She didn't even feel hungry.

She turned up the volume. Too much quiet made the room feel colder. She edged a little closer to the heater.

I know what my problem is. I'm lonely.

She had loved being alone before, taking a break from the pressure of human contact. She'd even breathed a sigh of relief when she cancelled her contract with the matchmaking service. But now that she knew what it felt like to be with someone she loved she couldn't go back. It just wasn't the same. She took another swig of her beer and tried not to think about him, but when she closed her eyes, there he was, sitting at his computer.

Her beer was finished. She crushed the empty can between her hands and put it on the table next to two others just like it – one from yesterday, and one from the day before. She'd recently given up trying to keep the house clean.

I'll microwave something, she thought, *it's the least I can do.* She was just standing up when the doorbell rang.

She opened the door to see an older man standing outside in a rumpled coat. He had broad shoulders and a sharp look in his eyes. Noriko immediately guessed his line of work and a bad feeling began to form in the pit of her stomach.

'Noriko Kurihara?' the man asked. He had an Osaka accent.

'Yes?'

'The name's Sasagaki.' He held out a business card, blank except for a phone number and his name. 'I was a detective with Osaka police until last spring.'

Noriko nodded, unsurprised.

'I was hoping I could ask you some questions, if you don't mind?'

'Right now?'

'If you don't mind. Maybe at the café down the street?'

Noriko frowned. She didn't feel like going out, but she didn't relish the idea of inviting a stranger in, either. 'Can I ask what this is about?' she asked.

'A few things, including your visit to the Imaeda Detective Agency.'

Noriko gasped.

'So you did go to Mr Imaeda's office in Shinjuku? That's the first thing I wanted to check on,' the former detective said with a pleasant smile.

Her unease began to spread, but it came with a glimmer of hope. Maybe this man would know where Akiyoshi had gone. She hesitated for a few more seconds before opening the door wider. 'Why don't you just come in?'

'You're sure?'

'It's fine. Pardon the mess.'

The detective stepped in. He had an old man smell to him.

Noriko had gone to the Imaeda Detective Agency in September, roughly two weeks after Akiyoshi suddenly vanished from her life. There hadn't been an accident, she knew that. He'd left his set of keys in an envelope in the mailbox. He'd also left most of his things behind, not that there was much to begin with.

The largest of his possessions was the computer, but Noriko had no idea how to use it. After debating with herself for some time, she finally invited over a journalist friend who was good with computers and had her check to see if there was anything on it. She found nothing. According to her, the hard drive had been wiped completely clean and all the floppy disks were blank.

Noriko racked her brains, trying to think of some way she could find out where Akiyoshi might have gone. The only thing she could remember was the empty file she had found in his duffel bag that night, the one with the name of the Imaeda Detective Agency on it. She looked in the phone book and found it right away. Noriko paid a visit to Shinjuku the following day.

Except the agency had been a dead end. The young woman there had told her there was no record of anyone named Akiyoshi, either as a client or a case. Which made the former detective finding her through the agency very curious indeed.

Sasagaki seemed a little surprised to hear that she had gone to check after a man who had been living with her and suddenly disappeared.

'It's odd that he'd have an empty file from the agency like that,' Sasagaki said when she finished explaining. 'And you have no idea where he might have gone? Did you contact his friends and family?'

She shook her head. 'I couldn't. I don't know any of them. I don't really know anything about him.'

'Interesting,' Sasagaki said, looking a little taken aback.

'Um, can I ask what you're investigating, Mr Sasagaki?'

He hesitated for a moment then said, 'This may come as a surprise to you, but Mr Imaeda has also gone missing.'

'What?'

'Yes. It's a bit of a long story. I've been trying to find out where he went, and haven't had any luck. Which is why I'm here, grasping at straws as it were.'

'I see. When did Mr Imaeda go missing?'

'Last summer, August.'

Noriko thought back and almost gasped out loud. That was right around the time that Akiyoshi had gone out for a night, taking the cyanide with him – the same night he'd come back with the empty file from the Imaeda Detective Agency.

'Something wrong?' the former detective asked, his eyes squinting.

'No, it's nothing.' Noriko shook her head.

'Incidentally,' Sasagaki said, pulling out a photograph, 'have you ever seen this man?'

Noriko took the photograph and nearly shouted out loud. He looked younger than when she had met him, but it was Yuichi Akiyoshi, without a doubt.

'Well?' Sasagaki asked.

Noriko tried hard to keep her heart from beating out of her chest. Her mind was racing. Should she tell the truth? Why would a former detective be walking around with his picture? Was Akiyoshi a suspect in some crime? Had he killed Imaeda? No …

'I'm sorry, I don't know him,' she said, returning the photo. Her fingertips were trembling and she could feel that her cheeks were red.

Sasagaki stared at her face for a long moment, looking through her. Noriko turned her head away.

'I see. That's unfortunate,' Sasagaki said softly, putting away the photograph. 'I suppose I should leave.' He stood. 'Actually,' he said after a moment, 'I wonder if you could show me anything that belonged to Mr Akiyoshi, anything that might help me find him?'

'What do you mean?'

'Something he left behind, if you don't mind?'

'No, not at all.'

Noriko showed Sasagaki into the back room where Akiyoshi's computer was still sitting.

'This was his computer?'

'Yes. He was using it to write a novel.'

'A novel?' Sasagaki said, looking over the computer and the desk. 'You don't have any photographs of him, do you?'

'No, I'm sorry. I don't.'

'Even a small one is fine. All I have to see is his face.'

'No, I really don't have a single photo. I never took one.'

It was the truth. Noriko had wanted to take a photo together several times but Akiyoshi always refused – another reason she had nothing left to remember him by.

Sasagaki nodded, but seemed clearly suspicious. Noriko swallowed.

'Would you have anything he wrote by hand? A memo, or journal?'

'I don't think so. If he had anything like that, he didn't leave it.'

'I see,' Sasagaki said, taking another look around the room. Then he smiled at Noriko. 'Right. Sorry to bother you.'

'I'm sorry I couldn't be of more help.'

As Sasagaki was putting his shoes on, Noriko stood, torn by indecision. The detective knew something about Akiyoshi and she wanted to know what it was. But if she told him who it really was in that photo he'd shown her, she worried she might be signing Akiyoshi's ticket to prison herself. Even if she never saw him again, she didn't want that for him.

Sasagaki finished putting on his shoes and looked up at her. 'Thank you for your time,' he said.

'Not at all,' Noriko said, her throat a little choked.

Just then Sasagaki's eyes looked back out at the room behind her, fixing on something. 'What's that?' He was pointing at a small shelf beside the refrigerator. 'Is that a photo album there?' he asked.

'Oh, that?' She looked back at the small plastic album sitting on the shelf. It was a cheap thing they had given her at the camera shop, free with her developed pictures.

'There's nothing in there,' she said. 'It's from when I went to Osaka last year.'

'Osaka?' Sasagaki said, his expression perking up. 'You mind if I take a look?'

'Oh, go right ahead, but there aren't any pictures of people,' she added, handing him the album.

All of the photos were ones Noriko had taken by herself on her trip to Osaka: strange buildings and houses, nothing interesting. She'd felt mischievous taking them and had never shown them to anyone, not even Akiyoshi.

The photos got a clear reaction from Sasagaki. His eyes went wide and his mouth hung halfway open.

'Is there something there?' Noriko asked, half afraid there might have been a photo of Akiyoshi in there that she'd somehow missed.

Sasagaki didn't answer right away but continued looking at the photos. Then he turned the album towards her, opened to a certain page.

'Why did you take a picture of this pawnshop?'

'Oh, I don't know. No particular reason.'

'And this building here. Any reason you thought to take a picture of that?'

'Why do you ask?' she asked, her voice trembling.

Sasagaki reached into his jacket pocket and pulled out the photograph from before, the one of Akiyoshi. 'Let me tell you something. The sign on your photo here reads "Kirihara Pawnshop", right? Well, that's this man's real name: Ryo Kirihara.'

Mika's toes and fingertips felt as cold as ice, and they weren't getting any warmer, no matter how long she stayed in bed. Mika buried her head under the pillows and curled up like a cat. Her teeth were chattering; her whole body was trembling.

She closed her eyes and tried to sleep. But as soon as she began slipping away there he was, the man without a face, attacking her. Her eyes shot open in fright. A cold sweat drenched her body and her heart beat so fast she was afraid it would burst.

She wondered how many hours she'd been lying here. She wondered if she would ever sleep again. She didn't want to believe that what had happened that day was real. She wanted it to be a normal day like the day before, or the day before that. But it wasn't a dream. And the pain in her lower abdomen was proof of that.

Leave everything to me. You don't have to think about anything, Mika. She could still hear Yukiho's voice ringing in her ear.

Mika couldn't remember where Yukiho had appeared from. She didn't even remember what she had told her. She probably hadn't said anything. But somehow Yukiho had understood and known exactly what to do. She had Mika dressed in moments and then they were riding in the BMW. Yukiho was making a phone call while she drove but Mika couldn't understand what she was saying, either because she was speaking too fast or Mika's brain was moving too slowly. The only thing she remembered was Yukiho repeatedly demanding that this 'be kept an absolute secret'.

Yukiho took her inside the hospital, not through the front door, but in through the back. Mika didn't think to wonder why at the time. Mika didn't think about much of anything.

She wasn't sure afterwards if they had examined her, or done anything to her. She just lay on her side, her eyes tightly closed.

An hour later they were driving home.

'The doctor says you're fine. You don't have to worry about anything,' Yukiho said gently as she drove. Mika couldn't remember how she had replied, or even if she had replied at all.

Yukiho never mentioned telling the police. She didn't even ask Mika for any details. The details weren't important to her, it seemed. Mika was grateful for that. She didn't feel as if she could talk about it and she was terrified that other people might find out.

At home, she saw her father's car in the car park and her heart stopped. What would she tell him?

'Tell your father you felt like you were coming down with a cold so I took you to the doctor,' Yukiho told her, as though lying to her father was no big deal. Maybe, given the previous events of the day, it really wasn't. 'I'll have Taeko bring you your dinner in bed.'

That was when Mika realised that what had happened could be – no, *would* be – their secret. A secret she'd share with the woman she hated most in the entire world.

Yukiho's performance in front of her father was brilliant. No sooner did she mention the hospital trip than she defused Yasuharu's worried look by telling him, 'Don't worry, we got some medicine.' He didn't seem suspicious about Mika's unusual gloom either. On the contrary, he seemed almost pleased that she had relented enough to permit her arch-enemy take care of her.

That night, Mika stayed in her room. Taeko brought her dinner as promised and Mika feigned sleep while she laid the food out on the side table. After Taeko left, she tried a little bit of the soup and the casserole, but it only nauseated her. After that, she just lay in bed, curled into a ball.

As the night grew deeper, her fear grew worse. All the lights in the room were out. She was scared to be in the darkness, but she was more scared for her body to be revealed by the light. She felt like someone was watching her. She wanted to live under a little rock, like a minnow in the sea.

She wondered what time it was and how much pain she would have to endure until the sun rose. She wondered if every night would be like this, and the anxiety pressed down on her like a weight. She bit her thumb.

Just then, she heard the click of the doorknob turn.

Mika froze, looking out at the door from under her covers. Through the darkness she saw it swing slowly open. Someone was coming into the room. She saw the hem of a silvery gown drift across the floor.

'Who is it?' Mika asked in a hushed, hoarse voice.

'I thought you might be up,' Yukiho replied.

Mika turned away. She didn't know how to act towards this person, the only other person who knew her secret.

She heard Yukiho step closer. Mika glanced at her out of the corner of her eye. She was standing by the foot of her bed.

'Get out,' Mika said. 'Leave me alone.'

Yukiho didn't answer. Wordlessly, she undid the cords on her gown. The silvery fabric dropped to the ground, revealing her white, naked body.

Before Mika could say anything, Yukiho crawled under the covers with her. Mika tried to escape, but Yukiho pressed her down. She was far stronger than she looked.

On top of the bed, she pushed Mika's legs apart and pressed down on her. Her large breasts swayed over Mika's chest.

'Stop,' Mika croaked.

'Did he do this to you?' Yukiho asked. 'Did he push down on you like this?'

Mika looked away. She felt Yukiho's fingers pressing into her cheeks, twisting her head back.

'Don't look away. Look here, into my face.'

Her mind screaming with fear, Mika looked at Yukiho. The large eyes staring down at her. The face was so close she could feel the warmth of her breath.

'You remember what he did when you try to sleep, don't you.' Yukiho said. 'You're scared to close your eyes, scared to dream. Aren't you.'

Mika nodded.

'I want you to look at my face. If you ever feel like you might remember the man, I want you to think of me instead. I want you to remember me doing *this*.' Yukiho straddled Mika's body, pressing her shoulders down into the bed until Mika couldn't budge an inch. 'Or would you rather see his face than mine?'

Mika shook her head.

Yukiho smiled. 'I thought not. It's OK. You'll be fine before you know it. I'll protect you.' Yukiho cupped her hands around Mika's cheeks. She moved her palms, rubbing, as if she enjoyed the feel of her skin. 'It happened to me too, you know. Only worse.'

Mika was so surprised she almost shouted. Yukiho put a finger to her lips. 'I was younger than you are now. Still just a child. But sometimes, demons come for children too. Many, many demons.'

'No ...' Mika whispered.

'When I look at you now, I see me then.' Yukiho lowered herself until she was lying on top of Mika, her warmth pressed against her, her hands cradling Mika's head. 'And it's sad. So sad.'

Then, Mika felt something twitch deep inside her, as though a nerve that had lain severed until now had suddenly been reconnected. Through that nerve, sadness came welling up from her heart like a flood. She began to cry like a baby in Yukiho's embrace.

It was on a Sunday midway through December when Sasagaki got in a car with Kazunari to pay a visit to his cousin Yasuharu. Sasagaki had come back up to Tokyo from Osaka for the occasion.

'Are you sure he'll see us?' Sasagaki asked in the car.

'I don't think he'll kick us out on the street, if that's what you're asking.'

'If he's even home.'

'No worries on that count. I get good intel from my informant.'

'Your informant?'

'The maid.'

It was a little after two in the afternoon when Kazunari's Mercedes pulled into the parking spot to the side of the guest gate.

'It's hard to tell exactly how big the house is from the outside of these places,' Sasagaki said, peering over the gate. Beyond the high walls, all he could see were trees.

Kazunari pressed the intercom button next to the gate. The answer came immediately.

'Hello, Kazunari. Good to see you,' said the voice of a middle-aged woman. She must be looking at them over a security camera.

'Hello, Taeko. Is Yasuharu in?'

'He's here. Just a moment.'

A couple of minutes later, her voice crackled over the speaker again. 'He says go around to the garden.'

'Right.'

There was a clicking sound from the gate as the lock opened.

Sasagaki followed Kazunari through. The long approach to the house was lined with cobblestones. Sasagaki felt as though he had stepped into an old Hollywood movie.

Two women were just walking out of the front of the house. Sasagaki knew who they were without Kazunari having to tell him: Yasuharu Shinozuka's daughter, Mika, and next to her, Yukiho.

'How do you want to play this?' Kazunari asked quietly.

'Just tell them anything you need to about me,' Sasagaki said.

They walked up the path slowly. The four of them stopped where they met on the path halfway to the house. Yukiho smiled and nodded to them.

'Hello,' Kazunari spoke first.

'Long time no see, Kazunari. How have you been?' Yukiho asked.

'Can't complain. You look well.'

She smiled and nodded again.

'Your shop in Osaka's opening soon, right? How's that going?'

'Not very well, but these things never do. I only wish there were a few more of me to go around. I'm heading to a meeting about that right now, in fact.'

'Well, I wish you the best of luck,' Kazunari said, turning to the girl. 'How have you been, Mika?'

The girl smiled and nodded. She seemed a bit withdrawn to Sasagaki. He'd heard from Kazunari that she didn't get along with Yukiho, but from what he could see there was no sign of that here.

'And I thought it might be a good chance to pick up something for Mika for Christmas,' Yukiho said.

'An excellent idea,' Kazunari agreed.

'Is this your friend?' Yukiho asked, her eyes turning to Sasagaki.

'Oh, sorry, this is Mr Sasaki. He's been helping us at the company for years,' Kazunari said without hesitation.

Sasagaki bowed and said, 'Hello.' When he looked back up, his eyes met with Yukiho's.

Sasagaki had seen her as an adult several times, but never face-to-face like this, not since that run-down apartment in Osaka. He could still see that little girl in the woman before him. She had the same eyes.

Remember me, Yukiho Nishimoto? I've been following you for nine-teen years, so much that I see you in my dreams. But I doubt you remember an old man like me. Just another one of your many, many fools.

Yukiho smiled. 'Are you from Osaka?'

'Indeed,' he said, a little flustered.

'I thought so. My new shop is opening in Shinsaibashi. You have to come visit.'

She pulled a postcard out of her bag, an invitation to the opening.

'Oh, thanks,' Sasagaki said. 'I'll make sure one of my relatives down there gets this.'

'It was your accent,' Yukiho explained, looking the old detective in the eyes. 'It's funny how little things can bring back so many memories.' Her lips parted in a smile. 'If you're looking for Yasuharu, he's in the garden,' she said to Kazunari. 'He wasn't satisfied with his scores on the course today, so practise, practise.'

'We'll try not to take up too much of his time.'

'Please make yourself at home,' Yukiho said, and with a nod to Mika the two set off. Sasagaki and Kazunari stood off to the side of the path until they had passed. Sasagaki watched her go, thinking maybe she did remember him after all.

They found Yasuharu in the garden hitting golf balls. When Kazunari walked over he put down his club and smiled – no trace of any guilt on his face over having sent his cousin to languish at a subsidiary.

But when Kazunari introduced Sasagaki, a wary look came into Yasuharu's eyes. 'A former detective from Osaka? OK,' he said, staring at the new arrival.

'He has something I need you to hear,' Kazunari said.

The smile faded entirely from Yasuharu's face. 'Let's talk inside.'

'No, here is fine. It's warm today, and we'll be leaving soon.'

'Really?' Yasuharu looked between their faces. 'Fine. I'll have Taeko bring us something.'

A white table with four chairs was in the garden, a place for the family to enjoy afternoon tea in the British style on the warmer days. The maid brought milk tea, and they sat to drink.

The mood couldn't have been farther from a pleasant afternoon tea. As soon as Kazunari started talking, Yasuharu's mouth twisted into a scowl where it stayed while he, together with Sasagaki, began telling the story of Yukiho Nishimoto. They told it all, every little event they had managed to piece together. Ryo's name came up several times.

Halfway through, Yasuharu slammed the table with his hands and stood. 'Ridiculous,' he scoffed. 'I wondered what you were going to say, but this – this takes the cake, Kazunari.'

'Please, hear us out.'

'I've heard more than enough. Look, if you've got so much free time on your hands that you're going digging for dirt that isn't there, why don't you spend it trying to fix that company of yours.'

'Actually, I have information about that, too,' Kazunari said to Yasuharu's turned back. He stood. 'I know who set the trap for me.'

Yasuharu looked around, a twisted smile on his face. 'Don't tell me Yukiho did that too?'

'You heard about the hacker that accessed the Shinozuka Pharmaceuticals network? It turns out that the hacker used a computer at the Imperial University Hospital to do it. And one of the pharmacists there was living with none other than Ryo Kirihara.'

Yasuharu's eyes opened a little wider at this. Then he said something the old detective didn't quite catch, but it sounded like 'so what'.

Sasagaki pulled a photograph out of his coat pocket. 'Would you mind taking a look at this?'

'What's this? A building?'

'This is the pawnshop where the murder happened twenty years ago in Osaka. The pharmacist took this picture when she went to Osaka with Ryo Kirihara.'

'And?'

'I asked when she made that trip. They went for three days, from eighteenth September of last year through to the twentieth. I believe those dates should be significant to you as well.'

It took Yasuharu a moment to remember, but he did. His light gasp indicated that.

'That's right,' Sasagaki said. 'On nineteenth September Reiko

Karasawa passed away. The hospital was at a loss to explain why her breathing suddenly stopped. This provides one possible explanation ...'

'Ridiculous,' Yasuharu said, tossing the photograph aside. 'Kazunari, I want you to take this crazy old man and leave. Pull something like this again and you'll never come back to our company, ever. You'd do well to remember that your father isn't on the board any more.'

He picked up a golf ball lying on the ground by his feet and flung it at the net. It hit one of the metal poles supporting the net and ricocheted back towards the house, where it struck a potted plant out on the terrace. There was a cracking noise like something had broken. Yasuharu didn't even look. Stepping up on to the terrace, he opened the sliding glass doors and went inside.

Kazunari sighed. He glanced at Sasagaki and chuckled dryly. 'That went well.'

'He's quite taken with the woman. That's her greatest weapon.'

'He's too angry to think straight right now, but once he cools down, the things we said will start to make sense to him. We'll just have to wait.'

'If that time ever comes.'

The two had turned to leave when Taeko came running out to see them. 'What happened? I heard a loud noise.'

Kazunari shrugged. 'Yasuharu threw a golf ball and I think it hit something.'

'Was anyone hurt?'

'Just a potted plant. No human casualties.'

The housemaid turned to inspect the plants on the terrace.

'My, it's one of her cactuses.'

'Yukiho's cactuses?'

'She brought them from Osaka. Dear me, the pot's completely destroyed.'

Kazunari went over to Taeko.

'Does she have a thing for raising cactuses or something?'

'No, I believe they belonged to her late mother.'

'Oh, right. She did say something about that at the funeral.'

Kazunari had stepped away when he heard the maid say 'What's this?' behind him. He turned to see her reach into the broken pot and pull something out.

'Look what I found,' she said.

Kazunari examined the contents of the woman's hand. 'Looks like a piece of glass.'

'It was near the bottom of the pot. It must have been mixed in with the dirt,' she said, shaking her head and placing the glass on top of the pieces of broken pot.

'What's going on?' Sasagaki said, coming over to see.

'Nothing much. There was a piece of glass inside the pot that broke.' Kazunari pointed to the broken cactus pot.

Sasagaki looked, his eyes falling on the slightly curved piece of glass. It looked like a lens from a pair of sunglasses. It was broken midway across. He picked it up carefully. A moment later he felt his blood stir. Memories came flooding back, tangled in his mind. Gradually, they resolved into a clear picture.

'You said she brought these cactuses from Osaka?' he asked in a hushed voice.

'That's right. They were at her mother's home.'

'In the garden?'

'That's right. She had them lined up by the side of the house. Is something wrong?' Kazunari asked, noticing the old detective's unusual behaviour.

'Maybe,' Sasagaki said, holding the broken lens up to the sky. It had a faint greenish tint to it.

It was nearly eleven at night and they'd been preparing for the opening of R&Y Osaka all day. Natsumi followed along behind Yukiho, making a complete circuit of the shop for a final check. Both in floor space and inventory the shop was considerably larger than its counterparts in Tokyo. They had pushed their PR campaign to its limits and beyond. Now all they had to do was wait.

'Well, I think we're ninety-nine per cent of the way there,' Yukiho said after they had finished.

'Only ninety-nine?' Natsumi asked. 'You mean it's not perfect?'

'No, but that will give us something to strive for tomorrow,' Yukiho said with a smile. 'Time to rest our weary bones. We should both go light on the drinking tonight.'

'The celebration's tomorrow, right.'

'Absolutely.'

It was already half past eleven when the two of them got into the red Jaguar.

Yukiho sat in the passenger seat, taking a deep breath. 'All we can do is our best. I, for one, am sure you'll be great.'

'I hope so,' Natsumi said, a little worried. She would be directly in charge of running the Osaka store.

'Be confident. You're number one. Got it?' She gave Natsumi's shoulder a shake.

'Got it,' Natsumi said, looking over at the other woman. 'But, to be honest, I'm scared. I'm not sure I can do it like you do it, boss. Aren't you ever frightened?'

Yukiho turned and looked at her directly. 'Natsumi? You know how the sun rises and sets at a certain time each day? In the same way, all of our lives have a day and night. But it's not set like it is with the sun. Some people walk forever in the sunlight, and some people have to walk through the darkest night their whole lives. When people talk about being afraid, what they're afraid of is that their sun will set. That the light they love will fade. That's why you're frightened, isn't it?'

Natsumi thought she understood. She nodded.

'You know,' Yukiho continued, 'I've never lived in the sunlight.'

'Hardly,' Natsumi said with a laugh. 'Boss, as far as I'm concerned, you *are* the sun.'

Yukiho shook her head. There was an earnest look in her eyes that wiped the smile off Natsumi's face.

'No, there never was a sun in the sky over me. It's always night. But not dark. I had something in place of the sun. Maybe not as bright, but enough for me. Enough so I was able to live in the night like it was day. You understand? You can't be afraid of losing something you never had.'

'So what did you have in place of the sun?'

'It's hard to describe. Maybe you'll understand someday,' Yukiho said. Turning her eyes back on the road. 'Let's go.'

Natsumi turned the key.

Yukiho was staying at the Sky Osaka Hotel in Yodoyabashi. Natsumi was already renting an apartment in North Tenma.

'The night's just getting started down here, isn't it,' Yukiho said, looking out of the window.

'There's certainly no lack of nightclubs in town, that's for sure. I used to go out a lot back in the day.' Natsumi said, and heard Yukiho chuckle in the seat beside her. 'What?'

'I heard you slipping back into the local accent,' she said.

'Oh, I'm sorry, it's just—'

'No, it's fine. You're in Osaka; you should talk like a local. I should probably switch back myself when I'm in town.'

'I think it would suit you, honestly.'

'Really?' Yukiho said with a smile.

She let Yukiho off in front of the entrance to the hotel.

'See you tomorrow, boss.'

'Sure thing. If anything comes up tonight, don't hesitate to give me a call.'

'It won't, but I will.'

'Natsumi?' Yukiho extended her right hand. 'Let's do this thing right,' she said, her voice a perfect Osaka drawl.

Natsumi shook her hand and smiled.

The hands on the clock had just passed midnight and Yaeko Kirihara decided it was time to close up when she heard the squeaking of the old wooden door opening and an older man in a dark grey coat stepped in.

When she saw who it was, the forced smile faded from her face and she gave a little sigh.

'Well, if it isn't Mr Sasagaki. Here I was thinking it was the God of Fortune come to give me a very belated blessing.'

'Don't say that,' Sasagaki replied. 'You know I'm your lucky charm.'

Sasagaki hung his scarf and coat on the wall and sat down at the counter. He was wearing a rumpled brown suit under his coat. He might not be a detective any more, but he still dressed the part.

Yaeko put a glass on the counter in front of him, opened a large bottle of beer and poured. It was all he ever drank at her shop.

Sasagaki took a sip, savouring it, and had a bite of the simple appetiser Yaeko put out for him.

'How's business? Getting to be time for those year-end parties, I should think.'

'Business is just what you see. The bubble burst here years ago. Not that I ever saw any bubble.'

Yaeko took down a glass for herself and poured. She drank down half in one gulp.

'I see the years haven't slowed you down at all,' Sasagaki said, reaching out for the bottle. He filled her glass to the top.

Yaeko nodded thanks. 'It's all I got.'

'How many years have you been running this place again?'

'Too long,' she said, counting on her fingers. 'Fourteen, I guess. Yeah, fourteen years this February.'

'That's a nice long run. Sounds like you found your calling after all.'

That made her laugh. 'Maybe so. The café I ran before this only lasted three.'

'Not helping with the pawnshop at all?'

'No. I hated that work. It was never a good fit for me.'

And still she had been married to a pawnbroker for almost thirteen years. That was the biggest mistake in her life, she had decided. She should have kept working at that bar in North Shinchi. She'd probably be the owner by now if she had, and business was always hopping there.

After her husband was killed, Matsuura ran the store for a while. But pretty soon there was a family meeting and the shop was entrusted to Yosuke's cousin. The Kirihara family had been in the pawnshop business for generations and a few of their relatives ran shops under the same name in different parts of town. Just because

Yosuke had died didn't mean his widow could do whatever she wanted with the store.

Matsuura soon quit. According to her cousin-in-law, he'd taken quite a bit of the shop's cash with him when he left, but she never heard any hard figures. In all honesty, she couldn't have cared less. She left the house and the shop to her in-laws and with the money they gave her opened a café in Uehonmachi. She hadn't known until then that Yosuke had never even owned the land the pawnshop had been built on; they'd been leasing it from his older brother.

Things went fine right after her café opened but about six months later the customers dropped off until they hardly came at all. She was never sure exactly why. She tried offering new menus, and redecorating, but nothing seemed to work. Soon she had to cut staff, which meant the service got slower, which meant even fewer people came.

The café closed without making it even for three years. She always took it as a personal affront that the *Space Invaders* boom had come along right after she left, sending young kids in droves to neighbourhood cafés.

She had managed to land on her feet, though. One of her friends from her old hostessing days got in touch with her to tell her about a shop in Tennoji that was up for sale. The terms were good and she jumped on it immediately. That was her current bar and she had managed to keep it afloat. When she thought about what she would have done without it, it gave her goosebumps.

'How about your son? Still no word?' Sasagaki asked.

Yaeko smiled faintly and shook her head. 'I gave up on Ryo a long time ago.'

'How old would he be these days? About thirty?'

'Something like that. To tell you the truth, I don't really remember.'

Sasagaki had started showing up every once in a while, from around the fourth year after she started the bar. She knew he had been the lead investigator in her husband's murder, but he rarely talked about that. He never failed, however, to mention Ryo.

Ryo had lived with her in-laws through middle school. It was a boon to her, busy as she was starting her café, that she didn't have to take care of a kid at the same time.

Around the time that she started her current bar, Ryo left the Kiriharas and came to live with her. It didn't mean much, however, she was soon to discover. She was always up late with the customers, after which she would sleep deeply, only waking up some time in the afternoon, after which she'd eat a simple meal, get in the bath, put on her face, and start opening the shop. Not once did she make breakfast for her son, and dinner was usually something from the bar. They barely saw each other for more than an hour a day, if that.

Ryo started spending more and more nights out. When she would ask where he was staying, he only gave vague replies. But she never heard anything from the school or the police, so she didn't pay it too much mind. She was too tired just getting through each day to worry about him.

On the morning of his high school graduation Ryo got ready for the day just like any other. Yaeko was awake that day, still in her futon. Normally he left without saying a word, but that day he stopped in the doorway and looked around. 'I'm leaving, Mom.'

'Yep, see you later,' she said, half asleep.

It was the last time they spoke. It was only several hours later that Yaeko found the note on her dresser that read, *I'm not coming back*. True to his word, Ryo never returned.

If she had wanted to, she might have been able to track him down, but she never really tried. She was lonely, true, but she felt like it was inevitable. She'd never been a real mother to him. And he'd certainly never thought of her as a mother.

Yaeko was fairly sure she had lacked any kind of motherly instinct from the very beginning. She gave birth not because she wanted a child, but because there wasn't any good reason to get an abortion. She had got married to Yosuke in much the same way – because she thought it would save her from having to work. Yet the role of wife and mother had been far more confining in its tedium than she had imagined. She didn't want to be either of those things. She wanted to be a woman.

About three months after Ryo left, she got into a serious relationship with a man in the import trade. He took away her loneliness. He let her be the woman she wanted to be.

They lived together for two years. When the split came, it was because he had to return to his other family. He was married, with a house in Sakai City to the south.

She saw other men after that but broke up with them. Now she was alone. It was easier this way, except for the lonely times. On those nights she would think of Ryo, except she forbade herself to want to see him. She knew she didn't have the right.

Sasagaki put a Seven Stars in his mouth. Yaeko quickly produced a disposable lighter and lit it.

'You know how many years it's been since your husband was killed?' Sasagaki asked, blowing out a stream of smoke.

'About twenty, I guess.'

'Nineteen to be exact. That's quite some time.'

'It is. I'm an old woman, and you're retired.'

'I was wondering if you might have anything you wanted to say, given how long ago it was.'

'What do you mean?'

'Something you couldn't say back then, but you could say now.'

A faint smile came to Yaeko's lips and she took a cigarette of her own. Lighting it, she blew smoke towards the dark stained ceiling.

'Still the same, after all these years. I'm not hiding a thing, detective.'

'Oh? That's funny, because there're so many things that don't quite match up.'

'You're still on that case? You have the patience of a saint,' Yaeko said, leaning on the shelves behind her, cigarette between her fingers. The faint sound of music drifted in from somewhere.

'The day it happened, you said you were at the shop with Matsuura and Ryo. Was that the truth?'

'It was,' Yaeko said, flicking ash into her ashtray. 'I thought you already looked into that one.'

'I did. But the only testimony I was able to really corroborate was Matsuura's alibi.'

'You mean to say that I killed him?' Yaeko blew smoke from her nose.

'No, I think you were there too. What I suspect is that there weren't three of you there. It was just you and Matsuura. Right?'

'What are you getting at, detective?'

'You and Matsuura had a thing,' Sasagaki said, draining his glass. Yaeko tried to fill it again, but he stopped her and filled it himself. 'You don't have to hide that any more, it was so long ago. Nobody cares but me.'

'Why do you care?'

'I just want to know what happened. Right around when your husband was murdered, someone came to your shop and found the door locked. Matsuura says he was back in the storeroom, and you were watching television with Ryo. But that's not the truth, is it. The truth is, you were in the back, in bed with Matsuura.'

'Maybe.'

'I'll call that a yes,' Sasagaki said, grinning a little as he drank.

Yaeko sucked harder on her cigarette. She watched the smoke hang in the air and let her mind wander.

She hadn't ever really loved Matsuura. It was just something to break the monotony. She had begun to get worried at one point that she might stop being a woman altogether. Which was why she'd readily agreed when Matsuura came on to her.

'And your son was on the floor above?' Sasagaki asked.

'What?'

'Ryo. You and Matsuura were in the back. He was on the floor above, right? That's why you locked the door upstairs, so he wouldn't barge in on you?'

'The lock?' Yaeko said vacantly, then she nodded. 'Oh, right. There was a lock on those stairs. You really are a detective, aren't you? Good memory.'

'So, Ryo was upstairs. But in order to hide your thing with Matsuura, you said he was with you. Right?'

'If that's what you want to think happened, then fine. What do I care?' She stubbed out her cigarette. 'Shall I open another bottle?'

'By all means.' Sasagaki drank the fresh beer with some peanuts. Yaeko joined him. For a while, the two drank in silence.

Yaeko's mind was tracing back across the years. It was just as Sasagaki said. The day it happened, she and Matsuura were right in the middle of it. Ryo was upstairs. The door at the bottom of the staircase was locked.

It had been Matsuura's idea to tell the police that Ryo was with them when they came asking after their alibis. He said that would head them off before they got their noses in any place they shouldn't be. They agreed to say that Yaeko had been watching television with Ryo – a science fiction show for kids. Ryo had a magazine he was reading that explained all about the show, which Yaeko read, just in case the detectives asked her about it.

'I wonder what's going to happen to Miyazaki?' Sasagaki said abruptly.

'Sorry? Miyazaki?'

'Tsutomu Miyazaki.'

'Oh.'

Yaeko brushed back her long hair. She felt some clinging to her hand and looked to see one white hair caught around her middle finger. She brushed it off on to the floor so that Sasagaki wouldn't see. 'They'll give him the death penalty, won't they?'

'I read an article about the case a few days ago in the newspaper. They say his grandpa died three months before he did what he did. Apparently, that's what broke him.'

'I'm not sure that excuses murder,' Yaeko said, lighting a new cigarette.

Between 1988 and 1989, a serial killer had abducted and killed four young girls in Tokyo and Saitama prefecture. It was all over the news. The defence was trying to plead insanity, but Yaeko was pretty sure that wouldn't hold.

'I wish you'd told me sooner,' Sasagaki muttered.

'Told you about what?'

'About your late husband's predilections.'

'Oh,' Yaeko said, trying to smile, but only succeeding in making her face go tense in a weird way.

So that's why he brought up Miyazaki.

'What good would that have done you?' she asked.

'What good? If I'd heard about that at the time of the investigation, it would have turned things around completely.'

'You don't say,' Yaeko said, blowing out smoke. 'Well, that's too bad, I guess.'

'Not that you could've said anything at the time.'

'No, I couldn't have.'

'Yeah.' Sasagaki said, putting a hand to his forehead. 'And now here we are, nineteen years later.'

Yaeko wanted to ask him what he meant, but she held back. Whatever the detective was thinking deep down inside, she didn't want to know.

Another silence followed. They had got the second bottle of beer down to about one third full when Sasagaki stood. 'Guess I'll be heading home.'

'Thanks for coming out in the cold. Don't be a stranger.'

'I won't,' Sasagaki said, paying the bill, putting on his coat, and wrapping his brown scarf around his neck. 'Oh, and I'm a little early, but happy New Year.'

'Happy New Year,' Yaeko said, with a smile.

Sasagaki grabbed the handle on the old sliding door, but before he opened it, he turned. 'Was he really upstairs?'

'Who?'

'Ryo. Was he really upstairs that day?'

'What are you talking about?'

Sasagaki shook his head and smiled. 'It's nothing. Next time.' He opened the door and stepped outside.

Yaeko stared at the door for a while before sitting down. She had goosebumps on the back of her neck, and not because of the cold air that had come streaming into the bar.

Sounds like Ryo's heading out again. Matsuura's words came back to her across the years. He was right there, on top of her, a bead of sweat running down his temple.

She had heard it too, the sound of footsteps on shingles. She'd known about Ryo's habit of leaving through his window and

walking across the roof to get outside. She'd never mentioned it
to the boy, though. Having him out of the house made it easier
for her to spend time with Matsuura.

He had left that day, too. She remembered hearing the sound
again when he came back.

*So he wasn't there. But so what? What does that detective think Ryo
did?*

Santa Claus stood by the doorway, handing out cards. Speakers
inside were playing classical arrangements of Christmas songs.
The combination of Christmas, New Year, and the grand opening
sale meant that the aisles were packed. Nearly all the customers
were young women. *Like insects drawn to a flower*, Sasagaki thought.

It was opening day at Yukiho Shinozuka's R&Y Osaka branch.
Unlike the shops in Tokyo, this one took up an entire building.
It was more than just clothes. There were accessories, bags, and
a whole floor for shoes – all luxury brands, not that Sasagaki
could tell the difference. Everything about the place seemed to
contradict what he had heard about Japan's economic bubble
breaking.

There was a small café next to the escalator leading from the
ground floor to the first. Sasagaki had been sitting there for about
an hour, looking down on the floor below. Even when night fell
outside, the customers kept coming. He'd had to line up for a
while just to get into the café, and there was still a long line at the
entrance. Sasagaki ordered a second cup of coffee to keep himself
on the good side of the staff.

A young couple sat across the table from him. To a casual
observer, they might have looked like a young man and wife out for
a day with grandpa. 'No show, huh?' the younger man said quietly.

Sasagaki nodded. His eyes focused on the floor below them.

Both of the people sitting across from him were officers from
Osaka Homicide.

Sasagaki looked at his watch. It was nearing closing time.

'There's still a chance,' he said, half to himself.

If Ryo Kirihara showed up, the two officers were going to take him into custody. The retired Sasagaki was only there as a spotter. Koga had arranged everything.

Kirihara was wanted for murder.

The moment Sasagaki had seen the fragment of glass from the broken cactus pot, a light had gone off in his head. He remembered the descriptions he'd read in reports of Matsuura just before he disappeared, in particular the comments they'd had from several people that he often wore Ray-Bans with green-tinted lenses. Maybe he hadn't been lying low after the pirated game bust after all. Maybe something worse had happened to him.

Sasagaki had Koga run a check on the glass. He was right. It was from a pair of Ray-Bans, and the slight fingerprint they found on it bore a strong resemblance to one they had taken in Matsuura's apartment. Forensics said there was a greater than ninety per cent chance it was his.

So why was a fragment of Matsuura's sunglasses in that pot? The most obvious explanation was that the glass had been in the dirt Reiko Karasawa used when she potted her cactus. So where did she get the dirt? Probably from her own garden.

They had needed a search warrant to start digging up the Karasawa garden. That was a difficult call to make, given the evidence they had, but Koga was willing to risk it. It helped that there were currently no residents at the Karasawa house. It also could have been grudging respect for an old detective's persistence, Sasagaki thought.

They had performed the search the day before and found a patch of soil in the tightly planted yard with no trees in it. They began to dig there first.

Roughly two hours later, they found a single white bone. Then the others. There were no clothes. They estimated that seven or eight years had passed since the time of death.

Osaka police then sent the remains to a forensic laboratory in an attempt to determine their identity. There were several ways by which they could do this, but each would take time. The odds were good, though, that they would be able to tell whether the bones belonged to Matsuura or not.

For his part, Sasagaki was sure they were Matsuura's once he heard that they'd found a small platinum ring on the right pinky finger of the skeleton. He could remember seeing it on the man's hand like it was yesterday.

The right hand was holding a piece of evidence, too: several strands of human hair wrapped around the bleached finger bones. Like hair he might have pulled out during a struggle.

Now the question was whether they could identify those hairs as belonging to Ryo Kirihara. Typically hair was identified by its colour, lustre, hardness, thickness, medullary index, pigment distribution and blood type, allowing a near one-to-one match with an individual. But given that the hair in question had been buried for years, it was uncertain how much of that information remained intact. Koga had promised to send it to a DNA lab for testing if it came to that.

DNA testing was a relatively new method, but they'd had some success with it over the last couple of years. There were plans to share the technology with every police station in the country within the next four years, but right now there was only one lab running the tests.

Times had changed in the nineteen years since the pawnbroker died. Everything was different now, even the way the police ran investigations.

The problem, then, was finding Ryo. No matter how much evidence they had on him, if they couldn't arrest him, none of it mattered.

It had been Sasagaki's suggestion that they keep a close eye on Yukiho Shinozuka's surroundings. *Watch the shrimp and eventually you'll find the goby*, that was his belief.

'He has to show up when she opens her new shop. Opening a place in Osaka has a special meaning for them. And Yukiho's been too busy with her shops in Tokyo to come down to Osaka all the time, so they're due for a reunion. Opening day is our day,' Sasagaki had told Koga.

Koga agreed with the old detective. From the moment the shop opened, several officers had taken turns watching from various

vantage points. Sasagaki, too, had been there since that morning
in a coffee shop across the street. Eventually, after hours of fruit-
less watching, he'd come inside.

'You think Kirihara is still going by Yuichi Akiyoshi?' the male
detective asked.

'Hard to say. He might have switched to a different name by now.'

While he answered, Sasagaki's mind was drifting off in another
direction – wondering about Ryo's choice of alias.

It had sounded familiar the first time he heard it, but it was only
recently that he had put two and two together. He had heard the
name 'Akiyoshi' from his informant Fumihiko Kikuchi. Yuichi
Akiyoshi was the name of the kid who had tattled on him about
the keychain, linking Fumihiko to the rape. Yuichi Akiyoshi, the
traitor.

So why had Ryo chosen that particular name as an alias? He
would have to ask Ryo himself to know for sure, but Sasagaki's pet
theory was that Ryo saw himself living a life of betrayal. His choice
of Akiyoshi's name was a self-deprecating inside joke.

Not that any of that mattered any more.

Sasagaki was almost certain he knew why Ryo had set up
Fumihiko. The photograph Fumihiko had showing Yaeko and
Matsuura's affair was a thorn in his side. If Fumihiko had shown
the photograph to the police, it might have spurred a reopening
of the entire case, making Ryo fear for his alibi. If Yaeko and
Matsuura had been in mid-tryst, that would have left Ryo alone.
Even if the police back then were unlikely to suspect an elementary school boy of murdering his own father, it was a piece of
evidence he'd rather not have out there.

It had been while he was drinking with Yaeko the night before
that Sasagaki had finally reached clarity in his own conjectures.
Ryo had been alone on the top floor that day, but he hadn't stayed
in the house. Just as it was easy for burglars to sneak in through
the upper-storey windows in those crowded neighbourhoods, a
boy could sneak out by the same route. Ryo had gone somewhere
that day, stepping across the rooftops.

And what had he done while he was away?

An announcement began to play in the shop announcing closing time. The flow of people shifted as more started heading for the door.

'No luck, I guess,' the man said. His partner looked similarly disappointed.

If they couldn't find Ryo today, they intended to take Yukiho Shinozuka in for questioning. But Sasagaki was against that. He was certain she wouldn't reveal anything of value. She would just give an utterly convincing expression of the purest surprise and say, 'What? Bones found in my poor mother's garden? I don't believe it! It can't be true!' And once she said that, they would have nothing. They knew from Makoto Takamiya's testimony that Reiko Karasawa had been visiting her daughter on New Year's Eve seven years ago when Matsuura was thought to have been killed. But there was still no proof that there was any connection between Ryo and Yukiho.

'Mr Sasagaki, over there,' the female detective said, subtly gesturing with her finger.

Sasagaki looked and saw Yukiho herself walking through the shop. She was wearing a white suit and a million-dollar smile. She was so beautiful she shone with a radiance that captured the eyes of every customer and even the floor staff around her. Wherever she walked, people turned to look, some whispering, some just staring.

'The queen makes an appearance,' the man whispered.

Yet when Sasagaki looked at Queen Yukiho, an entirely different image was superimposed in his mind. The little girl he'd met in that rundown apartment so many years ago. The girl who let no one close, closed off to everyone.

If only he'd heard about Yosuke Kirihara's predilections earlier he might have figured it out.

It had been five years ago when he'd first heard it from Yaeko. She was drunk, which was probably why she even talked about it to him at all.

'I can only say this now that he's gone, but my husband was never much in the sack. Well, not at first. He was fine at first, but gradually things got pretty quiet. See, he found something else, something better. Well, younger at least. Yeah, he liked little girls. He was always buying pictures of 'em. I threw them all away when he died, of course. Those things aren't right.'

In itself, this wasn't particularly surprising to the old detective, but it was what she said next that set his mind spinning.

'I heard something from Matsuura once. He said my husband was buying girls. When I asked him what that meant, he said he was paying money to sleep with them, really young ones, too. I asked if there was a shop that did that kind of thing, and why they didn't shut it down, and he laughed, saying that the wife of the pawnbroker should know more about these things. You know what he said? He told me it was moms selling their daughters for food.'

Her words set off a storm in Sasagaki's head. But when it passed it felt like a thick mist before his eyes had lifted.

Yaeko wasn't finished, either.

'You know, he even got it into his head that he wanted to adopt. He went so far as to ask a lawyer what it would take to formally adopt someone else's kid. When I started asking about it, he got real mad and told me it had nothing to do with me. He said if I kept bugging him about it he'd leave. To be honest, I think he was starting to lose it.'

Yet it was then that Sasagaki found the answers he had been looking for.

Yosuke Kirihara hadn't been visiting Fumiyo Nishimoto's apartment to see her. He'd been going there to see her daughter. He'd probably been there several times, with money, paying to sleep with her. The old apartment took on an entirely different image in Sasagaki's mind. It wasn't a refuge from a hard world. It was a place of business, illicit and contemptible.

This suggested another question to him. Was Yosuke Kirihara the only customer?

What about Tadao Terasaki, who died in the car accident? The investigation team had had him pegged as Fumiyo's lover, but wouldn't it make more sense if he had just been another pervert of the same persuasion as Kirihara?

There would be no way of knowing that now. There could have been any number of other customers and he would have no way of knowing.

The only one he knew about for sure was Kirihara.

Now the one million yen made sense. It was a final payment to Fumiyo so he could adopt her daughter. Paying for the privilege of being with the girl wasn't enough. He wanted her for his very own. Kirihara had gone to the library to pick up the object of his obsession, leaving Fumiyo to wander down to the park where she sat on the swings. Sasagaki wondered what kind of thoughts must have been going through her head.

He could paint a clear picture about what happened next. Kirihara had taken the girl into the abandoned building. He didn't think she would have resisted much, especially not when Kirihara told her about the million yen he'd given her mom.

Sasagaki didn't particularly want to imagine what had taken place in that dusty little room, but he did know one thing – Ryo had been there too. After leaving his house he had headed for the library. He probably went there a lot to see Yukiho and show her his paper cut-outs. The library was their sanctuary from the madness of the world around them.

But that day, near the library, Ryo saw something strange: his father, leading Yukiho by the hand. He followed them into the building. He might not have known what was going on, but he knew how to spy on them. Ryo had gone straight into the ducts. From his vantage point in the air duct near the ceiling he would have seen a nightmare unfold.

What sadness and hatred must have filled him, guiding the hands that gripped his favourite pair of scissors. Sasagaki pictured the wounds in the body – wounds that surely lay just as deeply on Ryo's heart.

After killing his father, Ryo let Yukiho escape through the door before jamming it with the cinder block – a smart move to delay discovery of the body. When Sasagaki pictured how the boy must have felt as he crawled back out through the darkness of those air ducts, it made his chest ache.

He couldn't say what Ryo and Yukiho had decided on afterwards. Maybe they had never decided anything – they were just trying to keep what remained of their souls intact. Yukiho shut herself off from the world, never showing her true self to anyone, and Ryo ... he was still crawling through the darkness all these years later.

Ryo's motive for killing Matsuura had been to protect his alibi. It was also possible that Matsuura had somehow realised the boy's guilt and held it over him when he coerced Ryo into pirating software.

But Sasagaki saw another motive there as well. Ryo would have seen a connection between his father's predilection for young girls and his mother's unfaithfulness. From his room on the upper storey of that old wooden building, he must have heard his mother with Matsuura on any number of occasions. To him, Matsuura could well have seemed like the thing that was driving his parents mad.

'Time to go,' the young detective said, bringing Sasagaki back to the present. He looked around, seeing the café had nearly emptied out.

A no-show.

A kind of emptiness spread in the old detective's chest. That morning he'd realised that if he didn't catch Ryo today, he'd never catch him. But sitting here in this empty café wouldn't help a thing.

'Guess so,' he said, slowly lifting himself to his feet.

Outside the café, Sasagaki got on the escalator with the two other detectives. Most of the customers were on their way out. The store staff looked happy, pleased with a successful opening. The Santa Claus from the door was heading up the escalator as they went down. He was slumped in his costume, exhausted from a long day of handing out cards.

Back on the first floor, Sasagaki glanced around the shop. Yukiho was nowhere to be seen. She was probably in a back office somewhere, tabulating the day's takings.

'Thanks for the help,' the man whispered just before they left.

Sasagaki nodded. The rest would be up to them, the younger generation. He wished them the best of luck.

Sasagaki went out of the store with a few other customers. The other two detectives broke out from the crowd and went to another of their co-workers across the street. They would regroup, then head in to question Yukiho.

Sasagaki pulled his coat tighter and started to walk. A mother who had just left the store before him was walking with her child.

'That's lovely,' the girl's mother was saying, looking at something in the little girl's hand. 'You'll have to show it to Daddy when we get home.'

The girl was about four years old. She was holding something up in her hand, a piece of paper fluttering in the wind.

Sasagaki's eyes went wide. The red paper in the girl's hand had been expertly cut into the shape of a reindeer.

'Wait, where did you get that?' he asked, suddenly grabbing the girl's arm from behind.

The girl's mother turned, shocked, her hands going to protect her daughter. 'What are you doing!?'

The little girl looked as if she was about to cry. A few passers-by stopped to watch.

'I – I'm sorry. I just wanted to know where your daughter got that,' Sasagaki asked, pointing at the reindeer.

'She got it just now, at the store.'

'From whom? Who gave that to you?'

'Santa gave it to me,' the girl said.

Sasagaki spun around and ran at full speed, gritting his teeth against the ache in his knees.

The doors to the shop were already closed. The few detectives standing outside looked surprised when they saw Sasagaki running toward them.

'What is it?' one of them asked.

'Santa Claus!' Sasagaki shouted. 'He's Santa Claus!'

Immediately grasping the situation, the detectives lunged forward and forced open the closed automatic glass doors, spilling into the shop. Ignoring the floor staff trying to stop them, they ran up the stopped escalator.

Sasagaki tried vainly to keep up with them, but then had another thought and instead turned back outside to head down the narrow alleyway that ran along the side of the shop.

I'm an idiot. How long have I been chasing this guy? How long has he been lurking in the shadows where no one would see him, watching over Yukiho?

Behind the building was a metal staircase with a railing that led up to a door. He ran up the stairs and yanked the door open to see a man standing in front of him, dressed all in black. He looked surprised to suddenly see someone appearing in front of him.

It was a strange, lingering moment in time. Sasagaki knew the man standing in front of him was Ryo Kirihara. And yet he couldn't move to grab him. He couldn't even speak. Meanwhile another part of his mind realised that Ryo knew who he was, too.

A second passed and the moment was gone. Ryo whirled around and began running in the opposite direction.

'Stop!' Sasagaki shouted, chasing after him.

He ran through the corridor and out into the first floor of the store. The other detectives were there in force. Ryo was running, weaving between shelves piled high with expensive-looking bags. 'It's him!' Sasagaki shouted.

The detectives turned and ran. Ryo was making for the top of the elevator. *We've got you now*, Sasagaki thought.

But just before Ryo reached the escalator he swerved, and without a moment's hesitation he leapt off the balcony.

A cry went up from the store clerks on the floor below. There was a loud crash of something breaking. The detectives raced down the steps of the escalator.

Sasagaki reached the escalator a few seconds behind them. His heart was racing painfully. Hand to his chest, he took the steps slowly.

Down on the ground floor, the giant Christmas tree was lying on its side. Ryo Kirihara was lying next to it, his arms and legs splayed out. He wasn't moving.

A detective ran closer and tried to pull him up, but then he stopped and turned toward Sasagaki.

'What is it?' Sasagaki asked. The detective just pointed down at Ryo. A pool of blood had started to spread on the floor beneath him.

Sasagaki walked over and knelt down. He started to roll Ryo over when he heard another scream.

There was something sticking out of Ryo's chest. It was hard to see through the blood, but Sasagaki knew exactly what they were. His scissors.

Someone shouted for an ambulance and he heard footsteps running, but Sasagaki had seen enough corpses in his life to know when it was too late for that. Sensing a presence, he looked up. Yukiho was standing nearby, her face as white as snow.

'Who is this man?' Sasagaki asked, looking her in the eye.

Yukiho was as expressionless as a porcelain doll. 'I don't know him at all,' she said quietly. 'The manager hired him.'

A young woman showed up, her face pale, and introduced herself as the manager.

The detectives were starting to move. One began roping off the scene. Another began questioning the manager, and another put his hand on Sasagaki's shoulder.

The old detective let himself be led away. He was walking a little shakily. He looked up and saw Yukiho going up the escalator, looking like a white shadow from behind.

Not once did she look around.

Keigo Higashino was born in Osaka. He started writing novels while still working as an engineer at Nippon Denso Co. He won the Edogawa Rampo Prize for writing at the age of twenty-seven, and subsequently quit his job to start a career as a writer in Tokyo.